THE CHARACTERS WHO ROCKED A NATION!

COLONEL "CONNIE" TRASKER
The commander of Planetary Fleet One—the astronaut who must overcome Russian sabotage as well as the treason of his own crew member

DR. "JAYVEE" HALLECK
The first black astronaut, race centered and moody, his deep shortcomings jeopardize the entire mission threatening the lives of the men

MONETTA HALLECK
Dr. Halleck's voluptuous wife, she finds love is sleeping with another man—Colonel Trasker

CLETE O'DONNELL
A former radical turned labor leader, he would do anything to prevent the success of the flight —and has some suspicious underground commitments as well

THE PRESIDENT
A torn, tired man, battered between powerful interest groups finally forcing him to abandon the astronauts in their greatest crisis

Available soon from Avon

ADVISE AND CONSENT
A SHADE OF DIFFERENCE

Alex
Sugzda
203-655-7280

The Throne of Saturn

A NOVEL OF SPACE AND POLITICS

Allen Drury

 AVON PUBLISHERS OF BARD, CAMELOT, DISCUS AND EQUINOX BOOKS

All of the characters in this book are fictitious, and any resemblance to actual persons, living or dead, is purely coincidental.

AVON BOOKS
A division of
The Hearst Corporation
959 Eighth Avenue
New York, New York 10019

First Avon Printing, March, 1972

AVON TRADEMARK REG. U.S. PAT. OFF. AND
FOREIGN COUNTRIES, REGISTERED TRADEMARK—
MARCA REGISTRADA, HECHO EN CHICAGO, U.S.A.

Printed in the U.S.A.

DEDICATED TO
THE U.S. ASTRONAUTS
and those who help them fly

Up from Earth's Centre through the Seventh Gate
I rose, and on the Throne of Saturn sate,
And many Knots unravel'd by the Road;
But not the Knot of Human Death and Fate.

—THE RUBAIYAT OF OMAR KHAYYÁM

MAJOR CHARACTERS IN THE NOVEL

At Manned Spacecraft Center, Houston:
  Dr. James Cavanaugh, Director of MSC ("Jim")
  Dr. Robert Hertz, Director of Flight Control ("Bob")
  Colonel Henry C. Barstow, Chief, Astronaut Office ("Hank")
  Colonel Bertrand L. Richmond, Director, Flight Crew Operations ("Bert")
  Colonel Conrad H. Trasker, Jr. ("Connie"), astronaut
  Jane, his wife
  Commander Alvin S. Weickert III ("Jazz"), astronaut
  Clare, his wife
  Dr. J. V. Halleck (*Jay*vee), astroscientist
  Monetta, his wife
  Dr. Petros S. Balkis ("Pete"), astroscientist
  Colonel Hugo S. Gaudet ("Gaudy"), astronaut
  Lieutenant Colonel Stuart Yule ("Stu"), astronaut
  Yo-Shin, his wife
  Dr. Emerson Wacker ("Em"), astroscientist
  Other astronauts, astroscientists, and their wives
  The medical staff
  Members of the media

In Washington, D.C.:
  The President
  The Vice-President
  Dr. William Anderson ("Andy"), Administrator, National Aeronautics and Space Administration
  Senator John Able Winthrop of Massachusetts, chair-

man of the Senate Aeronautical and Space Sciences
Committee

Representative James L. Satterthwaite of Wyoming,
chairman of the House Science and Astronautics
Committee

Senator Kennicut Williams of Indiana ("Kenny"), a
member of the Senate committee

Representative Cullee Hamilton of California, a member
of the House committee

Percy Mercy, editor of the magazine *View* ("P.C.M.")

Academician Alexei S. Kuselevsky, principal space adviser
to the Soviet Government

Marlon Holloway, assistant administrator for public
affairs, NASA

Members of the media

At Kennedy Space Center, Cape Kennedy, Florida:
Dr. Albrecht Freer, Director of KSC ("Al")
Bob Ellison, chief of public affairs
Clete O'Donnell, a union leader
Members of the media

*At George C. Marshall Space Flight Center, Huntsville,
Alabama:*
Dr. Hans Sturmer, Director

In Pasadena, California:
Dr. Vernon Hertz, Director of the Jet Propulsion Laboratory

At North American Rockwell, Downey, California:
Jim Matthison, manager

On the Moon:
The crew of Man in the Moon

WITH THANKS

Many are responsible for the facts and insights they gave me during the six months I researched this novel.

Most became, and I hope will remain after they read it, good friends.

None, of course, is responsible in any way whatsoever for what I did with the raw material about men and machines which they so generously provided.

Editorial space precludes listing them all. One group in particular, wrapped in its mantle of discretion and anonymity, I would not dream of naming. Suffice it to say that I am very grateful to those astronauts who talked freely— and told me a great deal. And I am equally grateful to those astronauts who were too cautious to talk freely ... and told me a great deal.

For the rest it comes down to many, many kind people in Washington, Houston, the Cape, Huntsville. I should be remiss indeed if I did not mention three above all. The first is the most astute and amiable Dr. George E. Mueller, then associate administrator for manned space flight, NASA, who was unceasingly helpful throughout, and who first passed the signal along the supersensitive NASA network that I really wasn't about to blow up the pads, and so people could probably relax and talk to me if they wanted to.

The second is the quietly knowledgeable and highly competent Gordon L. Harris, chief of public affairs, Kennedy Space Center, who helped immeasurably with technical information, insights into the program and details of Apollo missions which formed the basis for much of the verisimilitude surrounding the flight of Planetary Fleet One.

And the third is the delightful and supremely able Christopher C. Kraft, then director of flight control, now deputy director of the Manned Spacecraft Center, Houston, who patiently answered my technical questions, wrote me a genuine NASA-type technical description or two for use in the novel, and generally confirmed the logical parameters within which a novelist's mind might roam. I hope he will not be too upset that I decided to stick to my planned three-Saturn launch (and advance the timetable substantially, for reasons hereinafter made clear) instead of the four or five he contemplates, for the first flight to Mars.

And of course there are others, both inside NASA and out—Dr. Thomas Paine, then the Administrator of NASA; James E. Webb, the ex-Administrator; Dr. Wernher von Braun; Julian Scheer, administrator for public affairs in Washington; Dr. Robert Gilruth, director of MSC; Richard Johnson, his assistant; Dr. Kurt Debus, director of KSC; Jack King, chief press officer, KSC, and his most helpful staff to whom everyone covering the Cape is indebted; Bart Slattery, chief press officer, Marshall Space Flight Center; Alvin H. Bishop, Jr., then of RCA at Cocoa Beach, now with the executive staff, Hughes Nevada Operations, who very kindly and generously shared his many friendships in the astronaut corps; William Eichstadt, who assisted in research and then did a yeoman job of deciphering and typing a complex and much scribbled-upon manuscript; many friends in the working—as distinct from the pontificating—press at the Cape, such as Mary Bubb of Fairchild Publications; Julie Divine, formerly of Fairchild; and many, many others who, during some ten years in which I have attended launches at the Cape, and then during the final six months of intensive research, did much to give me the facts and feel of the program.

To them and to you I submit this novel: hoping that the story of Connie Trasker, his friends and his enemies, and how they all became involved in the flight of Planetary Fleet One of Project Argosy to the planet Mars, will stay awhile in memory.

ALLEN DRURY

Book One

1.

The satellite whirled around the globe, a tiny silver bubble lost in the sky's infinitude. With the perfect precision built into it by the Jet Propulsion Laboratory at Pasadena it photographed on every pass the changing features of the busy earth below. Nothing escaped it, as nothing escaped its many brothers from many lands, which also followed, each in its particular equatorial or polar orbit, the activities of the nations that launched them and the activities of those nations' enemies. All were on guard; and on this day as on many other days the vigil was rewarded, secrets were discovered, warnings were conveyed to important people whose responsibilities and suspicions required them to keep an eye on one another.

The calendar was pushing toward the eighties, and on the earth and in the sky there was, as always, little peace and less good will, toward men who had conquered almost everything but Man.

To see Connie Trasker walking toward the Astronaut Office across the vast green esplanade at Manned Spacecraft Center, Houston, was to see the nearest thing to a Space Age Casanova: or so said Bob Hertz, Director of Flight Operations, as he watched Connie's triumphal progress from his vantage point in the office of the Director of MSC, on the ninth floor of the Project Management Building.

It was a bright, sunny, non-windy day, a rarity in Houston in spring; and it was almost noon; and a lot of secretaries were on their way to the cafeteria; and many of them were obviously very much aware of Connie Trasker; and so Bob said it again.

"The nearest thing," he repeated, "to a Space Age Casanova. Look at that. It's a disgrace to the space program."

The Director, whose name was Dr. James Cavanaugh, laughed.

"You're just jealous. Colonel Conrad H. Trasker, Jr., is the happily married father of three and Jane trusts him implicitly. With, I am sure," he added somewhat wryly, "perfect cause."

"Is he going to be commander of Piffy One?" Bob Hertz inquired.

"Why not?" Jim Cavanaugh asked, a trifle blankly. "Bert Richmond and Hank Barstow think he's great. And you know the Astronaut Office: what those guys say, *goes*. Why don't you like him? They do."

"Oh, so do I," Bob Hertz said. "He's the most perfect All-American Boy since Frank Borman, and Neil Armstrong, rolled into one. I think he's beautiful. However: are you sure we should send all that to Mars? Can the secretarial staff let him go? Will Houston ever be the same?"

"Piffy One," the Director said, suddenly somber, "has a long way to go. Did you see the Houston *Post* this morning?"

He held it up.

"PLANETARY FLEET ONE IN TROUBLE," its headline said. "PRESIDENT FACES FIGHT IN CONGRESS ON FIRST MARS VENTURE. FATE OF SPACE STATION MAYFLOWER LINKED TO DEEP SPACE JOURNEY AS NEW RUSS PROBES HINTED. U.S. MAY LOSE LEAD."

" 'U.S. May Lose Lead,' " Bob Hertz echoed with something of the Director's somber unease. "Do they mean we still have it?"

"And do they mean he will really fight for it?" Dr. Cavanaugh wondered. "That's what worries me at the moment."

"He has so many priorities," Bob Hertz murmured, not without a trace of acid. "The blacks—the students—the cities—the peaceniks—the warniks—the demonstrators for this—the demonstrators against that—the North—the South—the East—the West—"

16

"—the Moon, the planets, the stars and us," Jim Cavanaugh finished for him. "And we come last, I sometimes get the feeling."

"He has to make everybody happy," Bob Hertz said. "There's always an election coming, and the cautious man, forethoughted and forearmed, fighteth with the strength of ten. I think," he added flatly, "he'd cut us in half in a minute if he felt he dared. There is some sentiment on the Hill, as noted. And there are all those pressure groups."

"Fortunately not too vigorous where we're concerned," the Director said. "But we've been lucky."

"Damned lucky," Bob Hertz agreed. "How are you going to the meeting in Washington tomorrow morning?"

"Hank and Bert are going to fly me over. Why don't you go with us?"

"Connie's already invited me," Bob Hertz said. "But I suppose we could combine forces and take one of the bigger planes."

"Let's," Jim Cavanaugh said. "We can organize our strategy before we have to face Hans Sturmer and the Huntsville Happybund."

"To say nothing of the empire-building sun-worshipers from the Cape," Bob Hertz remarked.

"Are you implying there are frictions and jockeying for power within the National Aeronautics and Space Administration?" Dr. Cavanaugh asked dryly. "Never let it be said."

"Never let it be said outside," Bob Hertz amended. "It spoils the NASA image. Anyway, we'll work it out the way we want it—Houston usually does, doesn't it? We have a few years, after all."

"Targeted for the mid eighties," the Director said thoughtfully, "if everything works as it should."

"And that's a big if," Bob Hertz remarked. "I suppose Huntsville will have some good excuses why the NERVA nuclear engine isn't going to be ready for testing until next year. They always do."

"And the contractors will be full of explanations as to why the modified planetary spacecraft aren't quite ready for testing yet either, but will be, any moment now." Dr. Cavanaugh sighed. "Everybody has his reasons, I've found, after a good many years in this outfit."

"I sometimes think the main reason is too many meetings," Bob Hertz said, "but of course that's treason and I mustn't even think it, let alone express it aloud. Why is it necessary to have another grand review right at this particular moment?"

"There really isn't any I can see," Dr. Cavanaugh said. "On the whole, everything seems to be progressing satisfactorily in spite of a few headaches here and there. We'll make launch date and no trouble, in my estimation. Connie's on his way to talk to Hank and Bert about the crew right now, in fact. Hopefully they'll come to some decision today and we can have at least the first four or five names of the projected twelve to tell headquarters at the meeting tomorrow. That will be one thing nearing readiness, anyway."

"So he *is* going to be commander," Bob Hertz said. "I'm glad it's all right for me to know."

"Your ears only," the Director said cheerfully. He smiled. "Hank only phoned and told *me* about two minutes before you came in."

"I sometimes think it's great, the way the astronauts run the program," Bob said with a mock wistfulness. "Why do they keep the rest of us on, I wonder?"

"Oh, we all contribute," the Director said. "But they're the ones who seem to have the most fun. As well as the most danger, of course."

"I think the fun makes up for it," Bob Hertz said. "After all, they've been given the greatest toy in history to play with."

"Haven't we all?" Jim Cavanaugh asked with a smile. "And don't we all love it?"

"We do that," Bob Hertz agreed with an answering smile. "Yes, I can't deny we do that." His expression changed, became again concerned and uneasy. "As long as it lasts, that is."

At that, he thought as he returned in musing silence to his own office overlooking Clear Lake at the opposite end of the building, was what concerned them all: *as long as it lasts.*

How long would it?

Looking back on almost two dramatic decades, Bob Hertz, who had been in the space program since the early days of Sputnik and the headlong drive to beat the Russians to the Moon, reflected that he had rarely known morale throughout NASA to be quite as blah as it was at the moment. It wasn't exactly low, it wasn't exactly depressed, the basic spirit was still strong, the protective we-against-the-world unity was still there, but some essential ingredient was missing, some essential impulse to keep everything going and hold everything together: "blah" seemed to him the right word. And this despite the valiant official attempts following the lunar conquest to arrive at a delicately calculated balance among the aspirations of man, the skills and energies of America, the desire for national prestige and security, the beckoning marvels of the universe, and the practical requirements of a budget torn ten ways from Sunday by the demands of a confused, contentious, potentially explosive yet still basically hopeful society.

He did not know exactly who was to blame for this—perhaps, he told himself wryly, the Russians, for just not being technologically good enough at the moment to provide the kind of competition that had largely been responsible for sending Americans with a single-minded dedication into space. But that it was a fact, he knew with a sometimes quite disheartening certainty.

"If we only had a goal," his colleagues constantly complained. "We wouldn't mind marking time if we knew we were going somewhere worthwhile at the end of it," the astronauts told him on numerous occasions. "We're losing all our best men and we don't know when we'll be able to get such a good team together again," his friends among the contractors reminded him almost every day. And he, and all of them, passed the word to headquarters in Washington. And from his office at 400 Delaware Avenue S.W., the Administrator no doubt passed it on to the President. And the President thought it all over and came to the conclusion that he couldn't give them a goal as dramatic as they wanted.

And so the blahs remained and, in many cases, became worse.

Not that he could blame the Chief Executive, of course, who did indeed have more priorities than mortal man should have to contend with. It was just that Bob Hertz felt—as the astronauts felt and the Administrator felt and nearly everyone else involved in the upper echelons of the space program felt—that theirs was the one priority that

19

should take precedence over everything but sheer national survival (and they were convinced that it included that, too). They could be sympathetic, as an intellectual exercise, toward the unhappiness of the minorities, the plight of the cities, and sometimes even the restless outcries from the campus; but when it came to what they really considered important above all, there was no contest.

"The program," they called it without other identification, as though after all, what other program could there be, worthy of men's deepest dedication and concern?

In that spirit they had carried America to the gates of the planets—and there they had been stopped. Or if not stopped, at least slowed to a pace that to many of them seemed the equivalent of stopping, so drastically had it reduced their resources, caused the inevitable attrition of many of their major talents, substituted for one clear-cut and shining aim a slow, methodical, inch-by-inch progression toward what might or might not be a valid and viable triumph when it was finally achieved.

He could give the President's predecessor high credit for doing the best he could with the funds and the political climate he had to deal with, but a space station for an immediate goal, and Mars off in the distance at some less controversial and more easily funded time, did not strike Bob Hertz as worthy of what America had done in the past or equal to what she could do now if all her potentials were once again unleashed. The goal of a Moon landing in a decade had grown out of a dismayed Executive's desperate search for some bauble to distract his increasingly critical countrymen from the disaster of his foreign policy at the Bay of Pigs, but still it had contained within itself the sort of inspiration that far transcended its initial rather hapless and forlorn motivation. It proved to be one of those quick decisions, based upon desperate political need, which amazingly transform both those who initiate and those who fulfill. The Moon, riding pure and high in the eyes and imaginations of mankind, imparted some of its purity to the program: and while (carefully shielded from public view) there had been impurities, uncertainties, faulty decisions, waste, incompetence and sheer, inexcusable stupidity in many aspects of Project Apollo, there had also been sufficient purity, dedication, skill, devotion and fine, unassailable genius at work to give the nation not only a triumph unsurpassed in history but a spirit of accomplishment and national unity sorely needed in a trying time.

This no Space Station *Mayflower,* vital though it was to future planetary explorations, could quite provide. Nor could a careful, cautious, step-by-step approach to Mars ever match that first dramatic, heart-lifting, mind-soaring goal of a landing on the Moon. Perhaps there could only be one such leap across space capable of seizing the spirits of men; perhaps inevitably all else, no matter how far the voyagers from Earth might travel down the distant highways of the galaxies, could only be, in some indefinable way, anticlimax. Perhaps nothing could ever again match the Moon.

And yet, Bob Hertz wondered as he riffled through the incoming calls his secretary had left on his desk and then swiveled around to stare down across the deceptively blue, polluted lake—who could know for sure, if it hadn't been tried? And was it quite fair to the astronauts who would venture there, to all in NASA who would work to send them safely on their way, and to Mars itself, to make the red planet in some sense second best?

He knew there were those, and many of them inside NASA's own jealously guarded citadel, who were quite content with the situation as it existed. One was his own brother, Dr. Vernon Hertz, director of the Jet Propulsion Laboratory in Pasadena. Out at JPL, at Ames Research Center at Moffett Field, California, at Goddard Space Center near Washington, D.C., at Lewis in Cincinnati, and at the granddaddy aerospace research center of them all, Langley Field, Virginia, the mood was not at all averse to just poking along in a leisurely fashion through the solar system, gathering scientific information via unmanned satellites, comfortably digesting its implications into an endless series of papers, reports, seminars and studies. The great division within NASA between the manned and unmanned sections, which had existed from the start of the program, continued unabated. For the moment, aided by the now definitely scheduled "Grand Tour" of Jupiter, Saturn, Uranus and Neptune, the scientists who managed the unmanned program seemed to be in the ascendant. Their one basic argument—why risk men when our technology will allow us to do the same experiments as well, and sometimes better, with our instruments?—had a powerful appeal in an era of tight budgets and heavy domestic demands.

It was bolstered further by the information that came steadily back from their increasingly extended probes of Earth's neighbors. Mars looked like the Moon, its only life apparently amoebic or bacterial, if it existed at all. Venus was too hot—Jupiter too gaseous—Mercury and Pluto too cold—and so on. The landscapes out there looked uniformly harsh, unfriendly and unproductive.

There were ways of correcting all these deficiencies, given time, sufficient skill and sufficient billions; but they were not the sort of projects that a public thrilled and cajoled by the immediacy of the Moon could be expected to support over the long haul. They were the sort of projects that had to grow in their own good time, as decades passed and it became obvious that man's destiny still, as always, lay forever outward from whatever safe center he had managed to establish. Many never wished to abandon the safe center, but fortunately there had always been those who were willing to dream and adventure. So the boundaries of the safe center were forever expanding, and would forever do so, as long as "forever" remained a concept man himself did not destroy.

In a semi-holding operation such as the manned program had now been forced into, the guardians of the unmanned sector were riding high. Send out our little gadgets for a tenth the cost and bring back at least ten times more, they argued, with the active support of his scientific adviser, to the President. Get more bugs for the buck. Don't send those nice clean-cut types out into the solar system to risk their handsome necks and superior brains: let a little piece of metal do it for you. Keep the boys at home!

The effect this had on the boys, Bob Hertz thought with a wry smile, was enough to drive some of them halfway up the wall. Over in the astronauts' building, where their memento-cluttered offices marched neatly side by side down the long white corridors, some of the vivid language lavished upon the scientists of the unmanned program would give the public an entirely new concept of the Model Astronaut, if the public ever heard it. Also, some of the comment on the public for being so gullible as to listen to the argument that machines could do the job better than men.

For some of the astronauts, Bob knew, a lot of things were riding on the program: not only patriotism, dedication to service and the great satisfying adventure of it, which were paramount with most, but also such more humanly measurable things as the desire for fame, fortune and future preferment. Several had departed for highly lucrative civilian employment. Two already sat in the United States Senate, secure in the calm inner conviction that they would rise in due course to the White House. The rest were profiting in many ways, personal and professional, from their association with the program. It was one of those "trade-offs" so beloved of NASA: all they had to do was put their lives on the line and the world would respond with many glittering rewards. It was not the major motivation, but for most of them, filled with more than the usual share of drive and ambition, and under the goad of such practical considerations as how best and most comfortably to raise a family and advance a career, it was certainly a practical and compelling impetus.

Considering the fact that they did indeed have to put their lives on the line, it was not, perhaps, too much to ask of the world in return. Thanks to the combined skills of several hundred thousand dedicated people, including themselves, and thanks also to the good luck of the United States, very few had been required to pay the final price for their daring. In some measure Virgil Grissom, Edward White and Roger Chaffee, whose fiery deaths on the pad in a simulated Apollo countdown at the Cape had been the all-time traumatic experience in NASA's history, had paid the price for all of them. On many occasions, such as Apollo 13, only the narrowest of margins had separated many of them from a fate either similar or equally horrible somewhere in space or on the Moon.

The fact gave them all a certain superstitious feeling: it made them all tread a little more carefully the dangerous pathways where they walked. They were better astronauts for it. It increased their dedication to the country and to the program. It made them more impatient with their critics both inside and outside NASA. It imparted a certain protective, defensive, hard-to-crack exclusiveness to them.

Behind the facade no group was more diverse or more human, yet to the public the succession of white-suited smiling figures who roared away from the Cape and re-

23

turned for triumphal parades across an awed and grateful land seemed all of a piece, immaculate, infallible, perfect and pure. "We have our usual three per cent of ass-draggers in the astronaut corps," one of the most glamorous had once remarked in a moment of private candor: the fact almost never escaped into public view. Even now, fed up as they were by the tantalizingly slow pace of the advance toward Mars, they managed to maintain the image. Their private foibles and private tensions, many of them brought on by the now almost interminable waiting for the Mars venture to begin, were for the most part successfully concealed.

Bob Hertz could sympathize with them because he knew them and understood them and most of them were his close and trusted friends. Many of them had been on the exploratory flights to the Moon that succeeded Apollo 11 and had participated in the Apollo Applications Program. Most had done their stint in modest little Space Station *Mayflower*, patiently undergoing the physiological and psychological tests devised by the medical division of NASA (which as usual was overcautious, overprotective, at times annoyed them intensely, yet still had their best interests at heart). But the goal for which they were training remained years away, and each week new rumors of resignations raced down the corridors, new conferences had to be held to appease frayed tempers, he and Jim Cavanaugh had to join Hank Barstow and Bert Richmond to confront some impatient and angry astronaut who professed to be fed up and ready to tell them where they could shove the whole damned program.

Nearly always these episodes blew over and things calmed down again. Aside from a few disgruntled astroscientists, attrition in the corps remained surprisingly small. There were "no unexpected anomalies," to use NASA's characteristically involved way of saying "everything's O.K." But he did wonder, Bob Hertz thought as he swung back to his desk and prepared to return the first waiting call, how long it could last.

The call was from his brother at JPL, and though he did not know it when that calm, steady presence appeared on the Picturephone, the news he was about to hear would within twenty-four hours change NASA's world and put all of them back again full-speed on the high road to the planets.

24

For Connie Trasker, no such welcome break in the future's apparent monotony would occur until much later in the day, when it finally became official throughout the program and everyone involved felt its exciting, all-compelling impact.

At the moment, Connie was passing the main pond in front of the administration building, whistling at the usual flock of contented mallard ducks that scattered at his approach. He had spoken cordially to five of Manned Spacecraft Center's top civil service employees, beamed winningly upon sixteen secretaries aged eighteen to sixty-three, autographed his official picture for five small boys, three little girls and two white-haired couples from Muncie, Indiana. His day's work, he thought wryly, was already half done. Now he was about to begin his ascent, as he often described it to himself with an irreverent irony, from the placid suburbanite surroundings of his home in nearby El Lago to the rarefied levels of the Astronaut Office where the crew selections for Planetary Fleet One of "Project Argosy" were about to begin.

Not be concluded, just begun.

More damned palaver would have to occur, more damned water would have to gush under the bridge, before the selections became final, than you could shake a Saturn at.

Colonel Trasker snorted.

The sound, fully expressive of his feelings as he contemplated the typically tortuous inner windings of NASA, brought an unexpected and not entirely welcome response from immediately behind.

"Gesundheit!" a familiar voice said cheerfully. He stopped and swung around so abruptly that Commander Alvin S. Weickert III, practically at his elbow, had to step nimbly to avoid bumping into him.

"Good morning," Connie Trasker said, extending his hand automatically. "It wasn't a sneeze, it was a snort."

"Same general idea," Jazz Weickert replied, giving him a vigorous and determinedly obvious handshake as a couple of scientists from the Lunar Receiving Lab stepped around them and passed by with smiles and nods. "What's got you snorting?"

"Life," Colonel Trasker said solemnly as Jazz fell into step beside him. "With a capital L. How was the Cape?"

"Still there when I left," Jazz said brightly. "The girls at

25

Ronnie's Merry-Go-'Round are still waiting for you, Connie."

"That's good," Connie said. "I wouldn't want to think you'd satisfied them all."

"Not all," Jazz said cheerfully. "One or two, though. One or two."

"Shame on you, you noble astronaut," Colonel Trasker told him. Commander Weickert grinned.

"There are astronauts," he said, "and sometimes there are astronaughties. This time I was an astronaughty. When are we getting crew assignments for Piffy One?"

"NASA would prefer," Connie Trasker said, sparring for time as he inwardly cursed Jazz's built-in radar whenever his own interests were concerned, "to refer to it as Planetary Fleet One, or at least 'P.F. One.' This in-house slang about 'Piffy One' spoils the whole image, you know."

"O.K., O.K.," Jazz said, and suddenly his eyes did not look at all relaxed, but quite strained and unhappy. "I said, when are we getting our assignments?"

"I don't know yet," Connie Trasker said.

It was Jazz Weickert's turn to snort.

"The hell you don't," he said in a bitter voice.

"I'm not lying to you," Colonel Trasker said. "One thing I've never done to you is lie. Isn't that right?"

"That's right," Commander Weickert agreed bleakly. "But you've done just about everything else."

"Now, see here, Jazz—" Connie Trasker began. Then he stopped, because what was the use? How could you ever unravel all the things that had gone into the complicated relationship with this fellow veteran of the program who had stopped walking, forcing him to stop also, and now stared at him from eyes filled with pain?

" 'See here, Jazz,' " Commander Weickert mimicked, dropping his voice to a bitter whisper as several tourists passed with worshipful and respectful glances, " 'See here, Jazz. Be a good boy, Jazz. Don't rock the boat, Jazz. Keep up the image, Jazz. Support the program, Jazz. Take the short end of the stick, Jazz, and don't say anything to anybody when your friends and colleagues screw you with it year in and year out.' God damn it, Connie, how long do you bastards think you can get away with it?"

"Jazz," Connie Trasker said, taking his arm firmly, making him move on, walking him determinedly forward

26

toward the Astronaut Office, "I know you think you have some legitimate gripes—"

"Think I have!" Jazz exploded in a voice that began loudly and then automatically sank to a savagely muted intensity as more tourists passed, suitably awe-struck. *Think* I have! You know damned well I have, so don't give me that wide-eyed, baby-faced, All-American-Boy innocence of yours. Ever since Gemini you bastards have been out to get me and time after time you've succeeded. But you know something, Connie?" An expression of unhappy satisfaction crossed his face. "I made up my mind 'way back that I was just going to stick around. I made up my mind you weren't going to discourage me or squeeze me out. I decided I was going to stay right here and rub your noses in it, and after a while I was going to win out. Because a lot of people wonder about me, you know, Connie. A lot of the public and a lot of people in the press and in Congress. They say, "What's become of Jazz Weickert? Why isn't he getting some of these good flights? Who's got it in for him? How unfair can you be?' And now we're coming up to the payoff, Connie-boy, and *this* time, Jazz Weickert's going to be on that crew. And he's not going to take any back seat, either. We all know who's going to be No. 1—not even *my* friends"—and he smiled without humor—"and I've developed a few these last few months—not even my friends can take that away from Mr. Perfection, here. But you're going to have a good second-in-command, old buddy. And that's me. And I *will* be good, too," he concluded in a tone suddenly drained of emotion, thoughtful, almost philosophic, "because I *am* good. Right?"

For a moment Colonel Trasker did not reply, automatically nodding to several more secretaries as they walked along toward the astronauts' parking lot, automatically checking the Corvettes, Porsches, Sting-Rays and Jaguars, noting that Hank Barstow and Bert Richmond were already there, noticing also that "Gaudy" Gaudet and Pete Balkis were on the premises, waving to Astroscientist J. V. Halleck as he unfolded his limber length from the Aston Martin he and Monetta had recently purchased.

Then he glanced directly at the angry colleague at his side.

"Certainly you're good," he said crisply. "Nobody's ever denied that. And I'll be happy to have you as second in command, if it comes out that way. But I tell you one thing, Jazz. If you think you can pressure your way in, you're wrong. It's going to be a big crew—NASA wants twelve, at least—and there's lots of room to hide you in it, you know, if you get headquarters mad. There's nothing says you've got to be No. 2. Not even your friends in the press and on the Hill. Now, why don't you calm down, and we'll talk it over with Hank and Bert—"

"*You* talk it over with them," Commander Weickert suggested coldly. "They're your pals, they always have been from the very first day we came into the program together. You tell them you want me, Connie. They won't say no."

"You know damned well they'll say no if they want to," Colonel Trasker said as they reached the other side of the parking lot and started across the street to the entrance.

"And anyway," Jazz said, "*you* don't want me. You don't want me on the crew at all, let alone as second in command. Isn't that right, old buddy?"

"Jazz," Colonel Trasker said as he pulled the door open for him, "all of this is an administrative decision. You know how it operates." He made his tone deliberately light and sarcastic. "The in-puts come from everywhere, and out of them all comes this miracle—*us.*"

"Yeah," Jazz said shortly. "Well. Some inputs are more powerful than other inputs. You tell Mr. God Senior and Mr. God Junior when you meet in that office upstairs that I intend to be on that crew and in just the spot I want to be in, or I'll scream so loud they'll hear it from here to Tranquillity Base and back."

Colonel Trasker sighed and shook his head.

"In all the years I've known you, you've never gotten anywhere this way. Why are you still trying?"

"Because I haven't always tried this way," Jazz Weickert said, and suddenly his face looked quite naked with pain, "and you know it. I've been a good boy, and I've been part of the team, and I haven't blown my stack in public, and I've taken more crap than anybody. And I'm just not taking any more. O.K.?"

"But it hasn't all been just us—" Connie Trasker began. And again he stopped as he had before, because in a sense it was hopeless, certainly hopeless to get through to a man convinced he had always been right and tell him that somehow, in some way nobody could entirely define, he had so often been wrong. "But I suppose," he amended quietly, "in large part it has been. I'll talk to Hank and Bert."

"Do that little thing," Commander Weickert told him coldly, turning away down the hall as they reached the elevator. "It could save a lot of trouble."

For a moment Connie Trasker stared after him before he responded.

"It could," he agreed, softly and to himself. "But it won't."

Above them in the cavern of the sky the tiny satellite came and went in a second, its message becoming more unmistakable and more insistent on each pass around the globe.

Yet the somnolent, uneasy calm so characteristic of NASA in these in-between years would remain unchanged for a few more hours, for the message, as yet, had not traveled very far. To Dr. Vernon Hertz at the Jet Propulsion Lab in Pasadena its possible implications were becoming clear as he read the first print-out from the computers and scanned the first hazy images taking shape from the steady transmissions of the high-resolution cameras on board the satellite. But even he was not quite sure what they portended, though he was beginning to have a good idea.

The knowledge, as he snapped off the Picturephone after passing the word to his brother—the one man to whom he always confided everything first, and who always reciprocated—gave him a gloomy feeling, for it simply meant that now Bob and his friends in Houston would be riding high again.

As a scientist, Vernon Hertz did not approve of this; and as Director of JPL, and so in a sense the paramount spokesman for the scientific community within NASA, he did not approve of it either, for it meant an abrupt intensification of the constant battle for funds and program priorities which the scientists had seemed to be winning in the past few years. It was obvious at once that Bob understood this. He had been disturbed, initially, by the implicit challenge to the nation. This reaction had been followed almost immediately by a barely concealed excitement as he realized that now his beloved astronauts and their beautiful monstrous missiles would once more be in command of the space program.

"Understand me," he had said earnestly, with something of the same innocent deviousness with which he had long ago concealed the "borrowing" of a baseball bat or the placing of a frog in his brother's bed, "I don't mean that the unmanned probes won't be even more important now. It's just that obviously, if this means what we think it does, my boys are going to have to have the major share of funds. At least for the next year or so."

"At least for the next decade or so, if I know you guys in Houston," Vernon Hertz retorted. "I guess it's back to beans and short rations for us test-tube types."

"Not at all——" Bob began stoutly. Then his eyes filled with their characteristic twinkle of amusement and he gave his infectious, lopsided grin. "Why, certainly," he agreed blandly. "Isn't that the proper balance of the universe?"

"Proper balance of my hat," his brother told him. "You know damned well without us scientists you wouldn't be able to make a landing on Catalina, let alone the planets. Our probes have to go there first and look it over, then you guys come along and rake off the glory. Some deal!"

"Very nice from our standpoint," Bob Hertz said cheerfully.

"This time, however," Vernon said, "things are going to be different. I want some scientists on that expedition."

"I think you have a perfect right to have them," Bob said, turning serious. "That's been the plan right along."

"It was the plan on the Moon expeditions, too," Vernon pointed out, "and then it got washed down the drain by the Astronaut office."

"Well," Bob said, "I wasn't for that, either."

"But it happened," his brother said. "How do we know it won't happen this time? After all, things are suddenly going to be pretty rough, now."

"All I can do is give you my word I'll fight for it," Bob said, "and so will a lot of others, including, I think, Connie Trasker, who is going to be in command."

"How does he feel about the astroscientists?"

"As near as I can gather, he judges them as all the astronauts do: on what they can do. Capability rates high around here, you know."

"Capability isn't everything on an eighteen-month

30

flight," Vernon remarked. "How do they get along personally?"

"Very well, on the whole," Bob said.

"What about my boys Pete Balkis and Jayvee Halleck?"

"Jayvee doesn't get along too well with much of anybody," Bob said promptly. "I'm not so sure you made a good decision that time. I can understand your motives, and all that, but I wonder in this case if the material matches the motives. Pete, on the other hand, is a great guy and everybody loves him. He's moody now and then, but he gets over it. Jayvee never seems to."

"He has a chip on his shoulder," Vernon Hertz admitted, "but that's understandable."

"Fully. But perhaps, here, there isn't much place for chips on shoulders."

"You mean there aren't any in the corps?" his brother inquired dryly. "That isn't what my spies tell me."

"We're human, behind the image," Bob said, his grin returning. "Anyway, I'll grant you there is a place for the Jayvee Hallecks of this world. Whether it's in this program, I'm not sure—and I know all the reasons, practical, historical, moral, ethical, religious, humanitarian and political, why there should be."

"He's an excellent scientist," Vernon said flatly.

"He is that," Bob agreed.

"I want him on that expedition."

"I'll try for you, but you know I'm just one voice among many—"

"Yes, I know," Vernon Hertz said. "I know how NASA works when it comes to crew selection. Hank and Bert and Connie put their heads together and come up with a decision and then you and Jim Cavanaugh shoot it along to Washington and the Administrator gets out that big rubber stamp that says APPROVED, BECAUSE THE ASTROS WILL RAISE HELL IF I DON'T, and that's that. Don't tell me you can't get Jayvee on that flight if you want to."

"I've said I'll do my best, and I will. With some misgivings but I will. Maybe the responsibility will calm him down."

"I'll talk to him," Vernon said. "He owes me a lot."

"They don't take kindly to being reminded of it," Bob said.

"Nonetheless," his brother said firmly, "he owes me the

effort to behave and co-operate. I'm going to cash in my I.O.U.'s with that boy, if I can get him on the flight."

"Good luck."

"Pete doesn't need any morale-building, does he?"

"Pete," Bob Hertz said, "is absolutely fine."

"He's reliable," Vernon said with satisfaction. Behind his shoulder Bob could see a harried-looking member of the JPL computer staff come in with a roll of tape from the machines and put it on his brother's desk. Vernon glanced down, then up into the Picturephone.

"It's getting more definite by the minute," he said. "I'd better call Washington. Take care, and keep in touch."

"Constantly," Bob Hertz said. "Give the Administrator my love."

"He'll be happy to have it," his brother said dryly as his face began to fade from the screen. "He's going to need all he can get from now on."

But in these last few minutes when headquarters, like the rest of NASA, and indeed the rest of political Washington, could relax in the knowledge that the space program was moving along with no particular headaches save the usual ones of money and morale, the Administrator was not aware that he was going to stand in need of any special affection and support from his colleagues.

Dr. "Andy" Anderson (The first name was really William, but NASA, without deliberately trying, seemed to nickname everybody. This had the happy effect of increasing the homespun, old-shoe image that formed such a perfect backdrop for fantastic heroism and achievement.) felt, with plenty of justification, that he was already a very popular and well-liked man. He had been in his job about two years, now, and everything he had done had seemed to add to his stature in Washington. He lacked Jim Webb's fireball enthusiasm and Tom Paine's good-humored flair for public relations, but in his own quietly amiable way he was equally tough, equally dedicated and equally determined that the program should get its fair share in the endless interagency jostle for funds.

To date he had been very successful, given the limitations placed upon NASA by the cautious former President and now by his more free-swinging and possibly less principled successor.

Like everyone in NASA, however, the Administrator

was not really satisfied with the rate of progress; believed with all his heart that the country should be engaged already in an all-out drive to get to Mars; could not abominate the carping voices in the press and on the Hill (he was about to entertain two of them now, as soon as he finished with his present visitor, and did not relish the prospect one little bit), that constantly derogated the program and clamored that its funds should be spent on the cities and the minorities; and in general took the straight NASA line that there was nothing on earth more important or more exciting or more worthwhile than to push the perimeters of mankind's venturings forever outward.

This made him a very popular man at headquarters, in Houston, Huntsville, the Cape and in all the many contractors' and subcontractors' offices around the country. "Andy will get it done if anybody can," had become a major article of NASA faith; and if neither NASA nor Andy were ever quite satisfied that he did as much as should be done, it was generally recognized that this was due to the inhibitions imposed by the White House and not to any lack of desire or drive on his part.

On the Hill he was also very popular, aided immeasurably, as his predecessors had been, by the fact that both the House and Senate space committees were headed by men as imbued as himself with the mystique of the program. In the House, "my committee," as he was wont to call it privately within NASA, was chaired by James L. Satterthwaite of Wyoming, a gentleman whose shrewd political sense and patient diplomacy were as impressive as his white hair and stately six-foot presence. In the Senate, "my committee" was led by the courtly, pleasant and quietly tenacious John Able Winthrop of Massachusetts, a man who said little and accomplished much for space, despite the increasingly open attacks of such younger opportunists as Kennicutt Williams of Indiana, who saw in space vs. the cities and the blacks the sort of issue from which presidential timber might be grown.

The thought of Kenny Williams made the Administrator frown. He and his most insufferable supporter in the press were due in about twenty minutes. Andy did not look forward to their visit.

Nor, as a matter of fact, did he regard with any particular relish the gentleman who faced him now across his desk; although, given various earnest calls for international brotherhood that had recently come from the White House—and the usual blandly equivocal response that had come back from Moscow—he felt it was his duty to do his bit, skeptical though he was of the whole business.

Round head, bushy hair, small face, little eyes, pug nose, a heartily tricky geniality that promised everything and delivered nothing: the map and manner of modernday Muscovy confronted him. Academician Alexei V. Kuselevsky had dropped by for a visit after a State Department-sponsored tour of Houston, Huntsville and the Cape.

Dr. Anderson was resigned to half an hour of the same sort of sparring that had gone on at every such meeting between spokesmen for the two space powers in the past twenty years. Never once in all that time had the Soviet Union offered one genuine piece of sincere cooperation with the United States. The United States, under the clamorous proddings of such as Kenny Williams and the journalistic pal who would be accompanying him here, had tired time and again to work out a genuine exchange of information: never once had there been anything but rebuff. Yet once again the President had bowed to the clamor and made the futile and foredoomed attempt.

Andy's reaction paralleled that of several of the astronauts when they were notified of Kuselevsky's impending visit to Houston. All-American Boys had used not very nice four-letter Anglo-Saxon words to express their impatience. "One more God-damned charade," Hank Barstow had summed it up, and Andy knew he spoke for his colleagues, because several of them told him so. Hank had spoken for him too, the Administrator had confessed, but it had to be suffered. Now they had done their duty, and he had to do his. He took out a pack of Safecigs and offered one to his visitor with a smile that he hoped would be accepted as reasonably friendly.

"Try these, Alexei," he suggested. "Officially declared 90 per cent nicotine-free but hopped up with a tiny trace of benzedrine, just enough to be non-addictive but still give you a little lift."

Academician Kuselevsky grinned.

"One more marvelous American attempt to have one's cake and eat it too. But, no, thank you, Andy. In my work, I must remain alert and as clear-headed as possible."

"Mine, too," the Administrator told him pleasantly. "I hope our people were kind to you at the various space centers."

"They could not have been more so," Alexei said. "They were superb. The visitor from abroad is always moved by your American friendliness and openness."

"Too bad we aren't equally moved in other places," Dr. Anderson observed, but if he had hoped to provoke some response from his visitor, he was disappointed. As of course he knew he would be. Alexei simply grinned again, looking more than ever like a big, amiable, roly-poly puppy dog.

"You are always welcome," he said blandly. "Always welcome, as we move side by side upon this great venture of mankind to the outer-most galaxies."

"Are you going there already?" Dr. Anderson inquired in mock surprise. "That seems a very ambitious undertaking, so early in the game."

"When, as Dr. Von Braun so movingly put it prior to Apollo 11," Kuselevsky said, "we are still at a stage comparable to 'that moment in evolution when aquatic life came up on the land.' Ah, yes. Well: one must always think ahead."

"To Mars, logically," the Administrator suggested, and decided to indulge himself in a blunt and straightforward question, since it wouldn't be answered truthfully anyway. "How near are you to launch?"

Alexei smiled and became suddenly earnest.

"Not as close as we would like to be." He sighed. "It is so difficult—the bureaucracy, the red tape, the problems with the military—"

"I thought you had appeased them with Space Station *Stalin*," Andy remarked. "Surely they can't complain about that, circling over your heads every two hours and spying on everything we do."

"We are not the only one with spies!" Kuselevsky retorted sharply. Then his tone became amicable again. "Be that as it may," he said with a deliberate lightness, "you know the military—they always want more. Except when, as is the case in your own country, there is such a close working relationship between so-called 'peaceful uses of space' and the desires of the militaristic-plutocraticimperialistic group who wish to dominate the skies and the solar system as well as the world."

I will not let him put me on the defensive, the Administrator told himself. Despite his resolve a slight but noticeable edge appeared in his reply.

"It is not we who rehabilitated the reputation of a mass murderer and gave his name to a space station that has every potential for threatening the nations of the world," he remarked, and now it was his visitor's turn to lose his careful congeniality. A distinct flush began to suffuse the round peasant face.

"And when have we threatened the world with it? It is entirely for peaceful, scientific purposes! Prove that we have ever threatened the world with it!"

"The mere fact that it is there, with your history behind it, threatens the world," the Administrator said flatly. "But," he conceded more calmly, "I will admit there has been no overt threat. Much to our surprise."

"Very well," Kuselevsky said, breathing a little heavily. "You admit it, then, there has been none. So why disturb our pleasant relationships with such unworthy suspicions? And why can we not talk about Space Station *Mayflower,* if you wish to discuss space stations?"

"Mayflower!" the Administrator said, and for a second his annoyance with his own people, a supercautious President and a budget-cutting Congress, broke through. "That puny thing one-fifth the size of yours! A couple of old Saturn third stages linked together and eight men shuttling back and forth on a series of poorly funded scientific experiments! What kind of worry is that to you?"

"We do not know it is all that innocent," Kuselevsky said with an infuriating smugness. "You say so, but we do not know it."

"Go up and look," Dr. Anderson suggested sharply. "We'll run you up any time you like and you can see the whole thing. That's how threatening we are! All we ask is that you reciprocate and let us see yours."

"Ah, *ha!*" Alexei cried, and the Administrator had a distinct mental picture of a Great Dane pouncing on a mouse. "Always there is a bargain! Always there is some deal! Always there is something to be gained, always some advantage; Always there is something devious, something tricky! Why do you not let us, as you put it, 'run up and see it any time we like' without all these strings and equivocations? Why are you always demanding things from us? Why are you afraid to be open and honest, as we are? Why, I ask you, old friend of the space program, *why?"*

For a moment the Administrator contemplated blowing his stack and aborting the mission, as his friends in Houston would put it. Then he shrugged, quite openly, because what was the use? His face relaxed in a smile, he looked at Academician Kuselevsky with an open and knowing grin that he knew must annoy. He meant it to.

"Alexei, old friend, you people take the cake, you really do. You win all the honors at double-talk, and I really know better than to try to compete. So: you're planning your launch to Mars about—oh, about next week, is that right?"

Just for a split second he thought he saw in the little, flat eyes the reaction he thought he might see if he watched them very, very closely; but then it was gone, if it had ever existed. Alexei relaxed into yet another of his amiable grins.

"Now, what a stupid idea!" he commented airily. "Really, how stupid. It will take us years to mount such an effort, as you know very well—just as long, probably, as it will take you. Really, Andy, you are indulging in space-dreams, now. Awake, dear friend! Come back to reality. Rejoin me here on simple, mundane, practical Earth."

"Yes," Dr. Anderson remarked. "I shall try to act very surprised, if it happens."

"My friend," Academician Kuselevsky said solemnly, "I give you my word, I give you the word of the Union of Socialist Soviet Republics, that no launch to Mars is planned for next week, next month, next year, or probably"—he smiled in a whimsical way—"next decade. Space Station *Stalin* will continue to conduct its experiments, Space Station *Mayflower* will continue to conduct its experiments, the Sun, the planets, the galaxies will keep moving on their appointed paths—life will go on. Is it not so, now and forever?"

The Administrator smiled.

"So it has always been assumed. What did you want to see me for, anyway, Alexei?"

"Courtesy," Academician Kuselevsky said, rising and extending his hand. "Merely courtesy. To thank you for the kindness shown me by all your people in NASA—to express gratitude for the tour you arranged for me so kindly—to 'touch base,' as you people say. And of course to invite you to come and see us at your earliest convenience."

"With pleasure, as always," Dr. Anderson said, rising also, shaking hands. "I'll be looking forward to that visit to Space Station *Stalin*."

"So tenacious!" Alexei V. Kuselevsky said with a merry laugh as he turned to the door. "So persistent! No wonder you are such a good and indomitable Administrator for America's space program!"

But good and indomitable was not what Andy Anderson felt as he returned to his desk to find Vernon Hertz and his news on the Picturephone. Instead he felt rather like a fool, though not exactly a surprised one.

He told his secretary to stall Senator Williams and his journalistic friend for a little while so that he could talk to the directors in Huntsville, the Cape and Houston. Then he began to feel angry. Which was not, perhaps, such a bad emotion with which to face what the country and NASA were now going to have to face.

In Huntsville, where the George C. Marshall Space Flight Center sits among the soft green fields and gently rolling hills of northeastern Alabama like some stately industrial plantation, nobody was very angry with anybody on this particular fateful day.

In "the Von Braun Hilton," as the administration building was still commonly called in in-house slang, the brilliant gentleman for whom it was named no longer guided its destinies from the huge office on the ninth floor, but his determined spirit lingered on. Control of Huntsville still rested firmly in the hands of what was known throughout NASA as "the Peenemünde Group," and its basic purpose was still to do the designing and technical work on the great missiles that sent Americans into the heavens. Here, too, a certain state of doldrums existed, brought on by reduced funds and the consequent necessity of working with a substantially reduced staff; but as single-mindedly, efficiently and impersonally as they had once worked at Peenemünde to send V-2s raining upon England, its top directors and managers now devoted themselves to the plans and drawings necessary to create new and dramatic vehicles for the United States journey to the planets.

They were all aware that it might be quite a few years before this could be accomplished, but they had learned from long experience with the Americans that you could never be sure. Sometimes the timetable speeded up amazingly and things got done much faster than anyone had believed possible. It was always well to be ready.

The present Director, Dr. Hans Sturmer, swiveling about in his chair to stare out across the spring-lush countryside that was one of the morale-building joys of Huntsville, did not conceive at this moment of any such breakthrough. But with the tidy and efficient spirit that characterized him and those who had come with him from the collapsing Nazi nightmare in the dying days of World War II, he made sure every day that, at least in the operation for which he was responsible, it would take only a few words of German snapped into five or six key Picturephones on the base, and Huntsville would be alert and ready to roll.

Here within the boundaries of the Army's Redstone Arsenal, where America's first missiles had been made ready to fly, and where something of the original exclusiveness of this fact still lingered on (fortified by the intellectual and racial clannishness of the Peenemünde Group), there was a certain amount of the usual NASA division between the dreamers and the engineers. But here the two conflicting points of view were brought as nearly into harmony as could be possible in the space program, for here the dreamers and the engineers were frequently the same. Here they knew dreams could come true, because here they had been given the funds and the freedom to make them come true. The funds, until recently, had never been a problem; and the freedom, after a few pitched battles in the early days with Houston, Washington and the Cape, had never really been in question.

Administrators and directors came and went at all the other centers, but at Huntsville the Peenemünde Group ruled on. It was true that its members were getting inexorably older, that some had already dropped away because of age and infirmity, that there were very few successors among the younger officials who came from the old country who had the old country's rigid dedication to duty and efficiency. The Peenemünde Group, before age brought inevitable dissolution, would still be around long enough to help America get to Mars. That was not too bad a return,

Hans Sturmer thought, for the things America had done for them.

For these, he and the Peenemünde Group were quietly but profoundly grateful. To those within NASA and outside it—and they were many—who could never quite understand the puzzle of men who in one moment of time were busily helping Hitler attempt to destroy democracy, and in the next had turned completely around and were with equal dedication helping democracy reach for the planets, Dr. Sturmer and his colleagues never bothered to comment or offer explanation. Many of them never made any conscious rationalization, for theirs was not the type of mind that needed rationalization to support what common sense proposed. But when they did, two factors seemed uppermost. The first was the money. They were scientists, and to them their dreams and experiments meant everything: whoever would give them the money to experiment was their friend, and for him they would work as devotedly and determinedly as they had for Hitler.

The second motivation was somewhat deeper and, to their credit, more worthy. There were many in NASA who, in moments of jealousy or annoyance, would refer to the Peenemünde Group as cold-blooded opportunists who had surrendered to the Americans rather than the Russians after World War II simply because the United States could give them more money. But thinking back on the frantic discussions that had finally persuaded them to follow Dr. Wernher von Braun into the American camp, Dr. Sturmer felt that there had been something more. An old historical fear and hatred of Russia, for one thing. More importantly, a genuine appreciation of the fact that the Americans, for all their haphazard ways and innumerable thoughtless and inexcusable mistakes, still possessed a basic decency and a very genuine devotion to intellectual and personal freedom that he and his fellow scientists felt they must have in order to live as functioning craftsmen and complete human beings.

Here in Alabama they had settled in, joined clubs, civic groups, little theaters and orchestras; sent their children to American schools and universities and, sometimes, been dismayed by the long-haired results. They had made a conscientious effort to adapt, to become part of the community, to become Americans; and if they and their wives still spoke mostly German among themselves, and if there was a certain air of intellectual and personal superiority that set them apart and made them sometimes seem smug and arrogant to this very day, then that, perhaps, was something inherent in them that could never be changed. At least they did their best to change it—did their best to be Americans—did their best to help America. And their help was not to be minimized. Without it, no American missile program could have gone so far so fast, or achieved so many technological triumphs unsurpassed in human history.

Secure in this knowledge, Hans Sturmer was preparing for what had become a typical Huntsville day: checking here and checking there, reviewing progress, making plans; plans that would not early see fruition, he believed, but which would be needed when the time came again, and should therefore be put in final form and neatly organized in Huntsville's many files, ready to go.

He was about to put in a call to one of his colleagues when his secretary interrupted on the voice override of the Picturephone to announce the Administrator from Washington. In a moment the pleasantly familiar face appeared. Dr. Sturmer could see at once that it wore an expression both disturbed and determined.

"Ja, Andy?" he said, concerned. "Is anything wrong?"

"Our meeting here in Washington tomorrow is going to be much more vital than we thought," Dr. Anderson said. "Vernon Hertz just called and he says—"

Two minutes later having listened gravely to the news, Dr. Sturmer permitted himself a small, rather spiteful smile.

"Albrecht," he observed, "is going to have to build himself another launching pad."

And as it happened, that was exactly what Dr. Albrecht Freer, Director of Kennedy Space Center on Merritt Island, in Florida, was contemplating at the moment, although not with any idea that he would soon see anything done about it. Right now, it was simply an excuse to get out of the office, even if it only meant plunging into the Florida heat. Already in mid-spring the climate was becoming heavy and oppressively humid, but at least it provided a change from the endless frustrating round of discussions with which the top officials of KSC managed to keep themselves busy and persuade themselves that it was worthwhile staying in the program.

The exciting era of Mercury and Gemini was long gone, the thrilling days when Apollos 7, 8, 9, 10, and 11 were all launched within the short space of ten months were far behind. The present schedule of a Moon expedition or two (if they were lucky) each year, interspersed with an occasional unmanned satellite, was hardly enough to keep either the launch crews or the management at top pitch. KSC was becoming too sleepy and somnolent for him, Al Freer often thought. But of course now that he had succeeded Kurt Debus as Director he could never leave it, because for him as for all his colleagues of the Peenemünde Group, rocketry was his first, most lasting and most absorbing love. He could not live without the hope of seeing the great birds lift off once more in steady procession, their first landfall Mars, and then the outer planets.

Right now, he told himself as the motor-pool chauffeur drove him slowly along toward the now almost deserted Apollo launching sites, Pads A and B of Launch Complex 39, it was foolish of him to even contemplate asking Washington for funds to build another. The idea was simply an excuse to get out of the office and think. He knew he would not do anything about it. With Pads A and B idle most of the year, who could possibly justify Pad C? It was a pipe-dream.

Nonetheless, quietly and strictly on his own, he had asked the launch director to prepare a set of tentative plans for him. The launch director had been more than enthusiastic. Already Dr. Freer had received preliminary sketches, delivered privately to his home in Melbourne, twelve miles south of KSC along the beach. The rough drafts had inspired an excited, far-ranging discussion that had lasted until almost 3 A.M. "This is absurd, you know," Albrecht Freer had said when he finally bade his exhausted guest good night. "There is no reason at all for us to be even dreaming such things at this time."

"You must have a hunch, Al," the launch director told him, and he had nodded, with his hesitant, almost shy, smile.

"Maybe I do," he said. But he could not have said why that night, nor could he say why now, as he smiled at the driver and said politely, "I think I'd like to visit Pad B, if I may."

"Certainly, sir," the driver said, and in a moment they were rolling slowly along the deserted roadway beside the track where the huge crawler laboriously carried the missiles from the Vehicle Assembly Building to the pads—when there were any to carry.

"Not so many these days," he said aloud, and the driver, a young fellow from Cocoa Beach who had only recently joined NASA, smiled somewhat ruefully.

"No, sir," he said. "Not as many as when I was growing up. We used to see lots of them, then."

"Is it a good idea?" Dr. Freer asked. The driver shot him a quick look and shook his head.

"Not the way I see it," he said. "I think we ought to be sending a lot more out."

"It costs money," Albrecht Freer observed.

"They'll beat us if we don't," the driver said, and Dr. Freer, who had no need to ask who "they" were, nodded and sighed.

"Yes," he said. "It's possible. Just drop me by the gate, if you like. I can call for someone else to come and get me."

"I'll wait," the driver said with a smile. "Give me a chance to eat my lunch. Take your time, Doctor."

"Thank you," Al Freer said. "I won't be very long."

But as he registered with the lone guard at the entrance, received clearance, and put on the special badge that still was necessary for access to the pad, even for him and even in these stand-by days, he was not so sure. The pads always tended to make him moody, he had found, which was why it would probably be better if he stayed away. But they also held an endless fascination, stimulated his imagination and made him think. He was convinced their present desuetude would not last forever.

He walked slowly up the long ramp in the steaming heat. Away from the car's air conditioning, he took off his coat, loosened his tie, rolled up his shirtsleeves. Thunderheads climbed in the east, off the Bahamas: later it might storm. In the swamp beyond the pad he could see egrets, herons, water-turkeys, ducks. High above the pad, buzzards and sea gulls swung. Across the Indian River that divides Merritt Island from the beach, he saw the gantries of Cape Canaveral. Two or three were occupied by Titans and Atlas-Centaurs being readied for unmanned scientific launches. The rest stood as forlorn and deserted as his own Apollo pads here at KSC. A great effort had been arbitrarily choked down to half speed—or less. The indignation he often felt but usually suppressed welled up suddenly. He muttered something in harsh and angry German before he continued his slow walk up the long incline where so many brave men had traveled to keep their dates with the gleaming white giants that carried them into space.

Well: most of the brave men were still around, he reminded himself, and so were a good many of the dedicated support teams that had built their missiles and helped them fly. Many were hanging on because their whole major working lives had been in the space program and they knew nothing else. Still more were remaining because with them the dream of space was a matter of absolute faith and they could not conceive of careers that were not dedicated to making the dream come true. This was his own motivation, of course, as it was the motivation of most of the top men in NASA: the dream of going ever outward, ever beyond, the hope of penetrating some final secret of the universe that would make all things fall into place and become viable in some great, orderly scheme of things. Even though, rationally, as men understood reason, there still seemed no real justification for believing that there was anything in the solar system but a succession of dead and inhospitable worlds.

But if that were true, then what was the rationale that could explain why this one world, this lovely Earth, had been singled out of all the universe to receive green grass and thinking men? It did not make sense that this was the only fertile globe, here the only developed life. Yet even if it were, then all the more reason for going on and on until, at last, the fact was proved beyond all question, and man, robbed of his final excuse, would have no choice but to turn back upon himself and really come to grips with the passions, desires, ambitions, cupidities. hatreds, jealousies and greeds that made of his inestimable heritage the beautiful Earth so unhappy and fearful a place.

The Director of KSC stood for a long, silent time at the foot of the tower on Pad B. Ghostly voices called out the countdowns for ghostly launches; a succession of smiling, white-suited figures, most of them his personal friends and good companions in the great adventure, passed him on the ramp, climbed into the elevator, ascended the tower, stepped into their command modules and roared away in thunder and flame upon their awesome journeys.

He came back down twenty minutes later, firmly resolved to prepare formally, and submit to Washington, his plans for Pad C. His driver met him at the gate and he could tell from his manner that there was some emergency.

"Your office has just called for you on the intercom, Doctor," the young man said. "The Administrator wants you. They say it's urgent."

"I'll take it in my office in the VAB," Dr. Freer said. He made the quick ride in silence, an excitement that did not dare dream too much growing in his heart.

So, too, did excitement grow a few minutes later in Downey, California, at the sprawling plant of North American Rockwell Aviation, home of the command and service modules for the Apollo-Saturn program. There the production manager, Jim Matthison, had been going through one of his periodic spells of the space glooms, as his wife Betty referred to them. He was another veteran of the program who had supervised the building of a dozen sleek monsters and sent them on their way, then seen the program dwindle, the production lines grind to a halt, the skilled manpower fall away save for a skeleton crew kept on in the wistfully stubborn hope that sooner or later they would be needed again.

Hope, but not really belief—until ten minutes ago. Then his secretary had buzzed, he had snapped on the Picturephone. Andy Anderson had appeared.

"We've run into a little problem you're going to be interested in," Andy said without preliminary. "Better grab the company plane and get on back here tomorrow. We're having a meeting."

"What's the matter?" Jim asked, rather stupidly, he thought later. But the call had taken him completely by surprise, he hadn't heard from the Administrator directly in months.

"Nothing to tell you across the continent," Dr. Anderson said pleasantly. "Just get your tail back here."

"Yes, sir!" Jim Matthison said with a big grin, which

the Administrator had returned before he faded from the screen.

Now there was excitement at North American Rockwell too.

And still in Houston (except for Dr. Cavanaugh, to whom the Administrator was even then confirming officially the words he had already received privately from Bob Hertz) there was no excitement, only the private tensions which this day surrounded the Astronaut Office—a place where, in any event, excitement was usually reduced to monosyllables as a matter of habit, temperament and training.

The news that would cause genuine excitement, and even some whooping and horseplay when it finally came, still had not been given the men charged with selecting the crew for Planetary Fleet One of Project Argosy, or to the men who would be selected. In the long white corridors decorated with pictures of astronauts, pictures of the Earth, pictures of the Moon, pictures of Mars, pictures of missiles being launched and missiles in flight, it was, for the most part, just another typical day.

Many of the offices, most of them shared by two or more astronauts or astroscientists, were vacant. Some of the corps were working out in the simulators, either here or at the Cape: the cumbersome, fantastic machines that could duplicate almost every possible aspect of space flight and simulate almost every possible visual aspect of the planetary surfaces over which the flights took place. Some others were out on the endless speaking engagements that all the astronauts are constantly asked to undertake, either by NASA for its own public relations, or by the White House and Congress for the bolstering of political goals.

Astronauts spoke to the local Lions Club to assist Senator X or Congressman Y; astronauts were invited to the White House for well-publicized family get-togethers, to fortify the image of a President devoted to the program and bosom-chummy with its heroes; astronauts addressed high schools and colleges, scientific symposiums and industrial conventions, to increase NASA's prestige and win NASA new recruits. Somehow in and around and between all this, astronauts managed to do some of the work for which they were hired and attend to some of the serious business to which they had dedicated their lives.

46

On this particular day, seven were in the simulators at Houston and eight were in the simulators at the Cape. Six were training in Space Station *Mayflower*. Six were absent on speaking engagements around the United States. Four were visiting the plants of North American Rockwell and other major contractors on morale-building junkets. Six were on goodwill missions to Europe and Asia. Ten were in their offices in the building, reading scientific publications, studying flight plans, or autographing pictures of themselves and answering the fan mail that still came in a steady flow from all over the world. Three of these ten were thinking seriously about resigning.

Of these, the most agitated at the moment was Commander Alvin S. Weickert III, still brooding over his angry argument with Colonel Trasker. But although they were less obviously upset than he, Astroscientists J. V. Halleck and Petros S. Balkis carried an equally unhappy burden inside.

For Jazz Weickert, Connie Trasker's comments epitomized exactly the attitude which, to his mind, made further service in the program almost impossible. Smug, arrogant, inconsiderate of other people's feelings, dutifully doing the hatchet work of the NASA establishment with a sort of smooth, ruthless perfection—these, to Jazz, were Connie's major characteristics. They were, he suspected, the characteristics that had constantly thwarted his own chances for really good flights. They were the characteristics that had encouraged Hank Barstow and Bert Richmond to favor Connie over Jazz from the first day they had entered the program together. They were the characteristics that had turned those three into the Holy Trinity of the astronaut corps, placing them in an alliance with headquarters that gave them virtually unassailable authority to handle the corps just about as they pleased: to make sure that their favorites got the breaks and to guarantee for mavericks the cold and unhappy position of being part of the glamour without getting any of the action.

There was a reason why certain smiling faces kept turning up time and again before the cameras, to wave and fly away on famous missions: there was a reason why others time and again found themselves ignored and passed over. The public knew nothing of this, being in no position to penetrate the strong defensive barrier of silence that NASA and the corps erected around themselves; but within the corps, they knew who the favorites were. It was no secret in-house who could be sure of being assigned to good flights, and who could be certain of getting only secondary or back-up crew assignments that would never bring them the public attention, the historic fame and the good fortune so many sought within the program.

Jazz had seen this happen in the selection of crews for Mercury, Gemini and Apollo. It had happened so often to him, he sometimes told Clare bitterly, that he had lost count. She was always counseling him to have patience, always telling him to keep hoping, reminding him of his responsibilities to her and to Michael, John and Joanna, and telling him he must stay in the program for the family's sake, putting on a bright face for the other wives when they met in the Nassau Bay shopping center or gathered in Taylor Lake Village or El Lago or Timber Cove to keep up the spirits of crew wives during a flight.

He owed Clare a lot, he was still objective enough to admit, even though he, like others in the corps, at times was an astronaughty when he visited the Cape for long weeks of training, or traveled around the country on speaking engagements.

With very few exceptions, these casual episodes meant little. There had been very few divorces and not very many long-time attachments—"the image" was always there, omnipresent and controlling. Certain things you might do privately as a human being, but you maintained the image in public. You maintained it for the sake of your family and your own career, you maintained it also because somehow you sooner or later became so much a part of the program that you found it almost impossible to jeopardize it deliberately by your actions. You helped maintain the glamour because it was part of you, and because, when all was said and done, you really believed in it, as much as any Boy Scout collecting autographs or any wide-eyed, available college girl or newshen eager to bed down with heroes.

The program placed a heavy burden on marriages, he often thought, and one of the great ironies of life was that most of this came about simply because John Kennedy had wanted to do something nice for Lyndon Johnson when the latter was Vice-President and head of the National Aeronautics and Space Council. There was absolutely no reason on God's green earth why a vast separate establishment should have been set up in Houston, when at the Cape they had all the land and facilities necessary for the entire program. It was the most conspicuous of all NASA's redundancies, and in many ways the most wasteful, unnecessary and inexcusable. Because of it, the space program cost untold extra millions each year. Because of it, astronauts had to leave their families and travel two thousand miles for training and for launches that logically should all have occurred in one place, the Cape. Because of it, more than one astronaut had from time to time been placed under almost intolerable strain, and more than one mission had come closer to human failure than the public would ever know. And all caused by politics, plain and simple.

Jazz Weickert, sitting in his cluttered office, made a sound of deep and impatient disgust.

Yet for one disgusted with politics, he had himself become increasingly involved in the last few months as the time for the selection of the crew of Piffy One drew near.

About a year ago he had made up his mind that there was only one way to avoid being passed over for the first Mars flight, and that was to enlist enough powerful outside support so that Hank and Bert and Connie wouldn't dare give him the shaft again. He had spoken in Indianapolis—the Administrator was always ready to have him speak, he thought bitterly, no matter how often he concurred in the misuse of his training and abilities—and after the banquet ended he had been invited by Senator Kennicutt Williams and his principal journalistic supporter to join them for a private drink and talk. Under their kind and sympathetic questioning, he had said rather more than he should have, perhaps, about his resentment of the internal politics of NASA and the corps.

From that evening may have stemmed the series of critical weekly editorials in Percy Mercy's hodgepodge publication *View*, which had given NASA and the program's supporters in Congress so much concern in recent months. From it too, quite possibly, had come the series of speeches by Kenny Williams in which he had begun to establish carefully for himself a position of pious concern about the space program's cost "when so many of our domestic problems cry out for adequate funds and urgent Federal concern."

Maybe what he had done that night, Jazz thought, had been wrong. But, damn it, if NASA didn't want people to be bitter, why did they treat people in ways that made them bitter? Specifically, why had they treated him that way?

He had tried many times to determine just where he had got off on the wrong foot with Hank and Bert and Connie, but for the life of him he never could. They had come into the program on the same day, had gone through training together, had even flown together on a couple of flights. Then Hank and Bert had moved into administrative positions, Connie had been put in command of an Apollo, and things had subtly but definitely changed. Possibly it had been because Hank and Bert had grown a little pompous in their new responsibilities, Connie a little ruthless in his fame, while to Jazz every one in his astronaut "class" was still on the same level and he could see no reason for treating them any differently. Possibly it was because to Jazz his personal life, which involved sports NASA considered dangerous for an astronaut, such as deep-sea diving and water skiing, was his own business and he made it clear in sometimes sharp terms that he was one astronaut who would have none of NASA's quivering mother-hen-ism. Possibly it was because he made no bones about taking his complaints to the press, when enterprising reporters broke through NASA's silken curtain to ask him. Maybe it was all of these, and more. But whatever it was, from that time on he began to get the short end of it, and no complaints behind the curtain or in public made any difference.

And yet along with it came a bland and infuriating recognition on the part of headquarters and his colleagues that he was indeed, as he had told Connie this morning, damned good. No one trained more rigorously, no one studied more diligently, no one was more cool and reliable on a flight. "If I were still flying," Bert Richmond had said with his slow, amiable grin, when *Newsweek* asked him, "there's no one I'd rather have beside me than Jazz." "Jazz is tops in efficiency, skill and reliability," Hank Barstow had said in the same interview (an inquiring but inconclusive little piece entitled, "Whatever Became of the Forgotten Astronaut?" which had appeared a couple of years ago). "We look forward to more great things from Jazz," the Administrator said with a friendly smile.

But here Jazz was, out in the cold.

This time, though, he wasn't going to take it.

This time, as he had told Connie, judged on ability, experience, seniority, reliability or any other standard, he deserved the No. 2 position on Piffy One and he either intended to have it or to make the final break and resign.

This was NASA's last chance with Jazz Weickert, he told himself grimly, unaware that news was on the way, and events were already moving, that would give him what he wanted in a strange, ironic, frightful way.

Elsewhere along the corridors in Houston where heroes found themselves brought down to size by the humdrum of endless paperwork, two others felt something of the same disillusion Jazz felt, though neither had been in the program a fifth of the time he had. J. V. Halleck and Pete Balkis were unhappy, too, and essentially their complaint came down to the same thing: a feeling that they weren't being used, a conviction that Mother NASA, aided and abetted by the Chief of the Astronaut office, Hank Barstow, and the Director of Flight Crew Operations, Bert Richmond, was deliberately wasting their skills, their abilities and their precious years of optimum vigor and accomplishment.

For Jayvee Halleck (somewhere along the way from Greensboro, North Carolina the nickname based on his initials had acquired the pronunciation *Jay*vee rather than Jay*vee*) this feeling was increased by a personality basically so taut that many of his fellow astronauts and astroscientists wondered how he had ever been accepted in the program in the first place.

"I'll tell you why," he had once snapped to Emerson Wacker when the subject came up, politely but pointedly, during an idle moment in the Mars Landing Module simulator at the Cape. "Because NASA needed a black for the sake of its precious public image, that's why." Em Wacker had given him a sidelong glance and an amiable smile. "Oh, really?" he had asked with a kindly but somehow skeptical air that had annoyed Jayvee even more. "Yes, really!" he said sharply and they had exchanged no further word that day aside from the impersonal queries and responses of the training.

Because of episodes like this, and for many other reasons, the program's only Negro had very soon acquired among his colleagues a reputation as a very prickly man it was generally wise to stay away from as much as possible. The disposition of the corps at first had been to welcome him with the same tolerance and friendliness that greeted all newcomers: the assumption was that since you had passed NASA's exhaustive mental, physical and psychological tests, you must be good to begin with. You were then given a few months of grace during which everybody kept an eye on you and it was up to you to make it or break it on your own merits. Presently—not in any formal way, but just in casual talk along the corridors, in the comfortable homes around Clear Lake and in the Astronaut Office—you were judged by your peers and placed in the proper category. You were one of the aces, one of the good guys, one of the reliables, one of the doubtfuls, one of the sad sacks or one of the "three per cent of ass-draggers." Once categorized, there you stayed, forever after.

Jayvee Halleck somehow didn't quite fit anywhere; and while his colleagues often denied vehemently to one another that his color had anything to do with their inability to decide where he belonged, he was convinced with an inner burning anger that his color had everything to do with it.

Given such an attitude, which was compounded of many typical hurts in his youth in North Carolina that had finally knotted themselves into one big permanent ball of hurts and resentments against the white world, it was probably indeed a miracle that he had been accepted for the program at all. If Vernon Hertz had not taken a direct personal interest, he probably would not have been; and, true enough, if his color had not been an extra recommendation to add to and increase Vernon Hertz' support, even then he might have been rejected. His mistake lay in thinking that his color had been the paramount consideration. It had helped, but without the initial impetus of Dr. Hertz' interest, he would never have made it.

This interest, at first quite impersonal when Jayvee had appeared at California Institute of Technology as a very bright church-scholarship student from Greensboro, had soon become more active when Vernon Hertz discovered that his new pupil possessed really unusual scientific abilities. His interest in aerospace and planetary sciences, Vernon's own field, made it almost inevitable that when Vernon was chosen to succeed Dr. Pickering as head of the Jet Propulsion Lab, Jayvee Halleck should have gone along as one of his bright young assistants. By then he was a graduate student with the highest academic honors, already married to Monetta Rudden, a fellow student from Los Angeles, and apparently well on his way to becoming one of the country's leading scientists in the increasingly important field of extraterrestrial exploration. It was an area in which he could operate virtually alone: the abrasive, self-defensive personality did not have too much chance to show itself to others, there.

For about a year he had been involved in what he now considered the happiest period of his life, assisting Vernon Hertz in the ever-expanding operatives of JPL as its unmanned probes roamed further and further into the solar system, photographed and recorded the unpromising secrets of the planets, gradually acquired increasing congressional and popular support as the planets appeared more and more to be inhospitable to man. During the course of this year he and Monetta formed a reasonably comfortable friendship with another of Dr. Hertz' protégés, Petros Balkis, a doctor involved in the medical-biological aspects of space exploration, and his wife Helen. About the time Pete and Helen got their divorce and Pete began to drift away from the friendship in some subtle but definite way, Vernon Hertz got the idea that was to rearrange drastically both Jayvee's life and Pete's: he decided it would be a great thing if they went into the astronaut program. Being, like his brother in Houston, a man in the habit of getting what he wanted, he had overwhelmed their protests with a flood of logical argument. Presently they found themselves reporting to the Astronaut Office to embark upon the activities that would change, in the final event irrevocably, both their lives.

Why he had succumbed to Vernon's persuasions, Jayvee was not quite sure now as he sat in his office and stared moodily out the window toward the Lunar Receiving Lab and the Space Sciences complex. The Director of JPL had been most persuasive as he argued that the manned space flight program was inevitably going to have to become more scientifically oriented if it wanted to retain its share of funds and public support. He had pointed out that the higher the caliber of astroscientists, the higher the caliber of science. He had predicted that brilliant scientists who had received the public exposure and fame that came with successful space missions would be in a much better position, either to dominate the program later on, or to return to much more influential roles in the scientific world after completing their service with NASA. He had mentioned with a jocular air that he thought it would be wonderful "if I have a couple of my JPL boys on the inside down there in Houston. You can help me keep an eye on my brother Bob."

The only thing he had not stressed was that he had also felt for a long time that the program was, as he put it privately to Bob, "color-blind—it can only see white." Surprisingly for one whose life was spent in science, Vernon Hertz was quite perceptively attuned to the needs and necessities of American politics in the concluding decades of the twentieth century. He was also a fair-minded man, and it simply did not seem right to him that all of America's space triumphs should be in one color.

It was true that there had been a couple of Negroes in the program in the earlier days. One had been killed in a plane crash, one had quietly resigned. The official explanation—that certain technical skills and abilities were necessary, and that those who were found not to have them simply did not remain in the program—had always struck Vernon Hertz as honest, factual—but more than a little heartless. He could understand that certain aspects of flight training required an absolute concentration and devotion to detail, an absolute self-confident ability to make split-second decisions, an absolute ability to move instinctively and move fast. And yet surely there were those who could qualify—surely NASA hadn't tried quite hard enough to find them and bring them into the program. Particularly now, when the program was becoming increasingly hospitable to the astroscientist, as distinct from the pilot-astronaut. Particularly now when Washington was contemplating Mars flights of twelve men or more. Surely now there was ample room in the corps for a reasonable proportion of qualified Negroes. And surely none could be more qualified than Jayvee Halleck.

Only once had Dr. Hertz expressed any such idea, even indirectly, to Jayvee, and that was to indicate cautiously that, "You can do a lot of good in the corps for the United States."

"As a pet black astronaut?" Jayvee had responded with an ironic smile.

"And for your own people," Dr. Hertz replied, unabashed. "It's about time the blacks had somebody in this show."

"It's too late," Jayvee said. But later he had thought it over; and now he could see that this had probably been the clinching argument in his own mind.

So he and Pete—upon whom Vernon Hertz had apparently used some other equally compelling argument that carried decisive weight with one who described himself quizzically as "a Greek loner from Tarpon Springs"—had sent in their applications. And with the help of Bob Hertz, who agreed with his brother's reasoning on most points, their papers had been processed with unusual speed and they had been rushed through the tests, which they had passed with outstanding proficiency. Two months after applying, they had been accepted in the program.

And here, ever since, they had sat, waiting for what they regarded as the promised use of Jayvee's scientific capabilities and Pete's medical skills.

By now they had been through their basic astronaut training, had qualified as pilots, had done their time in the simulators and in *Mayflower*, had performed their share of public appearances around the country, had studied flight plans until they could recite them backward—and still they sat. In this they were no different from most of their colleagues, but they felt they deserved something more. Veron Hertz' persuasions and Bob Hertz' assistance had given them both, perhaps unfortunately, the idea that they would receive preferred treatment.

Today Jayvee in his office, and Pete Balkis studying Mars over in the map division, had about reached the conclusion that this would not happen, and that they had better ways to use their time. Like all the corps, they were aware that the crew selections for Planetary Fleet One were about to begin, but neither had received the slightest indication that he might be considered. Neither was the sort to fawn, beg or play politics in order to get the assignment. Neither would have dreamed of deliberately seeking outside assistance as Jazz Weickert had done. Both were convinced they would be passed over.

In this, one would prove correct and one be mistaken, in the first event. Later, fates as ironic as those which toyed with Jazz would bring them all to their strange, and for the moment quite inconceivable, rendezvous with Piffy One.

"And now, gentlemen," the Adminstrator said, rising to greet his visitors with a cordial smile and a friendly handshake, "I think we can settle down to a little talk. It's been a rather hectic morning for me, and I appreciate your waiting so patiently."

"Hectic?" Senator Kennicut Williams asked with a certain alert surprise. "I never knew things were hectic down here at NASA any more. I thought you just drifted along. What's up?"

"He must know something we don't know," Percy Mercy agreed as he deposited his tidy little person neatly in a chair and clasped his hands about one knee. "He must certainly know something we don't know."

"Percy," the Administrator said with a carefully noncommittal expansiveness as he lighted a Safecig and settled back behind his desk, "all I know is that *View* is giving us one hell of a time these days. What I want to find out is, why? I hope you've come here to tell me."

"He doesn't have to explain," Senator Williams remarked somewhat belligerently. "It's a free country."

"And as for you, Kenny," Andy Anderson said comfortably, "it's getting so you give us hell every hour on the hour in your speeches up there in the Senate. You two haven't got an organized campaign going, have you?"

"Why do we have to organize?" Percy Mercy inquired. "Certain serious shortcomings are obvious about your program, and each of us has his responsibility to point them out. I hope it may never be said of me that I have abdicated my responsibilities as an editor."

The Administrator smiled.

"One thing nobody can ever say of you, Percy, is that you ever abdicated your responsibilities as an editor."

"I should hope not," the guiding light of *View* said with a certain smug complacency. "I should hope *not*."

And indeed, the Administrator reflected as he decided to interrupt the undeclared hostilities by offering them each a Safecig, no editor in the country, nay the world, exercised his responsibilities more diligently, or with more self-righteous arrogance, than Percy Mercy.

Every week in *View* there appeared a stern admonition about something, usually addressed to the United States (apparently, in Percy's mind, the only country ever guilty of anything) and always signed with the discreetly formidable and famous initials, "P.C.M." There were some irreverent souls who, inspired by the hysterical Doomsday tone of many of his editorials, said the initials "P.C.M." really stood for "Percy Comma Mercy." Others, noting the assumption of infallibility on all subjects that suffused his writings and his many speeches, said the initials really meant "Percy Christ Mercy." But whatever they meant—and Percy, who had adopted the "C." at sixteen, knew that particular letter, at least, meant nothing whatever—they did signify the pompous and in many ways insufferable minor literary personage whose haphazard catch-all of a magazine had given him perhaps rather more prominence and influence in certain highly vocal sectors of American opinion than his limited abilities justified or his narrow intelligence deserved.

The Administrator knew from long experience that Percy, under his guise of pious, above-the-battle nobility, was capable of being absolutely ruthless toward those with whom he disagreed. Always clamorous about his own right to express his opinions, he never hesitated to censor and suppress in his magazine all those with which he disagreed. Andy himself had published a collection of speeches, reasoned and calm in their defense of the space program, three months ago. He decided this would be as good a point as any on which to put his visitor on the defensive.

"About that book of mine, Percy," he said. "I see you haven't permitted *View* to review it yet."

To his delight, Percy, like all who dispense criticism but can't take it, bristled at once.

"I have given no instructions to anyone about your book," he said sharply. "I make no attempt to influence the book review editor. Such matters rest entirely with him."

"Surely," the Administrator said pleasantly. "I couldn't believe you more. Nonetheless, it hasn't been reviewed, has it? Meanwhile your own editorials attacking the program have been appearing almost every week for the last two months. Don't you believe in fair play, Percy? How about giving the other side a chance?"

"No one has ever proved that I am unfair!" Percy said, and Senator Williams shifted heavily in his chair, his pudgy young face creased with annoyance.

"That's right, Andy," he remarked. "Better watch those free-swinging allegations, I'd say."

"Your book no doubt will be reviewed at the proper time, in the proper course of things," Percy said more calmly. "But, as I say, that rests entirely with the book review editor. I don't know what he is going to have reviewed until I read it in the magazine."

"Per—*cy*," the Administrator said, but his visitor stared him straight in the eye.

"That is the truth," he said. A spitefully triumphant expression appeared briefly on his face, then was banished with an obvious effort of will. It clearly did not go with the image of "P.C.M."

"Of course you must realize that anything so obviously filled with special pleading and specious self-interested argument as your book cannot receive quite the attention we would devote to some more objective expression of opinion. We do, for instance, intend to review the Senator's speeches on the space program when they are collected and published—as I believe they will be?"

"That's right," Kenny Williams said with some satisfaction. "Next month."

"Oh, great!" the Adminstrator said happily. "Would you like me to do the review for you, Percy?"

"I assume," Percy said, not looking amused, "that we will find someone who is equally qualified but perhaps more objective."

"Mmmhmm," Dr. Anderson said. "I know what that means. 'Objective' in *View* means: 'I agree with P.C.M.' Well, Percy, let me know when you get around to ordering the hatchet-job on my book. That is, unless you plan to use your other method of attack, which is to continue to ignore it altogether."

"Now, Andy," Senator Williams said heavily, "that kind of talk isn't going to get us anywhere."

"Where do we want to get?" Andy asked pleasantly. "I'm still in the dark about the purpose of this visit. Is there one?"

"We believe," Percy Mercy said with a calm arrogance

that left the Administrator a little breathless, "that Commander Weickert should be given a top command post on Planetary Fleet One. We also believe that a black American, specifically Astroscientist J. V. Halleck, should be given a prominent assignment in the crew."

For a moment Dr. Anderson was tempted to let fly with all the anger and tension that were building inside him as a result of the news sent down so inexorably by the busy little satellite. But to do that, he knew, would be to indicate to two shrewd critics that something was at crisis-point in the space program. It was the last thing he wanted to reveal to these two at this moment. He forced himself to be equally calm and, he hoped, equally arrogant.

"The assignment of astronauts and astroscientists," he said with an aloof air, staring thoughtfully at a picture of the crew of Apollo 12 on the wall, "is a matter for internal decision within NASA and specifically within the Manned Spacecraft Center in Houston. It has never been, and it is not now, a matter for general public discussion or interference."

"Oh, yes it is," Senator Williams said bluntly, leaning forward to smack the desk with the flat of his hand for emphasis. "Yes it is, this time."

"Oh?" Andy Anderson said, an ominous coldness in his voice. "And who, may I ask, has reached that interesting conclusion?"

"The American people," Percy Mercy said blandly, and it was all Dr. Anderson could do to keep from laughing rather harshly in his face.

"Are you speaking for them these days, Percy?" he asked. The editor of *View* inclined his head slightly, thoughtfully, gravely.

"I believe I state their point of view on most things in my editorials and speeches. The American public thinks it is long overdue that so fine an astronaut as Commander Weickert should be allowed to assume the command responsibilities of which he is so obviously capable. Even more important, the American public believes it to be inexcusable that NASA should have waited so long to bring black Americans fully into the program. On this latter point, the world at large also shares a deep concern. I have an editorial appearing in tomorrow's issue which is going to discuss these matters in some detail."

"And I have a speech to deliver tomorrow afternoon," Kenny Williams said with a complacent smile. "So, you see, Andy, we rather have you boxed in, don't we?"

"Commander Weickert," the Administrator said, keeping his tone level at some cost, "has various problems which can only be worked out with the men who would have to fly with him on the mission. They cannot be solved by outsiders or, indeed, by pressure from Washington. They have to be solved in the Astronaut Office, by the very nature of these missions, which are intimate, dangerous and dependent upon absolute mutual trust and teamwork. I'm sorry he has seen fit to bring you into it—"

"No reprisals, now, Andy," Senator Williams said sharply. "Jazz didn't ask us to do this for him. It was our idea, to right a long-standing injustice. I warn you that we'll be watching to see there are no reprisals, Andy. They wouldn't be wise."

"There will be no reprisals from here," Dr. Anderson said, maintaining his unruffled tone with some difficulty.

"Or from the astronauts, either," Percy said.

"We don't control them."

"You should," Percy said shortly. "It's about time somebody did. As for J. V. Halleck—"

"J. V. Halleck is an excellent scientist," the Administrator interrupted. "Whether his particular skills will be needed on this mission, exactly how they will fit into the crew picture as we see it, whether he is sufficiently qualified as a pilot to be able to perform both scientific and flight responsibilities should the need arise—"

"Words!" Percy Mercy interrupted in his turn. "Just words, the same tired old words that have been used for generations to keep America's most sinned-against and deserving minority down! Why don't you say it honestly: you don't know whether J. V. Halleck will be on that crew because you don't know whether your precious lily-white astronauts will accept a black man's company on the trip to Mars. Isn't that the truth of it?"

"You sound like one of your own editorials," the Administrator remarked. "You also sound very unpleasant, offensive and insulting. I repeat, the nature of space flight is such that a crew has to be absolutely sure that all of its members are fully capable and that all can mutually trust each other."

His expression changed, the anger broke through for a moment.

"My God, man, these aren't patty-cake picnics these boys go on! They're matters of life and death. They can't take a chance on finding a goofball in the command module when they get out there. They've got to know before they leave the ground what each man's quality is."

"You're sure you mean 'goofball,'" Percy Mercy inquired with the nasty inflection he used on those who dared disagree with him. "You don't really mean 'burrhead'?"

"No," Dr. Anderson snapped, "I do not mean burrhead!" He stood up abruptly. "Now, if you will excuse me, I have some work to do before the White House announcement at 5 P.M."

"Just you keep in mind, Andy—" Kenny Williams began ominously. Then he caught himself. "What White House announcement at 5 P.M.?"

"Listen to it," the Administrator said shortly. "Everyone else will."

"Perhaps my editorial is already out of date," Percy Mercy said with the fatalistic and quizzical concern of the journalist whose product, already gone to press, may be overtaken by events.

The Administrator gave him a sharp, unfathomable glance.

"Oh no," he said with an odd bitterness in his tone. "You may be exactly right for what's going to happen."

And still in Houston men made leisurely plans on the assumption of the 1980's launch to Mars. But it was for the last time.

"Hi,"·Connie Trasker said, tossing his briefcase on the already cluttered table extending out from Hank Barstow's desk in the Astronaut Office. "What's the latest crap from headquarters?"

"Not taking any," Hank said with his quick, comfortable laugh; and Bert Richmond smiled his slow, unimpressed and unimpressible smile and said, "Not even accepting any C.O.D. at the post office."

"That's good," Colonel Trasker said, "because I'm in no mood for it. I've taken enough from Jazz today to fill an entire Saturn from top to bottom."

"Is he bellyaching again?" Hank asked with an expression of distaste.

"Not bellyaching," Connie said. "Telling."

"Who?" Bert asked.

"Us."

"What?"

"That he's going to be my second in command on Piffy One," Connie said. He paused and smiled the confident and appealing smile that had captivated so many during his years as an astronaut. "That is," he said with a modesty certain it could afford to mock itself slightly, "if it's going to be my flight."

"Was there ever any doubt?" Hank asked Bert.

"Could we make it any clearer?" Bert asked Hank.

Connie Trasker's face creased into a broad and happy grin.

"Well, thank God," he said in a tone whose lightness could not quite cover the genuine relief that underlay it. "I thought you were never going to drop that other shoe."

"Dropped weeks ago," Bert said solemnly. "Everybody seems to have known but you."

"The hell they did," Connie said. "Or if they did, they probably wondered why I'm crazy enough to want to leave my family and Earth for a year and a half."

"Don't tell 'em," Hank said, "let 'em guess. So what's with our boy Jazz today?"

"The same as every day," Connie said. "We've all been mean to him, he deserves better things, it just isn't fair, and he's going to weep all over the press and Capitol Hill if we don't put him on the flight."

"Tough," Bert agreed solemnly. He sighed. "When is that egotistical bastard ever going to realize that he queered himself years ago? It wasn't Hank's and my idea that he should come around demanding things from us as soon as we were appointed to our offices. It wasn't our idea that he should act as though the whole of NASA should bow down and worship him just because he was Jazz Weickert. We didn't ask him to skin-dive and water-ski and play saxophone in a combo. Combo, for God's sake!" His face wrinkled in an expression of distaste. "What kind of stunt is that for an astronaut to pull? What does that do to the dignity of the program? Who the hell does he think he is?"

"He's a poor little lamb who has lost his way," Hank

Barstow said dryly. "Bah, bah, bah. So he's demanding second place on Piffy One, is he? Now my ideas for that crew would be more along the lines of people like Gaudy Gaudet and Emerson Wacker and Bob Curtis and Stu Yule and Roger Webb and Dave McWharter and Bill Wheatley and——" He stopped and grinned.

"You've been thinking," Connie told him. "Oh, you have been thinking. I don't seem to find Jazz in there anywhere."

"We may have a place for him," Bert said comfortably. "It's going to be a twelve-man crew. We'll fit our sax player in somewhere. But it won't be as your right-hand man, old buddy."

"We hope you don't mind too much," Hank remarked.

Connie grinned.

"I'll try to bear up," he said. His expression became more serious. "Of course, I expect he *will* put up a howl, and I expect some people in the press and on the Hill will take up for him."

"That son-of-a-bitching Kenny Williams and that damned little twerp Percy Mercy." Bert Richmond said with a disgusted snort. "There's an unholy pair for you."

"They're sure riding the hell out of NASA right now, aren't they?" Hank agreed. "I guess Kenny thinks that's the way to run for President someday. I don't know what Percy thinks."

"He thinks it's the way to help Kenny and the way to increase the circulation of his damned catch-all of a schizophrenic magazine," Connie said. "But, we might as well make up our minds to it: there'll be some screaming if Jazz has to take a back seat."

"He'd better realize he'll be lucky to get on that crew at all," Bert said crisply. "And if they scream, so what? The astronauts don't have to defend themselves. We'll do what we always do: say nothing and let the bastards howl."

"Good," Connie said. "I'm not really worried about it. I just thought you ought to know."

"Duly recorded in the minutes of the office of the Social Director and Den Mother," Hank said. "How does that line-up sound to you, so far?"

"Pretty good," Connie said. He hesitated. "I assume we're going to have a medical officer."

"That's right," Hank agreed. He smiled. "Don't worry. You'll get your Greek."

"He isn't 'my' Greek," Connie said mildly, "but we are good friends. I'd feel secure with him along if anything went wrong."

"Add Pete Balkis," Bert said. He nodded. "He's a good man."

"The best," Connie Trasker said. He frowned thoughtfully. "There's one other matter that's occurred to me— you may not want to even give it a moment's thought, but then again, maybe you might. Do you think we ought to let Jayvee go along on this one?"

For a moment his colleagues stared at him without expression across the desk. Colonel Trasker was struck again with what a tough pair they were. And thank God for that, because however hard they might be on members of the corps at times, they were absolutely dedicated to the cause of the astronauts and fought their battles without fear or quarter against all comers.

"For what purpose?" Hank finally asked dryly. "To help the NASA image?"

"We aren't liberal enough?" Bert suggested softly. "We're restricting the right of a minority to go to Mars and maybe get blown to hell-and-gone?"

"Something like that," Connie Trasker said bluntly, for in his own way he was as tough as they were and didn't want them to forget it. "The NASA image could stand a little updating right there, it seems to me. You understand, I don't particularly want him along myself—"

"Then why suggest it?" Bert asked. "Haven't we got enough troubles?"

"You know damned well," Hank said, "that guy is an unco-operative, hypersensitive, race-ridden neurotic. You're asking for big trouble when you ask for that boy, Connie. Isn't the mission going to be tough enough without adding that?"

"Of course it is," Colonel Trasker agreed. "It also is going to be big enough, crew-wise, so that we can absorb Jayvee's little quirks if we have to."

"He isn't gung-ho," Bert said thoughtfully. "He just isn't with it. He isn't our kind of material, basically. He's never really fitted in here since the day he arrived. He makes me feel we've always got to prove ourselves with him, when, hell, he's really the one who's got to prove himself with us. He never has yet, in my estimation. I'd keep him on the ground if I were doing it."

"Which you are, of course," Connie Trasker said.

"You can't afford to have anybody in that crew you can't be absolutely sure of," Hank said. "Everybody's got to be an absolutely top-pitch astronaut as well as a good doctor or scientist, or whatever. And Jayvee just isn't that good. And you know it," he concluded quietly, "as well as we do."

Connie shrugged.

"You're right. I just wanted to raise the point, because I'm sure others will."

"Don't worry about it," Bert said.

"We'll take the flak," Hank added calmly. "We always do."

"We worship you for it," Colonel Trasker said with a grin, and dropped the subject. "You're going to have a pretty full list to submit to that meeting in Washington tomorrow, aren't you?"

"Never let it be said," Bert remarked, relaxing into his lazy smile, "that the Astro Office was unprepared."

"I suppose we'll go around and around and around in our usual tight little NASA circles," Hank said with a resigned air, "but at least we'll have something for them to chew on."

"It's a good thing," Connie said. "Otherwise we'd just sit and contemplate each others' navels all day."

But in this, as they and the whole wide world found out at 5 P.M. Washington time, 3 P.M. Houston, Connie was mistaken. At that hour it became apparent that the meeting at headquarters tomorrow would have much graver matters to discuss. The first inkling of this reached the Astronaut Office shortly before 2:30 P.M. their time, as Connie was preparing to leave.

He was halfway out the door when the voice of Hank's secretary came in on the override and announced that Dr. Balkis was on the viewer and Mrs. Trasker was waiting.

"Popular," Hank remarked with a smile.

"Always," Connie agreed. "Put Pete on," he ordered. The square, darkly handsome face of "the Greek loner from Tarpon Springs" appeared on the screen. Usually, whatever his restless inner feelings, he managed to conceal them with a quick-flashing smile. This time he wasn't smiling.

"There you are. I've been tracking you down for the

last half-hour. Hi, Hank, Bert. Have you guys heard the reports from Washington? There's a big special White House announcement coming up at 3 P.M. and they're all speculating it has something to do with space. Maybe Mars."

"The hell you say," Hank remarked softly.

"The hell I do," Pete agreed with a return of his smile. "Better turn on the tube and sit tight."

"We'll do that," Bert said.

"Thanks for telling us, Pete," Connie said. "You're a good man."

"We'll give you six Brownie points and a ticker-tape parade through beautiful downtown El Lago," Hank said.

Pete's smile became a grin.

"I'd settle for less, you guys. You know that. But, gee, thanks."

And he faded cheerfully from the screen. The pretty and intelligent face of Jane Trasker came on.

"There's a distinguished-looking body of men," she remarked. "I understand Pete got in ahead of me, so I suppose he told you the news, I will therefore confine myself to command decisions, Colonel Trasker. To wit: please stop at the shopping center in Nassau Bay on the way home and pick up a dozen eggs, some soap for the dishwasher and some steaks for us and Dr. Balkis and his lady friend. And, oh, yes, I almost forgot, four rolls of toilet paper."

"Because even astronauts," Bert remarked thoughtfully, "have to—"

Jane interrupted with a merry laugh.

"Stop that, Bert, you disrespectful old war-horse. Some things are sacred."

"Lady," Bert responded, "when you've spent two weeks in orbit, nothing is sacred."

"Janie," Hank said, "Louise and I want you folks to come over soon for cocktails. We'll have the Director and a few others. Can you make it?"

"Hadn't we better see what's coming from Washington?" Jane suggested. "Who knows where we'll all be after that?"

Hank tossed her a salute.

"Spoken like a true astronaut's wife," he said. "Connie, you have the prize of the program."

"I like her," Connie said, and his wife's expression softened with a genuine pleasure.

"It's mutual," she said. "And now I must run and turn on the television. Don't forget the shopping list."

Connie smiled.

"I won't."

"Well," Bert observed as the screen went dark, "that was nice."

"She's a good girl," Hank said. "You're lucky."

"She is that," her husband agreed. "And I am." He sat down again at the cluttered table, swiveled his chair, and began to fiddle with the television set. "Well, friends of the space program, what do you think's coming?"

The announcement was made by the President's Press Secretary, a selection that surprised a good many but was obviously the result of a deliberate decision to keep it relatively low-key at the moment.

"The President has asked me to tell you," the Press Secretary said, his round, youthful face staring solemnly into the cameras, "that intelligence reaching him indicates beyond all reasonable doubt that the Soviet Union today began preparing a series of major space launches apparently designed to carry large numbers of men and large amounts of material to Space Station *Stalin*.

"It is the President's belief, and that of his advisers in the space and intelligence communities, that this indicates the start of a massive and determined effort to launch a planetary expedition, probably to Mars, at the earliest possible moment.

"The President expects to meet with officials of the National Aeronautics and Space Administration at the White House tomorrow to determine the proper course of action this country should pursue in view of this major effort by the Soviet Union. He expects to discuss with you himself tomorrow night the results of this meeting."

"And what 'course of action' *should* we pursue?" Percy Mercy demanded scornfully in Senator Williams' office in the New Senate Office Building as the Press Secretary's earnest face faded from the screen. "Some sort of hysterical, demeaning attempt to scramble after the Soviet Union, wasting untold billions in the process, while our own cities and minorities suffer, and our own problems get worse and worse? It's insanity!

"And furthermore," he said, getting up and striding back and forth in his agitation while Kenny Williams watched him with a speculative eye, "I have an article by Alexei Kuselevsky running in next week's issue of *View* that's entitled 'Toward A Better World Through Space' and in it he absolutely denies they have any intention of trying a Mars expedition until, as he puts it, 'well into the eighties.' He says that 'The sole intention of the Soviet Union is to co-operate with the United States in bringing a better world to space and here on our own Earth.' He says 'the Soviet Union would be quite content to see the United States, home of space heroes equal to our own cosmonauts, make such a venture first. We and all mankind would applaud.' He says, 'I can categorically deny that the Soviet Union would make such a basically hostile attempt' as to try to beat us to Mars. He says, and he asked me to put it in italics, *'We will not do it!'* And now those insane fools in NASA are using the phony argument of a threat from Russia to persuade the President to start neglecting our own problems and start wasting billions again. It's absolutely criminal!"

"You tell 'em, Percy," Senator Williams said admiringly. "And so," he said, his chubby face settling into grimly determined lines, "will I. I don't see why we have to get so frantic just because the Russians want to run a few experiments at their space station. Hell, we do it all the time."

"Of course that's what it is," Percy Mercy said impatiently. "We *must* get this thing back in perspective."

"YIPPEEE!" Hugo Gaudet shouted as he and Stu Yule linked arms and went into an impromptu war dance in the midst of the excited group of secretaries and astronauts who filled the corridor outside the Astronaut Office. "We're on our way again!"

And as the afternoon wore on, and night came, and throughout NASA and Washington and America and the world all those who directly or indirectly would be involved in or affected by the flight of Piffy One absorbed the news, the reactions of Percy Mercy and "Gaudy" Gaudet seemed to sum up pretty well the two prevailing points of view.

In the Administrator's Office in Washington phones rang and excited messages flew as they had not done for six or seven years. In Houston, Bob Hertz could not resist another jubilant call to Vernon Hertz at JPL. Vernon kidded him good-naturedly and pointed out that unmanned probes would be even more important as launchtime neared. In Huntsville Hans Sturmer and his colleagues looked at one another with pleased smiles as they took out their blueprints and went over them with many excited comments in a jumble of English and German. At the enormous vehicle assembly plant at Michoud, Louisiana, and at the nearby Mississippi Test Facility, both standing silent and almost deserted through the doldrum years, the small managerial staffs broke out bottles and raised glasses in anticipation that they would soon be busy again. At Ames Research Center in California and at Langley in Virginia, at Edwards Air Force Base and Vandenberg Air Force Base, and all the other NASA installations across the country and around the world, the same excited conviction spread. At North American Rockwell, at Bendix and Boeing and Grumman, and all the plants of all the other contractors and subcontractors, men were jubilant. And at the Cape, Emerson Wacker, Roger Webb and the other astronauts in training left the Simulator Building, jumped into staff cars and roared out to the Vehicle Assembly Building, where they cheered and slapped upon the back a sentimental old man who stood at the huge glass window next to Firing Room I, staring out at the deserted pads of Launch Complex 39 with tears in his eyes.

And in certain offices on Capitol Hill, and in such mighty centers of the art of telling America what it ought to think as the offices of *View*—the editorial conference rooms of the *Times*, the *Post* and other major newspapers —the news magazines and television networks—men grim-faced and somber prepared to marshall all the words, photographs and propaganda techniques at their powerful command to thwart what they were convinced would be a wasteful and probably futile attempt to overtake the Russians. And at a reception at the United Nations, Academician Alexei V. Kuselevsky met the Ambassador of the United States, and they smiled and smiled and smiled and smiled upon one another.

Around Clear Lake as the night wore on, at the Cape

and at towns and cities around the country and across the world where their tours and speaking engagements had taken them, one small group of men in particular seemed to feel, with a sort of mass instinct, the same impulse. Wherever they were, they went outside and stared up into the sky.

The tiny new moon had risen and set, only the stars and planets in their infinite depths gave illumination to the heavens. Across them presently drifted and disappeared a quite large, brightly lighted object. After it in about five minutes came one much smaller, also brightly lighted, equally visible 132 miles below: Space Station *Stalin* and Space Station *Mayflower*, on their regular orbits around the earth.

The silent men looked up, and watching that arrogant first passage and that more modest, almost apologetic second, felt something they had never felt before. For the first time since America entered space, and for some primordial, instinctive reason they could not quite understand or define, they felt fear: not of space, but of their own kind.

2.

So the day of decisions came in Washington, and rarely had there been a more reported, televised, analyzed, admonished, advised and scolded gathering than that which met at 10 A.M. in the Cabinet Room of the White House.

PRESIDENT SAYS RUSS MAY PLAN QUICK MARS LAUNCH, MEETS WITH ADVISERS TO DECIDE U.S. COURSE, said the headline in the New York *Daily News*. NASA JUBILANT OVER POSSIBLE BOOST TO PROGRAM, said the headline in the Houston *Chronicle*. CONGRESS WARNS AGAINST "MORE MONEY DOWN DRAIN" IN MARS CONTEST, said the headline in the *Times*. MILITARY-INDUSTRIAL COMPLEX STANDS TO GAIN IN NEW MARS FLING, said the headline in the *Post*. And further down the front page, in all of them, a smaller headline which said, in essence, EDITOR FORMS ANTI-MARS COMMITTEE TO BLOCK NEW SPACE RACE.

Editorial comment ranged from the *Times*' somber beginning, "It is with much misgiving that we detect signs that the United States, instead of tending to its own badly neglected domestic needs, may once again be about to plunge headlong into the exciting but futile pursuit of a new space race with the Soviets," to the New York *Daily News*' flat assertion, "We say it is TIME TO BEAT THE RUSSIANS AGAIN." Polarized at those two extremes of opinion lay most of the newspaper giants in the country, with the greater majority, by far, siding with the *Times*. Somewhere in between lay most of the smaller metropolitan and rural dailies.

Vehemently agreeing with the critics were the major television networks. Kenny Williams was given twenty-five almost uninterrupted minutes by NBC to explain why the country should not attempt to compete with the Soviet Union in the try for Mars; Chairman Satterthwaite of the House Space Committee was allowed four minutes of rebuttal at the end, frequently interrupted by politely hostile questions from his two interrogators. Percy Mercy found his spiritual home with CBS, which gave him fifteen minutes of uninterrupted editoralizing at 8:30 A.M. to fan opposition to the Administration's presumed speed-up plans and to describe formation of his overnight inspiration, CAUSE: the Committee Against Unilateral Space Exploration. ABC presented a hastily thrown-together round table entitled, "Mars: Necessity or Fantasy?" The panel's membership was carefully selected to leave no doubt what ABC thought the answer was.

Lost in all the clamor was the point of view of the average American, at this point somewhat confused, somewhat uncertain, but basically quite determined that the United States should not again take a back seat to the Soviet Union. The happy euphoria of the Moon landings had given way in recent years to the constant fretful annoyance of having Space Station *Stalin* pre-empting the skies in ostentatious supremacy. The annoyance had not been alleviated much by Space Station *Mayflower*, smaller, less glamorous, less dominating. The Administrator in a number of public speeches had patiently pointed out that this calculated inferiority was what the country had apparently wanted and been willing to pay for. Characteristically, the country was not mollified: it wanted supremacy on the cheap and was upset when it didn't get it. Now supremacy might be within grasp again, if America moved fast enough.

As they took their seats at 10 A.M. around the cabinet table, the men of NASA were aware that if the country was not to be beaten again, a great, scrambling, desperate effort would have to be made to recover lost ground. All of this could have been prevented if they had been listened to five, six, eight years before; but they had not been. A careful President had opted for the mini-dream and the mini-goal. As a result, the United States stood in danger of a defeat whose full scope and ultimate implications could not accurately be assessed at the moment, except

72

that everyone in NASA's upper echelons had a blind, instinctive, absolute certainty that they would be ominous and far-reaching.

They did not, however, know how the present President felt; and so an uneasy silence fell while they waited for him.

The Administrator stared at the table and fiddled absent-mindedly with a pencil. Hans Sturmer and Albrecht Freer whispered together in German, their expressions intent and uneasy. The Director of MSC leaned back and studied the ceiling. Bob and Vernon Hertz stared thoughtfully at one another across the table. Hank Barstow, Bert Richmond and Connie Trasker sat side by side with a carefully casual air that did not conceal the tension in their eyes. Jim Matthison and his crew from North American Rockwell, last night's euphoric jubilation vanished in the morning's cold contemplation of the crash program that might lie ahead, scribbled and scrawled and nervously scratched-out on the pads of lined yellow legal notepaper that had been placed at every seat.

All of them stiffened for a moment as outside in the corridor there came that combination of businesslike bustle and hushed excitement that signifies in the White House that the President is on his way. Then he was in the room, they were on their feet, he was saying, "Gentlemen, please be seated," and they were down again, before they realized that the expression on his forceful face was grave and concerned. They immediately concluded that this was a hopeful sign for the space program. But he was too shrewd a man to let them know immediately if they were right.

"Well, gentlemen," he said with a sigh, "we seem to be in the middle of a pretty kettle of fish. The Vice-President, head of the Space Council, is on an official visit to Europe, as you know. He sends his very deep regrets he cannot be here. The problem rests with us. What do you think we ought to do about it? Andy?"

Dr. Anderson shrugged.

"That's pretty obvious, Mr. President, isn't it? Work like hell and beat them to it, is my attitude. How could I feel any differently?"

"And be Administrator of NASA?" the President asked with the start of a smile. "You couldn't. I suppose that applies to the rest of you?" He looked down the table, carefully studying them all as they nodded, each in turn.

The smile broadened. "Yes, that's my boys in NASA, all right. One for all and all for one, and everybody for the program." His expression changed, became serious again. To their dismay, his tone turned regretful. "Well: if only it were that simple."

"And why isn't it, Mr. President?" Dr. Anderson asked. "It doesn't seem to us that we have much choice."

"Nor to me," the President agreed, and instantly their hopes shot up again. "Except"—and down they came once more—"that there is a small matter of funding, a small matter of priorities, a small matter of a country whose domestic and defense needs are so great that I can't for the life of me see at the moment where the money is coming from. However"—and again his face relaxed into a smile and again they were encouraged—"don't all of you look so gloomy. There are ways of doing things and perhaps we can manage a few of them."

Down the table Dr. Freer cleared his throat.

"I think we can, Mr. President," he said, "if you give them your absolute and complete dedication." He paused and then added quietly, "Not otherwise."

For a moment they thought the President might be angered, but he was a shrewder and tougher man than that. He offered Al Freer a small bow, ironic but respectful.

"That is correct," he said. "That is absolutely correct. Now what I want you all to tell me this morning is what I can expect from you if I do give you my complete and absolute dedication in return. Start with yourself, Dr. Freer."

"Very well," Albrecht Freer said in a firm, precise voice. "We now have some 12,000 people still employed at KSC and the Cape. We have our two Apollo launch pads, A and B, at Launch Complex 39, idle most of the year but in excellent stand-by condition. I am confident that in a month, with the proper announcements and the proper financial inducement, I can restore a working complement of 25,000 men and women to the Cape. I have plans on the drawing boards for a possible Pad C that might be needed in a Mars flight—will, I think, be definitely needed, now that time is of the essence. Given funding for sufficient crews and overtime, I can have it ready in three months." (Somewhere down the table someone probably from North American Rockwell, whistled softly.) "Three months," Albrecht Freer repeated firmly. "I am not talking now, you understand, about child's play. I am talking about serious man's business, a real attempt to go all-out and win this thing. That, Mr. President, is what the Cape can do for you, if you say the word—and really mean it."

"And Huntsville?" the President asked.

Hans Sturmer leaned forward with a little smile that somehow looked patronizing, though he did not intend it so.

"Marshall Spacecraft Center, Mr. President," he said in his guttural accent, still heavy after more than three decades in the country, "is ready when you are ready. We have plans, designs, mock-ups, everything you could require. We must know, of course, the nature of the mission and what is demanded and expected of it: that I think we must determine here this morning, if I may suggest. But whatever it may be, you will find us ready."

"Very commendable," the President murmured with a slight smile.

"It is our job," Dr. Sturmer said, a trifle stiffly. The President nodded.

"And superbly done," he said matter-of-factly. "And the scientific sector, my distinguished friend down the table, there, from JPL?"

"As you know, Mr. President," Vernon Hertz said, "all through these years since the Moon landings we have maintained a steady program of unmanned probes of the planets. These have yielded very satisfactory results, particularly from Mars and Venus. We have very elaborate atmospheric analyses, surface soundings, photographs, maps, surveys—the lot. I agree with Hans that we have to decide here this morning exactly what we want this mission to be, and what we want it to do. Given that, I believe JPL will be found to have on hand almost everything you might need. If not, we can easily get it within any reasonable lead-time such as we will obviously have to adopt here. I know the same can be said for Ames, Langley and the other research laboratories, which are working on such things as waste elimination, food supply, life support and the like. We're in good shape."

"Excellent," the President said. "And the contractors?"

"We're like Al Freer, Mr. President," Jim Matthison said. "Give us the money and we'll recall the crews and do the job. In this I can say I've been authorized to speak for the other prime contractors, Douglas, Boeing, Bendix, Grumman, IBM and the rest. You tell us what the mission will be, what Huntsville and Houston want us to do to modify the Saturn for planetary flight, what's going to be required of the vehicle at launch and after, and we'll get it ready for you. Maybe not in three months"—he smiled and shook his head with an expression of disbelief "—but just as soon as we possibly can. The planets won't turn very far in their courses before we'll have the Saturn ready for them."

"Forbidding things, aren't they?" the President said with a sudden expression of distaste. "I don't envy the boys who have to go there. Which brings me, Houston," he said, and he looked down the table and smiled at Dr. Cavanaugh, at Bob Hertz and at the three astronauts sitting side by side, "to you."

"Yes, sir," Jim Cavanaugh said gravely. He looked down the table and back again and suddenly his face relaxed in a smile.

"Houston," he said, "is ready to go wherever you send us, whenever you send us, anytime, forever and always. We're ready. Man, are we *ready!*"

At this, as he had intended, they all joined him in laughter. Then he became serious again.

"Actually, Mr. President, we maintain such a steady course of training, even in the relatively stand-by era we've been in, that we could quite literally, I think, field a crew to Mars in three months. It would be close, but we could do it. Isn't that right, fellows?"

"I believe we could," Hank Barstow said.

"No doubt about it," Bert Richmond agreed.

"And what," the President asked, "says the captain of this gallant band? How do you feel, Colonel Trasker?"

For a moment Connie did not reply, staring thoughtfully off into some distance visible only to him.

"It all depends," he said, finally, "on the general time-table you set, and on how big a crew you want to send. Twelve men and twelve months—maybe. Three men and three months—maybe. Twelve men and three months— with all respects to Jim Cavanaugh and my colleagues— no, sir. We couldn't do it. The bigger the crew, the longer the time. It's one of those axioms. We could force a lot of things if we have to—and apparently, we do have to—but crew can only be forced to certain limits." He smiled at

Vernon Hertz. "It just goes to prove what the scientists are always telling us—men are so unreliable. If we were some of their little machines, we'd be off and flying tomorrow morning. But with us you run into the human factor—if you want the human factor. And I take it the Russians are aiming in that direction"—the President nodded—"and therefore, I would assume we are too. All I ask is that you not crowd my crew too much. First decide when you want to go, and then we'll decide how many we can send. There are certain parameters we have to work within, just by virtue of being men. You give us the job and we'll do it—but in terms of the job, not in terms of some dream of what would be nice if we were superhuman instead of human."

He stopped, looked embarrassed, and sat back, to the murmured approval of his colleagues from Houston and a good many others along the table. The President leaned forward and in the crisp tones that came next they could recognize why he happened to be where he was.

"Thank you, Connie. That was an admirable statement, and it brings me exactly to the point we have got to wrestle with here this morning. It's all very well for JPL and the research labs to be confident. It's all very well for Huntsville to tell me everything's ready and waiting, it's fine for Dr. Freer and North American Rockwell to assure me they can do the job in three months, or six, or whatever. But what I want to know is exactly what problems remain to be solved, exactly where we stand with them, exactly what, in your estimation can be done to speed them up without sacrificing quality and safety—in other words, exactly what we need, and how fast, to get ready. And without a lot of crap, I might add, about how you aren't sure how many billions it will take, but if I'll just give you as many as you ask for, it will all work out just dandy. I can't give you as many as you ask for, so get that through your heads right now. I can give you a substantial amount of it, and with that you will just have to make do. And if I decide to approve this, I shall expect you to make do.

"Now. From what we have received from the satellite in the last twenty-four hours, and from other intelligence sources we've called on since the pictures began to come in, the Russians have a certain lead-time problem, too. They aren't about to launch from *Stalin* tomorrow morning, either. They're still in the preliminary stages themselves, but since they do have a very substantial space station, and we have only our piddling little *Mayflower* up there, they can launch from there and it gives them a very substantial advantage. We are probably going to have to launch direct from Pad A, Pad B and"—he winked at Dr. Freer, who responded with a delighted smile—"Pad C. Which brings me, Huntsville, back to you. Dr. Sturmer, how soon is that NERVA nuclear engine going to be ready?"

"On a crash program," Hans Sturmer said with a crispness equal to his, "starting from the point we have already reached with our continuing experiments and planning, here in the late seventies, we can have the new engine ready in six months. It will give us all the propulsion to maintain a steady course to Mars, orbit and return. But again, we will have to know the size of the expedition, the length of it, and what will be asked of it. That, too," he could not resist adding, "is a practical consideration that must be decided."

"Before we leave this room," the President promised. "And the laboratories, Dr. Hertz? What about the food problem? What about life-support problems? What about the scientific instrument packages you will want to send on the expedition?"

"I repeat, Mr. President," Vernon Hertz said quietly, "we're in the same position Hans is in—that we're all in. We're beginning to see daylight on a lot of these things— we're in the home stretch. We can move faster and be ready in six to eight months—if that's what you want. You name it."

"The same with us in the plants," Jim Matthison volunteered.

The President nodded.

"And Houston?" he inquired. "How about the medical experiments, the physiological tests, the psychological tests, the experiments that determine how much the crew can take? The necessary modifications to the booster, the command module and the landing module?"

"Insofar as men can, Mr. President," Dr. Cavanaugh said quietly, "we have determined all these things. I still think Connie made the main point. When—and how much—and how long—and how many?"

"Eight months from this day," the President said.

There was a lengthy silence, during which they all looked at one another in a speculative, thoughtful way. It was broken finally by Bob Hertz.

"I assume that's the best estimate of when the Russians will be ready?"

The President smiled.

"A little short of it."

"Very well," Bob said, jotting notes on his yellow pad as he spoke. "That gives us something definite. On that basis, assuming everybody puts in a superhuman effort, I would say three vehicles and three or four men, for an expedition to last approximately eighteen months—eight months out, eight back, two in orbit around the planet conducting experiments. Vehicle I would carry the Mars Landing Module. Vehicle II would carry the Command-Service Module. Vehicle III, possibly manned by two men, would carry your scientific and medical experiments. Connie would be in command of Vehicle I and in overall command; Astronaut X in command of Vehicle II; and Astroscientists Dr. X and Dr. Y in command of Vehicle III. The modules would dock in space and proceed in tandem.

"A slight reduction from a twelve-man crew," he said, smiling at Jim Cavanaugh, "but still, a practical version of Planetary Fleet One that we can all live with if we have to. And I take it we have to."

The President chuckled.

"Have you ever thought of being Director of the Budget? I could use that kind of practicality and decisiveness right in that exact spot."

Bob Hertz smiled.

"No soap, Mr. President. I happen to love space."

"And thank God for that," the President said. He looked sharply down the table from face to face. "Gentlemen, are we agreed on that mission configuration and that timetable? If we aren't, say so." He smiled. "I'm not entirely unreasonable, you know. You can have an extra day or two, if you really need it."

"Huntsville can live with it, Mr. President," Hans Sturmer said.

"And the Cape," said Albrecht Freer.

"Speaking for the contractors," Jim Matthison said, "it will take some doing, but I think we can make it."

"We'll be ready," said Vernon Hertz.

"Houston can manage quite comfortably, I think," Dr. Cavanaugh said.

"Good," the President said. "That's decided. I shall go on television at 6 P.M. this evening and tell the country all about it."

"How much can we have for it?" Bob Hertz asked quietly. The President uttered a delighted laugh.

"Always my practical one! I have to have some secrets. Suppose you listen to television, too. I promise you it will be enough. Not enough to waste, but enough to do the job. Fair enough?"

"With some misgivings," Bob Hertz said, "I shall echo, 'Fair enough.'"

"Fair enough!" the President said, and laughed again.

There was a general stirring, a stretching and relaxing after tension, a general preparing to rise. The President held up his hand and abruptly it ceased. An attentive silence settled again.

"Now with that decided, I need your advice on one other matter, which is rather delicate. As you are aware, there are certain highly vocal critics of the space program who have long been opposed to any Mars expedition, and are especially opposed now that it appears that we may be entering a new competition with the Russians. I don't impart any invidious motives to them for this, it's just the fact: whenever the Soviet Union is involved, they become twice as frantic in urging their own country to take a back seat. I have never understood this, but there it is." He paused and gave them a candid look.

"There it is, for me as a President, as a politician, and as leader of this country. It creates certain practical problems, both politically and as regards the public climate in which we are to make this effort.

"You have all seen some of the papers this morning, and probably some of the television broadcasts. The usual wrecking crew is out full force against any attempt by us to overtake or beat the Russians. I, like you, happen to believe we must. I, unlike you, have to consider public opinion and the practical requirements of leadership in the kind of climate these people can create if I make no attempt to appease them and ignore their outcries completely.

"Now: let me ask you this, Bob, or any of you—have we ever received from the Russians any evidence of genuine co-operation in space since the whole space business began?"

"Never!" Hans Sturmer spat out.

Albrecht Freer nodded vigorous agreement.

"They always want to go through our plants and find out what we're doing," Jim Matthison remarked, "but they never tell us what they're doing."

"In fairness," Vernon Hertz said, "two or three vaguely worded scientific papers, at various international meetings each year, usually about some space achievement they made ten years ago. Almost nothing current, and nothing at all of any real substance."

"The cosmonauts sure believe in loading us with vodka when we go over there," Bert Richmond recalled with a reminiscent smile, "but they sure as hell don't tell us anything."

"They never co-operate," Hank Barstow said flatly. "We're wide open and they're tight as a drum. There's no argument: it's historical fact."

"Also in fairness," Bob Hertz remarked, "they did sign the space treaty."

Albrecht Freer gave a skeptical snort.

"Subject to cancellation without notice," he said dryly. "And launching themselves immediately, in violation of it, upon a constant program of testing weapons systems in space which continues to this day."

"Therefore," the President said calmly, "I take it you would be somewhat dismayed if I were to issue a formal invitation to them to participate jointly in the expedition to Mars?"

Bob Hertz shrugged.

"It's already been tried, years ago, and they turned it down. Why try again?"

"Particularly," Dr. Cavanaugh said, "when we start from behind the eight-ball and it would put us in the position of looking as though we were begging favors from them."

"To say nothing," Connie Trasker remarked, "of the fact that our technology is still a long way ahead of theirs, Space Station *Stalin* or no Space Station *Stalin*. So we give more than we get if we let them in. Right, Vernon?"

"That's right," Vernon Hertz said. "The American problem," he added wryly, "is very simple: lots of brains but no money."

"Then I take it you're unanimously against any such invitation," the President said. He nodded. "So am I. It won't be issued. But I thought I should get your advice." He smiled his most engaging smile. "I may have to quote you, if Percy Mercy or the *Times* or somebody like that gets too severe."

"Please do," Dr. Sturmer said. "I should be honored."

"So would we all," Bob Hertz agreed.

"Thank you, gentlemen," the President said pleasantly, and rose to his feet. "I think we have accomplished a good deal this morning. If I had some champagne on hand, I would propose a toast to Piffy One. Since it's too early in the day for that, you will just have to rest assured that you have my respectful and earnest good wishes and my every support."

And he left them happily aglow with the knowledge that though he had given them a hard and difficult task, they could rest confident and happy in the certainty of his support; not aware at that moment that to a President "support" means many things and takes many forms, not all of them exactly what his listeners may assume when, in the first bright enthusiasm of the moment, he utters words which to them appear as direct and unequivocal as words can be.

Immediately, things began to move; and as always with NASA, the first instinct was to hold a meeting. By 2 P.M. the Administrator was conferring at headquarters with the Associate Administrator for Manned Space Flight, the Program Director for Project Argosy, the Director of Space Science and Applications, the Director of Engineering and Development, the retired Air Force General who was Department of Defense representative to NASA and the Chairman of the Atomic Energy Commission.

In Huntsville, Hans Sturmer was leaning over the drawing board with six of his top colleagues chattering happily in a torrent of English and German as they swiftly sketched, swiftly destroyed and swiftly sketched again the ideas that came tumbling headlong for the final details of the new engines and the modification of the three launch vehicles.

At the Cape, Albrecht Freer was meeting in a state of jovial excitement with the Cape's manager of Project Argosy, the director of procurement, the director of engineering and the director of public affairs. They too were eagerly studying designs and drawings, maps of Kennedy Space Center, sketches of Launch Complex 39, the projected site for Pad C.

At North American Rockwell in Downey, California, at Boeing in Seattle, at IBM in Huntsville, Bendix in Fort Lauderdale, McDonnell Douglas in St. Louis and at several hundred other contractor and subcontractor plants and factories throughout the country, managers, engineers, technicians and directors of personnel were busily making plans to advertise for workers, rebuild their crews, retool their production lines, put the aerospace industry back into gear again.

At the Jet Propulsion Lab, at Goddard, Ames, Langley, Lewis and all the allied and associated research centers at more than 150 universities and colleges that did contract work for NASA, scientists, doctors and engineers prepared to resume or hasten experiments slowed to a walk by insufficient funding, and began to make serious plans for planetary flight, and for the really thorough study of Mars that at last seemed feasible.

And in Houston, the Director met with Bob Hertz, the director of space science and applications, Houston's manager of Project Argosy, the director of engineering and development, the director of procurement, the director of public affairs, Hank Barstow, Bert Richmond and Connie Trasker, to discuss with a revived and enthusiastic confidence, the great challenge and how they planned to meet it with the efficiency, skill and expertise that had always been the pride of the Manned Spacecraft Center.

All of this, which NASA had been unable to achieve in years of patient pleading with a cautious President, a critical press and a penny-pinching Congress, the Soviet Union had achieved in twenty-four hours.

Such is the marvelous nature of American foresight.

At day's end, most of the machinery required for the emergency launch of Planetary Fleet One was either under way or in an advanced state of preparation.

Only the President's final word to the country remained to make it official.

3.

"You really believed him, then," Jane said as they waited for the broadcast in the comfortable house in El Lago. "You don't think he'll let you down."

"My wife," Connie Trasker explained elaborately to Pete Balkis, who was lounging on the enormous sofa that stood along the two-story window looking out upon the garden, "is one of those inverterately suspicious women who give flesh to the clichés about marriage."

"She's cute, though," Pete pointed out with his cheerful grin. "You have to admit that."

"Yes," Colonel Trasker agreed, "I do admit that."

"It's one of those nice things he does," Jane said with a comfortable laugh. "It keeps me under control when the kids go on the rampage, or he has to stay up in *Mayflower* for a month's training, or he goes to the Moon for a couple of weeks. The little wife is happy at home, basking in the warmth of her lord and master's distant—but cordial, mind you—approval."

Pete Balkis smiled.

"I think he really means it, you know. He really does."

"Oh, I know he does," Jane said. "I just can't avoid a little spacewife's dig once in a while." She smiled. "Fortunately, I don't dig as deep as some."

Pete's expression changed and for a second his usual outward ebullience was shadowed a little.

"I know," he said gravely.

"I'm sorry," Jane said quickly. "I know you do."

"This program is very rough on wives," Connie remarked, twirling the ice in his glass and staring thoughtfully at the floor. "It asks an awful lot of them."

"The first year's the hardest," Jane said. "Some adjust and some don't."

"Helen didn't," Pete said.

"I know," Jane said. "But maybe you didn't either. Maybe the program was just an excuse. Anyway," she went on more lightly, as again some subtle sadness briefly touched his usually amiable and engaging face, "I can go through the Clear Lake communities right now and find you a dozen households held together by nothing more than devotion to the program. Along with many more, of course, that hold together because the husbands and wives really want them to."

"Almost no divorces," Connie remarked, "in almost two decades. Rather far," he added dryly, "from the national average."

"I was one of the bad boys," Pete remarked.

"Or one of the honest ones," Connie suggested.

Pete looked thoughtful.

"I'm surprised I got in, after being divorced. If it hadn't been for Vernon Hertz I probably wouldn't have. Now," he added quietly, "I'm not so sure I'm glad I did."

"Why?" Connie asked with a genuine concern. "I didn't know you were unhappy here."

Pete shrugged.

"I don't tell everybody everything." He grinned suddenly and his tone lightened. He reached over and slapped Connie's knee. "Not even you, old Daddy Confessor."

"Connie really thought you were eating it up," Jane said. "I can't remember how many times he's told me how well you were fitting in. I'm surprised, too."

"He's been very helpful," Pete said. His tone became completely serious, he looked straight at Connie. "Really, very kind." Then he smiled again and spoke more lightly. "A real great troop, as you military types in the program put it. No, I have no complaints about the way I've been received here. Everybody's been great to me. I just want to get busy and do something to justify all my training, that's all—and there just isn't anything to do. So I'm thinking very seriously about getting out."

"But things are going to change," Connie objected. He gestured toward the television. "The whole thing's going to pick up again. This is no time to run out on me."

"It wouldn't be running out on you, would it?" Jane asked, quickly and pleasantly. "It would be running out on the program, wouldn't it?"

"I'm not running out on anybody," Pete said before Connie could reply. "I'm just going to take my abilities, such as they are, where they'll be more appreciated and more used. It's a quite impersonal decision."

"Well, whether it's running out on me or the program or whatever," Connie said firmly, "this is no time to go. Sit tight, buddy. A lot of things are going to start happening as soon as we hear from our friend in the White House."

"Which," Jane said with a smile, "is even higher than Mars. Connie, why don't you get Pete another drink before the President starts?"

"Just time," her husband agreed. Pete gave him a level, searching look as he relinquished his glass.

"So you think I ought to stay around."

"I'm sure of it," Connie said quietly.

"I'll want a refill too," Jane said, rising also and moving to the television set. "Just time for both of us, Conn, if you'll hurry."

"Yes," he said with a certain dryness in his voice as he went to the bar in the corner. "I'll try."

"I think," Jane said, concentrating on the television set, "that with a little luck we should be able to get a really good picture."

"You've got one of the three-dimensional ones," Pete said in a politely interested tone. He got up and came to stand beside her. "How does it work?"

"Quite well," she said, flashing a smile up at him. "Want to try it?"

"No," he said, smiling back. "I'm content to be just a watcher."

"I wasn't quite sure."

"Oh, yes," he said, his eyes holding hers. "Watchers have their place. Otherwise, no admiring audience. Otherwise, no show."

"And this show," she said, turning back to the set, "is a good one."

"The greatest," he said, as Connie returned with their drinks.

"I'll drink to that," Jane said, raising her glass.

"I, too," Pete said, touching his glass to hers.

86

"And I too, whatever it is," Connie Trasker said.

His wife gave her merry laugh.

" 'The program,' " she said. "Isn't that what it always is—'the program?' "

"If you say so," Connie said with a rather puzzled smile. "Now, hush, everybody. Your great leader is about to address you."

"My," Jane remarked as they sat down in a dutiful row on the sofa, "he *is* a handsome man, isn't he?"

And so he was as the Great Seal of the United States faded slowly from the screen and his confident head and massive shoulders took its place. The hushed tones of the announcer introduced him, he folded his hands calmly on the desk before him, looked straight into the cameras and began in his usual direct and informal way—"just like he was a friend sitting right there in your own house," as so many of his admiring countrymen put it to one another after each performance.

"My fellow Americans," he said, "as you know, your government has received intelligence which indicates that the Soviet Union is planning a major space launch, probably to the planet Mars. In fact"—and he smiled comfortably—"we have received enough intelligence so that we know beyond any doubt that the goal is Mars.

"This has prompted us to re-examine some decisions of the past, and to make some new decisions for the future. I want to tell you about them now.

"First of all, we were confronted with the basic decision: should we, as some propose, simply ignore this new challenge in space and continue the low-key but ultimately certain time schedule that would in due course put us on the planet Mars in the mid 1980's—several years after what now appears to be a likely Russian landing there?

"Or should we institute an immediate crash program in an attempt to overtake and hopefully surpass our Russian friends, and so once again achieve the sort of national triumph we had when we landed first on the Moon?"

"Most of us can still remember the great thrill of that first step on the Moon. I don't believe it takes too difficult a stretch of the imagination to think how we would have felt if that had been a Russian step, a Russian flag, a Russian telecast.

"We have only to watch it against what we actually feel now when, as a result of past decisions that deliberately cut back our space efforts, we see Space Station *Stalin* pass over our country, as it has for almost two years, every couple of hours.

"It is not a comfortable feeling, even though there has to date been no overt Soviet attempt to use the space station to threaten us, either on Earth or in space. It still is not very pleasant to look up there and see that large object passing over, trailed by our little *Mayflower*."

He paused and took a drink of water, then returned with increasing gravity to his statement.

"I do not think Americans like to be second best. With *Mayflower* we made a deliberate decision to be second best. At the same time we made a decision that we might be second best with Mars. But that decision can still be reversed.

"I think," he said, and he gave the famed defiant toss of the head that always thrilled so many, "it should be.

"Now!

"I am assured by my advisers in the space program that we have on hand the scientific knowledge, the technology and the brave men——"

"Yaaaayyy, team!" Pete Balkis murmured, and Jane said, "You're being disrespectful!" with a muffled giggle. Connie asked rather sharply, "What's with you two?" and looked, for a moment, quite offended, before he decided to relax and smile a little.

"——to do the job. And to do it——fast.

"I have accordingly asked the National Aeronautics and Space Administration to be ready to launch Planetary Fleet One of Project Argosy on or about a date eight months from today.

"For this mission we have decided to select a crew of four men. They will be launched on three modified Saturn V vehicles from Kennedy Space Center. The mission will consist of a Command-Service Module, a Mars Landing Module and a Medico-Scientific Module. They will dock in space and then proceed in tandem, with a scheduled landfall on Mars approximately eight months later.

"Our intelligence tells us that this target, if successful, will put us on the planet perhaps a month before the Soviet Union. But whether it does or not"——and again the vigorous, challenging toss of the head——"at least they will know they have had some competition!

"They won't know it if we sit placidly by—and wait for their launch—and do nothing about it.

"For this purpose," he said, "I have decided to allocate—"

"Here it comes," Connie Trasker said with a sharp intake of breath.

"—out of emergency funds available to me, the sum of five hundred million dollars."

"That's ridicu—" Jane began indignantly.

"Listen!" her husband commanded.

"I have also decided," the President said, "to send to Congress tomorrow morning a special message requesting the sum of one billion, five hundred million dollars."

"Hot damn!" Pete said. "How's that for dropping the other shoe?"

"It'll be tight," Connie said happily, "but we can do it."

"Added to this year's budget of three billion, three hundred million dollars," the President went on, "this will provide NASA, with reasonable economies, somewhere in the neighborhood of four and one-half billion to devote exclusively to the scheduled launch of Planetary Fleet One eight months from today.

"I am confident this can and will be done.

"I will say," he went on, and his tone changed to one of more earnest discussion, more emphatic candor, "that there might be one way to avoid such a new space race, which is inevitably going to be very costly to both the Russians and ourselves. And that is for us to do it together.

"However, I must say to you, my fellow Americans, that there is virtually no evidence on the historical record of the past three decades that the Soviet Union has the slightest desire or intention to co-operate with us here on Earth, in any way. This is equally true of space. It would be nice if this were not so, and I know that many of you wish desperately that it were not so. But it *is* so, and no amount of sentimentalizing or wistful, wishful thinking can change the fact. They have never been overtly or actively hostile to our program—so far as we know—but also they have never been anything but secretive—exclusive—closed-off—completely unco-operative.

"They did sign the space treaty. So did many nations, including our own. Immediately thereafter they began systematically violating its provisions by testing bomb-delivery systems in space. They have continued those tests to this day.

"That is the historical fact.

"Therefore, with real reluctance, but acting on the situation as it faces me, I have decided that there would be little point, as things stand now, in issuing any invitation to the Soviet Union to join us in this effort.

"In space," he said, somewhat bleakly, "as on earth, it seems to be their preference to go it alone. So be it.

"Somewhat earlier than we planned, but still well within the capabilities of our present technology," he concluded gravely, "we are outward bound for Mars. I know you will all join me in prayers for the safe conclusion of this venture, and for all the brave and dedicated men who will, with God's good grace, turn the dream into reality."

And to the strains of the national anthem the distinguished, determined face faded from the screen.

"Specious, specious, specious!" Percy Mercy said angrily at Kennicut Williams' plush bachelor apartment at The Watergate. And, "Specious, specious, specious!" said all of Percy's friends in the editorial offices of the *Times,* the *Post,* the other newspapers that agreed with them, the magazines and the networks. And, "Specious, specious, specious!" said all the cautious, the earthbound, the unventuresome, the timid and the hostile, who for reasons monetary, self-interested or political, opposed the flight to Mars. "Oh, specious, specious, specious!"

"I told you he was for us one hundred per cent," Connie said with satisfaction.

"Never let it be said," Jane murmured, "that *he* was the man who deliberately let us fall behind the Russians."

"Do you think that's all it is?" her husband demanded. "Just politics? You should have been in that meeting yesterday. There wasn't any doubt about his commitment."

"Oh, that's obvious."

"Then what is it?" Connie asked with some exasperation. "Why are you so suspicious?"

She shrugged. "Just put it down to woman's intuition, I guess."

"You have it, doll," Pete said, and for just a second a wry little expression crossed his face and hers. He got up abruptly and stretched his arms full length above his head with a yawn and a whoop. "Thanks for the drenks, y'all, hear?" he said in an exaggerated Texas accent. "Ah've got to ru—uhn."

"Don't do that," Jane suggested. "Stay for dinner."

"Alice and I stayed until midnight last night and almost made him late for his Washington meeting," Pete pointed out. "Can't overstay my welcome again."

"Never that," she said.

"That's right," Connie agreed. "Stick around. It'll probably be hamburgers and beer, but—"

"No, thanks, really," Pete said. "I've got to go." A mischievous look came into his eyes. "Got to write out that resignation."

"Now—" Connie began. The mischievous look faded.

"Seriously, now. What chance is there for me, anyway? You heard him: four crew members. Just where does little Petros fit in?"

"Pete," Connie said with a certain annoyed frustration, "will you stop this guff? You have as much chance as anybody else."

Pete smiled.

"Four, the man said. Just four, out of all us eager beavers, each one breathing hot and heavy to get on board. I repeat, what chance—"

"I'm not so sure you're all breathing hot and heavy," Jane said thoughtfully. "Not everybody is as anxious as my husband to leave his wife and family to go off sixty million miles on a highly dangerous mission."

For a moment Connie studied her gravely.

"Some are less anxious," he said finally, "and some are more. Some don't want to get away at all, and they're eliminated right off as possibilities because NASA isn't in the business of forcing anybody who doesn't want to go. And some want to get away much more, because they can't stand it at home. That isn't why I want to get away."

"Why do you want to get away?" she asked quietly, as Pete became very still and looked at them both with an intent and speculative expression.

Connie spread his hands in an almost hopeless way.

"I don't know," he said slowly. "Why do I want to go? I don't know. Ambition, maybe, to be honest about it? Sure. But there's a lot more to it than that. The same things that brought me into the program in the first place,

I suppose. The challenge of it. The thrill. The fact that there it is, and nobody's ever been there before, and I'd like to be one of the first. The urge to explore and find out what it's all about. The feeling that my country ought to do it first, and I'd like to help her. The desire to find out what I can do, stretched to my limit. All of these things, I guess."

Again he made the curiously frustrated gesture.

"I don't know, it's—I can't give you a poet's reason, I'm not a poet. I'm a technician. I have a pretty good idea inside me why I want to go, but—it's difficult to spell out . . ." He smiled and his tone became lighter. "One thing, though, Janie—it isn't because I want to get away from my wife and family. Now surely you know that."

"I guess so," she said, and managed a small and not very convinced or convincing smile. Her voice sounded suddenly bleak. "But it's an awfully long way and an awfully long time."

"Well," Pete said decisively. "I really must say good night."

"Wait until you see the crew list before you start writing out that resignation," Connie suggested as they started with him toward the door.

Pete turned and faced him squarely.

"Am I going to be on it?"

"You know I can't tell you that. In the first place, it hasn't been decided, and in the second, I couldn't tell you if it were, until it was officially announced."

"Surely you could tell an old buddy like me," Pete said in an almost mocking tone.

"No," Connie said quietly, "I could not. I will say this: you were going to be on the original twelve-man crew. But now we don't have a twelve-man crew any more. What happens now—"

Pete smiled.

"You and Hank and Bert will decide tomorrow morning."

"That's right," Colonel Trasker said crisply.

"And somebody may blackball me."

"That's right," Connie repeated in the same crisp tone.

Pete gave his quick, engaging grin, white teeth gleaming, dark eyes snapping with amusement under curly dark hair: suddenly very handsome, boyish and engaging, as he

92

could be when whatever weighed him down got out of the way.

"I will say you're an honest bastard. I still think I'd better go home and draft that letter."

"O.K.," Connie said with an answering smile, "but don't be in any hurry to mail it."

"I'll give you"—Pete glanced at his watch with an elaborate severity—"twenty-four hours. That ought to be enough."

"For better or worse," Connie agreed, "twenty-four hours from now the crew of Planetary Fleet One will be selected."

"Can I sleep tonight?" Pete asked.

Jane placed her hand on his arm.

"Some won't," she said, "but I'm sure you will."

"I don't know," Pete remarked. "Dark things move beneath this sunny surface." He leaned down to kiss her lightly on the cheek. "But you must."

"I'll try," she said, with a return of some of her normal cheerfulness.

"Good girl," he said. He held out his hand to Connie.

"Captain Courageous," he said with mock solemnity. "I want you to sleep well, too."

"I will if they'll leave me alone," Connie said, returning the handshake with a firm pressure. He smiled somewhat ruefully. "But they may not."

And as he and Jane came back into the softly lit, comfortable, lived-in room to watch, through the tall window looking out across the garden, the long, red Jaguar XKE of Dr. Petros Balkis disappear rapidly down the quiet, tree-lined street, the phone rang once, twice, thrice. Connie knew instinctively who it would be as he went in the study and snapped on the Picturephone.

"Hi," Jazz Weickert said without other preliminary. "When are you picking the crew?"

"Tomorrow morning, I suppose."

"Everything I said day before yesterday still goes."

"Does it?" Connie asked in an ironic tone. "That's a surprise."

"Yes, it does!" Jazz snapped. "And I don't want any smart-ass evasions."

His face changed, lost its angry expression, looked for a second uncertain and much younger than his thirty-eight years. "Connie," he said in an almost pleading voice, "can't you be fair? Why is it so hard to be fair to me?"

"We're trying to be fair to you, Jazz," Colonel Trasker began uncomfortably, but Commander Weickert was having none of it. The little-boy look faded, the angry man returned.

"Oh, hell," he said coldly. "Trying, trying, trying! You don't have to 'try.' Just do it, God damn it."

"You know I can't promise you anything," Connie said quietly.

Jazz uttered a short, harsh laugh.

"Except a royal shafting. Well: remember one thing, Connie. I have more right than almost anybody in the corps to be on that crew. And I intend to be."

"We will decide tomorrow morning," Connie said, his voice cold.

"Decide right," Jazz suggested in an unpleasant tone.

Connie stared at him without expression for a long, thoughtful moment.

"We will decide," he repeated, and before Jazz could reply, reached over and snapped off the machine.

"I couldn't help but overhear," Jane said at the door. "I suppose he does have a case."

"He has a case," Connie agreed shortly, "but he ruins it. When are we going to eat?"

"Well, don't take *my* head off," she said. "I'll go get it right now."

"Good." He smiled. "I'm sorry. He always does that to me."

"I hope nobody else calls," she said. "I'd like a husband for dinner, not a bear."

"I'll try to be a real, nice husband," he said, slapping her on the rump as they started to leave the den. The phone rang again. "Oh hell!" he said.

"Now, be nice to whomever it is," she admonished as she went on into the kitchen. To his surprise the shyly smiling face of Monetta Halleck, big-eyed, high-cheekboned, patrician, appeared on the screen.

"Why, hello, Monetta," he said. "What can I do for you?"

"You're surprised aren't you?" she asked, the sly smile widening.

"I am," he admitted. "Beautiful girls don't call me every evening."

94

"That," she said lightly, "is not the way I hear it."

He laughed.

"It's true, I swear. What can I do for you?"

The smile vanished, the big eyes looked solemn and twice as big. He thought again, as he had on the two or three occasions when they had met briefly at NASA receptions on the base, that she had a thoroughly nice and patrician look. And why shouldn't she? he reproved himself automatically. Aren't many of them just as—and then his mind ordered, Oh, stop it, and he concentrated attentively on what she was saying.

"It's about Jayvee. I'm worried about him."

"He isn't there, I take it."

"He took Rudden to the movies to see the latest Walt Disney."

"Gramps and the Mars Buggy?" he asked with a smile. "I feel like Gramps, myself, right now."

"That's the one," she said, smiling also. Then the smile faded again. "I had to do something to make him stop brooding and get out of the house, even if it did involve Mars."

"Is Mars the problem?" he asked.

She hesitated and then said, with a formality that he found quite touching in some way he couldn't exactly define,

"Colonel Trasker, could we meet so I could talk to you frankly?"

"Sure," he said. "How about coming here tomorrow morning? It'll have to be early, though. I've got to get over to the office to work on the crew."

"Wouldn't Mrs. Trasker mind? I mean, if we—I mean—"

"Honey," he said, in a tone kindly enough so there was no sting in it, "she'd mind a lot more if we met behind her back, now, wouldn't she?"

Monetta smiled again, her shy, generous smile.

"I guess so," she admitted. "But I just don't know—"

"You come over here about 8:30, if you can." He grinned. "Tell Jayvee Jane wants to consult you about a party she's planning for the wives, if he catches you."

The shy smile gave way to a laugh, a trifle cautious, he thought, but genuinely amused.

"He wouldn't believe I'd be coming to a reception at your house."

"I'm damned if I know why not!" he said with a genuine indignation. "Nobody I know of at NASA has ever shown any——"

"I know," she said hastily, "I know. But you don't know Jayvee. He broods a lot."

"He has no cause here to brood on that subject!" Connie said sharply, looking and sounding every inch the protective astronaut.

Monetta looked deeply troubled and again she spoke quickly. "I know, I'm sorry. He really doesn't, I know that. It's just a part of—just everything. Maybe I could talk to you—we might be able to help him?"

"Certainly," Connie agreed, more quietly. "I've said you could talk to me. And I'm flattered you say maybe 'we' can help him. But I can't make any promises about crew assignments, if that's what you——"

"Oh no," she said quickly again, and he thought, Oh, yes, little girl. And maybe Jayvee put you up to this and knows all about it, after all. Bu he didn't say so, and his expression revealed nothing as he replied calmly,

"All right, then, come on over and I'll be glad to talk. I repeat, though—early. O.K.?"

"8:30," she said. "I'll be there."

"I'll be looking forward to it," he said. She smiled again her wide, shy smile and said softly,

"So will I."

And then looked quite embarrassed—which made him suddenly feel quite embarrassed—and faded from the screen.

Well, he thought, I'm damned. And told himself sternly, Now see here, Buster. Just see here.

"Janie!" he called as he went into the living room. "That was interesting. Do you know who that was?"

Later they watched television for a while: the factual reports of the President's talk, the not-so-factual analyses of the President's talk, the special programs that sought, through a careful selection of panelists and a careful slanting of questions, to tear down, derogate and minimize the new space effort. A few of those who appeared had a good word to say for it: some of the veteran space reporters, harking back sentimentally to the days of the great triumphs at the Cape, were obviously thrilled by the return of the old excitement. But for the most part it was, like all reports on matters that arouse the hostility of the networks, a querulous, nit-picking, ill-tempered, ungracious presentation. Running through it were two constant refrains: what right did America have to spend money to challenge the Russians again, when she had so many troubles right here at home? And, What was the point in going there anyway, when it was just one more barren planetary wasteland?

Finally Connie got up, crossed over, switched off the set.

"It's nice to know one is popular with one's fellow countrymen," he remarked dryly.

"The President isn't going to like it," Jane observed.

"Well, he isn't going to back down at this point," Connie said flatly. "He can't possibly."

"No," she said. "He won't back down directly."

"He won't back down at all!" Connie said sharply.

"I hope not, for your sake, and for all of you," she said. "Because I don't suppose," she added with a kind of wistful thoughtfulness, "that you will back down, either."

"No, I won't," he said calmly. "Why should I?"

"Perhaps because your wife would rather you didn't go," she said quietly, so quietly that they both were suddenly conscious of the stillness of the house, the hush of El Lago, the awareness that in many similar houses around Clear Lake men and women must be thinking and talking about much the same things in this late hour.

"Janie," he said finally, sitting down beside her on the sofa, "what is this, anyway? You've been the prize wife of the program for fifteen years. If there was ever anybody who was gung-ho, it was Jane Trasker." His tone became light and humorous. " 'Go get Jane Trasker,' they cried when a visiting Vice-President came on the scene. 'Go get Jane Trasker!' they cried when they needed someone to ride in a space parade. 'Go get Jane Trasker!' they shouted when a new wife in the program needed consoling. And now," he said, his voice turning serious and puzzled, "it seems to be Jane Trasker who needs the consoling. Why? What's wrong?"

"I know it's foolish, I know it's stupid. I know it doesn't make any sense at all. But anyway—I'm worried."

"There were more dangerous things in Mercury, Gemini and Apollo."

She gave him a skeptical smile.

"Maybe. But I doubt it. And so, my boy, do you."

He started to bluff—abandoned it—nodded.

"I'm not saying it's not going to be a dangerous mission. I can't say that. It's going to be a hell of a dangerous mission. And I'm not going to say that I'm going into it completely calm and confident and without any fears of my own, because that would be stupid. Of course I have some fears and worries. I'm human. Oh yes," he said with a smile as she made a little movement of mock protest, "I am, believe it or not. Even old Perfect Astronaut Conrad C. Trasker is afraid once in a while. But I'm not afraid to the point where it's going to blind my judgment, or cripple me emotionally, or destroy my confidence in my own ability, or the ability of my crew, to do what we have to do to come through safely. Because I've trained too long for this. I'm like most of us astronauts: I'm too good, basically, to be really, permanently scared of the job I've got to do. Scared once in a while, maybe, at given moments: but not scared over-all. And not to the point of letting it really mess me up."

"But you don't know the kind of crew you're going to have. You don't know who else is going to be with you—and how good *they* are—and whether or not *they're* afraid—and whether you can really depend on *them*." She smiled, again almost wistfully. "I know you all right, God knows, and I know you're just what you say you are. But I don't know them." She shivered. "And I don't know Mars."

"I don't either," he said, "except what JPL and the unmanned probes have told us about it. But it can't be any worse than the Moon, and we've mastered that. I've been there a couple of times, and this'll just be an extension. As for the crew—" He paused and stared thoughtfully into the empty fireplace.

"Yes," she said softly. "What about the crew?"

He shrugged.

"That we'll have to decide tomorrow morning. But it won't be a pack of babies."

"It ought to be the absolute best you can get, in character, in experience, in training, in ability." Her voice became flat. "And you're going to put Pete on it. Aren't you?"

He gave her a quick look, genuinely puzzled.

"What's this about Pete, all of a sudden? Why are you jealous of Pete? I'm not sleeping with him."

98

"Darling," she said with a laugh that managed to sound amused, "you can sleep with anybody you like. You can even sleep with Monetta Halleck, if that's who you—"

"Janie!" he exclaimed with a sudden real anger. "What *is* this? First you're worried about my going to Mars and now you're worried about my sleeping with everybody. What's it all about? I don't get it."

"I," she pointed out sweetly, "was not the one who introduced the concept of sleeping. Why did you?"

He sighed with a certain grimness.

"Now, see here. I know the wives in this program are jealous of a lot of things, and one of them is the time us little boys spend with each other—"

"And with little girls," she said, lighting a Safecig with a hand that trembled.

"—but," he went on calmly, "that doesn't mean us little boys are anything but just good buddies, even though by the very nature of having to depend so completely on one another, it gets closer than a lot of friendships. But that's all it is, and I'm ashamed you force me to defend it. As for spending time with little girls—some do and some don't."

"And you don't."

"Shall I really tell you?" he asked patiently. "Would it really make you a lot happier if I confessed a lot of things that weren't so?"

She smiled without amusement.

"Or are so."

"Good Lord," he said, and sighed again. "If you knew all the opportunities we have for all sorts of things—"

"Don't think we don't know!" she interrupted quickly. "Don't think we aren't all very much aware!"

"Well, how happy you all must be," he said bitterly. "How happy, sitting here in Clear Lake eating your hearts out while we're away." He tried to take her hand but she pulled it away. "For Christ's sake, Janie, and here all this time I thought you were one wife who didn't do that. I thought I was lucky enough to have a girl who kept her head and didn't spend all her time brooding about it. I thought I really had the wife they described in those articles they wrote during the Apollo flight. 'Calm and serene, lovely Jane Trasker has just two major interests in the world: her husband's career in the space program, and their delightful family in El Lago, Texas. Today with absolute faith and confidence in their husband and father, she and her three lively children are awaiting news of Col. Trasker's safe landing on the Moon—' "

"And I suppose," she said with a sort of weary humor, "I thought I had the husband they described at the same time. 'Colonel "Connie" Trasker may attract the adjectives "handsome" and "dashing" more often than most, but there's no more loving husband or devoted family man in the space program—' "

"And am I not?" he demanded sharply.

"You all have the image."

"And so do all of you," he said angrily. "So do all of you. And I for one am generous enough to admit that most of the time, it's the true one. You aren't generous enough to admit that about me, though, are you?"

"Oh, I do admit it," she said quietly. "I think you're perfectly capable of being a loving husband and devoted father at the same time you're being starry-eyed over what a buddy Pete Balkis is, while simultaneously bedding down with Monetta Halleck, and, no doubt, carrying on with eight or ten other people on the side, in addition. You men are all larger than life—it goes with the program."

"But we aren't," he said, trying to keep calm. "That's the point everybody misses. We're just ordinary guys like everyone else—"

"Ordinary guys don't go into space," she said flatly. "You like to think you're like everybody else, but you aren't. You work harder, and you play harder, and a lot of you have something nature built in that takes more than lovely Jane Trasker and her three lively children to satisfy."

"As for Monetta Halleck," he said, struggling to pick out some point of reference that would restore the conversation to a plane of relative sense, "I haven't seen Monetta in two months—and that, as I recall, was at the supermarket in Nassau Bay. She was buying dog food and I was buying cat chow for Tom-Toby. We smiled. We said hello. We remarked that Houston was having a rainy winter. We speculated briefly on whether it would clear the next day. I said, 'Give my best to Jayvee,' and she said, 'Give my best to Jane—' "

"But you didn't, did you?" she asked quickly. "I don't remember any greetings from Monetta. Ever."

"Janie, I repeat, what *is* this? And as for Pete Balkis,

he's a hell of a nice guy, and we work together very well, and I'm very fond of him——"

"He's fonder of you."

"That may be," he agreed calmly. "I'm aware of it. So is he. But that's where it stops—for him as well as me—and it's utterly ridiculous to even dream anything more. I repeat: Good—*Lord*. And as for eight or ten others on the side——" he began to laugh in quite genuine amusement. "You tell me how I can fit them into the program and I'll be glad to oblige, if you like. I sure as hell can't find the time on my own. Now, quite seriously," he said, and this time he captured her hand and drew her toward him, "what is this? You really are lovely, calm, serene Jane Trasker. You really are the prize wife in the program. You really are my girl, who has seen me through West Point, the Air Force, Mercury, Gemini and Apollo. You really are my good right arm who is going to see me through Project Argosy. What's with you, gal? You don't sound like yourself at all tonight. What's the problem?"

And, finally, she came into his arms and began to cry, in deep convulsive gulps that quite alarmed him.

"Shush—shush—shush—shush," he murmured softly, as he would to young Buddy or Jane Anne or Sue if they had a bump; "shush—shush—shush," stroking her hair and holding her tight.

"I know it's s-s-stupid," she said finally, drawing away a little to pull a handkerchief from her pocket and dab furiously at her eyes, "but I'm really scared of this mission. I d-don't know why, ex-exactly, but I just am. It scares me. I have a—a feeling—about it."

"Well, don't," he said gently. "It's going to be all right. We *will* have a good crew—and we have the technology—and I think the country as a whole will be behind us—and everything's going to move well——"

"And you," she said, still half-sobbing, but with a rueful little smile that acknowledged that life for him was a matter of ambitions and choices—"have to go."

"Yes," he said quietly, "I have to go. So: how about a smile and a kiss and a good roll in the hay, and we'll forget all about it, O.K.?"

"Lovely Jane Trasker," she said with a laugh still shaky but coming back fast, "is agreeable to all those things. But she won't forget all about it. How can she?"

"True," he said, serious again. "But at least don't let it

101

get you down, and don't let it make you say a lot of things you don't mean, because that doesn't help either of us. All right?"

"All right," she said as he leaned over to kiss her. She tucked away the handkerchief and stood up. "Just let me check the kids and then I'll join you for whatever you have in mind."

"Plenty," he said with a relieved grin. "Don't be too long."

"You either," she said, her face flushing in the way that always excited him.

And for the last time that night, the phone rang.

"Oh *hell,*" he said, jumping up and sprinting for the den. "I'll choke off the interfering bastard in a hurry, believe me!"

But he had no need to, for the interfering bastard was Hank Barstow and he was, as always, terse and to the point.

"Sorry to bother you at this ungodly hour," he said calmly, "but Dr. Cavanaugh just called me that he's heard from Andy Anderson, and Andy says there seems to be a lot of pressure building up. He's got hold of the *Times* and they have an editorial deploring the whole project but saying that if we're going to be such damned fools"—Hank's impassive face was crossed by the smallest of grimly ironic smiles—"as to try to get to Mars ahead of the Russians, the crew should damned well represent all sections of the American populace. And you know what that means. I understand they also put in a plug for Jazz Weickert, along the way."

"Has Andy heard from the White House?" Connie asked.

Hank shook his head.

"Not yet. But I think it would behoove us, buddy boy, to get our asses over to that office at the break of dawn tomorrow morning, choose our crew and announce it just as fast as we can, before anybody back there gets a chance to do some second-guessing."

"I have an appointment at 8:30—" Connie began, and then instantly corrected himself. "Sorry, nothing. What time?"

"How about 7? Or even 6?"

"I can make it at 6 if you and Bert can."

"We'll be there."

"Roger," Connie said. "Sleep well."

"You too," Hank said. For a moment his usual carefully cultivated calm cracked open. "I get so God damned sick and tired of these arch, irresponsible bastards in the press!" he snapped. "What the hell do they know about the chances we have to take, and what we have to have to make up a reliable and flightworthy crew?"

"Screw 'em," Connie advised. "Don't let it worry you. We'll do it our way, and we'll do it right."

"I wish I were as confident as you are. See you in the morning."

"Roger," Connie said again.

Half an hour later he stood by the bedroom window staring up into the great, soft Texas sky, where the stars at night are indeed big and bright. Inexorably across them there presently came huge, glowing Space Station *Stalin*, followed dutifully a few moments later by smaller, glowing Space Station *Mayflower*.

He sighed heavily.

A little sound of amusement came from the darkened bed, where peace and harmony had apparently been fully restored.

"Come along and stop worrying. I'm still available. And tomorrow, as Scarlett said, is another day."

"Scarlett," he said, trying to make his tone light but not really succeeding, "was right."

4.

But when tomorrow dawned, it appeared at first that all would go smoothly. It was 5:42 exactly—he looked at his watch with an instinctive glance that made him smile a little—when he drove the Porsche out of the garage and into the sleeping street. The quiet communities around Clear Lake were just beginning to stir, the first light was touching trees and lawns and well-kept houses. Even here, he thought with a certain wry humor as he began to pick up speed, the image prevailed: not even the occasional child's wagon abandoned by the curb, the odd bicycle leaning every-which-way beside a tree, could disturb it. Here, in this silent hour, all was dignified, substantial, almost stately. Here lived men with a Purpose, and their near and dear.

He drove through the deserted shopping village in Nassau Bay, stopped for the light, crossed NASA Road One and turned into the space center; was waved on by the guard, went down the road past the administration building, turned into the parking lot in front of the Astronaut Office. Hank's Mercedes and Bert's Corvette were aleady there. He turned in smartly alongside the Mercedes, cut the motor, got out. It was 5:58 in Houston, almost 8 A.M. in Washington, D.C.

"Andy?" the familiar voice said, and on the viewer the familiar handsome face materialized. "Excuse my unshaven and unshorn appearance."

"Mine, too, Mr. President," the Administrator pointed out. "What's the problem?"

104

"Not so fast," the President said with a chuckle. "Always straight to business, aren't you? It's not any crisis."

"That's good," Dr. Anderson said, with a certain wariness, for like many others in the government he had learned that with this President an apparently direct approach sometimes concealed an inborn love of intrigue.

"Nope, it's not a crisis," the President said with an air of satisfaction. He chuckled again. "It's a good and rare day when I can say that. No, it's just our friends in the press and some others around the country who seem to be a little excited."

"I see," the Administrator said cautiously. "You mean the *Times*."

"No, not just the *Times*," the President said, "though I must admit they sound rather severe. It's some of the others, too. And I'm getting some urgent wires. People like Percy Mercy, and so on . . ." His voice trailed away for a moment and he appeared to be in a brown study.

"What's Percy up to now?" the Administrator asked. The President came back abruptly from wherever he was. He grinned.

"He's frightfully upset. Simply frightfully. We're getting Percy Comma Mercy, in spades. He tells me he's rushing out an advance release on an article by Kuselevsky that denies the Russians have any intention of trying to launch to Mars. He says he's issuing a nationwide call for members in this new organization of his, this CAUSE thing, you know—the Committee Against Unilateral Space Exploration. He demands that we have a Negro on the crew in so many words—at least the *Times* shows a little delicacy, but you know Percy, he's about as subtle as a ten-ton truck —and he also demands that Jazz Weickert be selected. I wonder what you think of these suggestions?"

"I think," Andy Anderson said with a pleasant firmness, "that it is the astronauts' business who they select, and I think that neither Percy Comma Mercy, the *Times*, myself, nor, if you will forgive me, yourself, Mr. President, has the knowledge or the capability to tell them what to do."

The President looked thoughtful for a moment.

"Yes," he agreed. "You're of course entirely right. We do have, however," he added slowly, "at least you and I do—the authority."

"Which has only been used extremely rarely," the Administrator said, still pleasantly and firmly, "and then for only the most careful and cogent of reasons. Otherwise, we would have had a bunch of rebelling astronauts on our hands, long before this."

"You don't think the reasons that prompt Percy and the *Times*—and a good many others, I must tell you, according to the wires and calls we're getting here at the White House—are careful and cogent, then, I take it?"

"I do not," Dr. Anderson said crisply.

The President smiled.

"You're definite enough anyway," he said in a joshing tone.

"I intend to be."

"Well," the President said less jovially, "that's your privilege. And your job. And I admire you for it. It's your responsibility to be loyal to your own men. Even if you don't have quite the over-all responsibility I have."

"Mr. President," Andy Anderson said in a calm and impersonal voice, "if you were to make an attempt to influence the choice of that crew, I believe I would resign. And so would half the astronaut corps."

The President gave him a keen look.

"You're not threatening me now, of course."

Dr. Anderson shook his head.

"Certainly not. I'm projecting a likely situation for you, if certain things happen."

"Mmmmm," the President murmured thoughtfully. He smiled suddenly.

"Well! No need for us to get so solemn about it. I just thought you should know about some of the pressures that are beginning to come in on this thing."

"I hope they won't seriously influence the fate of Project Argosy," Dr. Anderson said. "I should hate to think our national purposes were so easily swayed by those who customarily attack everything their own country tries to do."

The President blinked and grinned.

"Wow!" he said softly. "You space people really don't like to be tampered with, do you?"

"Not especially," Andy Anderson said, relaxing a little and smiling, but not too much.

"Well," the President said comfortably, "don't worry about it, and I won't either. It will all blow over shortly, I'm sure. And don't worry about resigning, you and your boys. I'm not really such a big, bad ogre. After all, haven't I just laid it on the line and given you the go-ahead you wanted?"

"We're very grateful to you for that, Mr. President."

The President nodded.

"Fine, then. We see eye to eye." He paused. "You will get the word along to me, though, won't you, as soon as you hear from Houston?"

"Immediately."

"Good. I have every confidence the crew selected will be one worthy of the responsibility, in every way. Good-by for now, then, Andy. I'll be expecting to hear from you later in the day."

"Just as soon as I hear, Mr. President."

"Good," the President said comfortably. "Let's give 'em hell, Andy!"

"Let's," the Administrator agreed, as the confident, commanding presence waved and faded from the screen with a last cheerful smile.

But whether they would, he was now not at all sure. He realized suddenly that his organization was in a fight, and not only with the Russians. He did not know, at the moment, whether the pressures NASA could muster on the one side to influence a Chief Executive's political sensitivities would be enough to outweigh the pressures coming from the other side.

He went into his study, tiptoeing so he would not wake Louise, and punched the button on his direct line to Houston.

5.

"I don't want to influence you," Bob Hertz said, his face reflecting his concern, "but I thought you should keep all factors in mind when you make your decisions—"

"You aren't going to run out on us, are you, Bob?" Hank Barstow asked sharply.

Bob shook his head.

"I am not," he said quietly, "and you know it. But, there are these pressures—among them, I regret to say, my own brother—and I think you should be aware of them. Andy wanted me to pass the word on to you for whatever it may be worth."

"What does Andy think it's worth?" Bert Richmond demanded. "He seemed to be on our side when he called Jim Cavanaugh last night."

"He's still on our side," Bob Hertz said patiently, "but last night he had only read the newspapers. This morning he's heard from the President. You have to admit there's a difference."

"Only if the President is going to let himself be scared by the newspapers," Connie Trasker remarked.

"That's right," Hank said.

"That's for damned sure," Bert agreed.

Three stubborn astronaut faces stared at the director of flight operations from the little screen. Bob Hertz sighed.

"Now, don't get hard-nosed, you guys," he suggested with a calmness he did not feel. "You do what you think best, but just keep in mind that you aren't operating in a vacuum on this one. This time a lot of people, right on up to the President, are looking over your shoulder. Just be aware, that's all: be aware. That's all I'm asking you. All right?"

"Did you say," Hank asked softly, " 'be aware' or 'be ware'?"

"It's the same thing in Old English, isn't it?" Bob Hertz asked with an attempt at lightness that was not rewarded in the solemn faces. "Come on, now," he urged, dropping the humor. "Just take it easy. Get the chips off your shoulders and be damned sure you know what you're doing—and *have your reasons ready* if you get challenged. That's all I'm asking."

"Are we going to be challenged?" Bert asked with something of Hank's ominous quiet.

Hank made a disgusted sound.

"Of course we are if we don't behave."

"I know one thing," Connie Trasker said calmly. "I'm taking the crew I have to take to do the best job on this mission. And if we decide it's the best crew, then it *is* the best crew. And it doesn't matter who's on it or who isn't. And it doesn't matter who likes it or who doesn't. That's the way it's going to be, or I don't fly."

"And we quit," Hank said with an equal calmness.

"Pronto," Bert said.

"Now, see here," Bob Hertz said, in the no-nonsense tone he sometimes had to adopt with obstreperous astronauts. "Suppose you guys just calm down, all right? You act like a bunch of spoiled babies sometimes. In the first place, you have too much of your lives invested in the program, and it means too much to you, to quit. In the second place nobody's going to force you to quit, or create a situation in which you have to quit. Andy just thinks you should keep everything in mind, that's all. And so do I. I don't want us to get in a hell of a mess over this. I just want you to be aware, or *beware,* or however the hell you want to put it, of what's at stake here."

"What you're saying, actually," Hank Barstow remarked, "is that we give in and go against our best judgment—or there's going to be a fight and we may be overruled. Surrender gracefully or get shot down, isn't that the gist of it? What other alternative," he demanded sharply as Bob Hertz looked annoyed and shook his head, "are you leaving us? Tell us, Bob. We're just a bunch of dumb astronauts, and we don't get it."

"I've fought your battles from the day I entered this

109

office," Bob Hertz snapped, "and I'll fight them 'til the day I leave. You're damned ungrateful if you don't recognize that, so stop giving me this 'dumb astronaut' crap and all the rest of it! I'm trying to help you as I always have, and I'd appreciate a little acknowledgment of the fact and a little co-operation in working things out like mature men, O.K.? Now you let me know as soon as you get those selections ready, and the sooner the better. All right?"

For several seconds he stared angrily at them and they stared angrily back. Finally Bert spoke quietly.

"You wouldn't really let us down, would you, Bob?"

"You'll stand by us if we need you, won't you?" Connie asked in a tone that rejected any other possibility.

"It would be a hell of a sad day for Houston if you didn't," Hank observed softly.

Bob Hertz' expression remained unrelenting.

"Let me know," he ordered crisply, reached over and snapped off his machine.

There was a long silence after the screen went dark. Bert broke it.

"Well," he said in a matter-of-fact tone, going to the blackboard that is standard equipment in all major NASA offices, "that decides two crew members, anyway."

And taking a piece of chalk he wrote in large letters, JAZZ WEICKERT and J. V. HALLECK, and through them both he drew a large, slashing line.

"Now," he said briskly, returning to the table. "Who've we got here?"

"Just a minute," Hank said. He pressed the temporary disconnect on his Picturephone, stepped over and locked the door, came back to his desk and plopped down in his seat with a casual air as the sun rose full over Clear Lake.

"Connie wants Pete Balkis," he remarked in a tone as businesslike as Bert's, "and that's O.K. with me. I've been thinking about Gaudy Gaudet—"

"And of course there's Em Wacker and Stu Yule," Connie suggested, "to say nothing of Roger Webb and—"

"Oh, we've got plenty of material," Hank agreed.

"We're loaded," Bert said comfortably.

Shortly before 11 A.M. Joe Stevenick, director of public affairs, Manned Spacecraft Center, Houston, faced a press auditorium clamorous with more than three hundred reporters come from all over the nation and the world to

110

hear the announcement of the crew of Planetary Fleet One.

"Ladies and gentlemen," he began, and then raised his voice to surmount the gossipy hum, *"ladies and gentlemen,* if you please! If you will all kindly calm down, I can give you the news you've been waiting for."

"It's about time," the Chicago *Tribune* remarked to the AP. He groaned. "And all this on an empty stomach!"

"I know," the AP agreed. "I've been here since 6:30 myself."

"Haven't we all," the *Christian Science Monitor* remarked with a yawn.

"That's the way the mission crumbles," the Washington *Star* said cheerfully.

"Hush!" said the Manchester *Guardian.*

"The Administrator of the National Aeronautics and Space Administration," Joe Stevenick began when they had all subsided sufficiently, "has been advised by the Astronaut Office—"

("That's an odd locution," the *Guardian* murmured to the *Times.* "Yes, it is," the *Times* agreed with an alert nod. "I wonder what—")

"—that after due consideration of the records of all members of the astronaut corps, it has been decided to recommend the following for assignment to Planetary Fleet One, Project Argosy.

"With these recommendations"—Joe Stevenick's customary bland manner did not quite subdue the little murmur of questioning that flickered over the auditorium— "the Administrator of NASA, the Director of MSC and the Director of Flight Operations, MSC, are pleased to concur. The following crew members accordingly are approved:

"Colonel Conrad C. Trasker, Jr., U. S. Air Force, commander of the Mars Landing Vehicle, MLV, and commander of the flight.

"Commander Hugo S. Gaudet, U. S. Navy, commander of the Command-Service Vehicle, CSV, and second in command of the flight.

"Astroscientist Dr. Emerson Wacker, geologist, commander of the Medico-Scientific Vehicle, MSV.

"Astroscientist Dr. Petros S. Balkis, specialist in medico-biological aspects of space exploration, co-commander of the MSV.

"Biographies of these men are in the rack in the press office.

"We are hopeful the crew will be available to you for a press conference sometime later this week. We will have to work that out with the Astro Office and let you know as soon as we have something definite.

"Thank you very much."

"Joe—" somebody shouted. But he was already on his way, brisk and bland, off the platform and out the door.

"If you ask me," Fairchild Publications remarked to the AP as they walked back to the press office in the bright windy morning, "I'll bet there's been a hell of a fight about something."

And although she was, as usual, right, neither she nor any of them could imagine at that moment just how bitter and far-reaching the battle had been in these past four hours.

Nor could they possibly have imagined then the bitter, far-reaching, in some ways noble and in some ways terrible, consequences that would flow from the combination of human likes, dislikes, dreams, desires, ambitions, jealousies, weaknesses and strengths that had prompted this day's decisions and would inspire those in the days immediately ahead.

6.

"No," the Administrator said with an angry impatience his secretary had rarely seen him display, "I am not available to speak to Senator Williams, or Mr. Mercy, or anyone else!"

"The White House," the Press Secretary said calmly, "has no comment whatsoever to make at this time."

"I?" Dr. Sturmer said sharply to the Huntsville *Times*. "Why should *I* have anything to say? We have things to do, over here!"

"I'm afraid," the chief secretary of the Astronaut Office said sweetly, "that Colonel Barstow and Commander Richmond are not available right now. Neither is Colonel Trasker. *Nor* Commander Weickert. *Nor* Dr. Halleck."

"No, no," Dr. Freer protested to the Orlando *Sentinel*. "I really have no comment, I am too busy with plans for building the new pad, you know."

"Well," Vernon Hertz remarked when his brother's face appeared on the screen. "It looks as though your boys have got themselves in a hell of a mess, doesn't it?"

"I don't have anything to say right now," Jazz Weickert said, at home. "But," he added dourly, "I may have. Why don't you call me back later?"

"Oh, no!" said Alexei V. Kuselevsky with a merry laugh, at the UN. "If the Americans wish to ignore the black peoples of their own country and the world, that is their business. I have no comment on such imperialist neo-fascist racism."

"They asked for it," the editor of the *Post* said grimly to the editor of the *Times,* who nodded agreement, "and we're going to give it to them." "So," promised the *Times* in a pure and righteous tone, "are we."

"He isn't here," Monetta Halleck said nervously. "I don't know where he is. But I'm sure there will be no comment."

"He's not here," Jane Trasker said cheerfully, "and if he were, he wouldn't talk to you. You know better than that."

"Of course we're very pleased," said Hugo Gaudet, as Emerson Wacker smiled agreement. "But other than that, we can't comment."

"Me?" Pete Balkis said with an amiable grin. "I don't know anything. I'm just going along for the ride."

"I regard this as the blackest hour of the space program," Percy Mercy said angrily. "Blackest because whitest. I also regard the deliberate passing over of Commander Weickert as an inexcusable affront to one of America's greatest astronauts. And the failure to invite the Soviet Union to participate in this great venture is absolutely shameful."

"I think the Senate will want to go into this whole flight and examine it very closely, as a result of this racist decision," Senator Williams said. "Also, what they did to Jazz Weickert is a crime. To say nothing of the deliberate, provocative slap in the face to the Russians. I expect to discuss the whole mess when we go back into session tomorrow afternoon."

"The Astronaut Office has made its decision," Bob

Hertz said calmly, "and as far as this office is concerned, the matter is closed."

"I think, Andy," the President suggested with a pleasant smile, "that you had better come over here and talk to me."

7.

Looking down at the noontime secretaries spilling out of the jumble of Federal buildings along Delaware and Independence Avenues while he waited for his driver to come and take him to the White House, Dr. Anderson reflected that his own tone when he said, "Yes, sir," had been as pleasant as the President's. Which, he thought somewhat grimly, was something of a miracle considering all that had transpired in the past four hours.

His talk with Bob Hertz, immediately following the President's early-morning call, had been amicable enough, though he had detected in that able gentleman's attitude a much more adamant defense of the astronauts than Bob had shown, shortly after, in his talk with the astronauts themselves. To the Administrator, Bob had been a staunch defender of the right of the corps to choose whomever its members believed best qualified to fly on Planetary Fleet One. He had dismissed news of the presidential concern with a cavalier snort and a harsh comment about, "Damned politics!" Then he had unloosed an earnest and impressive eloquence upon the Administrator.

"Andy," he said, his face solemn and intent, "I have been in this program for almost twenty years, now, and in that time I have seen many men come and go. Not a single one of them who was genuinely dedicated to the program ever knowingly let politics get into it, or did anything but fight to keep politics out. It would be a great shame if this President turned out to be different, but it would be an even greater shame if this Administrator turned out to be different.

116

"Now, I know," he said, holding up a hand to forestall Dr. Anderson's indignant interruption, "that you don't think you will let politics come into it, but don't you see that by the very act of transmitting the President's concern and implying that he might take a direct hand in it, you are helping him put politics into it? You are putting pressures on the corps. And you are putting pressures on me. They won't like this. Neither do I.

"Always, the space program has represented the one fine thing in this country on which most people could agree, and which the great majority of Americans could take pride in, and be thrilled by. We've been remarkably free from the politicians and the kooks." Again he forestalled an interruption, with a quick, acknowledging nod. "I'm well aware we may be facing both this time, but I want us to remain as free and independent as we always have. It's the only way to keep our goals intact and our program pure. I don't think we should yield an inch to presidential pressure or any other kind. I think we should support our men all the way in what we know to be right. It's the only way, Andy. Anything else spells disaster for the program, in the long run if not right away."

"Why don't you tell all that to the President?" Dr. Anderson suggested, and Bob Hertz' chin came up as firmly as the Chief Executive's own.

"Let him ask me," he promised, "and I will. I may even volunteer."

"Well, good for you," the Administrator remarked. "I only wish it looked that simple from here. You don't have the responsibility of getting the funds for this program. There are ways of bringing pressure to bear on us that haven't even been mentioned yet." He sighed and shook his head. "They don't have to be. They're implicit."

"Only if we accept them," the director of flight operations said firmly. Again Andy Anderson sighed.

"Yes, I know you pure in heart. You want to assail all the citadels."

"That's why we've achieved what we have in this program. There are a lot of us."

"Nonetheless," Dr. Anderson said with a firmness of his own, "we are faced here with a lively and active presidential interest by a lively and active President who, I suspect, will not hesitate to be as ruthless as we are if he really deems his own interests to be at stake. So I want at least a reasonable show of co-operation in considering his point of view. It isn't all selfish—he said the other day, he has to operate in the climate created by these people. He is by no means an entirely free agent, himself. He wants to help us with our problems, I'm convinced of that, and so I think we should at least be tolerant and willing to help him with his."

"Only to the point where it doesn't jeopardize the safety of my men or the success of the program," Bob Hertz said quietly.

"Well," Dr. Anderson said, "suppose you give it a little try, O.K.? Suppose you make clear to your three prima donnas down there what's at stake in all this. They aren't completely perfect, either, you know: they can bend a little too. I want them to try."

"Is that an order?"

"I hope we don't reach a condition in which we have to consider it so." the Administrator told him calmly.

Then they had said good-by without further discussion and Bob had talked to the Astronaut Office along the lines Andy had suggested, and apparently quite forcefully, too. Hank and Bert and Connie had all complained about it when they called Dr. Anderson a couple of hours ago to announce their selections. Again the Administrator had warned of possible presidential displeasure, cautioned against too much independence just for the sake of proving they could be independent, pleaded for some consideration of the practical factors involved.

"Look, Andy," Hank Barstow had demanded finally, "do you want us to fly a safe crew, or don't you?"

"What kind of question is that?" Dr. Anderson retorted. "You must have a low opinion of me indeed if you think—"

"The best," Bert interrupted, "but we've also got to be damned sure this crew is flightworthy."

"Jazz Weickert is flightworthy, and you know it."

"All right," Connie agreed. "Put that one down to me, if you like. Maybe I just don't like him. Maybe I wouldn't feel safe with him as second in command. Isn't that my prerogative? Don't I have a right to have crewmates I'm completely comfortable with? I think so."

"If it's strictly a matter of ability," Andy agreed, "you certainly do. If it's personal dislike, that's something else."

"Is it?" Connie demanded. "On an eighteen-month mission to Mars, personal conflicts don't matter? Come on, now, Andy."

"They matter to a point," Dr. Anderson said. "With three modules flying, you can transfer around and get away from each other once in a while. You don't have to be together every minute."

"Almost," Connie said. "Enough so that it would cause frictions and I wouldn't feel easy about it."

"You aren't really telling me that Jazz Weickert would let you down in a crisis or do anything deliberately to hurt you, are you?"

"No, sir," Connie said soberly, "I am not. I wouldn't believe that of him, ever. He's a damned good astronaut and absolutely reliable in a pinch. I would never be afraid of anything with him along. But I just wouldn't be comfortable, that's all ... I guess," he concluded, "it comes down to which is more important, the commander's peace of mind or the ambitions and desires of the second in command. If you accept that I'll have enough on my mind so I shouldn't have to worry about his ego every minute, then that's one thing. If you think I won't, then of course you can force him on me."

"Nobody wants to force him on you," Dr. Anderson said impatiently.

"Then don't," Hank suggested.

For a long moment the Administrator stared at their determined faces with much the same feeling of frustration yet understanding Bob Hertz had experienced earlier. Unlike Bob, however, he did not decide to face them down; which, after all, had not done Bob any good, either.

"And what about Jayvee Halleck?" he asked finally. The three faces became, if anything, more stubborn.

"There," Bert said, "you really have a problem."

"Not only with me," Connie said, "but with everybody."

"He's not right for it," Hank remarked. "We don't think his color's all that important, but he does. It makes it impossible to relax around him, and the crew's got to relax. You can't fly up-tight for eighteen months. It would be criminally unfair to everybody. Including Mr. J. V. Halleck, whether he knows it or not."

"On the other hand," Dr. Anderson suggested, "it might well be the making of him and before you'd been out a month you might find him the best crew member you could ask for."

Absolute skepticism looked back at him from the little screen.

"If a man doesn't make it for himself and the program on the ground out here," Hank said, "he isn't going to make it in space. There's no magic in being up there, except everything is heightened a bit. If a man has good qualities they get better and if he has bad ones they get worse. This isn't a reform school, Andy. It's a flight to Mars."

"I don't think that's entirely fair," the Administrator retorted. "Men do get better under pressure, quite frequently."

"Sure," Bert agreed. "But there isn't time to take the gamble, this trip. Maybe you go up in Earth or Moon orbit for a week or two, it doesn't matter, your fellow crew members can carry you and hide your mistakes, the public thinks you're great, and you make out. Not to Mars. You have to be good when you leave the ground—then it's great if you get better, because you've got a lot going for you, right from launch. But if you haven't, then we can't take a chance on jeopardizing the rest of the crew and the mission while you acquire what you should have acquired in training."

"But he's an excellent scientist," Dr. Anderson said, "and in this kind of mission, does it really matter if he isn't the perfect astronaut?"

"He is an excellent scientist," Connie agreed. "In this kind of mission, everybody's got to be more than what his papers say he is. We're all going to have to depend absolutely on each other: everybody's got to be better than he is. We've never flown this far or this long, and *we don't know* what we will have to demand of each other. I'd rather take known quantities than a quantity I don't know very well—particularly when most of what I do know is touchy, unco-operative, suspicious and difficult.

"I still think you could carry him and he could do his job and turn into a real help to you," Dr. Anderson said. "And whether you like these mundane considerations or not, it would look better for the program and for the country to have him along. I only wish we'd landed a black man on the Moon, and I'm sorry you have apparently made up your minds we aren't going to land one on Mars."

"I wouldn't feel safe with him," Connie said. "It's as simple as that."

"Are you going to override us on it?" Hank demanded softly.

"We had hoped you would stand by us and endorse these selections, just as Bob has," Bert added.

"We really think you'd better, Andy," Connie said. "It would really look like hell if you didn't."

"I expect," the Administrator said quietly, "that I will. In fact, I know I will. Of course I'm not going to put you on a limb and leave you dangling. I'm a better Administrator of NASA than that, I hope. But," he added, and his face became grim, "it may take some explaining to the President, and he may not be so easy to convince."

"You've been recording this, haven't you?" Connie asked. Dr. Anderson nodded. "Why don't you take the films along and let him get our point of view for himself?"

But whether that would really convince a Chief Executive subject to the public clamor this one was going to receive, the Administrator was not so sure as his secretary told him his car was ready. He picked up his briefcase and the films of these and other heated conversations during the morning, and started for the door, a troubled man.

He was aware that NASA, under the goad of its determined astronauts, might be running headlong toward collision with forces that could seriously jeopardize, if not altogether destroy, the great mission of Piffy One.

He hoped with a certain sarcasm that everyone in Houston was happy.

Equally troubled, though he was not about to reveal it to the Administrator or anyone else, was the man who waited for him at 1600 Pennsylvania Avenue.

The President's personal inclination, as distinct from his political one, was to endorse the decisions made in Houston, and for exactly the reason given him by Bob Hertz when Bob had called after his argument with the Astronaut Office. The astronauts knew their own men better than anyone else, Bob said, and their judgment should be accepted. With this the President was in complete agreement, although he reminded Bob, as he had reminded the Administrator, that he had the authority to overrule the astronauts if he so desired. He had made no threats about this and given no indication that he might do so: he just wanted to place a notice on the record for everyone to think about.

"I doubt if it will impress them," Bob said. The President smiled.

"It won't unless it happens, and I really don't see any reason right now why it should."

As he expected, Bob picked up the key words.

"Neither do I, *right now*. And I would hope you wouldn't find it necessary later, either, Mr. President."

"I don't believe I will," the President said. He uttered a comfortable laugh. "Still determined not to come be my Director of the Budget? It's got even more headaches than NASA."

"And one tenth the fun. No, thanks, Mr. President. I'll stay here with my little charges, difficult though they may be."

"Yes," the President said, his expression sobering. "I've discovered that the more right people think they are, the more difficult they become. And your boys, I take it, think they're very right."

"I've just had a fight with them," Bob reminded him, "but in the last analysis, I'm with them. We have just one basic rule out here: the safety of the crew. Success of the mission—even," he said, a trifle dryly, "the political success of the mission—is all very nice. But what we have to come back to—and come back to—and come back to—and can never forget—is the safety of the crew."

"I hope you don't think I'd deliberately jeopardize it," the President said sharply.

"Certainly not," Bob Hertz said, "if you were aware of it."

"You just let me know," the President suggested. "If you ever have reason to think I'm jeopardizing the safety of that crew, you get on the line here and tell me about it. That's an order."

"Yes, sir," Bob Hertz agreed. "I shall regard it as such."

"You'd still be great at Budget," the President said, amiable again. "Call me about that, too, if you ever change your mind."

"Immediately," Bob Hertz said, and they parted with a reasonable show of amity.

But after the shrewd, intelligent face of the director of flight operations had vanished from the screen, the President had permitted himself a candid expression of opinion, aloud, in the privacy of his office.

"That damned Houston," he remarked to Thomas Jefferson, who stared down blandly from the wall. "They think they know everything."

As for him, what he knew already was that his Administration was in for a hell of a fight if the announced crew selections were permitted to stand. He had already received calls from a belligerent Senator Kenny Williams and a near-hysterical Percy Mercy, to say nothing of the other calls and information he was receiving as the news spread out across the country and the world. Already the first editorial comments were beginning to come in, righteous and sternly accusatory as the major figures of the media loved to be when chiding that ever-unworthy and vulnerable institution, the Government of the United States. More would come tomorrow when the *Times*, the *Post*, and all their chums and allies let fly. The networks were onto it already, and their anvil chorus would rage ever louder through the night and into the morning as the Administration got hammered in news broadcasts, commentaries and special presentations. All that he had received so far the Mars decision itself would prove to be only a warm-up for the great view-halloo with which they would go after a crew that did not include their pet neglected astronaut and his Negro colleague.

And as a matter of fact, the President was not so sure at this moment that they didn't have a point. He didn't know much about the crew selected, and he didn't know much about the one rejected. But he was a shrewd campaigner and he did know an issue when he saw one. He also had a pretty good sense of when an issue was unbeatable and you had best retreat before it. He was not sure yet that this was such a case—he wasn't really sure of anything, at the moment, except that he wanted to have a talk with the Administrator—but if it should be, he knew he was quite tough enough to handle it, and in the way that would be best for his Administration, which after all had responsibilities to many things besides NASA.

For all he knew, the two rejected men were excellent astronauts and had every professional right to be on the crew. Perhaps they also had a perfect moral right. Certainly it might develop that they had a perfect political right.

Contemplating the rapidly increasing hullaballoo caused by the crew announcement, he, like the Administrator, thought with a rather grim irony that Houston had apparently done exactly what it wanted to do, and now he certainly hoped everyone down there was happy.

But this, of course, was not the case: not for Jazz Weickert and Jayvee Halleck, certainly, and not even for Connie Trasker, though he maintained an outward appearance of calm and good cheer as he walked along the corridor toward the office he shared with Hugo Gaudet.

Gaudy, who retained an approximate French pronunciation of his name, "Gaw-*day*," was still at the Cape with Emerson Wacker and would not be back until late this afternoon. Connie hoped this would guarantee that he himself might have a quiet time in the office to review the decisions taken this morning and work out his own defenses of them against the inevitable moment later in the week when the crew must face the press and he must make public accounting. It would not be easy.

The President and the Administrator were not the only men aware that Colonel Trasker and his colleagues were on collision course; and while Connie understood the reasons to his own satisfaction, he knew there would have to be a more diplomatic presentation of them for the public than the blunt private exchanges that had taken place within NASA in the past thirty-six hours.

First of all, he decided as he walked along, smiling at secretaries and greeting fellow astronauts who tried not to look disappointed at being passed over, there would have to be more emphasis on the qualifications of Gaudy and Em Wacker, which had not really been discussed very much up to now. So much time had been spent by everyone arguing about Jazz' and Jayvee's weak points that the steady, quiet and thoroughly reliable personalities of the other two contenders had hardly been mentioned.

They were taken for granted in the Astronaut Office, but they would have to receive a big public build-up from now on.

Gaudy Gaudet, a native of Erie, Pennsylvania, had received his bachelor of science degree at the Naval Academy, transferred to the Air Force on graduation, gone on to get his master of science and doctorate in aeronautical engineering at the University of California. He had served on special projects at Wright-Patterson Air Force Base in Ohio, worked for a time at Ames Research Laboratory at Moffett Field, returned to full-time flying as a test-pilot at Edwards Air Force Base in California for two years prior to joining NASA as an astronaut. He was 35 years old, married to the former Ellen Sheffield, father of Mary Ellen, 12, and Hartford, 9; pleasant, comfortable, dedicated, determined; no strain to be around and a good second in command for anybody's crew.

Em Wacker, born in Chicago, had received his bachelor of science degree in geology from the Massachusetts Institute of Technology and his master's degree and doctorate from the California Institute of Technology. He had served on geological expeditions for the Algerian government in the Sahara Desert, won numerous special scholarships and grants, served with the United States Geological Survey's astrogeology department at Flagstaff, Arizona, worked with many of the Apollo crews on lunar geology experiments in the Arizona desert. He had been an astroscientist for five years. He was 38, married to the former Lucille Raudebush, father of Michael, 13, Janet, 12, Hilary, 9, and James, 6: easygoing, quick-witted, completely competent, completely compatible; gung-ho for Mars and an excellent man to have along on a lengthy and dangerous mission.

Both Em and Gaudy were thoroughly qualified for Planetary Fleet One—as, of course, were at least thirty other astronauts and astroscientists, when you came right down to it. It was easier to decide who shouldn't be on flight crews than who should, as a matter of fact: so many were so competent.

The final decisions here had come down to those indefinable inexpressibles that decided so many things in the Astronaut Office. Gaudy and Em were just a little easier than their fellows in their relations with Hank and Bert and Connie, just a little more amiable and alert, just a little quicker with the jest and the joke and the casual, no-sweat getting along together. In neither instance was this accident, of course. Both had decided long ago that they wanted to be on the Mars flight and both had taken pains to cultivate the men who could assign them to it. Everybody did this, and if they did it better than the rest, well, that proved something about their abilities, too. Connie was well satisfied with both of them.

He was also well satisfied with his medical officer, who had received the news of his selection with a big grin when they put through a call to his apartment in downtown Houston after making their final decision.

"Thank you, Daddy," Pete had said, and then corrected it with an even broader grin—"Daddies."

"You understand you're going to have to double in brass," Hank said. "You'll have to run scientific experiments with one hand and keep the crew healthy with the other."

"I'll manage," Pete promised. "I may have some trouble getting along with the commander, but otherwise everything should go well."

"He's a tough man," Bert agreed. "But I dare say you can handle him."

Pete chuckled happily.

"I think so." Suddenly he let out a gleeful yell full of sheer, exuberant, animal spirits.

"I'm really pleased as hell about this, you guys. Someday I'll write you all a letter and tell you so."

"Save it," Connie suggested with a smile. "We've got work to do."

And so they did, he thought as he neared his office door. Months of training, months of planning, months of hard, hard work before lift-off. He hoped they all would wear as well together as he thought they would, his engaging Greek included. You couldn't really tell at this stage, because previous training provided only indications, not certainties. Nothing could be certain, really, about this first Mars flight. A lot of things you wouldn't know until you were out there.

A little unconscious sigh, worried and surprisingly uncertain for calm, confident Conrad H. Trasker, escaped his lips as he entered his office. He noted automatically the empty clutter of Gaudy's desk in the outer room, noted also that his own inner door was closed. A puzzled expression crossed his face. He stepped forward quickly and opened the door. Monetta Halleck stared up nervously from big, wide eyes.

"I'm sorry," they said together. Then they laughed, somewhat awkwardly. Then they fell silent and looked at one another cautiously. Finally Connie smiled.

"*I'm* sorry because I got so swept up in our meeting about the crew this morning that I totally and completely forgot our appointment. What are you sorry about?"

"About practically breaking in here like this," she said, looking less nervous and more relaxed.

"They have big signs downstairs about that," he said with a mock severity, carefully leaving the door open, sitting down and facing her across the stacks of books and flight plans on his desk.

"Visitors are supposed to be announced."

"I know," she agreed, finally smiling. "But I didn't see anyone, so I just sneaked up in the elevator and came in."

"I dare say NASA won't collapse because of it. I really am sorry about this morning, but we had more or less of an emergency meeting and I had to leave the house before 6. It drove everything else out of my mind. I wouldn't have had a chance to call if I'd remembered. But I have to say I didn't. Did you see Jane at the house?"

"Oh, yes," she said. "She was very nice to me. We had coffee and a nice talk."

"Jane is nice. Was she any help with your problem?"

Monetta's eyes acquired a sudden veiled expression, followed by one of worried concern.

"I didn't tell her about that."

"I didn't expect you would, but Janie's pretty sharp. I thought she might have wormed it out of you."

She smiled her quick, shy smile.

"She tried, I think, but I wouldn't let her."

"You're better than I am," he confessed with a sudden grin. "She sees through me most of the time." He decided the best way through this was the most direct. "So: what can I do for you? You've heard the news about the crew, of course. We decided Jayvee should not be on it."

The veiled expression returned, shaded by an anticipatory pain, as though she expected to be hit. He felt a fleeting regret that he had been so blunt, then instantly dismissed it. This was the only way if things were to be kept on an impersonal plane.

"Why not?" she asked in a voice he could barely hear.

"Because we did not feel that he was qualified."

"As a scientist?" she asked. "Or as an astronaut? Or"— her voice dropped—"as a black man?"

Oh, hell, he thought: here we go again.

"As a human being who seems to find it difficult at times to get along with other human beings," he said crisply. "On a flight of this duration, that had to be the determining factor. It was."

"But he isn't like that, really," she said, her voice still low. "He wants to be liked and get along with people, but he—he just doesn't seem to know how."

"Does he get along with you?" he asked bluntly, impelled by some motivation he could not quite define and didn't want to analyze. She gave him a quick, startled look and then as quickly looked away.

"I don't see what that has to do with it," she said, in the same low voice.

"People live by patterns," he said, having received his answer and being curiously stirred by it. "It's all part of it. But perhaps you're right. It may be immaterial."

"I think so," she said, not looking at him, which in some odd way stirred him even more. Whoa, there, boy, he told himself abruptly: don't be crazy. Get back to business. "Anyway," he said, in a tone as matter-of-fact as he could make it, "that was the basic reason. We weren't sure how well he could stand the strain of the long flight, and how it would affect his relations with the rest of the crew. On the basis of his record here, we felt there were legitimate grounds to doubt that he could fit in smoothly with the rest of us. It had to be the paramount factor."

"I think he may feel that his color was the reason," she said quietly.

"If we had felt that we had to take him on the crew," he said, deciding with a sudden annoyance that he could play the race game too, "then it *would* have been because of his color. *That* would have been the really patronizing and hurtful thing to do, it seems to me. Or can't you and he see it that way?"

"I think," she said slowly, "I can see it that way . . . I think. But I don't think Jayvee can."

"Well," he said, his tone becoming more businesslike, "I sympathize with his feelings and I regret that other members of the corps possessed superior qualifications. Possibly on subsequent flights—"

"He won't stay around that long. You don't understand Jayvee. He hurts inside."

"Doesn't everybody?" he asked, almost flip, and then

regretted it instantly, because he could see it had angered her, though her tone remained soft.

"Does Colonel Trasker?" she asked quietly. "It seems to me Colonel Trasker has just about everything going his way. What does he know about hurting inside?"

For a second he almost flared up in anger, but, being honest with himself about most things, did not.

"All right," he said quietly, "I deserved that. So why does Jayvee hurt inside? Is there anything I can do to help, short of putting him on the flight? Can we make things easier for him here in some way? And," he added with a certain dryness, beginning to feel annoyed again, "is there any certainty he would respond if we did? We've tried to make him feel at home here, you know. With precious little co-operation or thanks, it seems to us."

"You could try to understand him," she said, still quietly.

" 'Understand!' " he said with a harsh little laugh. "One of the great clichés of our times. Sure, we'll understand him, but understanding is a two-way street. It won't do any good if he's at the other end of it hugging his grievance and enjoying his hurt more than getting along with people."

"He's got to feel more friendliness here," she said, her wide, dark eyes stubborn above the fine, high cheekbones, "or he isn't going to stay."

"He can resign," Connie said with a certain calculated bluntness. "Nobody would hold it against him for long."

"Or remember him for long, either," she said, a surprising bitterness in her voice. "You'd all be glad if he resigned, wouldn't you? It would solve your problem."

"Look," he said, trying to suppress the anger in his voice, "I don't think we have any problem. I thought it was Jayvee who has the problem. Isn't that why you're here? Why *are* you here?"

"I don't know," she said, in a suddenly defeated voice that, surprisingly, touched him very much. "I guess I really don't know. Because I thought maybe Colonel Trasker could help. Because I guess I thought Colonel Trasker was something special." She looked at him with a bleak little smile. "I guess maybe he isn't, though. I guess maybe he's like all the rest of them, smiling on the outside and hurtful on the inside. So I guess I'd better go."

"Not in that mood, I hope," he said quietly. "I don't

think I'm so bad and I do want to help. I'm sorry we didn't consider him suitable for this first flight, but there will be others coming and we'll try to get him on one of them as early as possible. But meanwhile, maybe you can talk to him a little—"

"I can't talk to him any more at all," she said and quite abruptly, startling them both, began to cry.

Lord save me, he thought with an exasperated sympathy, from crying wives. He hardly felt he could take her in his arms as he had Jane the night before, but he did get up and come around the desk, brushing the door shut with an apparent absent-mindedness as he did so.

"Look," he said, putting a hand, which she grasped with a sudden convulsive motion, on her shoulder, "I'm sorry if this upsets you, but you must remember we can't afford to be too sentimental here. I'll try to take more of an interest, myself—I'll see to it that we all try. Maybe that will make things easier for him and for us. And also," he concluded quietly, "for you."

The pressure on his hand tightened, but still she cried, and did not look up.

"Thank you," she said finally. "I'm sorry."

"So am I," he said. Then he uttered a rueful little laugh, in which she finally joined shakily as she released his hand. "That's the way we started, isn't it? Both of us being sorry. I hope the next time we talk we won't be so mournful."

"I hope not," she said with the return of a smile.

"We might talk again sometime, then," he said: not a question, a flat statement.

She looked up at him in the shy, hesitant way that now for some reason seemed to move him much more than it had before.

"Possibly," she said finally.

"Good," he said evenly, "I should enjoy that. Shall I call you, or do you want to call me?"

"Why don't we leave it that if it happens, it happens?" she said in a low voice.

"Things don't happen unless people make them happen," he said in the same even tone. "But it might be best not to talk here again."

"Oh, no," she said hastily.

"Then you will call me?" he said.

For a moment she said nothing, staring at him from the big dark eyes in whose depths many things now seemed to flicker as their glances held.

At last she gave the smallest of nods.

"Good," he said, turning to his desk and picking up his papers in a brisk, businesslike way. "Now perhaps you had better go find Jayvee."

"I would," she said with a return of bleakness, staring out the window over the white laboratories and neat glass office buildings of the Manned Spacecraft Center, "if I knew where to look."

And with a sudden wistful little smile she got up, carefully tucked her handkerchief into her purse, turned to the door and, after taking a deep breath and lifting her head high, walked out the door and swiftly down the corridor.

Conrad H. Trasker, he told himself, swinging his chair around to stare out the window in his turn, you are absolutely insane.

But he knew from experience that the insanity, now that it had begun, would probably last a while.

"Well, well," said a familiar voice behind him. "Are you counseling wives, now?"

He turned his chair back and held out his hand.

"Hi, buddy," he said calmly, thinking to himself, Boy, what is that fatal charm of mine that draws them in like flies? "Sit down and let's talk."

"I will," Pete said cheerfully, shaking hands and then dropping into the chair where Monetta had sat. "Is Jayvee going to give you problems?"

But whether he would give anybody problems, or just slink quietly away and try to be forgotten, was something that Astroscientist J. V. Halleck was in no frame of mind to decide at that particular moment. So bitter were the thoughts and emotions that swirled through his head and heart, so confused and confusing the things he contemplated and considered, that the bright windy afternoon seemed strangely clouded over and ominous to him. Not for the first time in his life for Jayvee Halleck, things just did not make sense.

It was not that he had really believed he had a chance to be on the crew of Piffy One, of course; yet hope, even after so many rebuffs, still lingered. Even if it had only been to satisfy Vernon Hertz' thesis that the image needed a Negro, he had thought there might be a chance; and patronizing and insulting as he might have considered his selection to be under that circumstance, he would have accepted without a murmur. He wanted to go, in a blind, visceral, atavistic way he could not explain or deny. He wanted to go.

He could not have said why any more clearly than Connie Trasker had been able to, though his basic reason would probably have been the same as Vernon's: he wanted to go as a black American, as a representative of his race, as a symbol that his people were worthy to participate in this greatest of all mankind's adventures. In addition to that, there were reasons much like Connie's—the challenge, the thrill, the mystery of Mars, the appeal of a new world, the chance to make use of his scientific abilities to their fullest; even the opportunity, though he often did not think much of America, to do something for his native land.

He would probably have had difficulty admitting it even to himself, but it would have been a proud day for Jayvee Halleck if the announcement that had driven him from his office in a dazed rage had included his name. Then there would have been no rage, no daze, no drifting about here aimlessly in a rowboat along the marshy edges of Clear Lake, as he was right now.

He was drifting along, he told himself bitterly, just like any other shiftless nigger. Just exactly like any other shiftless nigger in the sun. All he needed was an old straw hat, a fishing pole and a houn' dog sitting in the back, to complete the picture.

He did not think that anyone could see him or recognize him along these relatively uninhabited sections of the shore, but he was tempted to shout out, "Yes, here I am, Mrs. Colonel Trasker, lady! And here I is, Mrs. Commander Gaudet and Mrs. Dr. Wacker! And here's your ole frien', dear Dr. Balkis, buddy! Look at me, driftin' in the sun! Jes driftin' and driftin' 'cause they ain't no place for that *great* astroscientist Dr. J. V. Halleck to go, now. He jes' got to keep driftin' and driftin' 'til he drift right on down to de bottom ub de sea."

He shook his head hard, as though these were physical torments he could be rid of if only he attacked them with sufficient strength. But all the motion did was make him slightly dizzy and increase the headache that had begun as soon as he heard the crew announcement. Another headache. They never seemed to let up, and always the same dull, throbbing kind, brought on, he knew, by all the inner tensions that threatened to blow him apart. But the tensions kept coming and he could not seem to hold them back.

He uttered a little whimpering sound, sitting there in his rowboat, drifting in the sun. How had they managed to do such things to Jayvee Halleck? How had they ravaged his dignity and manhood so?

If he could have been honest with himself at that deeply unhappy moment, he would have had to admit that the ravaging had not been done any time lately, and he would also have had to admit that it was a pretty sorry thing to let oneself suffer for it so intensely so many years after it had been done. He would have had to admit that ever since he had entered Cal Tech, all through his postgraduate years, his year with Vernon Hertz at JPL and his three years in Houston, he had been treated with evenhanded courtesy as an individual and with very outspoken and flattering respect for his abilities as a scientist.

But he could not be honest with himself right now— nor, indeed, was he ever able to, being cursed with the angry, unbalancing burden of so many in his particular generation of blacks in America. He had received, on the average, one snub to a hundred praises during his lifetime. But, unforgiving and basically immature, quivering and desperately eager to be hurt, his mind could acknowledge only the snubs. The praises he was able to rationalize only as the attempts of the white world to ease its own conscience. He was never able to accept them for what they were, genuine tributes to his intellect. He always had to see an ulterior motive. He could never relax.

To some degree this was, of course, the fault of the white world as it appeared to be in the mythology of the blacks, and as, to some degree, it had actually been over the centuries. It was changing fast during the years of Jayvees growing up, but like so many of his race, he suffered a time lag in his appreciation of the fact. During the middle years of the century, the government of his country and the great majority of its white citizens tumbled over themselves in their haste to pass laws, improve conditions, right old wrongs. To an amazing extent, they succeeded. The fact of their good will and the proof of their sincerity remained on history's record and stood high among history's astonishments. But by all too many vocal and vindictive blacks their achievements were greeted with jeers and contempt and shrill, childish demands for more.

Inevitably many in the white world said, "To hell with it," and turned away again.

In large measure, this was the situation Jayvee had created for himself, first at JPL and then, in the last three years, in Houston. Of all the places in the world where a hypersensitive racialism would be out of place, NASA and the astronaut corps probably ranked near the top. "There just isn't *time* to worry about his thin skin," Roger Webb had remarked in frustration to Stu Yule one day when Jayvee had scowled out of the Simulator Building at the Cape, quivering under some fancied slight where none had been intended. "We've got too much work to do." "Forget it," Stu said shortly. "He's a child. Screw him."

The fact that to Jayvee the slights were not fancied but intensely real; that to him an inferiority complex was not something put on to get out of work but an absolute, inescapable, all-dominating, psychological necessity; that in his mind the world he lived in was an enemy, not a friend; that to him the camaraderie of the corps was a mockery, the basic spirit that linked even such antagonistic souls as Connie and Jazz Weickert was a fraud—none of these things could be understood by his colleagues.

"Of course you can't understand me!" he had snapped one day to Pete Balkis when Pete had ventured to act as intermediary in an attempt to ease things a little. "None of you are black!"

"That's right!" Pete had responded with a sudden, uncharacteristic anger. "None of us has that excuse, all right. And none of us would try to take advantage of it the way you do, either! Now why don't you come off it and try to act decent to people around here, as they do to you?"

But this of course was impossible for Jayvee, because to do that would be to face the fact that the whole underlying conviction of his life was mistaken. And a man couldn't do that without really spinning off into space.

So his years here had been unhappy most of the time, and the conviction had very soon developed among his colleagues that he was not flight material, except under the most controlled of conditions—that he was not, as Bert Richmond had put it, using that all-inclusive term which indicated the state of being completely acceptable, gung-ho.

Which, of course, created its own human, practical and political problems.

There had been many discussions in the Astronaut Office, many discussions between Bob Hertz and Jim Cavanaugh, about what to do with J. V. Halleck. There had been some thought of transferring him back to JPL with a top assignment: Vernon Hertz had squelched that, refusing to admit he had made a mistake about Jayvee, insisting that the program needed a Negro, promising to raise a fuss if he were not kept on. There had been some consideration of suggesting to Jayvee himself that he resign and return to the scientific community, where his abilities would almost certainly guarantee him a major and effective position: no one had quite dared broach the subject for fear that he would indeed resign, but with a bitter broadside to the press that could only harm the program. There had been the thought of assigning him to one of the relatively safe and controlled Moon expeditions: but they were being phased out by the time he had completed his training—and anyway, no one really wanted to fly with him.

None of these debates and arguments ever reached Jayvee, nor did they ever reach the public. They had to be kept private to NASA, and they were.

Until this week, he had been treated with kid gloves simply because he was black. Abruptly the Russian preparations and the reduction of the crew of Planetary Fleet One from twelve to four had changed all that. Hank, Bert and Connie had cut ruthlessly through three years of hypocrisy because they felt they must.

In effect, they had told the whole wide world that J. V. Halleck was not good enough to fly.

More devastating than that, they had in effect told the whole wide world that J. V. Halleck, black, was really not equal to his colleagues who were white.

It was this that had sent him from his office in a daze, as it was this which, even now as he drifted aimlessly along Clear Lake, was rousing distant forces he could not imagine that would come clamoring to his aid for pur-

135

poses and reasons of their own. It was this which had, finally, brought him to the point where he was deciding, through the whirling turmoil of his thoughts, that he must resign from NASA.

Many and many a time he had contemplated this, and almost always it had been his wife who had dissuaded him. He had married Monetta Rudden when they were graduate students at Cal Tech. Something about her gravely beautiful, patrician face, her shy, charmingly hesitant manner, and her tall, dignified bearing, had appealed to him greatly. She was a brilliant student, specializing in plant biology and hydroponics, so that he felt flattered to be marrying a brain almost as good as his. And she also had a quality of acceptance and stability that he knew instinctively he needed. During their courtship and in the early years of their marriage she had formed the quiet center of his life to which he had repaired for comfort, not only of body but of soul.

Early, however, they had begun to discover their differences on the matter of race. The years at the Manned Spacecraft Center had only served to exacerbate them. Monetta, he thought now with something close to contempt, was really nothing better than an ordinary Aunt Jemima, always rationalizing, always excusing, always forgiving. She could see slights and think that perhaps they weren't all deliberate, she could see failures of generosity and communication and find it in her heart to excuse many of them on the ground that his colleagues and their wives were rushed and hurried and harried by their own lives in the voracious maw of the all-domineering program. She took the world as it came, hoped it would improve, was grateful when it did, and did not let it destroy her when it did not.

She remained, for the most part, serene, even when his own frustrations goaded him into bitter arguments that left them both exhausted. She just went along, he thought, again with an impatience that edged contempt, bringing up little Rudden as best she knew how and meeting life with dignity and character.

He was, he realized suddenly, quite tired of her. Maybe he should resign from Monetta, too, after he got through resigning from the program.

He picked up the oars and began to row slowly back to

the cove where he had left the car. With each stroke the chaos in his mind seemed to lessen, his resolve become more firm. He wasn't really sure about Monetta—you didn't cut off half your life quite that summarily—but he had no doubts about NASA. They deserved to be left and he was going to leave them, with one big blast they could hear from Houston to D.C. and back again.

It was not until he got back to his office and returned the call that was waiting for him that he began to change his mind. But this perhaps was excusable, for the vistas that were opened up might well have confused a much steadier man than Jayvee Halleck.

They were not, however, enough to confuse Commander Alvin S. Weickert III, who *was* a much steadier man than Jayvee Halleck, and who had been waiting for years for just such a day. Now it had come to him and he intended to respond to it as effectively as he knew how. The two pompous faces confronting him on the little screen were apparently about to advise him. For what it might be worth, he was willing to listen.

"First of all," Percy Mercy said with a sort of primly disapproving indignation, "we just want you to know how very sorry we are that your colleagues should have seen fit to subject you to this kind of public humiliation. It is absolutely inexcusable."

"That's right, Jazzbo," Senator Williams said, annoying Jazz intensely by using a form of his nickname that he only permitted old friends. But he was prudent enough to refrain from comment. "They had no right to do that, and we think they should be punished."

"Well," Jazz said slowly, to give himself time to think—because, while they were on his side at the moment, he was basically as leery of these two as was everyone else in NASA—"that's very nice of you, to be so concerned. Of course in a technical sense they had the right. Maybe in a moral sense, considering my time in the program and my abilities as an astronaut, they didn't."

"I question that they even had the technical right," Percy Mercy said. Kenny Williams nodded vigorously.

"Absolutely. Doesn't the Administrator have the final say on crew selection? And doesn't the President have the right to overrule him?"

"It's almost never been done," Jazz said cautiously.

"Any reason why it can't be?" Senator Williams demanded.

Jazz smiled and shook his head.

"I think maybe you'd have to ask Andy and the President."

"We intend to do so," Percy said with a certain grimness. "Both directly, and through the various channels open to us."

There's going to be one hell of a stink," Kenny Williams promised with some satisfaction.

Jazz shrugged.

"What can you do? The decision's been made. About all that's left now is for me to resign, as I see it."

Percy Mercy looked shocked.

"Indeed you should not!"

"That's right," Senator Williams agreed with an equal vehemence. "That would be absolutely the worst thing you could possibly do."

Jazz looked skeptical.

"Why? You don't think having me mope around the corridors is going to change any minds in the Astronaut Office, do you?" He smiled a grim little smile. "God knows they've known how I feel about things for a long time. It hasn't made any difference."

"It may now," Percy said with a grimness of his own. "If the President intervenes, minds in the Astronaut Office really won't matter, will they?"

Again Jazz looked skeptical.

"What makes you so sure he will? He's got better things to do than worry about a personality clash in Houston."

"Not this time, he hasn't," Senator Williams said flatly. "Not this time, Jazzbo. Things are riding on this that you don't even dream of."

"What?" Jazz demanded. "The forgotten astronaut vote? The neurotic Negro vote?"

Percy looked offended and quite severe.

"I would think that you would not so cavalierly categorize a fellow astronaut who finds himself in the same unjust and inexcusable position as yourself."

"Jayvee?" Jazz asked with a contemptuous grin. "Neurotic is what he is and neurotic is what he's always been. I hope you don't put me on the same level with *that?*"

"You're together this time, Jazzbo," Kenny Williams told him, "so you might as well make up your mind to that. You stand or fall together, each for each and all for all."

"I don't blame Connie a bit for not wanting him on the crew," Jazz said tartly. "I wouldn't want him on it myself."

"Nonetheless," Percy Mercy said calmly, "if you want us to continue to organize pressure on the White House on your behalf, you must reconcile yourself to the fact that we are also going to be organizing it for Dr. Halleck. The two of you go, or neither of you goes. I should not," he added with a righteous air, "be true to a lifetime of battling for the cause of the black American, were I to abandon this most distinguished black American now."

"You're talking politics," Jazz said bluntly. "Here in Houston we talk facts. The facts are that he is not fully competent to fly—or at any rate, he is no more competent than thirty others who might have been chosen—and in a personal sense, he does not possess the mental and emotional stability, or the co-operative spirit, necessary to function as a completely reliable member of the crew."

"Good old American teamwork, eh?" Senator Williams asked with a sarcastic smile. "Old razzmatazz and hoooray for the team, eh? Can't be on it unless you're one of the boys, eh? Is that it, Jazzbo?"

"That's it."

"Is that why they didn't pick you?" Kenny Williams asked cruelly, and for a moment Commander Weickert looked at him with real anger. Then he shrugged with a deliberate contempt.

"Why don't you shove off?" he asked, and reached over and snapped off his Picturephone. But in a second, of course, they rang back.

"Apparently," Percy said when a picture had been reestablished, his face flushed, his voice quivering, "you have no comprehension at all of the factors involved here. This, I suppose, is typical of the rather parochial approach you people take in Houston. This is not just a personal squabble within NASA. It affects the whole of domestic politics, as well as America's international image, to boot. It is not something about which we on our side can afford to indulge in individual hostilities: too much is at stake. The fact that this crew does not contain a Negro, representative of America's most downtrodden and oppressed minority—"

"Bull," Jazz said. "Jayvee has had the red carpet treatment since the day he got here, and what good has it done us?"

"Not only," Percy repeated firmly, "does it not contain a representative of America's most downtrodden and oppressed minority, but it also deliberately excludes one of America's most supremely able astronauts, in a petty and vindictive action which poses a glaring question concerning the very foundations of NASA's reputation for honor and integrity."

"Maybe he thinks that's bull, too," Senator Williams suggested in an unpleasant tone.

Jazz snorted.

"You're a lovable son of a bitch."

"You damned astronauts are all alike," Kenny Williams retorted angrily. "Damned arrogant, high-riding obnoxious, insufferable bastards."

"Only when we're treated that way," Jazz said with a deliberately annoying blandness. "Treat us right and we're absolute dolls."

"Be that as it may," Percy Mercy said sharply, "we are going to get absolutely nowhere if we allow personal antagonisms to get in our way. I have already organized, as you know, the Committee Against Unilateral Space Exploration—CAUSE—and I have already received pledges of vigorous and enthusiastic support from a broad spectrum of the press, television and the academic, literary, theological and theatrical worlds. Our first full-page ad in the New York *Times* will appear tomorrow morning. We plan to run others just as soon as the money comes in. We also have an appointment tomorrow morning with the President, at which time we will convey our sentiments in person. Finally, the Senator here will speak in the Senate tomorrow afternoon."

"It sounds as though you have everything pretty well covered," Jazz said. "What's going to be in your ad?"

"A demand that you and Dr. Halleck be assigned to the crew, replacing Commander Gaudet and Dr. Wacker," Percy said. "A demand that the United States extend a formal invitation to the Soviet Union to participate jointly in the flight."

"It will never happen," Jazz said flatly.

"My contacts," Percy Mercy replied, "assure me that there is an excellent chance that it will."

"Your contacts must be better than the President's."

"In many areas," said Percy serenely, "I believe they are."

Jazz grunted.

"And to guarantee your support I have to stay here and take it, and also pretend that I have a high regard for the astronautical abilities of a man for whose astronautical abilities I do not have a very high regard. Is that it?"

"That's it, Jazzbo," Senator Williams told him with a certain relish. "That's the ball game. Want to play?"

Jazz frowned.

"Have you talked to Jayvee?"

"We have," Kenny Williams said.

"Did he give you any trouble?"

"I think we may safely say," Percy replied, "that Dr. Halleck, after a few moments' thought, was wholeheartedly in favor of our plans."

"I'll bet he was," Jazz said softly. "Yes, I'll bet he was."

"I'm damned if I understand you, Jazzbo," Senator Williams remarked, and he sounded genuinely puzzled. "Here we've been talking about just this sort of situation off and on for the past several months, and every time you've sounded all enthused about the idea of getting some outside support to help you. Now we come right down to it and you don't sound very enthused at all. Do you want to be on that crew or not?"

Jazz gave him an impatient look.

"Of course I want to be on it!"

"Well, then, what's the problem?" Kenny Williams demanded. "We're here, we're ready—"

"Do I have to issue some kind of statement?"

"Not necessarily," Percy said, "though we might wish to hold that in reserve for later, if it seemed advisable."

"I thought you've always wanted to issue a statement blasting NASA all to hell," Kenny Williams said, still puzzled. "Don't tell me you're having second thoughts on that, too?"

"I wouldn't mind issuing one at the proper time," Jazz said slowly. "If it wouldn't hurt the corps."

"Well, I'll be damned," Senator Williams exclaimed. "You make it damned difficult to help you, I must say."

Jazz smiled and looked as though he rather puzzled himself, at the moment.

"I'm still an astronaut," he said finally. "Maybe that's what you don't understand."

"I sure don't," Kenny Williams admitted. "I surely do not. Do you, or don't you, want us to go ahead with this?"

"You're going to anyway, aren't you?"

"Sure," Kenny said.

"But it would be more effective with your support," Percy told him. "If we are to advocate your assignment to the crew. Which we assume you want us to do."

For several seconds he and Jazz stared at one another without expression. Finally Commander Weickert nodded.

"Of course I want to be on the crew." He shrugged. "I suppose a few ads and speeches might help, and they probably can't hurt anything."

But that assumption, though he did not know it at the moment their solemnly determined faces faded from the screen, was made in a more innocent age, before the whole thing turned ugly.

The first indication that it might came an hour or so later, and it came first to the Administrator, after what he could only regard as a quite unsatisfactory talk with the President.

Not that there had been any overt hostility, of course, or even any open criticism, when he was first shown into the Oval Room. Nor was there any when he left. But there was no doubt that he faced a disturbed and very thoughtful Executive who was obviously considering many things and not revealing his hand on any of them.

"Andy," he had said cordially, rising and shaking hands when the Administrator approached his desk, "sit down and let's chew the fat a bit about this situation in Houston. Frankly"—and he smiled the sudden, intimate, just-between-us smile that always lighted up his face so pleasantly—"it's got me in a hell of a bind."

"I'm sorry for that, Mr. President," Dr. Anderson said cautiously. "But I'm not sure what we can do to—"

"Oh, yes, you are," the President interrupted calmly. "You know perfectly well what we can do, Andy. We can overrule your boys and force them to take Jazz Weickert and Jayvee Halleck on that crew."

"We can," Dr. Anderson agreed, less cautiously and more bluntly. "We can do that, in legal terms. What can we do in human terms that won't tear Houston and the program apart?"

"Now, there," the President said in a delighted tone, "is exactly why I made an awfully good decision when I decided to appoint you Administrator. You get to the heart of things and you aren't afraid to say so. That's good, Andy. I like that."

"I'm glad you do, Mr. President," the Administrator said. "I hope I have justified the confidence you had in my judgment when you appointed me."

"You have," the President agreed promptly. "You have."

"Good," Dr. Anderson said. "Then my judgment now is that we had best not interfere too openly and directly with this decision in Houston."

"Ah—*ha!*" the President said with the triumphant little laugh he liked to utter when he thought he had scored a point, "I notice you don't say we shouldn't interfere at all. Just not openly and directly—'too' openly and directly, I believe you said. That's a change from yesterday, when I was being threatened with mass resignations on all sides if I so much as raised an eyebrow in disapproval. How come, Andy? Why the retreat?"

"I'm not retreating," the Administrator said. "I'm just taking into account the possibility that you may go right ahead in spite of my advice and try to do something that could only have the most devastating effect on morale in Houston."

"What about morale in a lot of other places, Andy?" the President asked quietly. "Am I supposed to forget that?"

"Obviously you haven't, Mr. President."

"And obviously I can't."

Dr. Anderson nodded.

"That's why I'm beginning to adjust myself to the thought that you may find yourself forced to take steps I wouldn't want to see you take."

"And you won't resign if I do? You said you would, yesterday."

The Administrator sighed.

"I don't know. Probably not. I wasn't actually faced with it, yesterday. Now I am, and I have to stop thinking of a handful of men and their reactions."

"You have to think of the whole program," the President suggested. Dr. Anderson sighed again.

"Yes."

"As I," the President said gravely, "have to think of the whole country, and the whole world."

There was a silence while he swung around to stare out across the beautiful lawn to the street where the endless cars rushed by. The commanding head and shoulders loomed against the bright spring sunshine, massive, dominant, hard to challenge. Then he swung back and leaned forward.

"Andy," he said thoughtfully, "just what is the situation with that crew, anyway? Do you know?"

"There's always been a feeling," Dr. Anderson said frankly, "that Jazz is too arrogant and too ambitious and to self-confident and too independent—"

"Qualities," the President interrupted with a smile, "which are of course necessary to make a good astronaut." The smile increased. "Or a good President, for that matter. Why do they hold that against him? Because they're all alike?"

The Administrator smiled in his turn.

"Most of them," he said, "are pretty adept at smoothing out the rough edges. They are, in fact, pretty smooth all around. Jazz has never really bothered. He thinks he's damned good, and he is, and you can like it or lump it. Well, when you put him up against colleagues who are equally good but manage to refrain from rubbing your nose in it, you can imagine what the reaction has been from them. He deserves a lot of what he's received."

"But he *is* damned good," the President said.

"He is damned good."

"Very well. That answers one question, then: there's no problem of incompetence as far as he's concerned."

"None."

"All right. What about Dr. Halleck?"

The Administrator frowned.

"Jayvee is another matter."

The President gave a sudden grin and spoke with the mischievous candor that endeared him to so many, even when he most annoyed them.

"A black one."

Dr. Anderson laughed.

"A black one," he agreed. "But," he added more soberly,

144

"more from your standpoint than Houston's. The problem isn't black down there, except as it's his problem. He's very up-tight about race. They aren't. They couldn't care less—*except* as it affects his ability to work comfortably with them. Their main criteria are technical ability and professional competence—"

"And the ability to smooth out edges," the President suggested in the same mischievous way. Again Andy laughed.

"And the ability to smooth out edges. I think they forgive him even less than they do Jazz, because Jazz, whatever his edges, is on their level. I'm afraid Jayvee isn't."

The President looked serious.

"In what way?"

"Physical reactions—he isn't quick enough. Temperament—he doesn't seem to have the absolute singlemindedness they do. Emotional stability—the obsession with race seems to blow it, every time."

"Yet he's generally considered to be an excellent scientist."

"He is. In his field he's very close to the top ten or twenty in the country, I would say. That's why Vernon Hertz is so high on him and got him into the astronaut corps. But scientists, while they often work as teams, have a different kind of teamwork. It's more a matter of individuals working alone, on individual experiments, and then putting the results together into some kind of final pattern that makes sense. You can have a lot of personality problems and still make it all right in the lab. It's a little bit different on a mission to Mars, where everybody has to rely absolutely on everybody else with no time for emotional problems and racial hang-ups."

"You don't think the responsibility would impose its own discipline on him?"

The Administrator smiled somewhat wryly.

"I suggested that to our friends in the Astronaut Office and I seemed to meet with a lot of resistance. They don't think so. Hank Barstow, I believe it was, reminded me that they weren't running a reform school, as he put it, but a mission to Mars."

"Good phrasemaker," the President remarked with a smile. "Have to get his advice on a speech some day." He became serious.

"So as I understand it, then: if I were to insist that Jazz Weickert be on that crew, I might upset a few feelings but I actually would not be seriously jeopardizing the safety and success of the mission. But if I insisted that Jayvee Halleck be on it I might create really fundamental problems."

"That," the Administrator said gravely, "seems to me a fair summation."

The President looked thoughtful for a moment. Then he stood up and held out his hand with his customary forthright, pleasant smile.

"Well, Andy," he said, taking the surprised Administrator firmly by the arm and walking him to the door, "thank you very much for coming in. Your insights and advice have been very helpful and I appreciate them more than I can say. You make me prouder of my own good judgment in selecting you, all the time."

"But," Dr. Anderson said as he found himself at the threshold, "but—is there anything further I should do? Do you want me to arrange anything for you? Would you like to talk to Jayvee yourself, perhaps? We can always fly him up here to see you, if you think that would be of any value."

The President paused and rubbed his chin in a characteristic, thoughtful gesture.

"N—o," he said slowly. "No, I think not—at least right now. Possibly later if it became advisable—we'd have to think about that when the time came—if it came—but not right now." He gave the Administrator's hand a last, hearty squeeze. "Thank you again, Andy. We'll be in touch."

"But—" Dr. Anderson said again.

"You'll know anything I know," the President said, giving his puckish grin for the last time. "When I know it."

And having been briskly and efficiently removed, the Administrator found himself outside the office, not really knowing much more than he had known when he came in.

It was not until his car passed L'Enfant Plaza that he ceased for a while to puzzle over this, and became for a few short but hectic moments swept up in the darker currents of his time.

"Looks like something down there by the office," his

driver said abruptly as they stopped for a light a couple of blocks from NASA. "Wonder if I should go around the other side—?"

"Not yet," the Administrator said. "At least I should see what it is, I think"—though he was already pretty sure, after one quick glance.

BILLIONS FOR MARS—NOT ONE CENT FOR HUMANITY said one of the banners. TURN WHITE AND SEE THE PLANETS, said another. BLACK IS BEAUTIFUL, BUT, BABY, NOT ON MARS said a third. WHAT NEXT, UNCLE SAM? BOMBS FROM MARS? inquired another. IS THIS HOW U.S. CO-OPERATES IN SPACE? demanded a fifth. DON'T LET THE MILITARY-INDUSTRIAL COMPLEX GRAB MARS, TOO, advised a sixth.

Beneath the banners marched the same scruffy rag, tag and bobtail that had carried the banners of most protests in the United States for the past decade. Gleefully they shouted and pranced before the television cameras that dutifully recorded and encouraged their every antic; happily they screamed and wallowed in their own psychotic venom for the benefit of the reporters who hovered close. The underside of America was out on the streets again, Dr. Anderson thought, and in good old typical American style: dirty, demented, destructive—shrewdly and ruthlessly organized beneath their air of disheveled spontaneity—televised and reported with the most tender, loving care.

So foreign had all this always been to NASA that his first reaction was one of such violent repugnance that he almost ordered the car to stop so that he might jump out and personally challenge this willful desecration of his own front yard. But the impulse passed even as it came. He was no fool, nor was he about to give them any more headlines than they would get already. He had an instant vision of the *Post*'s happy ADMINISTRATOR MOBBED IN NASA PROTEST, the *Times*' pleased NASA CHIEF CLUBBED IN ANTI-MARS DEMONSTRATION. No, sir: not for him. But there was another way.

"Go around to the other side," he ordered, "and step on it!"

"Yes, sir!" his driver said, put the car in reverse, backed rapidly to the intersection they had just crossed, by some miracle managed to swerve around without running into any of the cars that were already jamming up, and shot forward again to deposit the Administrator at the other door.

He jumped from the car, ran up the steps, hurried to the security desk, grabbed a phone before the surprised Negro on duty could do more than greet him by name, and asked for the police.

NASA CALLS POLICE TO QUELL ANTI-MARS PROTEST, the *Times* subsequently reported. PICKETS ROUGHED UP AS POLICE STOP MARS DEMONSTRATION, the *Post* announced.

But at least it was not the devastating episode it could have been. That was some satisfaction to the Administrator, though he suspected, and accurately, that this was only the first testing of NASA's hitherto almost impregnable citadel.

8.

NASA CALLS POLICE TO QUELL ANTI-MARS PRO-
TEST, the *Times* reported next morning. PICKETS
ROUGHED UP AS POLICE STOP MARS DEMON-
STRATION, the *Post* announced.

It was not the best way, the President reflected as he
spread a half dozen of the nation's major papers before
him on his desk, to start the day. Particularly a day that
he was sure would bring still further tensions in the
growing dispute—he was not yet ready to term it "crisis"
—over the crew of Planetary Fleet One.

But dispute it certainly was. Already he had been
treated to an interview on NBC with Senator Kenny
Williams and some minor House member from Nebraska
who, like Kenny, apparently seemed to see in the issue a
chance to achieve a national prominence previously denied
despite valiant efforts to embrace all the Right Causes and
fawn on all the Right People. CBS had offered an analysis
in depth—the depth of the reporter's anti-NASA bias and
his desire to embarrass the Adminstration—of the situation in Houston. ABC had hired a lisping child of sixty
who wrote delicate books to give the whole thing a poetic
twist. His fragile thoughts on "The Mood of Mars" managed, in the sweetest way imaginable, to do everything
possible to increase the bitter mood of the moment.

And now the President's secretary had brought in the
newspapers, the newsmagazines and the new edition of
Percy Mercy's *View* and he had available, if he wanted it,
a whole feast of editorial goodies.

"The unfortunate episode at the offices of the National

149

Aeronautics and Space Administration yesterday afternoon," the *Post* began, "only serves to emphasize the growing national disillusion with the hurry-up, rush-rush plans to launch a frantic and ill-prepared expedition to Mars in an unworthy and unbecoming attempt to match or better an assumed Russian try in the same direction.

"Many Americans are not at all convinced that the Administration is right in its announced intention to telescope by at least a half-dozen years the carefully organized plans for a thoughtful, judicious and reasonable approach to the Red Planet. Many believe the President is letting himself be bulldozed and bamboozled by his space-happy advisers within NASA.

"This, bad though it is, would not be quite so ominous were it not for the apparent fact that these same individuals are apparently possessed of a deep-seated racialism which has led them to reject arbitrarily for crew membership the brilliant young black scientist, Dr. J. V. Halleck. They also apparently hate Russia . . ."

"Yesterday's potential riot at NASA headquarters," the *Times* said, "fortunately did not turn into the kind of all-out major protest against the agency which its handling of the new 'instant-Mars' mission could very logically invite.

"For this, NASA can thank its lucky stars—or lucky planets, if it has any. It cannot thank any innate goodness or rightness of its own which saved it from such an ugly challenge—such a challenge as may yet come, at any moment, unless recent NASA decisions are swiftly and drastically changed.

"Not only has the agency apparently gone racist to the point where its astronaut selection board is willing to deny crew membership to a thoroughly fine and thoroughly qualified Afro-American, but it has also ruthlessly excluded, apparently for some petty jealousy, one of the major astronauts of the earlier days of the space program, Commander Alvin S. Weickert III. And it has compounded these errors by apparently advising the President that he should reject out of hand the very real possibility that the Soviet Union might very well be willing to enter upon a generous and truly hopeful sharing of this great venture with the United States.

"It is on this last point, it seems to us, that the Administration is most vulnerable, and rightly so, to criticism and
150

to the type of protest which occurred yesterday afternoon and may very well occur again at any moment as the true enormity of the hasty and poorly-thought-out decisions of the past several days begins to sink in to the American people, and to the world . . ."

But it was in *View*, of course, that the chorus of denunciation reached its shrillest, most self-righteous pitch. P.C.M. was at his rarest. Hysteria provided by Percy Comma Mercy vied with noble appeals to the Higher Morality produced by Percy Christ Mercy. There were moments when it was hard to believe that the only thing at issue was a flight to Mars. It could well have been a Second Coming, or the decision of an implacable Jehovah to destroy the latest version of the Cities of the Plain.

"Now," he began, "has NASA done it.

"Now at last has the whited sepulcher been revealed in all its ugly, unseeing, unimaginative, true colors.

"Now has the Administration, falling all too supinely into the trap laid for it by the little gnomes who counsel it on space, made that one, fatal misstep which can so swiftly reduce great states and humble proud men.

"Not content with displaying for the world to see a vicious and deliberate racism—not content to pass over perhaps the finest and most experienced astronaut in the entire manned space program—not content to reveal shamelessly at last the rotted hulk that lies behind the gleaming white facade—NASA and the Administration have gone that one inch further that turns disaster to doom.

"They have rejected, flatly and crudely and with the sneering air that spells the death of hope, the hand of the Soviet Union, proffered in friendship, good faith and the true spirit of world brotherhood as it confronts the awesome mysteries of space.

"Writing in these pages in this issue, Soviet Academician Alexei V. Kuselevsky dispels forever the American myth that the Russians do not desire to co-operate in space. He reveals it for what it is: the myth of children, the myth of infantile, sick minds. Because the Soviet Union wishes, with perfect right, to conduct a new series of major scientific experiments aboard Space Station *Stalin*, this myth has suddenly received official imprimatur. The United States has suddenly been switched violently off-course. A whole national effort is being stamped out of context. Vast sums are being taken from America's desperate domestic needs to squander on an hysterical speedup of a hitherto sane, sensible, carefully funded and carefully planned program to go eventually to Mars.

"Now we must go to Mars immediately. Now we must drop everything and throw good money after bad, down the endless pathways of the universe. 'One giant step for mankind,' Neil Armstrong said when he set foot on the Moon. But he, and all of us, meant it to be one giant step *forward* for mankind in its quest for brotherhood, peace and a decent life for all.

"It was never intended to be one giant step for mankind into further suspicion, further hatred, further futile and foredoomed competition in the name of an outdated nationalism and a no longer valid (if it ever was, which we doubt) desire to wave the American flag in the face of the world and flaunt American arrogance in the eye of God.

"No: it is not thus that America will be saved. It is not thus that we will find that new dedication to the cause of mankind that we must have, to be redeemed for our sins of arrogance and pride. It is not thus that we will signify ourselves worthy to sit with the Children of God.

"It is time to end these futile suspicions, these bitter rivalries that destroy the harmony of the world. Let us pray—and truly pray—that we may reverse these dreadful decisions taken in these past few hysterical days, and so cleanse ourselves of our self-begotten, self-destructive blindness and bad faith.

"Let us hold out our hands to the Soviet Union and say, 'Brothers! We are with you! Let us go forward together for mankind, to Mars and ever beyond! Let us love one another and be secure in our love! Let us be worthy of what we *are*, as we, with you, reach out and explore together *what we can be!*'

—P.C.M."

And now, the President thought with an impatient inward sigh, he had an appointment to see the author of this high-sounding paean, ostensibly devoted to the higher glories of love with the Soviet Union but essentially and actually, most deliberately designed to destroy his Administration's purposes and restrict his own ability to maneuver.

He touched the buzzer, told his secretary to bring in

Mr. Mercy and Senator Williams. When she had done so, he decided, without rising, to sail right into it.

"Percy," he said, gesturing to the magazine, "do you really believe this crap?"

It seemed for a moment that the pompous little man before him must explode, so affronted was his expression, so purple and apoplectic his face. When he spoke, it was in a low voice that quivered with the anguish of the righteous mocked.

"Never in my life," he said, almost gasping for breath, "have I been addressed in such a fashion, Mr. President. Never have I—never—have I—never—"

"It's good for you, Percy," the President said cheerfully. "Now you know how your victims feel when you write something like this: completely stripped of all human dignity. It's great stuff to dish out, isn't it, Percy—not so easy to take. I repeat: do you really believe this crap?"

Again he thought the little man might burst. But after some great and obvious internal struggle, he spoke with a strained but rather impressive solemnity.

"I assure you, Mr. President, I believe it. If you think that I have exaggerated, then that may be due to my alarm and dismay that your Administration could so willfully take so desperate and destructive a step. If I have entered a harsh indictment, perhaps it can be attributed to the nature of the crime."

"You really think," the President said in a tone of deliberate skepticism, "that it is a crime."

"*I* do," Kenny Williams said belligerently. "A damned crime and a damned shame. And I intend to say so in the Senate this afternoon. May we sit down, incidentally," he asked with an elaborate politeness, "or had you rather we stand?"

"I'm sorry," the President said. "Sit if you like, stand if you like. I take it you won't be here long."

"Long enough to tell you what we think," Senator Williams said, dropping his youthful bulk into a chair with an insolent casualness.

"And for me to do the same," the President replied crisply. "Sit down Percy," he directed, not unkindly. He leaned forward. "Now I want you to tell me why you believe a smooth-talking liar like Alexei Kuselevsky rather than the intelligence estimates of your own government."

"I haven't believed my own government," Percy Mercy said bleakly, "for fifteen years."

"How sad for you," the President said softly. "And how very sad for your country, which has had to suffer from your disbelief in editorial after editorial, speech after speech, issue after issue, all those years. What infinite damage have you done to America, professing all the while to love her and claiming that only you know what is best for her."

"Then why has she betrayed me?" Percy Mercy demanded, and for a moment it seemed to the President that there was a genuine anguish in the little man, under all the righteous poses. "Why have we never done what we should have done, why have we always destroyed the hopes of mankind, why have we made of our stated goals a mockery and of our greatest dreams a shambles? Why have we not done what I, and not only I but many millions, have believed to be best for the world? How could we have destroyed so many hopes and been so false to ourselves? *How could we?*"

"That's what I want to know too," Kenny Williams said, and the President was thankful for his heavy-handed intervention, for it gave him time to think. He did not for a moment minimize the forces in the country these two represented, so he framed his answer with some care.

"Of course you know perfectly well," he said with a flat calm he hoped would restore some semblance of everyday reason to the conversation, "that I am not responsible for the policies of my predecessors. I have had to take the situation as I found it and go on from there, just as they did in their time, and as my successors will do in theirs. Sometimes this has not been easy, but always it has been inevitable. I also have had to act, as they have had to act, on information which is not known to the general public, or even to a small fraction of it, or even, hard though it may be to accept, Percy, to you. And I have had to act bearing in mind that nations nowadays do not get many second chances, and that if I do the wrong thing, my nation may not survive it. Why, good God, man!" he exclaimed with a sudden, bitter asperity. "You prattle on in your little editorials about the ideal things America ought to do, but *I* am responsible for what America actually has to do in order to survive. Survival isn't always pretty and perfect and ideal. Sometimes it's a damned grubby, serious business. Sure, it would be great if America could be the noble, humble, meek, turn-the-other-cheek country you would apparently like her to be, but if she were, she'd be dead in a minute.

"Now, I tell you," he said, and his voice became level and grim, "that regardless of what your friend Kuselevsky wants you and your wishful-thinking readers to believe, the Soviet Union *is* preparing a launch to Mars, and it *is* attempting to gain an advantage over this country again, and I don't give a damn how gullible you and your pals may be, that *is* the fact, and anybody who helps the Soviet Union in this by weakening his own government is playing the Soviet Union's game and will live to regret it. If, that is, he really cares what happens to America. Or did you," he concluded with a deliberately savage sarcasm, "give up on that fifteen years ago, too?"

"Now, see here," Senator Williams began. "If you're accusing *me* of—"

"You were still wetting the bed fifteen years ago," the President said. "Let this man answer for himself, if you please."

"You may use all the old clichés," Percy Mercy said with a certain serene disdain that he seemed to have recaptured during the President's reply, "but the basic facts do not change. You cannot prove to me that the Soviet Union is doing anything but what Alexei says it is, preparing to conduct a perfectly reasonable series of experiments at Space Station *Stalin*—"

"But I can prove it," the President said. "I can show you the reports."

"I should not believe them," Percy said in the same serene fashion, "for reports can be doctored and documents can be faked, when it suits the purpose of a suspicious and fearful government that wishes to deny the hopes of mankind for peace and co-operation in space."

"But you have it turned upside down," the President began. "It is not *we* who are the suspicious and fearful government—" But then he dropped it, for something in the smug and self-certain face that confronted him told him its defenses could not be penetrated, so convinced was Percy of his own infallibility, so closed, illiberal and intolerant his mind to any ideas that did not agree with his own.

"Very well," the President said. "And what do you

155

propose to do about it, just write more drivel like this and fly in the face of the facts?"

"I have already gone beyond that," Percy said calmly, "as you know. CAUSE is already a functioning organization and our temporary headquarters downtown on L Street is absolutely swamped with incoming phone calls, telegrams, letters and pledges of support. You saw our ad in the New York *Times* this morning, demanding assignment of Dr. Halleck and Commander Weickert to the crew, and demanding that the Administration invite Russia to participate as an equal partner in this unilateral attempt on our part to launch a hasty and ill-advised expedition to Mars——"

"You and your kind just won't believe the facts when they are unfavorable to Russia, will you?" the President asked in a wondering tone. "You just simply *will not believe.*"

"The word of a government in which we have no faith?" Percy asked calmly. "No, sir, we will not."

"How invaluable people like you are to the Communists," the President said, still in the same almost awe-struck way. "How infinitely invaluable, placed as you are and with the influence you have."

He swung his chair around to cut off the start of Percy's indignant reply; stared out across the lawn hunched and thoughtful for a long moment; apparently came to some decision; swung back. "I suppose there is no point in asking you to restrain these efforts a little until I have time to review the situation further?"

"What good would that do?" Percy asked. "The choices are simple enough."

"They will be when I get through presenting them to the Senate," Kenny Williams promised dourly.

"There is nothing I can do to make you change your minds?" the President asked, with what appeared to be the beginning of capitulation, and was taken by them to be such. "Nothing to even get you to grant me a little time?"

"Mr. President," Percy Mercy said, and his voice held the start of triumph, "there need be no time to make the decision so patently just."

"Perhaps you're right," the President said thoughtfully. "Then perhaps there will really be no need for that fighting speech of yours this afternoon, either, Kenny. Right?"

Senator Williams gave him a sudden sharp look.

"I—don't—know," he said.

"Well, think it over," the President suggested with a certain tartness. "You'll look a little foolish if you launch a clarion-call for action I've already taken, won't you?"

"How do I know you'll take it?" Kenny asked.

The President leaned forward.

"Look," he said, "be a little realistic, you fellows, will you? I have a lot of touchy personalities involved here, and it's going to take me at least a few hours to get them all in line. Now, suppose you hold that speech for twenty-four hours, at the request of your President—which," he said dryly, "ought still to carry a little weight with you—and then if you think it's still needed, fire away. But in the meantime—ease up. Give me a chance. O.K.?"

"Well—" Senator Williams said doubtfully.

"What do you want?" the President asked, still dryly. "Some dam or other? A new highway project? My job?" He smiled at Kenny's involuntary start. "It takes a big man to fill it. Prove you are: give me time."

"How do I know—" Kenny began, but the President stared him down. "Well," he said grumpily, sounding like the spoiled child his older Senate colleagues often considered him. "All right. If you say so. But only for twenty-four hours."

"Twenty-four hours," the President agreed promptly; so promptly that it immediately revived their doubts, as he intended it should. He stood up and began to move them firmly toward the door.

"Then we have your word, Mr. President—" Percy began, trying to hang back. But the President's hand on his elbow was polite and irresistible.

"You have my word," the President said as they reached the door, "that during the next twenty-four hours I shall do my best to reach the fairest possible decision in this difficult situation. Isn't that, really, all you have the right to demand?"

"Twenty-four hours," Kenny Williams repeated uncertainly. "After that—"

"After that," the President said cheerfully, "who knows what hell may not break loose?"

Which, he told himself as he closed the door behind them with considerable relief, might well be true; although, having successfully convinced his guests and himself that he still had independence of choice in the matter, he did not really believe it.

Percy, however, did; and when he returned to *View*'s hushed and elegant offices on Connecticut Avenue just below Dupont Circle, he resumed without a moment's hesitation the planning interrupted by his visit to the White House.

He did not trust the President, and he did not approve of him. Like so many in his particular sector of the political spectrum, Percy had gone through a series of changing attitudes toward the Chief Executive which were as fixed and inevitable as the orbit of Mars itself.

These had begun with initial fanatic support which had progressed to inevitable later disillusion as the President had proved to be, not the doctrinaire liberal Percy and his friends had at first assumed, but a hard-working pragmatist forced to accommodate himself to the realities he found in the White House.

For Percy, for his friends on the *Times*, the *Post* and similar self-appointed guardians of the True Grail, the metamorphosis—which had occurred with monotonous regularity in the case of each of their candidates down these latter decades of the Twentieth Century—had produced with this President, as with others, its inevitable corollary. It made them disillusioned, bitter, intolerant and suspicious of their former idol, overreactive in their opposition to the things he did.

It also made them, on an issue such as the Mars mission, a formidable, unrelenting, vindictive and destructive political force behind which could, and did, gather every element in America which wished America ill.

It was necessary to understand this recurring political dismay of Percy and his pals in order to understand why it was possible for them to get involved in the kind of protest that now was being mounted all across the country against NASA, the President and their plans for Planetary Fleet One. Only in this context did it make sense that Percy Mercy, presumably responsible editor of a presumably responsible magazine, could deliberately associate himself with the sort of sinister scum that was rushing to join the many decent and genuinely concerned citizens who were responding to the appeal of the Committee Against Unilateral Space Exploration.

158

He could perceive easily enough the way in which the decent and genuinely concerned were responding, when he reached for the Picturephone and checked with his organization's wildly excited headquarters on L Street. Behind the happily confused face of the youthful director he could see on the little screen the bright-eyed college kids, the bearded professors, the clever clerics, the self-conscious authors, the pompous movie stars and the little old ladies in hippie beads who had formed the working backbone of every campaign organization from Eugene McCarthy to the President himself. It was like old times, he realized, the contagion catching him a little, too, for all his sophistication and experience. This outpouring of native idealism was one of those things that restored one's faith in America.

It was good to be engaged in a campaign against the government once more, and to have such honest support for it. It made a man feel Right to be blackguarding his own country again and to know that many millions of his good-hearted, innocent fellow citizens were with him one hundred per cent.

For Percy, as for many of his colleagues, it resolved a lot of doubts.

Because they did have doubts, and they too were quite sincere and quite genuine. They epitomized that most peculiarly American product, the Americans who despise America because she isn't as perfect as they think she ought to be.

Thus they were impaled forever on the anguished knife of a most genuine and most desperate belief in their country—and a most genuine and most desperate dismay that she did not always, on every occasion, in every situation, live up to the ideals she was supposedly in the world to represent. Percy had not been engaging in sophistry when he had cried out bitterly to the President, "Why has she betrayed me?" It was an absolutely sincere and personal wail.

Since he felt betrayal as he did, it was therefore logical that Percy, like his friends, should on many occasions work with, and advance the cause of, less idealistic and less loyal souls whose attitude toward America was far more sinister. Percy and most of his friends were not Communists laboring, as Communists had for more than half a century, to destroy America: they were simply

159

well-meaning and deliberately self-blinded fools who did Communism's work for it.

They were, as Lenin had described them many years ago with a cruel contempt, the "useful idiots of the West" upon whom Communism could rely to scornfully reply to its critics, scathingly denounce its enemies, eagerly smooth its pathways and, with a fatal complacency, willingly open its doors.

Thus in utter stupidity but quite good faith and innocence, Percy could eagerly publish, devoutly believe and bitterly defend the cynical lies of an Alexei V. Kuselevsky. And he could with equal stupidity, innocence, and good faith call Miami, as he proceeded to do now, and talk to the individual who appeared on the Picturephone with all the customary ease and friendship of two old campaigners who had championed many a cause, sat on many a committee, agreed in many a seminar, linked arms on many a march.

It would have shocked him and provoked his virulent scorn if anyone had suggested that his friend was not loyal to America. Indeed, he had written one or two bitter editorials in *View* defending him against even the vaguest imputation of such a thing when it had been raised, years ago, by some obviously vicious, reactionary and demagogic member of Congress.

His friend said he would be happy to accept appointment as one of the national co-chairmen of CAUSE.

He would also be happy, though he did not tell Percy the extent of his pleasure, to interrupt his vacation at the Fontainebleau and fly up to the Cape immediately on the errand he had been contemplating all morning without knowing quite how to find a logical way to go about it. Now Percy, all crusading innocence, had given it to him. He was properly grateful.

"Thanks very much, old pal," he said with a fervor Percy found a little excessive and puzzling for a second. "You've just handed me a great opportunity."

"We must all stand together against this crazy, mismanaged adventure," Percy told him solemnly.

"We sure must," his friend said cheerily, and Percy forgot his puzzlement in the face of such satisfying enthusiasm. "You can count on me!"

After he faded from the screen, Percy sat back with a feeling of righteous satisfaction. He did not believe for a

160

moment that the President intended to do anything constructive in the next twenty-four hours. And so hell might indeed break loose. And justifiably so, in Percy's estimation.

He knew he could perhaps be considered to be helping it along, but he did not regret it for a second. It was probably the only way to restore some sanity to the situation and rescue the Administration and the country from the disastrous errors that were developing around the unfortunate mission of Planetary Fleet One.

9.

What a foolish old man you are, he told himself as he went humming about his office, or checked and rechecked the rapidly expanding personnel lists, or had himself driven out, as he was now, to the area where the workmen were placing the first preliminary stakes for Pad C. What a foolish, sentimental old soul, to be skipping about inside his head like a schoolboy, jumping and kicking his heels and hugging himself for joy in a world suddenly made glorious and exciting and young again. All because stakes were being driven in the ground, scientists and technicians were being rehired, plans were beginning to move off the drawing board into reality. All because he was going to be allowed once more to perform, to the fullest extent of his great administrative abilities, the job he had been put on earth to do. All because his beautiful, monstrous birds would soon be flying again.

"You are a fool, Albrecht Freer," he told himself in a gently chiding whisper as he got out of the car, told the driver to wait, and walked slowly across the hot earth of Florida, under the steaming Florida sky, toward the busy workmen. "You are absolutely an old softhead, with Saturns where brains ought to be . . . But," he added happily, "so are we all. So are we all, in NASA today."

And this he knew to be generally true, even though he was as aware as anyone of the personality difficulties in Houston, the bothersome disturbance yesterday in Washington, the hostile criticisms echoing across the land. Over and beyond these things, which he knew to be just "the growing-pains of an unexpected rebirth," as he had de-

162

scribed them to his wife this morning, he could literally feel the space program beginning to move again.

It was in the clipped tones of his old friend and competitor Hans Sturmer in Huntsville, trying to be businesslike but not quite hiding the excitement in his eyes as he chatted briskly on the Picturephone. It was in the newly confident smile of Andy Anderson in Washington, as the Administrator assured him cheerfully after yesterday's demonstration, "Don't worry, Al, no little gang of unwashed thugs is going to stop us now." It was in the pleased tones and quick suggestions of Jim Matthison at North American Rockwell as he called to discuss some minor but necessary change in the vehicle. It was in the engaging grin of Bob Hertz from Houston as he called to offer personal congratulations, "Because you and I, Al, we *really* know the fun of this thing." And it was in the happy faces of Stu Yule and Roger Webb, Dave McWharter and Bill Wheatley and the other astronauts in training at the Cape, as they came out of the simulators to wave and grin and give him thumbs-up when they saw him beaming down upon them from the glassed-in visitors' catwalk, high above.

Yes, the program was moving, and whatever the reasons for it, whatever the complications it might be creating in some places along the long, long network of NASA, he knew that basically and essentially the movement was vital and enthusiastic and good, as happy for the great majority of his friends and colleagues as it was for him. There were worries, there were annoyances, there were problems, but no one who had been through the years of Mercury, Gemini and Apollo had any real doubts about the end result. They had always licked their problems before, and whether they expressed the certainty aloud or simply hugged it to themselves as a matter of almost subconscious, instinctive faith, they were perfectly sure that they would lick them again.

"How are you coming along?" he called to the nearest workmen. White teeth flashed from white faces, black faces, sunburn-red faces.

"Give us a chance, Doc!" somebody called back. "We've only been on this job a day and a half."

"Long enough," he responded with a jovially chiding mock-severity. "Long enough to build twenty pads. You must work faster!"

"At least give us until tomorrow morning," someone else suggested. "Maybe we'll have it by then."

"That's good," he said with a laugh. "You just keep at it, now!"

"Yes, sir, Doc," they agreed. "We'll have it for you soon, Doc!" And more quietly as he turned away, with a genuine admiration that pleased him deeply, "The Old Man, he sure does love his rockets, doesn't he?"

Well, so he did, as much as Hans and the others loved them in Huntsville, as much as Bob and the astronauts in Houston, as much as Andy in Washington, as much as anyone could possibly do. They were his reason and his life; and he knew that nothing, now, could really deter them from flying again on the great adventure to Mars.

He could not remember exactly when he had first fallen in love with rockets, but it must have been sometime in his eighth or ninth year after an uncle gave him a book about them for Christmas. The drawings in those days were crude, the theories oversimplified, the tone highly romantic. Many years of hard, patient work lay between the fascinated child and the director of Kennedy Space Center. But from that moment there was no doubt in his mind what he wanted to do.

He came of a reasonably wealthy manufacturing family in Cologne, schooling was no problem even in the threadbare times between the wars, and upon graduating from high school he had enrolled at the Berlin Institute of Technology. There he became, first a competitor, and then—when he perceived that he could not outdo that coruscating figure in public appeal and effective charm—close friend and colleague of Wernher von Braun. This was in the days when Professor Hermann Oberth was making his first experiments with a liquid-fueled rocket engine (its thrust 15 pounds compared to Saturn's 7,500,-000) and the young Albrecht, like the young Wernher, was a fascinated and willing assistant.

From that point on, like many of the leading members of the Peenemünde Group, he found his life and career inextricably linked with Wernher's; and while they had their frictions from time to time, he, like the rest, presently settled into a reasonably comfortable relationship in which Wernher captured the headlines and smoothed the way, and the rest provided the technical follow-through that gave Wernher's brilliance its solid foundation.

With Wernher he did experimental work for the German Society for Space Travel at "Rocket Field Berlin," moved on into work for the Ordnance Department, became one of the principal members of the Group when Rocket Center Peenemünde was established in April, 1937, as a joint project of the German Army and Air Force. The V-2s were developed and successfully launched upon England; pleasing to the desperately dying Hitler regime, more or less incidental, in some curiously cold-blooded way, to the Peenemünde Group: their dreams continued to lie beyond. When the chance came to join the Americans in 1945, his was one of the strongest voices upholding the decision. Everything since had confirmed the wisdom of that choice.

With Wernher he had gone to Fort Bliss, Texas, to work for the Research and Development Service (Sub-Office Rocket) of U.S. Army Ordnance, and then, in 1950, to the Army's Redstone Arsenal in Huntsville. There the Peenemünde Group, aided and frequently abetted by General John Medaris, commander of the Arsenal, developed the Jupiter, Jupiter C, Juno II and Pershing missiles. There they successfully patched together and launched Explorer I, America's hasty answer in January, 1958, to the Soviet Union's first Sputnik in October, 1957.

In 1960 the Army relinquished control of space, NASA took over, the George C. Marshall Space Flight Center at Redstone Arsenal was formally dedicated by President Eisenhower. Wernher became director, the Peenemünde Group assumed command, the great years began. Saturn I, Saturn IB, and finally majestic Saturn V were designed in Huntsville, successfully launched at the Cape. Mercury, Gemini, Apollo, had their successes and their glories; the Moon was conquered, Space Station *Mayflower* rose to join Space Station *Stalin*; the great days passed, the program dwindled. Al Freer, dutiful and effective right-hand man, superb administrator, stayed for some years at Huntsville, moved on to the Cape to assist Kurt Debus, succeeded to the directorship of Kennedy Space Center shortly after Hans Sturmer took over in Huntsville.

By a happy circumstance the Peenemünde Group, which had done so much to help America master space, was still in charge and ready to help her again now that she had decided to try for Mars. A little bit grayer, Dr. Freer told himself, a little bit older, quite a bit wiser—but

165

still at heart the space romantics they had always been. And thank God for that, because without dreams, men got nowhere.

Already since the White House conference he had issued a nation-wide appeal for engineers and technicians. Its peroration—"Your Cape needs you! We want you with us once again! *Come back to the Cape!*"—was displayed on posters being distributed across the country to all NASA installations and to all major contractors and subcontractors. Already he had approved the preliminary plans for Pad C, already presided at an informal but quite emotional little ground-breaking ceremony yesterday morning. And now, after what must be at least his tenth inspection visit in the past thirty-six hours, he was on his way back to his office to go over the hundreds of telegrams and letters that had already reached him from the men and women, many of them personal friends, who used to work in the space program and were now responding, as eagerly and youthfully as he, to the thrill of being part of it again.

He was a happy man as his driver deposited him at the door of the administration building, happy because fulfilled. The mood lasted until he reached his office, saw waiting in it another old friend, shook hands eagerly and said, "So we are all together again!"

Then the mood changed and there began for Albrecht Freer a dark, unhappy time, for the old friend was not as friendly as he used to be.

"Andy," said Hans Sturmer in Huntsville, his voice troubled, his expression concerned, "have you talked to Albrecht?"

"No," the Administrator said in a puzzled tone. "Should I have?"

"I thought perhaps he had called you also."

"Not since yesterday after the protest. He seemed all right then. What's on his mind? Should I call him?"

"He was not really very clear," Hans Sturmer said. "He was, in fact, very obscure. But he was obviously fearful and very agitated. I don't know why he didn't tell me fully what it was," he added in an aggrieved tone. "We are, after all, old friends."

"What did he say?"

"He said we should all be warned. He said there may be trouble."

"Where, at the Cape?"

"Presumably," Hans Sturmer said, "though he was really rather incoherent."

"I'll call him right now," the Administrator said. "Thank you, Hans."

But when he reached Dr. Freer's office a minute later, the secretary said he was on another line, talking to the White House.

"Have him call me as soon as he's free," the Administrator ordered and turned back to his desk, puzzled and upset. As he did so he instinctively glanced out the window. But all was quiet around headquarters. Nothing was going on here.

"So you see, Mr. President," Albrecht Freer said, and his voice held a desperate urgency, "you must issue a statement right away, and you must furnish me with federal troops at once."

"Now, Al," the President said, his tone respectful, but tolerant and gently amused. "That sounds to me like rather drastic talk. Don't you think? Surely the situation isn't as serious as that. After all, you know Clete—he's apt to be something of a blowhard sometimes."

"I have known Clete O'Donnell for ten years," Dr. Freer agreed, his agitation not decreasing. "We have talked together many times since he organized his coalition of unions down here seven years ago—"

"The 'One Big Union'?" the President asked, and now his kindly amusement was directed at Clete O'Donnell, inviting Dr. Freer to join him. "He does have the Cape pretty well organized, doesn't he? I always admired his enterprise in that. Particularly," he added, and now his tone invited Dr. Freer to relax with him and put the whole thing in perspective, "since to my knowledge he has never once threatened a stoppage down there, or been anything but co-operative with the space program. Isn't that correct?"

"That is correct, but, Mr. President, this time he is not friendly. He is very hostile. This time he is threatening—"

"Why should this time be different?" the President inquired, allowing a touch of genuine skepticism to enter his voice.

Dr. Freer hesitated and then spoke with a dogged stubbornness.

"This time, perhaps, the stakes are higher."

"But in what way?" the President asked. "Surely you are not implying that he would willingly assist the Communists by attempting to block our mission. Now, that's a serious charge, Al. It really isn't worthy of you, my friend."

"Mr. President," Albrecht Freer said, with the same dogged stubbornness, "it may be because I was not originally of your country, but we who grew up in Europe are not as reluctant as some Americans seem to be, to call Communism honestly what it is."

"That is a far different thing," the President said sharply, and his face on the Picturephone became stern in a way that might have intimidated a man less frightened already, "from alleging that a perfectly loyal American citizen is deliberately and knowingly aiding his country's enemies. What proof do you have of this very serious charge? Anything that would justify my taking the action you suggest? Anything that would stand up in court, if it came to that?"

"It might not be the kind of evidence that would stand up in court," Dr. Freer said in a low voice, "but it is the kind that would stand up in men's minds, if they were aware—"

"Of what?" the President demanded. "Of something only you heard?"

"Of what is going on," Dr. Freer said.

The President uttered a short and scornful laugh.

"Now you sound like every hysterical witch-hunter in this country for the past thirty years. Just what is 'going on'?"

"I cannot always cite you proof and court evidence," Dr. Freer said, sounding harassed and upset but doggedly determined still, "but I do know that this man, as you say, has been co-operative with the space program for seven years during which he and his union have had a virtual stranglehold over the Cape. Those were also years in which there was no real competition with the Soviet Union: in which the Soviet Union, indeed, in Space Station *Stalin*, was allowed by this country to acquire a temporary advantage in a major area of space. Now suddenly we are engaged once more in a real competition,

168

where it will really help the Soviet Union if we can be stopped. And suddenly this man is no longer friendly. Suddenly he comes to my office and threatens to disrupt the program at the Cape. Suddenly he is an enemy."

"Oh, come now," the President said, and he was amiable again, exercising his famed powers of persuasion over troubled men. "Surely you are exaggerating again, Al. And are you sure you understood him? Couldn't you have been misinterpreting? It's easy to do, when one is overly protective of something, as you are about the program— and rightly so, Al, I admire you for it. But we musn't let it lead you into exaggerations, or unfounded and unfair charges against a fine and loyal American citizen. That would be too bad, Al. That would really be too bad."

"I know what I heard," Dr. Freer said bleakly. "I know the voice in which he said it. This man is not friendly to the United States. I must repeat, I think you should issue a statement and furnish me with federal troops."

"Why?"

"To protect this installation!" Albrecht Freer said in an indignant and frightened voice. "To protect the Mars mission! To protect America!"

"I protect America," the President said, more mildly than would perhaps have been justified, "and I will protect your installation, and I will protect the Mars mission. But only if they are genuinely threatened, Al. Not on a one-sided report of a conversation to which, I gather, there were no witnesses?"

"No," Dr. Freer said in a voice suddenly tired. "I did not think I would need witnesses. I thought he was a friend."

"And I'm sure he is," the President said. "Say!" he said, obviously struck by a placating thought. "He isn't part of this CAUSE thing Percy Mercy is putting together, is he? I'll bet he is, they're old friends. Maybe that's why he came in to talk to you, and he just went overboard and sounded more threatening about it than he should have. Couldn't that have been it?"

"He is part of CAUSE, yes," Dr. Freer said in the same tired voice, "but he did not 'go overboard.' He meant exactly what he said."

"I'll tell you what I'll do," the President suggested. "I'll call Clete O'Donnell myself and we'll have a little talk. I'll get to the bottom of this, and then I'll call you back. I'm sure it's all a misunderstanding."

"But what will he say to you, Mr. President?" Albrecht Freer asked sadly. "He will not threaten you. He is one of your supporters, I believe, politically, is he not? He will be most amiable to you. But soon he will do what he threatens down here. And then you will be sorry."

"Now, Al," the President said, and his voice became soothing and comfortable, "you just let me work this out in my own way, and we'll get by without any ugliness, or any statements by me that would be libelous and I'd just have to retract, and without any federal troops that I couldn't get there anyway, at least in time to do any good. You just relax and trust me. We'll be in touch. Everything is going to be all right. O.K., Al?"

"Mr. President," Dr. Freer said in one last, desperate attempt, "I must beg of you to help us. I must beg of you to issue a statement and furnish troops."

"I can't do it, Al," the President said. "It would make me a laughingstock. It would be political suicide. And also, as far as I can determine, I wouldn't have anything to back it up. There's no logic to it. Now, you just take it easy down there and go ahead with Pad C, and after it's under way perhaps you and Lise can take a little time off and get away to Bermuda or Europe or someplace for a real rest. This business is more of a strain on all of us than we realize, I suspect."

"Mr. *President*—" Albrecht Freer began but with a smile and a wave and a toss of the happy, leonine head, the Chief Executive faded from the screen.

"The Administrator wants you to call him right away," his secretary's voice informed him.

"Yes," he said in a tone of bitter determination, "yes, I will. Get him for me at once, please. Andy will listen. Andy will back me up."

And Andy did, after hearing him relate his conversation with Clete O'Donnell, which this time he recounted almost verbatim, his voice trembling frequently with a mixture of indignation and fear.

It had begun as soon as he reached his office and found Clete waiting, his usually amiable face serious and stern. He had permitted himself the briefest of smiles when Dr.

Freer hurried forward eagerly to shake his hand and exclaim, "So here we are all together again!"

"Maybe," he had replied tersely.

Albrecht Freer, momentarily nonplussed but still too filled with the euphoria of his visit to the pad to understand this as a warning, took him by the arm and urged him toward his private office.

"Come in, come in, old friend," he said heartily, signaling "no calls" to his secretary and closing the door firmly behind them. "Isn't it wonderful to be embarked on exciting times again!"

"Exciting for you, maybe," Clete O'Donnell said somberly, staring out the window over the flat scrubland with a distant, closed-off expression that instantly sobered his host. "Damned worrisome for me."

"Why?" Dr. Freer asked blankly. "We have our go-ahead from the President, everything is moving, and already"—he gestured to the mound of papers on his desk—"I am getting a tremendous response from old friends. What is the matter? Where is the worry?"

"You have heard of CAUSE," Clete O'Donnell said: not a question, a flat statement.

Albrecht Freer nodded.

"Yes," he said with a scornful little smile. "Our friend Percy is up to his usual tricks, I see. What of it?"

"He has asked me to serve as one of his national co-chairmen," Clete said. He looked solemn. "I've accepted, Al. It's as simple as that."

"But I still don't see—" Dr. Freer began.

Clete held up a restraining hand.

"I've accepted because I believe in what he's doing."

"You *oppose* the mission?" Albrecht Freer asked, and his astonishment was so evident that Clete O'Donnell almost dropped the solemnity and laughed right out loud. But discipline held and he did not.

"He asked me to come and talk to you," he said gravely. "He wanted to make clear that there might be serious consequences here at the Cape if certain things are not done."

"Certain things?" Dr. Freer echoed. "Certain things? What 'certain things'? This fuss about the astronauts, perhaps? An invitation to Russia which we all know would be a useless fraud? What can we do about those things here? What 'certain things'?"

"You can use your influence with the program and the President to get them changed," Clete O'Donnell said.

"I have no influence with the program and the President," Dr. Freer said.

Clete O'Donnell looked skeptical.

"Now, Al. Now, Al. Don't be disingenuous. You have as much influence as anybody, and more than most. He'll listen to you. Why don't you give him a call?"

"What would I say?" Albrecht Freer demanded. "That Clete O'Donnell thinks we should change our plans, so why doesn't he listen? Really, you know! He is stronger than that."

"Tell him Clete O'Donnell will strike the Cape," Clete said, his tone suddenly cold, his face grim. "Tell him Clete O'Donnell cannot be responsible for the kind of violence that might happen then."

Albrecht Freer looked at him with an expression of absolute shock.

"You would not dare," he whispered. "You—would—not—dare."

"Try me," Clete said in a tone almost of indifference, and turned away to stare out again across the steaming flatland.

"What would you use for excuse?" Dr. Freer inquired finally, his voice filled with the great anger that was beginning to fill his heart. "What possible excuse? The hours are good, as they have always been, the pay is high, as it has always been, working conditions have not changed, we are providing extra bonus incentives for old employees who wish to return—what excuse? What excuse?"

"Perhaps just the excuse that what is being done in this mission is completely immoral and unjust," Clete said. His voice became heavy with sarcasm. "There are some people in this marvelous country, you know, who have a conscience."

"That is specious," Dr. Freer said with a flat contempt that caused Clete's eyes to narrow. "That is utterly and completely specious."

"Is it?" Clete asked in a tone as savage as his. "Tell that to the millions in the cities who have to suffer from inadequate housing and poor living conditions. Tell that to the blacks, who are second-class citizens in the space

172

program as they are everywhere else. Tell that to the Russians—"

"*You* tell that to the Russians!" Dr. Freer shot out. "Maybe they will listen to *you,* who seem to be playing their game so well!"

Clete's eyes narrowed further and with what appeared to be a genuine anger—appeared to be, but Dr. Freer was suddenly as sure of him as he had ever been of anything— he brought his fist down hard on the pile of telegrams and letters, scattering them across the desk and over the floor.

"God damn it, Freer," he said in a voice as menacing as he could make it, "if you weren't twice my age I'd knock you down for that."

"Go ahead," Dr. Freer spat out. "I'm not that old. Communist!"

For a moment Clete O'Donnell stared at him, almost without expression. Then he smiled.

"Who would ever believe it?" he asked softly. "Who would ever believe it about that fine Clete O'Donnell, that fine young leader of American labor? Nobody, Al. Not nobody, no-how. And you know it."

"How long?" Dr. Freer asked, again almost in a whisper. "How long?"

"Longer than you could imagine, old man," Clete O'Donnell said. "But don't try to tell anybody, because they'd laugh you off the face of the earth. It's so absurd. It's so ridiculous. Clete O'Donnell?" He laughed out loud. "Good God, how crazy can you be?"

"You are a monster," Albrecht Freer said, his voice still almost inaudible. "But I will tell them. I will. Whether they believe me or not, I will. I have to."

Clete shrugged.

"Go ahead," he said indifferently. "Make a worldwide fool of yourself. I'll have fifty-nine major editorials and twenty-three nationwide telecasts on my side before you can say Lenin-Stalin-Ho Chi-Mao. Try it and see, Al. You'll find out." He leaned forward, his eyes suddenly stripped of laughter, completely cold and ruthless. "If you try anything," he promised softly, "my friends will destroy you. And if you don't get on that machine and call the President, I will destroy this Cape. And if he doesn't do what we want him to do, I will anyway. So get busy."

"Monster," Dr. Freer said, finding himself somehow on his feet, voice rising, arm outstretched, finger pointing.

"Monster, monster, monster! Get out of here, Communist! Get out of here, scum! Go on! Get out!"

"They'll laugh at you, Al," Clete O'Donnell said stooping to pick up the papers he had dislodged, replacing them neatly and unhurriedly on the desk before he turned to the door. "Oh, how they'll laugh!"

And the President had, and so probably would many others, but not the Administrator. Andy looked after his own in NASA, and Andy believed. Dr. Freer could see that as he concluded his story, so shaken he was almost in tears.

"He won't help us, Andy," he said desolately. "He won't help us. But we've got to do something. What shall I do? Issue my own statement?"

Dr. Anderson hesitated for just a moment. Then he spoke with complete firmness and authority to his distraught lieutenant.

An hour later in Washington the NASA pressroom came to life. Downtown in the wire service offices, moments after that, the message began to chatter out on the teletypes:

"BULLETIN. NASA ORDERS CAPE GUARDED, 'SHOOT IF NECESSARY.'

"Washington—The National Space and Aeronautics Administration announced this afternoon that NASA installations at Kennedy Space Center have been threatened with strikes and violence if plans for the Mars mission, Project Arogsy, are not immediately revised and curtailed.

"Acting with the full concurrence of Administrator Dr. William Anderson, the director of Kennedy Space Center, Dr. Albrecht Freer, has ordered establishment of a strong armed guard at all entrances to KSC and around the site where work has begun on the new Pad C of Saturn Launch Complex 39, from which one of the three mission vehicles will be launched.

"The guards at the Cape are furnished by the George C. Wackenhut Agency of Miami. Dr. Freer announced that they have been given orders to use weapons up to and including guns, if necessary.

"He said the threats were made to him personally today by Clete O'Donnell, head of the union which controls most of the Cape's labor force.

" 'I do not know why Mr. O'Donnell has taken a posi-

tion so hostile to the best interests of the United States,' "
Dr. Freer said. 'But he has. Therefore NASA feels we
have no choice but to take adequate steps to protect ourselves. This is being done.' "

Half an hour after that, from Miami Beach, another
story:

"Miami Beach—Clete O'Donnell, union boss of Kennedy
Space Center, this afternoon ordered a complete work
stoppage on all projects currently under way, including the
new Mars mission Pad C of Launch Complex 39. The
stoppage takes effect at 6 P.M.

"O'Donnell said his action was taken in retaliation for
statements hostile to him made by Dr. Albrecht Freer,
director of KSC, and because he and his union 'do not
believe in this ill-advised, essentially racist, internationally
hostile, unilateral attempt to send men to Mars.'

" 'Dr. Freer has the right to call names if he wishes,'
O'Donnell said. 'Neither he, nor this Administration, has
the right to send this nation on a wild goose chase to Mars
that by its very nature is harmful to our domestic needs
and inimical to true space co-operation with the Soviet
Union.

" 'As free citizens of a democratic America, we feel we
have every right to make our position known and to make
it effective.' "

Twenty minutes after that, Dr. Freer issued a statement
through the Chief of Public Affairs at KSC:

"Stoppages and interferences with the work of Kennedy
Space Center as it prepares for Project Argosy will not
be tolerated.

"I have asked the Wackenhut Agency to furnish immediately as many extra men as possible for guard duty. I
have also asked police authorities of our neighboring communities of Cocoa, Cocoa Beach, Melbourne and Titusville to give me as many men as they can spare. I have
similarly asked the sheriffs' offices of Brevard, Seminole
and Orange Counties to give me additional men.

"I am proud and happy to say that all of these agencies
have responded with pledges of the fullest co-operation.

They are already dispatching assistance to KSC.

"Our work shift changes at 6 P.M. I appeal to all administrative and technical personnel, and to all other loyal
workers, to come to their jobs as usual. They will be pro-

tected. I do not anticipate trouble, but if it occurs, we are ready."

(LITTLE CIVIL WAR THREATENS CAPE, the Orlando *Evening Star*, first publication in the nation to carry the news, declared in the banner headline of its early edition.)

Ten minutes after that the President of the United States was on the Picturephone to the Administrator of NASA.

"Andy," he said, and there was no amicability left in the forceful, commanding face, "what in *hell* is going on down there?"

The Administrator hesitated. Then he took a deep breath (*You can always go back to MIT*, a mocking voice somewhere in the back of his head told him dryly) and said crisply, "Exactly what appears to be, I guess."

"I cannot conceive," the President said coldly, "of two otherwise sane men like yourself and Al Freer deliberately putting their government in such a position."

"I believe Clete O'Donnell bears some responsibility, Mr. President," Dr. Anderson said with equal coldness. "In addition to which, Dr. Freer requested you to intervene and assist him in this situation. You refused, I believe. So I decided to do it myself. He has my complete backing."

"I've been in a National Security Council meeting for the past two hours," the President said. "None of this hysterical hullaballoo reached me until fifteen minutes ago. I am sorry," he said with a biting sarcasm, "that such minor matters as the Middle East, Asia and South America have to take precedence over the mighty affairs of NASA, but now and then they do. I can assure you, however, that had this not been done behind my back we would not be in this situation now."

"Nothing was done behind your back," Dr. Anderson said. "I did not know you were in a National Security Meeting. Even if you had not been (*Yes, MIT, here I come*) I should have done what I felt I had to do to protect NASA and the mission."

"I want to protect them, too," the President said in a somewhat milder tone than would perhaps have been justified, "but not this way. It wasn't necessary to force the issue. I had intended to call Clete and work it out as

176

soon as I could get rid of the Security Council. I didn't know Al Freer saw Communists under every bed."

"I believed him on that."

"Obviously. Why?"

"The old man doesn't lie," Dr. Anderson said. "No one could dream up that conversation out of whole cloth without some basis for it."

"You see, that's part of the trouble," the President said. "He didn't tell me the whole conversation."

"Dr. Anderson shook his head with a sort of tired frustration.

"He started to, but you obviously didn't believe the first word of it, so he stopped."

"That's right. I didn't."

"Let me ask you, Mr. President—why not?"

"Clete O'Donnell?" the President said in a tone of absolute skepticism. "It's absurd. It's utterly ridiculous. Don't make me laugh, Andy . . . well." His voice became once again cold and commanding. "I am very much afraid that I have no choice but to ask you to relieve Dr. Freer of his duties."

"Under fire?" Dr. Anderson asked with complete disbelief. "With the mission threatened?" His voice became very quiet. "Very well. Relieve me too."

There was a moment's silence during which they stared at one another from the little screens, the President's expression stern and unyielding, the Administrator's strained but equally unyielding.

Presently the President smiled.

"Now, Andy," he said, his expression relaxing, his voice relaxing, the whole mood shifting with the lightning skill at which he was so adept. "Let's don't add to the hysteria, shall we? Perhaps I'm a little hasty myself. Maybe I would be better advised to at least wait and see how we get over this 6 P.M. deadline, which is now, as I make it"—he glanced at his huge gold wristwatch—"roughly an hour away. If there isn't violence, then perhaps I'll have time to defuse it. If there is"—his expression became more sober—"then maybe I'll have to insist that Al be assigned some other duties, or go on vacation, or something of the sort. I won't embarrass or chastise him publicly. I can see your point on that."

"I would hope not," Dr. Anderson said, "because I'm

177

very much afraid it would look as though you were abandoning the whole project under fire."

"Oh, I'm not doing that," the President said. "I'm not doing that at all." He looked at his watch again. "O.K. then, Andy. Join me in a little prayer. I guess that's all we can do up here, right now."

And, basically, it was about all they could do at the Cape, Dr. Freer thought as he moved nervously about his office while the long flat rays of sunset slanted eastward across the palmettos and the launch pads, and the hour of 6 P.M. drew near. Just pray and hope for the best, knowing that what had to be done had been done, and that now the event was in the hands of more cold-blooded men than he.

He had issued his statements and taken his action with a strange mixture of anger, determination and fear such as he had never known before. Now the reaction was setting in. He was feeling very shaky and as though every minute of his sixty-odd years was hammering away at his legs, his arms, his shoulders, his back, his head. His head in particular was aching fiercely and several hastily gulped aspirin had not seemed to help. He also thought his churning stomach might betray him at any moment. He was a peaceful and peace-loving man, and having to take up arms, as he quite literally regarded it, against the enemies of his beloved Cape was bringing heavy toll.

It was not, however, deflecting him in the slightest from his decision to stand firm. He was fortified by a call from the Administrator, calm and encouraging; by similar calls from Hans Sturmer and Bob Hertz; and, just a moment ago, from Connie Trasker, Hank Barstow and Bert Richmond. Somehow the sight and sound of these last three, so different yet so alike in their essential alert, clean-cut, pragmatic efficiency, encouraged and strengthened him most of all.

"If we had time, Doc, we'd be there," Connie assured him. "You know that."

"The corps is behind you one hundred per cent," Hank said crisply. "Give the bastards hell."

"Tell Stu and Roger and the rest of the boys who are there that we said to rally 'round," Bert said laconically. "You're our hero, Doc."

"Thank you boys," he replied, touched and quite choked

up. "You can rest assured the Cape won't be pushed around."

"Spoken like a true son of NASA," Connie told him with a smile. "We'll all have a drink to that, after this nonsense is over."

"Get that Stu Yule to help you," Bert suggested. "He's a hot-headed little son of a bitch. He'd just love to take a few pot-shots at friend O'Donnell and his crew."

"Well, I don't want that," Albrecht Freer said with a smile, "but already, you know, the boys are here and helping. It makes the Director feel happy."

"You can count on the astros to stand by the dear old flag every time," Hank assured him. He grinned, rather dryly. "We aren't All-American Boys for nothing."

"Thank God for it," Dr. Freer said fervently. "Thank God for it."

And he did, too, for here they were, those astronauts who were at the Cape, sitting in with him and his top staff members in their hastily organized little council of war, running errands, making calls, coordinating plans, turning his office by their very efficiency into an impromptu but effective command post. Roger Webb, Dave McWharter, Bill Wheatley and Bob Curtis were already at the gates checking the arrival of guards and the outflow of workers going home from the just-concluding shift. And Stu Yule, sure enough, just by sheer brains and vitality, by his anger with Clete O'Donnell and his enthusiasm for the task of defeating him, was already acting as a sort of informal aide-de-camp upon whom Dr. Freer found himself relying without hesitation or reserve.

For the moment, things seemed to be proceeding smoothly with both the incoming carloads of guards, police and deputy sheriffs, and the outgoing workers. Closed-circuit television conferences with the various project and division managers half an hour ago had disclosed a considerable reluctance on the part of many employees to leave KSC, but Dr. Freer had appeared on the screen in person to urge them to go as soon as possible.

"The quarrel of Mr. O'Donnell is not with you," he said. "Nor do we have any quarrel with those of you who may belong to Mr. O'Donnell's union and may want to turn right around and picket us, as long as you do it peaceably. The first thing is to leave the Center. Then you may each do as you please. I am sure Mr. O'Donnell will let you go."

With this, Mr. O'Donnell apparently had no disagreement, for so far there had been no known interruptions of the outgoing traffic. Nor had there been any attempts to interfere with the inflow of security men, who had already established road blocks a mile outside each of the gates.

As of 5:47, Dr. Freer could reflect with a shaky but growing confidence that all was going smoothly. It appeared that Clete's threats might fizzle out into no more than a sensationally headlined but quickly dying protest.

But that, of course, was not what Clete intended; and in this instance, having the controlling hand, what he intended came about.

At 5:51 a call from the northernmost gate, Gate 3 leading to Titusville, brought the first intimation of real trouble. Several truckloads of armed men were halting incoming cars beyond the barricades, forcing their occupants to get out and submit to search, forcing all those who were not members of the union or professed sympathizers with the strike to turn back. Two minutes later a similar report came in from Gate 2 giving access from Cocoa, Cocoa Beach and Orlando. And at 5:57, looking out the Director's office windows north across the scrub, the men at headquarters could see a pillar of smoke and flames rising from the temporary construction trailers at the site of Pad C.

At this, something cold and frozen came to life inside Dr. Freer, perhaps not to be dissipated for a long, long time, and with it a blind rage that sent him rushing from the office, Stu Yule and the rest in troubled pursuit close behind.

"I want my car!" he shouted as he hammered impatiently on the elevator buttons in the hall. "Get my car at once, please, get my car!"

"Doc," Stu Yule said. "Doc! *Doc!* Stop it! Where do you think you're going?"

"I'm going out there and tell those—those *people*," Dr. Freer cried in a tone of absolute contempt, "to take their filthy hands off that launching pad and *get out of here*, just *get out!* Aaaaah!" he added in a tone of furious impatience with the elevator's slowness in coming, and flung away down the stairs, Stu again close behind as the others began to fall back, willing but winded.

180

"I want my car!" he shouted as he raced through the lobby. But at the moment, either because the dirvers were all on temporary guard duty or because they had decided it was wiser to be elsewhere, there was no car.

"Stuart!" he shouted, almost crying with rage and frustration. *"Stuart!"*

"I'm right here," Stu Yule said, overtaking him. "And the car's right across the street."

Dr. Freer hesitated for a moment.

"If you had rather not—" he began, but Stu Yule wasted no time on argument.

"Come on!" he said, grabbing Albrecht Freer's arm and propelling him out the door toward the parking lot. "Let's go!"

Much later, when they could laugh about it again, he and Stu would agree that probably no Corvette had ever been driven so fast, even by Stu's colleagues in the astronaut corps, some of whom would have qualified rather favorably alongside Parnelli Jones, Mario Andretti and other giants of the Indianapolis 500. Stu probably did not take all corners and all curves on two wheels, it just seemed that way; and he probably did not miss other cars by less than a sixteenth of an inch as he roared north on Kennedy Parkway past the VAB, the press site and the Crawler trackway on his headlong plunge to Pad C. But he gave as good an imitation as it was possible to give in their frantic dash toward the fire, whose flames and smoke mounted steadily higher in the damp, lifeless air.

Half a mile south of Pad B, they turned off onto the new dirt road just cut through the palmettos. The car rocketed north, unopposed for the first mile and half. Then as they approached close enough to see that all three construction trailers were brightly burning, their progress came to a halt in a scream of brakes and a wrenching swerve that almost overturned them.

Squarely across the road was a line of trucks, bulldozers and halftracks. In their cabs, along their sides, and on their roofs stood a jeering line of pickets bearing signs. And miraculously but quite inevitably, sprung no doubt full-panoplied like Minerva from the Florida scrub, a dozen television cameramen busily photographed their angry placards and recorded their bitter cries.

STOP THE RACIST MISSION! their broadsides said; and, BILLIONS FOR MARS, NOTHING FOR U.S.

SLUMS; and, NO MORE SPACE JUNKETS, UNCLE SAM; and, NO CO-OPERATION, NO FLIGHT.

And the voices Albrecht Freer heard now were far different from the voices he had heard five hours ago.

"How do you like your Pad C now, Doc?" they jeered; and, "How's this for a launching?"; and, "Hey, Nazi, too bad you aren't still working for Hitler!"

For several moments, while the cameras swung around to study him impersonally, he did not try to reply. Indeed for a little while he could not, so filled was he with fury and contempt. Furthermore, Stu was at his elbow and his advice, murmured in a low voice, was far less hot-headed than Bert Richmond would have imagined.

"Don't answer, Doc," he kept saying, over and over. "Don't give them the satisfaction. Don't answer."

But there came a moment very swiftly when Albrecht Freer decided he must; and calling out "Help me!" firmly to Stu, who perceived he evidently had no choice and so obliged, he clambered awkwardly onto the hood of the Corvette. There he stood, precariously balanced, one hand gripping Stu's for support, the other raised high above his head for silence.

"Sieg heil!" someone shouted mockingly, but he ignored it and began to speak in a voice that was shaking with anger, not fear.

"This strike," he shouted, "is a completely illegal attempt to interfere with the work of this Center." There was an angry murmur, but he went on. "It is an attempt to intimidate NASA and the United States Government. It is a politically motivated plot to stop the Mars mission so that the Soviet Union may successfully take the lead—"

At this there was a sudden roar of boos, but he continued to shout through it.

"I repeat, a political plot to give the Soviet Union the lead by stopping the Mars mission. It is a plot by traitors and Communists—"

Now the roar of boos became a bellow, and against it, red-faced, quivering with anger, almost incoherent, unheard, he continued to shout. But not for long.

Suddenly out of the crowd he had a vague impression of something hurtling, turning, spinning, toward him in the air. He was conscious of a sudden movement from Stu, a powerful yank on his arm which dragged him off the hood of the car and sent him staggering. There was a flash of

182

flame, a sound sharp, powerful, solid, a heavy physical impact somewhere near. He tripped over a rock, fell, hit his head on another. Blood spattered from his temple, the bright dream of rockets went out for a while.

Fifty feet from his prostrate body in the sudden silence there was an automobile that would never run again and on the ground beside it an astronaut who would never fly.

Happily the cameras ground on.

SPACE DIRECTOR, ASTRONAUT BLASTED IN CAPE STRIKE, the busy headlines said. FREER SUFFERS HEAD INJURY, ASTRONAUT YULE LOSES LEG IN BOMB VIOLENCE. UNION LEADER CALLS OFF STRIKE, DEPLORES "UNNECESSARY TRAGEDY CREATED BY UNNECESSARY FLIGHT." CONTINUATION OF HARD-LUCK MARS MISSION UNDER FIRE.

"Andy," the President said quietly, and the Administrator nodded in a tired, strained way.

"Yes, Mr. President," he said with an equal quietness. "I've been expecting your call."

10.

Of the writing of savage editorials, the concocting of hostile news stories, the fashioning of hostile headlines, the production of bitterly slanted television "specials" and "reports" and "commentaries," there was no end as that night dragged to its long, unhappy close and a long, unhappy day succeeded. Criticism harsh, unyielding, unforgiving screamed from major newspapers, wailed from major networks, spewed from major figures. Those who favored the mission were muted, uneasy, uncertain, appalled by the tragic violence at the Cape, frustrated by the general air of confusion and controversy skillfully created around Planetary Fleet One by its enemies. For a time it did indeed seem possible that continuation of the mission could be in doubt.

At 9 A.M. the White House press secretary appeared to set that to rest with a terse two-line statement which apparently answered one question. But as Senator Williams remarked in a shouting, ranting, bitter Senate speech an hour later, it left all the rest unresolved.

"The President wishes it to be known," the youthful secretary read in a nervous voice to two hundred clamoring reporters, "that there has been no change in the target date for Planetary Fleet One of Project Argosy. The President will speak to the nation on this and related matters at 9 o'clock tonight."

"And what will he tell us then, Senators?" Kenny Williams demanded, while over in the House his friend from Nebraska cried out with equal bitterness, both of them speaking from texts written during the night by
184

Percy Mercy. "What fiction will be offered to cover up the terrible reality that lurks behind the frightful tragedy at Kennedy Space Center last evening? What smooth story will be used to turn the minds of the nation and the world away from the ghastly mistake of the Mars mission, growing more ghastly by the hour?

"A distinguished scientist," Kenny Williams said, and his voice dropped to a low, respectful note in the hushed and crowded chamber, his eyes staring intently up at the television cameras that now were permitted during major debates, "a leader for a generation in the space world, lies unconscious, gravely wounded, in Orlando. A fine young American astronaut, pilot, war ace, happily married father of three, brilliant star of the astronaut corps for the past five years, lies near him in the same hospital.

"Senators," Kenny said, and his tone dropped even lower in a hush yet more profound, "there may be a chance—we all pray God there is, and the doctors assure us we may be answered—that the great scientist will recover.

"But, Senators!"—and his voice held a thrilling ring— *"We know the fine young man will never fly again. We know he will walk on crutches or an artificial limb to the end of his days. We know he has been stricken from the skies he loved by this insant, foredoomed mission. We know his government has ruined his life forever as surely as though it had taken an axe and chopped him down.*

"O what insanity, Senators! What folly! What perversity! What unforgivable guilt!

"Surely the President cannot be serious in announcing the continuation of this foredoomed venture. Surely there is time to change his mind. Surely all of us who believe in decency, in sanity, in peaceful, non-competitive cooperation with the Soviet Union, have still the time and the chance to let him know what we believe.

"I urge all Americans to wire, phone, write your President. Do not let Dr. Albrecht Freer lie unconscious in vain! Do not let the brave sacrifice of Astronaut Stuart Yule go unrewarded!"

"In the names of these two brave men, stop the Mars mission!"

For a full minute after his staring eyes and pudgy, sagging baby-handsome face faded from the screen, there was silence in the Astronaut Office. Finally Hank Barstow broke it, very softly.

"Well, I'll be God damned. I will be God *damned*. So Al Freer and Stu Yule are now the heroes of the stop-Mars campaign! If ever there were two men more whole-heartedly dedicated to the cause of Piffy One—well," he said softly again, and this time he shook his head in absolute wonder, "I will be God damned!"

"They're beyond belief, that crowd," Connie Trasker said. "Really beyond belief."

"And you know something?" Bob Hertz asked wryly. "They're going to get away with it, too. Unless the President is a lot tougher than I think he is."

"He'd better be," Bert Richmond said grimly. "Otherwise this whole program is going to be shot straight to hell."

"That's exactly what they want," Bob said. "We can't let them do that."

"The White House did say one thing," Connie said, trying to put more hope in his voice than he felt. "They said there's no change in the target date."

"'*Has been* no change,'" Bob Hertz corrected. "Nobody said there wouldn't be."

"But the clear implication was—" Connie began half-heartedly. Then his voice trailed away.

"Here's Andy," Bert said as the Picturephone began to light up. "Maybe he'll have the word."

But after the Administrator had spoken to them, relating his two conversations with the President, one last night immediately after the tragedy, the other this morning shortly after the White House announcement, they did not know much more clearly than before where the Chief Executive stood. The only thing they knew definitely was where they stood. The ball, as Bob Hertz remarked grimly when Dr. Anderson said good-by, "is in our corner now."

11.

"I can't believe he's that political," Jane said as she put a quick soup-and-sandwich lunch on the table. "I just can't believe he would be that—that *frivolous* with the program. Surely he wouldn't just abandon the flight, would he?"

"Oh, no," Connie said dryly. "He won't abandon it. He'll just change it all around so it isn't the same thing any more. But he won't abandon it. I don't think he'd dare."

"Then maybe it won't be so bad," she suggested, joining him in the pleasant alcove that looked out upon the back lawn. "It may work out all right, after all."

"Dear girl," he said, not unkindly. "My eternal optimist. No wonder Jane Trasker is Mrs. Manned Spacecraft Center, our laughing, golden one who rallies the troops in times of darkness and need. How can it possibly be all right?"

"Well, I don't know," she said, "but I just think it will. He has some sense of responsibility, after all. He isn't going to do anything that would affect the safety or success of the mission. He's American. He wants to be first."

"If it doesn't cost him too much politically, yes," Connie agreed. His expression became grim. "He didn't do much to help Stu and Al Freer."

"We don't know all the story on that, yet," she said, and suddenly his expression softened.

"You're a very charitable person, really, you know that? I like you."

187

"Well, I should hope so," she said, looking pleased. "I try to be."

"You do try. You really do. That's more than most people do."

"Most people here, anyway," she remarked, with a smile that removed some of the sting. "Astronauts get pretty fierce when they're challenged."

"I suppose it's the nature of the breed," he admitted. "We're dedicated, and I suppose it limits us, in some ways." He looked thoughtful. "It makes us good in others, though."

She laughed.

"You look so serious, thinking about it. Like a little boy."

"Maybe we're that, too," he said, more lightly. "When you come right down to it." Then worry returned, he frowned. "Did Pete say what he wanted to see me about?"

"No, he just said he knew you'd be home for lunch today, and he wanted to see you here. I invited him to join us but he said that after touring the West Coast with the three Russian cosmonauts last week, he was going to have to diet for a while."

"They're a strange breed, too," Connie said soberly. "He told me he practically had to beg them to sign the guest book at Jet Propulsion Lab. They're so suspicious of everything and everyone, behind those jolly smiles. It gives you a little insight into the system they live under."

"Maybe they feel we've given them cause to be suspicious," she said. He laughed.

"Even charitable to the Russians—that's my Janie." He listened for a moment. "I hear a Jag. Our boy must be arriving."

"Your boy," she said, but he noted with relief that the comment appeared to be without tension.

"Whose-ever he is," he said, "I'd like to know what's on his mind."

But he was not prepared for it, when he found out.

Look at me, he thought as he drove the Jaguar carefully along the comfortable shaded streets of Nassau Bay toward El Lago. Look at the Greek loner from Tarpon Springs, about to lay down his dreams for his friend. Greater love, he told himself dryly, hath no man.

188

That it was love or something very close to it that he felt for Connie Trasker, he had faced and stopped worrying about some time ago. It had been a little rough at first, but it had soon settled into a comfortable friendship without, he felt, any real strain. At least, very little on his part or Connie's, though it had been clear enough from time to time that it was upsetting Jane.

Why this was, he could not really understand, unless it was just some feminine sense of exaggeration that had put two and two together and come up with ten. God knew he wasn't in the business of seducing husbands or breaking up homes, and he felt with a certain masculine impatience that Jane should know it too. Yet there had always been a little edge to their relationship, an instinctive hostility, muted but alive—again, more on her part than his.

"You can have your boy," he said aloud; adding, although it might not have been altogether true some other time, some other place, some other circumstance, "I don't want him."

When he had come to Houston from JPL, still unhappy and uncertain from the collapse of his marriage (because, he had told himself then, before he got to the point where he could be really honest with himself about it, he was too independent and really too much of a loner to settle easily in that particular harness), the first astronaut he had met had been Connie Trasker. Connie was standing by the elevator waiting to go up to his office when Pete came in the front door with that unmistakable air of the newcomer. Connie spotted it at once and held out his hand.

"You must be Pete Balkis," he said. "I'm Connie Trasker. Welcome to Houston, the Moon, outer space and the local Safeway. Just checking in?"

"Yes," Pete said with the quick, attractive grin under humorous dark eyes and curly black hair that was his trademark. "Which should I contact first?"

"I'd suggest the Astronaut Office," Connie said. He gave Pete a quick, appraising glance, made some instant, instinctive decision. "Come by my office when you're free. Down the corridor on your left. We'll talk."

"Thanks," Pete said, genuinely pleased. "I'll do that."

Thus easily had begun his friendship with one whose picture he had seen for years, whose Gemini flights and Apollo moon walks he had watched on television, whose name and fame were perhaps the brightest and most glowing in a bright and glowing company. And thus easily, almost before he knew it, had he cut moorings and set forth on a new and frightening sea.

Frightening for a while: then common sense, discipline, integrity, his own innate pragmatism and the pragmatism of the corps, which soon rubbed off on all its members, had brought him back to safe harbor again.

For six months or so, while Connie, perhaps suspecting and perhaps (though Pete would never know for sure) not entirely unflattered or entirely adverse, had treated him with a cordial intimacy, his day's activities and his nighttime thoughts had revolved around his new-found friend. Nothing had ever come of it, he was convinced nothing ever would, he was convinced further that he did not really want it to—and yet he could not conceal from himself that for a while Connie, so kind and sympathetic and helpful to the awe-struck newcomer, was the center of the world.

He still was, but not quite in that first idealized and impossible way. There had come a long, dark night, after Pete had fought himself to a standstill with too much liquor and too many easy bar hostesses in Houston, when he had finally gone in the bathroom, turned on the light, and forced himself to look straight into his own exhausted eyes.

"You, Pete Balkis," he said aloud, "are not a school kid with your first crush. You are a grown man of 30, a doctor, a scientist, an astronaut of the United States, and you are too fine a person to keep yourself tied up in knots like this. You like him, he likes you, you're friends forever and you both know it, and that's enough. Now, *snap out of it.*"

He returned to bed, dropped instantly into a profound and untroubled sleep. In the morning, perhaps luckier than he knew, he awakened to a safer world.

From then on, the friendship had entered upon the easygoing, affectionate, jesting intimacy he hoped it would always have. He suspected that there might be other close friendships in the corps that might at one time or another have gone through—and successfully surmounted—stresses similar to his: it was not surprising or so uncommon among men thrown together and dependent upon one another for great and dangerous enterprises. But the spirit of the corps, the hold of the image, the basic good sense, the level heads, the innate stability and necessary pragmatism—all combined to preserve the balance and keep things steady. And so they had for him.

So he continued to work with Connie; became friends, and he hoped ultimately it might be really good friends, with Jane; brought dates faithfully to the occasional social gatherings of Nassau Bay and its related suburbs; slept with them efficiently when he felt like it, which was fairly often; made no promises, undertook no involvements, kept himself separate, independent and free. He knew his heart was in large measure committed and always would be; but now he could live with it. No sweat, as they said in the corps. And thank God for that.

Out of it, he honestly felt, there had come something finer than there had been before—because what was he about to do now, if not sacrifice his greatest ambition for his friend? And what could a man do more selfless than that?

"Hi," he said when the door opened. "Is this the home of the world's greatest astronaut?"

But he might have known, the bantering tone did not fool Connie.

"What's the matter?" he asked sharply, shaking hands and drawing him into the living room where Jane was waiting with coffee. "You sound funny. What's up?"

"Hi, Jane," he said, to give himself time.

"Hi," she said. "Cream and a little sugar, coming up." She too gave him a searching look. "Are you all right, Pete?"

"Sure I am," he said, though absurdly he found his breath starting to come short. "I came here—to tell you—"

And quite irrationally his voice began to tremble and tears, humiliating, childish, unavoidable, came into his eyes.

"I came here to tell you," he said with a careful slowness that did not help much, "that since you are under such pressure about the crew, I am going to—get out of the way and request that I be—reassigned—to some other mission—so that you can have—my place—for Jazz or Jayvee—"

"But you don't want to do that!" Jane protested, her eyes filling with sympathetic tears.

"You're damned right you don't." Connie said in a

deliberate tone of disgust, "and for God's sake, are we all going to stand here and bawl like a bunch of babies?"

"Probably," Pete said with a shaky little laugh. "Probably we are."

"Well, then stop it," Connie said in the same stern tone. "Just God damned stop it, if you don't mind. Sit down and have some coffee and stop this nonsense. You aren't going to do any such thing and you know it."

"Who says so?" Pete asked, still shaky.

"I do," Connie Trasker said, "and I am still the commander of this lousy flight, such as it is. I never heard such a thing in my life. Of all the damned noble, self-sacrificing, holier-than-thou—" he shook his head in deliberate outrage. "You *want* to go to Mars with me, don't you?"

"More," Pete started to say, "more than I could—possibly—"

"All right, all right, all right!" Connie snapped. "Jesus! What have I done to deserve this sentimental waterfall? You *are* going, and that's that. Now have some coffee or some booze or something and simmer down!"

"Is that an order?" Pete asked, beginning to grin a little and sounding more like himself.

"It's more than that," Connie said, and suddenly he gave him a direct and kindly smile. "It's a request," he said quietly, "of my friend."

"Well, on that basis," Pete said, though still a little shakily, "I guess I don't have any choice."

"That's right. Janie, hand my crewman some coffee."

"With extra sugar," she said, still a little shaky herself, "for needed energy."

"I will tell you what you can do, though," Connie said in a tone all business again, sitting down in a favorite chair with his coffee and leaning forward intently. "You can bring one little boy into line. I won't use you on the other one, because it's going to take somebody higher up than me to take care of him. But you can go to Jazz Weickert and tell him what you've just offered to do, if you like."

For a moment no one said anything. Then Jane said softly,

"My goodness, don't I have a shrewd husband!"

"He hopes he is," Connie said. "So what about it, Petros? Will you do it?"

192

"If you think it will do any good," Pete said slowly. "I don't know that it will—"

"I don't know, either, but the tactical problem is to separate those two from each other and from their supporters, if possible. Unless I have old Jazzbo figured entirely wrong after twelve years, this may do it. And the sooner the better. Shall I find out where he is?"

"Clare tells me he usually eats home for lunch like you do," Jane said. "Shall I call her?"

"Please," Connie said.

While she was out of the room, their eyes met. Many things were in them. They held for a long time before Connie, with a little sigh he probably did not know he uttered, looked away.

"They're there," Jane reported.

"Up and at 'em, buster," Connie said, standing up briskly and holding out his hand. "Appeal to all his finer instincts about the dear old program. Give him hell."

"Poor Jazz," Jane remarked with a comfortable little laugh. "He doesn't know what's going to hit him."

"My secret weapon," Connie said. "Come on, I'll see you to the door."

On the threshold, with the door shut behind them, alone in the dignified, deserted noon-hour street, he held out his hand again and took Pete's in a firm, affectionate grip.

"Thanks, buddy," he said quietly. "I appreciate your offer. I know how hard it was for you to make. I know what you were trying to do for me. I won't forget."

"Good," Pete said with equal quietness. "Then I won't either."

"I wouldn't want you to," Connie said. "I really wouldn't want you to."

Back in the living room as the Jaguar moved out and away toward the Weickerts' Tudor house in Nassau Bay, he looked at his wife and smiled.

"Well," he said, "that makes him happy again, I hope—and it will make Jazz straighten up and fly right, I hope—and maybe—just maybe—we'll do it my way on the mission, yet."

Jane looked at him for quite a long time. Then she smiled.

"You're quite something. You know, you really are."

He grinned.

"Make you wonder sometimes what you married?"

"I'll probably never know," she said in the same humorous way. "I probably never really will."

He uttered a wry and cheerful laugh.

"I'm not always so sure myself, sometimes. But it seems to work."

But whether it would work with Jazz Weickert, Pete did not know as he brought his car to a halt in the circular driveway in Nassau Bay. Joanna, four, was riding her tricycle up and down between the doorway and the curb with a determined frown as he got out.

"Hey, honey," he said. "Are your daddy and mommy here?"

"I'm Joanna," she said, not looking up from her firm grip on the handlebars.

"I know," he said. "Are your mommy and daddy here?"

"I can go fast," she said, turning at the door and putting on a sudden burst of speed as she started down the drive again.

"I see you can," he said. "But not too fast, now!"

"Why not?" she asked, turning to look at him finally and at the same moment instinctively yanking the front wheel to the left.

"Look out!" he said, but to no avail. Loud lamentations broke the quiet of the placid street.

"There, there," he said, and other sounds of condolence. Joanna was not to be distracted. He picked her up carefully, kissed a badly scratched elbow, touseled her hair, and carried her carefully to the door. Clare, looking, as always, sweet, vague and a little disheveled, opened it and greeted him with a grateful smile.

"Thanks so much, Pete," she said. "Here, I'll take her. She *will* do things like this."

"I went too fast!" Joanna wailed from her mother's arms.

"And Uncle Petey told you you went too fast, too," he said.

Joanna stopped wailing and spoke firmly between subsiding sobs.

"I *like* to go fast."

He laughed.

"Guess that puts me in *my* place."

"I'll say it does," Clare agreed. "I thought you got along with women better than that, Pete."

"Usually. But, then, not too many of the ones I know drive tricycles."

"I suppose that's true," she agreed with a smile. "Come on in. Jazz is in the den if you want to talk. I have some laundry to look after, so just go ahead—"

"Oh, no," he said, "this isn't all that private. In fact, I'd like your thoughts on it, anyway."

"Is it about the flight?" she asked, her eyes suddenly shadowed.

"It is," he said, startled but not too surprised at feminine instinct.

Her troubled expression increased. She looked, if possible, even more than usual like an harassed little waif.

"Jazz is so worried and upset. Are you sure you want to—?"

"I'm sure," he said, and now that Connie had resolved his problem for him he found he felt a surprising serenity: which, he told himself wryly, he should, since he was going on the flight and Jazz was still out in the cold. "I just want him to know about—my feelings about it, that's all."

"Well," she said doubtfully. "If you really want to—"

"I do."

She hesitated a moment longer, then gestured down the hall.

"The end door on the right. I really do have to check the laundry, then I'll be in. Would you like some coffee?"

"No, thanks. I had plenty at Connie's."

"Oh, that's right," she said, and something more unhappy and protective of Jazz came into her eyes. "You were just with them, weren't you?"

"Yes. Shall I go in?"

"Oh, yes," she said hurriedly. "Yes, please do."

Inspite of his new-found serenity and apparent outward calm, it was with some tension that he rapped on the door and called out, "Jazz, this is Pete. Can I come in?"

For a moment there was silence. Then the door opened and Jazz held out his hand, his eyes guarded but his expression reasonably friendly.

"Sure, pal. Come on in."

"Thanks," Pete said, shaking hands. His eyes moved to

the newspapers spread out on the floor around the big leather chair by the window. Jazz gave him an ironic glance.

"Quite a story, isn't it?" His expression became somber. "Doc badly injured and Stu without a leg. I hope somebody thinks it's worth it."

"Do you?" Pete asked, sitting down on the sofa, staring thoughtfully at the shouting headlines, deliberately not looking at his host.

"What kind of question is that?" Jazz demanded, dropping heavily into his chair. "Just what in the hell kind of question is that?"

"Just what I said," Pete replied, lifting his eyes in a level, unyielding glance. "Do you think it's worth it, what your"—he hesitated a second, then went on—"what your friends are doing to try to stop the mission?"

For a moment he thought Jazz would explode into some physical response, but he did not. Instead his eyes became cold with anger.

"They are not," he said, snapping out the words, "my friends. And don't you or Connie or anybody else around here ever say anything like that again! Understand?"

Pete did not flinch.

"I understand," he said gravely, "but I wonder if the country does. They claim to be your friends. You don't seem to be objecting. If you and Jayvee have agreed to play along with them, how is anybody on the outside going to get the distinction?"

"I'm not 'playing along with them,' " Jazz said harshly. "And as for Jayvee, I haven't talked to that—I haven't talked to him since this all began. He's got his own problems and I've got mine. He can meet his in his way, and I"—his tone dropped and became coldly emphatic—"will meet mine in mine."

"But nobody outside knows that," Pete said patiently. "All the public can see is that you two are the heroes of this drive to stop the flight. It's your route, Jazz, but a whole lot of people who are no friends to the program are claiming you."

Jazz frowned and looked out the window for several seconds before he spoke.

"I know that," he said finally. "Damned if I don't."

"Then cut loose," Pete suggested quietly. "It wouldn't be so hard."

"But I want to go on this flight," Jazz said in a sudden anguished tone, his voice low, almost a whisper. "*I want to go on this flight.* It's fine for you to talk—you've got Connie in your corner. But I'm on my own, and he sure as hell isn't going to give *me* anything, if he can help it."

"I want to tell you something about Connie and me—" Pete began, and at once Jazz' expression became ironic.

"Oh?"

"—about Connie and me," Pete repeated flushing a little but keeping calm, thankful that Clare was coming into the room before he snapped back something in anger that would end the conversation, "and I'm glad you're here. Clare, because I want you to hear it too.

"I've just been talking to Connie and Jane, as you know. I went there to tell him that I was resigning from the mission"—he was conscious of Clare's intake of breath, Jazz' suddenly intense quiet—"and wanted to be reassigned to something else. So that you could go in my place. Jazz. So that you could go. And if you think that was easy—if you think *I* don't want to go"—he drew a long, sighing breath which indicated that perhaps the inner man wasn't so serene, after all—"then you're just crazy, Jazz. You're just crazy."

For a long moment Jazz studied him carefully while Clare tried to make herself even smaller at the other end of the sofa. Finally Jazz spoke softly.

"Of course he wouldn't let you do it."

"No," Pete agreed quietly. "He wouldn't. But that doesn't change the fact that I really offered, Jazz. It doesn't change the fact that I really wanted to help this mission. And if he changes his mind, I'll still do it, Jazz, and you can go. Because I'd rather do that than have this—this"—he gestured toward the headlines on the floor—"this human *crap* succeed in what they're trying to do to the program. That's how I feel, Jazz." His voice dropped, became even quieter. "How about you?"

Again there was silence, in which he became conscious of wind in the trees, swift clouds chasing over, birdsong. Everything—NASA, Washington, Piffy One, the world—seemed very far away: though of course they were right here, waiting like lions in the soft spring weather.

At last Jazz spoke, with a careful slowness.

"I believe what you say, Pete, and I know how you feel about the program. God, don't you think I do, too? But

I've got to think about it. I've just got to think. There's so much involved, here. I've—I've taken so much. I really have, Pete. You'll never know it all. And now when I see maybe there's a chance I can finally have what I've wanted for so long—" His voice trailed away. Suddenly he pounded his palm with a fist clenched so tight the knuckles shone. "I've got to think, Pete. I've just got to."

"O.K.," Pete said quietly, standing up. "I'll go. No, don't get up, Clare. I know my way out." He turned back for a moment at the door. Clare stared at him from large, worried eyes. Jazz, head down, hands still tight together, did not look up. "Whatever you decide, Jazz," he said, "I respect you for it."

But Jazz only gave a half nod and did not look up. Pete walked down the hall, let himself out quietly, and drove with a quick, automatic efficiency back to the Simulator Building, his thoughts somber and far away.

After the sound of his car died out, silence held the comfortable room in the comfortable house for a long time. Clare did not speak, Jazz did not move: the lions walked and were frightening in their power.

Finally Jazz looked up, his face ravaged with pain and hurt and many old, unhappy things.

"What do you think I ought to do, baby?" he asked; and because it had been a long time since he had called her that, it took a while for Clare to answer.

"I can't advise you," she said at last. "It's your decision." She paused, her eyes bright with held-back tears. "I know what I would do, but maybe—maybe you would consider that running away."

Again he was silent, for several more minutes. Then he uttered a sigh so profound it seemed to come from the depths of the years, unclenched his rigid hands, and stood up.

"No," he said quietly, "it wouldn't be running away, baby. It wouldn't be running away."

On the Picturephone a moment later he looked tired but determined when Joe Stevenick, director of public affairs at the center, came on the screen.

"Joe," he said, "I want to issue a statement. Can you get it out for me as quickly as possible?"

"Why sure, Jazz." Joe Stevenick said, concealing his surprise and excitement in the smoothly efficient gesture of snapping on the tape recorder on his desk. "Go ahead

198

and dictate and we'll shoot her out just as fast as we can."

The little bells rang on the teletype, his secretary called him to the outer office in quick excitement. Vernon Hertz at JPL, like most other top officials of NASA in their offices across the country, read the news direct as it came over the AP leased wire:

"HOUSTON—Commander Alvin S. 'Jazz' Weickert, III, today removed himself from consideration for the crew of Mars-bound Planetary Fleet One and strongly repudiated 'the dividers, the haters, the crackpots and the kooks' he alleged were attempting to subvert the mission.

"In a statement issued through the public affairs office of the Manned Spacecraft Center, Weickert, who has not been assigned a mission for six years, said he did not want his name considered 'since I am apparently being used by forces hostile to America's success in space.'

"Weickert did not identify the 'forces.' But he said recent protest demonstrations in Washington and violence at Cape Kennedy had convinced him that the national controversy surrounding Planetary Fleet One was 'something more than just ordinary citizens upset about spending too much money.'

"'When I learned,' he said, 'that two of my close associates, Dr. Albrecht Freer and Astronaut Stuart Yule, had been gravely injured in a deliberately staged riot at the Cape, I decided to reconsider my position. I realized that there must be some sinister motive in the minds of those who have been insisting that I be assigned to the crew of Planetary Fleet One. I have concluded that they are hostile to the whole idea of the mission and also to this country's supremacy in space. I think they are just using me as an excuse to make trouble.'

"Weickert said his whole life was 'devoted to American success in space exploration.' He took note of the fact that he had been 'almost excluded from this effort in recent years.'

"'But,' he said, 'that fact does not change my devotion to my country or to the program. I still want to fly and I am hopeful that I will be permitted to. I do not, however, wish to become the pawn of outside groups seeking to bring pressure upon NASA and the program.

"'It appears to me that the dividers, the haters, the crackpots and the kooks have gotten behind me in an attempt to prevent the projected Mars flight. Therefore, since I am apparently being used by forces hostile to America's success in space, I want to make it clear that I completely repudiate them. I also want to make it clear that I do not want to be considered for the crew of Planetary Fleet One on any such basis.

" 'The crew has been selected. The decision has been reached. I accept it and I support it. Any attempt to reopen the matter is done without any consultation with me or any approval by me.'

"In an obvious reference to Dr. J. V. Halleck, the black astro-scientist who is also favored by many as a replacement for already-announced crew members, Weickert concluded:

" 'I speak only for myself in this statement. But I suggest that others in a similar position might give the matter the same thought and the same resolution that I have.' "

And that, Vernon Hertz thought wryly, puts it squarely in your lap, Dr. J. V. Halleck, and what are you going to do about it?

He returned to his inner office unsmiling and concerned. Like many of NASA's scientists, he had not been able to escape a certain I-told-you-so satisfaction when Piffy One began to run into trouble. He had been against the mission. He was still against it. It was his absolute conviction that unmanned probes could do twice the work for half the price and none of the danger. He thought the whole thing was a gigantic, unnecessary stunt, and he had told his brother Bob so to the point where Bob would hardly take his calls any more.

He also still thought that if the Administration was going to go the route of a manned probe, it at least ought to have a Negro along, and he was still determined to bring this about if he could. But he had been as alarmed as Jazz Weickert—if that had really prompted Jazz' statement, which he wondered—by the well-organized and increasingly violent opposition. It seemed to him, too, that there was more behind it than "just ordinary citizens upset about spending too much money." And it seemed to him that Jayvee, for many reasons—his future relations with his colleagues, his integrity, his conscience, his self-respect—would be in a much better position if he, too, would issue a similar statement. Then if he were selected to replace

200

any of the announced crew members he would be his own man, his hands would be clean, and he could go into the mission in a much stronger position than if he were crammed down NASA's throat by outside political pressure.

But whether Jayvee could see this, Dr. Hertz did not know. It was with considerable misgivings and some trepidation that he asked his secretary to get Dr. Halleck on the Picturephone. And when she notified him in about ten minutes that she had, he took a deep breath and switched on his machine with a little private prayer that he could speak with sufficient conviction to sway a stubborn man.

"Afternoon, Jayvee," he said as the handsome head and troubled eyes of his protégé took form on the screen. "How's it going?"

"All right, I guess," Jayvee said cautiously. "How are you?"

"I'm fine, thank you," Vernon Hertz said. "Did you hear about Jazz?"

"Yes," Jayvee said. "I heard about him."

"What did you think?"

Jayvee did not reply for a moment. Then a contemptuous little smile crossed his face.

"Houston *Post* called me about that a little while ago. I didn't tell 'em. But I have some thoughts about it."

"You've always been able to talk things over with me," Dr. Hertz suggested. "Try it now."

Again Jayvee hesitated.

"I won't tell anybody. I'm as good a friend as you've got. You can level with me."

"What did you call for?" Jayvee asked, his eyes filled with suspicion and pain. "Probably want to lecture me about something, right? Well, I don't want any lectures!"

"I want to know," Dr. Hertz said with a careful patience, "what you think about Jazz." He made his tone deliberately tougher. "If I want to lecture you after that, I will, and you'll listen. But maybe I won't. Why don't you try me?"

"I don't see why he had to cop out like that," Jayvee said sullenly. "I don't see why he had to duck and run. He didn't have to be a coward about it. He didn't have to leave me to take it all."

"Since you are left," Vernon Hertz said, seizing upon it

at once, "what are you going to do about it? Don't you think you'd be smart to do the same thing?"

"What?" Jayvee demanded in a tone of such outraged dismay that Dr. Hertz thought he had probably destroyed reasonable discussion right there. "Give up my chance to be on the flight? I will not!"

"No," Vernon Hertz said with a deliberate disgusted patience, as though he were talking to a child, as perhaps he was, "I don't mean give up your chance to be on the flight. I mean put yourself in a better position to go on it. I mean cut yourself loose from all this human junk that's getting behind you. I mean be your own man, for a change."

"I am my own man!" Jayvee snapped with a fearsome scowl.

"Are you?" Dr. Hertz inquired, unimpressed. "Prove it."

For a second he thought Jayvee might explode into open anger and go off the screen. But the habit of years of deference proved controling. He looked sullen but remained.

"As for 'human *junk*,' " he said finally, I don't know what call you have to be so harsh about it. These people sincerely believe they have a good point—"

"Some of these people do."

"All right," Jayvee said sharply. "Don't you, Dr. Hertz? Haven't you told me right along a black man ought to be in this program? Didn't you get me into this to be your symbol?" His expression became sarcastic. "Some symbol! First chance that comes up, I get the same old treatment. How's that for symbolism!"

"I don't mean that," Vernon Hertz said. "I mean the organized national campaign against the flight—I mean the demand that Russia be invited—I mean the tragedy at the Cape—I mean the whole obvious attempt to stop the mission altogether. You're incidental to these people, Jayvee. You're nice to have around as a weapon they can use, but they don't really give two hoots in hell for J. V. Halleck, black man. I do." Instantly an unmistakable skepticism shot across Jayvee's face and Vernon Hertz responded with real anger. "All *right!* You look me straight in the eyes and tell me I don't, damn you! Go on and tell me! I'm waiting."

For several seconds he glared straight at his recalcitrant

202

young friend. Finally Jayvee dropped his eyes and said in a muffled voice,

"All right, I apologize. I shouldn't have said that. You've done more than you should for me and I'm not forgetting it. But, Dr. Hertz"—and he suddenly looked very naked and young—"I don't believe that these other people don't care about me. I think they mean it when they say a black man ought to be on the flight. And I'm the only one there is. I think they're sincere. I believe that."

"I said some of them are," Vernon Hertz conceded. "I expect millions of them are. But not the ones who are really behind this. There you get into something bad, Jayvee."

"Communists?" Jayvee asked with a return of sarcasm. "Like Dr. Freer said? Is that what you mean?"

"I'm not calling any names," Vernon Hertz replied. "I'm just telling you they're bad business. The whole thing smells, Jayvee. And as long as you stick with them and don't disassociate yourself from them, you smell too. Why don't you be smart like Jazz and cut yourself loose? It isn't going to hurt your chances to get on the flight, and if you do, you'll be in a lot better position. You'll be your own man, not theirs."

Again the sullen, closed-off look came into Jayvee's eyes, the look that Dr. Hertz knew from experience meant he was losing him.

"How do you know it won't hurt my chances to get on the flight?" Jayvee asked slowly. "I can't say as I have so many friends in NASA who are pushing me—except for you, of course. I can't say any of my white *buddies* in the astronaut corps are breaking their tails trying to get me in. In fact, they've already made their decision. Their decision is, I'm out. So why shouldn't I get help where I can?"

"If you get on that flight, there's one man who will do it, and not a mob."

"Yes," Jayvee said with a dry shrewdness in his voice, "but he'll do it because the mob makes it hot for him."

"I don't believe he's that kind of man," Vernon Hertz said quietly, though he was not so sure.

"I do," Jayvee said, and he obviously was sure. "I'll stick with my 'mob,' as you call them. They'll get me there, if anyone can."

"You'll sacrifice the respect of your crewmates if you do," Vernon Hertz said. "And when you get out there, you'll have to have it."

A look of genuine and complete contempt came over Jayvee's face.

"*Respect*," he said bitterly. "Have they ever done anything to make me respect them?"

Vernon Hertz studied him as though he had never seen him before, as perhaps he never had.

"If you really feel that way," he said at last, "then I fear for this mission if you get on it."

"I intend to get on it," Jayvee said in a level voice, "any way I can."

"For the first time since our friendship began," Dr. Hertz told him quietly, "my wish for you is that you fail."

For a second Jayvee looked as though he had been struck in the face; he looked as though he might cry. Then his expression hardened into one of bitter anger.

"Thanks," he said. "I thought you were different, but you're not. You're all alike." And abruptly his face did crumple, he did cry out in pain and anguish as he went off the screen, "Oh *damn* it to hell, to *hell*, you're *all alike!*"

But when Vernon Hertz, deeply troubled, called his brother in Houston and told him about it, Bob, equally troubled, could offer little comfort.

"There's nothing we can do with him here," he said. "We're still hoping against hope that the man in Washington will let the crew selections stand. If he doesn't . . . well," he concluded bleakly, "I just hope to hell he does."

For a long time after Dr. Hertz faded from the screen, Jayvee sat motionless before it, staring moodily into its opaque depths as though he might find therein some answer to the devils that beset him. One of the few whites he genuinely respected had laid it on the line, and naturally he had grown defensive and flared up, saying things he probably shouldn't have and rather regretted now. But that didn't change the fact that he knew them to be true, any more than it changed his uneasy feeling that maybe some of the things Dr. Hertz had said might be true, too. He was all torned up, as his grandmother used to say a long time ago back in North Carolina: all torned up and not much chance in sight of becoming untorned. Not, anyway, as long as his color and his own savage resentments made him the inevitable football for contending forces.

But, damn it, he thought, becoming angrier and more self-defensive by the moment, why should that have to be? Why couldn't the astronauts judge him on his ability, as they did each other? Why were they so—so damned *impervious* about it all?

It was this, he decided (forgetting that it had been different when he first came into the corps) that probably embittered him more than any other single thing: this exclusive, closed-off quality of theirs, this little-band-of-brothers attitude, this we-and-them state of mind that divided the world and left him on the outside looking in. NASA said he was one of them, but NASA damned well didn't act like it when the chips were down. He hoped the damned racists got what was coming to them. He didn't care if it did upset Colonel High and Mighty Trasker and Commander Hank Patronizing Barstow and Colonel Bert Contemptuous Richmond and all their buddies. It would serve them right.

Maybe there were some rough elements involved in the campaign to get him on the flight. What of it? Things were rough all over. Let them try being black for a while: they'd know what rough was.

And Dr. Hertz wanted him to issue a statement like Jazz, did he? That would make it nice for NASA. That would take off the pressure, all right. Again a contemptuous little smile crossed his face for poor, stupid Jazz. He'd cut himself loose from his friends and now he wasn't anything. He was *nothing*. Now he didn't have his friends and he didn't have the flight. NASA could keep right on kicking him in the face the way it always had. That's what happened when you repudiated your friends. Poor, stupid, hopeless Jazz.

But not poor, stupid, hopeless Jayvee. Oh, no. He was too smart for that. Powerful people in this nation had offered him support and he was glad to have it. He wasn't going to cut loose from them with a lot of bitter words that would make them hate him. He was too smart. Nor was he about to listen to any blandishments from Dr. Hertz, though he still had enough respect left to think Dr. Hertz probably meant them sincerely. Dr. Hertz was conditioned by NASA. He couldn't help it if he tried to soft-talk Jayvee. He was a loyal NASA man. But not Jayvee. What had NASA done to deserve his loyalty?

Jayvee, who had been treated with excessive care by conscience-stricken whites all his professional life until he came into the corps and found its unimpressed members giving him exactly what he earned and no more, hugged his grievances and swore vengeance on the world.

In such foul mood he greeted Monetta when she came in from lunching with Mary Webb and Belle Curtis, wives of two of his fellow astronauts. She, too, thought he should issue a statement and follow Jazz' example. He demanded to know if they had been discussing him at lunch. She admitted they had. Their argument was short, sharp, bitter and furious. She left in tears and he didn't give a damn where she went. He got himself a beer and slouched in front of the television set. Lots of important people were saying lots of harsh things about Piffy One. He gave a savage grin and toasted them with his beer. He wished them well—unless he was on it.

With a shrewd and ruthless understanding of white man's politics, he knew that the more they talked, the more likely he would be.

Not only for Jayvee and his troubled colleagues of the corps was Piffy One an obsession on this warm spring afternoon when the wind raced and the white clouds scudded across the mild blue sky of Houston. For many others, in many places and in many ways, it dominated the world.

For Percy Mercy and Senator Williams, congratulating each other on the responses to Kenny's touching speech that were already beginning to flood in from across the country, it was both a cause and a political opportunity. They promised one another grimly that they would continue to attack and prepared to do so with a vindictive and relentless skill. They had been a little shocked by the violence at the Cape, but Percy in particular recovered quickly. He had behind him thirty years' experience rationalizing the evils committed by his friends. He had long ago found that he could always swallow their methods providing their stated purposes were noble enough to meet his own high standards.

For the Administrator, Piffy One was also a cause, and

one he wanted to protect from politics. He was concluding sadly that this would not be possible.

For the President it was a political problem he had to place in perspective against many other pressing things. This was not easy and he was not considering it lightly or happily, though to his visitors on this day of decisions he managed to appear his usual commanding, imperturbable self.

For Albrecht Freer, returning gradually to full consciousness at Orange Memorial Hospital in Orlando, Piffy One was still what it had been before, the dream and the goal from which nothing could detract and with which nothing must be allowed to interfere. He was already insisting impatiently that he be allowed to telephone his staff at the Cape, and his doctors, though dubious, were about to agree. It would be better, they thought, than the risk of an embolism brought on by excessive emotional rebellion against their cautious restraints.

For Stu Yule, lying motionless in his darkened room nearby, staring unseeing at the ceiling, Piffy One was now part of another world that he was forcing himself with great discipline and great anguish to relinquish. From time to time a sob, harsh, strangled, unexpected, rose abruptly from some cavern of endless desolation in his heart. Then he was still again. Beside him Yo-Shin Yule, whom he had married in Viet Nam and brought home to untroubled years of happiness, loyalty and devotion, held his hand, and prayed, and said nothing.

For Clete O'Donnell, Piffy One was a task to be accomplished and he felt he had gone a good way toward bringing it off with yesterday's strategic show of violence at the Cape. His swift cancellation of the strike had won him all the points he needed to offset the whispers of subversion that had sprung up following Dr. Freer's peculiarly worded statement of defiance. Many influential journals had joined the *Post* and the *Times* in strongly worded editorials mocking the "peddlers of polarization" who implied that "this great American might in some weird, mysterious way be linked to elements unfriendly to the United States." This made Clete smile: they reacted so beautifully on schedule, his friends of the media. CBS had asked him to appear on its news round-up this evening. He was already practicing, gravely and with great dignity, the fine statement on patriotic dissent that he was going to give the nationwide audience so kindly and generously offered him. He felt very good about things.

For Alexei Kuselvsky, winging home to Moscow with a pleased, ironic smile, Piffy One was a project the Russians didn't have to do much about. The Americans, with their customary penchant for self-destruction, were doing it for them.

And at home and overseas, for journalists, columnists, broadcasters, commentators, students, professors, politicians, preachers, doctors, lawyers, labor leaders, authors, actors, organized America-baiters everywhere, Piffy One was the excuse for one great, gleeful, envious, universal yawp of condemnation, derision, skepticism and scorn for the United States and all its works.

For Monetta Halleck, walking blindly down quiet streets toward the lake shore, Piffy One had a very direct, personal meaning. It meant a frightful quarrel with her husband and a desperate, aching pain inside. It meant worry. It meant tension. And it meant fear.

Fear for Jayvee, to whom she still felt some loyalty despite his increasingly savage tendency to take out on her his frustrations with NASA. Fear for little Rudden, fortunately away today at nursery school but all too often, lately, present at their bitter arguments. Fear for the astronauts chosen to fly on what could only be an extremely dangerous mission. Fear that Jayvee might be one of them. Fear for her country, which she liked better than he did. Fear that he was moving farther and farther away from reality about it, rushing headlong toward some dark future she could not imagine but which she sensed instinctively might be awful for all of them. Fear for her marriage, with which all these other fears were inextricably entwined.

That her marriage might be collapsing was a possibility she had forced herself to face with increasing honesty for the past six months. The program did many cruel things to marriages, and it was never possible at the beginning to predict how the individual astronaut and his wife were going to handle them. Some were models of rectitude and integrity. Others were faithful to rectitude and integrity in their fashion, which preserved the family for the children and turned it hollow for the parents. Still others grew embittered and fell apart. She had never dreamed at the beginning that the third way would be theirs.

When she had met Jayvee at JPL, both scientists, both highly intelligent, both young and eager and excited by the possibilities of space, there had appeared to be no obstacle to happiness. Their attraction, courtship and marriage had a quality of inevitability that seemed to guarantee a future loving, secure and unshakable. For a couple of years this had continued to seem true. Then had come the move to Houston, undertaken partly at the request and through the influence of Vernon Hertz, partly because both of them felt an almost mystical sense that they were carrying the banner for their race into a great and exciting new area where it ought to be.

Thus had begun diaster.

Jayvee's acceptance into the astronaut corps had come swiftly and with a minimum of red tape, thanks to Dr. Hertz. They had arrived in Houston to be greeted by colleagues and their wives who perhaps felt that they were carrying a banner for their race, too, and so gave them an extra cordiality and acceptance. At first Jayvee had been treated with an evenhanded and, as nearly as she could tell, helpful friendliness. Everyone was on his side. Then he had gone sour. And the whole thing had gone sour.

She was startled, as she walked along, hardly seeing where she was going through the tears that kept welling up, to realize that she had used in her thinking the phrase "*he* had gone sour," and to realize the priority she had given it. First *he* had gone sour and only then had the program gone sour for him. But she knew at last and beyond denying that it was true.

She had never quite admitted it to herself before, but that was really the way it had been: Jayvee had done it himself, because he was cursed with devils that made it impossible for him to mature sufficiently to meet the challenges the corps imposed. And not only the corps: the challenges of being a responsible black man in a white society. This was a task that required a stability and maturity that many blacks, turning to the easy, sick-child's cop-out of violence and hatred, had given up trying to achieve. That was Jayvee's problem. He had been given his chance and he had ruined it, because it was easier to be bitter toward the white man than it was to measure up

209

to what the white man expected of him—and, in this instance certainly, had a right to expect of him.

Few Negroes, Monetta knew, had been as favored as she and Jayvee. Few had been given more praise, more advancement, more respect, more prestige, more reward. She had adjusted to it beautifully. Why hadn't Jayvee?

How was it that she had grown up black and been able to come through it without hatred, without rancor and without tension? She had suffered the same insults—and received the same praise—as Jayvee. Why was she emotionally direct and uncomplicated, tolerant where he was intolerant, steady where he was erratic, compassionate where he was cruel?

It could only be—and this was the thing that was finally forcing her to the conclusion that the marriage might not last—that simplest yet most complex of reasons: character. She was one kind of person, her husband was another. She had come through her testing: she and life were on good terms with one another. Jayvee and life perhaps would never be.

There came to her, like a flash of revelation in the placid springtime street, the absolute conviction that Jayvee must not fly on this mission. Their violent quarrel just now had shown her why. She was convinced that Jayvee knew perfectly well what Jazz was talking about in his statement—he was too intelligent not to. But he was deliberately selling himself to forces hostile to the project in order to achieve his ambition to be on it. She, too, had wanted him to be on it; but not at that price. Jayvee was flawed, and she did not think he would recover.

Suddenly she saw Jayvee as his fellow astronauts must see him. And because she still was not sure she had given up loving him, and because she felt suddenly so sorry for him, with a deep, dragging pity that clouded the charming sunny day and threw the world in shadow, her expression became desolate, sad and lost.

It was thus that Connie Trasker saw her as he drove along on the way back to the office and whatever new crises awaited him there: standing on a quiet residential street corner in Nassau Bay, looking as though the world had ended. For a split second his mind had an argument with itself. Then the argument was over. He braked to a halt, leaned over, opened the door.

"Get in," he said. "Life can't be all that bad."

For a second her mind argued too. She looked startled, glanced hastily up and down the streets, hesitated.

"Get in," he repeated. "The more time you take, the worse it's going to look. If you get in at once, I'm offering you a ride to the shopping center. If you hesitate, God knows what our friends will say. Or, rather," he added with a cheerful grin, "we both know damned well what they will say. Get in. Maybe I *am* going to take you to the shopping center. I hope you have your list."

She did not reply as she complied, but he was pleased to see that a little smile was beginning to invade the desolation on her gravely beautiful face: not a pretty face, but a dignified, almost stately, thoroughly nice face.

"That's better," he said; reached across her to slam the door firmly shut, and gunned the motor and turned off down along the lake. "Now," he said when they came to a little wooded point where fishermen sometimes tied up their boats, "we will stop here for a few decorous moments and you will tell me all about it. Incidentally, you haven't called me. Why not?"

She gave him a quick glance, hesitant and shy, then looked away.

"Perhaps I didn't feel I needed to. Anyway, you've been busy."

He sighed.

"Yes. I have, that. I've thought about you, though."

Again she glanced at him as she spoke, and this time waited for his answer and did not look away.

"Why?"

"Well," he said. "That's a question: why?" He grinned suddenly, in a way he had always found effective. "I honestly can't tell you." But it didnt work this time.

"Why can't you?" she asked quietly, still looking at him. He smiled candidly and without guile.

"Perhaps I can. Because I hoped to see you again. Is that bad?"

She shook her head quickly.

"I didn't say it was."

"You looked it."

Her expression became quiet and contemplative.

"It could be."

"Oh, yes," he agreed with equal gravity. "If there weren't so many reasons why it couldn't be ... But," he said briskly, experience telling him it was time to drop that subject, "you haven't told me what the matter is. Are you worried about Jayvee?"

She nodded and again the profound sorrow touched her face.

"Frankly," he said, "he worries all of us. Particularly me. I may have to fly with that character. I don't like it. Although I suppose I shouldn't talk to you like that about your husband."

She looked out across the lake, her face shadowed and unhappy.

"We had a terrible fight a little while ago," she said finally, her voice low. "I told him he ought to issue a statement like Commander Weickert."

"And he won't do it."

"He won't do it."

"And he was angry with you."

"Terribly."

"And he struck you."

"Yes," she said so quietly he could barely hear it, a heavy sorrow in her voice. "Not bad, but—he shouldn't have at all. I was only trying to help him."

" 'Netta," he said, and where the nickname came from he couldn't say, though it seemed very natural on his lips, "some people you can't help. All of us realize that now and then, I guess, in our lives. You come up against somebody who just can't be helped, no matter how you try. I think he's one."

"But somebody's got to help him!" she said desperately. "Help him, and—and help you-all. You fellows don't want to fly with him if he's in that mood."

"We're in better shape than you are," he said dryly. "We have ways of taking care of moods, in the program— not always successfully, but we try. Anyway, this may all be a needless worry: the crew may not be changed. Although," he added grimly, "I wouldn't want to place any bets." He frowned. "But that isn't the problem right now. What about you? Are you safe?"

She gave him a quick, sidelong glance and for just a second he saw real fear in her eyes. But she managed to keep her voice reasonably steady.

"I think so, I don't think Jayvee would really do any-thing—bad—to me. Anyway"—her expression became bleak—"I don't expect he'll have the chance, pretty soon."

"Why?" he asked quickly; and realized suddenly that he

was more interested than he had really intended to be. Her answer somehow was very important. "Are you going to leave him?"

Again the profound sadness, more moving than tears, touched her face. Instinctively his hand reached for hers, even as a saner voice, the pragmatic, cautionary voice of the program, said: *Don't.* But his move was instinctive, and more. She did not draw away.

"I may," she said finally, in a small, remote voice he could hardly hear. "I'm thinking about it."

"I suppose," he said, his voice a little uneven as the other voice said coldly: *What is this?*, "that I should tell you not to. I ought to tell you to stick with him a while longer for the sake of the program. But I'm not going to. Some things are more important than the program." *Who are you kidding?* the other voice said. *You'd drop this in second if it interfered with the program, and you know it. This is a nice girl. What kind of a bastard are you?*

"Are they more important?" she asked shyly, as though she had heard it. "To you?"

"Yes," he said, still holding her hand, telling the voice triumphantly, *Well, she isn't taking it away,* "to me. I'd rather see you out of this mess and feeling happy again. It would probably be better for Jayvee, too. It might be the thing that would straighten him out." *Oh, yes,* said the voice, "It might," he repeated, almost defiantly, and she gave him an odd little look.

"I don't know," she said, turning to stare out the window and gently but firmly withdrawing her hand. *That's better,* the voice said, over his protest. "I don't know . . . and I'm beginning to wonder if I care, any more. He's so—so—closed off, now." She sighed, a profound, and to him profoundly moving, sound. "I'm afraid for him, Colonel Trasker."

"Connie," he said. She gave him a sad little smile.

"Maybe . . . I *am* afraid. I'm afraid for what he might do to himself, and what he might do if he's on the mission. And I guess I'm just afraid for all of you. It's so dangerous. And so far away."

"We'll manage," he said, a simple statement of fact. "It's our job." Experience told him the moment was over, it was best to leave it and let it go to work on its own. *If you think that's wise,* the other voice said, ignoring his assurances. "Let me say this, Monetta"—and he turned and looked fully at her, steady and kind——"if things come to a crisis in some way, don't hesitate to call me. I'll do anything I can to help you. You know that."

She smiled, a slow, rather wistful smile.

"I wouldn't bother you. You have so much to do, so many things on your mind. You don't want me there."

"You're there already," he said quietly.

Again she smiled, in the same wistful way, and gave him a glance of complete and unflinching candor.

"I know where I am. It doesn't mean much alongside your family and the program."

"You're wrong," he said, and was surprised at the vehemence of his own protest. *Colonel Trasker's over the slope*, the voice said. *Colonel Trasker's losing his grip. And*, it added firmly, *that's the way it should be*. "You're wrong. I'm your friend and I want to help you. You must let me, if I can. Promise me you will."

The smile faded, the quiet sadness he found so moving reclaimed the high-boned, patrician face.

"If I need you, Colonel Trasker, I'll call. I promise I will ... Now maybe you'd better take me back. I think I'm ready to see Jayvee again."

"Then, you see," he said with a triumphant little laugh, "I've helped you, already. Haven't I?"

"Yes," she said, and this time the smile was not sad but, finally, relaxed. "Yes, you have."

"Good!" he said. *Score for you*, the voice said. *But we don't approve*.

"I wonder," he remarked thoughtfully as he turned the car around and started away from the lake. "Maybe I should drop you——"

And now she laughed quite genuinely and without offense.

"I don't know what you usually do, Colonel Trasker, but maybe in my case you'd better let me off in the street back of the shopping center and then drive right on. Nobody will notice. I do have to get some groceries, and then I'll call a cab."

"Well," he said gratefully, "if you don't mind——"

She laughed again and said, with a little mischievous twinkle that both surprised and intrigued him, "I wouldn't want anything to interfere with the program."

"Me, either," he said, joining her in laughter. "God forbid!"

Ten minutes later as he drove briskly toward the Space Center she was already beginning to slip to the back of his mind. The beautifully trained machine that was Astronaut Conrad C. Trasker, Jr. was at work again on the myriad problems of Piffy One. He found they had not diminished when he walked into the Astronaut Office.

"Where the hell have you been?" Hank demanded. "We were just about to send out an all-points bulletin for you."

"What's up?" he asked calmly.

"Our friend in Washington wants to talk to us in half an hour," Bert said. "Our big friend."

"Oh?"

"Plus Bob Hertz and Dr. Cavanaugh," Hank told him. "Plus Pete. Plus Gaudy and Em Wacker. Plus Jazz. And," he added grimly, "plus Jayvee."

Connie Trasker sighed and spoke with an equal grimness.

"It looks as though the fix is in."

"It do that," Bert Richmond agreed. "It sure do that, indeed."

12.

The massive head and powerful shoulders filled the screen. The attitude was commanding, the charm under tight control. He was not in much mood for persiflage and no more were they.

"Gentlemen," he began without preliminary, "I have asked you to talk with me this afternoon as your Commander-in-Chief"—Bob Hertz and Connie exchanged the briefest of glances—"because I have reached a difficult decision. It is a command decision, and as such, I expect it to be obeyed willingly and without rancor, in the best traditions of your respective services and of the space program. I also expect any complaints or comments about it to be reserved to yourselves and not to be spread all over the press and the networks—all of whom," he said with the slightest of wry smiles, "are as eager to get my hide as they are yours. Can I expect this co-operation?"

For a moment there was silence, a little stunned by the direct approach and the tone which permitted no argument. Instinctively they deferred to Bob Hertz. After a moment he replied.

"Those sound like rather stringent conditions, Mr. President," he said with a rather nervous smile, "but I imagine we can live with them. I particularly hope we can abide by the no-comment proviso. I couldn't agree with you more."

"It would be a help," the President said. "Since we're on the subject, I do especially want to commend you, Jazz, for your fine statement. It was a great assist to me and to the program."

216

"Thank you, sir," Jazz said. He too smiled, without much humor. "It wasn't easy."

"I know it wasn't," the President said, "which is why I was particularly grateful for it. I believe you will find, however, that it will make the months ahead much easier for us all."

"I hope so," Jazz said, though his tone did not sound too sanguine.

"I only regret," the President said quietly, "that Dr. Halleck did not see fit to do the same. Not to do so was, in my judgment, an unwise and immature decision which has raised substantial questions in my mind."

Again there was a silence, during which Jazz, on one side, and Connie, on the other, shifted slightly but noticeably away from Jayvee. At first it seemed he might reply, as anger succeeded shock and a sullen scowl succeeded anger. But he did not, only lowering his eyes and studying the floor with a grim, unhappy intensity.

"Nonetheless," the President resumed calmly, "I have decided, for various reasons you know—some reasons you think you know—and some reasons you can't know—to take the action I am about to take. I do so in the hope that everyone present will realize the sacrifice this imposes on some and the great responsibility it places on others. I have no doubt the sacrifice will be accepted as befits brave men. I intend," he added with a slow, emphatic emphasis, "that the responsibility will be discharged in the same way . . .

"If it is not," he said, as they became, if possible, even quieter and more solemn in their semicircle around Hank Barstow's worktable, "then I want to remind everyone present that in this White House it is possible to give and it is possible to take away. It is not always so easy to take away, once one has given; but it can be done. And if necessary, I am quite prepared to do it. Is that clear to everyone?"

He paused and again stared straight at them, allowing the silence to grow while they sat in absolute stillness save for one. Jayvee began to fidget in his chair, his body twisting almost as if in physical pain. Presently his head came up defiantly and he stared straight back with a frightened angry air.

"What are you trying to do, Mr. President?" he asked,

217

his voice high and strained but unyielding. "Put me on the spot?"

"Don't you think you deserve to be?" the President asked calmly. Jayvee flinched as though he had received a physical blow.

"I don't see why I—" he began, his voice beginning to tremble, "I don't see why everybody is stomping on me. I don't see why you have to pick me out to lecture!"

"Because," the President replied promptly, his tone measured and cold, "you have good qualities, I think, but you are not living up to them. I am one who is genuinely concerned about you, Jayvee. Your so-called friends who have been raising hell around the country don't really care whether you are capable or not. To them you're just a symbol and a useful tool with which to embarrass the United States and my Administration. I think better of you than that. I think you have great capabilities, not only as a scientist, but as an astronaut. I just want to be sure you understand your responsibilities and obligations. If I am to put you on that flight—"

There was perceptible stirring around the table. Now Emerson Wacker and Gaudy Gaudet, hoping against hope they would not hear what they knew they were going to hear, were the ones who looked as though they had been struck.

"If I am to put you on that flight," the President repeated calmly, "I am taking upon myself the responsibility of overriding the carefully considered judgment of the men who know you best. I am giving you what you apparently want to have: the chance to prove that an American Negro is competent to go into space. I believe you are competent, and I intend to see to it that you don't let me—and more importantly, your crewmates—down. I intend to hold you to your capabilities, Jayvee. I'm not going to permit you to cop out on them."

His voice turned, if possible, colder, his manner became more measured and more final, he spoke like a sledge-hammer.

"In the presence of these witnesses, Jayvee, I am telling you that I am going to put you on this flight and if you don't measure up I am going to take you off. And not all the yaps and all the yawps from all the newspapers and all the networks from here to Mars and back are going to help you one little bit if you force me to that decision. So I hope you will not. I do sincerely hope so ...

"And now," he said, not waiting for a response, speaking more briskly and in a more kindly way, "I come to the really hard part of this, which is to convey my thanks and my appreciation to two fine men whom I am going to ask to step aside—for this mission only. I want Commander Gaudet and Dr. Wacker on the back-up crew for this mission and it is my intention that they will fly without fail on the second Mars mission. I hope I have the agreement of the Astronaut Office to that."

He paused and looked at them expectantly. Hank and Bert, grimfaced and unhappy, gave the barest of nods.

"Good. And Gaudy, and Em—I want you to know this has been no easy decision for me. I know how much this mission means to you, and I know how much I am asking when I ask you to step down. I know Jazz understands, and will accept his assignment with full appreciation of what you are giving up, I hope Jayvee does, too. Certainly the rest of us do.

"There were many reasons for this decision, and I know that when our little talk here ends, most of you will say bitter things about me and you will all be convinced that it's nothing but politics and a President who gives in under pressure.

"Well," he said, and his face too looked grim and not very happy, "you can say what you like about me, but just try to remember things aren't always that simple. There are lots of reasons why people do the things they do, and a President, who has responsibility for the whole country and for many, many things that interlock almost inextricably with one another, probably has more reasons than most.

"I know you dislike and despise me right now, but I hope that in time, as you have a chance to sit back and think about it, you won't hate me too much. I give you my word that I will not endanger this mission. I think you can work together, and I expect you to. If you can't, I will change the assignments again.

"I am going on the air tomorrow to discuss this and other aspects of the flight. At that time I shall announce the crew changes and I shall say that I am making them with the consultation and the concurrence of the Astronaut Office. I expect you to support me in this and I expect you to keep our conversation confidential. I expect Piffy One to go on schedule with a mutually trusting, co-operative and unified crew. I wish you well."

And he reached over and snapped off his machine, his strong, determined face fading slowly away, its expression firm and confident of their compliance.

For probably two full minutes no one moved and no one spoke. Finally Connie cleared his throat and broke the silence, his voice a little unsteady.

"Gaudy—" he began. "Em—I'm sorry—"

But both his friends had taken all they could for now.

"I don't want to talk about it," Gaudy said in a muffled voice, standing up abruptly and starting out of the room.

"Me, either," Em Wacker said unsteadily, following him. "We'll see you guys later."

Again there was a silence, broken this time by Jayvee, who suddenly pushed back his chair, got to his feet and walked out, looking at no one.

"Keep in touch," Hank called after him sarcastically.

"That doesn't do any good," Dr. Cavanaugh told him.

"I think," Bob Hertz said in a businesslike tone, "that we had better call a meeting of the entire corps tomorrow morning and explain it to them, don't you? Otherwise morale is going to go to hell."

" 'Otherwise'?" Bert echoed wryly. "What an optimist!"

"You just do as I say, if you will, please," Bob Hertz suggested shortly.

"Roger," Hank agreed. "You're right, of course."

"It's almost five," Connie said, glancing at his watch. "I'm for home."

"My car's at the Texaco station," Jazz said. "Can you drop me off?"

"Sure thing," Connie said.

But it was all they said to one another, except for "Good night" at the station.

"What happened?" Clare asked before he even got the door closed. "Are you on the crew?"

"I'm on," Jazz said.

"Oh, dear!" she said, and began to cry.

The door was slammed hard, the feet sounded heavy down the hall.

"Did the President put you on the crew?" Monetta

asked quietly, looking up from the stove as he paused in the kitchen doorway, scowling and grim.

"Yes."

"Aren't you happy?"

"Don't talk to me," he said, flinging away into the bedroom. "Just don't talk to me!"

"If there's anything I can do to help—" Pete said on the Picturephone, his smile gone, his dark eyes worried and concerned.

"Just stand by me," Connie said. "Just be my good, steady, right-hand crewman, and stand by me. We'll work it out. I'm not worried."

"Much!" Pete said with the start of a skeptical smile.

"You just stay steady and stick by me," Connie said in a level tone, "and that will be the biggest help you can give me. O.K.?"

"Yes, sir," Pete said, instantly sober, "I'll do my best."

"I can see why the President did it . . . I think," Jane said as his troubled face faded from the screen. "But it's going to be hard to explain in Houston."

"You can say that again," Connie said grimly. "You can say that eight or ten times."

The quiet, comfortable room where they met the press for private interviews each Friday was filled for a few moments with their greeting and talking and getting settled, but the air of lighthearted joshing and horseplay that usually preceded all-crew meetings was absent this morning. Faithful to Bob Hertz' injunction, no one had alerted the grapevine. But it did not take men as intelligent as these more than a few seconds to sense that something was wrong. Perceiving the unusual presence of both Bob and Dr. Cavanaugh, noting the not-quite-concealed strain on the determinedly unconcerned faces of Gaudy Gaudet and Em Wacker, studying Jazz' uneasy look and Jayvee's withdrawn expression, they were hoping against hope that what they suspected was not true.

Knowing his men, the Director of the Manned Spacecraft Center let them have it straight.

"Gentlemen," Jim Cavanaugh said, and the room instantly became very still, "I expect you have a pretty good idea of why we've called crew meeting this morning. The President has intervened to change the assignments for

Piffy One. Gaudy and Em are off the crew and Jazz and Jayvee are on."

There was a sudden intake of breath, exclamations, disbelief. Roger Webb said "Oh, *Christ!*" in a tone of anguished disgust.

"You know," Dr. Cavanaugh said quietly, "that Bob and I feel just the same as you do. There was no necessity for the change, as near as I can see, except a political necessity. To my mind that wasn't enough. But I'm not the President."

"Too bad," Bob Curtis said dourly, and for a moment there was a little tension-releasing ripple of laughter.

"I can also say," Dr. Cavanaugh continued, "that Andy Anderson in Washington also feels as we do. We talked at considerable length last night, and his word to Houston is that he is with us 100 per cent—but he isn't the President, either."

"Why doesn't he quit?" Tom Andretti asked.

"Why don't we all quit?" Dick Ohlman suggested.

"That," Roger Webb said softly into the sudden silence, "might be a damned good idea."

"No, sir," Dr. Cavanaugh said firmly, looking at clean-cut faces turning stubborn and belligerent, "it would not. And I'll tell you why. Offhand, it's a great idea"—he smiled with a deliberate humor—"you have all the makings of an A-1 organizer, Rog, I can see that—but in practical fact it's nonsense, as we all know. That isn't the way we do things in NASA. That isn't our mission and it isn't our character. It wouldn't be us.

"Furthermore, it would be running away. It would be letting the bastards know they'd really gotten to us. It would be playing the game the same way they do, and that's a damned dirty way in a damned dirty game. It would be giving up, when what we've got to do is stand firm and hang on.

"Now, I know this thing isn't easy. It violates every principle and every tradition on which we've operated here in Houston since the program began. It's a direct and, to my mind, inexcusable intervention by the Commander-in-Chief. But he *is* the Commander-in-Chief, and I'm quite sure he hasn't arrived lightly at this decision—" There was a stir of skepticism and he interrupted himself sharply. "You weren't there yesterday afternoon when he spoke to us. We were, and I repeat: he didn't arrive at it lightly. But for many reasons—"

"The next election," Bill Desey said, just loud enough to be heard.

"For many reasons," Jim Cavanaugh repeated, ignoring it, "he thinks this is best. He is, after all, the President. He does, after all, favor this program. He is not, after all, about to endanger its success or its personnel. He said so in so many words. And I think"—and he looked at Bob Hertz, who nodded, but refrained from looking at Hank and Bert, who did not—"that all of us who heard him believed him. So it comes down to whether you believe us when we say that, or not. You suit yourselves.

"Anyway, here we are, and that's the decision, and we've got to live with it. I know"—he smiled again—"that I don't have to caution anybody about talking to the press about how we feel in-house about it. But maybe"—he stopped smiling—"I do have to caution some people about how we handle it among ourselves.

"This decision was made from outside, and while there may be some doubt in some of your minds about the way one or two of you may have been involved in it, still there's no point, and probably no justice, in blaming anybody. As soon as Jazz here realized the sort of thing that was developing, he issued a statement disassociating himself from it which was just about as clear and definitive and final as any statement could be."

"Hear, hear," Rick Johnson said, and there was a scattering of generous applause. Jazz looked grateful and not quite so strained.

"Jayvee," Dr. Cavanaugh said quietly, "did not do so."

There was the faintest suggestion of a hiss from somewhere in the room. He reacted with genuine anger.

"Now, stop that! You're not children here, you're astronauts with some self-respect and some pride, I hope! So cut that stuff! ... I'm sure," he resumed more calmly, not looking at Jayvee, who seemed to diminish and hunch down in his chair although actually he sat like stone and made no move, "that Jayvee had his reasons—"

"What were they?" Roger Webb interrupted bluntly. "Maybe he'd like to tell us."

And as if on command they all turned and stared at Jayvee, who did not meet their eyes but stared unseeing at the floor.

Dr. Cavanaugh hesitated a moment, then decided to switch tactics.

"All right," he agreed. "Maybe he would. Jayvee?"

But into the sudden silence that grew and lengthened Jayvee spoke no word. At first it seemed he might—his face changed, his jaws worked, he seemed on the verge of blurting out some word of protest, anger, supplication— they would never know, for it did not come. The most they could hear was an almost animal mumble, some- where far down inside. It did not last long. Silence re- claimed them.

"Well, as I say," Jim Cavanaugh resumed quietly, "we must assume that he had his reasons and we must assume that to him they were sufficient. We must also assume," he said, and his tone became more stern and more pointed, "that now that he has been selected, he will be a full and co-operative and reliable member of the crew, in every sense. For him to do anything else would be to betray the confidence placed in him, betray us his colleagues, and betray the country whose hopes and prestige ride upon this mission." He paused and measured each word while Jayvee still stared at the floor, giving no sign, uttering no sound.

"We do not expect this to happen . . .

"And now," he said, in a more matter-of-fact and businesslike voice, "I guess that's about all, except to say one final word to two men whose loyalty to the program, whose character and patriotism, were never better shown then in their willingness to accept what to them must be a very bitter—"

"Dr. Cavanaugh," Gaudy Gaudet interrupted, getting to his feet, his voice a little unsteady but managing to get it said all right, "I think maybe Em and I would prefer if you not say anything about us. That right, Em?"

"That's right," Emerson Wacker said, his voice too a little unsure, but determined. "We got it, and got it good, but"—he shrugged, not meeting their sympathetic eyes— "that's the way the mission crumbles, I guess. We would have done our best, and if we get the chance next time, we'll still do it. That's all I have to say about it."

"That goes for me, too," Gaudy said. "If this decision is best for the flight, then that's the way it is and we're not griping. It would have been great to go, but as Em says, we'll go next time and really give it hell. Now it's up to all of us to pitch in and help Connie and the new crew to get ready and do the best job they possibly can for the United States and for the program. God bless them."

And he sat down and blew his nose heavily as the applause began and continued for several moments, deep, heartfelt, admiring and sad.

"Then this meeting is adjourned," Dr. Cavanaugh said. "Thanks for coming, and let's get on with what we have to do."

"As they left the room in twos and threes, talking quietly to one another, a few giving Jazz' shoulder a squeeze or a slap as they passed, all of them walking wide around Jayvee, who still sat silent, unmoving and alone, Colonel Trasker took his first step on the new road to Mars.

"Jazz," he said, going up to his old colleague, friend and enemy as he stood a little uncertainly in the rapidly emptying room, "come on over to the office with me and let's talk for a while, O.K.?"

"Sure thing," Jazz said. "I want to talk to you."

"Good," Connie said. He looked across the room.

"Jayvee," he said, "can you stop by and see me after lunch? About 1330?"

For almost the first time since the meeting began, Dr. Halleck showed some sign of life, stirred, shifted, looked directly at him.

"I'll have to see what my schedule—" he began, his expression hostile, his voice unyielding.

Connie Trasker's face froze and his eyes became colder than anyone in Houston had ever seen them.

"God damn you," he said in a level voice, *"you be there.* Come on Jazz," he said shortly, turning his back, not waiting for an answer, "let's get out of here."

But by the time they reached the office, still talking in cautious generalities though a little easier with one another than they had been last night after the President's ultimatum, the mood had passed. Inside, door closed and locked, Jazz seated across the desk from him, he uttered a sad and disgusted sound.

"That was a hell of a thing to say," he remarked glumly. "That was a *hell* of a thing to say. I shouldn't have said a thing like that to him, annoying bastard though he is. I should be better than that. I *am* better

225

than that. Why the hell do we let that type pull us down to their level?"

Jazz shrugged.

"He deserved it. Why sweat?"

"Yes," Connie said, staring out over the parking lot to distant Clear Lake gleaming in the sun, "he deserved it. But I've got a crew to put together and I'm very much afraid little Mr. Jayvee has got to be patted and petted and made much of, if he's to fit into it. He could just turn stubborn, you know."

"On the other hand," Jazz said, "we—" he hesitated over the pronoun, smiled a little, glanced at Connie.

"All right," Connie said, beginning to relax, returning the smile with a certain irony. "*We.* What?"

"We can't afford to let him get away with too much, either. Otherwise we're just going to become the con trail on Jayvee's rocket—some nice white boys who happen to be going along so this great black hero can get to Mars. At least I expect that's how his friends like Percy Mercy and the press and television crowd will try to present it. You and Pete and I may have a little trouble reminding the folks we're here. I think we ought to be as tough with Jayvee as the President was. Certainly he didn't mince any words."

"No," Connie agreed thoughtfully, "he didn't. Maybe that does give us our warrant to be as tough as we please—but I just have a hunch that all it does is give the President the warrant to be as tough as *he* pleases. We may be expected to treat Jayvee with kid gloves."

"As far as I'm concerned," Jazz said calmly, "I going to treat him as I would any of the guys who happened to be going along. He's a crew member, he shapes up or ships out. I'm not going to waste time washing his diapers for him. And I'm not going to hesitate to recommend his removal direct to the President if I think it's justified."

"Well," Connie said a trifle tartly, "I hope you don't think I'll hesitate either. To recommend anybody's removal who doesn't shape up."

"I'll shape up," Jazz responded with a tartness of his own. "You don't really doubt that, I hope."

"No," Connie agreed, more mildly, "I don't doubt that. As a matter of fact, I have absolute confidence I can rely on you implicitly."

"Then why did it have to come to this to get me on the

226

crew?" Jazz asked quietly, and the old pain and resentment were back in his eyes.

"Jazz—" Connie began. Then he stopped, frustrated once more by the impossibility of explaining so many little things and the ways in which, over the years, they had become such big things in the eyes of Jazz' critical, image-conscious colleagues. "Why don't we just drop it? I couldn't explain. Maybe I don't even know any more."

"You and Hank and Bert sure put me through hell for something you can't explain!" Jazz snapped.

Connie sighed but his eyes did not drop before the angry ones confronting him.

"O.K.," he said. "So we were probably unjust. I'm sorry. But we're here now—we're on the crew together—Piffy One is going to go and we're it—and we'll just have to forget it. I know the bigger burden lies on you, because you have more to forget and forgive—or maybe not forgive, maybe you can't, but forget. If you're going to go through this final training period—and go through the launch—and go through the trip—resenting me every minute, Jazz, you're going to be a hell of a co-pilot, and you know it. So," he concluded quietly, "stop letting it eat you. You've won. Now let's get to work."

"I didn't win with you," Jazz said bitterly. "I had to be forced on you. What kind of winning is that?"

"I repeat," Connie said quietly, "don't let it eat you. Or you won't have won. Anything. Inside."

"Easy for you to say."

"And not so easy for you to do," Connie agreed. "But you don't have much choice, do you? Hell!" he said, suddenly impatient. "What have you got to worry about? You made a fine statement, Jazz. It brought you all the way back, with the corps. You're on top with us. You've won all along the line. You've *really* won. The President just made it possible for us to acknowledge it. What more do you want? Relax and enjoy it, man!"

"I do regret bouncing Gaudy," Jazz said slowly.

"It's unfortunate somebody has to get hurt," Connie agreed. "But he and Em can take it. They're younger in the program than we are, and they'll be on back-up for this mission and fly the next. We're going to abandon the old Apollo hopscotch system where you were back-up this time and flew three missions later. The President wants them to fly the next mission and we do too. So don't worry about Gaudy and Em. They'll be all right ... What about you, though? Will you be all right?"

For several moments Jazz did not reply, staring out the window in his turn, eyes brooding, expression hooded. Then he reached his decision. His face relaxed, he spoke in a matter-of-fact tone.

"When do you figure we should really begin to bear down on the training?"

"Tomorrow morning."

"Let's make plans."

"Roger," Connie said.

At 1:47 Jayvee appeared. Connie glanced at his watch.

"I got tied up in traffic!" Jayvee said sharply. "I didn't do it deliberately. Though I should have, considering what you said to me."

"That's right," Connie agreed calmly, not getting up, not offering his hand, gesturing toward the chair across the desk. "I was an absolute son of a bitch. Under provocation, but still, I'll admit, an absolute son of a bitch. I'm sorry. I apologize. I shouldn't have let you provoke me to such a response. The response didn't become me. The provocation, I suggest, didn't become you. What do you think we should do about it, crewmate? Hate each other all the way to Mars and back? Or get with it and get this mission on the road? Sit down and tell me. I'm open to your suggestions."

Jayvee made no reply as he sat slowly down in the chair and leaned forward, elbows on its arms, hands clasped tightly together. But his eyes remained fixed on Connie's with an antagonistic, analytical, musing expression, as though he were trying to decide what to say, or even whether to speak at all. Connie returned his gaze impassively. Finally Jayvee shook his head impatiently and looked away. But still he did not speak, only uttered a heavy and frustrated sigh.

"Come on," Connie said. "I mean it. We're all alone here and you can say exactly what you think. I'm telling you we'd better have it out now, because once we start training, namely at 9 A.M. tomorrow morning, we're committed and I'm not going to stand for any hanging back or any malingering or any personal emotions. All of that is out as of 0900 tomorrow. So get it out of your system now. I'm telling you."

"Who are you," Jayvee demanded finally, his voice bitter, "to 'tell' me? Just who are you, Connie?"

"I am the commander of this flight," Connie said evenly, "and I have behind me the Commander-in-Chief of this flight, and he says if you don't hack it, you get grounded. You heard him."

"Why do you hide behind him? You're the one who has to get along with me, not him."

"Oh," Connie said softly. "So *I* have to get along with *you.* How about you getting along with me, and with the rest of us? How about your responsibility to us, Jayvee? It seems to me we've tried to do right by you since you came to Houston. When do you start doing right by us?"

"0900 tomorrow," Jayvee said in an unpleasant, mimicking voice, and for a second it seemed that Connie might explode into genuine anger. But he was too smart and too tough for that.

"What's your gripe, Jayvee?" he asked reasonably. "What have you got against us here in the corps? It seems to me we've done everything we could to make you feel at home, to make you part of us, to—"

"To make me the perfect little astronaut," Jayvee concluded for him in the same unpleasant tone. "To make me your grade A little black astronaut. That's what you've tried to do."

"And what's wrong with that?" Connie inquired blandly. "Which do you object to? Being an astronaut? Or being black?"

Much to his surprise he saw that he had hit home. It was obviously Jayvee's turn to restrain himself from open anger. Connie could see it was a fierce struggle, and he decided he was not going to let him recover his balance until they had really gone to the bottom of this.

"What have you got against being black, Jayvee?" he asked softly. "Some mighty fine people have been, you know, and they've managed to do great things for themselves and their race. Why is it such a tough problem for you? You can do it. You have the ability. What's the problem?"

"Don't talk to me," Jayvee said, and his breath wasn't coming right and he appeared to be almost on the verge of crying with rage, "don't talk to *me* like some damned patronizing white man! I'm not ashamed of being black! I'm proud to be black!"

"I don't believe you," Connie said. "I think that's at the base of your trouble. If you were really proud of being a black man, you'd make up your mind that you were going to be the best damned astronaut that ever went on a flight, because that's the way to make all black men, and all white men too, proud of you. You'd cut yourself loose from this rabble that's behind you and you'd be your own man. You'd pitch in and make this the best mission ever—and pal," he said softly, "that's what it's *got* to be, if you and I are going to come back alive—and there wouldn't be any temperament or any sulking or any playing the racial game. If you're not ashamed of being black, then *be* black, and be part of this team, and show us you can do your job, and let us know we can rely on you and be proud of you."

He looked away from the tortured face before him and stared out the window.

"Show you've got some real self-respect, Jayvee, not this phony stuff of demanding respect just because you're black. Respect is earned, it doesn't come just because you're a color. *Real* self-respect, that's what we ask of you. We're not holding you back. Nobody's created this problem for you but you yourself. It's inside you."

He turned back and held the anguished eyes with his. His final tone was blunt.

"You solve it."

For a long moment their eyes locked, Jayvee's furious, pain-filled, wild, his own as steady, calm and unflinching as he could, with considerable effort, keep them. This was not as easy for Perfect Astronaut Conrad H. Trasker, Jr., he thought grimly, as anyone seeing him might suppose. He didn't like this sort of thing, though fortunately he was tough enough to be able to do it when it had to be done.

At last Jayvee spoke in a slow, strangled, at times almost inaudible voice.

"So I'm to earn respect, am I? So I'm to be one of the team and make you all proud of me, am I? So it's all so easy to be black, is it, and I'm supposed to cut loose and say 'Rah, rah!' and 'Hail to the flag!' and you'll all pat me on the head and let me be your good little old buddy, will you? Well, hell with that! The only reason I'm on this crew is because he forced you to put me on it, and the only reason he did that is because my *friends,* as you call them, forced *him* to. And I'm supposed to be grateful for that? I'm supposed to roll over and knuckle under and be your little old Uncle Tom Fly-Boy, that great black astronaut you can all point to and say, 'See, we made him into an astronaut! We made him"—and his voice held a withering sarcasm—" 'just like us.' Just like *you!* I'm supposed to be proud of that? I'd rather be just like me, thank you very much! Can't you see that's what I want to be—just like *me,* Connie Trasker! Just like *me!* I don't want any part of your damned perfect white-man astronaut image. I want to be what I am—*me!*"

He stopped, out of breath, and Connie asked calmly,

"Are you through? Because if you are, I have a few more home truths I want to give you."

"No, I'm not!" Jayvee said harshly. "I want to give you some. Ever since I came into this program you've never judged me, any of you, on my own merits as a person. You've always regarded me as *the* Negro in the program, NASA's own little pickaninny, the black side of the mirror that would make the white side look tolerant and broad-minded. Dr. Hertz knew what he was doing, all right, when he got me in here. He knew NASA needed me to make itself look good. He just made one mistake. He thought I'd be the patsy for it and not stand up for my rights."

"Oh, that wasn't his mistake," Connie said quickly. "He thought you were a grownup instead of a crybaby. That was his mistake."

It seemed for a moment that Jayvee might try to swarm across the desk and hit him, and Connie instinctively braced himself to spring out of his chair and chop him down if he did. But with a great effort Jayvee remained where he was, hands gripping the arms of his chair as though he would break them, face suffused, breath gasping, eyes glaring. And Connie stayed where he was, face cold and deliberately contemptuous. Once again they were in a staring match, and this time, again, it was Jayvee who gave way and turned to look out the window, his eyes suddenly blank, unresponsive, faraway.

"You were about to get us into a real old-fashioned melodrama for a moment there, weren't you?" Connie asked dryly. "It might have been interesting but it wouldn't have proved very much ... Now, you listen to me, Jayvee, because I'm going to say a few things to you and I'm never going to say them to you again.

"You and I and Jazz and Pete are on this crew together by direction of the President, and there isn't anything we can do about it unless you want to resign, which might be the best thing all around since you seem to hate the program so. But if you want to stay, you stay on the same terms everybody else does. You forget your damned precious black skin and your damned precious 'rights' that nobody here to my knowledge has ever done anything but respect, and you play ball. You get on this team and you stay there. You stop this crap and you get down to work and you do your job as you can do it, which is damned well if you'll just stop waving the race flag and pay attention. Nobody here has ever judged you on anything but your ability, and we all respect you for that. Where you got off the road into thinking anything else, or where you got off the road into judging us on anything else but *our* ability, I'm damned if I know and I don't want to know. I said that was your problem and it is. From now on you keep it to yourself, because neither I nor your other two crewmates have the time, nor the patience, to stand for it.

"We've got a job to do—it's the biggest job we've ever been called upon to do—we have all got to do our part of it to the very best of our ability—and we just haven't got time for this sort of thing, Jayvee. We just haven't got time.

"You apparently don't want to resign. You apparently intend to stay with it. The chances are, as you rightly estimate, that it would be a damned difficult business forcing you out unless you gave us an awful lot of public excuse, and you're too clever for that. So you're with us and you're probably with us all the way. But I just suggest to you, Jayvee, that you do a lot of serious thinking; because while it would be hard to break you, I think the three of us could manage if we had to.

"Suppose we just don't any of us try to find out, O.K.?"

"Are you through?" Jayvee asked in a remote voice, as though coming back from some area where he had been residing, shut off and perhaps not even listening, while Connie talked. "Can I go now?"

Connie shrugged and leaned forward to pick up the tentative flight plan he and Jazz had started to develop before lunch.

"Who's to stop you?"

232

"You said 0900 tomorrow?"

"That's what I said," Connie answered, not looking up.

"That's what I thought you said," Jayvee said; stood up abruptly; and was gone.

After the door had slammed behind him, Connie Trasker sat for a long time in some closed-off world of his own, staring out at the distant lake, his eyes unhappy, his face a study in tiredness and strain. He felt physically exhausted, emotionally drained, empty and worthless. Their talk had gone just the way he had not wanted it to go. Hostility had snarled from every sentence and flared in every glance. He hadn't accomplished much for Piffy One this day. Or had he? He didn't know . . . probably wouldn't know until tomorrow morning . . . might not know then . . . might never know. He felt loathing and contempt for Jayvee, but more for himself, for not handling it more skillfully. He was better than that.

For the first time in his forty-two years, he felt old.

When the bell rang on the Picturephone he swung back to his desk and with considerable effort managed to look reasonably alert. Jazz appeared on the screen, studied his expression, looked worried.

"How did it go?"

He sighed.

"Not too well."

"Maybe the flight will straighten him out," Jazz said, trying to sound hopeful.

"I doubt it very much. I don't think the flight is going to ennoble him any. I think he's going to be a race-sick child when he goes up and a race-sick child when he comes down."

"Looks like our friend in Washington has really handed us a problem."

"Yes," Connie said. "Somehow we've got to work it out without letting it look like three to one."

"We'll manage," Jazz said, again sounding determinedly optimistic.

"We'll get a better fix on it tomorrow morning," Connie said. "Get a good night's sleep."

"You, too," Jazz said.

"And thanks for calling."

"Sure."

After the screen went dark again, Connie got up and went to the window to stand and stare out once more across the parking lot to the lake. Cars passed up and down, tourists wandered, scientists, staff and several of his fellow astronauts passed below. The life of Manned Spacecraft Center went on. Presently it would be quitting time, then dinner time, then listen-to-the-President time. What rabbits would come out of that clever hat tonight? He couldn't imagine there were many left, though he was sure there would be a smooth, comfortable public paste-up job that would conceal the tattered remnants of the morale of poor old Piffy One.

Thinking of his recent conversations with Jane, Monetta, Pete, Jazz, Jayvee and the rest, thinking of Gaudy Gaudet and Em Wacker, thinking of Al Freer and Stu Yule, he realized suddenly that Piffy One seemed to be carrying quite a burden of tears. He felt rather like crying himself, in fact, as he stood staring out, not really seeing, and contemplated the present state of the great bright mission which had begun with such excitement and such unity, so short a time ago.

13.

None of this melancholy, of course, was noticeable in the presentation from the White House. There all was confidence and good will. And there were some new rabbits from the hat, too. Connie should have known.

"My friends," the President began promptly at the witching-hour for Presidents—9 P.M. Eastern Standard Time, 8 P.M. Central, 7 P.M. Mountain, 6 P.M. Pacific— "I am speaking to you briefly tonight to keep you informed of events in connection with the Mars flight of Planetary Fleet One. I am speaking to you so soon after my original talk on the subject because there are major announcements to be made about it and it seemed advisable to me that I should be the one to tell you about them, since I am the one who brings them about.

"The first is a change in crew assignments."

("*Good!*" Percy Mercy exclaimed with a triumphant excitement to Kenny Williams in the latter's apartment in The Watergate. "Oh, *good.*")

"The second is the selection of a back-up crew.

"And the third is an announcement of more general nature, which I hope may open the way for a new era in space exploration."

("He's going to invite the Russians!" Percy cried happily to Kenny. "My God," Jazz said unhappily to Clare. "I'll bet he's going to invite the Russians.")

"It is with considerable reluctance," the President said solemnly, "that I have reached the conclusion that a change in the crew assignments will be necessary. The change is in no way whatsoever a reflection upon the two

235

fine Americans whom I have asked to step aside. In fact they will be on the back-up crew" (Gaudy Gaudet glanced up at Ellen and his air of profound dejection eased a little) "and they will fly on the second Mars mission. Their relief from this flight and their assignment to the next flight has nothing to do with competence or character. Both are superb.

"It has to do, rather"—and he looked directly into the camera with an open, candid expression—"with the practical necessities that face me as President of the United States—and with the need to send out to Mars, as representatives of the United States, a crew that reflects *all* the people and *all* the interests that make up this great democracy. Specifically, the great black people of this nation have a right, it seems to me, to be included in this greatest of all space adventures. And fortunately they already have in the astronaut corps a fine, and wholly worthy, representative."

("And what about the Indians, the Mexicans, the Polish, the Germans, the Italians, the Japanese, the Chinese?" Connie asked dryly. "To say nothing of us poor Greeks," Pete agreed with a grin. "Hush," Jane said. "It isn't an easy situation for him.")

"There was also one other astronaut, a veteran of the space program of many years' standing, whose qualifications, it seemed to me, warranted the most serious consideration. After consultation with the appropriate officials in Houston, I took it upon myself to request that these two men be assigned to the crew.

("Not one word about violence or pressure," Bob Hertz remarked glumly to Jim Cavanaugh. "Isn't he going to at least warn against it?" Dr. Cavanaugh looked quizzical and shrugged.)

"This intervention was somewhat unprecedented," the President admitted with a frank smile, "but it was fully within my authority and my responsibility for the mission. The consequences, it seemed to me, would be a more representative, a more closely knit—

("*What?*" Hank Barstow exclaimed. " 'Closely-knit,' meaning 'all screwed up,' " Bert Richmond said.)

"—and a more representative American crew. I thought the country—I knew I—would feel better about it.

"I have been assured by all the men involved—I talked to them yesterday at some length—that these changes in

236

the mission are agreeable to them, and that they will proceed forthwith in full unity and co-operation to make this the greatest space venture of all time. Therefore, it is with satisfaction and with confidence that I announce that the primary crew of Planetary Fleet One will consist of Colonel Conrad C. Trasker, Jr., U.S. Air Force, commander of the Mars Landing Vehicle and commander of the flight; Commander Alvin H. Weickert III, U.S. Navy, commander of the Commander Service Vehicle and second-in-command of the flight; Astroscientist Dr. J. V. Halleck, geologist, commander of the Medico-Scientific Vehicle—"

(*"He's demoting me!"* Pete exclaimed in anguished disbelief. *"I* should have had that slot, if Em isn't going to go!" "I'm sorry, buddy," Connie said unhappily. "I didn't know.")

"—and Astroscientist Dr. Petros S. Balkis, specialist in medico-biological aspects of space exploration, co-commander of the MSV."

"The back-up crew for this mission, and the prime crew for the second Mars mission, will consist of Commander Hugo S. Gaudet, U.S. Navy, commander of the MLV and commander of the flight; Colonel Roger Webb, U.S. Air Force, commander of the CSV; Astroscientist Dr. Emerson Wacker, geologist, commander of the MSV; and Astroscientist Dr. Robert Curtis, specialist in medico-biological aspects of space exploration, co-commander of the MSV.

"Now I come," the President said, and his expression became solemn and intent, "to the third matter I wish to talk to you about tonight. It involves the future of space exploration and possibly the future of world peace—and, possibly, the future of the world itself."

("Not a word about violence," Bob Hertz repeated glumly to Jim Cavanaugh. "Not *one single solitary word.*" Again Dr. Cavanaugh looked quizzical and shrugged.)

"It has been proposed," the President said with a portentous slowness, "that the United States invite the Soviet Union to participate in this mission. After long and serious consideration, I have decided to take this step."

("Oh, *marvelous!*" cried Percy Mercy. "Oh *Christ!*" groaned Connie Trasker.)

"I have this day addressed the following letter to the

Honorable Valerian Susnev, Chairman of the Council of Ministers, U.S.S.R.—Mr. Chairman:

" 'I write you to propose a revolutionary and unprecedented step for the betterment of all mankind. I do so in the spirit of brotherhood and co-operation which should unite all peoples of the Earth as they confront the continually expanding frontiers of the universe.

" 'Both our countries are now embarked upon a major effort to reach the planet Mars.

("They haven't admitted that," Pete said. "And they won't, either," Connie replied.)

" 'This effort is enormously expensive in terms of money—

("When they have always spent twice the percentage of their budget on space that we have, from the very beginning?" Hans Sturmer asked indignantly. "Does he really think they care about the expense?")

" '—in terms of man hours and man energy, and in terms of concentrated national effort that might better be applied to the pressing needs of both our countries.

" 'This new space race was not the decision of the United States. If pursued as it has been begun, it can only contribute to further suspicion and hostility between our two countries, with consequences for mankind that could be tragic if not disastrous.

("And who started *that?*" Kenny Williams asked in a disgusted tone.)

" 'Therefore, Mr. Chairman, in the hope that the journey to Mars might truly prove a new path to friendship and harmony here on Earth, I am pleased on behalf of the United States of America and its people, to invite the Soviet Union to join us in full co-operation and amity in pursuit of this great objective. This would include combined personnel, combined crews, combined missiles, combined launches. It would be a truly co-operative, genuinely friendly project.

"Because this will require agreement on many technical matters, I am asking the Vice-President, as chairman of the National Aeronautics and Space Council, together with such of his scientific advisers as he feels necessary, to meet with any representatives you wish to designate, in the city of Geneva—

("That's bad," Percy Mercy said with a frown. "Why impose conditions?")

" '—not later than three days from today—

("Don't *do* that!" Percy protested angrily. "We have no *right* to ask them to meet any requirements from us!")

" '—to begin immediate, substantive talks. It is my hope and wish that these might be concluded within three weeks.

" 'The United States, Mr. Chairman,' " the President concluded solemnly, "is prepared to enter into such an undertaking with full co-operation, full trust, full enthusiasm. We believe it would enormously benefit mankind if our two countries were to work in harmony together on this greatest of all space adventures. We are prepared to do our part. We respectfully invite your great country to join us. The result can only be good for Earth and all her peoples. Yours with sincere regards.'

"This letter," he said, "I have this day transmitted to Moscow. I urge you to join me in my hopes that it may be accepted, and that our two great nations can go forward together, in amity and in peace, to meet this awesome challenge."

And his earnest, powerful presence faded from the screen to be followed immediately on all three networks by analysts and commentators babbling with a happy excitement, tumbling over themselves with praise for this great, this noble, this most farsighted of men and his marvelous idea.

And thus there came unto them great victory; and there was joy and dancing in the land.

"It is with a profound sense of relief," the *Times* said in its lead editorial, reaching the streets shortly after the President spoke, "that we greet the Chief Executive's decision to change the crew of Planetary Fleet One.

"With even greater relief, and with a great sense of anticipation and hope, we welcome his farsighted and statesmanly decision to invite the Soviet Union to participate as an equal partner in the great drive to conquer Mars.

"From a narrowly chosen, racially oriented, Houston-dominated body of men, the crew has been changed to a broadly based, fully experienced, truly democratic group of astronauts, worthy in every way to represent the finest purposes, hopes and aspirations of the United States.

"We applaud the selection of Astronaut Alvin S. Weickert III. We are sure his abilities as an astronaut will soon mercifully bury the memory of his naïveté as an analyst of the American social scene. Still more do we applaud the selection of Astroscientist Dr. J. V. Halleck, a black American whose character, maturity, idealism and integrity make him a magnificent representative of his race and of us all. To him in particular we say: God speed.

"But even more magnificent than his selection of the crew is the President's decision to open the way at last to the full space co-operation with the Soviet Union which holds such great promise for the future of all mankind. It seems safe to say that both nations have long desired this. Now an American President has broken through the chauvinistic barriers of timidity and suspicion which have so long bound this government to a policy of non-co-operation and has held forth his hand to our great friends and allies in the conquest of space.

"We await with confidence Moscow's reply.

"We feel, with a singing hope, that it will be favorable.

"With this courageous decision by a courageous man, a new day has dawned in space.

"Let us welcome it with open arms."

The *Post*'s arms were also open and it was singing too:

"The President's decision to place a black American on the crew of Planetary Fleet One, and to invite the Soviet Union into full participation in the flight to Mars, must rank as one of the major turning-points of our time.

"At last the racial barrier which has so long crippled and cast a sorry shadow upon the activities of NASA has been broken by the selection of a fine and wholly admirable American Negro, Astroscientist Dr. J. V. Halleck. The nation may rejoice that a young man of such ability and such human worth was available for this assignment, so long overdue one of his race. We are proud of America, that it has such fine black citizens in it, and proud of the President for at last giving them their due in the space program.

"We are also pleased with the selection of Commander Alvin H. Weickert III, whose skills as an experienced astronaut fortunately outweigh the rather naïve and simplistic approach to American social realities disclosed in his statement in Houston yesterday. We hope the callow indiscretion of his statement will be soon forgotten in the glory of his performance on Planetary Fleet One. We are

240

confident that, as with so many technicians who venture into political areas they know nothing about, he will presently recognize his incompetence in this field and return, perhaps a trifle shamefacedly, to the one in which he is unsurpassed.

"The President's invitation to the Soviet Union is an event of such majesty and such awesome grandeur in the long story of mankind that we can only say it matches the concept of the Mars flight itself. With one swift executive action he has broken through the miasma of delusion, fear and chauvinistic pride which has for so long prevented the American people from accepting the great opportunity offered by co-operation with the Russians in space.

"Nothing has more become us than this invitation by our President. Nothing can do more to erase the tensions that divide and terrify the world than the sight of the two great space powers linked at last in a joint endeavor to achieve the neighbor planet. We can forget that we waited so inexcusably and so long. We can congratulate ourselves that Tomorrow dawns."

In similar mood and prepared to write in similar vein, Percy Mercy returned in great excitement to his silent office on Connecticut Avenue. His taxi was one of the few cars moving on the capital's deserted, fear-haunted streets. He thought vaguely as he paid the nervous driver that he must do an editorial on crime in Washington, sometime, when other, more globular matters were not so pressing.

But tonight he knew he had weightier things to discuss, as the watchman let him into the empty building and he took the elevator up to his softly-carpeted, luxurious sanctum. "Percy's Think Tank," his friends called it; "Percy's Piffle Pot," his enemies said—but how much circulation, how many stations, how much exposure did *they* have? Not very damned much, compared to the powerful legions who marched side by side with Percy C. Mercy and that marvelous publication, *View*. He sat down at his desk and drew his typewriter toward him, content.

He would, he decided, stress the themes stressed by the *Times*, the *Post* and all the other Right Thinkers whose editorials, commentaries and analyses would flood the country and the world in the next few days.

The simple, thrilling, wonderfully noble *blackness* of Jayvee Halleck—the utter naïve political stupidity of Jazz Weickert (but a few gracious, saving words for his

241

great ability as an astronaut, too)—the marvelous, ecstatic, almost-beyond-belief statesmanship and leadership of the President: these were good themes. They were *great* themes. And Percy Christ Mercy—calm, judicious, fatherly and all-knowing, now that the horrible mistakes of the past few days which had so aroused the awesome fury of Percy Comma Mercy had been washed away—was prepared to do them justice.

He would do so with the sort of dreamlike denying of the known facts which so easily afflicted himself and his colleagues in their patient, unending endeavor to bring some sense to their poor, stupid, wayward countrymen.

He would do so knowing perfectly well that Jayvee Halleck was a difficult, immature, neurotic, potentially dangerous man to send into space—but Percy would always describe him in his pages as a man co-operative, reliable, steady and mature.

He would do so knowing perfectly well that both Dr. Freer and Jazz Weickert had touched on something that privately made Percy himself profoundly uneasy, namely a really serious doubt about the loyalty of Clete O'Donnell and some others opposed to the flight—but Percy knew that in his pages Clete O'Donnell and those others would always be described as fine, patriotic, decent and loyal Americans inspired only by the noblest motives.

He would do so knowing perfectly well that the Russians had always flatly refused to co-operate in space, and that if by any chance they were smart enough to accept the President's invitation, they would join Project Argosy with no other aim than to block, thwart, subvert and destroy it in every way they possibly could—but Percy knew that in his pages he would always describe the Russians as fine, noble, upright, trustworthy and honest allies whose only aim, ever, was to work sincerely and helpfully with the United States of America.

So it had always been, with Percy and his particular element in the media. So, presumably, it would always be. A sort of deliberate insanity gripped them, a sort of willfully upside-down logic that miraculously transformed the world they knew into the world they wished, every time they wrote, reported, commented upon or pictured it.

Moved by this sweet, deliberate euphoria with which he and his friends had contributed so much to the misinformation and confusion of their countrymen over so many years, Percy began to write his editorial for the upcoming issue of *View*.

Around him his domain was hushed and silent. The only sound on the whole floor of the building in this late, deserted hour was the steady tapping of his typewriter and the jubilant little hum that now and then burst unconsciously from his lips.

He was elated almost beyond his considerable capacity for expression by the knowledge that Planetary Fleet One—bright and shining at last, thank goodness—had been rescued almost miraculously, by the concerted efforts of himself and his friends, from the shabby, disgraceful, ruinous disunity with which it had begun, so short a time ago.

Book Two

1.

There now began, for the crew of Piffy One, for the administrators and staffs of NASA, for the contractors and subcontractors and for all their families, friends and relations, that period of intensified pre-launch activity that veterans of the program knew so well from the great days of Mercury, Gemini and Apollo. Practical men made practical plans. Pragmatic decisions followed upon pragmatic decisions. Hours grew longer, lives more selfless. With a spirit befitting the bravery of the men who would fly and the skills of the men who would help them do so, all segments of the nation united in a great, selfless, noble dedication to the cause.

Perfect, shining and pure, Project Argosy moved on its majestic way in harmony, happiness and peace.

Politics and human emotions were banished and allowed no more to trouble it.

Much.

It was not, the Vice-President thought, that he was a fussy man: but he did like a little more advance warning than his vigorous superior had given him in his address to the country last night, if he was to mount a full-scale negotiation with the Russians. It was all very well for the President to say grandly, in effect, "I have asked the Vice-President to do the dirty work," but it didn't look that easy in the baroque, baronial office in the baroque, baronial old gingerbread Executive Offices Building next door to the White House on Pennsylvania Avenue. There, it caused problems.

247

Not, of course, that the Vice-President objected to the task, though he was extremely skeptical of its success. He was not about to violate the basic rule of Vice-Presidents, which is never to comment in any way, shape, manner or form upon the wisdom of what their Presidents do or do not do. But had it been his responsibility, he might have handled it differently. To begin with, he would certainly have stated a few conditions. He would not have made it quite such a grandiose "Come and get it, boys," type of invitation—although, he supposed with a certain wryness, the President had to satisfy the shouters and screamers. But he didn't really see why he had to go as far as he did, when he had already thrown them the bone of the new assignment to the crew of Piffy One.

Like all Vice-Presidents of the space age, the incumbent was slightly more Catholic than the Pope when it came to supporting the program. "This job of being chairman of the Space Council," one of them had remarked privately, "is about the most fun there is in this job. Maybe," he added, only half-joking, "the only fun." His boys, as the current Vice-President liked to call them, were among the most pleasant and exciting people he knew in his curious and generally thankless occupation. He felt they had been most cavalierly treated by the President and he regretted deeply that he had been away at the time.

Had he been in Washington instead of gallivanting around Europe on a good will jaunt the Chief Executive had asked him to undertake, (more or less, he suspected, to give him something to do) he might well have thrown his weight on the side of the Astronaut Office in the conferences and strategy sessions that had preceded the crew change. As it was, he had arrived back last night shortly after the President's talk to find everything decided, two good men booted off the crew and two—or at any rate one—doubtful quantity added, and morale, he had no doubt, generally shot to hell. This was too bad, the Vice-President felt, and he decided he would call Houston soon and get a rundown on the situation from his favorite astronaut, the amiable and redoubtable Colonel Trasker.

Meanwhile, he must decide how to approach these talks with the Russians. Already the State Department was giving him assistance. One of its ablest negotiators, a man wise and experienced in the methodology of yielding ground to the Communists while maintaining for the folks

248

back home the illusion of American achievement, had been waiting on his doorstep when he arrived. All brisk, bright, shiny and suave, he had begun to advise the Vice-President candidly on how to handle the Russians.

The Vice-President was to be soft, he was to be gentle, he was to be respectful, he was to be mild, he was to accept each Soviet insult—"And they will come, Mr. Vice-President, oh yes, we all know they will come!"—as simple strategy concealing kind and willing hearts. He was to smile and smile and agree and agree and accept and accept. He was not to demand, not to insist, not to raise his voice, not to present conditions, not to ask concessions, not to—

"How am I to negotiate?" the Vice-President interrupted, deliberately sounding like the dullard he knew they all thought he was. "I mean, if I just accept everything they suggest and agree to everything they demand—well, where's the negotiation? I don't get it."

"Mr. Vice-President," the State Department's clever one said, "*sir:* the negotiation comes in the skill with which the representatives of the United States adapt themselves to the rather crude ways in which the Soviet Union states its demands. It's not that they're basically unreasonable. They're just a little—unpolished, sometimes, that's all. You have to be sympathetic and see things through their eyes. It was our thought that if you were just *aware* of this, if you were just *forewarned*, if you were *alert* to the real *purposes* behind their sometimes rather flamboyant words—"

"I'm aware of their real purposes," the Vice-President said. "They want to do us in. Are you telling me I should let them?"

"Mr. Vice-President," the State Department's expert said, "Mr. *Vice-President!* Certainly we do not advocate that. We simply want to be helpful, that's all. We think that style and method are so important in arriving at an accommodation to their views, Mr. Vice-President. They are *so* important."

"I want them to arrive at an accommodation to our views," the Vice-President said. "What's the style and method for that?"

"That is such an impossible goal," the State Department's expert confessed with a charming smile, "that we don't even worry about *that.*"

After he had wound up that interview with an amiable but implacable speed, the Vice-President was subjected to several more of a similar nature from the CIA, the U.S. Information Service, the chief press officer at NASA and the White House communications director. Finally he had remarked to the last gentleman, somewhat tartly, "I don't see why everybody is telling me all this. The President wants it, so that's the way it's going to be. What's the fuss?"

"We just thought you should be briefed," the communications director told him. "It's quite a delicate matter."

"If my humble homespun ways aren't delicate enough just as they stand in all their stark, naked simplicity," the Vice-President said, "then perhaps he should get somebody else. Why don't you suggest it?"

"We wouldn't think of it," the communications director assured him hastily.

But the next move, the Vice-President knew, would be to surround him with a crew of advisers whose whole aim would be exactly that of the State Department: to agree, to accept, to accommodate, to make no fuss and to do it, by God, with style.

Basically, he supposed, this was the right thing to do, from the standpoint of the historical record. Despite the paeans of joy from the media, he did not believe for one minute that the President had the slightest illusion that the Communists would accept his invitation. No more did the media, he suspected, but they were putting up such a happy hullaballoo you would never guess it. So his job was to make the attempt in good faith for the record and await the inevitable rejection that would permit the United States to say to the world, "You see? We made the offer and they turned it down. What more can you ask?"

Of course he knew, and so did the President, what a good many of the watching nations would ask if they thought they could get it. Already ninety-seven members of the ruling party in the British Parliament, having nothing better with which to engage their energies in the aftermath of empire, had adopted a resolution calling on the United States to abandon the flight altogether. The premier of lucky Sweden, always in the middle, had led a protest march through downtown Stockholm demanding the same. Not to be outdone, though they couldn't possibly do any better than that, the Communist nations behind the

Iron Curtain were joining the chorus. India and the Maldives formed a mighty duo crying the same.

The poor old United States, the Vice-President reflected ironically, just couldn't win. Somehow it would just have to struggle along and survive in spite of it, the way it always did.

And somehow he had to help his boys and do what he could to guarantee the success of their mission. He regretted that his own mission would be taking him out of the country again just as they were beginning their long, intensive grind. But given a three-week limit such as the President had suggested, he should be back in ample time to assist if needed. He prided himself that he could contribute something, even from his strange Constitutional limbo. He was respected in the program and, he thought, respected in the White House. In an office whose influence depended largely upon the personal character and strength of the incumbent, he was not the weakest ever, by any means. It gave him a comfortable if not overwhelming clout when he wanted to use it.

Before he left for Geneva, he decided, he should check the bases, not only with Connie in Houston but with people like Jim Matthison at North American Rockwell, Hans Sturmer in Huntsville, Al Freer and of course Stuart Yule, in Orlando. He could generally find out a good deal on a need-to-know basis. He felt he did need to know how things were going in these opening days of the new Piffy One.

There were no real worries, as he soon found out, at North American Rockwell, at Boeing, at Bendix, at IBM, at Grumman. Nor, Jim Matthison and his colleagues reported, were there any major problems with the various subcontractors—except, of course, the overriding problem of recapturing lost personnel, particularly in the higher grades.

"I've kept in touch with quite a few over the years," Jim explained, "and so have we all. But the trouble is, you see, we're all competing with each other: these guys can practically name their own tickets now that the government has suddenly decided we need them back, and brother, they *are*.

"Furthermore, Mr. Vice-President, there's a certain amount of aging process here, too. Everybody's grown

251

older, they're settled in other jobs, their families have roots in other places, they're usually making a great deal more than they did when they left the program ... It's just a damned shame," he observed sadly, "that the Administration and the Congress didn't decide about ten years ago that we were going to maintain a steady, active, relatively high-achievement program, with salaries to match, that would have kept these fellows in. We're suffering for it now that we need them, and we're going to suffer more before we get it sorted out."

"And yet," the Vice-President said thoughtfully, "the Administration and the Congress had ample warning from everybody in a position to know, as I read the record. I can say this," he added with a smile, "because I wasn't in the government then, I was just a lowly governor. But it certainly was clear enough at the time."

"The trouble with us," Jim Matthison said, "as a government, as an Administration, as a Congress, and as a people, is that we never look an inch beyond our noses. We never think ahead, we never plan, we never really believe we're going to have to do the things that ordinary common sense, at any given moment in time, tells us we're going to have to do. We're just not farsighted and we're not prudent. We'd rather pretend it isn't so, because to admit it would cost money and sacrifice and make us work. Then comes the big crisis and everybody demands instant miracles, and Lordy, Gordy, the overalls land in Mrs. Murphy's chowder and there's hell to pay. Why are we so stupid? Do you have a good explanation?"

"I don't," the Vice-President admitted. "I wish I did. Not that anybody would pay any attention, of course. The thing that really worries me," he said with a frown, "is that we might suffer for it in some mechanical way that will hurt the astronauts—that because we didn't keep on top of it when we had the chance, we're going to get sloppy workmanship in this emergency situation that could really endanger lives. How does that strike you?"

"Well . . ." Jim Matthison said, frowning too. "That could be a problem. I won't pretend it couldn't. But I think we're going to come out all right. I won't deny that sabotage is a worry, though. You take a crash program such as we've let ourselves get boxed into, and it could be tight in that area. It could be."

"What are you boys going to do to prevent it?" the Vice-President inquired.

"Build back our security force to where it was, as near as possible, and re-establish all of our regular security procedures, starting with personnel investigations, badging, the whole bit. We've of course kept them up to some extent in these slack years, but inevitably we've been a lot more relaxed about it than we were when Apollo was at its peak. We haven't had the need."

"No," the Vice-President agreed, somewhat glumly. "I hope we really won't have the need now. I'd like to think, fondly and romantically that we didn't—but of course we do."

"Oh, sure," Jim Matthison said. "I'm afraid so, particularly with Clete O'Donnell throwing his weight around the way he is."

"What do you make of him?" the Vice-President asked. "Have you ever had any thought that—?"

"Once or twice," Jim Matthison said, thoughtfully. "Once or twice. Nothing I could quite put my finger on—I don't know him very well, we've only really talked once, when he was out here as part of one of NASA's VIP tours of the major installations—but there was just . . . something. I couldn't quite tell you, I couldn't tell you now, but something just didn't ring quite true. To me, that is. Now to most of the country, the press, television, newspapers, the rest of them, he's apparently a great hero. Maybe he is. I don't know. He's a very smart boy, there's no doubt about that."

"What do you think of his performance at the Cape the other day?"

"Well, he got out of it clear, didn't he? I heard him on CBS after he called off the strike. It was certainly a fine statement, a real clarion call for the right of patriotic dissent." Jim Matthison smiled, a trifle ironically. "Made me feel I'd be damned *un*patriotic to disagree with him. Didn't you have the same feeling?"

The Vice-President nodded.

"We have a lot of those in this country. The words are just fine. The actions—" his smile, too, turned ironic. He shrugged. "I think I'd like to keep an eye on him. You might do the same. I imagine you have some pretty good contacts on the working level at the Cape."

"Sure," Jim Matthison said. "I'm in and out all the time. I'll make it a point to get chummy."

"Be careful," the Vice-President suggested. "Don't want to talk like a spy novel—seems ridiculous to suggest it—but the stakes are big, here. The bigger they get, the more ruthless some people become."

"I'll start with golf," Jim Matthison said. "I understand he loves it. So do I. I'll get a confession on the nineteenth green."

"Nothing sensational required," the Vice-President told him. "Just keep in touch with the situation . . . Do you anticipate any mechanical difficulties out there? Any manufacturing problems that we can help you with from here?"

"Thanks very much," Jim Matthison said, "but I don't think so. The other boys may have a few, but I expect we're all in pretty good shape. As you know, NASA still has two Saturns in storage at the Michoud assembly facility just outside New Orleans. They're already getting them ready to send out here, probably within the week. Then we'll get to work and make whatever modifications Houston and Huntsville tell us are necessary. Meanwhile we're already tooling up again to produce the third—and very likely three more, if headquarters gives us the go-ahead."

"They will," the Vice-President promised. "Redundancy, redundancy, redundancy—it's the great NASA theme song."

"And sometimes a damned good thing, too."

"Sometimes," the Vice-President agreed, "a damned good thing. There's another mission coming, and of course we have to have back-ups for this one, just in case."

"There won't be any 'just in case,'" Jim Matthison said comfortably, "but it's good to know they'll be there, anyway."

"Correct. I'll try to get out and see you in a couple of weeks, as soon as I get back from Geneva."

"That'll be a couple of hours, won't it?" Jim Matthison inquired with a smile.

The Vice-President chuckled.

"Probably. But we're taking it very seriously, around here."

"Really?" Jim Matthison inquired with some skepticism. "Just between you and me, I hope you fail abysmally."

"I will," the Vice-President said comfortably. "The Russians will help me."

"I'll be as disappointed as you are," Jim Matthison said.

"I expect that's a rather common sentiment around NASA," the Vice-President said.

But he did not find it common with Clete O'Donnell, whose initial expression of surprise when the Vice-President came on the Picturephone yielded instantly to a comfortably patronizing air. It was obvious that Clete thought he was concealing this, but the Vice-President was accustomed to this sort of thing from a certain element whose members thought they were smarter than he was. They weren't, but it often served his purposes to let them think so. He decided a respectful dumbness would be the best way to open the conversation.

"Good morning, Clete," he said with a smile. "How are things in Miami Beach?"

"Hot," Clete O'Donnell said with a smile. "How are they in Washington?"

"Hotter," the Vice-President said. He shook his head with a baffled amiability. "Especially where I sit right now."

"How's that?"

"The Russians, and all. It's quite a responsibility the President's given me. I don't know whether I can handle it."

"I'm sure the country has no doubts, Mr. Vice-President. Obviously the President hasn't."

"He flatters me, I'm afraid," the Vice-President confessed with a sigh. "It's a big job, dealing with those people. I'm not sure I—" he broke off and frowned thoughtfully. "Clete, how would you handle them? Could you give me a little advice? I'd certainly appreciate it."

"Is that why you called?" Clete asked, and the Vice-President got the impression that he was relaxing from some inner tension. "I didn't know—"

"Oh, that wasn't the only reason," the Vice-President said comfortably. He was intrigued to see Clete almost visibly tensing up again. "I wanted to talk to you a little about the trouble at the Cape, of course. That's part of my responsibility as chairman of the Space Council."

"Did the President ask you to talk to me about it?" Clete asked sharply.

"Nope," the Vice-President said. "I just thought I'd raise it on my own. It seemed a curious little episode and I thought I'd like to get the story from the man who was responsible and find out whether we can expect the same sort of thing again. Any objections?"

"Certainly not," Clete said. "I don't really consider myself responsible, however. If Dr. Freer hadn't seen fit to put it on such a personal basis, if he hadn't attempted to attack my loyalty and smear me as—a—I don't know what—then we might have been able to avoid the unpleasantness."

"I wonder why he did that?" the Vice-President asked thoughtfully. "Can you imagine why he would say such a thing?"

"Senility, perhaps," Clete O'Donnell suggested coldly. "Or hysteria brought on by too much obsession with space."

"Apparently he did have some grounds to think you might be trying to interfere with the mission," the Vice-President suggested mildly. "You did call a strike to try to stop it, after all."

"Only under provocation," Clete pointed out with a certain smugness. "Only after he put on extra guards and attacked me personally as being hostile to the United States."

"Which you aren't," the Vice-President said gently.

"No, sir!" Clete said with a harsh indignation that sounded genuine.

"But you did threaten a strike," the Vice-President said. "You evidently had some conversation with him and you did threaten a strike. And you apparently gave him some reason to think your motives might be not quite as disinterested as the public was subsequently given to understand."

"Are you charging me with disloyalty, Mr. Vice-President?" Clete asked with a dangerous quietness.

"Oh, no," the Vice-President said. "Oh, dear, no. But I'm a little bit puzzled by Al Freer, nonetheless. It hasn't been my experience of him that he's either senile or obsessed with space—at least to the point where the obsession would lead him to make what is really quite a grave allegation about a loyal fellow American. I heard your talk on CBS, incidentally. I thought it was a fine statement of your point of view."

"Thank you," Clete said, somewhat mollified. "If you want my explanation of Al Freer, it's that he's been around space too long and he's seeing ghosts under the bed. It's the only sensible conclusion I've been able to come up with."

"Except, of course," the Vice-President insisted gently, "that you *did* call the strike you had threatened to call. And it did get very nasty."

"Not my doing," Clete said blandly. "I didn't know the old man and his astronaut would get in the way."

For a second the Vice-President had all he could do to keep his tone impersonal. But he managed.

"Do you feel any sorrow about that?" he inquired presently. "Any regret for Al Freer? Any compunction about Stuart Yule?"

"Mr. Vice-President," Clete said, "I'm not really a monster. I'm not really cold-blooded. Naturally I regret the old man got hurt, and I think it's most unfortunate that Stu Yule had such bad luck. But still—they *were* attempting to interfere with a perfectly legitimate protest."

"They were trying to stop a fire, as near as we can determine up here," the Vice-President remarked. "Was that 'perfectly legitimate protest'?"

"Oh," Clete said comfortably, "one or two of the boys may have been a little careless. But after all, Mr. Vice-President, *they* weren't responsible for the climate that surrounds the project. It was just something that happened in the heat of the moment"—he grinned cheerfully—"if you'll excuse the pun."

"It *was* unfortunate," the Vice-President said, permitting a certain acid in his voice for the first time. "What's going to happen next? Another strike?"

"Well, I don't know," Clete said with an earnest slowness, ignoring his tone. "There wouldn't be much point now, would there? I mean, the essential things we were striking for, we've achieved, haven't we? The crew's been changed, and now that the President's invited the Russians—well, it's just going to be a much finer, more sensible and more worthwhile thing, that's all. We don't have any objections to co-operating with that. On the contrary, we're going to show you some real production records at the Cape. When are you coming down to see us?"

"I think I'll make a swing around after I get back from

257

Geneva. But you still haven't told me how you think I should approach them."

"You didn't let me," Clete pointed out with a smile. "You got me off on this other thing. I thought you'd forgotten it."

"No," the Vice-President said, "I don't forget things. What kind of concessions do you think they ought to make if we're to let them participate?"

"*They* ought to make!" Clete said, and he sounded quite genuinely shocked. "We're issuing the invitation. Why should they make concessions?"

"Well, we can't have it just an open-end invitation to come in and take over the mission, can we? It ought to be a partnership, or it will be meaningless."

"Mr. Vice-President," Clete said earnestly, "speaking for myself, and I think for all the many thousands who have been flocking to join the Committee Against Unilateral Space Exploration in these past few days, I think that right there you have illustrated what we are all afraid of in the next stages of this. If the United States goes in with a whole set of preconceived notions and impossible demands, then we're going to blow it, Mr. Vice-President. You're going to come home without an agreement and without a space partner, and we're going to be right back where we've been all these weary decades of wasteful and futile competition."

"Wasteful sometimes, maybe," the Vice-President conceded, "but not futile. After all, we do have a lot of firsts to our credit, don't we?"

"It depends on how you interpret 'credit,'" Clete said. "If you use it in the old-fashioned, imperialistic sense, then maybe, yes, we do have some historical firsts. But if you speak in the broader sense of what has been best for the world and for mankind, then I'm not so sure. It's just been naked competition, and often bitter competition, at that. What good has it done? It's only made the Communists more suspicious and more hostile, hasn't it? It hasn't made the world any safer."

"The world isn't any safer," the Vice-President agreed. "Then what would be a good partnership agreement, in this situation? Should we ask them to make any concessions at all?"

"I think you'd be both wise and enlightened, Mr. Vice-President," Clete said earnestly, "if you didn't ask for a

258

single one. Just make it an honest, straightforward, good-faith bid to them to join in. They're not fools, Mr. Vice-President. They're very smart people and great space technicians—we have to admit that. They'll know what's needed and how to go about it."

"Yes, I'm sure."

"As far as our unions are concerned," Clete went on earnestly, again ignoring the irony in his voice, "we don't have any doubts at all about our ability to work with their people. Just let them come in, freely and without hindrance—and also, I might suggest, without a lot of stupid interference by the Immigration Service and the FBI—and we'll take it from there. That's how to make it a truly great mission for all mankind, Mr. Vice-President. *Don't hold back.* It's been the curse of America in her relations with the Communists for as long as the world can remember. We've always been afraid to meet them as brothers. Now we must."

" 'Must'?"

"If this mission is to succeed," Clete O'Donnell said calmly, "and if it is not to encounter further unpleasant difficulties along the way."

"I see," the Vice-President said.

"I hope so, sir," Clete said, looking his most intent and solemn, "because we look to you as our agent to do what is right."

"Oh, I'm going to try," the Vice-President said. "And I do thank you for your suggestions. You've given me a lot to think about."

And so he had, the Vice-President thought a few moments later while he waited for his secretary to get the channels cleared to Dr. Freer's bedside in Orlando. Clete had obviously been prepared for an attack and the Vice-President had to admit his defenses were good. He had been the alert, intelligent, earnest and responsible citizen his friends and supporters liked to describe. Only once or twice had there been any indication of inner tensions, only once or twice a word or turn of phrase that didn't ring quite true. No one who was not suspicious, the Vice-President admitted to himself, would have sensed a thing. But he was suspicious. And he had.

He was not going to forgive Clete O'Donnell for the strike, he promised himself stubbornly, despite the fact that somehow there seemed to have been a general consensus of forgiveness in the media, on the Hill, and possibly—though he did not like to think so—in the White House. It was almost as though the strike had come and gone so fast that no one found time to really absorb its implications. It had been so brief that everyone could almost pretend that it had never happened—could almost forget that Al Freer had raised a question of loyalty that could be most serious—that Clete's official excuse for the strike was a blatant and deliberate attack upon the entire concept and success of Planetary Fleet One. The strike had begun in an hour, ended in an hour. It was easy to forget.

But not for him, the Vice-President thought, deciding that he would continue to reflect upon it patiently, add little bits and pieces together as he found them, and keep an eye on Mr. Clete O'Donnell. He had an ally in Jim Matthison and he knew he had one in Dr. Freer. He was pleased to find the Director of Kennedy Space Center in relatively good shape and relatively good spirits when his face appeared on the screen against the antiseptic background of his hospital room.

"Al," he said cordially, "my good old friend of space—how are you?"

"I have been better," Dr. Freer said, managing a small smile which, peeking out from among the bandages that swathed his head from crown to chin, made him look rather like a pinched, but amiable, Santa Claus.

"How soon are they going to let you go back to the Cape?"

"They say a week. It will be two days."

"Come on, now," the Vice-President said. "Take it easy. There's no point in being foolish."

"The foolishness," Albrecht Freer said somberly, "lies with those who did not protect us when we needed protection."

"I'm sorry I was out of the country when that occurred," the Vice-President said gravely. "I might have been able to help you."

"Not without the President's support. He was against us."

"Why do you say that?"

"Because I asked for his assistance," Dr. Freer said, "and he refused it." His eyes darkened, Santa Claus disappeared in a surge of indignation. "He refused it!"

"Why would he do a thing like that?" the Vice-President asked, though he suspected he knew.

"He refused to believe me when I said Mr. O'Donnell was not a friend to the United States. Mr. O'Donnell," Dr. Freer remarked with a spiteful air that was quite unlike him, "has many votes in this country."

"Do you think that was the reason," the Vice-President asked, "or was it something more fundamental than that?"

"That is not fundamental?" Albrecht Freer demanded scornfully. Then his expression softened. "I may not be fair," he said, sounding more like himself. "He simply did not believe me. He simply could not imagine that Mr. O'Donnell is what I said he was."

"What's that?"

"A Communist," Dr. Freer said. "Yes," he repeated defiantly, "a Communist. He told me so. He said no one would believe me if I told them." His face became bitter. "He was right."

"He seems to be a popular man," the Vice-President observed.

"He is false, vicious, completely amoral and completely worthless," Dr. Freer said.

"But he is a popular man. How do you think we could convince anyone that he is not what he appears to be?"

"You believe me, then."

"Oh yes," the Vice-President said. "But this, you know, is very old-fashioned. It's a tired old cliché. Communists aren't bad men any more. They've reformed. They're good. They're kindly. They're enlightened. It's absurd to worry about them. It's a sad old reactionary hobgoblin, this Communist myth. They are no longer a major threat in Europe, Asia, South America or any other damned place you can name. They're our buddies. They're the salt of the earth. They're great guys. *You* know that, Al."

"Yes," said Dr. Freer bleakly. "And so does Stuart Yule."

"Yes, not to mention a good many millions of others. But not our great thinkers here at home, you know. That's our problem, as far as Clete is concerned. He is so deliciously *in*, so perfectly One Of The Bunch. You haven't been in shape to notice, but he's had quite a strong defense against your attack from some pretty powerful sources."

"He told me he would," Dr. Freer said. "I am not surprised."

"Do you think he will attempt anything further at the Cape?"

"Not if the Soviets come to this country to destroy the mission for themselves. He will not have to. If they do not, he will be active for them again."

"Why, do you suppose?"

"God knows why some Americans do the work of those who wish to destroy them," Dr. Freer said, "and He turns His head away in fear and disgust of them."

"So should we," the Vice-President said, "but many of us, being fools, do not. Therefore it is incumbent upon the rest of us to be on guard against them."

"How can we break his union?" Dr. Freer inquired with a tired shrug. "He is entrenched across the path of Project Argosy."

"We will simply have to convince the President of it. Then there will be action."

"The President is not a fool, but he is a willfully self-blinded man. If you can make him listen, more power to you. He paid no attention to me."

"But now he has the proof you were right," the Vice-President said. "He has the affirmation of two brave men."

"Completely discounted, apparently, by all the most influential voices in the country. That schweinhund Senator Williams, I believe, has made me and poor Stuart his heroes for a campaign *against* the mission. My God!"

"The gall is colossal," the Vice President admitted. "And," he added somewhat glumly, "it works, too. CAUSE is apparently gaining adherents by the thousands every day."

"I shall soon be back on the job," Al Freer said firmly, "and then we will put things in perspective and we will have no more nonsense about what the motives were in that work-stoppage or any other that may occur. But whether we can actually prevent them from happening . . ." His firmness faltered, his face looked sad among its bandages.

"I would hope," the Vice-President suggested quietly, "that when you return home you will take some precautions about your own personal safety. No more dramatic charges into the thick of battle, if you don't mind—you're too valuable to us and too necessary to the program. And also, lurid though it may sound, I think you should have a personal bodyguard and a guard on your house. When you get back to the Cape you'll be quite a symbol. There could be those who would like to see you permanently removed."

"Not Clete, surely," Albrecht Freer said dryly. He gestured to the flowers that lined the top of the service shelf behind him. "Two dozen of these pretties are from him 'with sincerest wishes for your swift recovery, old friend. Your Cape needs you!' " His smile became deeply ironic. "There are times when one is speechless."

"If one is not Clete or Kenny Williams," the Vice-President said. "They are never speechless . . . How are things going over there in your absence?"

"Back on schedule. The burned trailers were removed yesterday and the new ones installed. We have extra guards assigned to the site now, with orders to shoot if necessary to stop arson or sabotage. Work is proceeding. Everyone is happy. You would never dream a foolish old man and his headstrong young astronaut had caused such an unnecessary rumpus the other evening."

"How is Stu?"

"He is a brave man like most of his colleagues. Talk to him. He will be glad to hear from you."

"I shall in just a moment," the Vice-President said, "now that I have satisfied myself that you are indestructible."

"I'm a tough old bird," Al Freer said wryly. "It will take more than this to cook me."

"Unless you persist in jumping in the pot again," the Vice-President said. "Have sense enough to stay out next time, please."

"I was angry and hot inside, then. Now I am angry and cold. It is a better combination."

"Much."

"God speed with your mission to Geneva. Of course it will fail at once."

"Perhaps."

"Make it fail."

The Vice-President smiled.

"No, I can't quite do that, I'm afraid. But I can swallow my disappointment gracefully when *they* make it fail. Which they will."

"Inevitably," Dr. Freer agreed. His expression changed. "My God," he asked softly. "What if they don't?"

"Then," the Vice-President said grimly, "we're in for it. But I think we can count on them to be as stupid as they have always been in these matters."

"I shall pray for it."

"I shall join you. Now: be good, and mind your doctors, and they'll have you back at the Cape right on time, a week from now."

"Two days," Dr. Freer said calmly, peering out with a serenely confident smile from among his bandages. "Two days only."

"Stuart," he said gently to the pain-filled eyes that stared with a desperate intensity from the Picturephone, "how goes it?"

"Oh," Stu Yule said in such a sad and uncertain voice that the Vice-President felt like crying inside, "pretty good, I guess."

"I hope so," the Vice-President said. "Is Yo-Shin there?"

"She's here," Stu said, and for a moment a gravely beautiful little oriental face appeared next to his, smiled shyly, and vanished. "I guess I couldn't make it . . . if she weren't."

"We know you're going to make it," the Vice-President said. "There's no question of that. You'll walk again and you'll fly again."

"Don't say things like that," Stu said in a voice so low the Vice-President could hardly hear it. "I know I'll walk again . . . somehow. But I . . . but I won't fly."

"What do you mean, won't fly?" the Vice-President demanded. "We're getting to the point very soon, now, you know, where everybody isn't going to have to be a full-fledged astronaut to go out there."

"But that's what I was," Stu said, still very low. "I *was* a—a full-fledged astronaut. What am I now? *What am I now?*"

"You're a very brave man who is going to go right on being brave because we all expect him to and because there isn't anything else he can do and remain true to Stuart Yule, Astronaut. Isn't that right?"

"That's easy to say," Stu Yule said, and suddenly he

gave a heavy sigh, staring somewhere far away. "That's easy to say."

"Have they told you how long they think it will be before you can walk again?"

"A month or so, I guess. My leg"—he gave a sad little smile—"or whatever's left of it—has to heal over, and then I have to be—fitted—and then—then I can try it, I guess. Quite something," he added, and for a second his face threatened to crumple entirely. "Here I've traveled 235,000 miles to the Moon and 235,000 back, and I was hoping someday I could go 60,000,000 to Mars, and 60,000,000 back—and now it's going to take all I've got to—to walk across the room. That's really something, you know, Mr. Vice-President? It's really something."

"Cape security is still trying to find the man who did it and see he gets a good long sentence for it," the Vice-President said. Stu made a weary dismissing gesture with his hand.

"What good would that do? Anyway, they'll never find him. He didn't throw that bomb. The enemies of Piffy One threw it. The climate of that particular moment threw it. Who created the climate? Millions of people."

"Not so many millions," the Vice-President said grimly. "Just a little handful, working in the media and through their friends on the Hill. Of course if you put a bomb in the hands of Percy Mercy or the *Post* or the *Times* and said, 'Here, throw this and tear off the leg of Stuart Yule,' they'd be absolutely horrified. They don't really want violence: they just want the fruits of violence. And maybe if they ever really have to come face-to-face with those, they wouldn't want them either."

"They're insulated," Stu Yule suggested with a wry little smile.

"Wrapped in rationalization until it covers them like a cocoon," the Vice-President agreed. "Remote and smugly safe from the horrors they encourage others to perpetrate ... No, I suppose you're right. Whoever the dupe that threw the bomb may have been, it wouldn't help much to catch him, except as a small example, maybe, to discourage others at his level. It wouldn't get at the people who really did it, the ultimate criminals of our age."

"One of the nurses who has a brother at the Cape was telling me," Stu said with the same wry, almost listless sadness, "that Clete O'Donnell has actually offered a reward to anyone who catches the guy."

"Now, I didn't know that," the Vice-President said. "Then we will find him. And Clete will turn him over to justice. And all the world will worship Clete."

"Who was probably the last link in the chain and the guy who gave him his orders anyway," Stu said. He sighed. "Mr. Vice-President—do you ever just get tired of the world we live in? I mean really, altogether tired?"

"Frequently," the Vice-President agreed. "But then I stop to think about a lot of corny old-fashioned things like—well, like you, for instance. A young man, a brave man, with a lot of his life still before him, who is going to come back strong and continue to devote his life to his country just as he has right along, and continue to help us in the program—"

"How?" Stu Yule asked with a sad skepticism. "What can I do? Really, now, will you stop trying to build up my morale and start being honest with me? I can't do the one thing I've trained for and dreamed about for almost half my life. I can't fly a mission to Mars. And I don't want to stay on the ground. I couldn't take it."

"Plenty of people have," the Vice-President remarked. "They haven't been able to fly, or they have flown already, so they've decided to serve elsewhere." He concluded with a deliberate bluntness: "You've been to the Moon, after all. Stop pitying yourself."

He was delighted to see that Stu Yule for the first time responded with a real animation and a real anger. The dull sadness lifted, he responded with a dangerous snap in his eyes.

"I'm not pitying myself! I'm doing my best to—"

"You're doing your best to sit there and luxuriate in your own misfortune," the Vice-President said sharply. "You aren't doing your best to think about the country or the program and what you can do for them. You're thinking about poor old Stuart Yule and what a tough break he's been handed. All right! It is a tough break! It's damned tough! But you've got more with which to pull out of it than nine tenths of the people in this world. Now, you just stop worrying about what you're going to do or aren't going to do when you get back to duty. First of all, somebody has to be Capsule Communicator for the mission, right? Somebody has to sit there in the control room in Houston and be the ground link with Connie and the boys. That's a pretty big job. This time it's practically next to being on board, it's so important. Do you think you could handle it, Stuart Yule, or shall we let you sit there in a bog of self-pity and get somebody else?"

For a moment Stuart Yule did not reply because he was unable to. Finally he uttered a shaky little laugh.

"I don't want to sit here in a bog of self-pity, I might get wet. Anyway, I'll bet this is all your own kind idea. I'll bet you haven't cleared it with the Astronaut Office."

"I have indeed," the Vice-President said stoutly.

Stuart Yule stared at him solemnly for a moment. Then a little twinkle broke through.

"Things like that aren't official for us guys until we hear them from Hank and Bert."

"I think I can promise you," the Vice-President said, thinking grimly, *By God, they'd better*, "that before the day is out, you will hear it from Hank and Bert."

"Well, thank you," Stu Yule said, still not entirely convinced but no longer, the Vice-President was relieved to note, sunk so desperately deep in sadness. "You are very kind."

"I try to be," the Vice-President said. "It's one of the small fringe benefits of this job. If you are very quiet and unobtrusive about it, so that nobody notices and criticizes you for having an ulterior motive, now and then you *can* be kind. I hope," he added, more lightly, "that at least you're going to wish me bon voyage on my trip to Geneva."

"I'm sure all us in NASA do," Stu said soberly. "There isn't any chance they'll accept, is there? I sure hope to hell not. It would completely destroy the mission. And the program."

"Myself," the Vice-President said, "I don't think they're clever enough. But I am going to go in good faith and make the attempt. Like you, I shall be most dismayed if it succeeds."

"If they should accept," Stu said glumly, "I suppose I'd have to have a little Ivan sitting beside me as CAPCOM."

"Yes, you would. And so on, right down the line."

"*Jesus*," said Stuart Yule. "Whatever got into the President, anyway?"

But to that one, the Vice-President reflected as he ended the conversation with a brief farewell to a now much relieved and much happier Yo-Shin, there was probably no single, clear-cut answer. Politics, pressure, the lingering hope—still lingering, in spite of all these decades of Communist deceit and Communist betrayal, of ruthlessly dashed American hopes and brutally rejected American friendship—that possibly this time, things might be different. He supposed all these elements entered into the decision to send him on this strange, improbable journey, which his own instincts and the instincts of those he valued most among his current associates told him was foredoomed.

He called Hans Sturmer in Huntsville, learned from him that things were humming happily at Marshall Spacecraft Center, received yet another bit of urgent advice to steer clear of the Russians; called Connie at home in Houston, heard about his plans for the first crew meeting scheduled for a couple of hours from now, asked him to pass along to Hank and Bert the idea, which Connie thought a great one, of appointing Stu CAPCOM; and received yet another profane suggestion about what to do with the Russians.

The one person from whom he had not received instructions, he thought ironically as he cleared the last papers from his desk prepared to walk over to the White House to take the helicopter to waiting Air Force 2 at Andrews Air Force Base in nearby Maryland, was the President himself. And he expected, quite accurately as it developed, that no word would come from the Oval Room, not even a farewell handshake at the helicopter.

But the Vice-President, contrary to the by now automatic allegations of his critics, was not a fool. He recognized deliberate strategy when he saw it. He knew he had received his instructions as surely as if they had been written out.

He knew his plane would be followed to Geneva by a rage of indignant editorials, a sneer of nasty broadcasts. He could hear the threnody now: "Does the President deliberately mean to downgrade this desperately important conference, perhaps the most vital in which the United States and the Soviet Union have ever participated?" The wail would be absolutely predictable, a parody of itself.

The Vice-President, who was not normally a vindictive man, thought of their dismay with pleasure. That was exactly what the President intended. He departed on the President's errand a much happier man than he had been when first advised he was to undertake it.

2.

But of course there was no way to transmit this feeling of his to Houston, nor would the Vice-President have done so had one existed. He was not entirely sure of the President—who ever was?—but he thought he understood him. If he was correct, events and the Russians would have to confirm it. He could not risk an open hint even to such trusted and obviously troubled friends as Connie Trasker.

And Connie was troubled, there was no doubt of that. In fact, he thought grimly as he stared out at the crisp green lawn in El Lago, he was damned if he knew how this whole thing was going to go, messed up as it was by the President and everybody else—including, he supposed, himself.

When it had all begun he had been fired up, eager to go, serenely confident of his ability to command and control Earth's most daring challenge yet to the universe. Now it had become so eroded by personalities and politics that he found himself afflicted with an uneasy melancholy, a disturbing self-doubt—not of his technical abilities or of his courage, but of his capacities to weld the mission into the kind of unified, mutually trusting and mutually dependent human organism that it would have to be to successfully accomplish the year and a half round trip to Mars.

Though not customarily given to many regrets or much self-criticism, he found this morning that Perfect Astronaut Conrad H. Trasker was inclined to think perhaps he had been too harsh, too hasty and too arbitrary in some of his statements and actions in the opening days of the controversy that now swirled incessantly around Planetary Fleet One.

Poor old Piffy One had seemed at first to be almost the private preserve of himself and the Astronaut Office. Hank and Bert had encouraged him in this feeling by the very unity with which the three of them had gone about defying Washington, making their own crew selections, giving their critics the defiant gesture, in effect challenging the world to take a flying jump if it didn't like what they did.

It could be, he thought now with a moody sigh, that he and his old buddies had been just a trifle, just a wee trifle, arrogant, ruthless and high-handed—maybe as ruthless, arrogant and high-handed as their critics had told them.

Well, two of their critics were not on the crew, and therein lay probably his major problems. Jazz was half solved, but Jayvee might never be. What then?

It was obvious that for Jazz the pull of the program, the spirit of the corps, his great if unexpressed gratitude that his ambition was finally to be satisfied, were going to be sufficient to bring him back into line. There might still be some lingering reservations, undoubtedly old disappointments and bitternesses would continue to rankle for a while, some things he would never forget and perhaps never forgive. But when the showdown came he had returned to the ranks, issued his statement, put himself irrevocably on NASA's side.

It had been, Connie had to admit, an act of great generosity and quite amazing selflessness, considering how bitterly Jazz had felt about it. It awoke a responsive gratitude and emotion in himself: it was quite conceivable that he and Jazz might end up being real friends before this was over. Certainly he had no doubts whatsoever that he could rely upon him to be an absolutely co-operative and reliable crew member and second in command. Jazz, as he himself had pointed out so acidly a few days ago when this had first begun, was exactly what he said he was: damned good. Now human warmth had finally been injected into the combination. There were no basic worries left where he was concerned.

And then, of course, there was Jayvee. Jayvee was apparently going to keep on playing it sullen and hard to get, right down to the wire. Connie didn't think he would quite dare stay away from crew meeting this morning, because, for one thing, that would really be spiting himself to spite the rest of them. He had to know what the plans were and what was going on. For the sake of his own job and his own safety, he had to be there. But that didn't mean he had to be pleasant about it.

Nor did it mean that he would ever be pleasant about it as long as the mission lasted. Which was endurable, provided that underneath there was some understanding of basic personal responsibility and the overriding needs of the flight. Connie was prepared to deal with sullen mono-syllables for the next two years if he had to, but he was not going to waste time on any deliberate malingering or any real refusal to co-operate with orders and flight plan. Orders in NASA had always been an informal thing, matter of mutual understanding and agreement, because everyone had the same dedication, the same concern for his own safety, and the same goal. Real orders, in a military sense, had almost never been necessary. But Jayvee might conceivably force a situation in which they would be, just to see if he could get away with it. Connie was grimly determined not to put up with this more than once. Four lives and the mission were at stake: there was no possible room for nonsense. The President had said Connie could call on him if necessary, and he would, without hesitation.

In the kitchen he could hear Jane saying good-by to the kids, and the bustling domestic sound made him think with a sigh, as all the astronauts did from time to time, that he really must try to spend more time with them. The pro-gram picked you up and hurled you into the skies. Back home, if it didn't do things to you as a husband, it certainly did as a father. He couldn't count the number of times he had heard the wistful phrase—in the Simulator Building here, in the Simulator Building at the Cape, on field trips to the moonscapes of Arizona and Hawaii, in classroom, in gymnasiums, on speaking trips, at banquets, during parades—"I'm going to try to work it out so I can spend more time with the kids." But few ever managed, so extensive and all-consuming were the demands of the program. And little strangers underfoot rapidly became bigger strangers underfoot, and in due time they would be no longer underfoot, and they would still be strangers.

It created a constant little fretting regret that lived underneath somewhere, one of those things that worried a man but with which he could somehow never quite come to grips.

For himself, he tried to make a point, when he was in Houston, of taking Jane Anne, Sue and Buddy, to the beach, the ball game, picnics, the movies. He tried to make himself available, when he wasn't tied up at the Space Center, to hear small complaints and mediate small battles. He went through the motions as best he knew and as best he could. But always he had that elusive yet harrying sense that they were slipping away from him, that three bright little beings, busy and happy about their own affairs, were running, running, running, away and away and away from him, never to be stayed, never to be recaptured, never to be known again.

"Jane Anne!" he called, his mood lending a little edge of sharpness that he recognized and regretted at once.

"Yes, Daddy?" she called, sounding alarmed. "What is it?"

"Nothing, baby," he called back, trying to cancel the impatient note, passably succeeding. "Aren't you kids going to say good-by to me, too?"

"Yes, we are, Daddy," Sue shouted gleefully, running in and throwing herself into his arms.

"Yes, we are!" Jane Anne and Buddy echoed, swarming over him too until in a second they were a laughing tumble of arms and legs and kisses and hugs.

But in another second, as abruptly and as swiftly, the birds had flown again, they were racing out the door, it slammed, the house was instantly still, echoing and re-echoing with a bittersweet, regretful silence.

"Where do they go?" he asked Jane, almost stupidly, when she came to the door, and for a second they looked at one another with a sudden sadness, suspended and helpless before the relentless, incessant assault of the irrevocable, unyielding years.

"School," she said with a wistful little smile, her eyes suddenly bright with a touch of tears. "And then college—"

"And then the world and then marriage—and then good-by." He sighed heavily. "Too fast—too fast, Janie."

"I'll have your breakfast ready in a couple of minutes," she said gently. "Take your time."

"Thanks," he said, turning back to stare out, not too clearly, at the placid lawn again. "Thanks for everything."

And that was really what he meant, too: thanks for

everything. Thanks for being a good wife and thanks for being a good mother; thanks for being a good bride, a good helpmeet, a good partner and a good companion along the way; thanks for taking care of, looking after, putting up with, loving, tolerating, suffering ,enduring, Conrad H. Trasker, dashing young man about space.

How was it, then, he wondered gloomily, that he could even now, along with all his other worries and problems revolving around Piffy One, be idly, and not so idly, contemplating the very real possibility that he might be drifting into an affair with the wife of his biggest headache? It didn't make sense.

But of course it didn't have to.

He had learned in an observant and reasonably active life that such things never did make sense, really. There was no sense in certain areas of living, and that was one of the most nonsensical of them all. But it was fiendishly clever. It immediately gathered around it a mass of rationalizations and intellectual acrobatics that passed for sense, and that were very comforting in replying to the bothersome carpings of moral responsibility. You could forget very quickly that they really weren't sense. They were just the Great Excuse, which soon became the Great Reality.

And they were powerfully strong when allied to something as powerfully strong as the physical urge. They could provide full-formed a whole philosophy and a whole program for action, instantaneous in conception, overwhelming in logic, ruthless in execution. They could be, and often were, unbeatable.

And what did he have with which to hold them off? Jane—the family—the program—and the innate common sense which told him—if he could listen—that these were more important by far than anything to be gained on the other side.

Not that he was worried about consequences, of course: who, among the daring, ever is? Consequences were not the issue. The dashing young man about space had dashed before, on occasion, as had some others in the corps. But he had not dashed very long or very far, and never in his own backyard. Traveling the world in triumph after an Apollo, relaxing along the Strip at Cocoa Beach, things had happened now and then, as quick-flashing as desire, as quick-dying as dreams. One or two had left a lingering affection, a lingering regret: the rest, for all they meant to him, had never been. And never had they occurred in Houston, for there he drew a line that was not always drawn by some of his colleagues. And certainly never had they occurred within the corps itself.

But, said the voice he wanted to hear, *Monetta is different.*

And that is why, said the voice he didn't want to hear, *you had damned well better stay clear, buster.*

No, said the first voice, *she really is. It isn't just physical, though right now she herself seems to think it is. Because she isn't beautiful, exactly, though she has an inner serenity and strength and dignity that make her beautiful. It's more her personality. She has character.*

Ummhmm, said the other voice. *Oh, yes, sure. Don't they all, when you want them? They have to, don't they, for the sake of your own self-respect? Connie Trasker, Perfect Astronaut, couldn't settle for less. Connie Trasker, P.A., couldn't consider them otherwise. That wouldn't fit his concept of Connie Trasker, P.A.*

Oh, I don't know, said the first voice. *Connie Trasker isn't all that perfect. Connie Trasker has played catch-as catch-can on occasion. Connie Trasker isn't as particular as all that.*

Aha! said the other voice. *But Monetta is different. You said so yourself.*

Stop trying to trap me, said the first voice. *I know what I'm doing.*

Yeah? inquired the other voice. *You sure as hell sound like it, pal. You really sure as hell do.*

Oh, cut it out, the first voice said. *Stop trying to get me all confused. I've got a crew meeting to conduct in forty-five minutes and a mission to plan. I can't be bothered with all this crap. Leave me alone. I'll do what I think best. You all don't have to keep after me.*

All? said the other voice. *All? Who's "all"?*

Just everybody, said the first voice. *Just everybody. And everything. And I've got it all on my shoulders, and I just can't—can't—can't be bothered with—with this kind of stuff.*

That's what we're saying, the other voice pointed out. *Why complicate things? Haven't you got enough problems? Most people would have quite enough to do with crew meeting in forty-five minutes, mission to plan, Jane,*

kids, program, image, Connie Trasker, Perfect Astronaut—
Perfect Astronaut—Perfect Astronaut—Perfect Astro-
naut—

"For Christ's sake!" he said aloud. "God damn it!"

"What did you say, Con?" Jane called from the kitch-
en. "Were you calling me? Did you want something?"

"No," he called back. "Not really. How's breakfast coming?"

"You can sit down. It's almost ready."

"Good," he said, managing to sound casual as he
walked down the hall and into the breakfast nook. "I'm
starved."

"Got to get up your strength for that meeting," she said
cheerfully, putting the coffeepot and toaster on the table.

"Got to get up my strength for a lot of things, Janie,"
he said with a quite successful smile. "A lot of things."

But the first and most important, of course, was the
crew meeting, and as he drove swiftly toward it through
the bright spring morning he found his thoughts gradually
calming, gradually rearranging themselves into the pattern
of carefully managed foresight and intelligent anticipation
that would be his really dominant and overriding mood
from now to launch, and beyond. Other things might ebb
or flow, grow in importance or diminish, but essentially
nothing would be more important to him than the care
and feeding of Piffy One. Beleaguered the mission might
be, surrounded by enough human problems and difficulties
to founder a hundred projects, but it was his job to get it
on the track and make it move.

His self-doubts of an hour ago seemed to diminish
rapidly and steadily as he turned in the gate, waved to the
sentry and drove on toward the astronauts' parking lot. By
the time he had placed the Porsche neatly in alongside
Bob Curtis' Stingray and Roger Webb's Corvette, he had
almost persuaded himself that he was invincible. Except,
of course, that he knew with a wry little inward smile that
he was not.

Nonetheless, nobody would have guessed it to see him
enter the building just as Tom Andretti and Allan Samson
converged upon it from the other side of the parking lot.

"There he comes," Tom called out cheerfully. "Ta-da-
da-da!"

"Our hero," Al agreed, opening the door with an elaborate bow. "All aboard for Mars, Alpha Centauri and the outer galaxies! Make way, Earthlings! The King of Space approaches!"

"Do you get paid for that?" Connie inquired. "Do you mean NASA actually compensates you for that kind of—"

He broke off with a thoughtful frown. "But on second thought, I guess *somebody* has to provide the laughs. Probably it's worth it to have a couple of house clowns."

"We aren't the only ones," Tom remarked.

"But with us," Al said, "it's official." He gave Connie a sudden poke in the arm. "How're you doing, buddy? All ready for the big push?"

"I'm reasonably calm at the moment," Connie said as they approached the elevator, "but don't talk about it. I may get queasy and have to reach for my oops-bag."

"That'll be the day," Tom Andretti said dryly. "When Connie Trasker—"

"Everybody's hero," Al said respectfully.

"—let's a mission get him up-tight. Buck up, my boy! We *believe* in you!"

"You two jokers," Connie said as they stepped in. "You're really something."

"Hey!" someone shouted just as the door closed irrevocably; and, startled, they saw that it was Jazz, hurrying to catch up. Just behind him was Jayvee.

"Well, well," Tom said softly into the silence as they started to ascend to the third floor. "That should be an interesting little cageful."

"Let's wait and take bets at the top on who comes out alive," Al suggested.

"I'll take Jazz," Tom said promptly. "Then old Connie's problems will be automatically cut in half."

"I'll take Jayvee," Al said. "He's a much nastier son of a bitch. I didn't used to think so when I first came in the program, but I do now."

"Let's hope they both come out alive," Connie said, "because I don't want any more problems than I have already, thanks."

"We shall see," Tom said solemnly, stepping out first as the door opened. "Your Majesty, tarry a moment. We shall see which of yon felons—too bad!" he said as the other elevator arrived and Jazz and Jayvee stepped out, carefully looking as though they weren't together but otherwise unruffled. "Nobody hurt."

276

"Pity!" Al murmured.

"You guys get along or I'll report you to Hank and Bert and have them put you on bread and water," Connie said.

"Good luck," Tom said fervently.

"Good *luck*," Al agreed.

"Good morning, Jazz," Connie said easily as his two junior funsters gave him a couple of jovial farewell jostlings and walked off down the corridor toward their own offices. "Good morning, Jayvee. Seen Pete?"

"No, I haven't," Jazz said. Jayvee said nothing.

"He's probably already in my office," Connie said. "Why don't you two go on along to the room. They've got it set up for us. We'll join you in a minute."

"Roger," Jazz said. Jayvee said nothing.

But he went when Jazz did, and watching them walk off, stiff and unyielding like a couple of cats about to jump one another, Connie opened his door with a little sigh and went in. As he had expected, the one crew member he was sure of greeted him with an amiable if somewhat shadowed grin.

"You're worried," Pete said with the intuition of affection that doesn't hesitate to express itself. "What's the matter?"

"Two distinguished and able astronauts," Connie said, beginning to riffle quickly through his mail and messages, "have just arrived on their way to the briefing rooms: friends, brothers, comrades, lovers—"

"Hey!" Pete said cheerfully. "That's for us."

"Not this trip," Connie said matter-of-factly, wondering for a second why he had not thought of this along with his other problems a while ago, and deciding because it wasn't a problem: being, as it was, under such firm control. But he found himself softening his response with a concerned, attentive glance. "You look a little peaked yourself. What's the matter? Still brooding about that demotion?"

"Yes," Pete said soberly, "I am. I really am unhappy as hell about it, Conn. *I'm* commander of that Medico-Scientific Module." He spoke with a rare bitterness: "That black bastard isn't."

"Oh, yes, he is. By order of the Commander-in-Chief. And that, my boy, is an order that is an order."

"But why?" Pete demanded angrily. "What have I done to deserve the short end of the stick all of a sudden?"

"Just got yourself born the wrong color, that's all," Connie said, sitting down for a moment to peruse his mail in greater detail.

"Us Greeks are dark as hell," Pete said with a rather rueful return of his grin. "All over . . . anyway, I think it's a damned unfair shame."

"So do I," Connie agreed, "but I'm not in much position to do anything about it. Nor, laddie, are you. So I'd suggest a stiff upper lip and make the best of it."

"But I've got to share that damned capsule with him *eighteen months,*" Pete said, his tone dejected again.

"Have fun," Connie suggested. "Match skin-tones."

Pete laughed right out loud, a genuinely amused sound.

"That'd be the day. That would really be the day . . . You don't think maybe the decision can be changed somewhere along the line before we go—?"

"If it can be," Connie promised, "I'll do it and you know it. But if he behaves himself and co-operates there won't be any grounds for it that I can see."

"That's fine," Pete said with a sudden renewed bitterness. "That's just fine. As if poor old Piffy One doesn't have enough troubles without getting me all upset too. How'm I supposed to feel now?"

"Just like me," Connie said. "Damned annoyed—damned tired—and damned responsible. Come on," he said in a businesslike tone, standing up abruptly, getting a firm grip on a handful of curly black hair and pulling Pete to his feet with it. "Our soulmates are waiting. Let's get on down to the training room and have at it."

"Ouch!" Pete said, slapping his hair into place again with a hasty hand as they went out the door. "That's real."

"So's Piffy One," Connie said. "All too."

And as they walked together down the corridor, seeming almost to carry about them a presence and a light larger than life, a glow that to the watching secretaries and their envious fellow-astronauts did almost seem golden, he realized that he wasn't kidding in even the remotest way. Piffy One *was* real, and suddenly—here she was.

He took a deep breath as they approached the training room door, pulled it open quickly, gestured Pete in and closed it firmly behind them. Two pairs of uncommunicative and wary eyes stared up at them in a silence that immediately became as heavy and oppressive as though it were a stifling, implacable tarpaulin actually weighing down upon them all.

Without speaking he took his place at the head of the table while Pete started to take his alongside Jazz, hesitated (*Don't do that*, Connie ordered sternly in his mind, but of course Pete couldn't help it) and then sat down beside Jayvee. For just a second a dry, ironic gleam came into Jayvee's eyes. Then it passed.

"Gentlemen," Connie said, sitting back and letting a level gaze travel across them one by one. "I give you Planetary Fleet One, Project Argosy. Here she begins and here she stands or falls . . .

"I've asked for this room," he said slowly, "and I've asked us to have this meeting, because this is where we make it or break it. If Piffy One goes or doesn't go, she goes or doesn't go right here in this room—right here in us, in these four minds and these four hearts and these four personalities which seem to have come to this point"—his tone filled with an rionic dryness of his own—"through rather strange and divergent paths. But: here we are. And here we are, for better or worse, until touchdown, two years, and two months, from today . . .

"Now, what we do with that time is pretty much up to us, because NASA, as you know, exercises a rather light hand once a mission has been assigned. Jazz knows this and I know it, but it's new to you two, so that's why I'm spelling it out. How much time you study, how much time you concentrate, how much time you spend in the simulators or the gym or whatever—over and beyond what anybody would consider the reasonable norm, that is—is up to us. We'll have some field trips, of course, to Alaska and Hawaii for simulated surface work, probably to Antarctica for isolation duty, probably Space Station *Mayflower*—and we will have regular crew meetings to review things, whenever I consider them necessary—or for that matter," he added smoothly as Jazz shifted ever so slightly in his chair, "whenever any of us considers them necessary. Don't hesitate to call one if you want one. We're all in this together.

"Which leads to another thing: I'm commander because somebody has to be, but that, too, is fairly flexible—at least up to the point when we actually take off. After that, things will get tighter, because out there, somebody's really ly got to be in charge.

279

"For that," he said simply, but with a certain steel entering his voice, "I have been selected. It is my responsibility—and I shall discharge it—and if anybody has any objections, or wants to modify it in any way, the time and place to do it is while we're on the ground. We've got to understand very clearly that once we're up, I'm the guy—within reason, of course, in all normal contingencies. But if we get into a real emergency, which I hope to God we won't, then there won't be time to question. Obedience to orders will have to be instinctive and instantaneous if we're to come out alive. I hope I can rely on you for that. I hope we can all rely on each other for that—and for everything else we have to face. Because by God, we're going to have to . . .

"There," he said, and he turned toward the spectacular photograph taken by Viking II from 9000 miles out, blown up and shimmering before them against the blackboard, "is Mars . . ."

His voice became soft and he repeated with an intonation that moved even Jayvee,

"There is Mars . . ." and for a few seconds said no more, while they all turned and looked at it, finally seeing it as they had never seen it before, the sheer enormity of what they were going to attempt at last striking home to them all.

"You know, it's a funny thing," he resumed presently. "The second time somebody lands there, the world is going to say, 'Oh, hell, they're on Mars again,' and shrug, and go about its business. But they won't say that for us. And it won't be like that for us . . . Look at that baby!" he said in a hushed and wondering tone. "Just *look* at her! . . . Mars . . . and it's up to us. Just—us . . .

"Jazz," he said, breaking the mood deliberately with a brisk and businesslike tone, "you're well checked out on your job, I guess, which is essentially to backstop me, assist with training programs and flight plans and be thoroughly familiar with everything I'm thoroughly familiar with. I guess you already are, to a considerable extent, right?"

"I have the drill pretty well in mind, I think," Jazz agreed. His voice edged a little almost in spite of himself. "I've had plenty of time to think about it."

"That's right," Connie said calmly. "Jayvee and Pete—you can probably tell Jazz and me more than we can tell you about what your duties are going to be. We're not scientific and doctor types like you are. Enlighten us."

"Is that an order?" Pete asked with a smile, as Jayvee made no response other than an uneasy shifting in his chair.

"Official," Connie said.

"And endorsed by No. 2," Jazz said. "You guys live in a world of mystery to us technical types. Tell us about it."

"Well—" Pete began. Then he hesitated. "I'm not commanding the MSM," he said quietly. "Maybe Jayvee ought to talk."

"We're asking," Jazz said shortly, and he looked at Jayvee with an expression that prompted Connie to lean forward and intervene in a tone unhurried but firm.

"Now, right there is where we watch it, Jazz, if you don't mind. As I said before, we happen to have arrived here by various routes and for various reasons. But we *are* here, and for the sake of the mission this is where it's got to begin. Not yesterday or last week or ten days ago or ten years ago, but right—now. So let's don't look back and let's don't get into a lot of things that are better left untouched. Let's move on. All right?"

"Well, then, let him say something, God damn it!" Jazz said angrily, glaring across the table at Jayvee who still, though with some difficulty now, remained impassive. "He's not inarticulate and he's not a fool. He can speak! Let him do it!"

"Yes, Jayvee," Connie said quietly. "It seems a reasonable request. If you have a gripe, let's have it right now, because after this—no more. Not ever. So come on. We're waiting."

For a long moment no one moved and no one spoke. The crew of Piffy One stared at one another with a moody and relentless tension that twisted them all like a giant hand. Finally Jayvee spoke in a thick and difficult voice that at least sounded unhappy, Connie recognized with an instantaneous perception: at least Jayvee was conceding that it wasn't easy for him, either. That was possibly something gained.

"I'm not here," he said slowly, "for you-all to sit in judgment on me. I'm not here to be lectured like a schoolboy. I'm not here to take crap I stopped taking when I was—when I was"—his voice trembled, some violent inner crisis or memory ravaged his handsome face for a second—"sixteen, maybe. I'm here to do my job on this mission and that's all. Hear me? That's all!"

"All right," Connie said, still quietly. "That's all we're asking you to do."

"No, it isn't," Jayvee said, his eyes as tortured as his voice. "You're asking a lot more than that. It isn't enough for me just to do my job. You-all won't be satisfied with that. You're asking me to respect you. You're asking me to like you. *You're asking me to love you,* because we're all part of the same crew and people like you just can't stand not being loved. I can't satisfy you just doing my job, I've got to love you, too. Well," he said, still thick and still unhappy. "I won't, hear me? I won't. I'll do my job but I won't love you. Not ever."

"Christ!" Jazz said in a disgusted tone into the silence that followed. "An amateur psychologist, yet."

"No," Connie said soberly. "Maybe he has a point."

" 'No,' " Jayvee mimicked, 'maybe he has a point.' Yes, maybe I do. Just maybe I do!"

"All right," Pete said with a sudden sharpness, pushing his chair away from Jayvee with an abrupt angry motion, sounding as rough as Jazz. "Are *we* supposed to love *you?*"

"You don't have to love me," Jayvee said. "You can respect me—"

"Why?" Pete demanded angrily. "You've just told us you don't respect us, you don't like us, you don't love us, you hate us. Why should we do anything for you? Just why, now?"

Jayvee spoke almost in a whisper, so low they could hardly hear him.

"Because you have the bigger debt to pay."

"Crap!" Pete said flatly. "What debt do I have to pay? My dad came to Florida from Mykonos forty years ago." He too lowered his voice and with a most uncharacteristic venom spat out the words: "What debt do *I* owe *you?*"

"The debt of being white," Jazz said with a harsh, disgusted laugh, looking deliberately away at the haunting blow-up of their mysterious objective, ghostly and elusive. *"That's* the debt, and what place that crap has on a mission to Mars, I can't see. Look here, Jayvee!" he said, swinging back and leaning forward as far as he could across the table, slapping the flat of his right hand hard upon it. "You and I both got on this crew through outside pressure, baby, and don't you forget it. Just because being black put you here doesn't mean it will keep you here or make you a crew member fit to fly with the rest of us. We're both damned lucky to be here, and you remember that. And get this too, buddy: maybe we don't *like* you. And maybe we don't *respect* you. And maybe we don't *love* you. But we've sure as hell got to know that we can depend on you—and rely on you—and trust you—and know that you'll be there when we need you. Hell!" He hit the table again with his hand, a sharp, unyielding crack. "I don't give a good God damn what you think of me, but when I'm out there and I'm relying on you to do something, buster, *you do it.* O.K.?"

Again there was a prolonged silence while the crew of Piffy One, that glamorous body of men who were the envy of their colleagues and the cynosure of all, stared at one another across many chasms, peering with a curious bemusement out of their own personal agony that the world knew nothing of.

Finally Jayvee spoke.

"Our experiments in the Medico-Scientific-Module," he said in a flat, almost monotonous voice, "will be directed basically, I believe, toward ascertaining much the same broad scientific and medical spectra as those first conducted on the Moon. In addition to a number of tests to analyze atmospheric conditions and basic gravity, we will also be concerned, of course, with the possibilities"—he sighed, ever so softly, and went on—"with the possibilities of establishing and maintaining some of the simpler life-forms over a feasible period of time, say until the next landing, until Piffy Two. For these, we will be taking equipment of a suitable nature which—"

Twenty minutes later—a strange twenty minutes, Connie thought, perhaps the strangest he had ever spent or hoped to spend, a sort of time-capsule suspended somewhere without feeling or emotion, completely empty, completely drained, and finally, at last, really concerned with the needs of the mission—the flat, competent voice stopped and silence again enwrapped them. He was determined not to let it grow and spoke into it at once in a matter-of-fact, concluding tone.

"Very good," he said quietly. "Thank you very much, Jayvee. That gives us a very thorough picture of what you two will be doing and we appreciate it. It will help us a great deal to help you and that's the most important thing. Petros?"

Pete shook his head.

"Nothing to add." He hesitated. Then he said one of the hardest things he had ever said, not really sure he meant it but sure it was the right thing to say at that moment. "Maybe the right decision has been made. Maybe the right guy is commander of the MSM, after all."

For a startled second Jayvee looked at him with some unfathomable, almost unbearable emotion. Then the mask came down again.

"Thank you very much, Pete," Connie said quietly. "That—I hope—will be the spirit of Piffy One."

He glanced at his watch and stood up.

"O.K., Jazz," he said briskly. "Why don't you come on back to the office with me and we'll do some more work on the training schedule. You two, fan out, if you want to, and do whatever doctors and scientists do until 1500 this afternoon. Then let's regroup and by that time Jazz and I should have our timetable lined out on field trips, simulator duty, and so on. O.K.?"

And when they met again at three, after a long, arduous but profitable session that ran straight on through lunch, and in which he and Jazz got the over-all framework fairly well blocked out, he was pleased to find that the other two had been busy also and that their plans were coming along in good shape and apparent co-operation if not amity. Amity aboard his flight was something he had given up hoping for this morning, but he would be glad to settle for impersonal competence, as long as it was impersonal and as long as it was competence.

When they took their plans to Bob Hertz in a day or so, and to everyone else who had to get into the act before a mission could be formalized, he wanted it to be a unanimous presentation with a united front and no emotionalism. He saw just a faint glimmer of hope for this, as Piffy One's first day drew to a close—providing, of course, the world would now leave them alone.

Of this, he was not too sanguine; a doubt the tiny satellite, still whirling faithfully above, might yet confirm.

3.

Yet for a few days—actually for the next two weeks, while the Vice-President's mission went forward in Geneva with great fanfare, no obvious frictions, and no real accomplishment that anyone could see—things appeared to be moving with a reasonable speed and efficiency throughout NASA. Or so it seemed to Andy Anderson, as he completed the first of the progress reviews he intended to conduct periodically until Piffy One had completed its mission and was safely home again.

Considering all the problems that had surrounded the project from its inception, the Administrator was satisfied that things were proceeding about as well as anyone had a right to hope. There were still some vague hints in the media of discontent within the crew, but Connie had managed to clamp the lid on pretty well and not even Jayvee had so far violated what Dr. Anderson knew to be a fragile truce at best. How long this would last no one could say—Connie in their several private conversations had been extremely cautious about any long-range predictions—but while it did it was that much gained.

On the scientific side, the brothers Hertz were working together with a single-mindedness that both delighted and amused the Administrator. He had never had the slightest doubt that they would, but he knew there was just enough jealousy of the latest drama in the manned space program, at JPL and the other scientific centers, so that there could have been a certain amount of bickering and some more or less deliberate delays. Nothing of the sort had occurred. Vernon Hertz was apparently satisfied with his part in getting Jayvee on the crew—or if he wasn't satisfied, Dr. Anderson thought with some irony, at least he was stuck with it and had to pretend he was satisfied—and now he was snapping the reports, studies, analyses and projections out of Pasadena so fast that Houston was swamped with them. And as for Bob, Andy reflected with a smile, he was back in his heaven now that he had the biggest launch of them all to worry about. In his shop, too, the pressure was on and the word was out to move and move fast. The Mars trajectories that had orginally been planned back in the late sixties and early seventies when Chris Kraft was Director of Flight Operations had already been substantially revised by Bob and his staff in accordance with the new target time and the conditions that would prevail in the galaxy on that date. Much remained to be done, both in the scientific preparations for the flight at JPL, Ames, Goddard and the rest, and in the plotting of trajectories, emergency abort plans and all the other educated guessing that had to be done in Houston before a flight plan could be finalized. But with great harmony and enthusiasm the Hertzes were going about it. The Administrator knew he could rest easy on that score.

In Huntsville, Hans Sturmer and the Peenemündians were happy as little clams, to hear Hans tell it, as he did several times a day via Picturephone. There, too, there were no substantial worries. All the hard work and careful preparations of the decades past were paying off, everybody was fired with a new enthusiasm, Andy Anderson could almost hear them singing, "Hi, ho! Hi, ho!" as they rollicked and frolicked off to work. Or such was the mental picture conjured up by Hans' frequent bubbling reports: reports which sounded a little smug and self-satisfied, but which Dr. Anderson knew were justified by the progress achieved. The achievements of Apollo, Apollo Applications and *Mayflower* made it a relatively simple matter to calculate the necessary changes in the launch vehicles and the modules. They would be on paper, Dr. Sturmer felt, within the month. Then it would be up to the prime and subcontractors to produce the vehicles—Huntsville would supervise their testing at the Mississippi Test Range —final corrections would be made—and they would be ready to fly.

"Two months from now, in a dream world," Dr. Sturmer said cheerfully. "Eight, if we simply must wait for North American Rockwell and the others to get busy."

"Oh, they're busy," Dr. Anderson responded. "I've been out already, and I've seen them."

And so he had, a personal inspection trip which had taken him to Grumman on Long Island, where the Mars Landing Module was being constructed; to IBM in Huntsville, where the instrument unit that controlled the infinitely complex life of the Saturn V was assembled; to Boeing in Seattle where portions of the Saturn were manufactured; and finally to North American Rockwell in Downey, California, where the command module and the third stage of the Saturn were produced.

He had found a universal mood of determination and drive, a releasing and rechanneling of energies that had genuinely thrilled him. Only from Jim Matthison had he received any indications of doubt or inkling of possible trouble. Somewhat more guardedly than he had expressed himself to the Vice-President, Jim had confided to Dr. Anderson, too, his worries about possible dangers in a crash program after so long and deliberate a national slowdown. He had warned that speed might produce sloppy workmanship, though everything humanly possible would be done to prevent it. And he had raised with Andy also the thought of sabotage, and the enigmatic and peculiarly elusive character of Clete O'Donnell.

To the thought of inadequate workmanship, the Administrator had responded with a hearty confidence that all such problems could be solved as they always had been in the program, by vigilance, care and dedication. To the thought of possible sabotage he had responded not quite so confidently, for there of course the program had always been vulnerable and vigilance had succeeded because it was accompanied by a genuine loyalty on the part of the great majority of workers and administrators. As for Clete O'Donnell, after a few moments Jim talked more freely and Andy discovered that they shared a common worry with the Vice-President.

"About all I can say, though," he told Jim, "is that things seem to be proceeding quite smoothly at the Cape now. Apparently it was just a—just a—" He hesitated and Jim supplied the words.

"Show of strength? Or warning?"

"Both, I suppose."

"The Vice-President thinks he'll act up again if the conference fails in Geneva."

"Quite possibly. Does he have any affiliated unions here?"

"No," Jim Matthison said. "But," he added soberly, "he may have affiliated friends."

"Yes," Andy agreed. "Well. About all we can do is be vigilant, I suppose. And keep an eye on him."

"You won't get much done at the Federal level," Jim remarked. "Too many friends, up there."

"We'll see," the Administrator said. "I'll raise the question."

"Good luck," Jim Matthison said dryly. "You'll need it."

"May be," Andy Anderson said thoughtfully. "May be."

He had found much the same skepticism when he had gone on from Downey to the Cape, arriving there the day after Dr. Freer came back, not quite as soon as he had predicted, in an ambulance from Orlando. The old man was in his office, having traveled there by ambulance also, and although he looked pale and a little shaky and still wore a rather horrifying bandage swathed around his head, there was no doubt that he was back on the job and in full command of his domain once more.

"Andy," he said, holding out his hand. "How nice to see you. You will forgive me if I don't get up."

"I think I probably will, yes," the Administrator agreed with a smile. "How are you, Old Unsinkable?"

"I'm all right," Albrecht Freer said. "I tire, I get a little dizzy now and then, but I do not surrender. I fight it. And I win. And every day I improve, so"—he shrugged—"all is well. How do you find things in NASA?"

"Very good, on the whole," Dr. Anderson said. "I am very pleased, really. You know Huntsville, of course: they're buzzing. You know the industry: it's humming. You know Houston: they're clicking as smoothly as their computers—I think."

Dr. Freer nodded.

"Ja. I can imagine Connie clicking with certain people on his crew."

"They'll be here before long and you can judge for yourself," Andy Anderson said. "Hopefully," he added with a wry little smile, "they will still be together by then. How are things at Pad C?"

"I have not been out since I got back," Al Freer said. "When I heard you were coming I decided to wait. Come, give me your arm. My ambulance is ready. We will go right now."

"But I thought you couldn't get up—"

"My doctors think I am crazy," Dr. Freer said complacently. "Come."

"Fine," Dr. Anderson said with a laugh. "I wanted to take a look anyway, and no better company. Is it safe?"

Dr. Freer gave a disgusted snort.

"They tell me it is a picnic out there. Simply a picnic. They sing hymns to NASA every morning and pray for Piffy One every night. Did we ever have trouble here? What gave you that idea?"

"Nonetheless," Andy Anderson said as they took the elevator down, "I think you should be very sure that all security precautions are at the maximum. I don't trust these smiling faces any more."

"We are very aware," Al Freer said, moving slowly, leaning heavily on Andy's arm but apparently feeling a steadily increasing strength. "Orders are in effect, the guards are armed and alert, we have enough at the site now to handle most things, I believe. But you will see. All is brotherhood and co-operation."

"Pending the outcome in Geneva," Dr. Anderson suggested dryly.

"A typical blind and reactionary comment," Dr. Freer told him as they reached the ambulance, "which will do you no good in truly enlightened and progressive circles. However," he added quietly as they got in and came into the driver's hearing, "we hope we will be ready for what we think we can expect."

"Good," the Administrator replied, taking his seat in front while Dr. Freer lay down in back; and said no more until they reached the pad.

But he thought a good deal, as they rode along in amicable silence, out past the VAB and on out to Launch Complex 39. It was another steamy day, thunderheads climbed high from the Bahamas, Florida's somnolent summer peace was already beginning to hold the natural world. In contrast to his last visit six months ago, however, there was a marked increase in human activity. A steady procession of trucks and cars shuttled back and forth along the road beside the crawler track. An air of purposeful bustle accompanied their busy parade.

A sudden pride, a sudden excitement, a sudden sense of achievement and accomplishment he had not known for a long time, struck him so forcefully that he could actually feel the hairs on the back of his neck begin to rise.

In imagination he could see three great white monsters standing against the cold blue sky of December. Liquid oxygen floated in gentle white trails around their sides, and over loudspeakers important voices boomed. There was a mounting excitement in the firing room, a mounting tension at the press and VIP sites. The moment was near.

Abruptly Piffy One was reality at last, never to leave him until the great dream was accomplished.

Al Freer chuckled and gave his arm a nudge.

"You see them, now," he said. "I was watching your face. I saw you see them."

"Yes," Dr. Anderson said softly. "I see them. They will go, Al. *They will go.*"

"Oh, yes," Al Freer said calmly. "Anything else would be—unacceptable . . . Come now," he said, a certain dryness entering his tone. "We are here. Let us alight and receive my hero's welcome."

And sure enough, when he got out slowly and moved forward, again on the Administrator's arm, the sight of his white-bandaged head and still-erect old figure produced a magical change in the busy scene surrounding Pad C. There was a shout of, "There he is! There's the Old Man!" and with joyful cries shovels, tools and work-gear were flung down, work was abandoned, two or three hundred happily excited men crowded around, slapping his back, shaking his hand in warm, affectionate greeting. For just a second his eye caught Andy's with a dry, ironic gleam. Then he was hoisted swiftly but gently onto one of the flat-bed trucks. A respectful hush fell.

"Thank you, my friends," he said calmly into the silence, broken only by the scream of a gull flying by on some urgent private business. "It is good to be back, and it is good to see you all at work with such enthusiasm on our new Pad C." The ironic gleam returned but they could not see it. "You have made great progress since I was here last. It is a fine sight for an old man to see. Many of you," he went on, as more trucks drew up and more men came running to join the friendly, encouraging crowd, "have probably never met our Administrator of NASA in Washington, Dr. Anderson. Andy—" He gestured, and quickly Dr. Anderson was assisted onto the truck to stand beside him. "Perhaps Dr. Anderson would like to say something to you also, if you would like to hear him."

There was a cheer, hearty, quickly stilled. The silence returned, attentive now, and a little wary.

"I too," Andy said, "would like to join Dr. Freer in congratulating you on the progress you have made since he was"—he hesitated deliberately and then went on— "last here. It is a fine tribute to the spirit we hope will continue to prevail here at the Cape from now until the day the job is done.

"And done," he said quietly, "it will be. We in NASA are determined to see it through—on the timetable we have set—to achieve the goal we have established. I know you all join us in that determination.

"On behalf of the program, and more particularly on behalf of the four men who will fly the mission, I bring you greetings from Planetary Fleet One, Project Argosy, and I wish you well in your work on this pad—this very spot—from which one of its three units will be launched eight months from now. Here on this actual ground from which these enormous forces will be let loose in flame and smoke and frightful thunder to take our men to Mars, I say to you—long live Piffy One!"

And, "Long live Piffy One!" they dutifully echoed, with cheers and shouts and fine, companionable laughter, as he and Dr. Freer were helped down from the truck and escorted cordially back to the ambulance.

As they drew away to the sound of a last, prolonged cheer, Dr. Freer permitted himself just one short, eloquent, sound.

"Ha!" he said, and was silent until they arrived back at the administration building. There his secretary told them with some excitement that Clete O'Donnell was on the Picturephone.

"Al!" Clete exclaimed, not even pausing in his haste to speak to Dr. Anderson. "My good friend! The boys just phoned and told me what a fine thing you did. That was magnificent, Al! That was simply magnificent!"

"I am glad you approve," Dr. Freer said with a noticeable dryness. But Clete was not to be discouraged in his buoyant, boyish happiness.

"It was *wonderful*. It's done so much for morale—I could tell it in the way the boys talked about it. They thought it was just grand, your coming out and talking to them like that. And you too, Dr. Anderson," he added, finally acknowledging the Administrator's presence. "Both of you," he said in an admiring tone, "really know how to get the best out of your workers, all right."

"Better that than get the worst out of them," the Administrator remarked.

"What's that?" Clete asked with a politely puzzled smile. "I don't get it."

"Oh, I think you do," Dr. Anderson said.

"I—really," Clete said, and he gave a baffled little laugh. "I don't know what you're talking about."

"It has to do," Dr. Freer said calmly, "with bombs."

"Bombs?" Clete repeated, still baffled, still wondering. Then illumination came. "Oh!" he said. "You mean you think I—Al, how could you? You know I issued a statement after that unfortunate episode, condemning it and deploring any such use of violence." He shrugged. "After all, you know—it wasn't I who provoked a crisis. It was intended to be just a peaceful protest, until you and poor Stuart Yule got into it. How is poor Stu, by the way?"

"He is recovering," Dr. Anderson said coldly. "Why don't you stop by and see him if you're going to be anywhere near Orlando?"

"You know, I might just do that," Clete said with a pleased smile at the thought. "I just might."

"You are disgusting," Albrecht Freer said and deliberately turned his back and began going through the papers on his desk.

At this the mask dropped for a moment and an expression cold, venomous, vicious, passed briefly across Clete's open, sincere, patriotic face.

"I hope," he snapped, "we will have no more trouble with you, old man!"

"You will have just as much trouble as you ask for," Dr. Anderson said evenly, "and that's a promise. So be advised."

Many things, none of them pleasant, gleamed briefly in the face before him. Then Clete relaxed and smiled in a comfortable, almost pitying way.

"I don't anticipate any more trouble. I think everything is going to work out all right."

"It had better."

"Oh, I'm sure it will," Clete said confidently. "When the Geneva Space Accord is signed and we begin real co-operation with the Russians, everything will go like clock-work. You'll see."

"I don't know anything about any 'Geneva Space Accord,'" Andy Anderson said, "but I do know work at the Cape is going to proceed right on schedule, no matter what happens elsewhere."

"Are you sure?" Clete asked with a smile that was about as sarcastic and smart-alecky, the Administrator figured, as he could possibly make it. "Does the President agree with you?"

"Yes," Andy said calmly. "He does."

Clete gave him a slight, contemptuous bow.

"Very good. I'm so glad for you."

"Now, I think if you'll excuse me," Dr. Anderson said, "Al and I have some things to discuss."

"Me?" Clete asked with an elaborately pleased smile. "That will be nice."

"Good-by, Clete," the Administrator said. "Watch your-self."

For just a second the venom glared out again. But he did not wait to find out whether it would be accompanied by words.

He snapped off the machine and turned away to find Dr. Freer regarding him with a patient, sympathetic expression.

"He is a very bad man and a deadly enemy to this country."

"Yes, I believe you," the Administrator said. He frowned. "But how we convince those who have to be convinced, I don't quite know."

"Surely you will try," Dr. Freer said with some alarm in his voice.

"Oh, yes. I will try."

And now that he was back at his desk in Washington, he was going to. He had an afternoon appointment with the President. The ostensible purpose was to furnish a progress report on Piffy One, but there would be much more than that. NASA was in good shape but other things were obviously not. He would talk about Clete O'Donnell and Percy Mercy and all the conglomeration of opposition that had been temporarily lulled by the crew change and the Vice-President's trip to Geneva. He was under no illusions about this seeming quietus. Clete's deliberately flaunted hostility had convinced him his continuing concern was correct. The lull was probably a very temporary thing.

And in the hushed and reverent offices of *View*, uptown off Dupont Circle, it was, indeed. The editor and publisher was restive, and when Percy Mercy was restive, another blast from "P.C.M." was usually imminent.

Now as he sat behind the enormous desk that apparently compensated in some way for his rather small size, he was reviewing without much satisfaction the events of recent days in the area that concerned him most: namely the world. Uusally he carried it with so judicious and effective a care upon his shoulders that he never paused to worry about it, knowing it was in such good custodianship. But today, as the Geneva conference continued to drag on without outward progress of any kind, he was beginning to build up quite a head of steam.

In Percy's mind, Geneva was infinitely more important than the changes in the crew, though he had made the crew his immediate target, as the easiest to achieve. He thought now with a certain contempt of the way in which the President had bowed to the pressure exerted by himself and his friends. They could always do it, he told himself triumphantly: they could always do it! Situated as they were, in control of the major news media of the country, they were ideally equipped to browbeat Presidents, change or destroy policies, create or destroy reputations. An organized howl from Percy and his friends could usually do wonders.

So it had been with Planetary Fleet One.

They had decided, by that sort of group osmosis that works its wonders from Manhattan Island to the Golden Gate, that they wanted the crew changed to something more democratic and representative of the great American Republic whose destinies they guided so well—and they had succeeded. They had wanted to bring the Soviet Union at last into full partnership with the United States in space—and they had succeeded.

Or had they?

It was right there that Percy Christ Mercy began to

wonder and Percy Comma Mercy began to grow indignant.

Certainly there wasn't much out of Geneva yet to indicate any such happy consummation of their organized desires. At Soviet insistence the talks had been secret, but thanks to almost daily reports from his old friend Academician Alexei V. Kuselesky, who was principal adviser to the Soviet delegation, he was fully informed. He had learned with wrathful amazement of the disgraceful twistings and maneuverings of the Vice-President and his advisers as they attempted to weasel out of the President's firm commitment to begin an equal partnership with the Russians in space. It was a sorry picture for any one who truly believed in peace and world friendship based upon a genuine and tolerant understanding of the Soviet Union's perfectly justifiable ambitions. It was enough to make a man lose faith in his own country, so barefaced and shameless had been the attempt to establish conditions the Communists could not possibly meet.

Thus to the perfectly understandable and reasonable Communist demand that they be allowed to furnish 60 per cent of the technical personnel to run the firing room at the Cape and the control room in Houston, in return for permitting the United States to have 60 per cent of the personnel controlling the laboratories at JPL and the tracking network at Goddard, the Vice-President had presented a most unreasonable and obdurate opposition.

And to the equally valid Communist insistence that, as the first to orbit man in space two decades ago, they should be allowed to have four members of an enlarged crew of six, the Vice-President had been equally adamant.

And when the Communists had insisted that all immigration and security checks be suspended on all Russian or Iron Curtain personnel they might bring into the United States, and also on all native Americans they might wish to hire to assist them, the Vice-President had been simply impossible.

In fact, looking at the situation as the truly impartial and objective observer he knew he was, Percy could not help feeling a great shame for his country. Such a sorry figure it was cutting in Geneva! So vainly and viciously was it opposing mankind's chance for peace through space co-operation, and so blindly and shortsightedly was it attempting to thwart the perfectly reasonable Soviet proposals that were attempting to achieve that highly desirable goal. It was enough to make a man cry. Or write an editorial.

Many of his friends were giving signs of a similar disquiet. The *Post* had been edgy this morning—"Are We Stalling in Geneva?" it had entitled its lead editorial. Walter Dobius' column had also raised "grave and serious doubts about the sincerity of American intentions." And the *Times'* reports from the conference were beginning to display that snide biliousness that always crept into the news columns when its proprietors had reached the conclusion that editorials were not going to be enough to take care of some pet hate or personal enemy.

Wasn't it about time that they all let fly again, before the Vice-President completely ruined what might well be the first, last and only chance for genuine co-operation with the Communists in this desperately important field?

Shifting the phrases, alternately singing and savage, that whirled through his busy little head, P.C.M. was tempted to begin writing at once. He had been patient with the United States Government quite long enough. He had given it almost two weeks to make good on its pious pretensions of international good will; it had failed; and it must be judged. Yet some inner concept of the practical and possible, some innate caution, made him hesitate. It was not that he was an egotistical man, but he knew he had some influence. Perhaps it might be better to make one last private try at changing the course of events in Geneva before he made it a public issue. The editorial would keep, and perhaps, hopefully, it would never have to be written. He wasn't interested in puffing himself up, after all: he was interested in results.

After a moment's thought he nodded brightly to himself and, calling his secretary, requested her to get him an appointment with the President. He was not at all surprised when she reported back promptly that the President would see him after lunch. P.C.M. knew how to get things done.

So also—he thought—did Conrad Trasker. But as the days had gone on with only the absolute minimal courtesy from his most difficult crew member, he had begun to wonder. Jayvee remained a stubbornly sullen and unknown quantity. Despite the impersonal even-handedness with which Connie tried to treat him, and despite obviously efficient way in which Jayvee was proceeding with his own part of the mission, there was a dragging dead weight of hostility and dislike that Piffy One's commander found more wearing than he hoped Jayvee would ever know. If he did know it would give him too much satisfaction. If he had the satisfaction it would be only a short time until he tried some gesture of genuine insubordination. And this Connie was grimly determined he would not allow.

In this determination he was joined by the other crew members, most actively, he thought with a wry annoyance, by his second in command. Jazz had never been noted for his patience, and his normally short temper had been on even shorter fuse ever since the first crew meeting. It was true that Jayvee had finally appeared to fall in line on that disputatious day but Jazz had not forgiven him his bitter reluctance to do so. Jazz' suspicions and dislike had, if anything, increased as the days passed and Jayvee showed no signs of any real, fundamental, human unity with his colleagues.

Jazz had already demanded on several occasions that Connie start thinking seriously about requesting Jayvee's removal from the crew. When Connie demurred, Jazz exploded. Their argument the last time had become so heated that Connie had begun to wonder if Jayvee might not succeed, in some perverse, indirect, inactive way, in splitting up the rest of the crew simply because they would get to fighting over him so bitterly that their own sometimes fragile unity would be irrevocably destroyed.

He said as much to Jazz but Jazz was not particularly impressed.

"Hell," he said, "if our co-operation rests on a basis so flimsy that we can't do what we have to do to get that bastard straightened out, then we'd better forget the whole thing."

"I'm doing what I can to get him straightened out," Connie said with more patience than he felt.

"How?" Jazz demanded. "By letting him act like Little King Sambo all over the place? I don't go for this smart-ass silent treatment, myself."

"Do you think I enjoy it?" Connie inquired sharply. "It gripes my tail, if you want to know. But I'll be damned if I'm going to let it provoke me into the kind of retaliation the two of you would like me to take. Look," he said sharply as Jazz gave him a sardonically skeptical glance. "Suppose I did what you want and went bellyaching to the President two weeks after the mission begins. What the hell am I going to sound like? I'll tell you: some damned cry-baby. 'Jayvee doesn't smile at us, Mr. President. Jayvee won't play with us, Mr. President. Jayvee's a *bad* boy, Mr. President.' Why, hell. He'd laugh me out of the room and he'd be right. You can't nail a guy on that sort of thing. You have to have something definite and something big. You know that, Jazz. Or you ought to know it."

"Oh, I don't know," Jazz said, and some of the old bitterness was back in his eyes and voice. "It never took very much to nail me, as I recall."

"I won't reply to that," Connie said, "because it would get us into exactly the sort of wrangle I expect Jayvee wants us to get into. We aren't talking about you, we're talking about him. How do we handle him? You say raise hell without anything to go on but dislike and annoyance. I say wait until we have something a lot more solid than that."

"He won't give us anything more solid than that."

"Then we'll just have to suffer him, because if he doesn't, he stays and there's not the slightest chance of getting him off the crew."

"You sound as mealy-mouthed as the President," Jazz said scornfully. "If I were commander of Piffy One—"

"Well, you're not buster," Connie snapped, "and don't forget it."

"I can't," Jazz retorted. "You won't let me."

Momentarily they looked at one another with some of the old hostility. Then Connie with a real effort of will forced himself to speak in a calm and level tone.

"Jazz, what in the hell good is it going to do for you and me to have a falling-out with each other over him? What's the point in jeopardizing Piffy One for that? I don't get it."

"I'm saying *he's* the one who's jeopardizing Piffy One," Jazz said, also speaking more calmly. "I just don't want you to let him get away with it. If he thinks he can walk all over us, babe, he'll tromp. You know that as well as I do."

"Well," Connie suggested, "maybe we ought to try to see it from his point of view for a change. At least it might help us understand him and be able to handle him better. He's got a gripe against the white world, and being white we don't appreciate it much. But at least we ought to try to understand him, it seems to me. He doesn't strike me as a particularly happy guy, you know. I don't think he enjoys it any more than we do, basically. But he seems to feel he doesn't have a choice."

"That's why he ought to be off this crew," Jazz remarked. "Keep talking."

"Not without real cause," Connie said stubbornly. "And nobody's going to move on it unless there is one. And that's final, Jazz. Whether you like it or not."

"There's a limit to how long you can keep the lid on, Connie. Even you."

"It's been on two weeks," Connie said tartly, "and that's hardly what I'd call a long time."

"Of course if you're afraid to do anything about it—" Jazz began unpleasantly, but Connie's sudden angry look stopped him. "Well," he said. "You do it your way and we'll go along if we have to. But don't kid yourself you're doing anything but store up trouble."

"Not without cause," Connie repeated coldly. "And that's final."

And that, he thought as Jazz gave him a skeptical, unyielding glance and went out, was how he really felt about it, and be damned to him. He didn't know whether Pete felt so strongly about it—he was being very discreet on the subject, right now—and he wondered a little whether Jazz actually did. Jazz might be testing him too, with Jayvee as the excuse. If so he hoped Jazz had his answer.

He was not, as a matter of fact, as upset about Jazz as his concluding statements and present mood might have indicated to an outsider. He could handle Jazz, he always had, and he was confident he always would. On the whole, Jazz had embarked upon the mission with far more good will and co-operation than Connie had really anticipated. He had expected that a reaction might set in once Jazz was actually on the crew, and that he would be faced constantly with challenges to his own authority. Aside from their running argument about Jayvee there had been surprisingly little of this. Jazz had joined in planning the mission like the highly competent technician he was. His attitude had been constructive, his suggestions valid. Connie had been well pleased with him as a crew member and as his second in command. There was still the occasional stab about the past, the old bitterness would flare now and then as it had a few moments ago, but on the whole it seemed to be lessening. In many ways Jazz seemed to have come to terms both with himself and with his colleagues. Even his concern about Jayvee could be interpreted as excess of zeal rather than a means of testing Connie. Perhaps that idea, Connie acknowledged as his annoyance ebbed, might be unfair.

He did not like to be knowingly unfair to anyone and he particularly did not want to be unfair to Jayvee, who had a problem that Connie recognized must be terrible and almost overwhelming for him. Connie was neither professional black-lover nor professional black-hater; he prided himself on being simply a man who judged other men as shrewdly and impersonally as he could. It was a state of mind that went with his profession and it was a state of mind he had always instinctively and inherently possessed. As he grew older he had consciously cultivated it. Nowadays he applied it to most people, and, he thought, with some success.

So he had spent a good deal of time in these recent days trying to analyze and understand Jayvee, and he had done it without being influenced, consciously at least, by the fact that Jayvee was the husband of a girl for whom he felt an attraction stronger than he had felt in quite some time. The ability to separate was another of his characteristics: Jayvee as a problem for Piffy One was an entirely distinct entity from Jayvee as Monetta's husband. And it was Jayvee as a problem for Piffy One that had concerned him almost constantly since the mission began.

He wondered, sometimes, if Jayvee had any concept of the forces national and international that had gathered around him in his drive to get on the crew. He suspected that Jayvee understood them partially and used them cold-bloodedly according to the quite limited, quite selfish view he apparently held of his own ambition. He did not, Connie suspected, understand them in relation to his position with his crewmates. In that area Jayvee, Connie thought, was operating almost entirely on blind emotion.

The causes for this he could only partially comprehend, and then almost entirely as an intellectual exercise. Obviously he could not completely understand emotions that sprang from being black. But as a reasonably kind and sympathetic human being he could at least give them some tolerance and compassion—providing they did not get out of hand and did not jeopardize Piffy One.

Jayvee had apparently suffered some wound, or many, along his way from North Carolina to Houston, and he was apparently determined to make the white world suffer for it. Maybe the wound, as Connie had suggested to him, was just the wound of being black: maybe it went too deep for him ever to get over. If that were the case, then Jazz of course was right and Jayvee should be removed before his feeling erupted in some way that would harm them all.

If on the other hand it were something more superficial in the sense of something that could be alleviated by time and patience, then that was the way Connie wanted to handle it. Infuriating as what Jazz described as Jayvee's "smart-ass silent treatment" might be to his crewmates, it was not something that could not be broken down, given sufficient strength on their part. Sullenness and impersonal hostility were hard things to maintain forever if they were not constantly recharged by active opposition. The more they allowed Jayvee to provoke them into angry responses, the more strengthened he would be in his own determination to be unfriendly. The more patience and charity they could show him, the less sure of himself he would become and the less able to maintain his pose of frigid aloofness. He had accused them bitterly of wanting him to love them, but Connie suspected, now that he had given sufficient thought to it away from the tensions of that harsh moment, that what Jayvee really wanted was for them to love him—without reservations, without consciously working at it, and without patronizing him in the process.

This was a tall order, Connie had to acknowledge, but he thought it could be done providing he and the others were really willing to do it. He knew he was and he thought it might be relatively easy for Pete, the easygoing, decent, friendly and goodhearted. It was obviously a lot tougher for Jazz, who had his own problems, and now that he had solved them, was not disposed to show much charity to Jayvee.

But easy or no, Jazz had to join the effort or it wouldn't work. Connie hoped their conversation had at least given

301

him something to think about. He hoped his plug for a little understanding might take root in Jazz' mind. It was a stubborn mind but it was basically a pretty fair one, underneath the trained technician's impatience with those who appeared to be falling short. It would take a little time, but he thought maybe he could persuade Jazz to co-operate.

For himself, he would go right on doing what he had done every day since the first crew meeting had rubbed all their emotions raw: swallow his own impatience and perhaps his own pride; maintain an even-handed, friendly courtesy toward Jayvee; be decent, just, steady and kind. He was not very proud of himself for the way he had lashed out at Jayvee on that particular day and on the days preceding: he should have had more understanding and more maturity then. But he hadn't and he admitted it. Fortunately the crew meeting had provided some sort of catharsis for him and since then it had been easier. He was supposed to be mature and understanding, after all. He told himself with a certain wryness that this was one of the principal things Uncle Sam was paying him for: it was part of his job as commander to have character.

In this mood he heard a familiar rat-a-tat-tat on his door and looked up to find himself involved in a conversation which began innocently enough and then, in several respects, suddenly demanded all the character he had.

"I hate to interrupt the profound thoughts of my leader," Pete remarked, dropping into the chair across the desk with a cheerfully accustomed ease, "but I thought I would consult on a little problem, namely Jayvee."

Connie smiled.

"By a happy coincidence that seems to be Topic A on today's agenda. I've just beaten Jazz into line on it and I'm ready for you. What's up?"

"He's getting on my nerves," Pete said soberly, "and I know he shouldn't. But at the moment I'm a little stymied what to do about it. He's giving me the usual arms-length politeness bit, but in the last couple of days he seems to be in an unusually foul mood about it."

"Is it interfering with his work?"

"Not that I can see," Pete conceded. "We're moving right along in our sector and everything's as it should be, I think. It may interfere with mine a little, though, if it keeps up. What do you suppose is the matter? He and

302

Monetta aren't having trouble, are they? I wouldn't blame her if they were."

"Not that I know of," Connie said, startled but managing, he thought, to conceal it.

"You don't know of anything," Pete said, giving him a shrewd and thoughtful glance.

"Why should I?" Connie asked blandly. "I'm not privy to what goes on in that household. Am I?"

"No, I guess not," Pete said backing down before his challenging gaze, though Connie could sense he wasn't really giving up on whatever his instinct was telling him. "Anyway," he went on, dropping it for now, but not, Connie suspected, forever, "it's increasing the problem. I don't want to blow up at him again, I'm going to do my damnedest not to, but—it's a problem. Isn't there anything you can do to quiet him down?"

"Why come to me?" Connie asked, somewhat tartly because he was annoyed by Pete's perception and by the inner trepidation it seemed to be causing him.

"You're our leader," Pete said with a smile that requested forgiveness for whatever presumption he might have shown.

"And you're the crew," Connie said bluntly, not ready to admit there had been any grounds for presumption. "We're all the crew and we all have to work it out together or it won't be worked out. I'll tell you the same thing I told Jazz, who wants me to go to the President right now and get Jayvee booted off the mission. It won't happen like that without real cause. My recommendation for the rest of us is to sit tight, be patient and try to understand."

"Turn the other cheek," Pete said dryly.

"Unless you two have something more constructive to offer, yes."

"Well," Peter said slowly, "it ain't gonna be easy, Daddy, but I'll try if you say so."

"Please do," Connie said, still somewhat tartly, turning back to the flight plan spread before him on the desk in a gesture he started to make dismissing. But that wouldn't do, either. "How's everything else going?" he asked, more amicably.

"Oh, fine," Pete said, relaxing into humor because he, too, decided it was the best thing to do for the sake of friendship. "I think I have everything I need. My red woolen undies, my ear muffs, my N.S. pills—"

"All right," Conine said patiently, not looking up from the flight plan but going along with the mood. "What are N.S. pills?"

"No Sex," Pete said cheerfully.

"Yeah," Connie said, glancing up with an elaborate sufferance. "Very clever."

"Well, something has to be done. I mean, eighteen months—"

"And you can't be quiet for eighteen minutes," Connie said dryly. "I know. Well, I'm afraid it will just have to be every man for himself, Petey boy."

Pete laughed.

"Are you sure?"

Then his eyes changed—the laughter faltered—he started to say something.

Just in time, he stopped.

But Connie decided he had better answer anyway.

"Pete," he said quietly. "Just don't back me into a corner, O.K.? I've got too many other things on my mind. Honest I have. And so should you."

For a long moment their glances held. Then Pete flushed and nodded with an expression in which self-contempt, self-disgust, regret, dismay, struggled painfully. The dark eyes became shadowed, the engaging boyish face was suddenly unhappy and bleak.

"Yeah," he said. "Sure. Of course I do." He turned and stared out across the white, antiseptic buildings and the wide green lawns. "I'm sorry," he said finally. "I was just going to say something funny—I thought. But I guess it wasn't . . . though," he added very quietly, "I still think—"

"I don't think so," Connie said with an equal quietness. "At least, I hope not. Not that I'm shocked or offended or antagonized. And"—he gave his friend a level, candid gaze—"not that I'm afraid. But—we do have an awfully big job. And it's got to be done. And nothing else matters, really. Does it?"

There was silence for a moment. Then Pete spoke in a low voice, still staring unseeing out the window.

"I guess not."

"You know it," Connie said. "Now," he inquired calmly, "what about those stress-tolerance studies we're supposed to be getting from *Mayflower?* Have they come in yet?"

"Probably on my desk now," Pete said, glancing at his watch and standing up. "I'd better go on back and get at them." He managed a reasonably steady smile and held out his hand. "Thanks, leader. It was an impulse."

"What isn't?" Connie asked, smiling also and returning an affectionate, reassuring pressure. Again he gave Pete the level, honest glance. "I'm really not afraid, Pete. And if I'm really honest with you, maybe I'm not all that unwilling either. You're my friend—and I like you a hell of a lot—and life's life—and one lives it as best one can. Maybe some other time, some other circumstance— But right now—really—" He sighed and shook his head with an unhappy frown, his mind already back on the mission. "We *do* have so damned much to worry about, without—"

"I know," Pete said quietly. "I'm sorry."

Connie smiled.

"Don't be. We'll both survive."

"I hope so," Pete said with a brave try at returning humor. "I'd hate to think I was the guy who gave the commander of Piffy One a case of the heebie-jeebies."

Connie laughed.

"If they're all as mild as this one, buddy-boy, I'll get by all right."

But after Pete left he sat for a long time staring out the window himself, seeing nothing, thinking many things, none very coherent.

Life *was* life, all right.

And sometimes it wasn't so easy.

Nor was it easy an hour later when the buzzer sounded on the Picturephone and he switched it on to find Monetta, obviously upset, looking at him with an anxious shyness from the little screen.

He was not, at the moment, in a very good mood to talk to her; but perhaps this was best. Perhaps it would save him once and for all from something he really knew he should not do or even contemplate. Maybe it was just as well Pete had come along and with an unpremeditated, inadvertent, and quite devastating spontaneity, forced the issue. The reaction might not be such a bad basis from which to talk to Monetta.

Even so he must not be unkind.

"I'm sorry, Colonel Trasker," she began nervously. "I didn't intend to call you at the office, but—"

"I'm glad you did. And it's still Connie, if you like."

"Connie," she said with a fleeting little smile; and in spite of his new-found resolution, the familiarity lifted his heart a little. But in the face her obvious distress he did not linger over it.

"What's the matter? Same thing?"

"I'm afraid so," she said, and her eyes began to fill with tears. "Colonel Trasker—Connie—I think I am going have to leave him."

"Well, now," he said, stalling for time to sort out the conflicting thoughts and emotions that this aroused. "I think we should talk about it a little before you do anything so drastic."

"Oh, I wouldn't do anything to embarrass you," she said with a sudden fierce, quick pride that flared through the tears. "I have relatives in California to go to."

"Now, just a minute," he said quietly. "Just a minute. I hope you think better of me than that."

"I don't know what I think of you. I really don't."

"You obviously think I can be of some help or you wouldn't have called me," he pointed out calmly. "Now, can I or can't I? If not—" and he started to turn back to the books and papers on his desk.

"No," she said hastily. "No, please, I'm sorry. He's—he's got me so confused I just don't know what I'm saying, I guess. Colonel Trasker—Connie—I think I'm afraid of him, now. I really am."

"I'm sorry to hear that," he said quietly, leaning his chin on his hands and concentrating his full attention on her beautiful, tragically worried eyes. "Tell me about it. Has he been threatening you? Or beating you?"

"Not any more. Now he's just—still."

" 'Still.' He's like that around us, too."

"He goes away somewhere, inside . And he acts as though he might really hurt me if I tried to make him come out. Really hurt me." She placed a long, graceful hand along her cheek in a forlorn little gesture that touched him deeply. "I don't know how to reach him any more. I really don't."

"Nor do we," he said in a puzzled tone. "It's very strange, this business of his. He's got what he wanted, he's on the crew, he's doing his job on the surface, but something's missing underneath. As you say, he goes away. But why? And where?"

"I don't know," she said helplessly. "He won't say."

"And you really think he might try something violent with you. You really feel you and the boy are in danger."

"I can't be around him without wanting to help him," she said simply. "He's my husband, I loved him—some ways still do, I guess. If I'm in his house I can't help wanting to help him. But he warns me off so I know he'd do something really bad if I kept on."

"How do you know that?"

"He's my husband," she repeated. "I know, much as anyone can with another person, I guess. So that's why I think I'd better leave. Before he does something to me and Rudden that would be—really bad."

"Well, now," he said slowly, aware, with thanks, that the prospect of her leaving her husband did not stir any particular pleasure in his heart, "I wonder if that would really be the best thing to do."

"I wouldn't hurt the program," she said quickly, almost scornfully, with something of the prideful flare she had shown earlier. "I know you always think of that. But no one would have to know about it. I'd be quiet."

"It isn't that," he said, still slowly, ignoring the challenge. "I know you would. And really, you know"—he tried a smile and was pleased to see her unyielding expression soften just a little—"I'm not really as heartless as all that. I do think of other things besides the program. You, for instance."

At this her expression softened still more and his smile was finally returned, though somewhat tentatively and without conceding a great deal.

"I know. That's why I called. I thought I could trust you to give me good advice."

"I hope you can," he said quietly; and made his decision. "It may not be what you want to hear, though. Or even," he said, with something of the same candor with which he had tried to comfort Pete, "what I want to hear. But I think you should stay with him."

"But—" she said with a dismay so deep it shook his heart and almost overturned his resolution then and there, "but, Connie—"

"I think you should," he repeated gravely. "I think he needs you. And I don't really think he would hurt you.

He's a very mixed-up guy right now, but he does need help—ours and yours. Particularly yours."

"But," she said, and it was almost a whisper, "I really am afraid, Connie. I really am."

"I don't think you need to be," he said, praying to God that he was correct, knowing he could never forgive himself if he weren't. "Of course you know him better than I do, but I don't think Jayvee is really bad inside. Terribly mixed up, as I say, but not really bad. We have to help him work his way out of this. We can do it."

"He won't," she said, still in the same almost inaudible voice. "He can't. He's sick with being black and he won't ever recover. Not ever."

Despite his best intentions a sharp little edge of impatience came into his voice.

"But he's being given everything he could possibly want. What more are we supposed to do?"

"Some of us," she said, "are sick like that. We just are. For some of us, it's all been just too much—just too much. It haunts and cripples and destroys—it just never goes away. He's like that."

"And why aren't you?" he asked, the impatience gone, a compassionate sympathy in his voice. "How have you and so many others escaped?"

"I guess I'm strong," she said simply. "And I guess he isn't."

"Then don't you see that's why he needs us?" he asked quickly. "Don't you see that's why you've got to stay with him, for his sake, and why we've all got to help him?"

"Not if it means hurt for my baby," she said with a sudden fierceness. "Not if it means hurt for me."

"I don't think it will," he said, and tried to find for her some proof to support the vigor of the affirmation; and found it. "Do you think I would tell you to do this— caring for you as I do—if I thought it would mean harm for you and the boy?"

She was silent, the enormous dark eyes under the high, intelligent forehead staring into his with a pleading intensity that stirred him profoundly. Presently she uttered a deep, shuddering sigh and said, very low,

"No, I guess you wouldn't."

"No," he responded quietly, aware that he had won— although what, he would have to wait for time to tell him—"I would not."

When she had gone from the screen, still troubled and uneasy but apparently somewhat reassured and willing to try a while longer for his sake, he turned to his desk and attempted to lose himself again in the mission. But this was not so feasible, given his own uncertainties about the wisdom of his advice. It had solved his own problem, or so he thought, but despite his confident air, he was not so sure it had solved hers.

He was honest enough with himself to acknowledge that his basic motivations this day had been two. Both, in human terms, might have been selfish; both, in the context of Planetary Fleet One, could be considered selfless. For all the calmness he had forced himself to show Pete, and for all the genuine affection that had prompted the effort, he had been deeply shaken and disturbed. The overriding reaction had been to divest himself of everything that might in any way complicate his life further and thereby affect the success of Piffy One.

If he had responded to Pete, which in human terms might have been entirely possible, he would, as he had said, have acquired an additional burden to add to those he already carried as commander, to say nothing of the probably unsettling effects upon Pete. If he had encouraged Monetta to leave Jayvee—as he had before Jayvee joined the mission and became his responsibility—certain things could have been much easier. But they would also have complicated his life and affected the mission, and they might also have spun Jayvee completely off-balance, whereas now the chance was good he could be helped back to stability, and so perform his full share of the mission. Therefore Connie had acted as he did, and now he was home scot-free, or so he thought, relieved of complications he had tacitly, and in some ways actively, encouraged. And Piffy One was the principal beneficiary; which, given his major responsibility in the world right now, was as it should be.

Nonetheless, a nagging doubt persisted: had he really been fair to either of them or had he simply suited his own selfish convenience?

He decided, because he must, that he had indeed been fair. If he had really believed for a moment that Jayvee was capable of doing his wife real harm he would never have urged her to stay. If he had really believed for a moment that Pete was incapable of measuring up to his own inner challenges and mastering them he would never have been so gentle. And because in both cases the opposite course would have been to further burden a mission already burdened enough, he had acted as he did. Or so he told himself.

It did not occur to him that there were moral issues involved in either episode. Moral issues had their place in the world, and as a father he did his best to impress them upon his children—when he could find time to talk to them. But in his profession and in the context of the mission, moral issues were not the question right now. The question was what was best for Piffy One: to send his life and Jayvee's into a tailspin over Monetta, to send Pete's life into a tailspin by being too harsh—or to try to hold everything together as best he could and keep the mission moving. Like all intelligent men of strong conviction, he felt that in the last analysis he had no choice, and had done the right thing.

Thus when the buzzer sounded for the call he had been expecting, he handled it in the same way. Pete was in an agony of humiliation and embarrassment and Connie was correspondingly gentle. That this might be twice as devastating as something more impersonal did not occur to him, either. Nor would it, perhaps, have changed his approach if it had. Acting as far as he knew with the best will and intentions in the world, he followed straight on the trajectory devised by Conrad H. Trasker, Perfect Astronaut: unaware that it might, like all trajectories if carried to their ultimate mathematical conclusions, turn back upon itself in ways that Conrad H. Trasker, P.A., could not then suspect. Whether this would have made any difference to him was a question he did not think of, and of course was not at that point called upon to answer.

"Now, buddy," he responded calmly to Pete's first hesitant words, "I told you to relax and you do it, O.K.?"

And although for Pete relaxing was something he thought he was not going to be able to manage again very soon with Connie, their brief conversation went off fairly well. Pete apologized once more for a stupid, kid impulse, was told once more to forget it; received assurances of affection and support that moved him to protest wryly, "You're very kind—which of course doesn't make anything any easier"; and left the screen apparently feeling a good deal better. For which, Connie thought with a mixture of sympathy, affection, pity and something else he could not quite define, they could both be damned thankful.

That accomplished, he took what he hoped would be his last call for a while (This is really my morning for being Mother Hen, he told himself in some annoyance when the buzzer sounded yet again.) from his volatile second in command.

"I've just run into Jayvee," Jazz said without preliminary, "and he's acting damned peculiar. Even more so than usual, if that's possible."

"Oh? What did he do?"

"Snarled. Right out loud. I was walking down the hall talking to Roger Webb, didn't see Jayvee coming out of his door and literally ran right into him. He said, 'God damn it, watch where you're going!' Which was a lot, these days, for Jayvee."

"At least now you know he's alive," Connie said dryly. "What did you do, knock him down?"

"Not quite," Jazz said, sounding as though he regretted he hadn't. "But it makes me wonder. He seemed really upset. Unusually so. Actively. You don't know any reason why he would be, do you?"

"No," Connie said cautiously.

"Hmm," Jazz said thoughtfully. "I wonder if he and Monetta—"

"Everything's all right as far as I know," Connie said crisply, though he was not really sure what he had to be crisp about. "Maybe it was just a mood. Maybe it means he's going to talk to us again. Don't knock it, Jazzbo. Be thankful."

"I still wish you'd let me handle him my way."

"You will not," Connie said flatly. "That's final, now. Drop it."

"O.K. But watch out for him. Something's working."

"All right. Thanks for the warning. I'll be ready."

But as the morning moved on with no further calls and no indication of anything from Jayvee, he began to relax. He thought that with a little luck they might all come through all right. The difficult human cargo of Piffy One might adjust itself, after all. He might just have succeeded in removing some major obstacles, both for the mission and for himself. If so it was a good day's work.

So he thought, unaware that a sometimes whimsical

Lord might yet have in store for Conrad H. Trasker, Perfect Astronaut, as He did for many unsuspecting and hopeful men, a few ironic surprises.

Certainly He did for the President and his visitors of the afternoon, each of whom approached the Oval Room with his own particular ax to grind. Percy Mercy and Senator Williams came first, the Administrator followed. For a little while the President thought he could congratulate himself that he had all their complaints under control. Then the Vice-President called from Geneva and the Lord had his little joke.

P.C.M. and Kenny Williams of course were properly indignant, properly menacing. The President decided he had better drown them with oil instead of vinegar, much as he would have liked to call a White House cop and have them bodily thrown out. Too many votes and too much emotion were piled up behind these two pompous visitors and both were too adept at taking advantage of the fact. He could not afford at the moment to be that candid about his feelings. At least that was the idea with which he began.

"Well, Percy," he said, rising with the quick, flattering cordiality he knew how to muster on a moment's notice, coming rapidly from behind his desk, surprisingly light on his feet for a big man, "it's always nice to have you drop in and tell me how the country's going. And as for Kenny here, there isn't a day that goes by that I don't read in the *Post* and the *Times* how he's saving humanity for us. It's good of you both to come by."

And although he thought his tone was broad enough to slay an ox, he saw that they were actually taking him seriously. They actually looked flattered. Ego, Ego, he thought. Thy name is Omnipotent.

"Why don't you sit over here on the sofa," he went on easily, "it's much more comfortable. And it gives me an excuse to use the rocker. Now: how goes it?"

"Mr. President," Percy said firmly, "we think you should know that there is a very rapidly growing national uneasiness about the course of events in Geneva."

"Growing damned fast," Senator Williams agreed with a frown on his pouchy, fading baby face, melting away almost visibly under the twin erosions of too much liquor and too many willing congressional secretaries. "*Damned* fast."

312

"What is the course of events in Geneva?" the President inquired innocently. "I didn't know anything had been made public."

"It hasn't," Percy Mercy said in a disapproving tone. "Keeping the conference secret, it seems to me, was a most unwise and undemocratic move."

"You really think it would have helped the Russians to have those demands made public?" the President asked quickly. "Come, Percy!"

"They haven't seemed so unreasonable to me," Percy replied tartly; and then paused, flushing.

"I'm glad we've kept you informed," the President said dryly. "And I'm glad somebody thinks the Russian demands are reasonable. I must say I don't."

"I can't say I know too much about them myself," Kenny Williams said, hesitated a moment as the President gave him a cheerfully skeptical glance and then went stoutly on, "but from what little I've been able to gather, I can certainly see their point of view."

"Oh, I can see that," the President said. "I'm trying not to forget ours."

"And what exactly is it, Mr. President?" Percy inquired, swiftly recovered from whatever minimal embarrassment so self-contained and self-contented an ego could allow itself. "I haven't been able to ascertain, unless it's just complete obstruction."

"I'm tempted to blow the conference and disclose the entire Russian text right now," the President said with more sharpness than he had intended to let himself display. "I'd like the country to judge who's being obstructionist."

"This government has given its word that the details of negotiations will remain secret," Percy said serenely. "Only the final agreement is to be made public."

"Except to a few important souls," the President couldn't resist, "on a need-to-know basis."

The editor of *View* gave him the solemn, owlish, intent stare that he was accustomed to use on those he wished to disconcert. The President, not being a disconcertable type, stared back. Presently Percy spoke with the gravity he was accustomed to use for matters of great national and world import.

"Mr. President, the Senator and I did not come here today to indulge in intellectual fencing. We came as supporters of your Administration to tell you that a very serious political problem is developing very rapidly around Geneva. Not only political, but moral, ethical—humanitarian, if you like, in the very broadest world-sense of the term."

"Good phrases," the President agreed. "Next week's editorial?"

"Mr. President—" Kenny Williams began in an indignant voice. But Percy raised a small, neat, commanding hand.

"Don't worry," he said calmly. "The President knows what I am talking about."

"I do," the President said amicably. "I surely do. The next step is for you to cry, 'Havoc!' and let slip the dogs of the media. When can I look for the barrage to begin?"

"There's no need for that," Percy said calmly, "providing there is some sign of genuine progress at Geneva. But if there is further stalling by the United States, Mr. President, then I must warn you our patience is wearing very thin. You saw the *Post* and the *Times*. You saw what Walter Dobius had to say."

"I did," the President said solemnly. "I was withered."

"Nonetheless," Percy said sharply, for, as with all the pontific, ridicule was the one weapon he could not stand, "my colleagues and I are reaching the end of our tolerance. The training stage of Planetary Fleet One is under way. The production lines are rolling. Can mankind's dream of peace in space be allowed to fall behind?"

"Use that language, man." the President urged. "Use it!"

"Now, Mr. President," Senator Williams said again. But again P.C.M. needed no defense.

"Very well," he said icily. "If this represents the attitude of the Administration toward the most pressing problem now confronting the world, then every responsible commentator in this land must speak out through every channel that is open to him. We must begin, and begin at once. We had hoped that the change in the crew and the invitation to the Communists to participate meant a real breakthrough. Obviously the latter, in particular, was simply a grandstand play—simply window dressing in an attempt to relieve political pressure. But it won't work, Mr. President. It won't work. We who genuinely have the interests of the nation and the world at heart must now speak out. You permit us no choice."

"What will you speak out about?" the President inquired with an iciness of his own. "Impossible Russian demands for a 60—40 control of launch operations? Impossible Russian demands for four men out of a crew of six? Impossible Russian demands for a waiver of all security checks on everybody who comes in with them and everybody they hire here? Good God, man, act your age."

For several moments it seemed that P.C.M., instead of acting his age, would simply pop. But with a great effort of will, and after a titanic struggle between ego and abandon, he managed to retain control of himself and speak in a determined, if quivering, voice.

"Every thinking American who truly believes in world co-operation and peace can only conclude that the Russian 'demands,' as you call them, Mr. President, are entirely reasonable and warranted suggestions on their part.

"Naturally they do not wish to risk a failure in so great an undertaking: hence the request for a preponderant control, by scientists and technicians who have amply demonstrated, particularly in Space Station *Stalin*—so much more sophisticated than our little Space Station *Mayflower*—their competence in this field.

"Naturally they believe, and in all justice, that as the first nation to successfully place man in orbit around the earth, they should have a majority of the crew.

"Naturally they feel, in view of all the shameful harassments of their nationals and of Americans friendly to co-operation with the Soviet Union by the FBI, the Passport Office and other agencies of this government over so many years, that they cannot join with us wholeheartedly unless these absurd and punitive harassments are removed.

"They are not asking for the shadow of co-operation, Mr. President. They are seeking the substance! And the United States quibbles and hesitates while humanity's great opportunity hangs in the balance. For shame, Mr. President! For shame!"

There was silence as he concluded his moving statement, which displayed the best of Percy Mercy: emotional, passionate, sincere—*involved*. Into it the President uttered one awed expletive and a cordial farewell.

"Well," he said softly, "I'll be God damned. I genuinely will ... Percy—" and he rose to his feet and extended his hand, and perforce Kenny Williams, looking slightly

dazed, and a P.C.M. still looking nobly exalted, did too—
"Percy and Kenny—thank you so much for giving me this
fine statement of your concern for the country. I appreciate your views. I shall treasure them and take them under
advisement. They will assist me greatly. I urge you not to
be too hasty in your judgments. I urge you to be patient
yet a little longer. Give us a day or two more. Let us keep
trying in Geneva." His voice became husky, his eyes
became larger and brighter; almost they could imagine
tears. *"Give us your help!"*

Wordless, bemused by Percy's rhetoric and the President's, his visitors moved dreamlike out the door. The
moment it closed behind them he collapsed into the rocker
again, laughing helplessly. It was thus the Administrator
found him a moment later, wiping the tears—of laughter—
from his eyes.

"Andy, Andy!" he exclaimed. "Have I ever had a funny, phony afternoon!"

"How's that?" the Administrator asked, somewhat cautiously, for he did not know how the President's mood
might affect his own business. "Did the two musketeers
give you a hard time?"

"Oh, you saw them, then," the President said, his laughter subsiding. "Yes, they were, as usual, threatening me
with all sorts of consequences, mostly dire. They aren't
happy with the way things are going in Geneva. Apparently Percy has an inside line. Frankly," he added with a
frown, "I'm not happy myself. He thinks the Russian
demands are great."

"He's a fool."

The President nodded.

"But fools in his position are very dangerous fools, for
they have the means of loosing their foolishness upon the
entire populace. They are so desperately afraid of any real
firmness with the Communists, so frantically committed to
some sort of impossible dream of balance of power with a
system whose sole aim is to tip the balance entirely its
own way, that they are beyond reason. They would literally rather see their own country destroyed than see it act
harshly toward the Russians. It's a state of mind almost
beyond belief but in Percy and his friends it actually does
exist, beyond all reason and all rationality. And America
suffers for it, dreadfully, as she has ever since the end of
World War II."

316

"What is going to happen in Geneva?" Dr. Anderson asked. "Is anything at all going to come out of it?"

The President gave him a cynical, candid look.

"No. A scramble for headlines, a scramble for propaganda advantage. Nothing concrete, no agreement, no co-operation. The same old pattern the Communists always follow. An exercise in futility for us."

"Then why—?" Andy Anderson inquired though he knew the answer. The President shrugged.

"Political necessity. Perhaps for many Americans a psychological necessity. For Percy and his friends a bone tossed by me to try to keep them quiet for a little while." He smiled ironically. "It isn't going to work. They really want us to surrender to these demands. Percy just came by to tell me that if we don't they're going to raise hell again. He needn't have bothered. It was implicit and inevitable in everything they've done for thirty years."

"If Geneva collapses without result," the Administrator began, and then amended it: "when Geneva collapses without result—we're going to face more than a few screams from the media, I'm afraid."

"Mostly talk. It will blow over."

"I'm not so sure," Andy Anderson said slowly. "There could be more than talk."

"Now, Andy," the President said. "NASA isn't seeing ghosts under the bed, is it? What are you afraid of?"

"Clete O'Donnell for one," Dr. Anderson said, deciding to meet the problem head-on. "He's pulled one wildcat strike to try to stop the mission and he's as much as told me in so many words he'll pull another if the Russians don't get their way."

"Andy," the President protested, and the Administrator could tell, with a sinking feeling, that he was about to meet the standard skepticism again. "You don't mean to tell me *you* believe all those hobgoblin tales about Clete? *You're* not going to tell me he's a secret Communist, I hope!" He shook his head with a humorously baffled air. "You and Al Freer!"

The Administrator hesitated but decided to stand his ground.

"Has he ever been investigated, Mr. President?"

The President looked almost offended for a second but answered in a reasonable tone.

"Why, I suppose so. Hasn't anybody of any prominence at some time?"

"I'd like to see his record," Dr. Anderson remarked.

"I think I can assure you," the President said dryly, "that if there were anything subversive in it, it would have come to my attention."

"Perhaps."

"Now, see here, Andy," the President said with some asperity, "it's always fashionable when somebody does something some people don't like to charge him with being a Communist. That doesn't make him one. Clete O'Donnell has served on government commissions, official boards, national organizations of all kinds, for the past ten years or more. Surely you don't believe he could have escaped detection all that time if he were really disloyal?"

"People have," the Administrator said stubbornly. "From Alger Hiss right on down the line. A great skepticism goes to work for them, powerful friends in the press and in public life get committed to them. If there's anything questionable about them, it gets swept under the rug. If there's anything embarrassing, it gets carefully glossed over. If anything shows up in the record it gets a fast shuffle and lands in a locked file to be deliberately forgotten. It's happened many times in this town. And," he added, though he knew he was risking real displeasure from his powerful host, "we both know it."

"But not Clete," the President said, more mildly than Dr. Anderson expected. "Not Clete, now, Andy. Really!"

"There it is, you see," the Administrator said bleakly. "That great skepticism again. How can one ever fight it?"

"With Clete O'Donnell, why should one?" the President inquired. "It's true he's involved with Percy in this CAUSE organization of theirs, but so are a great many perfectly fine and loyal citizens. I may not agree with it but it's a legitimate activity, after all. And that little strike of his—"

"Which almost cost Al Freer's life and did cost Stuart Yule's leg," the Administrator could not help interjecting with some bitterness.

"—which did," the President agreed calmly, "do those things, and nobody regrets them more than I—nonetheless could be regarded as an understandable, if somewhat excessively emotional, attempt to make a point. I don't think it could really be regarded as a genuinely subversive attempt to stop the mission. Otherwise, why did he call it off if that was the motive? Why didn't he just go right on and really try to wreck things?"

"Because you agreed to invite the Russians. He gained his objective, didn't he?"

"Andy," the President said, "if you really think I offered to go to Geneva just because Clete O'Donnell pulled a strike, you have a strangely naïve view of things, I must say."

"Clete was the symbol. It was what he represented that turned the trick. You said yourself you had to throw them a bone."

"But there's a limit to how big a bone they can get," the President said quietly. "Which is something they may not know."

"Mr. President," Dr. Anderson said soberly, "if we leave Geneva without an agreement for Russian participation, mark my words, we will have very serious trouble from Clete O'Donnell at the Cape and from other elements at other NASA installations around the country. I'm convinced of it."

"Obviously you are, Andy," the President said, "and I don't blame you. It's your job to worry about NASA. But it's mine to worry about the whole country and I tell you frankly"—he gave the sudden challenging, engaging grin that was one of his chief strengths with his countrymen— "I'm not worried. Certainly not about Clete O'Donnell, who may be a little emotional and headstrong sometimes, but who really isn't a Communist, Andy. Honest he isn't. So don't let him keep you awake nights. He doesn't me."

"I'm glad," the Administrator said and he could not resist a sharpness in his voice. "It's nice to know one of us is resting easy, anyway."

"Now, Andy," the President said with a chuckle as the buzzer sounded and he rose from the rocker and went back to his desk to answer, "don't get acerbic with me. My hide's too thick for it to penetrate . . . Yes? Oh, good, put him on. Andy, come over here with me. It's Our Man in Geneva, right now . . . Well, well," he said cheerfully. "How goes the battle today?"

"Lousy," the Vice-President said grimly; and as he told them what had just occurred in the Palais des Nations, the President's ebullience faded and the Administrator's fears increased.

4.

It had begun, in what he had come to recognize as the standard routine for such things, with the motorcycle-flanked, siren-screaming procession of sleek black limousines to the Palais des Nations, arriving promptly at 2 P.M. each day. There trumpets sounded, rifle stocks cracked as soldiers standing rigidly at attention presented arms, lights flashed, cameras whirred, reporters scribbled. The mighty of the earth dismounted from their rented chariots and the affairs of man stood still, awaiting their august attentions.

Three hours later to the minute, after competing statements, competing claims and much sound and fury signifying nothing of any positive value to the world, trumpets sounded, rifle stocks cracked, lights flashed, cameras whirred, reporters scribbled. The mighty remounted their rented chariots and rolled away to quibble again another day.

Promptly at 8 P.M. each night they met for free-flowing cocktails and sumptuous dinner, at Soviet headquarters on even-numbered days, at United States headquarters on odd-numbered days. At 11 P.M. sharp they bade one another farewell and went to their hotels to compare notes, contact their governments and prepare for tomorrow's futility. And promptly at 2 P.M. the next afternoon, motorcycles roaring, sirens screaming, rifle stocks cracking, lights flashing, cameras whirring, reporters scribbling, they arrived once more at the Palais des Nations.

Out of two weeks of this, as the Vice-President reported to his vigorous superior each day, nothing so far had been accomplished. The Communists had presented their demands, he had taken them under advisement with an air of file-and-forget that was not lost on the Russians, and the time had passed in charge and countercharge.

All of this had taken place in secret, though of course Alexei Kuselevsky, principal adviser to the Soviet delegation, had seen to it that his friends in the Western press received all the titillating scraps of misinformation they needed upon which to build a running story of noble Russian willingness to co-operate and stubborn, inexcusable American refusal to let them do so. To Percy Mercy and a handful of others in America and Britain, Kuselevsky four days ago had confided specific details of the major Communist demands, with the understanding that they were confidential and for background only. Since then the tone of editorials and broadcasts in the West had noticeably sharpened toward the United States.

He had seen to it that journals such as the *Christian Science Monitor*, the *Wall Street Journal*, the Chicago *Tribune*, the New York *Daily News*, *Women's Wear Daily* and anyone else who might be able to throw a little counterweight on the other side, were excluded from this favoritism. The Vice-President and his advisers, abiding in good faith by the secrecy restrictions demanded by the Russians at the opening session, did not help their friends. Consequently the voices raised for the United States were uninformed, vague and uncertain, unable to sound any very clear note of positive support.

The world, and particularly the American people, received an overall impression of flat, stubborn, hostile, inexcusably bull-headed American intransigeance.

Alexei Kuselevsky had not been scientific adviser in the Washington embassy for six years for nothing. He knew his American friends of the media and he played them like a violin. With obliging skill and the conviction that they were helping to save the world, they carried the tune.

Now, on this fourteenth day and tenth formal morning session of the conference, he and his colleague the Foreign Minister, acting on instructions received from Moscow after last night's particularly delicious feast, decided, in the Vice-President's annoyed words, to blow it all to hell. Their move came when the Foreign Minister, following the alternating schedule which gave him today's opening statement, deferred to "my dear friend, Academician Alexei V. Kuselevsky, for a procedural matter."

"Mr. Vice-President, Mr. Foreign Minister, distinguished delegates," Alexei said promptly, his round little face creased by a thoughtful frown, "it is the belief of my government that we have now reached the stage at which these proceedings should be public. Accordingly on behalf of the U.S.S.R., I do so move, distinguished delegates."

For several moments there was a stunned silence, while the Vice-President, chairman for the day under the alternating rule, did his best to remain impassive. He had always believed secrecy was bad in principle and probably disastrous to the United States in application, but the President and the State Department had insisted he go along with it, the State Department with its usual reason: it would upset the Russians and jeopardize negotiations if the United States insisted upon maintaining its own principles. When the Vice-President called for instructions the President had been more pragmatic: "Let's jolly them along for a bit and not get into an argument on the first day." The result had been the same.

And now here it was, just as the Vice-President had anticipated, playing directly into their hands. He could see the headlines now: U.S. BALKS AT RUSS DEMAND WORLD BE TOLD OF GENEVA TALKS. REDS CHARGE AMERICANS NEED SECRECY TO CONCEAL SPACE IMPERIALISM.

And that, of course, was exactly what Alexei did charge five minutes later, after the Vice-President, impatiently brushing aside the bright young men from Washington who immediately buzzed in his ear with frantic and impossible advice, had reminded the conference coldly of the unanimous agreement on secrecy reached the first day.

"Mr. Vice-President," Alexei replied in a tone of deep reproach, "the government of the U.S.S.R. did not understand at that time that this was to be an inflexible and eternal restriction, Mr. Vice-President. My government did not understand that it was to be used to deny the peoples of the world their perfectly justifiable right to know what we are doing here in our work toward space co-operation. My government wonders, Mr. Vice-President," he added severely, "what the Government of the United States is afraid of? What is it trying to conceal? Is it some new and sinister form of space imperialism, Mr. Vice-President? The Government of the U.S.S.R. wonders this."

322

"The Government of the U.S.S.R.," the Vice-President snapped, "knows perfectly well that it is raising an utterly phony issue, I will say to Delegate Kuselevsky. This is a bare-faced and blatant attempt to get world headlines and win a propaganda advantage. The Soviet Union, as usual, is not interested in co-operation. It is interested only in propaganda."

"Mr. Vice-President," Alexei Kuselevsky retorted, his round face flushing, his pudgy little hands clenching and unclenching before him on the table, "the delegate of the United States is making unwarranted and unworthy charges here. The Government of the United States for some sinister space-imperialist purpose of its own is choosing to deny knowledge of our proceedings to the peoples of the world. *Why, why, why?* That is what I ask the distinguished chairman, the delegate, the Vice-President of the United States!"

"The distinguished chairman, the delegate, the Vice-President of the United States," the Vice-President replied in a tone so scathing that his bright young men visibly cringed and wilted like dying flowers at his side, "says to the delegate of the U.S.S.R. that he is talking nonsense. Further, he knows he is talking nonsense. Blatant, deliberate, crude, vicious nonsense."

"The United States is trying to keep these proceedings secret!" Alexei cried, pounding his tight little fists furiously upon the table. "The United States is seeking an imperialist advantage in space. Space imperialism, Mr. Vice-President, space imperialism!"

"Very *well!*" the Vice-President said, raising his voice and drowning Alexei into silence for the moment. "Throw open the doors! Bring in the press and television! Put your ridiculous demands on the table in front of the whole world ('Oh, my *God!*' murmured one of his young men, turned pale and appeared about to faint) and see what the world makes of them. See what the American people make of them, when they get the truth! The United States," he went on more calmly, "has been trying to protect you from your folly, I will say to the delegate. We did not think you would want the world to see how truly impossible you are."

"Impossible?" Alexei demanded, apparently getting a second wind while the Foreign Secretary maintained his usual dourly frowning silence at his side. "Impossible?

What is impossible? We make a perfectly reasonable request for a percentage of the launch teams that will reflect our scientific achievements in this field. As the first nation to orbit man successfully in space, we make a perfectly reasonable request that we be given four members of a crew of six. And because we have always been hindered and hampered in our search for co-operation with the United States by your morbidly suspicious security procedures, Mr. Vice-President—such 'security,' more like crazy witch-hunting!—we have asked that these stupid and unnecessary procedures be suspended so that we may work freely with you on this great adventure to Mars.

"And this is 'impossible!' This is 'folly!' The United States should know what impossible folly is, Mr. Vice-President! It has destroyed this conference with it!"

And with a quick glance at the Foreign Minister, who nodded and followed his lead, he picked up his papers and marched sternly toward the door. After him, frowning and looking as ostentatiously severe as they could manage, marched the twenty-seven other assorted scientists, clerks, secretaries, spies and propaganda experts of the Soviet delegation.

"So can I come home?" the Vice-President inquired into the silence of the Oval Room.

"At once," the President said.

"I think that would be best," the Vice-President agreed. "I apologize, Mr. President. They never intended to negotiate, and we didn't want to. But I'm afraid I let them beat me to it. I should have thought of a way to avoid that."

"But of course," the Administrator said, "we couldn't have moved first. Imagine what the reaction would have been."

"Watch it now," the President suggested dryly.

In a handful of major publications and a few smaller ones, here and there throughout the world, some balance and perspective were maintained:

RUSS END GENEVA TALKS WHEN U.S. OPPOSES GIVING FULL CONTROL OF MARS FLIGHT . . . U.S. CALLS RED DEMANDS RIDICULOUS AS CONFERENCE COLLAPSES . . . SOVIETS WALK OUT WHEN U.S. REJECTS ONE-SIDED MARS PLAN.

But overwhelmingly from America's most influential

journals and from the great majority of the newspapers of the world there came another story—the story Alexei and his friends had counted upon. Their confidence was not misplaced:

U.S. BOMBS SPACE TALKS . . . U.S. SECRECY RULE BRINGS RUSS WALKOUT AT GENEVA . . . REDS DEFEND WORLD RIGHT TO KNOW SPACE PLANS . . . SOVIET DELEGATION TERMS U.S. SECRECY "IMPOSSIBLE FOLLY" . . . RUSS CHARGE U.S. SEEKS SPACE IMPERIALISM . . . SOVIETS END CONFERENCE AS U.S. BLOCKS MARS COMPROMISE . . .

And on the editorial pages and in major news broadcasts and commentaries the theme of American intransigeance and iniquity expanded and grew as it had on a thousand other occasions in these peculiar decades when derogating America had become the pastime not only of the world, but of a highly vocal and self-important portion of America's own citizenry:

"We do not for a moment, of course," the *Times* declared solemnly, "hold any great brief for giving the Soviet Union absolute control of the Mars mission. Nonetheless, we cannot escape the conclusion that if the United States had not gone to Geneva so obviously adamant in its intention to dynamite any kind of agreement, the world might today be in much better shape and feeling much more secure on this difficult issue.

"There are arguments to be made, perhaps, against the Soviet suggestion that its technicians be given a numerically (but perhaps not scientifically) greater amount of control over launch operations. But equally, it seems to us, there are arguments that can be made for it. Certainly it did not warrant any such harsh and out-of-hand rejection as this government's somewhat odd delegation, headed by the Vice-President, gave it.

"But this was in a sense only a minor dispute compared to two other matters on which the conference foundered: the refusal of the United States to waive internal security measures which past experience has shown to be ill-advised and punitive to the point of insanity, and the insistence of the United States upon an iron-clad secrecy rule at the conference which is repugnant to the world's right to know and to all the instincts of this free people.

"We have opposed for many years the petty ways in

which the FBI, the Justice Department, the Passport Office and all the other peek-and-pry agencies of the government have pandered to the shabbiest fears of America's more timorous and easily frightened citizens. We do not believe in witch-hunts and we have said so on many occasions going back to the high-riding days of the late Senator Joseph McCarthy and beyond. We believe America has nothing to fear from a free interchange of persons and ideas with the Russians. We can understand the Soviet resentment that now, at this late date and in connection with this great enterprise, the United States should still be acting like a terrified child afraid of the dark. On this ground alone we can appreciate why the Soviet Union decided to terminate what was obviously a futile attempt to instill some sanity into these matters.

"But it is on the ground of secrecy and this government's adamant refusal to permit the peoples of the world their fair and basic right to know the inner truths of a venture that could drastically affect all their lives and futures, that we think the United States is most gravely to blame for what has happened in Geneva . . ."

"With an infallible instinct for the wrong thing," the *Post* began, "this government has once again destroyed the chance—perhaps the greatest chance—to arrive at a genuine working arrangement with the Soviet Union. This time the occasion was the Mars flight. In the past it has been other proposals for co-operation and unity. Every time, American fear or American stupidity or outright American intransigeance has brought a sad collapse to bright and shining hopes. How long can this go on? How long, indeed, do we have left?

"It may be, as the United States seems to maintain, that the Soviet suggestion that they be allowed a majority of the technical personnel in charge of the Mars launch is a somewhat exaggerated claim. But surely it would not have been rejected outright. Surely there is present in the United States (if not, perhaps, in the delegation headed by the Vice-President which went to Geneva) the intelligence, the patience, the broad world view, and the skill, to come to some reasonable determination on this issue. In our estimation it was not something to kick overboard summarily. It was worthy of better than that.

"On the issue of the removal of the petty and punitive internal security regulations which have hampered U.S.-

Soviet co-operation for many decades, we could not agree more with the Russian position that they are ridiculous, inhibiting, self-defeating and inexcusable, particularly when applied to so great an enterprise as the mission to Mars. This is not some monumental attempt to keep a bushy-bearded Bolshevik from infiltrating the Senior Citizens' Bowling League in St. Petersburg, Florida. This is a solemn and serious attempt by a great scientific power to achieve a genuine co-operation with the United States in space. And still we find the witch-hunters of the FBI, the Justice Department, the Passport Office and all the other peek-and-pry agencies of a timorous government trying to impose their frightened little rules upon the great project of sending an expedition successfully to Mars. We cannot say we blame the Soviet Union for its reaction.

"Nor can we blame it for its condemnation of the United States insistence upon a secrecy rule which flies completely in the face of the traditions of this free democracy, and completely in the face of a worried world's right to know what is going on in the project which could have such dramatic impact upon the future of all mankind. Nothing can justify so undemocratic, so arbitrary and so harmful a stand . . ."

And from Frankly Unctuous and the great majority of his colleagues of air and tube, from Percy Mercy, Walter Dobius and the great majority of their think-alikes of column and commentary, there came the same insistent hammering upon the same self-righteous themes. Competing voices, even those which said nothing more startling, in effect, than, "Hey! Let's stop and look at this thing objectively!" were drowned and lost in the clamor. It was, after all, as some of the most famous members of the media had often blandly told the country, an article of faith that "there is no such thing as objectivity." Those who justified giving free rein to their own intolerant and illiberal prejudices by claiming so, roared on.

Much of this ill-tempered yawp, of course, was standard procedure and the sort of thing that every American administration in an intolerant and truth-twisting century was used to and shrugged off. But enough of it struck home to the less sophisticated to worry and alarm those who bore the major responsibility for Planetary Fleet One. By next morning in Houston they felt themselves to be under a steadily mounting pressure from which they were not protected by the thick skins and dogged determination of those more accustomed to public life.

Once again in the velvet night they had gone out to watch brightly lit, arrogant Space Station *Stalin* pass on its cold, inexorable rounds. Once again they had watched modest little Space Station *Mayflower* come trailing along diffidently behind. And once again they had felt fear.

It was in no easy mood that they met next day to consider the implications for themselves and their mission of the events, so misrepresented and so ominous, of Geneva.

5.

Jazz asked for the meeting in a call to Connie shortly after the 6 P.M. news broadcasts with all their sly and not-so-sly condemnations of the United States and their indirect and not-so-indirect musings as to whether Piffy One should be allowed to fly at all in view of the new world situation.

"I don't quite see what we can do about it," Connie told him, "except go on about our business and keep our mouths shut. It seems to me that's the best answer to these bastards from where we sit."

"I'm not saying we should answer them," Jazz said impatiently. "I'm saying we've got to protect ourselves."

"We can't stop them from talking."

"That's not what I mean. Do I get my meeting or don't I?"

"Nine tomorrow, my office?"

"Thank you."

"Not at all."

But though he said good-by with a certain dryness in his tone, Connie was not sorry Jazz had precipitated a meeting. He felt some psychological need to be with his crew, whatever their differences, in the face of what seemed to be almost universal attack. When he told Jane about it she looked at him with a wide-eyed, serious stare.

"He's afraid for you all. And frankly so am I. There seems to be so much criticism and so much bitterness—it's almost as though there were an active force in the air wishing things would go wrong. I'm a little superstitious about that sort of thing: I think there can be such a thing

329

as a universal malevolence. I think lots of our own countrymen are helping to create it right now."

"Lots," Connie agreed, "but I can hardly believe all. There's a certain group that always fouls its own nest but I still think the great majority is with us and for the mission." He smiled. "Three months from now, when all the damage has been done and it no longer matters, somebody will publish a public opinion poll showing this to have been true ... No, Janie, I wouldn't worry, if I were you. It will work out all right."

"Aren't you worried?" she asked, her eyes shadowed with concern. "How can you hear all these bitter statements and not be? Some of them are practically demanding that the mission be cancelled. They sound as though they don't want Piffy One to fly at all."

"I thought you agreed with that," he suggested, though, in fairness, she had said nothing further on the subject since their argument a month ago. She gave him a sudden glance.

"Only if you yourselves decided not to go. I wouldn't want a lot of—of—*outsiders* interfering with Piffy One."

"That's my Janie," he said with a laugh, pulling her toward him and giving her a quick kiss. "You really sound fierce, gal. Spoken like the wife of an astronaut, and that's for sure. True to the corps and all that stuff."

"Well," she said, smiling a little but standing her ground, "it's the way I feel. I want them to keep their sneering tongues and lying pens off Piffy One. Piffy One belongs to us, not them."

He sighed, suddenly sober.

"I'm afraid that's not the case, Janie. She's theirs and they can ruin her if they try."

"Well, I don't want them to hurt *you*," she said fiercely. "I want you to be safe."

"We're safe enough. There isn't much they can do to us except turn us back to pasture."

But with this, he found next morning, neither Jazz nor Pete agreed. They expressed a concern that had already occurred to him, though he had refrained from alarming Jane. Jazz came right out with it the minute Connie closed the door of his office and the four of them were alone.

"What do we do if the damned Russians try to shoot us down?" he demanded. "And don't tell me I'm crazy just because it's never happened. They have the capability."

Jayvee uttered a snort of mingled skepticism and disgust and looked at him as though he were insane.

But Pete nodded soberly.

"Ever since they successfully tested Cosmos 248 in the fall of 1968 they've been able to destroy satellites in earth orbit and presumably in moon orbit also. They must have quite a few killer-satellites in the stockpile by this time. We've just been damned lucky they haven't quite dared use them on us, I guess."

"Do you really mean to tell me," Jayvee said slowly, and since it was the first general comment he had made to them in quite some time they followed it intently, "that you *actually* want me to believe that the Russians could *actually* shoot us down—and that they might do it?" He stared at them one by one with an expression of tired scorn. "You're something. You're *really* something."

"We may be," Connie said, trying to keep the sharpness out of his voice as much as possible, "but it is a definite possibility. As far as we know, they can do it. As a matter of fact, Andy called me last night and we had quite a talk about it. But I wasn't going to alarm anybody for a while, yet."

"Alarm anybody?" Jayvee echoed. "With hobgoblin stuff like that? I should hope *not*."

"Listen—" Jazz began, but Connie hit the table with the flat of his hand.

"Stop it, Jazz. Cut it out. I know it's hard for someone like Jayvee, who hasn't been informed on these matters to believe anything like this—"

"Why wasn't I informed?" Jayvee demanded dourly. "If everybody else seems to have heard it, why didn't I?"

Connie shrugged.

"I don't know where Jazz and Pete picked it up."

"We listened," Pete said dryly. "We paid attention. We stayed around. And we talked to people. You can pick up an amazing amount that way."

"Well," Jayvee said flatly, "I don't believe it."

"You'd damned well better," Jazz said harshly, "because it's your precious black skin if you don't."

"All right, I said," Connie remarked in an exasperated voice. "Damn it, Jazz, lay off, will you? It isn't going to do any good to berate him if he doesn't want to take our word for it. The practical issue is, *we* believe it, so what do you want us to do about it?"

"Not talk about it in public, I hope," Jayvee remarked. "Piffy One would be the laughingstock of the world."

"Nobody said anything about talking about it in public," Connie said sharply. "Jazz, what do you think we should do?"

"First of all," Jazz said, "keep our mouths shut—and not because Piffy One would be a laughingstock, either—but because if we do anything I *assume*"—and he stared at Jayvee, who stared back—"I *assume* we don't want the Communists to know about it. Or do we?"

Jayvee gave a shrug of elaborate disdain.

"Don't ask me. This is your idea. I don't believe it, remember?"

"More fool you," Jazz said shortly and, deliberately ignoring him, spoke directly to Connie. "I think we ought to request that the spacecraft be armed. And not just defensively, either."

"It seems to me offensively is the only way they could be armed," Connie said thoughtfully, "if we really wanted to protect ourselves. I'm afraid there isn't much room for defensive maneuver in space. At least not enough to make much difference. Whoever strikes first probably wins. I doubt if there's a second chance."

Pete looked at him soberly.

"*I'd* feel a lot better."

"So would I," Jazz agreed.

"That makes three of us," Connie said. "So I'd suggest we rally the troops here and brace headquarters on it. Suppose I get hold of Hank and Bert and Bob Hertz and Dr. Cavanaugh and we all meet back here in an hour and put through a call to Andy." He turned to Jayvee. "Is that agreeable to you?"

Again Jayvee gave them the look of tired and disbelieving disgust and slowly shook his head.

"*No*," he said finally, "it's not agreeable to me. I don't believe it, can't you understand that? I think you're acting like a bunch of hysterical babies. I think the Russians have succeeded in scaring you to death, which is probably one of the things they want to do. You assume they're hostile to us. I don't believe that either. I can understand why they walked out of the conference when our great Vice-President and our great President wouldn't negotiate, but that doesn't mean they're hostile. Anyway, I don't blame them if they're annoyed, the way we act so suspicious of them all the time. They've got a gripe coming. They ought to be arming against *us*. I wouldn't blame them."

"Then I take it you don't agree with this crew decision," Connie said evenly, forestalling Jazz' angry comment with a firmly raised hand.

"It isn't my decision," Jayvee said tersely, "and I'm part of the crew." And with a sudden contortion of hate on his face, so unexpected, so inexplicable and so personal that it astounded them, he added, *"Mister* Commander."

There was silence for several moments until Connie finally answered. (*Now what the hell* he wondered. *Surely he didn't overhear her talking to me. And if he did, I was only telling her to stay with him.*) He managed to speak with a reasonable calmness though it cost him a real effort.

"Then I'd suggest that you be here with the rest of us an hour from now and make your pitch. You have the right: go ahead. Maybe you can convince everybody."

Jayvee uttered a tight and scornful laugh.

"Oh, sure. Sure I can. Your minds are made up. You can't be convinced of anything."

"Then get off the crew," Jazz suggested coldly. "Nobody said you couldn't resign."

Again there was silence during which they returned Jayvee stare for stare, his changing from furious to inscrutable, theirs determinedly impassive.

"Oh, no," he said softly at last. "I wouldn't give you that satisfaction."

"Then be here in an hour, will you?" Connie repeated in a tone deliberately impersonal and businesslike. "We have important matters to discuss with Washington."

But an hour later Jayvee, who had made no reply but simply stood up and stalked out without a glance, was nowhere to be found. His absence got their conference off to exactly the start Connie suspected Jayvee had intended: they spent the first ten minutes discussing him.

Finally the Administrator demanded in an exasperated tone, "Well, what do you want to do about him, fire him? It can't be done without a reason."

"That's what I keep telling these hotheads," Connie remarked with a rueful laugh, "but I can't seem to get the point over to them. Thanks for helping me, Andy."

"You're welcome," Dr. Anderson said. "And I hope we won't have any further discussion about it."

"O.K.," Hank said. "We'll stop talking. But we'll watch."

"You damned well bet your retro-rockets we will," Bert said grimly.

"So watch," the Administrator said. "And when you have something, shout. But don't worry it every minute in the meantime. Now, what's the real reason you called?"

"The crew feels," Dr. Cavanaugh said, "and as director of the Manned Spacecraft Center I agree with them, that in view of what happened at Geneva they had better be armed."

"They had better be armed or the spacecraft had better be armed?"

"Both," Bob Hertz, Connie and Hank said simultaneously. The Administrator smiled.

"Sounds pretty universal. What about the rest of you?"

"Aye, aye," Pete said.

"Roger," Bert and Jazz replied together.

"Hmm," Dr. Anderson said, his expression thoughtful. "Jayvee, I gather, disagrees."

Connie nodded.

"So he tells us."

"But he'll go along with it."

"Who knows?" Jazz asked. "I don't trust that sneaky son of a bitch one inch."

"We'll have to assume he will," Dr. Anderson said. "If he doesn't, you have your reason ... Well: I shall take it up with the proper quarter. I warn you, though, I have no idea what the response will be."

"Surely he won't send us out there naked, will he?" Connie demanded with a genuine annoyance.

"Not if he's convinced there's a real danger," the Administrator said. "Certainly not."

"Are you?" Dr. Cavanaugh inquired, and they all leaned forward intently and waited for his answer.

"Enough so that I'd rather have you safe than sorry," Andy Anderson said. There was a little sigh of relaxed tension around the table in Houston.

"Good," Bob Hertz said with his comfortable lopsided grin. "That's our boy."

"You know I am," Dr. Anderson said. "But I don't have the final say. I'll do my best. In the meantime, I'd suggest we keep this absolutely to ourselves. Nothing

334

could make a bigger mess or raise more hell than to get the wrong impression out to the public prematurely."

"We won't talk," Connie said, with an emphasis on the "we"; knowing, as did they all, that someone might, and that if he were going to, he was probably at it already. And knowing also, with a certain instinctive inevitability, that there was probably nothing at all they could do about it in time to prevent the kind of uproar Andy Anderson foresaw.

But for all that they thought so little of him at the moment, it was not a decision lightly arrived at or a show of defiance blithely embarked upon. If there had not been so many bitter, conflicting things swirling through Jayvee's mind—swirling and still swirling, after more than two weeks of agonizing so intense he had wondered sometimes at his own ability to stand it—he might have been able to decide upon a course of action and follow it through with some peace of mind. As it was, the emotions he felt as he did what they expected he would do were not satisfying or comforting or conducive to even a minimal peace of mind. He thought with some vestige of ironic self-judgment that he couldn't even enjoy paying them back: so tortured and self-defeating had his thoughts become.

Still he felt he had to do what he did, even if it didn't give him much real satisfaction. It would show them they couldn't count on him: it would make them sit up and take notice. It would make them take him at his own evaluation as an important man who was not to be trifled with. And this at least was not to be minimized.

Why he should still feel this way after having achieved his ambition to be on the crew he could not entirely analyze, but he knew it revolved around a couple of things. The most important, up to a couple of days ago, had been his general resentment of the arrogant superiority he thought they must feel toward him simply because they were white. The second had been his discovery that something was apparently going on between his wife and that great, glamorous, shining knight in armor, Colonel Trasker. He felt that the combination would have justified anything. Anything.

His response to what he believed to be their general attitude toward him—and in Jazz' case, certainly, it did

335

not take much imagination to support belief—had been to "Go away somewhere inside," as Monetta had described it to Connie in the conversation he had overheard. That was what he had done, all right, he thought now with a grim amusement as he sat in his office waiting for his call to go through—he had gone away somewhere inside and he had extracted a savage pleasure out of watching them try to guess where. He hadn't told them and he never would. He wanted to see it get on their nerves, and it had, as probably few other things could have.

It was true, what he had told them in that first bitter crew meeting: they couldn't stand not being loved, these great boyish figures who got their kicks out of bounding about space. They just couldn't take the silent treatment, which was twice as devastating if you were accustomed to the adulation of everyone you met. He had embarked upon a psychological gambit so simple it constantly amazed him that they fell for it. But they did, he could tell that. He got on their nerves dreadfully just by not responding with anything but the tersest comments on the most banal and businesslike subjects. The slightest attempt on their part to establish some lighter, more humanly normal intimacy, and he froze. He froze and they got tense. It worked like clockwork every time.

How long he could have kept it up, he couldn't say, for aside from being a satisfying means of getting vengeance for their presumed feeling of superiority toward him, it was wearing on him too. He had to admit that. Always to be watching, always to be defensive, always to be on guard against relaxing, even in the slightest degree. Up to a couple of days ago he had thought that while Jazz was insufferable, Connie and Pete at heart weren't so bad. He had actually been contemplating softening up a bit with them: their patience, though they would never know it and he would never admit it, had finally been about to achieve results.

Then had come Monetta and Connie's chummy little talk in which he had heard himself being discussed with a rending candor he had never experienced, to say nothing of its indications of a much more than casual intimacy on their part. And then had come the fiasco in Geneva, which had been so contrary to everything he believed about peace and the need for co-operation in space as a major

336

step toward it. The combination had sent him into a rage that seemed to him to call for and justify almost any act of retaliation, no matter how destructive it might be to Piffy One and his own ego and ambitions that rode upon it. And then had come this morning's meeting with its insane and hysterical idea that the Soviets would in some way attempt to destroy the Mars mission and that therefore the American spacecraft and astronauts should be armed. That did it, he told himself grimly. That really did it. At that point they lost him, and for good.

And he had not yet even begun to feel the full impact of what he had discovered about Connie and Monetta. It was true that Connie had appeared to be urging her to stay with him, but there had been an intimacy about the tone that would have alerted the instinct of a man far less intelligent and perceptive than he. They were either lovers or had thought about it: the understanding was implicit in the voices. He didn't think his marriage would last, either, but he wanted the option of terminating it. He didn't want Monetta to have the privilege: it was too ego-destroying for him to be rejected like that. And he certainly didn't want old high-and-mighty glamour-boy Connie to come along and speed the process, either. That would really be rubbing Jayvee's nose in it; and this, too, he was grimly determined would not happen.

So for all these reasons he was in no mood to co-operate with NASA or Connie or Piffy One or anything but his own driving emotions on this turbulent day. What he was now doing was an inevitable result of his own character and the recent stresses it had given and received.

When the buzzer sounded he reached over and snapped on the Picturephone without a trace of compunction.

"What would you do," he asked abruptly, "if I told you Connie Trasker and the rest of them out here in Houston want to arm the crew and the spacecraft because they *say*"—he gave the word a heavy sarcastic emphasis— "they *say* they're afraid of a Russian attack?"

What he would do, the editor of *View* told him grimly, and what he was now doing as fast as he could to the best of his considerable ability, was arouse all the friends he could think of to oppose this latest and most insane of all the insane things that had occurred in connection with Planetary Fleet One.

P.C.M. was on the rampage, and when P.C.M. was on the rampage administrations trembled, strong men quaked and great leaders looked to their own salvation. It was not that he was egotistical, he often told himself approvingly, but he did have power. And when he could use it in a high moral cause, as he was absolutely sure he was doing now, it was doubly delicious and satisfying because then he could convince himself that the ruthless methods he so often employed were righteous, noble and pure.

The conviction of his own righteousness, purity and nobility was very necessary to Percy Mercy.

He could not, in fact, have lived without it.

So now there were no hesitations in his voice, no restraints upon his wingèd words as they sped across the country, north, south, east, west, up, down and sideways, to all the seats of power where his like-thinking friends controlled the major media.

Their response, as he had anticipated, was immediate and inevitable.

Typewriters still hot from condemnations of Geneva blazed up anew.

Microphones scarcely dry from the spew of sarcasm heaped upon America were hastily wiped off and put back in service.

Dour deans denounced, proud prelates pronounced.

CAUSE roared, the UN deplored.

From Academe to Thespia, with an occasional input from the American Medical Association, the American Bar Association and the National Council of Churches, the statements alarmed—appalled—opposed—poured forth.

Pickets marched at the White House, at Houston, at the Cape.

Every Right Thinker worth his salt from Berkeley to Bombay sounded off and the media were right there to carry the message to the ends of the earth with the speed of light.

It was fun, fun, fun, and Percy and his friends went at it with a will. And the nice thing, the great thing, the absolutely marvelous thing about it all was that it was so right.

The thought of arming the Mars mission *was* repugnant and horrible.

The Soviet Union *was* friendly and *did* want to co-operate.

The implication that the Communists might actually have hostile intentions *was* insane and an outrageous affront to the peaceful hopes of mankind.

It *was* an egregious and inexcusable insult to a great and responsible power.

It *was* a most shameful and horrible example of all the fear-ridden stupidities of ignorant, middle-class, silent-majority America.

It *was* the right and duty of all far-seeing lovers of humanity to attack it with all the venom, vitriol and viciousness at their command, for it was indeed an example of the infantile suspicions that could end the world.

And were they not the world's protectors?

Today they were on the side of God and angels, and if they were incidentally on the side of the Communists, too, well, that was happenstance, and happenstance, moreover, which their wayward countrymen had brought upon themselves.

It was a happy, thrilling, deeply satisfying occasion for them all.

So the full floor, hardly abated in the past twenty-four hours since Geneva, broke anew upon the Administration, NASA and Planetary Fleet One. All afternoon, into the night and on into the next day the torrent of editorials, broadcasts and stern condemnations raged. By the time Kenny Williams rose in the Senate shortly after 1 P.M. to demand that "the crew and administrators of NASA be required to appear at a public press conference so that the country and the world may know the real truth about this strangely motivated and strangely mismanaged mission," he spoke a universal word.

Even the journalistic and congressional friends of Piffy One—and there were some, though a wan and wobbling minority—agreed now that there must be a public accounting.

At 6 P.M. the White House bowed and NASA bowed with it:

"BULLETIN—NASA Administrator Anderson announces press conference crew and managers Planetary Fleet One Houston 10 A.M. tomorrow."

6.

It had been the place for many proud press conferences in the past but there was a good chance NASA and its glamour boys might be humbled now. The exciting possibility drew the keepers of the world's conscience in like flies.

The auditorium at the Manned Spacecraft Center was so full by 9:30 A.M. that Bob Hertz, looking out through the curtains at the back of the stage, remarked dryly to Andy Anderson that if they let in any more the building might collapse and bury the lot.

"Which," he added with only a partial humor, "might not be such a bad idea."

"That's not a very friendly attitude to take," commented Connie Trasker, overhearing.

"And anyway," Dr. Cavanaugh joined in, "they'd say we did it on purpose."

"We can't win," the Administrator agreed in mock dismay. "This just isn't going to be NASA's day."

"It had damned well better be," Jazz said. "This is make-or-break, this time."

"That's right," Pete agreed. "Where's our friend?"

"I'm sure he'll be here," Hank said. "As unco-operative as he dares."

"We'll tend to him later," Jazz promised grimly.

Connie nodded, not very happily.

"Yes. I'm afraid we have to, now."

"Jesus!" Bert Richmond remarked with a sudden explosive violence. "I wish to hell this were over."

But it would be a while, yet, before it was, and in the

340

meantime things were being readied for what promised to be the biggest and perhaps the most controversial of all NASA's many confrontations with the media. The men behind the curtain were as certain that the men and women out front were out to get them as the men and women out front were. Mutual hostility crackled in the air beneath a covering blanket of outward cordiality. Objectivity, being impossible, did not have to be remembered: its delightful absence opened the door to all sorts of thrilling and dramatic contingencies. Maybe Conrad Trasker could be driven into a public rage—maybe J. V. Halleck could be encouraged into a real attack upon Piffy One. It was a moment when anything could happen; and the majority, bearing in mind objectivity's impossibility, were cheerfully determined that it should.

On the surface, of course, in these final pre-conference moments, everyone went through the motions of hearty good fellowship. In some cases, such as the little hard-core group of veteran newspaper and television reporters from the Cape, these motions were quite sincere: they were, and always had been, one hundred percent for the program. They were sympathetic to NASA, dedicated to its purposes, aware of its problems and tensions, willing to defend it and able to do so with a clear conscience and a friendly conviction. From them the men behind the curtain could count on questions good-hearted, encouraging, sincerely designed to bring both sides before the public. If NASA could justify its position they were ready to give it generous publicity.

Elsewhere throughout the auditorium, prospects were not so kindly. P.C.M. and Walter Dobius were there, looking ineffably self-important, eagerly listening while pretending not to, to the running whispers of, "There's Percy Mercy! ... Well, well, this *must* be important, to bring Walter 'way out here!" Frankly Unctuous was present, hatchet in hand, ready to tell his millions of network viewers what they had just seen, in the bland assumption that they had not seen what he had, which was entirely true. The *Post* and the *Times*, severe accompanying editorials already written and waiting back home to be rushed into print, were ready with questions needling, nasty, self-serving of their particular point of view which was not NASA's. From overseas came the supercilious British scold, the draggled Italian witch: NASA need expect no charity from them. Busy, bright and bustling, a little knot of Soviet and Iron Curtain reporter-spies jabbered happily in a corner. An acrid wit from Canada told his dullard cousins below the border about their country's shortcomings and his cousins eagerly agreed. The stage was set for a lively and probably bitter clash of wills and personalities which would be, as Jazz accurately stated, make-or-break.

Promptly at 10 A.M. the Administrator, inwardly tense but managing to look reasonably relaxed, led his colleagues on stage. Five hundred pencils busily scribbled, while a dozen cameras peered and transmitted—

"Anderson, Cavanaugh, Hertz, Barstow, Richmond, Trasker, Weickert, Balkis, Stevenick—"

"Where's Halleck?" the *Wall Street Journal* hissed to the Chicago *Tribune,* and the *Tribune* hissed back, *"out in de co'n fiel', bringin' in de sheaves."* The British scold looked deeply offended, the Italian witch made one of her countrymen's standard gestures. And of course when Joe Stevenick, looking somewhat intimidated, announced the formal opening of the conference, it was the first question out.

"Dr. Anderson!" a confident, determined voice called out, and there was a turning and a buzzing and a hey-hey-hey as everyone recognized the small, trim, determined figure who spoke thus forcefully. "May we inquire: where is Dr. Halleck?"

"Dr. Halleck has been informed of this conference," the Administrator said calmly, "as far as I know, Percy, he is on his way—"

"I'm here," Jayvee called from the back of the room, and came down the aisle with an ostentatious slowness while necks craned, eyes looked, pencils scribbled, cameras zeroed in upon his leisurely, just-this-side-of-insolence saunter.

"Good," Dr. Anderson said as Jayvee finally stepped up onto the platform and took his seat at the end of the table, next to Pete but carefully separated from him by at least two feet. "Now we can proceed."

"I should like to ask Dr. Halleck," Walter Dobius said, rising beside his colleague, "whether he has been conscious of any attempt to punish him for his lack of conformity."

"Now, just a minute," Andy Anderson said, a genuine annoyance in his voice. "Suppose you specify, Walter. What 'lack of conformity'?"

"There have been well-substantiated rumors," Walter Dobius said calmly, "that Dr. Halleck is not in agreement with some of the policies adopted for the Mars mission. I repeat, Dr. Halleck, have you been conscious of any attempt to—"

"He has not been punished," Dr. Anderson interrupted coldly.

"Will he be?" Percy asked like a quick little ferret from his seat.

There was an uneasy stirring along the table, over the room an amused little ripple. Checkmate on the first move out would really be too much to hope for. But how delicious!

The Administrator stared thoughtfully down upon his two blandly waiting inquisitors and decided to give as good as he got.

"What lack of conformity has Dr. Halleck been guilty of, gentlemen?" he inquired. "You seem to be better informed than I am on his activities. Has he done something we should know about?"

But Percy was equal to him. In a tone equally bland he asked,

"Can you give us assurance that Dr. Halleck will not be disciplined because of his disagreements with official NASA policy?"

Again there was a little stirring along the table; five hundred pairs of eyes assessed its significance in five hundred different ways, few friendly to NASA. Dr. Anderson visibly checked the start of a quick rejoinder and rubbed his chin thoughtfully.

"What is this," he asked finally, "an attempt to trap me? Is that the purpose here?"

"I'm sorry," Percy said, getting to his feet again, "that NASA seems to be so sensitive that it feels every legitimate inquiry is in some way hostile or designed to entrap." An elaborate patience came into his voice. "I simply wish to ask whether there is any desire or intention within NASA to discipline Dr. Halleck for disagreeing with certain policies concerning this mission. Why is NASA trying to evade an answer, Dr. Anderson? I'm sure the country doesn't understand it."

"NASA is not trying to evade an answer!" the Administrator snapped. "By the same token," he went on more calmly, "NASA is not going to let itself be trapped, as I

343

think you quite obviously wish to trap it, into a pledge that it will never discipline one of its astronauts if he gives it good cause to do so. To accept that premise would be to abandon control of the program altogether."

"Has Dr. Halleck given you such cause?" the *Times* inquired, rising from his seat at the other side of the auditorium.

"Or do you expect him to?" the *Post* added, from down front.

For a moment the Administrator said nothing, while the tension in the room rose swiftly. Four bland, polite, courteously insolent faces looked up at him. He surveyed them deliberately, one by one.

"I do not think," he marked finally, "that any purpose is to be served by pursuing this line of questioning. If Dr. Halleck deserves to be disciplined, he will be. If he does not, he won't. I don't really know how I can make it any plainer than that."

"You don't know," Walter Dobius echoed heavily, "how you can make it any plainer than that. Very well. It will be interesting to follow Dr. Halleck's progress and see how you apply this rather flexible rule to him. And we will all, of course, be following his progress."

"As I hope you will the progress of all our astronauts," Dr. Anderson said blandly. "They're a fine group of men." Suddenly he gave a cheerful grin, inviting them to laugh. "Are there any other questions? If not——"

And laugh they did, a brief unyielding jollity. Then the atmosphere congealed again. The AP stood up, not himself hostile, but sounding so in line of duty.

"Dr. Anderson, what is the decision on arming the mission?"

"There has been no decision."

"But the matter is under discussion?"

"There has been some mention of the idea," Andy answered calmly.

"Nothing official?"

"Well——" He hesitated and they were on it at once. The Italian witch was on her feet.

"Dr. Anderson," she said in her heavy, dramatic accent, managing to sound patronizing, supercilious and bitchy rolled into one. "Dr. Anderson, is it not true that it is being discussed at the highest levels? Is it not true that the crew is badly divided over the question? Are they threatening to resign because of it?"

"Jayvee," Dr. Anderson said like a flash, turning to stare down the table, "are you threatening to resign?"

For a moment Jayvee looked completely taken aback, jolted out of the carefully sullen expression he had been maintaining since taking his seat. He frowned, looked at some distant point out over the auditorium while the cameras zeroed in to transmit his handsome, brooding face across the globe. Finally he uttered one word.

"No."

"Good," Andy said crisply. "Connie? Jazz? Pete?" And he looked with an elaborate concern along the table. "Do tell Fortunata whether you intend to resign. God knows we'd better find out right this minute if you do!"

Connie leaned forward to the microphone in front of him on the table.

"Not I," he said cheerfully. He pushed the microphone to Jazz.

"Here for the duration," Jazz said cheerfully. He pushed the microphone to Pete.

"Likewise," Pete said cheerfully. He pushed the microphone back to the Administrator.

"Fortunata," Dr. Anderson said cheerfully, "it must be just another of those delightful things about NASA that neither NASA nor anybody else ever knows until you tell us. As usual, there appears to be nothing to it."

"Very funny," Fortunata said, and sat down with a muttered comment in Italian which received uproarious chuckles from several of her countrymen seated nearby.

But the diversion of course did not deflect anyone from the main point.

"Dr. Anderson," the UPI said politely, "I assume this is an open press conference—I mean, we can ask questions of anyone—"

"Oh, it's a free-for-all," the Administrator said cordially. "We're all your victims this morning. Fire away."

"Good," UPI said. "My first question is to Colonel Trasker: are you in favor of arming the spacecraft?"

"I am," Connie said crisply. "And the astronauts."

"Are you, Commander Weickert?"

"You damned betcha."

"Dr. Balkis?"

"Absolutely."

"Very well, then, Colonel Trasker, could you tell us why you all feel this way, please."

"Certainly," Connie said, drawing the microphone to him and leaning forward with an intent, serious expression. "Gladly. I think I can speak for Jazz and Pete and myself when I say that we have been very gravely concerned about what happened at Geneva and about the obviously hostile attitude of the Soviet Union toward our Mars flight. I guess that sums up the reason as well as anything."

"You regard what happened at Geneva as the Russians' fault, then," the Los Angeles *Times* said.

"Don't you?" Connie inquired with a bland surprise.

"There seem to be differing opinions," the Los Angeles *Times* replied. "Anyway, it scared you, is that it?"

"I wouldn't say any of us is exactly scared," Connie said with a certain acid in his voice. "You have to remember we are all experienced fliers and astronauts. I wouldn't say we scare very easily. But concerned, you could say. Yes, concerned."

"To the point," the British scold asked, with his usual don't-give-me-that-guff tone, "where you actually believe it necessary to arm yourselves against this presumed awful Russian attack?"

"Whether or not presumed," Connie retorted, the acid if anything heavier, "I think even you might grant it would be awful if it occurred. Therefore we believe adequate precautions should be taken both for our own safety and for the success of the mission."

"Which comes first?" the *Times* of India asked with a nasty inflection.

"Obviously," Connie said with an I'm-being-patient-with-a-fool expression he took pains to make apparent, "if we aren't safe the mission isn't safe. If the mission isn't safe we aren't safe. The two are the same, aren't they?"

"Not necessarily," the St. Louis *Post-Dispatch* said. "Couldn't an unmanned probe be sent to Mars and accomplish the same results you will get, without risking human lives?"

"And couldn't an unmanned probe be shot down much more easily than a manned probe whose members were equipped to defend themselves and on the alert against attack? You tell me."

346

"That isn't our job," the *Post-Dispatch* said blandly. "We're just here to ask questions."

"It seems to me some of you have been getting into speeches," Connie remarked dryly. "Anyway, you asked our reason. That's it. We don't trust the Russians, we believe them to be hostile to the success of this mission, and we intend to protect ourselves. Can I make it any clearer? If so, tell me how and I will."

"That's quite clear," the *Times* commented with an equal dryness. "Now tell us, if you will, whether you have received assurances of support from Washington for this position."

"I believe we have," Connie said, glancing down the table at the Administrator, who nodded matter-of-factly.

"From the highest level?" the *Post* inquired quickly.

"That's all we're authorized to say today," Dr. Anderson replied calmly.

"Then you don't have support from the highest level," the *Post* said with a broad, insinuating smile.

"I'm sorry," Andy Anderson said with a smile equally broad. "We've told you all we can on that point today."

"Then I would like to go to Dr. Halleck, if I may," the UPI said politely, "and ask him what he thinks. If NASA doesn't object, Dr. Anderson."

"Not at all," Andy said cheerfully, only a little tightening along his jaw betraying to Bob Hertz at his side the rising tension with which he awaited this line of questioning. He chuckled comfortably. "I think we'd like enlightenment on that subject, too."

At this there was general laughter, but there was tension in it and a rising excitement. Jayvee was the pay-off, if there was to be one. And from all they had heard, gossiped, rumored and reported, he was in a mood to blow Piffy One sky-high.

But for a moment just before the UPI asked his opening question it was impossible to say what might happen. They were all suspended in time waiting for something to push them into action again: the reporters leaning forward intently, the men at the table doing the same, eyes, minds, hearts, cameras, notebooks, poised and concentrating upon the handsome black face that scowled forth upon them all with a sullenly resentful, unyielding expression.

"Dr. Halleck," the UPI said, and the room became very still, "you have heard your crewmates express their fears about Russia and their desire that the mission be armed. Do you agree with this?"

There was a silence during which Jayvee shifted uneasily in his chair, looked out across the room, stared up at the ceiling. With an elaborate consideration Pete moved the microphone along in front of him. Finally, still staring into space somewhere above the level of the highest bank of cameras, Jayvee replied in a voice so low they could hardly hear it, even with the microphone.

"No," he began, "I don't agree—"

"Louder!" someone shouted. He leaned forward and spoke with a sudden burst of anger that made his voice blast in a roaring harshness over the room.

"NO, I DON'T AGREE! . . . I believe," he went on, more quietly, "that the Soviet Union went to Geneva in good faith and tried to work something out. I believe the United States Government rejected the Soviet position too fast. I don't say, now"—and the pens and pencils that had been scribbling so happily hesitated a little—"that the United States is entirely to blame and I don't say the Soviet Union was entirely right. But I think the United States should have stayed and negotiated and tried to work it out instead of forcing an end to the conference. I think the world would be a lot better off right now if that had been done.

"About arming Planetary Fleet One—" again he hesitated, and five hundred pairs of eyes suddenly left scribbled notepads and lifted to focus with an almost painful intensity upon him—"and arming us—the crew . . . I have told my crewmates what I think."

And abruptly he stopped and sat back as though that would end it. If he really thought so, he was quickly disabused.

"But you haven't told us, Dr. Halleck," Percy Mercy said quietly but with a firm authority that carried clearly across the silent auditorium. "That is the question."

"Yes, Dr. Halleck," Walter Dobius agreed with a heavy importance. "That is what we want to know. Do you or don't you?"

Again Jayvee was silent while the tension grew. Finally he spoke in a defensive, almost resentful tone.

"I've said I wasn't going to resign. I'm going on the mission."

"But do you agree," Percy said patiently, "with the

position of Colonel Trasker and the others that the mission should be armed?"

"I'm going on the mission," Jayvee repeated. "If it's armed, I'll go armed. I guess it doesn't much matter what I think."

The *Times* stood up with an impatient air.

"Are you afraid of punishment by NASA if you tell us honestly what you think, Dr. Halleck? Is that why you're being evasive?"

"No!" Jayvee snapped with a show of genuine anger.

"Then why don't you tell us honestly that you disagree with the policy and are against the arming?" the *Post* joined in bluntly. "Isn't that what you have told certain distinguished members of the press in private? (There was a stirring along the table but he went firmly on.) Why don't you tell us in public? Or *are* you afraid of NASA?"

"Dr. Anderson has given us his word there will be no disciplining," Percy said, not bothering to conceal the triumph in his voice. "There's nothing to fear."

The Administrator leaned forward quickly.

"I said I would not be put in the position of saying we could not discipline one of our astronauts if he gave us good cause," he said sharply. "I said if Dr. Halleck deserved to be punished he would be, if he didn't he wouldn't. That's all I said."

"Do you think he would deserve to be if he opposed arming the mission?" the *Post* asked quickly, and from somewhere to his right the *Wall Street Journal* said impatiently,

"Let Dr. Halleck answer the question! We don't know whether he opposes it or not!"

"That's right," Andy Anderson said promptly. "Let him answer. You haven't given him a chance."

"But—" Percy began, but there was a general chorus of boos from his colleagues and he dropped it with a glare at the Administrator, who bowed blandly. "All right, then! Dr. Halleck"—and he spoke with a firm, unyielding emphasis—"do you or do you not oppose the arming of this mission?"

Once again the room became very still. Again it was a while before Jayvee answered. At last he spoke in a slow, almost muffled, still resentful voice.

"First of all," he said, "I didn't tell 'distinguished members' of the press about my feelings. (Again there was a stirring along the table, an exchange of glances accompanied by a murmur of obvious surprise over the room.) Second of all, I think it's my business what I—"

"Oh, no, Dr. Halleck," the *Guardian* interrupted quickly. "No, that would be too much. The whole world thinks you don't agree with something with which the whole world, I suspect, or at least a major portion of it, also does not agree. Therefore you are a very important man to the world right now, over and above your position on the crew of Planetary Fleet One. We want to know your views, Dr. Halleck. What are they, if you please?"

"I think the arming of the mission," Jayvee said at last, "may not be wise. It may not be necessary. But I said before and I'll say it to you again, I'm going on the mission and if it's armed, that's the way it'll be. I don't know what else you want me to say."

("Oh, yes, you do," the *Times* murmured to the AP. "But you just ain't agonna do it," the AP murmured back. "They've got him scared to death," the *Times* said with a bitter disgust. "They've got him absolutely beaten down.")

"Is that all you intend to say?" the UPI inquired.

"That's all," Jayvee said and looked away toward the ceiling again.

"Then, ladies and gentlemen," the Administrator began, "if you have no more questions—"

"One last question, Dr. Anderson, please," the AP said into the susurrus of whispers and excited half-audible comments that now filled the room. "Do you intend to present the request for arming the mission to the President?"

"Obviously he would have to approve," Dr. Anderson said.

"Do you intend—" the AP began again patiently.

"Yes," the Administrator said with an anger that showed how wearing the tensions of the morning had finally become. "Yes, yes, yes!"

"Thank you, gentlemen!" the *Times* called out with an ironic inflection; and talking, arguing, gossiping, comparing impressions and confirming one another's notes, he and his colleagues began to move slowly out of the auditorium into the hot Houston morning, already pushing toward new levels of heat and humidity in the quick-dying spring.

Behind them on the platform the men of NASA stood about for a few moments exchanging their own impressions, a recapitulation in which Jayvee, standing by himself to one side, did not join. The consensus was that it had not gone too badly, considering everything. But no one tried to pretend that it had left anything other than a sour taste and more trouble.

"They'll be on us like vultures in the next edition," the Administrator said with a grim sigh.

"When are you going back to D.C., Andy?" Bob Hertz asked.

"Immediately," Dr. Anderson said. "Connie," he said, "come over here a minute—" and he drew him aside for an exchange so brief the others hardly had time to notice their absence from the group.

Then they were all on their way off the stage and out through the now-deserted auditorium. At the door Connie drew Jazz and Pete aside.

"My office at 1300," he said. He raised his voice at the ostentatiously unconcerned back ahead of them on the walk. "Did you hear that, Jayvee? Crew meeting in my office, 1300."

"I—" Jayvee began, swinging around with a defiant look.

Connie returned him look for look but did not raise his level voice.

"1300. O.K., Jayvee?"

For an appreciable length of time Jayvee stared at him with a look in which many things, all resentful, were inextricably mixed. Then he said, *"Oh—!"* and flung away.

Behind him the faces of his crewmates were a study in the hot, heavy sun: a grim little smile from Jazz, Pete troubled and uneasy, Connie regretful but determined.

In these same moods they gathered again at 1 P.M. in Connie's office. Jayvee made his usual point by appearing at 1:09. They greeted this without comment and without emotion. He understood, with a sudden agitation that bravado could not quite overcome, that the time for emotion had passed.

"Jayvee," Connie said quietly, when he was seated, "there is no need to prolong this. You saw Andy take me aside after the press conference. His exact words were, 'O.K., we've had it. That's the end of Jayvee. Start the process rolling and I'll back you up.'

"Accordingly, I have called this meeting to notify you,

351

in the presence of the crew of Planetary Fleet One, that you are no longer a member of it. As of this afternoon you are assigned to the extraterrestrial sciences lab here, and if you so desire you may be reassigned to JPL in Pasadena as soon as you put in an application. Or you may resign entirely from the space program. The prime decision has been made. Any subsequent decisions are up to you."

He concluded as quietly as he had begun and sat back in his chair, his eyes fixed impassively upon the dark eyes that stared back at him, dismayed, astounded, appalled, arrogant, beseeching, defiant, proud, humble, furious, desolate, angry . . . angry . . . angry.

Pete and Jazz said nothing, sitting very still, tensed for whatever physical violence might explode, bracing themselves for whatever psychological battering they might have to take.

For a good two minutes no one broke the silence. Outside in the corridor two secretaries greeted one another cheerfully. Roger Webb and Emerson Wacker went by talking in vigorous tones about yaw and transmartian injection. The world drifted: stunned, stilled, suspended, out of time and nearly out of context.

At last Jayvee started to say something, seemed to strangle on it, could not for the moment articulate, made some sort of wounded-animal sound, subsided. The others did not speak, did not move—almost, they felt, did not breathe.

Presently Jayvee tried again.

"So," he said, gasping for breath, his voice trembling, his words tumbling and almost disjointed, "you finally managed to do it, didn't you? You had to tell a lot of lies and do a lot of things, but you did it, didn't you? You got me fired—or you think you did. Because you don't think you're going to get away with it, do you? You don't think my friends are going to stand for this, do you? *Do you?*"

"I don't think we had to tell any lies or do anything, Jayvee," Connie said, still quietly. "I think you did it all yourself. I think you came on this crew from the very first determined you weren't going to be helpful, determined you weren't really going to be a part of it. It seems to me the result has been inevitable."

"Particularly," Jazz said, "after your performance in the past twenty-four hours. Talk about lies! No, you didn't talk to distinguished *members* of the press, did you, but you damned well talked to little jerk Percy, *a* member of the press, didn't you? And that after we specifically agreed no word to anybody. You created that press conference and the latest flap for Piffy One. Did you really think there wouldn't be any response from NASA? Did you really think you were going to get away with it, for Christ's sake?"

"All right, Jazz," Connie said patiently. "For the last time, hold it down, O.K.? It isn't necessary for anybody to shout. In fact, it isn't even necessary to stay here talking, as far as I can see. The word's been given. We can go."

"Oh, no!" Jayvee said, his voice still coming with great effort, shaking with anger, quivering with dismay. "No, you don't! You can't just do your damage and get away without paying for it. There'll be a reckoning, oh yes, there'll be a reckoning, you damned, arrogant bastards! You say I haven't co-operated. You just point to one single way in which I haven't done my work to get ready for this mission. You just tell me one! You know I've co-operated. You know I've done my job. You can't tell me I haven't done my job!"

And he paused, almost crying with rage, to give them a challenging glare.

"That's right," Pete said quietly. "You have done your job."

"Then *why*—" Jayvee demanded, "*why*—"

"Jayvee!" Connie said sharply. "You know why. Now stop shouting like a child. Do you honestly think you've been a loyal, co-operative, willing member of this crew? Do you really think you've made us feel we could trust you, with this prolonged fit of the sulks you've put on? And do you think we should trust you now, after you betrayed us—yes," he repeated angrily, over Jayvee's attempted protest—"betrayed us, by running to the press and getting the whole world stirred up? You talk about reckonings. All right, there's a reckoning for that kind of behavior, too, and this is it. You think you can do any damned thing to hurt Piffy One and hurt us and get away with it. You *are* a child. I'm finally convinced that really is your problem. I think we're a damned sight better off without you."

Jayvee stared at him with a look that made them all instinctively tense up again for some raging physical violence that might explode at any second. But his words when they came were very soft and very sneering.

"And Colonel Trasker is a damned sight better off without that sweet little Monetta's husband around, isn't he?"

There was silence for a while, broken only by their heavy breathing, the sound of a chair as someone shifted, the sharp cracking sound of a plastic model of a Saturn 5 falling to the floor as Pete accidentally brushed it off the desk with his elbow: the little scuffling sound as he hastily reached down to retrieve it.

When Connie finally replied it was in a quiet tone that cost him much. But he managed.

"Jazz and Pete can tell you that I have consistently defended you and have repeatedly told them to be more patient with you. I have sincerely and honorably tried to protect your place on this crew, in the hope that you would gradually prove yourself worthy of it—yes!" he said, with his only show of sharpness, as Jayvee made an angry movement of protest—"*worthy of it!* Because it *is* something to be worthy of, and you haven't shown the slightest sign that you appreciated that fact one little bit. But I've been patient, and I've been protective, and I've tried. Believe me, Jayvee, I've tried. You can say what you like—think what you like—do what you like—and it won't change what I've honestly tried to do for you. And I'm not the only one.

"From Vernon Hertz right down the line, we've tried to help you, in this program, and all we asked of you was that you meet us halfway—maybe not even halfway, because you had our guilty consciences on your side, whether they should have been guilty or not, and you wouldn't even have had to come halfway. Maybe just one little inch, Jayvee—just one little inch. But you just haven't had the character to do it. That's your trouble. You're a child without character, and I'm very much afraid you're never going to grow up. And I'm sorrier for you than words could possibly say.

"Now I think you'd better get out of my office and out of my sight. You will do everything you can to wreck Piffy One, I'm sure of that. But we'll just have to stand that, I guess . . .

"Jayvee!" he said sharply as Jayvee half rose with an

354

almost animal moan and words, jumbled, bitter, incoherent, incomprehensible, began to come. *"Get out!"*

And after another mumbled moment or two whose sense they could not determine except that it was bitterly furious and antagonistic, he did, looking back for one last raging, crippled glare at the three implacable faces that watched him go.

"Poor Piffy One!" Pete said softly into the silence that echoed to the slamming door. "Do you think we'll ever fly?"

"Oh, yes," Connie said grimly.

"You damned betcha," said Jazz.

7.

The house in El Lago seemed deserted as he hurled the Aston Martin into the driveway and entered with an angry rush. But when he passed the kitchen he saw her out of the corner of his eye, standing rigidly silent by the refrigerator, her hand arrested on its half-opened door. Apparently she had frozen where she was: as if, he thought contemptuously, she could escape him that way.

On an impulse as abrupt as they all seemed to be in the last few minutes, he spun into the kitchen, brushed her roughly aside, took out the water jar.

"Excuse *me*," he said elaborately. "I've got to have a drink."

And without waiting for her reply—without even realizing she offered none—he yanked open the china cabinet, yanked out a glass, sloshed in the water. It overran the edge and spilled on the floor around his feet.

Automatically she walked over to the rack of paper towels, pulled off a couple, stooped and wiped it up. He could see she was so insolent and uppity he almost kicked her in the face.

As if she sensed the thought, she was up like lightning and across the room by the wastepaper basket, where she tossed in the used towels and then turned to face him, wide-eyed, obviously frightened but also obviously standing her ground. If he needed anything more to infuriate him, it was this dramatically defiant stance.

"What call you got to be so smart and sassy with me, girl?" he demanded with a harsh irony. "Is this how you treat fine ole Massa Trasker? I'll bet you're nicer than that to *him*."

She looked as though he had hit her and he wished he had. But though she flinched at his words, her gaze did not flinch.

"What's the matter, Jayvee?" she asked quietly. "What's happened?"

"Haven't you been listening?" he demanded loudly. "What you been *doing*, girl? Haven't you been *listening?*"

"I watched the press conference," she said. "I haven't heard anything since."

"Have you had it on?" he demanded quickly, and as quickly turned away and hurried down the hall to the den. "Haven't you had it *on?*"

He paid no attention to her reply, again unaware there was none. He turned on the machine, spun the dials, brought in a couple of afternoon soap-operas, cursed violently, spun the dials again: a mid-afternoon news broadcast on one of the Houston stations began to come in.

"—question of whether or not to arm Planetary Fleet One apparently now goes to the President for final decision," the newscaster said. "In Bonn today, it was disclosed that the West German government's plans to test atomic weapons in co-operation with the Japanese government at the Japanese underground testing site on Okinawa have moved a step nearer completion. Japanese Foreign Minister Hidashi, on an official visit to Bonn, told newsmen—"

He turned it off with a savage sound and whirled upon her as she stood, knowing she should go but mesmerized, at the den door.

"They haven't got it!" he said with an angry incredulity. "It hasn't been announced!"

"What do you mean, Jayvee?" she asked with a still frightened but almost weary patience. "What are you shouting for?"

"Me!" he said in a crazily mixed tone of triumph and dismay. "Me! They fired me! They kicked me off the crew! Your nice colonel, he said, 'Jayvee, *scat!*' But," he said, and his voice dropped to a bitter defiance, "I'm not scatting. You can tell him that for me. I'm not *scatting!*"

"I'm sorry," she said, raising a hand in a characteristic gesture to place it alongside her cheek. "I'm sorry it's come to this, Jayvee. I was hoping maybe things could work out all right—"

"You be nice to that smart little colonel for me, and everything will work out all right," he said with a fleering sarcasm, and again she flinched. But again she did not yield, and the quiet adamancy of her strength provoked him further.

"You like that white colonel, don't you? You like that white—"

"Jayvee!" she said sharply. "You stop that! At least he's kind and decent and that's more than you are lately!"

"Is that right?" he demanded, rising and moving toward her. "Well, why is that, Miss Prissy? Just *why* is *that?*"

"I don't know, Jayvee," she said with a tired sadness. "I really don't know."

"Well, I do!" he snapped, and came still closer; but she stood her ground. "Because they've resented me, and looked down on me, and hated me because I wouldn't Uncle Tom 'em, ever since I came to Houston! And now they hate me because the biggest damned hypocrite of them all wants my wife! And I'm supposed to stand for it. I'm supposed to let them do anything they please! So they're trying to kick me off the crew. They're trying to disgrace me and put me down in front of the whole world. *Well,*" he said, and he smiled with a savage satisfaction, "they aren't going to get away with it. No, sir. No way. They aren't going to get me off the crew and"—his tone became ugly—"they aren't going to help old Connie get my wife. Or maybe I should say—" his smile was as ugly as his voice—"*keep* my wife. I guess he's already got her."

"That isn't true," she said quietly, though with a great effort which took its toll in her strained face and tightly clenched hands, a toll he obviously misinterpreted with his continuing unpleasant smile. "It just isn't true."

"Got her or thought her," he replied softly. "Got her or thought her. It's all the same to me."

"Well, it isn't to me!" she retorted with a sudden flash of anger. "And it isn't to him! You think whatever you want to with your crazy mind, but it isn't that way to either of us!"

"Tell me that again," he demanded, his contorted face within inches of hers. "I come home here the other day, and what do I hear? I hear *my* wife on the box with that pure little lily-white Connie, and maybe they don't say anything with their words, much, but I can *hear* what they say with their voices and *see* what they say with their eyes. Why, hell, girl! You mean you *haven't?* You're missing a big bet. That boy's ready for you, baby. That boy's *ready.*"

She slapped him so fast and so hard that it momentarily knocked him off balance. But only for a second: he returned it as hard and as fast. Breathing heavily, inches apart, they stood glaring; and now she was so angry that she no longer felt afraid.

"You stop," she said furiously. "You stop that talk, you trash. I won't have it."

"*You* won't have it?" he shouted. "*You* won't have it? Well, I'll be *damned. You* won't have it!"

"No, I won't," she said, flinching no longer; and abruptly the harshness went out of her voice and a compassionate note he mistook for weakness came into it. "Jayvee, what's the matter? *What is* the matter? You used to be so nice and so steady, but you've gone off these last few months, way off. And all the time everybody's been trying to help you—"

But she could see from his expression, even before she heard his words, that compassion was useless. He was gone, and she knew with a sudden inward flare of fear that she had better go too, before something dreadful happened to them both.

His words when they came were cold and measured and as cutting as he could make them.

"Nobody's been trying to help me, least of all my sweet little wife, catting around behind the bushes with precious Colonel Conrad H. Trasker, Junior, that big hero. Nobody's been helping me! And they aren't going to, either, because I'm going to help myself. I'm going to stay on that crew and I'm going to fly that mission and I'm going to live my life the way *I* want to, by *my*self. And you can get out, hear me? Just get out! Call *me* trash! At least I don't spread my legs for every whitey that says, Good morning, black pet, let's roll. Now—*get!*"

"I'm sorry for you, Jayvee," she said at last in a thin, strained, uneven voice; and this time when he slapped her she did not slap back, but only staggered away toward the door, crying hysterically, moving blindly out of the room, out of the house, out of his life, at last, forever.

For perhaps five minutes he stood where he was, his breath coming in great sobbing gasps, his fists clenching and unclenching, his eyes staring wildly at the door she had slammed behind her, seeing nothing, thinking nothing, almost feeling nothing.

Then gradually the storm began to ebb, passions died. He began to think again. It was over.

Swiftly he went to the Picturephone and placed a call to Percy Mercy. It hadn't been entirely true that nobody would help him. There were plenty who would. He was going to give them their chance.

Upstairs in the guest bedroom she had moved into a month ago she packed her suitcase and Rudden's with an almost automatic, desperate haste. The boy was at nursery school until 5 and she could arrange for him to stay overnight until she decided what to do; she herself could go to a motel. The immediate future did not worry her, nor did Jayvee's presence in the house. She felt instinctively that he would not come near her again, and presently, after several long, muffled phone conversations whose tone was violent but whose import she was unable to determine, he slammed out of the house as he had slammed in, and was gone.

Somehow she got the suitcases packed, somehow called the nursery school, somehow spoke calmly to the matron and soothingly to Rudden: somehow called a taxi, somehow got out the door, somehow said good-by to her home and reached the motel. There for several hours, as afternoon drew on into evening, she lay on the bed helplessly, hopelessly, crying until, around 6 P.M., she was cried out.

She managed to dress, bathed her eyes, put on her make-up, got to dinner; returned to the room. Then she did what she knew she should not do, but in her desolation and despair was unable not to do.

She suspected he might be working late in his office and it was there that she called him. Presently he came to her, knowing also that he should not, knowing that it made a mockery of all his careful rationalizations so short a time ago.

But he was in the grip of pity, an emotion more terrible and more devouring than love. He could not, in that unhappy hour, have kept himself from responding to the appeal of her tragically haunting beauty if his whole life, career and reputation depended upon it.

Fortunately they did not: they would be decided by other means in other places. By the time he returned home shortly before 11, he and his mission, as he soon realized, were in serious trouble. Jane met him at the door, deeply alarmed by what she was seeing and hearing on the insistent, ubiquitous, implacably demanding tube.

"What's the matter?" he asked, alarmed himself by her expression.

"Just come listen," she said, "they're having a field day."

And so, it appeared, they were, as he hastily got a beer from the refrigerator and settled himself in his favorite armchair in front of the set. Frankly Unctuous was holding forth at the moment, and he was giving it his purse-lipped, disapproving best.

"There appears to be an almost universal condemnation tonight—" he said in his pompous, indeterminate accent (born fifty-one years ago in Buffalo Wallow, North Dakota; resident of Washington, D.C., and New York City for the past thirty years; simple, homespun, American non-sophisticate, untouched by the crafty wiles of "the Eastern Establishment"; fresh, innocent, pure as the day he left the prairies) "condemnation for the strange and peculiar things that seem to be going on within NASA in connection with the men and mission of Planetary Fleet One.

"Many of you watched this morning when the crew of P.F. 1 and the top men of NASA held an extraordinary press conference in Houston. Out of it emerged one simple, clear-cut fact: there is a sharp division among these men over the question of whether or not the mission should be armed, presumably to guard against some sort of attack by the Soviet Union—an attack, we might add, which seems to be more a figment of rather hysterical imaginations within NASA than it is any real, or actual, or even possible, threat from the Russians.

"You will remember that Dr. J. V. Halleck, the only black member of the crew, ventured to raise a word of skepticism about this fancied 'attack'—and you will remember that he seemed strangely reluctant to do so openly, though it has been well-known in the press for the past twenty-four hours that he viewed this so-called 'threat' as an absurd and impossible hobgoblin.

"Tonight his strange reluctance is explained. Despite firm pledges by the Administrator of NASA, Dr. William Anderson, that Dr. Halleck would not be disciplined for his views, it appears that he is about to be disciplined, and in the harshest and most decisive way possible—by being fired summarily from the crew and removed from all association with the Mars mission."

("Is that the decision?" Jane asked.

Connie nodded.

"Is it wise?"

"It's inevitable," he said with a trace of impatience. She started to say something and stopped, as Frankly's words flowed smoothly on.)

"This blatant act of arbitrary punishment has understandably aroused a nationwide outcry seeking justice for Dr. Halleck, whose only crimes, apparently, were to refuse to become hysterical, and to state his honest views. Those views are violently opposed by his militarily trained and militarily minded crewmates and by the apparently rather martial type of thinking which seems to dominate the higher echelons of NASA.

"Taking into account the misfortunes that have plagued the Mars mission from the start, this newest episode has raised a very grave and fundamental question in the minds of many Americans: should Planetary Fleet One be allowed to fly at all?

"Should it not be scrubbed, and should this nation not return to the careful, steady, well-planned progress that was originally slated to send Americans to Mars as much as a decade from now? This is what many Americans are wondering tonight."

(Connie snorted.

"The hell you say!"

"It's true," Jane said.

"That's what he and his friends would like us to believe."

"They're making *me* wonder," Jane admitted with a wry little smile.

"Don't," he said tersely. "If they get to enough people like you, then they will stop us—and that's exactly what they want to do.")

"Already—" Frankly Unctuous said, and he raised and

held before the camera the *Times* and the *Post*, with their glaring headlines (HALLECK FIRED FROM MARS CREW FOR OPPOSING ARMS, the *Times* said; BLACK'S OUSTER BRINGS CALL TO END MARS FLIGHT, the *Post* declared)—"already America's most influential journals are expressing the grave doubts that are plaguing Americans of good will everywhere.

" 'In view of the unbroken series of controversies and disasters which have haunted unfortunate Planetary Fleet One from the beginning,' the *Times* says in its lead editorial, 'it seems to us a fair question whether this ill-conceived and ill-fated project should not be abandoned altogether, and the sooner the better.'

"And the *Post* comments, 'In any normal ball game the rule is three strikes and out. It seems to us that Planetary Fleet One, foolish, foredoomed and futile, has had more than its share of strikes. We think it is time for the President to show the decisive courage his partisans claim for him and stop the nonsense now.'

"And so," Frankly concluded gravely, "it seems to this reporter, too. Planetary Fleet One began as an unworthy and unbecoming attempt to revive the space race with the Russians and gain some sort of empty prestige advantage over them. It had caused nothing but trouble since. It has been hostile to the Soviet Union abroad, racist and undemocratic at home. It has brought controversy, bitterness and disaster. Its cost is fantastic, and because of it, desperate domestic needs have been slighted and forced to take a back seat. Millions go hungry while Planetary Fleet One swallows billions—"

("My *God!*" Connie exclaimed. "The unfairness of it!")

"—and now the final disaster has befallen it. Its crew is disintegrating, and its purposes are made even more suspect by a basically military decision to seek arms against the Soviet Union, a nation which has clearly indicated that it wants only peace and co-operation with us in space.

"There may be arguments for continuing Planetary Fleet One, but if so, its proponents bear a heavy burden of proof tonight. It appears to many millions, both in America and abroad, that it is time to abandon once and for all this ill-advised and disaster-prone project and get back to a decent, steady, peaceful and non-provocative space program that we and the world can live with."

And prune-prim, disapproving, self-righteous and smug,

his face faded from the screen, leaving behind it for several minutes a brooding silence in the home of the ill-advised and disaster-prone project's commander which his wife did not dare break.

Presently with an unintelligible but thoroughly disgusted explosion of pent-up angry sound, he jumped up and hurried to the Picturephone.

"Bob," he said urgently when Bob Hertz came on, "you know what I think we ought to do?" I think—"

"My thought exactly," Bob interrupted. "Couldn't agree more. I'll call Andy and Jim, you call the rest."

"Ellington Field, 0600?"

"We'll make it," Bob Hertz promised.

Above in its swift inexorable orbit, the little satellite, reporting routinely for a month, came alive again. Half an hour later at JPL Vernon Hertz and his assistants were studying the first batch of photographs and the first computer readout. Within an hour he was on the phone to Washington and within an hour after that busy men in the basement of the White House were putting together photographs, readouts and intelligence reports from many other sources.

At 4 A.M. Bob Hertz, Dr. Cavanaugh, Connie, Hank, Bert, Pete and Jazz rose from their respective beds, and at 6 A.M. on the minute their plane took off from Ellington, Connie and Hank at the controls. It was a fast flight and a silent one. Above in the sky and below in the White House, the skilled and impersonal work went on as they hurtled east.

8.

On days like these, the President reflected with a rueful sigh, he should have stayed in the governor's mansion. The White House had its attractions, Lord knew, and he had fought hard enough to get there, but there were times ... there were times. And this, with a planeload of angry astronauts about to land at Andrews and come on full tilt to his office, was one of them.

Not that he was afraid of their visit or had any real doubts about how to handle it; but it was just another, and major, complication in a day already heavily burdened by the national and world-wide clamor about Piffy One, by the growing hints of a more active unrest concerning the mission, and now by the reports from JPL and his intelligence people that were arriving at his desk in an ever-mounting stack. Add to this the angry conference that now impended and it was enough to give even the blithest and most self-confident of Presidents pause.

Andy Anderson had called him near midnight last night to transmit Houston's formal request for the meeting. His quick response had been the only one possible under all the circumstances.

"I'm delighted," he said, quite truthfully. "I think it's about time we sat down and talked it out together. There seem to be developments I haven't been told about."

"They've happened rather suddenly," Andy said somewhat defensively.

"Indeed they have," the President agreed.

"There really hasn't been time to reach you," the Administrator said, "You've been busy all day, and then with the state dinner tonight—"

"It's been a busy day," the President conceded. "Possibly just a two-minute phone call, though, somewhere along the line—?"

"I tried."

"More than once?"

"No, I must admit," Andy said with a not very repentant smile. "Only once. But I figured you'd hear about it all soon enough from the media."

"So I have," the President said. "I have indeed. You know"—his tone became philosophic—"people imagine a President is instantly informed on all subjects. They imagine his appointees *want* to inform him instantly on all subjects. This isn't always true."

"What time shall we come to the office?"

"Are you coming too? Yes, I suppose you should. Let's make it 11, and let's get the Vice-President, too. We might as well really let our hair down."

"Shall I call him, or—"

"Oh, I will," the President said. "He's not a protocol sort of Vice-President, thank heavens, and his feelings don't get hurt too easily, but on the other hand—maybe I should be the one. I'll see you all tomorrow at 11 then." He gave his sudden, charming smile. "Don't be too rough on the poor old piano player. He's doing the best he can."

"My only worry," Dr. Anderson said, "is that he'll be rough on us."

"Hardly likely," the President said with a bland humor he knew would give the Administrator a few restless moments before he dropped off to sleep. "Hardly likely at all, Andy."

He had apparently awakened the Vice-President when he called the beautiful house in Georgetown, but his reaction was cheerful enough as he came quickly alert.

"I've been thinking this should be done," he said, "but it wasn't my place to suggest it. I'm glad."

"I'm afraid you're all going to be against me," the President said in a mock-rueful tone that really sounded quite cheerful about the prospect. The Vice-President smiled.

"I don't really think we worry you in the least, Mr. President."

366

"Oh, I wouldn't say that," the President said more seriously. "I have a lot to think about."

And within five minutes after their brief conversation ended, Vernon Hertz had called from JPL and the things he had to think about abruptly increased.

But in spite of that he had spent a reasonably restful night, being possessed of some innate facility, for which he thanked his lucky stars, that enabled him to put the day away until tomorrow and go quickly and soundly to sleep. There had been brooders in the White House in the past but he didn't see how they had done it. Things were tough enough when you worried about them all day long. He could only imagine how rough they must be if you worried about them all night too.

He had, however, risen early, shortly before 6 A.M., and gone padding downstairs in bathrobe and slippers to the Situation Room, hoping against hope that something new and encouraging might have come in during the night. But no such luck, of course. The pattern of reports was exactly the same as it had been when he went to bed. He padded back upstairs again, ate a quick breakfast, dressed and went to the Oval Room. There the reports continued to come in, unchanging, insistent, disturbing.

And now the Houstonites were on his doorstep and an argument polite, intense and fundamental was about to begin. He acknowledged his secretary's message, told her to show them in, rose beside his desk to greet them: calm, confident, blending his impressive physical presence with the dignity of his office in a way that would have intimidated lesser men.

It did not, he could see, intimidate the men of Houston. They were respectful and properly deferential when they came in and shook hands, but there was something about them that signaled the world that these were men with a responsibility and an obligation, too.

"Why don't we go along to the Cabinet Room?" he suggested, and led the way with an easy banter that fooled no one, though the Vice-President and Bob Hertz entered into the spirit of it without noticeable strain. The rest were inclined to be silent and remained so when the door closed and they were seated around the end of the long elliptical table: the Vice-President on his left, the Administrator on his right, Connie, Hank and Bert next to the

Vice-President, Dr. Cavanaugh, Bob Hertz, Pete and Jazz next to Dr. Anderson.

"We seem to be in trouble, gentlemen," he said, dropping the banter, speaking gravely. "I'm glad you're here: we should talk. Jim, maybe as director of Houston, you ought to start the discussion. What do you want of me?"

"Most simply and directly stated," Dr. Cavanaugh said, "I suppose we want two things: we want your O.K. on removing Jayvee Halleck from the crew, and we want your authorization to arm the spacecraft."

"Yes," the President said slowly. He looked down the table to his right, down the table to his left. "Is there anyone here who disagrees with that?" No one replied. "Anyone at all?" And again he looked slowly and carefully along their sober and intent faces. "Those are pretty grave requests," he remarked thoughtfully. "I could wish," he added with a certain tartness, "that they hadn't been made through the media."

"That's exactly why we want to get rid of Halleck," Jazz said. "He made them public property. We didn't."

"He apparently felt he was fighting for his professional— and perhaps for his racial—life," the President said. "It can make a man desperate."

But to this charitable remark there was no charitable response: rather a noticeable tightening of jawlines and hardening of expressions all along the table.

"Well," he observed, "I can see I'm alone in that ... Now, before I decide anything on that particular subject, I want an honest answer to a fundamental question: has he given you any cause—any cause whatsoever—to be dissatisfied with the work he has been doing for the mission?"

"No," Connie responded slowly, after a moment. "No, I think we must say honestly that he has not. Which," he added with a rather grim little smile, "is a limited answer to a limited question."

"Well, then, what is it?" the President inquired with a slight show of impatience. "What are the grounds on which I am to support the action you apparently want to take—have already taken, I guess, to hear the press tell it."

Connie nodded.

"We've told him."

"I told them to," the Administrator said.

"Without consulting me," the President remarked thoughtfully.

"The situation had deteriorated to the point where decisive action had to be taken," Dr. Anderson said quietly.

"He did, after all, violate an agreement to keep our discussion about arming the spacecraft confidential," Connie pointed out. "Plus a lot of other things. But that was the decisive one."

"What other things?" the President asked.

Connie gave a humorous, rather helpless shrug and looked across the table.

"Tell the man, gang."

"He's been a hostile, unfriendly, damned un-cooperative bastard," Jazz said, "and that's a fact."

"In what way?" the President asked patiently.

"Mr. President," Pete said, "it isn't a simple black-and-white"—he smiled slightly—"if you'll forgive the expression—proposition. I've been working with Jayvee on the scientific side of it, now, for several weeks, since you put him on the crew. In that time I would estimate that, aside from a couple of rather lengthy and bitter exchanges that we've all taken part in, on crew matters, he hasn't said more than ten words to any of us on anything that wasn't strictly and rigidly associated with the flight. Now, you can say—and no doubt," he remarked, "when the media get hold of it, they will say—that this is damned little on which to fire a man. But it's plenty, it seems to me, on which to judge him. He's been sullen—hostile, as Jazz says—resentful—un-cooperative in all the *human* aspects that have to go into the making of a mutually trusting and mutually dependent crew—a really successful crew, which this has got to be, because there isn't any room for error.

"Now, to us," he concluded slowly as they all followed him intently in the silent room, "that seemed sufficient. Then you add to it his open and deliberate defiance of our agreement to keep our differences to ourselves, in the face of what you will admit, I think, has been a generally hostile reaction from the media since the very beginning—and you have a situation in which we felt we had to act ... I know I haven't expressed it very well, Mr. President, but that's how it's looked from inside the crew. Right, fellows?"

Jazz nodded.

"You said it."

"And very well," Connie observed.

"Yes, very well," the President agreed. "Very, very well. The fact remains, your differences with him and your desire to get rid of him are now public property—and the heat is on—and what do I say to justify removing him? I'm not afraid to do it, if I have to, don't misunderstand me—you will recall that I told him exactly that when I put him on the crew. But what shall it be? 'Incompatibility?' 'Pouts in the hallway?' 'Frowns in the dining room?' 'Leaves the john dirty?' I mean—I don't really intend to be too frivolous, but you see my problem."

"Betrays crew confidences, destroys crew trust," the Vice-President offered quietly. "Isn't that sufficient?"

"Ah," the President said. "Yes. But violates crew confidences on what? On something that probably 70 per cent of the major media, and 70 per cent of this country's most vocal citizens, and 70 per cent of the rest of the world, agree is absolutely wrong and should be stopped. He's on the popular side."

"Whose side are you on, Mr. President?" Hank Barstow asked quietly and wondered forever after how he had dared to do it. But the President's response when it came was surprisingly mild.

"I'm on yours. You know that. But I'm not just President of NASA, God damn it, I'm President of the whole United States. And a lot of its people are convinced that Jayvee Halleck is right when he opposes arming the Mars flight."

"Do you think he is, Mr. President?" Connie asked. "I don't mean to be disrespectful, but I really want to know."

For a moment the President looked at him, a shrewd, patient, knowledgeable glance. Then he stretched his powerful hands out flat upon the table.

"If I really thought," he said quietly, "that I was sending you boys out there unprotected to face a real, active, hostile threat from the Soviet Union, I wouldn't hesitate for one minute to arm those spacecraft. But again—what *do* I know? I know more," he admitted soberly, "than I knew last night, I can tell you that, and tonight I'm going on the air and tell the country what I know—and in a few minutes," he added as their expressions filled with concern, "I'm going to tell you—but I still don't have any evidence of any arming of their satellites and spacecraft, though I know and have known from the time I assumed this office that they have the capability."

"Then why," Bob Hertz protested, too upset to be polite, "*why* is there any question? Why haven't you from the very first—"

"Because I don't have proof," the President said quietly. "Can't I get that through to anybody? Because I don't have proof—and because without proof, I cannot jeopardize the at best very flimsy and very fragile remnants of friendliness and co-operation with the Soviet Union by openly taking an action that they could only, and legitimately, regard as hostile to them."

"How about doing it secretly?" Jazz suggested. "Does it have to be open?"

The President lifted his hands in an ironic shrug.

"Jayvee has made it open. It's impossible to do it in secret, now. We literally cannot move to protect you because the media literally will not let us—unless they have open and absolute and completely undeniable proof that the Communists are doing the same. And of course the Communists have a closed society and they don't let those things get out, and you can't convince our media of them on their own government's say-so and so: there—we—are."

"But surely, Mr. President," Jim Cavanaugh said, "surely you have intelligence at your disposal which tells you whether they are or not."

"And I release the intelligence and I blow the cover and there goes our means of keeping tab on them," the President said. "I tell you, it's a vicious circle—about as vicious as a circle can be. But I also tell you"—and his voice lowered and became graver and more emphatic—"and I give you my word upon it—that as of this moment, no intelligence I have received indicates in any way that the Soviets are preparing or have prepared an attack of a military nature upon Piffy One. I give you my word. A propaganda attack, yes, an attack in the sense that they are apparently attempting to advance their launch by at least two months—"

"Oh, no," the Administrator said in a tired and disgusted tone.

"Oh, yes," the President said, "and that means"—and he looked again carefully along both sides of the table at faces that instantly understood—"that means just exactly what you think it means, my friends. But without the fear, I honestly believe, of any type of hostile physical attack ... My God," he said quietly, "you don't actually *believe* I'd send you out there unarmed if I thought any differently, do you?"

"No, Mr. President," Connie said quickly into the silence because somebody must. "Of course not. But we would feel a lot better if you'd let us have the capability to protect ourselves if we need to."

"I can't," the President said simply. "I'm sorry—I sympathize—but I can't."

"I wish you could," the Vice-President remarked quietly. "I really wish you could."

"You wouldn't in my place," the President said, and for a rare moment the two men who between them were the guardians of such great power gave one another look for look. Finally the Vice-President said gravely,

"Who can say? I wouldn't want to presume to, because I can't."

"I don't think you would," the President said. "Maybe I have to think that, but anyway, I do ..."

"And what about Jayvee?" the Vice-President asked.

"I have nothing substantial," the President pointed out again. "What could I say?"

"Well—" the Vice-President began. Then his voice trailed away and down the long table there was silence.

Finally Jazz shifted in his chair, seemed to gather himself together, started to speak, found it difficult, cleared his throat.

"Mr. President," he said at last, and it obviously did not come easily, "if that is your final decision, then I am afraid I shall have to submit my resignation from the crew."

"I, too," Pete said quietly and without hesitation.

Again silence fell while they all looked at Connie, who did not return the look but sat in his place holding a pencil between the fingers of his two hands, twirling and twirling it, slowly, thoughtfully, as though mesmerized.

At last he let it drop to the table, where it made a loud, clattering sound exaggerated by the tense quiet in the room, as it rolled away.

"Yes, Mr. President," he said then, looking up directly and calmly into the attentively studying eyes of the Chief Executive, "I think I would too."

The President nodded as there came a little rush of pent-up breaths released around the table.

"I have received threats of resignation since the speed-up of this project began," he said quietly. "None of them has been carried out. If you wish to resign, I will remove Jayvee and we will start over with an entirely new crew. You are welcome to leave if you wish. You will not be penalized. Others are waiting and anxious to take your places. He gave them each a long thoughtful stare. "Feel free."

Again there was silence, in which the three of them felt as though the physical world were actually drawing away; that they were on some far, receding shore, mystical and hazy—on Mars, perhaps, distant, shimmering, elusive and now, apparently, vanishing forever.

It would take them a long time later to analyze, each for himself, the tumult of thoughts and emotions that assailed them. Pride, desire, ambition, dreams—challenge, hope, self-confidence, shame—the infinite satisfaction if they went, the eternal regret if they did not—pride, desire, ambition, dreams . . .

The President waited, the others looked from face to struggling face in unhappy, agonizing, sympathetic silence. Presently there came the words the President knew would come.

"You don't leave us much leeway," Connie observed, very low.

"None," the President said.

"You make it very hard," Pete remarked, also very low.

"I do," the President said.

"O.K.," Jazz said in a sudden, angry burst. "You know we want to fly. You know we will fly. But if that bastard gives us any more trouble, he's dead. And I mean, that could be literal."

"No, it couldn't, Jazz," the President said, unperturbed. "You're all too decent and too imbued with the program for any nonsense like that. But I will talk to him again, I promise you that. And severely. Now," he said, and he leaned forward with a pleasant firmness as though no crisis had occurred at all, "is there anything else?"

"How will you handle all this?" Dr. Anderson asked in a wondering tone.

The President displayed his confident, commanding smile.

"Geneva—Jayvee—the question of arming—the fact that we must now speed up the mission even more than before—I'll cover them all in my talk tonight—you'll see. I think you all know pretty well what I'll say. But you might listen."

Bob Hertz uttered a little laugh that did not sound very amused.

"I expect we will. One good thing, anyway—from the way you talk about speeding it up, I take it you have no plans to cancel Piffy One."

"No," the President said with an expression both wry and determined. "That is one thing I am not going to do."

The flight home was as swift and silent as the flight to Washington. By noon Houston time they were on the ground at Ellington Field. They drove off in their respective cars at carefully spaced intervals, to the astronauts building, the administration building, the flight control building. As far as they knew, none of the newsmen wandering the center saw them arrive, as, hopefully, none had seen them depart. Already the whole episode seemed almost dreamlike—except that they had been forced to face what Piffy One was up against, and in the process face themselves, and it was not.

Shortly after 2 P.M. Connie received a call in his office and was away for a couple of hours. When he returned another was waiting, from Jayvee. For a second his pulse began to race guiltily. Then he thought, What the hell, and snapped on the machine.

"Yes?" he said coldly. "Did you want me?"

"The President called," Jayvee said, trying to keep his voice flat, declarative, unemotional, but not quite managing to conceal the triumph. "He says I'm still on the crew."

"You are," Connie said, his voice carefully devoid of feeling. "He told you to shape up, too, didn't he?"

"He—" Jayvee began indignantly. Then as Connie stared at him his eyes dropped. "He said I should try harder to get along with you-all," he amended sullenly.

"I hope so," Connie said, voice unchanged. "Is that all?"

"Are we going to have another meeting?"

374

"Do you want one?"

"No."

"Good. There's no reason, for a while, that I can see. Just carry on as you were. We'll go to the field in a couple of weeks. I'll let you know."

"O.K.," Jayvee said and without farewell left the screen.

And screw you, too, buddy, Connie thought savagely as he turned back to his desk. I'll believe you're part of this crew when I see it.

But later, in the President's accounting, everything was right as rain and smooth as pie. It was a study in technique by a master of the art of politics, and as such, did much to strengthen his own position. Whether it really helped to solve any of the problems of Piffy One was not so clear to its crew and administrators.

"My countrymen," he said at 9 P.M., "again I have asked for the gift of your time and the courtesy of your attention to discuss with you the most recent developments concerning Planetary Fleet One, the mission of our four astronauts to Mars. I do so because recent events, both national and international, may have led some of you to wonder, not only whether this mission can be successful, but whether it will be possible for it to fly at all.

"Let me make clear at once," he said firmly, staring straight into the cameras with a calm, confident candor, "that Planetary Fleet One will go to Mars. Let no timid voices persuade you otherwise. P.F. One will fly. And it will be successful."

("I *knew* it," Percy Mercy said angrily in his apartment at Prospect House. "He seems awfully sure," Clete O'Donnell observed with a tight little smile.)

"It will also," the President said, "fly at a substantially earlier date than my space advisers and I had originally thought feasible. It will be launched on or about six months from today, instead of the eight previously announced."

("Good God," Connie said explosively to Jane and Pete in El Lago, "what does he think we are?" And at North American Rockwell in Downey, California, Jim Matthison looked around his silent office at the shocked expressions on the faces of his division managers, shook his head in sober dismay and uttered a long, low whistle.)

"The reason for this is very simple. In the past forty-eight hours we have received new intelligence reports, from many sources scientific and otherwise, that the Soviet Union is drastically increasing the rate of preparation for its own launch to Mars. Coming as these preparations do in the immediate aftermath of the Russians' abrupt termination of the conference in Geneva, they can only be regarded as a direct and deliberate attempt to beat us to the next great objective in space.

"I feel, and I think a majority of you, my countrymen, feel, that the United States cannot afford to let this prize go without a determined effort to meet—and surpass—any Soviet effort to be first on Mars.

"I am confident our men can do it. I am confident our industry can do it. And I am confident we as a people can do it. I urge you all to give our brave men and skilled manufacturers your utmost support in this great adventure."

("It is easy to say," Albrecht Freer remarked to Stuart and Yo-Shin Yule, who sat beside him in his office at the Cape. "He's a great one at words," Stu agreed, grimacing a little with pain as he carefully shifted his bandaged stump in the chair.)

"The events in Geneva," the President went on, his expression turning somber, "would seem to indicate—to all but the most willfully self-deluded—that the Communists really have no sincere intention at all of co-operating with us in space. They never have, and despite the opportunity afforded them by our invitation to meet in Geneva, this traditional attitude of theirs apparently has not changed.

"Their demands seemed to your government to be unwarranted and excessive. They wanted majority control of the launching and flight control staffs. They wanted a majority of four men on a crew of six. They wanted your government to waive security regulations on all Soviet and Iron Curtain nationals to be brought by them into this country for this project. And they wanted your government to waive security regulations on all American citizens hired by them in this country to work on this project.

"Although some superficial support was apparently generated for these propositions in some circles in this country, no responsible American Administration, having in mind our own great achievements in space and the security of our own country, could have accepted these conditions.

"I do not really think," the President said, and he looked into the cameras with a direct, challenging stare, "that any sane American among you would have wanted us to accept these conditions. While some may have seen a superficial appeal in a willing surrender to Russian control by this government, we in the Administration could not. I don't believe most of you could either.

"Our purpose was equality, not submission."

("Why didn't he say that in the first place?" the Vice-President inquired dryly of the Administrator in the big house in Georgetown. "It would have saved a lot of fuss." "Technique," Andy Anderson said with equal dryness. "A matter of virtuosity.")

("So chauvinistic!" Percy cried with an angry despair. "So blind, so stupid, so destructive of international good will and world peace!" "This isn't the last word," Clete promised grimly. "A lot of us have something left to say.")

"Therefore," the President went on, "Geneva ended, with a Communist pretext which had something to do with trying to blame us for maintaining a secrecy rule they themselves had originally insisted upon. In some circles they apparently blamed us rather successfully. But again, I think the majority of common-sense Americans understood the facts.

"Their action, however, did precipitate two rather unfortunate consequences. It aroused within the National Aeronautics and Space Administration, and more particularly among the members of the crew of Planetary Fleet One, an anxiety lest Soviet lack of co-operation result in active Soviet hostility, of some physical nature, against the mission. And because there were sharp differences concerning this possibility within the crew, it resulted in a temporary feeling that perhaps one or all of the crew should retire from the project.

"I am happy to report to you," he said, and his expression was cheerful and calm, "that this temporary worry has been alleviated. The crew remains as before and will go forward confident and unified to carry out its successful mission.

"As for the possibility of any Soviet interference with the Mars flight"—his face changed and became grave—"I do not believe that it exists. But I do wish to make it clear that no such interference could possibly be tolerated by us. Because the Soviet Government knows this, I am confident no interference will be attempted. If the Soviets wish to launch their own mission, that, of course, is their privilege, and we wish them God speed. May they go, as we go, in peace. I am confident, knowing the consequences of the opposite course, that they *will* go in peace. For them to do otherwise would be unthinkable—and unacceptable."

("How do you make good on this threat?" Hans Sturmer demanded of placid Helga in Huntsville. "How do you police it? *How do you make sure?*" And Helga, as on so many occasions with excitable Hans, did not even look up as she murmured, "Ja, ja," and went on reading *Der Spiegel.*)

"So the Mars mission goes on," the President said, "more swiftly than we had planned but with no less assurance of unity and success. We regret that the Soviet Union has seen fit to reject this latest opportunity for co-operation in space. But we do not let it dismay or intimidate us. If we cannot have a friendly teamwork we offer a friendly competition. Let us both move forward and expend our best efforts and see who wins.

("Winning!" Walter Dobius said to the editor of the *Post* as they listened in Walter's study in the Virginia countryside. "That tired, old-fashioned concept again!" "Incredible, isn't it?" the *Post* agreed. "After all these years.")

"The United States is not worried about the outcome," the President concluded with a rising cheerfulness in his voice. "Planetary Fleet One is on the way and nothing can stop her now. Our crew is united, our industry is in high gear, our administrators of space have made their plans. Mars lies just ahead.

"May we all go there with our brave men in spirit, if not in flesh; and may our journey be safe and our homecoming happy. And may all mankind profit from our generous and far-reaching endeavors."

"Great stuff," Connie said as the forceful visage faded from the screen and the commentators began their snide, corrosive work. "Sing hallelujah."

"Is that really the mission we know?" Pete inquired with a matching irony. "How nice if it were."

"It isn't *really* so terribly far from it, is it?" Jane asked, quite seriously.

Her husband shook his head.

"You see?" he said to Pete. "He's a wonder, that guy."

But as the hours wore on and night tumbled into day, and day raced on into succeeding nights and days and weeks and months, it appeared that the President's magic wand might not be quite enough, in the face of the bitter opposition of some of his more determined countrymen, to waft away all the obstacles in the path of Piffy One. There were a few left to go, as he well knew, before the beautiful great birds could thunder with their uneasy human cargo into the Florida sky.

Book Three

1.

But for a while, Piffy One proceeded with relative ease and quiet.

The first wild rush of reaction to the collapse of Geneva was tempered by the President's "cool and statesmanlike refusal to let himself be stampeded into the fantastically hostile act of arming the spacecraft." The fact that the "military-minded, disturbingly racist white members of the crew" had been "thwarted in their stubborn and inexcusable attempt to exile one of America's finest and most responsible black citizens from the mission" also helped. And there was the now unmistakable certainty, which not even Percy and his friends dared challenge, that the Soviet Union was definitely and with increasing openness rushing preparations for its own launch. This helped too.

Piffy One dropped from the headlines, the world turned for a time to other concerns. An outward if possibly deceptive serenity settled over the issue. Everyone involved had a chance to get down to serious work. If the President had done nothing to alleviate the private worries and tensions of the crew, he had to a considerable extent defused the public issue. For this, most of those concerned felt themselves lucky and were properly grateful.

Planetary Fleet One enjoyed a breathing spell. Tentatively, and perhaps not too wisely, the men of NASA thought they might be through with crippling outside attacks and on the way to smooth completion of their task.

The Lord, incurably ironic, might have news for them. But for the time being, things seemed to be moving forward with a steady and increasingly successful momentum, at last.

Not the least important aspect of this, the Administrator presently had occasion to note with some amusement, was the vast publicity machine of NASA, which had ground into action for every major launch since the program began and was now grinding ponderously—and inexorably—into action again.

He had just finished an hour-long conference with the Assistant Administrator for Public Affairs. With his usual shrewd decisiveness and sharp-tongued skill, that able gentleman, whose name was Marlon Holloway, had presented a program that pretty well covered all contingencies—starting with the customary biographical releases on the crew, providing for the special interviews, press conferences and television appearances that were always demanded by the media, running right on through to the plans for what would undoubtedly be the most numerous and overwhelming news corps ever to descend on the Cape.

"If there's anything I haven't thought of," he said with his usual sleepy smile—sleepy like a cat, Andy Anderson had found over the months—"I'll think of it an hour from now. So don't worry."

"I'm not worried at all," Dr. Anderson said with an answering smile. "I'm breathing a little easier for the first time in many a day."

"Don't draw those breaths in too fast," Marlon Holloway suggested. "It's still possible to strangle."

"Oh, very possible," Andy agreed. "But at least we can take advantage of the lull while it lasts. And I must say you're doing so, excellently as always. You want me to check over this release on the mission and have it back by this afternoon, then."

"I don't want to rush you," Marlon said gently, "but if I have it by 3 o'clock it can go to the printer this afternoon and be ready for distribution tomorrow. A lot of the press is already clamoring for it."

"I don't see why," Dr. Anderson said. "It's something they've had a thousand times already. We must have issued enough slush over the years to float a battleship."

"Sink it," Marlon corrected. "But each time is new, you see. So each time we do it over again."

"Half of the NASA budget——" Andy Anderson began in humorous exasperation.

"Call me King of the Mimeographs," Marlon said with another sleepy smile. "It's how we keep them happy. Or try to."

"Or try to," Dr. Anderson echoed. "O.K., leave it and I'll get to it right away. It will be back by 3."

"Thank you," said the Assistant Administrator for Public Affairs, and departed: quick-witted, acrid, quietly and thoroughly capable. Like all of them, he had taken a rough pounding from the clamoring media in the early crisis weeks, but Dr. Anderson had never known him to utter an ill-considered statement or perpetrate one hasty blunder. And this had not been easy.

Taking up MISSION OPERATION REPORT—PLANETARY FLEET ONE/PROJECT ARGOSY, that handsome multi-paged document that would presently tumble forth in thousands of copies from the Program and Special Reports Division, Executive Secretariat, NASA Headquarters, the Administrator buzzed his secretary and told her to hold all calls. Then he crossed to his conference table, sat down in a comfortable leather armchair beside a window facing west, and began to skim with a practiced eye.

The official picture of a planetary mission, so smooth, so sure, so perfect, so mechanical and free from all human foibles, began to unfold.

In these pages, he told himself with a sardonic little smile, everything was neat, scientific, inevitable and pure. Here he would find no Connie Trasker and Jayvee Halleck—and by the same token, no Percy Mercy or media either. Perhaps that was boon enough, he reflected, the smile growing: maybe he should just read, and not complain.

In concise, familiar words, the profile of Piffy One took shape:

SPACE VEHICLE

The primary flight hardware of the Argosy planetary flight program consists of a Saturn V Launch Vehicle and an Argosy Spacecraft. Collectively, they are designated the Argosy-Saturn V Space Vehicle. Three such vehicles will be launched to form Planetary Fleet One.

SATURN V LAUNCH VEHICLE
The Saturn V Launch Vehicle is designed to boost up to 285,000 pounds into a 105 nautical mile earth orbit and to provide for planetary payloads of 100,000 pounds. It consists consecutively, starting with the base of the vehicle, of three propulsive stages (S-IC, S-II, S-IVB), two interstages, and an Instrument Unit (IU). Above them come the units that form the spacecraft.

S-IC STAGE
The S-IC stage is a large cylindrical booster, 138 feet long and 33 feet in diameter, powered by five liquid propellant F-1 rocket engines. These engines develop a nominal sea level thrust total of approximately 7,650,000 pounds and have an operational burn time of 159 seconds. The total loaded stage weight is approximately 5,031,500 pounds.

S-II STAGE
The S-II stage is a large cylindrical booster, 81.5 feet long and 33 feet in diameter, powered by five liquid propellant J-2 rocket engines which develop a nominal vacuum thrust of 230,000 pounds each for a total of 1,150,000 pounds, The stage's approximate loaded gross weight is 1,064,600 pounds.

S-IVB STAGE
The S-IVB stage is a large cylindrical booster 59 feet long and 21.6 feet in diameter, powered by one J-2 engine. The S-IVB stage is capable of multiple engine starts. Engine thrust is 232,000 pounds for the first burn and 206,000 pounds for subsequent burns. This stage is also unique in that it has an attitude control capability independent of its main engine. The launch weight of the stage is 259,160 pounds.

MODIFICATIONS FOR THE MARS MISSION-MODULES AND NERVA
For the Mars mission of Planetary Fleet One of Project Argosy, certain modifications have been made in

the Saturn V launch vehicles and the spacecraft to satisfy the environmental and scientific requirements of the crew, and to accommodate the NERVA nuclear engine. One of the vehicles, designated the Command-Service Vehicle, has been extensively altered to provide greatly increased space for food supplies and life-support equipment. Another, designated the Medico-Scientific Vehicle, will, in addition to providing substantial space for extra food supplies and life-support equipment, also have ample space to accommodate necessary medical supplies for the crew and the large amount of scientific equipment that will be needed for experiments during the Mars orbit period of the mission. The third, designated the Mars Landing Vehicle, has been configured to carry the Mars Lander, a Command Center for the major instrumentation of the flight, and four nuclear rocket stages powered by the NERVA nuclear engine.

The nuclear rocket stage is a multipurpose stage capable of performing lunar or interplanetary missions. For lunar missions a single nuclear rocket stage is required. For interplanetary missions, at least four nuclear rocket stages are needed.

The nuclear rocket stage is a large cylindrical stage, 142½ feet long and 33 feet in diameter with 15 degree half angle conical aft dome, powered by one NERVA engine. The engine thrust is 75,000 pounds and the stage is capable of multiple restarts. Launch weight of the stage is 388,320 pounds plus interstage weight. For the Mars mission of Planetary Fleet One, one NERVA engine will be launched with the Mars Landing Vehicle, one with the Command-Service Vehicle and one with the Medico-Scientific Vehicle. The fourth NERVA engine is already at Space Station Mayflower, where it was assembled for experimental purposes two years ago. It will not be needed for the initial Moon test phase of the mission but will be added when Planetary Fleet One returns to Mayflower for check-out prior to final departure for Mars.

INSTRUMENT UNIT

The Instrument Unit (IU), is a cylindrical structure 21.6 feet in diameter and 3 feet high installed on top of the S-IVB stage. The IU contains the guidance,

*navigation and control equipment for the Launch Ve-
hicle. In addition, it contains measurements and telemetry, command communications, tracking and emergency detection system components along with supporting electrical power and environmental control
systems.*

SERVICE MODULE

*The Service Module (SM), atop the Instrument Unit,
provides the main spacecraft propulsion and maneuvering capability during a mission. It provides most
of the spacecraft consumables (oxygen, water, propellant, hydrogen) and supplements environmental, electrical power and propulsion requirements of the Command Module.*

COMMAND MODULE

*The Command Module (CM), the top of the Sat-
urn except for a small emergency Launch Escape
Tower above, serves as the command, control, and
communications center. It is capable of attitude and
directional control. Supplemented by the Service
Module, it provides all life support elements for the
crewmen in the mission environments and for their
safe return to Earth's surface.*

Which will be, the Administrator wondered as he
stopped for a moment to stare down upon the throngs of
lunch-bound government workers in the sweltering early-
summer heat—when? About a year and eight months
from now, if the flight went on schedule—if the mission
were successful—if every one of 6000 parts functioned
perfectly—if the human cargo aboard could stand a journey for which there was no precedent and for which there
could be, in the last analysis, no real preparation.

The trip would not be easy no matter how many plans
were made. It would be even more difficult with the crew
that was to fly. He realized with a smile that he couldn't
keep the human element out, after all. Their faces took
form for him through the print as he returned to his
reading: Connie confident and intent, Jazz impatient and
determined, Pete easygoing and competent, Jayvee closed-
away and determinedly impersonal still. He could not

repress a little involuntary shudder as he read the description of the familiar vessels on which they would make their awesome journey. The modules would be linked together for comfort and leg room, and the description sounded practically houselike until one stopped to realize how very small and confined they were, closed in against the myriad hostile challenges of space:

CREW COMPARTMENT

The crew compartments have a habitual volume of 210 feet each. Pressurization and temperature are maintained by the Environmental Control System. Each crew compartment contains the control and displays for operation of the spacecraft, crew couches, and all the other equipment needed by the crew. It contains two hatches, five windows, and a number of equipment bays. The equipment bays contain food supplies, scientific instruments and other items needed by the crew, as well as much of the computers, navigational, telecommunications and other equipment needed for operation of the spacecraft. Each module has five triple-pane windows: two side, two rendezvous and a hatch window. Each pane has an antireflecting coating on the external surface and a blue-red reflective coating on the inner surface to filter out most infrared and all ultra-violet rays. Aluminum shades are provided for all windows.

TELECOMMUNICATIONS

The telecommunications and radio frequency systems provide voice, television, telemetry, tracking and range communications between the spacecraft and earth, between the Command Vehicle, the Mars Landing Vehicle and the Medico-Scientific Vehicle, and between the spacecraft and astronauts wearing the Portable Life Support System on extra vehicular missions. The astronauts' headsets are used for all voice communications. Each astronaut has an audio control panel which enables him to control what comes into his headset and where he will send his voice. Two methods of voice transmission and reception are possible: The Very High Frequency/AM equipment is used for near-Earth phases of a mission. The S-band equipment is used during both near-Earth and deep-space phases of a mission.

And what would the voices say on their way to Mars, and what would their message be from the red planet?

Andy Anderson could remember many voices down the years, some awestruck and gleeful like Alan Shepard on Freedom 7 and John Glenn on Friendship 7; some filled with a tightly-controlled emotion like Frank Borman, Bill Anders and Jim Lovell reading their Christmas message from Genesis on Apollo 8; some upset and concerned like Tom Stafford and Gene Cernan spinning temporarily out of control in Apollo 10's Lunar Module; some solemn and dedicated like Neil Armstrong of Apollo 11 setting foot for mankind on the Moon; some carefree and kittenish like Pete Conrad and Alan Bean of Apollo 12 loping about the lunar surface like a couple of kids; some quietly alert like the voice of John Swigert of Apollo 13 saying quietly, "Houston, we've got a problem"; and through them all, the voices that still haunted NASA and would never be forgotten, crying, "Fire in the spacecraft!" as Gus Grissom, Ed White and Roger Chaffee died on the pad at the Cape.

What would be the burden of the voices that would come back from the long, long journey of Planetary Fleet One? What would they have to say, after the first exhilaration and thrill had worn off and the prospect of eighteen months of fearfully lonely travel finally became real? After the initial scientific measurements had been made, the first experiments had been run, the busy-work was over and they had to face the prospect of nothing but each other—and themselves—for all the length of that vast and silent highway through the universe?

And what would they really feel, confident as they were of their equipment, when they realized that not only the success of their journey, but the very breath of life itself, depended upon a fragile shell and the fragile wires and systems that fragile human hands had put together? When they finally knew, farther from home than any men had ever been, that the slightest malfunction could trap them, lifeless but preserved forever, in the endless grave of space?

He sighed and read on:

ENVIRONMENTAL CONTROL SYSTEM

The Environmental Control System (ECS) provides a controlled environment for the astronauts. For Planetary Fleet One, this environment includes 3 pressurized cabins (five pounds per square inch), a 100 per cent oxygen atmosphere, and a cabin temperature of 70 to 75 degrees Fahrenheit. The system provides a pressurized suit circuit for use during critical mission phases and for emergencies.

The ECS provides oxygen and hot and cold water, removes carbon dioxide and odors from the cabins, provides for venting of waste and dissipates excessive heat from the cabins and from operating electronic equipment. It is designed so that a minimum amount of crew time is needed for its normal operation.

GUIDANCE, NAVIGATION, STABILIZATION AND CONTROL

The Argosy spacecraft is guided and controlled by two interrelated systems. One is the Guidance, Navigation and Control System. The other is the Stabilization and Control System. The two systems provide rotational, line-of-flight and rate-of-speed information. They integrate and interpret this information and convert it into commands for the spacecraft propulsion systems.

Guidance and navigation is accomplished through three major elements: the inertial, optical and computer systems. The inertial subsystem senses any changes in the velocity and angle of the spacecraft and relays this information to the computer which transmits any necessary signals to the spacecraft engines. The optical subsystem is used to obtain navigation sightings of celestial bodies and landmarks on the earth and moon. It passes this information along to the computer for guidance and control purposes. The computer subsystem uses information from a number of sources to determine the spacecraft position and speed and, in automatic operation, to give commands for guidance and control.

The Stabilization and Control System operates in three ways. It determines the spacecraft's attitude (angular position); maintains the spacecraft's attitude; and controls the direction of thrust of the service propulsion engine. This system is also used by the computer in the Command Module to provide automatic control of the spacecraft. Manual control of the spacecraft attitude and thrust is provided mainly through this equipment.

And what of the comfort of this intrepid group, Dr. Anderson wondered, and could not resist a certain amusement, for the report made it all sound so comfortable—or at least, if not exactly comfortable, at least quite livable. He had heard many astronauts express themselves on the subject of clothing and food and waste material. Some of their comments had been both uproarious and unprintable. Many new methods had been devised in these recent years of experimentation, but life in the module was not exactly life in the astronauts' favorite Acapulco hideaway, Las Brisas. Yet for the public some of the main questions, which he himself received many times on the public platform, were the same now as they had been from the start of the program:

"Is the food good? How do they eat it? What they do when they want to—er—what do they *do* with it?"

Well, on planetary flights, as the astronauts already knew but the public could not quite believe, the food would be reasonably good and the methods for its ingestion relatively comfortable. As for what they would do when they wanted to—er—and what they would do with it, NASA had news for them. Solid waste would be compressed, incinerated and disposed of in space. But a sizeable proportion of the liquid would be run through chemicals, reconstituted, dressed up with pretty flavors and served all over again.

That, the Administrator thought with a wry little smile, was the sort of item that did not fit too well with the picture of heroes. But on second thought, maybe that was more heroic than most of the things they would be asked to do. He chuckled and read on:

CREW PROVISIONS

APPAREL

There are three basic configurations of dress: Unsuited, suited and extravehicular.

UNSUITED

This relatively informal, "long underwear" mode of dress is worn by crewmen under conditions termed "shirt-sleeve environment." This unsuited mode is the most comfortable, convenient, and consequently, the least fatiguing of the modes. When unsuited the astronaut relies upon the environmental control system to maintain the proper cabin environment of pressure, temperature and oxygen.

SUITED

This mode enables a crewman to operate in an unpressurized cabin up to the design life of the pressure suit of 115 hours. The intravehicular configuration includes: a torso-limb suit, pressure helmet and pressure gloves; the fecal containment system; constant wear garment; biomedical belt; communications carrier; urine collection and transfer assembly.

EXTRAVEHICULAR

In the extravehicular configuration the constant wear garment is replaced by a liquid cooling garment and four items are added to the pressure garment assembly: extravehicular visor assembly, extravehicular gloves, Martian overshoes and a connector cover which fits over umbilical connections on the front of the suit. The addition of the portable life support system and oxygen purge system back-pack completes the equipment. This equipment protects the astronaut from radiation, micrometeorite impact and planetary surface temperatures.

COMMUNICATIONS CARRIER AND BIOMEDICAL HARNESS

The communications carrier is a polyurethane foam headpiece which positions two independent earphones and microphones. The biomedical harness carries signal conditioners and converters to transmit heart beat and respiration rates of the astronauts.

URINE COLLECTION AND TRANSFER ASSEMBLY

The urine collection and transfer assembly is a truss-like garment which functions by use of a urinal cuff, storage compartment, and tube which connects to the external collection system.

FECAL CONTAINMENT SYSTEM

The fecal containment system is an elastic underwear with an absorbent liner around the buttock area. This system is worn to allow emergency defecation when the pressure garment assembly is pressurized. Protective ointment is used on the buttocks and perineal area to lessen skin irritation.

PORTABLE LIFE SUPPORT SYSTEM

The portable life support system is a portable, self-powered, rechargeable environmental control system with a communications capability. It is carried as a backpack for extravehicular activity. It weighs about 68 pounds. It supplies pressurized oxygen, cleans and cools the suit atmosphere, cools and circulates water through the liquid cooling garment and provides radio communications with a dual very high frequency transceiver. It can operate for up to four hours in a space environment before replenishment of water and oxygen is required.

FOOD AND WATER

Food supplies are designed to supply each astronaut with a balanced diet of approximately 2800 calories per day. The food is either freeze-dried or concentrated and is carried in vacuum-packaged plastic bags. Each bag of freeze-dried food has a one-way valve through which water is inserted and a second valve through which food passes. Concentrated food is packaged in bite-size units and needs no reconstitution. Several bags are packaged together to make one meal bag. The meal bags have colored dots to identify them for each crewman, as well as labels to identify them by day and meal.

The food is reconstituted by adding hot or cold water through the one-way valve. The astronaut kneads the bag and then cuts the neck of the bag and squeezes the food into his mouth. A "Feed Port" in the pressure helmet allows partaking of liquid food and water while suited. Food preparation water is dispensed from a unit which supplies 150 degrees F, and 50 degrees water.

Drinking water comes from the water chiller to two outlets: the water meter dispenser, and the food *preparation unit. The dispenser is in the form of a button-actuated pistol. The pistol barrel is placed in the mouth and the button is pushed for each half-ounce of water. The meter records the amount of water drunk. A valve is provided to shut off the system in case the dispenser develops a leak or malfunction.*

COUCHES AND RESTRAINTS

The astronaut couches are individualls adjustable units made of hollow steel tubing and covered with a heavy, fireproof, fiberglass cloth. These couches support the crewmen during acceleration and deceleration, position the crewmen at their duty stations and provide support for translation and rotation hand controls, lights and other equipment. The couches can be folded or adjusted into a number of seat positions. The astronauts may sleep in their couches or in bags under the left and right couches with heads toward the hatch. The astronauts sleep in the bags when unsuited, and sleep restrained by straps on top of the bags when suited.

HYGIENE EQUIPMENT

Hygiene equipment includes wet and dry cloths for cleaning, towels, toothbrushes, and the waste management system. The waste management system controls and disposes of waste solids, liquids and gases. The system disposes of feces, removes odors, dumps urine overboard and removes urine from the space suit.

OPERATIONAL AIDS

Operational aids include data files, tools, workshelf, cameras, fire extinguishers, oxygen masks, medical supplies and waste bags. The fire extinguisher weighs about eight pounds. The extinguishing agent is an aqueous gel expelled in two cubic feet of foam for approximately 30 seconds at high pressure. Fire ports are located at various panels so that the extinguisher's nozzle can be inserted to put out a fire behind the panel. Oxygen masks are provided for each astronaut in case of smoke, toxic gas or other hostile atmosphere in the cabin while the astronauts are out of their suits.

Medical supplies are contained in an emergency medical kit, about 7 x 5 x 5 inches, which is stored in the lower equipment bay. It contains oral drugs and pills (pain capsules, stimulant, antibiotic, motion sickness, diarrhea, decongestant and aspirin), injectable drugs (for pain and motion sickness), bandages, topical agents (first-aid cream, sun cream and an antibiotic ointment), eye drops and emergency feeding equipment.

Each crewman is provided with toothbrushes, wet and dry cleansing cloths, ingestible toothpaste, a 64-cubic-inch container for personal items, and two-compartment temporary storage bag. A special tool kit is provided which also contains three jack screws for contingency hatch closure.

It was almost noon and he had a luncheon date with the Vice-President in the latter's office. He wondered if he should put off further reading until afternoon, decided he could accomplish in ten minutes the remaining highlights he felt he had to read; pressed on. "Mars Landing" the next subhead announced: a tiny white spider spun down in mind's eye toward the fog-shrouded, mysterious surface of the far-off planet.

Connie would be at the controls. Someone—it had not been decided yet, probably Pete—would be beside him. Above, Jazz and Jayvee in the linked modules would continue their inexorable, predetermined orbit. The planet, two thirds the size of Earth, would turn slowly below them as they flew; they would have lost visual contact with the tiny white spider almost at once. Only the precious voices, probably fuzzed and distant in the atmospheric conditions of Mars, would come faintly back to them, and from them to Houston, and so to the waiting world.

The tiny spider might or might not land, that too had not yet been decided. But—a mass of wires and systems hopefully infallible, and two humans as infallible as skill, nerves and training could make them—it would get as close as it dared before its commander fired the ascent rockets and he and his companion, and the world, found out whether everything was infallible or not.

To the red planet, slumbering through the eons, the tiny spider would matter not at all. Only if someone were waiting would it matter. And of that, for all the work of Vernon Hertz' JPL, there was, as yet, virtually no indication and even less proof.

But again, man was as prepared as he knew how to be. And nothing was going to stop him now. Watch out, Mars, Andy Anderson thought wryly: here we come, ready or not.

MARS LANDING

The Mars Landing Module (MLM) is designed to transport two men safely from Planetary Fleet One in Mars orbit to the Martian surface and return them to the mother craft. The MLM provides operational capabilities such as communications, telemetry, environmental support, the transport of scientific equipment to the Martian surface and the return of surface samples with the crew to the mother craft.

The Mars Landing Module consists of two stages: the Command Center and the descent-ascent stage.

For Planetary Fleet One the stages have been fused as a single reusable unit. There will be no separation, and no abandonment of the descent stage, as occurred on Apollo missions to the Moon.

COMMAND CENTER

The Command Center accommodates two astronauts and is the control center of the MLM. The stage structure provides three main sections consisting of a crew compartment and mid-section, which comprises the pressurized cabins, and the unpressurized aft equipment bay. The cabin volume is approximately 235 cubic feet.

DESCENT-ASCENT STAGE

The descent-ascent stage is the unmanned portion of the MLM. It provides for major velocity changes of the MLM to deorbit, land on and ascend from the Martian surface. The major structural material is aluminum alloy.

GUIDANCE, NAVIGATION AND CONTROL SYSTEM

The GNC system provides all equipment required

*for a manned Martian landing mission and return to
Planetary Fleet One. It includes a landing radar
which provides slant range and velocity data for
control of the descent to the Martian surface. Slant
range data is available below Martian altitudes of
approximately 25,000 feet and velocity below approximately 18,000 feet.*

COMMUNICATIONS SYSTEM

*The communications system provides the links be-
tween the MLM and the Manned Space Flight Network, and between the MLM, the mother craft and
any extravehicular astronaut. The CS includes all
S-band, VHF and signal processing equipment necessary to transmit and receive voice, tracking and ranging data, and to transmit telemetry and emergency
keying.*

ENVIRONMENTAL CONTROL SYSTEM

*The environmental control system of the MLM
provides a habitable environment for two astronauts
for the maximum assigned Martian stay time while
the MLM is separated from the mother craft. It also
controls the temperature of electrical and electronic
equipment, stores and provides water for drinking,
cooking, fire extinguishing and food preparation.*

But before Mars would come the long flight out, and
before the flight would come the launch; and before the
launch, the drama would have moved to Florida. There
Al Freer would be in his glory again after all the drab,
drear years of penny-pinching, science-crippling, mind-
hobbling drought.

The Administrator had been down just a week ago. He
had been able to congratulate himself that all appeared to
be going well as of now. Clete O'Donnell had not interfered again—so far.

Pad C was moving fast. Already its great concrete massif,
riddled with underground tunnels and honeycombed with
electrical systems, loomed above the flat scrubland beside
its two older brothers. Hardhatted workmen, their cover-
alls white against the merciless sun, swarmed over it.
Jackhammers and pneumatic drills chattered in the sultry
air. A constant stream of trucks filled with support equip-

ment and electronic gear ground up the ramp along which the ponderous Crawler would presently carry Piffy One to her marriage with history.

He could imagine the three great missiles now, white and perfect in the sun. The thought of that beautiful sight, whose like he had seen so often in the great days of Apollo, made his pulse beat faster and brought a sudden touch of moisture to his eyes.

"You *will* go," he assured them again softly in the silence of his office. "You *will* go."

At the Cape, in the domain of Albrecht Freer, they were getting ready to do the endless, detailed, painstaking jobs that had to be done—the thousands of patient, necessary things that thousands of patient, necessary minds and hearts and eyes and hands would bring as their contributions to the success of Planetary Fleet One of Project Argosy.

The report, as usual, reduced it all to a straightforward march of statistics. But they were statistics fantastic and almost too much for the mind to grasp:

LAUNCH COMPLEX

GENERAL:

Launch Complex 39, located at Kennedy Space Center, Florida, is the facility provided for the assembly, checkout and launch of the Argosy Saturn V Space Vehicle. Assembly and checkout of the vehicle is accomplished on a mobile launcher in the Vehicle Assembly Building. The space vehicle and the mobile launcher are then moved as a unit by the Crawler to the launch site. The major elements of the launch complex are the Vehicle Assembly Building, the Launch Control Center, the mobile launcher, the Crawler, the crawlerway, the mobile-service structure and the launch pad.

LC 39 FACILITIES AND EQUIPMENT

VEHICLE ASSEMBLY BUILDING

The VAB provides a protected environment for receipt and checkout of the propulsion stages and Instrument Unit, erection of the vehicle stages and spacecraft in a vertical position on the mobile launch-

er, and integrated check-out of the assembled space vehicle. The VAB is a totally enclosed structure covering eight acres of ground. It is a structural steel building approximately 525 feet high, 518 feet wide and 716 feet long. The principal operational elements of the VAB are the low bay and high bay areas. A 92-foot-wide transfer aisle extends through the length of the VAB and divides the low and high bay areas into equal segments. The low bay area provides the facilities for receiving, uncrating, checkout and preparation of the S-II stages, S-IVB stage and the Instrument Unit. The high bay area provides the facilities for erection and checkout of the S-IC stage; mating and erection operations of the S-II stage, S-IVB stage, IU and spacecraft; and integrated check-out of the assembled space vehicle. The high bay area contains four checkout bays, each capable of accommodating a full-assembled Argosy Saturn V space vehicle.

LAUNCH CONTROL CENTER

The Launch Control Center serves as the focal point for overall direction, control and monitoring of space vehicle checkout and launch. It is located adjacent to the VAB and at a sufficient distance from the launch pad (three miles) to permit safe viewing of lift-off without extra protections. The center has four firing rooms, one for each high bay in the VAB, and each containing control, monitoring and display equipment for automatic vehicle checkout and launch.

MOBILE LAUNCHER

The mobile launcher is a transportable steel structure which, with the Crawler, provides the capability to move the entire Argosy Saturn V vehicle to the launch pad. The ML is divided into two functional areas, the launcher base and the umbilical tower. The launcher base is the platform on which a Saturn vehicle is assembled in the vertical position, transported to one of the launch sites and launched. The umbilical tower provides access to all important levels of the vehicle during assembly, checkout and servicing. The equipment used in the servicing, check-

out and launch is installed throughout both the base and tower sections of the ML.

The launcher base is a steel structure 25 feet high, 160 feet long and 135 feet wide. The upper deck, designated level O, contains, in addition to the umbilical tower, the four hold-down arms and the three tail service masts. There is a 45-foot-square opening through the base for first stage exhaust. The umbilical tower is a 380-foot-high open steel structure which provides the support for eight umbilical service arms, spacecraft access arm, 18 work and access platforms, distribution equipment for the propellant, pneumatic, electrical and instrumentation subsystems and other ground support equipment. Two high-speed elevators service 18 landings from level A of the base to the 340-foot tower level. The structure is topped by a 25-ton hammerhead crane. Remote control of the crane is possible from numerous locations on the launcher.

LAUNCH PAD

The launch pad provides a stable foundation for the Mobile Launcher during Argosy Saturn V launch and pre-launch operations. The three pads at LC 39 are located approximately three miles from the VAB area. Each launch site is approximately 3,000 feet across. The launch pad is a cellular, reinforced concrete structure with a top elevation of 42 feet above grade elevation. Located within the fill under the west side of the structure is a two-story concrete building to house environmental control and pad terminal connection equipment. On the east side of the structure, within the fill, is a one-story concrete building to house the high-pressure gas storage battery. On the pad surface are elevators, staircase and structures to provide service to the mobile launcher and mobile service structure. A ramp with a five per cent grade provides access from the crawlerway. This is used by the Crawler to position the mobile launcher housing the Saturn V and the mobile service structure on the support pedestals. A flame trench 58 feet wide by 450 feet long bisects the pad. This trench opens to grade at the north end. The 700,000-pound, mobile,

401

wedge-type flame deflector is mounted on rails in the trench.

MOBILE SERVICE STRUCTURE

The MSS provides access to those portions of the space vehicle which cannot be serviced from the mobile launcher while at the launch pad. The MSS is transported to the launch site by the Crawler where it is used during launch pad operations. It is removed from the pad a few hours prior to launch and returned to its parking area 7,000 feet from the launch pad. It is approximately 402 feet high and weighs 12 million pounds. The tower structure rests on a base 135 feet by 135 feet. At the top, the tower is 87 feet by 113 feet.

CRAWLER

The Crawler is used to transport the mobile launcher including the space vehicle and the mobile service structure to and from the launch pad. The Crawler is capable of lifting, transporting and lowering the ML or the MSS, as required, without the aid of auxiliary equipment. It consists of a rectangular chassis which is supported through a suspension system by four dual-tread, crawler-trucks. The overall length is 131 feet and the overall width is 114 feet. The unit weighs approximately six million pounds. It is powered by self-contained, diesel-electric generator units. Maximum speed is 1 mph with full load on level grade and 0.5 mph with full load on the five per cent grade to the pad. It has a 500-foot minimum turning radius and can position the ML or the MSS on the facility support-pedestals with ±2 inches.

VEHICLE ASSEMBLY AND CHECKOUT

The Saturn V Launch Vehicle propulsive stages and the IU are, upon arrival at Kennedy Space Center, transported to the VAB by special carriers. All components of the space vehicle, including the Argosy spacecraft and launch escape system, are then assembled vertically on the Mobile Launcher in the high bay area. Following assembly, the space vehicle is connected to the launch control center via a high-speed data link for integrated checkout and a simu-

lated flight test. When checkout is completed, the Crawler picks up the ML with the assembled space vehicle and moves it three miles to the launch site via the crawlerway.

At the launch site, the ML is emplaced and connected for final vehicle checkout and launch monitoring. During the pre-launch checkout the final system checks are completed, the mobile service structure is removed to the parking area, propellants are loaded, various items of support equipment are removed from the mobile launcher and the vehicle is readied for launch.

And at that point, the Administrator thought with a fond smile—for everyone was fond of Bob—Bob Hertz would come into his true glory.

Already, of course, he had come into a good deal of it, for he and his highly skilled group of scientists and technicians at Mission Control Center in Houston had already spent many long days and nights and weeks and months on specific plans for pre-launch and launch operations, on plotting trajectories, on devising crew exercises, on abort procedures and on all the many other advance coordinations that had to be done before the great birds and their passengers could fly. Bob Hertz loved space and his contributions to it were mighty. It was at launch and after that it all paid off.

How would Bob feel, Andy wondered, as he stood in the glassed-in observation booth above the big Mission Control Room looking down upon its four banks of busy computers and its restless occupants as the countdown neared its end? More likely he would be down on the floor in the thick of it, standing beside Stu Yule at the Capsule Communicator's desk, his hand resting easily on Stu's shoulder as the seconds ticked away. Outwardly he would be calm, joking, unconcerned as always. But the pressure of the hand would be growing—growing—growing. Stu would know how Bob really felt inside; and Stu himself would not be exactly calm either, although outwardly he too would probably laugh and joke and parry, now that he was beginning to walk comfortably again and had regained some of his sense of life and humor.

It would be a great moment for them, and great for everyone else in Mission Control, when Planetary Fleet

One took off for Mars. They would guard and protect her all the way through the flight plan Bob and his staff had established: the launchings, the rendezvous at Space Station *Mayflower* for the docking of the three modules, the checkout journey to the Moon, the practice lunar orbits, the practice lunar surface descents and ascents of the Mars landing Module *Adventurer*, the return to rendezvous with Space Station *Mayflower* for final checkout and then the engine firing to put them into trajectory for Mars. And after that, almost constant hellos and goodbys, suggestions, corrections, agreements, objections, experiments and changes, for eighteen long months, until at last, at very long last, splashdown and the emergence from Planetary Fleet One into the glaring eye of the world, of—what?

No one really knew, Dr. Anderson thought with a little shiver, for no one had ever tried it. But whatever emerged—and prayerfully, it would be the same personalities that left, a lot older in many ways, a lot more knowledgeable of secrets never unlocked before, probably more tired and physically strained than they had been upon departure, but essentially the same men, in good shape—it would not be for lack of care and protection by Bob Hertz and his faithful crew. Not only in Houston but literally around the world, the controllers and their network would keep pace with Piffy One; and though the signals might grow a little faint far, far out on the distant planet, the care and concern, the helpfulness and encouragement, the affection—the love—would keep them company.

It was not so bad a companionship, Dr. Anderson reflected as he turned to complete his reading: not many were so fortunate. Love was not a concept one thought of very often with skilled, impersonal, scientific NASA, but love was there—and had been—and would be—on every occasion when brave men and their brothers worked together to fling their challenge into the face of the universe. This was Bob Hertz' world, and few could have guarded it better.

MISSION PLANNING, EXECUTION AND MONITORING

Mission planning begins with the receipt of mission requirements and objectives. The planning activity results in specific plans for pre-launch and launch operations, pre-flight training and simulation, flight control procedures, flight crew activities, support by Mission Control (Houston) and Manned Space Flight Network (worldwide), recovery operations, data acquisition and flow and other mission-related operations. Numerous simulations are planned and performed to test procedures and train flight control and flight crew teams in normal and contingency operations.

Mission execution involves the following functions: pre-launch check-out and launch operations; tracking the space vehicle to determine its present and future positions; securing information on the status of the flight crew and space vehicle systems via telemetry; evaluation of telemetry information; commanding the space vehicle by transmitting real-time and updata commands to the onboard computer; voice communication between flight and ground crews; and recovery operations on return to earth.

The flight crew and the following organizations and facilities participate in mission control operations:

1. Mission Control Center at the Manned Spacecraft Center, Houston, Texas. The MCC contains the communication computer, display and command systems to enable the flight controllers to effectively monitor and control the space vehicle.

2. Kennedy Space Center (KSC), Cape Kennedy, Florida. The space vehicle is launched from KSC and controlled from the Launch Control Center (LCC), as described previously. Pre-launch, launch and powered flight data are collected at the Central Instrumentation Facility at KSC from the launch pads, CIF receivers, Merrit Island Launch Area (MILA) and the downrange Air Force Eastern Test Range stations. This data is transmitted to Mission Control, Houston, via the Argosy Launch Data System. Also located at KSC is the Impact Predictor, for range safety purposes.

3. Goddard Space Flight Center, Greenbelt, Maryland. Goddard manages and operates the Manned Space Flight Network and the NASA Communications networks. During flight, the Manned Space Flight Network is under operational control of Mission Control, Houston.

4. George C. Marshall Space Flight Center, Huntsville, Alabama. By means of the Launch Information Exchange Facility and the Huntsville Operations Support Center, Huntsville provides launch vehicle systems real-time support to Kennedy and Houston for pre-flight, launch and flight operations.

COMMAND SYSTEM

The Argosy ground command systems have been designed to work closely with the telemetry and trajectory systems to provide flight controllers with a method of "close-loop" command, The astronauts and flight controllers act as links in this operation. With a few exceptions, commands to the space vehicle fall into two categories: real-time commands and command loads (also called computer loads, computer update, loads or update.)

Real-time commands are used to control space vehicle systems or subsystems from the ground. The execution of a real-time command results in immediate reaction by the affected system. Real-time commands are stored prior to the mission in the Command Data Processor at the applicable command site. The CDP, a general-purpose digital computer, is programmed to format, encode and output commands when a request for uplink is generated.

NASA COMMUNICATIONS NETWORK

The NASA communications network is a point-to-point communications system connecting the Manned Space Flight Network stations to Mission Control in Houston. NASCOM is managed by the Goddard Space Flight Center, where the primary communications switching center is located. The MSFN stations throughout the world are interconnected by landline, undersea cable, radio and communications satellite circuits. These circuits carry teletype, voice and data in real-time and may be activated as needed at any point during the mission.

And so it stood, as he finished reading and put the report aside to stare out into the heavy sky, threatening storm, that lay over Washington. So it stood, in this fourth month of their preparations, two months from launch.

How mighty is man, he thought, with an irony he sometimes found he could not avoid; and how brave in the face of the infinite.

Listen to him, Lord, as he assures You how magnificently he will be housed, how astutely he will conduct himself, how comfortable he will be as he travels across Your universe. Note the perfection of his machines, the beauty of his science. Note how carefully he will be clothed, how efficiently his needs will be tended to, how skillfully he will meet Your problems, how shrewdly he has thought of and provided for every possible threat to his safety and ease—except the threat of his own nature and all the things You can devise to test it.

See him as he prepares to challenge. You, wired—encapsulated—suited—unsuited—experimenting—communicating—urinating—defecating—carrying his life about on his back in a portable pack—scientifically eating—sleeping—doctoring himself—peering into Your hidden places—while he glides in unbelievable machines at unbelievable speeds over unbelievable distances just beneath the corner of Your eye.

Look very quickly and You will see him pass through Your shadow. Perhaps he will return and perhaps he will not, but he goes equipped with all the precautions You have permitted him to achieve in all the millennia of his life upon Earth.

Will they be enough?

Don't tell him.

Let him go.

He would not believe You anyway.

Book Four

1.

Just a little more training, Connie told himself with some satisfaction, a little more preparation, a little more polishing of routine to the point where it became truly and entirely instinctive, and the crew of Planetary Fleet One would be as ready as it would ever be. As he talked the details into a tape-recorder for his secretary to transcribe and transmit to the Administrator, Bob Hertz, the Vice-President, he could see them in mind's eye: the crew and the back-up crew, tiny figures in many landscapes, practicing their experiments, practicing their routines—practicing life:

The desert stretched rocky and shimmering, far in the distance the mountains danced in the dry, relentless heat. The surface of Mars, courtesy of Arizona, lay before them. For two weeks, grotesque yet familiar, their white-suited figures clambered slowly down the gullies and up the ridges, air-cooled and protected against the heat. Alongside, stripped to khaki shorts, protected only by sunglasses and pith helmets, sweating, shouting suggestions, making notes, a dozen technicians from Mission Control kept them company . . .

All about lay the hostile white plains of Antarctica, insanely blinding in the sun when they were not ominously hidden by roaring snow. For a month of complete isolation, talking only to one another and to distant Mission Control, they lived in three tiny module-sized huts at the edge of the world, going patiently about their set, daily routines, testing, checking, retesting, rechecking, running gradually out of small talk, confining themselves more and more to the terse, necessary, verbal shorthand of their fantastic profession, eating, sleeping, performing their duties—surviving . . .

In the weightless stage of Space Station *Mayflower* for another month they lived, practiced, performed, observed their own reactions, were observed—survived . . .

For two intensive weeks in classrooms at JPL, MIT, Stanford, Harvard, Houston, they received quick refresher courses in the subjects they had studied in their initial astronaut training when they entered the program: geology, astronomy, digital computers, flight mechanics, meteorology, guidance and navigation, physics . . .

For two more weeks they received further refreshers in a tour of space facilities, familiar to them from early training, familiar from daily reference, familiar in the cases of Connie and Jazz from earlier flights, but now alive with the new urgency of Piffy One: the Cape for launch preparations and countdown operations; Huntsville and the Mississippi Test Facility for a review of the exhaustive tests that would guarantee the performance and safety of their vehicles; briefings on the operations of Mission Control which they still found absorbing; instruction in the Argosy spacecraft systems including the prime and subsystems of the Command-Service, Medico-Scientific and Mars Landing Vehicles . . .

For yet another two weeks they traveled the country visiting contractors and subcontractors, checking on the progress of the equipment being built for their use, making suggestions that were often accepted, giving necessary and effective boosts to the morale of the hastily recruited work crews that were on around-the-clock, three-shift schedules to meet the President's deadline . . .

And now, for the last two months preceding launch, they were on home ground again, about to return to the simulators of Houston and the Cape for the steady, repetitious, monotonous, life-supporting, life-saving exercises that would make of survival a habit so automatic they would not even have to think about it.

On the whole, Connie congratulated himself, they had all come through so far in very good shape. He had been careful to give Jazz all the responsibility and authority he deserved and needed for purposes of his own morale, and Jazz had responded without spoken gratitude but with a willingness and general good nature that were a long way from the sour sorehead who had challenged him so bitterly on a morning that now seemed long ago. He was not exactly a riotously jovial companion, Connie reflected with a smile, and never would be: that wasn't his nature. But in his blunt, impatient way he was becoming a good companion who would wear well on the voyage.

Pete, too, had settled back into the wise-cracking, easygoing, comfortably reliable pattern that had prevailed before what Connie thought of as "that conversation." There had been no repetition of that conversation and he was pretty confident there wouldn't be. Certainly he hoped not and was thankful there were no signs of it. The initial embarrassment had long worn off, they had worked together on their various field trips as closely and impersonally as though it had never occurred. They wouldn't have been human if somewhere under the surface the memory had not been there: now and again a fleeting look, a tone, an unspoken familiarity for which he was probably as responsible as Pete, would momentarily shatter his complacency; but for the most part he was convinced that it was far beneath the surface and would not come back. He had made up his own mind it would not and he was sure Pete had too. Pete, he told himself, was a great help and no problem.

And then there was Jayvee, and to this day, four months after his triumphant return to the crew, he remained an enigma they were no closer to penetrating than they had been before. He was a little more pleasant—or perhaps, in response to the President's warning, a little more cautious in expressing his resentments—but it never went beyond the minimal requirements of training and enforced proximity. They were resigned to the fact of a permanent outsider in their midst, and when they discussed it among themselves had to admit honestly that they had probably not helped matters much by their own impatient annoyance in the opening days of the mission. Yet they always concluded that there was something more than that to Jayvee's isolation: something deliberate, inherent, alien, not to be bounded by comfortable clichés about brotherhood or brought within the uncertain confines of enforced companionship. "He thinks differently and he acts differently," Jazz finally said with a shrug. "He just is different." And although it went against the grain of all the careful teaching and frantic exhortations of the days

413

of their growing up, they finally found themselves forced to the conclusion that yes, maybe he was.

But as Pete commented. "We don't really have to understand him if we can just rely on him to be where he's supposed to be when we need him." And in that regard Jayvee, once he had won his battle to remain on the mission, had given no trouble. He did his job, he made his plans, he prepared and conducted his scientific experiments with an impersonal skill and attention to detail that made them realize at last why Vernon Hertz had been so determined to have him on the crew. He seemed to have resolved something within himself as a result of having his own way and his work showed it. If there was still some deep-buried unexpressed, instinctive uneasiness on their part, some lingering fear of something unknowable that might yet explode and do them all damage, they could not prove it by Jayvee as he appeared to be now. He was there when they needed him and that was all they perhaps had a right to ask. It was very evidently, at any rate, all he was going to give them.

He had never again mentioned Monetta to Connie in any way, nor had he ever again indicated by so much as a look that he entertained the suspicions he had snarled forth when they tried to fire him from the crew. Whether he knew that the suspicions were now true, Connie could not determine. After a time he stopped worrying. They had not been true very often after that first night when his pity and her desperation had brought them together with an inevitablity they could not deny in a union neither had really wanted. Since then there had been four occasions in four months, spaced out because of the demands of his training and her hesitancy. A genuine affection and tenderness had come to exist but never any illusions of permanence. Mutual kindness, he supposed, could be the word for it: a help to her while she readjusted her life, took up residence in nearby Galveston, got a job as a laboratory technician; a help to him while—what?

While his wife left him, his home collapsed, his life tottered and he had to start over to support himself and a child? While he went through emotional storms and physical brutality and saw the careful edifice of years come toppling down?"

Hardly, the voice he didn't like to hear advised him. *You haven't got that excuse. You haven't got any.*

414

She needed me, the other voice said. *I was sorry for her. I couldn't say no.*

So now you're blaming her, the first voice said. *A real gentleman, Conrad Trasker. A courageous one, too. You're brave, kid. We'll give you medals.*

I *didn't need* her! the other voice said. *I could have gone on just as I was and been perfectly happy. I could stop it now and be perfectly happy.*

She might be too, the first voice said. *Did you ever think of that?*

She would not!

Did it ever occur to you that she may have been drawn to you in the first place because she felt you were getting older and needed somebody to tell you you weren't? Maybe she pitied you, buster. How about that?

That's a lie! That's a real damned lie.

Maybe this all began because you felt you were getting over the hill and you just wanted to prove to yourself that you weren't. Maybe it all began as an exercise for your own ego, just to make it feel better. Just to prove you still could. Just to prove the skirts will still come running when Conrad Trasker lifts his little finger.

That's not true. That very definitely simply is not true.

But, he suspected with a frustrated self-distaste as he left his office and started over to the simulator building for the first all-crew exercise, it probably was.

What, then, was he to make of Conrad H. Trasker, Perfect Astronaut, as he seemed to draw up and away in some disembodied, brooding fashion and watch himself walking briskly, a trim, compact, self-confident figure, along the concrete path in the sweltering summer sun? What was he to say about himself, captain of the crew, reasonably shrewd analyzer of men, quite competent manipulator of their hopes and ambitions, leader of their enterprises, unifier and co-ordinator of their abilities and their skills?—highly competent forty-two-year-old machine, getting ready for the greatest challenge of its glamorous, publicized, thus-far-successful life?

Why, he supposed—and he did not apologize for it—that it was human. That behind the outward image, the happy, confident, white-suited figure of a million photographs, the smiling rider in parades, the relaxed testifier before committees, the unruffled interviewee of television and press, the easy, commanding speaker to Congress—there was a human being as complex, inconsistent, unpredictable, inexplicable as any other; as full of noble impulses and ignoble instincts, great ideals and small realities, as all the rest. A bundle of opposites a little more intelligent than most, a little more highly trained than most, a little braver than most—perhaps, adding it all up, a little finer than most, whatever its private imperfections. But still human, still a man.

And one, he told himself with a certain defiance as he neared the simulator building, who might have weaknesses but also had plenty of strengths. And for this he and his country could thank God, considering what his country expected of him and what he would have to demand of himself.

So he thought, Connie Trasker, P.A., as he entered the simulator building and his mind began to abandon introspection and shift over to the module-docking routine that would be their first intensive exercise; aware that this was a very good thing but not yet aware of how soon the dormant enemies of Piffy One were going to rouse themselves and put his strengths and the strengths of all of them once more to bitter test.

"Andy," said Jim Matthison at North American Rockwell, and the Administrator could sense his worry immediately, "we've got trouble here."

"Oh?" he responded cautiously, thinking, *I might have known things were going too smoothly*. "What's the matter? Sloppy workmanship because you had to let so many good men go during the budget-cutting years?"

"More than that," Jim said soberly. "As you know, a lot of them have come back; we're able to manage, there. No: we're beginning to run into definite sabotage, just in the last couple of days. Bolts not tightened properly, wires slightly out of place, circuits not quite right. Nothing really bad yet, but—almost as though somebody were trying it out. Getting ready. Practicing."

"Anything to do with our friend?" Dr. Anderson asked. Jim Matthison frowned.

"I don't know. His unions are concentrated at the Cape but of course he could have friends here. They get around, that kind. What do you hear from Al Freer? Everything all right there?"

"No word yet," the Administrator said. "I trust he's got

plenty of informants on the inside who would tip him off. At least, I hope he has."

"You might call him," Jim suggested, "and check with the other contractors and subcontractors too. We're on to it here and I think we'll lick it all right, but I'm not being alarmist, there's a problem. One of the engines didn't check out right this morning. I think we came very close to an explosion, as a matter of fact. You'd better get on to Boeing and the rest right way. And tip Huntsville and Mississippi, too. They start testing tomorrow, don't they, on the first shipment?"

"Day after, I believe," Andy said. "Have you had a chance to talk to Clete at all in these past months?"

"We've played golf a couple of times, when he was out here speaking on behalf of CAUSE. He wanted to see the plant, so I invited him over. We socialized a bit."

"And what did you find out?"

"Nothing much. He's very close-mouthed, you know. Outwardly he runs on like water but it's a millimeter deep. Nobody gets under the surface. At least I didn't."

"But he's still active in CAUSE."

"And CAUSE is still active. I thought they'd fold when the President refused to budge but they're still going."

"Yes," Andy said. "It gives Percy Mercy and Kenny Williams something to do. I get the feeling it's sort of on stand-by—they'll stir it up again if it suits their purposes.

"Maybe we're getting to the point in the mission where it's going to," Jim suggested. "Maybe things are beginning to tie in to one another. They couldn't stop it before but now it's narrowing down to a few points where it can be blocked again."

"You could be right," the Administrator agreed thoughtfully. "But Clete didn't give you any indication."

"This is strictly hunch. Clete doesn't give indications, at least to me."

"I'll get on it right away," Andy promised. "Be careful."

"We are," Jim said. "I hate like hell for the mission to have trouble again, but—I guess that's the way it is."

"I guess so," the Administrator agreed grimly. "People like that never rest."

"And they only succeed when we do."

"That's right. This time, we're not going to."

But even before he had a chance to start checking,

other calls began to come in from McDonnell Douglas in St. Louis, Grumman on Long Island, IBM in Huntsville and the rest. He began to discover a pattern that made him wonder whether they had not already rested too long. No one had any big specifics to report but several had small ones; and in a machine as infinitely complex as the Saturn V, in which the tiniest malfunction could become the greatest disaster, even one small thing wrong was one too many. Yet after he had received worried assurances that security would be tightened and procedures made more stringent everywhere, he talked to Al Freer at the Cape and found that everything was still, apparently, as peaceful as he had found it on his visit two weeks ago.

Perhaps Clete and his friends were saving up for the Cape. Perhaps that was where the big battle would come, if all the little sabotages down the line were successfully thwarted. He would give a lot to know what Clete was up to right now. But he decided he would let him show his hand a little more clearly before he made any attempt to challenge him direct.

At the moment, however, Clete could not have been more innocent, lying suntan-oiled and apparently sleepy in the sun at his favorite hotel on Miami Beach; outwardly oblivious to the world, inwardly, as always, thinking, thinking, thinking. "Clete never stops," one of his co-conspirators had said admiringly back in college days. "He's always working on something." And so he was, and so, he supposed, he always would be, until the day when all the rotten society around him collapsed and he could move into his rightful position as one of the managers who would make it over into the Model State.

Unlike so many of the mindless, incorrigibly infantile anarchists who had attempted to destroy America in the past decade, Clete knew where he was going and what he intended to do when he got there. He was one of those who had been vouchsafed a revelation of the Plan and to it he had long since sworn absolute and undeviating loyalty. He despised the anarchists with their gibberings of "Revolution!" which meant nothing but chaos: that was not how real revolutions were made. He could use that type and now in this problem of Planetary Fleet One he was getting ready to. But never for a moment would he really trust or rely upon them. They were there to be used

418

and after they were used, disposed of. He and his friends knew all about that: they had done it in half a hundred countries already. It had not always brought them control of the countries, but it had almost always successfully eliminated the "revolutionaries."

You had to have a plan to succeed in an enterprise so vast as the crippling, looking toward the ultimate destruction, of the United States of America. Otherwise sheer numbers and the sentimental loyalties of the great middle areas of America's population would defeat you. These loyalties were not geographic nor were the middle areas: they spread across the whole spectrum of land and people. It would take many combinations of craft, fear, national embarrassment, disillusion, mistrust, despair, disappointment, uncertainty, before the morale of the country could finally be reduced to a state in which takeover would become feasible.

Somehow, despite all the stout attempts that had been made by some very shrewd minds in the past few years, America had survived them all and was still here. It was disappointing but it was not disheartening. No one had ever said it would be a short and easy battle. Only true patience and an absolutely unshakable determination, extending over many years and even decades, could bring success.

Patience and determination were something Clete and his friends possessed in ample measure. They had perceived many years ago that the way to destroy America was not by childlike frontal assaults or by infantile posings in front of television cameras, or by a destructive and terrifying but essentially wasteful and pointless use of bombs and guns and frightfulness. The way to destroy America was to get inside and play the game and move up the ladder and acquire respectability within the system until finally you arrived at a fulcrum from which you could topple the world. That was how to do it and that was the way he had done it. Clete O'Donnell, lying in the opulent sun by the opulent pool in opulent Miami Beach, outwardly the perfect symbol of wealth and power and liberal respectability, was worth a hundred thousand sick children playing with terror. He was the real terror because he was in the arms of the system, holding a knife at its throat even as it embraced him.

He had known for a long time that the destruction of

Planetary Fleet One was to be his particular project but neither he nor those with whom he conspired could have known that he would be called upon so soon to do his damage. Probably no one had known until there had been one of those convulsions within the Kremlin, a decision long deferred had been suddenly reached, those who had not yet reached the category of being-permitted-to-know were abruptly informed, and a predetermined plan was put into action.

He had not been aware that the Soviet Union was capable of an early launch. He did not really understand why it had been decided to make one. He had learned over the years that such decisions could sometimes be as abrupt, irrational, emotional and human as any decision in a democracy.

He was willing to bet that somebody in Moscow had suddenly become scared to death that the United States was planning a secret early launch. He had received queries about this, he had checked, he had ascertained the truth, he had knocked the rumor down. He could not convince whoever the skittish souls were back there. The ponderous machinery of Communist decision, like a pachyderm suddenly frightened by a mouse, had gone trumpeting off despite all the evidence he had given them, all the evidence others had given them, and the evidence of their own spy-satellites. They lived by the theory of conspiracy in Moscow and so they constantly believed conspiracy of others. They began feverish plans for launch—the United States immediately learned of it and began feverish plans for launch—and here they were.

Here they were and it was up to him to do what he could to interfere with, inconvenience and if possible destroy, Piffy One. To aid him in this enterprise, which he approached without the slightest hesitation or regret, he had the solid standing and reputation he had laboriously created with the opinion-molders of the country over the past ten years. As an extremely shrewd and intelligent student of his own country he had early perceived that there were certain causes and certain people who were the key to acceptance by the media. If you faithfully endorsed these causes and people, faithfully supported them, faithfully praised them and worked for them, you had an automatic ticket to headlines, editorials, coy little friendly references in society and gossip columns, constant and

420

flattering mentions in political columns and commentary, and a guaranteed permanent invitation to be on all the major television programs which provided so sure and effective an access to the minds and emotions of your countrymen.

If you combined this with an effective power base of your own, you very rapidly became one of the movers and shakers of America. You became part of the Group. You were In.

The power base had come easily, more easily than he had anticipated when he first began the task of putting it together. Its creation had been aided by his standing with the media, his standing with the media had been aided by its creation: the two formed a whipsaw that he used with great effect. Because he backed certain causes and people he in turn was supported by certain causes and certain people. It was considered very sensible, in all the publications and columns that Really Mattered, that there should be a young, vigorous, dynamic Right Thinking leader of the unions at the Cape, and it was considered very sensible that he should be assisted in his drive to break the hold of the older, more traditional organizations and remold their fragmented parts into the "One Big Union" of his official slogan. It had taken him the better part of a decade to do this but he had received a fine assist from all the publicity he received in all the right places. A couple of years ago the goal had been won: he was ready to keep his date with Planetary Fleet One.

Since the announcement of the crash program for the launch, an extra dimension had been added. Now he was put in touch with others around the country. Another phase of the program was put into operation. Sabotage, which had never succeeded with the veterans of NASA in the old days but might with the green hands whose hasty recruitment had been made necessary by previous penny-pinching, was to be attempted. So it had always been in the sick, kindness-destroying world to which he belonged. And so it would be now.

And not once in all these years had anyone who Really Mattered given the slightest credence to the occasional rumors or charges that he might be a Communist. As cheerfully as the President, as scornfully as Percy Mercy, they had laughed it off. Clete O'Donnell? It was impossible. Good old Clete, who worked so hard for Presidential Candidate A, who was so devoted to the civil rights campaign of Soul Brother B, who attended so many Waldorf-Astoria banquets for the agricultural strikes of Professional Innocent C, who had such a well-publicized collection of the paintings of With-It Artist D, who lolled about the baths of Palm Springs with Very-In Author E?

A Communist? Our Clete? How crazy-fool-ridiculous could you be?

No one, he had found, could be so easily duped as the self-congratulating clever. And so with an utter comtempt for those who fawned upon him, and a completely cold-blooded and ruthless manipulation of their naïve and eager support, he had moved along until he was virtually unassailable. Not even his quickie strike against the Cape four months ago had done him any real harm where it counted. There had been some grumbling here and there over the country, a few reactionary newspapers and minor columnists had mumbled, but, again, those who Really Mattered had quickly forgiven and forgotten. The whole episode was hazed over now in the public mind. Dr. Freer was long since back on the job. Stu Yule was up and around again, his tragedy never mentioned except within NASA, which was reactionary and old-fashioned in its emotional loyalties anyway. And Pad C was nearing completion. There had been a chance to nail him but nobody had. So who remembered any more? Clete O'Donnell was as popular and invulnerable as ever.

In fact, he thought with a cruel little smile as he signaled the pool attendant to bring a portable Picture-phone to his cabana, he owed a great debt to fools such as the one he was going to talk to now, because without them he would never have been where he was, potentially able to do such devastating damage to the plans and morale of the country they shared and despised together.

"Hello, Percy?" he said easily when the self-important face appeared, "I hope you're working as hard as I am."

"You look it," Percy said with a smile. "Aren't you absolutely boiling in the sun down there?"

Clete chuckled.

"I'm like a lizard on a rock. The hotter it gets the more I like it. I suppose that comes of growing up in northern Michigan. What's new with Planetary Fleet One these days?"

422

"I was going to call you and find out. Apparently everything is proceeding on schedule."

"Are we going to let it go without doing anything more about it?" Clete inquired. "It seems to me CAUSE ought to be giving some serious thought to what we're going to do around launchtime."

"Oh, very definitely," Percy agreed. "If you've noticed, I've had an editorial about that every two or three weeks for the past couple of months."

"I know," Clete said in an admiring tone. "And Percy, I think they've been among the best you have ever done. I just don't think this nation realizes how much it owes you for the way you've helped to keep major issues in perspective. It has been a magnificent job, all the way."

"You're too kind," Percy said, and Clete thought with a withering contempt that the monstrous little ego was lapping it up as usual.

"I really mean it," he said solemnly. "It has been a public service virtually without parallel. In my humble estimation."

"I have done my best," Percy said solemnly. "It is all a man to whom God has given a modest talent can do."

"It has been magnificent," Clete repeated. "Simply magnificent. What do you think we should do about the launch?"

"I would think some sort of nationwide moratorium, wouldn't you? Possibly combined with mass picketing at the White House and NASA headquarters."

Clete smiled.

"All NASA installations, why not? Why be exclusive?"

"Well, do you think—I mean, as far as the Cape is concerned—do you think—?"

"I didn't say *strike* it," Clete said, his smile broadening. "I just said picket it."

"I don't know that we want more violence, though," Percy said. "I mean—do *you*?"

"I never wanted violence," Clete said blandly. "Nor do I want it now. If peaceful, legitimate protesters are subjected to it, then they will probably respond. But I can't be responsible for that, can I?"

"N—o."

"Can I?" Clete repeated and their eyes met. After a moment Percy's dropped. His doubts were resolved as Clete had known, contemptuously, they would be.

"No, you cannot," he said firmly. "I suppose we should begin some serious work on organization, then."

"Shouldn't the Executive Board of CAUSE pass an official resolution calling the moratorium?" Clete asked. "Just a suggestion, but it might be better to make it legal."

"You're so right," Percy agreed.

"You can probably poll by phone. I vote Yes."

"You don't want to leave Miami," Percy remarked with a smile.

"I may be needed in Florida," Clete said with a lazy grin. "Anyway, I like it in the sun. I hope you're thinking in terms of a really big moratorium."

"Oh, yes," Percy said quickly. "I think we should make it very impressive. Then even though we can't stop the launch, we'll at least register a protest that will make the government think twice before it contemplates another."

"Oh, maybe we can stop it," Clete said in the same lazy way. "If it gets that far."

"Why won't it?" Percy asked quickly. "You don't know —I mean, there isn't anything—?"

"Just a hunch," Clete said soothingly. "But it is a big project, and they've been moving awfully fast, and a lot of the personnel are green and inexperienced, and—well, you know. Many a slip, and all that. A lot of things can happen through just sheer carelessness. We'll see."

"I wouldn't want anyone to get hurt," Percy said somewhat nervously, "but I *would* like to see it stopped."

"We'll see," Clete repeated. "Maybe," he added lightly, just to give the little twerp something to think about, "sooner than we think."

"I hope so," Percy said. "I hope there will be some accident that won't hurt anyone but *will* stop it."

"Accidents aren't always that particular," Clete pointed out dryly. "But maybe somebody can arrange one that will be."

But when it came, two weeks later, it appeared that whoever had done the arranging had not been that careful.

FIVE DIE AS PLANETARY MISSILE SECTIONS EXPLODE AT TEST SITES, the headlines said. MISSISSIPPI, HUNTSVILLE ROCKED BY BLASTS. NASA

424

HINTS SABOTAGE, MARS FLIGHT MAY BE DE-
LAYED.

And P.C.M., deliberately putting out of his mind the
dreadful and impermissible thought that had crossed it
when the news came—and with it, like a flash, an instantaneous mental picture of his self-satisfied and arrogant
friend lying bland and lazy in the sun—wrote the words
he had to write for the next edition of *View*:

"The twin tragedies at NASA's Huntsville and Mississippi test sites have called into grave question once again,
after several months of relative quiet, the wisdom of the
American attempt to beat the Soviet Union in the race for
Mars.

"That it should be a race at all is a disgrace to this
country and a blow to world brotherhood. That it should
now have resulted in new disasters which have taken the
lives of five Americans is a shame for which the Administration bears a heavy burden.

"It was with great misgivings that this publication, in
common with all thoughtful Americans, acquiesced finally
in the President's determination to go ahead with Planetary Fleet One despite the difficulties that had plagued it
from the beginning. Memories are still vivid of the controversies that surrounded the decision to challenge the Soviet Union to another improvident and wasteful contest in
space; the selection of a multiracial crew truly representative of all the nation; and the argument over the absurd
and hysterical proposition that the spacecraft should be
armed because the Soviets might, in some mysterious and
unexplained fashion, seek to attack them in the skies.

"Any one of these issues standing alone was enough, in
our estimation, to warrant cancellation of the mission.
Together they appeared to us, and we believe to the
overwhelming majority of the American people, to present
an insurmountable argument for terminating it without
delay.

"But the President, encouraged by certain individuals in
NASA and possibly by his own desire to appeal politically
to shortsighted and reactionary elements among his own
countrymen, plowed on. And so once again we have
disaster for Planetary Fleet One and a renewal of all the
grave questions that continue to make of its flight a most
foolish exercise in American egotism and a most inexcus-

able waste of American dollars that could better be used for pressing domestic needs.

"In the wake of new disaster and misfortune all sensible Americans must register once more their vigorous protest against this Caesar's-circus of blood and treasure.

"There is still time to stop the Mars flight.

"It must be done.

"There exists, in the Committee Against Unilateral Space Exploration (CAUSE), a powerful medium through which immediate and effective protest can be made. CAUSE drew the support of many hundreds of thousands of concerned citizens during the opening weeks of the Mars mission. Many thousands more have joined its ranks in succeeding months. Many of America's most informed and most outstanding citizens and organizations have placed themselves unreservedly in the forefront of its continuing activities.

"Never were its purposes more valid and its chances for success greater than they are now.

"Two weeks ago, the National Executive Board of CAUSE voted unanimously to hold a nationwide moratorium of protest against the Mars flight at the time of launch. It was intended then that this should be a symbol to the world that many millions of Americans do not, and cannot, support their government in this ill-fated venture. Now symbol must become reality—the reality of the end of Planetary Fleet One as it now exists and a return to a steady, unhurried, sensible Mars program that will take its place over the decades in proper priority *after* the many other pressing problems of the United States have been fully and adequately met.

"We urge all Americans truly concerned for the welfare of their country to join CAUSE. We urge its Executive Board to authorize not just one, but several, massive protests between now and launchtime. And we suggest that in the days immediately preceding that event, CAUSE and all other Americans truly interested in the long-range good of their country register in unmistakable terms their determination that this fearful folly should come speedily and completely to an end.

"The scheduled flight of Planetary Fleet One can be stopped.

"It must be.

"Reason, common sense and the highest type of patrio-

426

tism—the patriotism that thinks of *all* Americans, not just a handful of glory-seeking men in NASA and the White House—demand it."

To this, and to many other sentiments like it that screamed from headlines, roared from editorial pages, insinuated from news stories and preached from television screens, the President's rejoinder was terse and to the point.

Two days later at 9 in the morning the White House issued a brief statement:

"The President wishes to make clear to the country that Planetary Fleet One of Project Argosy, the flight to Mars, will continue as planned.

"The tragic disasters which occurred at the test sites in Huntsville and Mississippi damaged but did not destroy important space equipment.

"The damage can and will be speedily repaired.

"Those responsible for the explosions will be found and punished to the fullest extent of law.

"Planetary Fleet One will be launched on schedule."

Grimly and anxiously, and with a newly embittered determination, those who were directly concerned with Piffy One moved ahead.

2.

And now, soon, they would be leaving for the Cape and the final weeks in the simulators there, and suddenly Piffy One loomed directly ahead, enormous and inescapable. Up to now it had somehow never seemed quite real despite field trips and training and the many crises that had surrounded it. But here it was.

The feeling of being on a steadily accelerating toboggan from which there was no escape began to grip them all.

It was an odd mood, filled with many things. If he had to define the single overriding element, Connie decided, it would probably be a curious melancholy; arising, he supposed, from the fact that they were finally face to face with the thought, and the very real possibility, that they might not come back.

Plans were fine, training was splendid, machinery and equipment—now that they were being rigidly and thoroughly checked—were apparently reliable, but the harsh red planet was still mysterious and forbidding and it was becoming more so each day as the time of challenge neared. Maps, studies, photographs by the Mariner probes, landings by the Vikings, scientific computations, analyses, projections—they were good as far as they went. But they still did not answer the fundamental questions that only men could answer: *What's it like? And after we find out, can we get away from it and get home?*

"All this stuff is great," Jazz had remarked recently, pushing aside a stack of reports a foot high, "but it's a little different when you know that baby out there is waiting for *you*, personally."

"You don't regret it, do you?" Pete had asked and Jazz had given him a scornful glance.

"Are you kidding? Hell, no."

But while that instant rejoinder probably reflected accurately the public mood of all of them, even Jayvee, Connie knew from his own feelings that privately they were not so cavalier about it as all that.

To Jane, who had felt from the beginning that this mission carried the possiblity of something ominous and unkind to those who would fly it, the now hurrying days only seemed to increase her underlying uneasiness. She was not giving in to it, she was still, as he told her jokingly from time to time, Mrs. Space Program in all her public appearances, but underneath there was a rising tension she could not entirely conceal at home. Even the kids, who had dismissed his Moon flights and *Mayflower* visits with a matter-of-fact acceptance, were quieter and more loving now. Lately they had taken to hanging around when he was home; they were not so apt to go rushing off pell-mell on their own pursuits. He found all this touching—more than he could bear sometimes, almost—and under the pressure of it he had gradually come to a decision that made him feel better about himself and perhaps, in a sense, better able to meet whatever Mars might have in store for him.

By a sort of unspoken agreement, and with a mutual respect and consideration he knew would always leave a residue of affection and good will on both sides, he and Monetta had decided several weeks ago to stop seeing one another, at least on the previous basis. He had been amazed at how gently and with what grace and instinctive dignity she had carried off her part of it, and he only hoped his own conduct had been as becoming to him. Apparently it had, for they had parted friends and would, he knew, continue friends. In fact, he had already begun the process of bringing her into his family life; and, he congratulated himself, successfully.

"I imagine Monetta Halleck's a little lonely down there in Galveston," he had suggested casually one day to Jane a couple of weeks ago. "Why don't we have her over for dinner next Friday when we have Jazz and Clare and Pete and the Yules?"

"Do you think Jazz can refrain from commenting on

429

her husband?" Jane asked with a smile that indicated nothing but a genuine friendly interest of her own.

"Oh, Jazz isn't all rough edges," he said. "And anyway, I guess she must be going to get a divorce. What does Yo-Shin Yule say, aren't they rather close?"

"I don't know," she said. "I'll have to ask. Sure, let's have her, I think it would be nice. And maybe she'd like to join the Book Club too."

"I heard some place that she's working, but I imagine if she could get away, she'd really like to."

"I'll ask her," Jane said, and gave him an amiable glance which he knew from long experience he was never going to quite figure out. "I wonder why I didn't think of it before?"

"I'm sure I don't know," he said, and returned the smile in the sudden instinctive knowledge that they understood one another perfectly; but also sensing instinctively that he was over the danger point and it was all right. "It's a great idea."

She chuckled and to his surprise came over and kissed him.

"I'm a great girl."

"You are that," he agreed with a laugh that told her a door in his life was closed as finally as she had hoped it was. "You really are."

Whether all doors were closed, he did not know as he went methodically about the routine tasks of clearing his desk at the office, putting his things in order at home, getting ready to say good-by to Houston and all it meant, for eighteen months—or perhaps forever. But he thought so. It was necessary conviction, for now life was narrowing down to just one thing and nothing at all outside its predetermined parameters could be permitted to interfere with it in any way whatsoever.

For Jazz and Pete and Jayvee; for Al Freer at the Cape and Hans Sturmer in Huntsville; for Bob Hertz in Mission Control and all his network of guidance and communications around the world, on Space Station *Mayflower*, and on the surface of the Moon; for the President, the Vice-President and the Administrator in Washington; for Percy Mercy and Clete O'Donnell and Senator Kenny Williams and all their friends; for Jim Matthison at North American Rockwell, for his colleagues at Boeing, Grumman, Bendix, IBM, General Dynamics, McDonnell Douglas and all the other contractors and subcontractors around the country; for Alexei Kuselevsky in Moscow and all his assistants and helpers and sympathizers at home and abroad who wished the mission ill; and for all the millions and billions around the globe who either wished it ill or, if they were Americans or in some measure possessed of a reasonable friendliness and good will, wished it well—life also narrowed down in these final racing weeks.

As it had with all previous missions, "T," meaning "Time of launch," became the metronome of the world; and as T minus two months passed into T minus six weeks and then to T minus five weeks and so finally to T minus one month, the final things were done according to routines and traditions established and perfected in the great days of Apollo; not lately used, in these recent arid and penurious years, but quickly re-established by those who remembered and placed their remembrance, almost reverently, at the service of Planetary Fleet One.

The ritual of a launch, as set and unchangeable as the rite of some mystical religion—which, perhaps, in a sense, it is—entered its concluding stages for the greatest launch of all.

"Beautiful," Albrecht Freer said reverently as the metal screens of three of the great doors of the Vehicle Assembly Building rolled simultaneously up with a slow and impressive grinding. "They are beautiful."

And so they were as they stood ready at last for the roll-out to the pads, on the three Crawlers: thirty-six stories high, enfolded in the arms of the three mobile launchers, draped with cables, laced with umbilicals, white and almost ghostly against the cavernous depths of the VAB behind them; carrying high above, on the spacecraft that looked so tiny and vulnerable from below, the names chosen by a majority of the crew:

Nina, Pinta, Santa Maria.

"You've done it Jim," the Vice-President said, trying to keep the emotion from his voice but not succeeding very well.

"Yes," Jim Matthison said huskily. "So far, so good."

In front of the enormous building, on a special flag-draped platform erected for the occasion, surrounded by some two hundred of the already gathering news corps, they watched in silence as the engines of the Crawlers turned over with a simultaneous roar. For a moment there was no other sound, no other movement anywhere, save for the whirring television cameras that were photographing the roll-out live for world-wide distribution. Then ponderously, mightily, inexorably, the Crawlers began to inch forward.

Still there was no other sound, no other movement. For five minutes they watched, hushed and immobile, only the cameramen busily working.

Then the Crawlers approached the thresholds of the three bays. The first rays of the chill autumn sun fell slanting across the *Nina*, the *Pinta* and the *Santa Maria*. And from most of them, even from some who were determined not to be affected, a great and emotional cheer went up.

"Well," Bob Hertz said to the Administrator when it had died down, "somebody seems to like us, anyway."

"They can't help it," Andy Anderson said. "Second thoughts will set in about one minute. Or less. Come on, let's climb aboard. We've got a four-hour ride ahead."

"I shall enjoy every minute of it," Bob Hertz said. "Which Crawler are we riding?"

"We're on *Nina*," Andy said. "We've given the Vice-President and the crew the *Santa Maria*, and Al Freer and Hans Sturmer will be on the *Pinta*."

"And so in triumph we will ride our antediluvian monsters down the crawlerway like Caesar in his prime."

The Administrator chuckled.

"To be followed by cocktails and a buffet luncheon in Firing Room I of the VAB. No Caesar ever had it so good."

"I think it was a smart decision to do it this way," Bob remarked as they left the platform with the others and walked toward the Crawlers, now stationary two hundred feet away, their giant burdens looming above. "It symbolizes something that needs to be symbolized, I think. Particularly having the Vice-President here."

"It was his idea, bless his heart. He said it would show the world how much importance the Administration attaches to the mission."

"Too bad the President couldn't come," Bob said dryly. "But we can't have everything."

432

"No," the Administrator said, waving to the others as they began to climb up to the cabins of their respective Crawlers. "And you must admit we have a good deal on this day, in spite of everything."

"Oh, yes," Bob agreed. "I think we should have a little talk after lunch about a few things. It will probably be the last time we're all together before the launch."

"That's the Vice-President's idea," Dr. Anderson said as the engines started again with a growl that made further conversation difficult.

"Four hours of this?" Bob shouted quizzically.

"Just routine," Andy Anderson shouted back cheerfully. "Relax and take a nap."

But a nap was not what they had, nor did they have much relaxation. Things that should not have happened did happen, things that had never happened before happened. To the media, which suddenly, to the horror of many, found some of its own members involved, it was absolutely fantastic, improbable, impossible, lurid, melodramatic and insane. But it was an insane age, in America, and those who had helped to coddle the unbalanced should not really have been too surprised to find insanity unloosed. It just wasn't supposed to be unloosed among *them*. And quite suddenly and desperately, it was.

Reconstructing it later when the official party was back in Firing Room I at the VAB, drinking their cocktails rather unsteadily and trying to settle down, the blame, if any, appeared to attach to some degree to Marlon Holloway and his colleagues of the news staff at Kennedy Space Center. But as he pointed out with unassailable logic and a certain amount of temper he knew how to get away with, he could not be responsible for every damned crackpot who showed up asking for press credentials. He could check and check and check and so could the news staff at KSC, but short of running complete FBI scans on everybody, there was a limit. He pointed out tartly that 251 press and television newsmen, newswomen, cameramen, and technicians had already been accredited and were on site, and that there awaited processing on his desk in Washington, and on the desks of his colleagues in Florida, the applications of some 3000 more. And the end, he predicted with considerable annoyance, was not yet. So how could he know if half a dozen subversive screwballs got

433

in under cover of a press badge? They could probably all be thankful there hadn't been more.

"We assume you'll tighten up considerably from now on," the Vice-President suggested.

"Yes, sir," Marlon said promptly. "Whatever the government gives us money and staff for, we'll do."

"Mmmm," the Vice-President commented. "I'll see what I can do for you, Marlon, but whether there's more money or no"—his expression turned serious and determined—"we have got to have complete security from now on at the Cape."

"Yes, sir," Marlon said again. "We'll do what *we* can."

"And so will we," Dr. Freer remarked. "But you cannot outguess *all* the crazy people in this world."

"No," the Vice-President agreed somberly. "No, you can't."

Enough of them had been present midway in the Crawlers' majestic clanking progress to the pads to cause quite a sufficient stir for one day, though they had not, fortunately, been allowed to do any serious damage. It could be said for the guards at KSC that they had reacted promptly and without hesitation after the first shocked second or two, and it could also be said for most of the newsmen present that they had turned on what they had thought to be their own with a commendable and courageous speed. Together the forces of impromptu law and order had brought the invaders down, but not without a real risk to their own persons. The risk to the three Saturn V's, of course, had been potentially even graver.

The Crawlers, inching slowly over the ground with their towering cargo at less than one mile per hour while reporters, guards and technicians walked alongside, had been roughly half the three-mile distance between the VAB and the launching sites when without warning there had come a sudden movement in the casually straggling ranks of the press. At the heart of it had been two conservatively dressed youths later identified as having claimed badges as representatives of something called, "The Student Liberation Scientific Free Press"; a middle-aged, rather frowzy woman who wore a badge saying, GENERAL GUIDANCE MAGAZINE; a scrawny long-haired youth who had managed to get himself accredited as a messenger for the Associated Press; and an elderly, nondescript, insignificant looking man whose badge said simply, MIDWEST NEWS.

434

The two conservatively dressed youths had begun running suddenly toward the base of the first Crawler, carrying *Santa Maria*, the Vice-President and the crew. The frowzy woman and the insignificant man had run for the second Crawler, carrying the *Pinta*, Dr. Freer and Dr. Sturmer. The long-haired youth had charged toward Crawler No. 3, bearing the *Nina*, Andy Anderson and Bob Hertz. Fortunately they had begun shouting as they ran.

Instinctively the reporters closest to them had thrown themselves in the way, tripped them, grabbed their upflung arms, tackled them, buried them in a mass of bodies.

The guards rushed forward, the Crawlers ground slowly and gently to a halt. By the time the passengers were able to descend from the cabins the five had been subdued. In the shaking hands of guards and reporters, taken from the woman's huge purse, the man's empty typewriter case, the pants and coat pockets of the three youths, a sizable and quite sufficient arsenal was displayed: seven homemade bombs of various types and two .45-caliber pistols. Any one of them, thrown or fired with a reasonably accurate success, could have shattered the thin metal skins of the Saturns and probably have crumpled them enough to bring them toppling down, total losses and carrying death with their deaths, upon the Crawlers and the crowd.

For several minutes while the five screamed obscenities, press, guards and dignitaries stood about almost paralyzed with shock. Then the Vice-President stepped forward and took charge.

"First, stuff something into the mouths of these individuals to stop their noise," he said firmly. Several reporters promptly wadded handfuls of copy paper and obliged with enthusiasm. "Now, ten of you guards handcuff them and take them back to the security office in the VAB and hold them for the police."

When that was done and the two official cars had swept away with their wildly glaring prisoners, still mumbling and making animal noises through their impromptu gags, he turned to the tense crowd and managed a reasonably comfortable and relaxed smile.

"Fortunately," he said calmly, "that type always has to yell to get up its own courage. Now I'd suggest that we all carry on."

And nodding to Connie, Jayvee, Jazz and Pete, who

were standing tensely alongside, he led the way back to *Santa Maria* and clambered, a rather fat, rather elderly, rather awkward, but at that moment undeniably most impressive man, back up into the cabin of the Crawler.

And now the *Santa Maria,* the *Nina* and the *Pinta* were firmly on their pads and final levelings and boltings and adjustments were being made, a process that would proceed for the rest of the day and probably well into the night; and on the glass-walled landing outside Firing Room I those who had escaped dying with them on a cool autumn morning in Florida were getting ready for their lunch. It was a somber and angrily frustrated group which argued rather pointlessly with Marlon Holloway and gave up when he stood his ground. Most of its members did not entirely disagree with Hans Sturmer when he abruptly blurted out,

"I sometimes feel this mission is damned by the gods!"

But Bob Hertz, ever the optimist, was not prepared to be so gloomy.

"That's very Germanic and Wagnerian, Hans, but I don't think Piffy One is in quite that bad shape."

"There's never been one like it," Dr. Sturmer said darkly.

"That's just because it's never been to anybody's interest to make a real, genuine, determined attempt to stop it. This time somebody has tried and is still trying. But he—or they—or it—haven't succeeded yet."

"Too close for comfort today," Andy Anderson remarked grimly.

"Too damned close," Jazz agreed. "I hope to hell your people on the pads have their security in good shape, Al."

"I repeat, we cannot guard against all the crazy people." Dr. Freer said, somewhat testily. "But we are doing our best for you boys. We will be even more careful from now on. I have done *my* best to capture Clete, the guilty one. No one has paid any attention to me."

"Do you think he was responsible for what happened today?" the Vice-President inquired.

"His country was," Dr. Freer said.

Connie looked puzzled.

"The country of his mind," Albrecht Freer explained coldly. "The country that destroys all decent things and all hope for mankind. The country that deliberately wrecks whatever it touches. That country."

"How are they doing on their launch?" Pete asked. "Has anybody heard?"

"Coming along," the Vice-President said. "But still behind. We'll beat them by about a month, I would think."

"That much," Jayvee commented; and because it was the first time he had entered the general conversation in all the long and hectic morning, they turned and looked at him with a sudden concentration.

"That much," the Vice-President said.

"So we don't need to worry, Jayvee," Jazz told him calmly. "We're going to be all right."

"I'm not worried," Jayvee said, a little edge coming into his voice. "I was just surprised."

"Glad you asked," Jazz said, his tone unchanged. "I was wondering myself."

"What *is* being done about Clete?" Connie inquired, after a moment's hesitation: but Jayvee had received his warning and surely would not violate confidence at this late date. "Anything?"

"Nothing I can tell you much about," the Vice-President said, hesitating also for a second but apparently reaching the same conclusion. "But I think I can say this: steps are being taken to find out certain things."

"You mean the President is doing something at last?" Al Freer asked. "I find that very hard to believe."

"The President is not a fool," the Vice-President said with a certain sharpness.

"But he is hard to convince," Dr. Freer said dryly. "I am very surprised. Stuart Yule and I were injured here. Five died in Huntsville and Mississippi. It has taken him a long time. Too long, in my judgment."

"No thanks to him we're alive right now," Pete agreed. "And the birds on the pads."

"All I can say," the Vice-President repeated, his voice still sharp, "is that the government has begun to follow up very vigorously certain leads. But it's a long way from that to something definite that will stand up in court."

"And meantime——" Bob Hertz said in a quizzical tone.

"Meantime," the Vice-President said crisply, "we will continue to do exactly what we've been doing, only more of it. Tighter security—greater alertness—more precautions—"

"And good luck, one and all," the Administrator said.

"That's about it," the Vice-President agreed bluntly;

and for a while they all fell still, looking very thoughtful and saying nothing.

"Well," Dr. Freer said finally, with an attempt at heartiness that did not entirely succeed. "I believe we should not be so gloomy, for I see them signaling across the hall, so luncheon must be ready. Let us go in and celebrate. After all"—and he gestured with his glass through the floor-to-ceiling window toward the distant gantries with their three precious burdens, small and shining in the sun—"Piffy One is still there. And she will go."

"I'll drink to that," Connie said. "And confound her enemies!"

And with a conviction they did not entirely feel, they joined him; aware, as they went in to lunch, somewhat more relaxed and beginning to joke a little, that in three vehicles, each containing some six thousand parts, all of which must be perfectly protected for the next month and then work perfectly at launch, there lay so many possibilities for disaster that all they *could* do was drink to good luck and the confusion of enemies, and hope for the best.

Yet that night, after an afternoon of hectic activity in Al Freer's office and at the News Center in north Cocoa Beach while the story of the mysterious five grew and proliferated in Washington and around the world; after a visit by the crew to the simulators and the quarters they would soon fly in from Houston to occupy, in virtual isolation, in the final days; and after the Vice-President, the Administrator and Bob Hertz had managed to sneak away unnoticed for a quick couple of hours of golf at Patrick Air Force Base, south along the coast below Cocoa Beach, they all found themselves feeling in some curious way a returning confidence and optimism.

He could not have said quite why, the Vice-President remarked to Andy as they took off from Patrick in Air Force Two shortly after 9 P.M. for the return trip to Washington. But he did feel better and less worried about things.

"Maybe it's because we're just beginning to realize what a miraculous escape we and the mission had today," the Administrator remarked with a smile. "We're probably just coming out of shock. We're thinking that if Piffy One can survive *that*, by God she can survive anything."

"Maybe that's it," the Vice-President agreed with an answering smile. He looked out the window as the plane

438

swung north and spoke with a sudden emotion. "Look down. Isn't that a beautiful sight?"

And on an impulse he picked up the intercom and asked the pilot to circle over the pads.

Below them in the full moon, three small candles held back the night. They were bathed in searchlights and around them tiny ants that were men and trucks and cranes and automobiles came and went in constant activity. Beyond them on the one side stretched the dark masses of the Florida scrub, on the other the lazy Atlantic curled in upon the shore, slow waves tipped with silver in the haunted light.

Symbols of man's dreams, aspirations and hope, symbols of his bullheaded determination to go where men had never gone before, proof of his folly, proof of his pride, affirmations of a foolhardiness and courage beyond belief, the candles signaled their challenge to the darkness and the darkness drew back. The monstrous men and forces who sought their destruction and the destruction of all they stood for were far away on this night; and on this night, defeated.

Perfect and pure, they made their statement to the universe and were not to be denied.

The Vice-President and the Administrator watched in hushed silence while Air Force Two swung slowly around. Soon the lights of another, smaller plane appeared slightly below and to their right, making the same slow circle to see the same fantastic sight.

"Sir," the pilot said over the intercom, "that's Mr. Hertz and the crew on their way back to Houston. They say hello and God speed."

"And say God speed to them," the Vice-President said softly. "From both of us."

A moment later the small plane dipped its wings twice, put on a sudden burst of speed, swung wide and out and around and disappeared rapidly toward the west.

"We can go home now," the Vice-President said, still softly.

For a few more minutes he and the Administrator remained at their windows, staring back as long as they could while the candles dwindled and dwindled. Finally they disappeared altogether, swallowed up at last in the vast velvet night of Florida, between the palmettos and the sea.

3.

T minus three weeks, and it was a time for hurryings and packings and the saying of farewell. At the house in El Lago in the concluding days before departure for the Cape, Connie, Jane and the kids stayed home for dinner five nights running: somehow nobody wanted to go out, away from familiar surroundings that seemed to promise some security, however fragile, against the unknown dangers of the unknown planet. Jazz and Clare Weickert had the same reaction; they too stayed close to home with their children. Pete was with the Traskers three nights out of the five, with Jazz and Clare one night, and with his older sister and her husband, who flew down from Denver, the fifth night. Both Connie and Jazz, feeling a surge of crew spirit as time fled, invited Jayvee to join them on the nights Pete came to dinner; the invitations were firmly, but politely, refused. Around Clear Lake along the tree-lined streets in the quiet, substantial neighborhoods, and in the stores and supermarkets, dry cleaners and movie houses where they ran into one another, the other astronauts and their wives began to be gripped by that spirit of intense involvement that always claims the astronaut community before a major launch. There but for the grace of God, the President, the Astronaut Office, the media and a few other things, they might be going; indeed, would be in due course, if Piffy One succeeded and the conquest of the planets went on. Jane and Clare got the calls that always came in from other astronauts' wives at such a time.

"One more crying session with the girls," Jane finally

remarked, not altogether humorously, to Connie, "and I'm going to climb the wall. They all mean so well, and I've done the same thing myself, but it's wearing me down."

But the calls, of course, kept coming.

Neither Connie nor Jayvee saw Monetta in person during these days, but both heard from her on the Picturephone. On the afternoon of the farewell banquet tendered them in the Astrodome by the Houston Chamber of Commerce, the buzzer sounded in Connie's office. He turned it on to find, still with considerable emotion, the gravely beautiful face he had come to know well in the past four months. She did not detain him long.

"I just wanted you to know I was thinking of you," she said quietly, "and wishing you well. Take care of yourself."

"I will," he said with equal quietness. "Your thoughts will help. I appreciate it. And take care of yourself, while I'm gone."

"I will."

"Stay well."

"And you."

Her conversation with Jayvee was not quite so short and not quite so pleasant. But it was something she felt she should do and she felt better for it when it was over. How he really felt was, as always lately, a mystery, and one whose solution she found no longer cared about.

"Hello," he said shortly when her face appeared on the screen. "What do you want?"

"I just wanted to wish you luck," she said, flushing a little at his tone but standing her ground. "So does Rudden.'

"Is he there?"

"I'll call him in a minute," she said. "I wanted to say my piece first."

He shrugged.

"Go ahead."

"Just that," she said. "Good luck. Have a good flight. Come home safely."

"Why?" he asked, and for the first time looked directly at her. "Do you care?"

Again she flinched a little but again stood her ground.

"I've been married to you for six years, Jayvee," she said quietly. "I can't just see you go off, 'way out there, and not have some feelings about it."

"Why don't you go ahead and file for divorce when I'm gone?" he suggested.

"Now, how would that look!" she demanded, and for a moment a genuine anger came into her voice. "How would that look, me filing for divorce while you're gone on the flight, like it was behind your back?"

"I suppose you're right," he said with a certain smugness. "The public wouldn't stand for it."

"And I wouldn't do it," she said coldly. "But I can tell you this, I'll get it the moment you get back. And that's for sure."

"Thanks," he said.

"Don't mention it!" Then her voice softened, she made one last attempt to part friends. "Jayvee—do take care of yourself. I know it doesn't matter to you any more what I think, but you need good wishes to take along. You can't go without some to help you."

"Don't worry about me. I've got plenty, girl. Plenty."

"Not from real friends."

"And that's you? Don't make me laugh!"

"It was," she said quietly. "It was. Fly safely, Jayvee, and come home. Now I'll get Rudden."

But not even with his son did her husband relax, though the boy cried sadly for him. For a moment she thought Jayvee might respond, do something human. For a tenuous moment, so did he. But he caught himself in time. The mask came down.

"Stop that, child," he said, not unkindly but without much real emotion. "Stop your blubbering, now. Your mother needs you to be strong. You take care of her and be a big boy."

"I don't want you to go!" Rudden wailed.

"Well, I've got to," he said and reached over to snap off the machine.

"Good-by, Jayvee," she said.

"Thanks for calling," he said impersonally.

But that night, when she watched the banquet in Houston on television, he was surprisingly adequate, and, in fact, surprisingly good. So were they all, in this their formal good-by to their friends and fellow workers of the Manned Spacecraft Center and their first formal joint appearance before the world as the crew of Planetary Fleet One.

Around the Astrodome floodlights slashed the Houston sky. Limousines, official cars and ordinary motors drew up in steady procession at the door, thousands of people entered in long, amicably excited lines, thousands more who did not have tickets stood about outside talking, laughing, joking in the cool fall air. This was the city's good-by and NASA's good-by, and although many extra policemen, guards and sheriff's deputies were on duty, it began to seem, as the minutes moved on toward the arrival of the astronauts and their families, that this would not be a crisis night, after all. There had been a lot of worries about this in Jim Cavanaugh's office at MSC, in Andy Anderson's office in Washington, and in the White House, but there was something in the air that indicated that this would be the happy occasion it ought to be. There was something that said that anyone who tried to make it otherwise would receive short shrift and no mercy.

Shortly before the crew arrived there was proof of this. One tiny group of demonstrators, jeering and carrying signs, appeared at the edge of the crowd and tried to force a way through. Its members were set upon with an angry shout, their banners ripped down, their heads beaten, their noses bloodied. In five minutes' time they were in police vans on their way to jail. The astronauts were Houston's own and Houston tonight was having no nonsense. No others, if there were others, dared show themselves.

Which did not, of course, as Dr. Cavanaugh and Bob Hertz, arriving together in an official limousine, were well aware, preclude the silent murderer with the gun or the bomb; and with a mutual, unexpressed understanding, they delayed going in when they got out of the limousine and instead turned back to wait outside the door.

"I won't feel easy until everybody's inside," Jim Cavanaugh confessed.

"I won't feel easy until we're all safely home in our beds," Bob Hertz said grimly.

But very shortly it began to appear that perhaps they were worrying too much; although, looking back, every one of them who had an official position or was connected directly with Piffy One realized that he had not really felt secure that night until he was indeed, as Bob Hertz put it, safely home in bed. It was a sad commentary on the state of their country in these recent mixed-up years, but it was true. Fortunately character, discipline, training and the sort of fatalism that has to accompany prominence in a sick and insane century, came to their assistance. None of those watching received the slightest hint that anyone was troubled or uncertain or uneasy.

And the crowd helped. Some distance away, a steadily rising swell of sound, Bob and Jim could hear the welcoming roar begin. It grew and grew, happy, excited, friendly, warm. When it seemed about to overwhelm the world, the first of the three limousines carrying the astronauts arrived in the midst of a motorcycle police escort, engines sputtering, sirens screaming.

The limousine stopped. Connie, Jane and the children got out. The world exploded in happy sound while they stood in the glaring eye of the spotlights, the television cameras and the flashing strobes, Connie with one arm around Jane, the other waving, Jane waving too, the children waving in front of them.

"Get inside," Bob Hertz said fiercely beside Jim Cavanaugh. "Damn it, *get inside.*"

"They're all right," Jim replied. "They're O.K."

And so they were, as, after a couple of minutes, they gave their final waves and moved along toward the door. There Bob and Jim shook hands with Connie, kissed Jane, patted the children, shooed them in.

The second limousine drew up. Jazz and Clare and their three dismounted. The world again went wild. They too posed, waved, went in. Pete and Jayvee followed together in the third limousine, posed, waved, went in. With sighs of relief that no one else heard, and with rather shame-faced smiles at one another, Bob and Jim followed.

The doors closed for an hour and a half, during which the banquet was to be held at long harvest tables covering the floor of the Astrodome. Then the doors would be opened, the bleachers would be filled with as many of those waiting outside as could be accommodated, the formal proceedings would take place.

At the head table, where Hank Barstow and Bert Richmond held down the anchor positions at each end, with Bob Hertz next to Hank on the right, Dr. Cavanaugh next to Bert on the left, then Pete, Jazz, the mayor of Houston in the center, Connie and Jayvee, the meal proceeded with reasonable dispatch and only the most casual of conversation. The families were at tables directly below, and waving at them for the group of photographers who lurked just under the edge of the dais took up a good deal of time.

"Christ," Jazz muttered out of the side of his mouth at one point to Pete, "I can't get a bit in edgewise."

"Don't knock it," Pete said cheerfully. "Three weeks from now we'd give our eyeteeth for roast beef under *any* conditions."

"That's right," Jazz agreed with a grin and turned to oblige one more importunate photographer.

Before them across the great floor were the employees and families of the Manned Spacecraft Center, many representatives of contractors and subcontractors such as Jim Matthison, most of the civic and social dignitaries of Houston. Ticket price had been kept at a mimimum just sufficient to cover expenses, a generous Dutch treat bar service had been arranged and was being generously patronized. Steadily the jolly and convivial hum increased as the meal went on. If there were enemies of Planetary Fleet One in the world they were snarling elsewhere this night. The men of NASA were among friends.

At 8:45 the doors were opened, the crowd outside jostled eagerly in and filled the bleachers. The mayor, slightly but very amicably the worse for wear, arose, wobbling a bit, at 9:02.

"Ladies and gentlemen," he said into the rustling, clinking, murmuring hush that fell over the amphitheater as the lights were gradually dimmed, except for the brightly glowing head table, "this is Planetary Fleet One's night and Houston's night. God bless you all for coming!"

There was laugher, applause, a Rebel yell or two. He waved them down with a happy smile and continued.

"We have said good-by to many brave men over the years and we have said hello to them again when they have come back. And that's exactly what we're going to do this time!"

Again there was laughter and applause.

"Only this time, I guess maybe they're the bravest of them all. Because they have the farthest to go—about from here to Waco, Texas"—he grinned and was rewarded with a shout of laughter—"and they have the toughest job to do. It's going to be a while before they eat good Texas beef again ('You see?' Pete murmured to Jazz) and a while before they see their homes and loved ones again. I

445

guess they can stand that all right but I just don't see how they can stand being away from Texas that long! . . .

"Now, seriously," he said, when the laughter had subsided again, "now, seriously, it isn't my purpose to make a speech here——"

"Then sit down, God damn it!" a voice roared good-naturedly from somewhere on the floor. The laughter welled obediently up.

"That must be my good friend James Xavier Garvey," the mayor said with a chuckle. "Jimmy X.'s oil-wells would *reach* from here to Mars. Anyway, as I said a moment ago before I was so rudely and characteristically interrupted—as I said a moment ago, I won't make a speech. We just want you men to know"—and abruptly his voice became solemn and began to tremble a little with emotion, assisted by the Dutch treat bar but basically perfectly genuine—"that all your friends here in Houston are with you one hundred per cent, all the way. We'll be thinking of you. Our prayers will be with you. Our *hearts* will be with you. God bless you, every one."

There was a great emotional burst of applause while he wiped a tear, part feeling, part Jack Daniels, from his eye.

"And now it gives me great pleasure to introduce to you the man who guides the careers of these fine young men, the man who has been responsible for the past four years for all the many activities that go on down there at that fascinating place we all know so well and are so proud of—my friend Dr. Cavanaugh, Director of the Manned Spacecraft Center!"

The applause started, and as it did, Connie on a sudden impulse stood up. Jazz, Jayvee and Pete followed suit, Hank and Bert and Bob did likewise. In a moment the entire assemblage was on its feet. Jim Cavanaugh smiled and waved, genuinely moved. They sat down, the Astrodome fell silent again. He began to speak in a crisp, decisive tone.

"My friends of Houston, my fellow workers of MSC: thank you for coming tonight and thank you for all you have done to make Planetary Fleet One the great success we know it will be.

"NASA is many things and some of them"—he smiled—"are so scientific and so complicated that even I can't understand them, though I'm supposed to be in a position where I know what they're all about. But basically, NASA

446

is something much simpler than that. NASA is people and the space program is people. And without the dedicated and loyal efforts of all those people, neither NASA nor the program would be anything.

"Many of you who are here tonight play major roles in Goddard and JPL and all the other NASA installations at home and around the world, play equally vital and necessary roles. Without all of you there would be no program, no Project Argosy, no Planetary Fleet One, no mission to Mars.

"God bless you all, all of you everywhere, you in this room and you who are watching on television. You serve your country well and it owes you much.

"And now, enough of patting ourselves on the back and on with what we're here for. There is no formal program tonight—just an informal farewell to four brave men. I know you want to hear from them and then we will be through.

"Ladies and gentlemen, it gives me great pleasure to introduce to you a most distinguished doctor and scientist, a man whose contributions to the success of Planetary Fleet One have already been great and will be much greater as the mission moves on: Dr. Petros Balkis, co-commander of the Medico-Scientific Vehicle. Pete—"

For a moment, as once again the assemblage rose and the applause rolled up, Pete stood at the lectern staring out almost without expression at some far distance only he could see. Then he seemed to come out of it, smiled, waved, broke finally into a grin of pure pleasure.

"Jim," he said, when silence came, "Connie—Jazz—Jayvee—Bob—Hank—Bert—our wonderful friends of NASA and our wonderful friends of Houston:

"I don't suppose the baby of the bunch—and I think I am, Jayvee, by a couple of months"—and he smiled in apparent perfect friendliness at his crewmate down the table—"has much right to say anything in the presence of his elders, here, so I'll be brief.

"It's a great privilege to be on the crew, a great fulfillment of my ambitions and my dreams, and a great challenge. Like all of us, I wanted this assignment. Like all of us, it's now up to me to produce. I give you my word that I, like all of us, will do my best. With your support and your prayers we cannot fail."

And with a graceful little bow and a glance once again

447

along the table at his crewmates and colleagues on both sides, he waved and sat down while the applause, deep, warm, enthusiastic, roared up around him.

"Thank you, Pete," Dr. Cavanaugh said with a smile. "At MSC, we train 'em to be brisk, bright and brief. You can see he's been a perfect pupil. Let that be an example to the rest of you"—he almost said 'boys,' remembered whom he would introduce next, and with a little inward sigh of exasperation that nobody knew, corrected himself smoothly—"fellows . . .

"Ladies and gentlemen," he said when their comfortable laughter subsided, "again I introduce to you a most distinguished doctor and scientist, one on whom Planetary Fleet One has depended, and will depend, for many things: Dr. J. V. Halleck, commander of the Medico-Scientific Vehicle. Jayvee—"

And with the misgivings they all shared, but having known right along that this moment was inevitable and would have to be met, he shook hands with Jayvee as he reached the lectern, and sat down.

Again the applause came: possibly, to a sensitive ear—and it fell on a sensitive ear—just a little more dutiful, just a little less genuinely hearty and emotional and warm, than that accorded his teammates. But although he, too, stared for several moments almost unseeing over the again-standing audience while his colleagues held their breaths and newsmen and television commentators in the press boxes watched with an avid expectancy, his words when they came were reasonable, dignified and mild. For once in his life—maybe only once, nobody could be sure, but at least for this once—Jayvee lived up to the image.

"Ladies and gentlemen," he said quietly, looking young and leonine and very handsome in a light tan sport jacket, white shirt, dark blue tie and blue slacks, "I thank you very much for your warm greeting and farewell to my crewmates and me tonight. I know it means a great deal to all of us.

"I am very proud to be here tonight, both as a scientist and as a member of my race."

There was a sudden uneasy stirring in the audience, a quick exchange of glances along the table, a gleeful tension in the media. But having raised it, he left it.

"As a scientist, the flight to Mars presents challenges beyond anything a scientist has a right to hope for. As a

448

black man, it gives me a chance to show that I, too, can do a job for you in space. Both of these opportunities I intend to meet to my fullest abilities."

Applause, relieved, gratified, satisfied, began and mounted around him. He waited for it to subside and concluded.

"Again, I say thank you to all of you. As Pete says, we need your support and your prayers. Without them, Planetary Fleet One would have a hard time. With them, we will go to Mars."

And he returned to his chair while they gave him a final round; smiling a little, with a grave, judicious air; waving, once.

"As I said," Jim Cavanaugh remarked at the lectern, looking after him with a gaze in which only his colleagues at the table could see a certain ironic relief, "brisk, bright and brief, that's the way we like 'em. And now I know I'm going to present to you one of the briskest, brightest and briefest of them all—a man of few words and many accomplishments—Commander Alvin S. Weickert III, commander of the Command-Service Vehicle and second in command of Planetary Fleet One. Jazz—"

For several minutes, while he, too, received his standing ovation and the hearty, friendly applause filled the Astrodome, Jazz stood at the lectern looking out with a pleased and amiable grin—in a mood somewhat akin to the mayor's, for he alone of the crew had not limited himself quite as strictly as he might have on this gala evening, but perfectly coherent and capable nonetheless.

"Are you trying to tell me something, Jim?" he asked when silence returned. "All this 'few words and many accomplishments' stuff? Do I get your message?"

When they had laughed at this and again subsided, he looked around the hall and suddenly a great, big, undisguised grin broke out.

"Ladies and gentlemen," he said, "it took me a long time to get here and I want you to know I'm damned glad I am!"

At this there was a shout of delighted laughter and a wave of applause that rose and lasted and took quite a while to die down. For a moment his colleagues felt some concern about what would come next. But Jazz was too happy to say anything really drastic.

"Yes, sir," he repeated, "damned glad I am! And

damned glad that such fine and marvelous people as all you folks of NASA and Houston have turned out to be with us tonight. It really makes your crew feel great, I can tell you that. It's just wonderful.

"You've heard from two of our brightest—and briskest—and briefest already, and they've said pretty much what I feel, too. As soon as I've stopped shooting off my mouth, you're going to hear from our smoothest—and blandest—and most spellbinding—old Conn—and he's going to say it some more. So I'll just say this:

"You've all heard that there was some trouble about getting a crew together—yes, I know," he said, as there was a visible stirring along the table, to the delight of the press, and Clare cringed below, "but they *have* heard it, and we might as well get it out in the open—and you all know I wasn't an original choice to go. But I'll say this and I know Jayvee will back me up: once we were on the crew, there couldn't have been a more closely knit or better-working bunch to work with. We've pushed this mission through with real co-operation all the way, we've all done our jobs and now we're just about ready to fly. And that's a real tribute to the spirit of the space program, I'll say to you, and America can be proud that her astronauts have that spirit and can work together and do these things when we have a job to do!"

Once again, led with great vigor by his colleagues at the table, most of whose expressions were studies in quizzical amusement, applause approved him.

"And so I say to you," he concluded, "God bless you! God bless you for your support and help all the way, God bless you for being our countrymen who we can do this job for! We're proud of you and we hope you're proud of us! Good night and God bless you!"

("Jesus," the *Times* said to the *Post* in the press box, "isn't anybody going to tell the truth in this love feast?" "He started to," the *Post* said dryly, "but the spirit of Mother NASA overcame him. Isn't it sickening the way they all pledge allegiance to the space flag?")

But there was one left to go, and by the time Jim Cavanaugh had introduced him and he in his turn had received his ovation, had smiled his smiles and waved his waves, he had decided on a course that soon had the *Times*, the *Post* and their brother and sister skeptics of the media quite busy scribbling notes and taking film.

"Jim," he said gravely when a noisy, rustling hush returned, "Jazz—Jayvee—Pete—Bob—Hank—Bert—my friends of Houston and NASA:

"Jazz says you know certain things and they ought to be in the open.

"I agree."

There was something about the way he said it that brought an instant attention out of the amiable haze. Abruptly the hush deepened, became complete save for the whirring of the television cameras, now suddenly audible, that were trained intently upon his face.

"There was, to begin with, the controversy over selection of the crew which he mentioned. It did exist. Many people and many forces far beyond the normal confines of NASA became involved. The President himself finally had to intervene. The present crew was selected.

"With none of this do I or my colleagues have any quarrel. It was only when outsiders who know nothing of the problems of a flight deliberately brought pressure upon us that we became resentful. It was only when those who we believe do *not* have America's best interests at heart got themselves involved, that we complained.

"But we are used to doing our duty, and when the decision was made we accepted it. As Jazz says, the crew has worked in successful co-operation ever since. If we have not all of us been as personally close as some of the Apollo crews were, that has been our problem and one we have learned to live with. We can live with it to Mars and back. It has not affected, and I believe will not affect, the mission.

"Another controversy arose, over whether or not the mission should be armed. Three of us thought so, one did not. Again outside forces brought pressure, again higher authority intervened. We were overruled. We go unarmed and we hope we go safely. If we do not," he said, and now the vast amphitheater was deathly still save for the ever ubiquitous cameras, "there will be some heavy reckonings to be made. By that time, of course, they may not concern us. But they will have to concern the rest of you. That, too, was the decision, and that, too, we have accepted.

"Apparently, though, that was not enough for some of the critics and opponents of Planetary Fleet One. It is all very happy and jolly here tonight, but I remind you that

451

the lives of five Americans"—there was a gasp from his audience, an alarmed look from Jim Cavanaugh and Bob Hertz, but he continued grimly on—"the blood of another, and the leg of yet another, have been the cost, to date, of Planetary Fleet One.

"There have been riots, there has been sabotage, there has been violence, there has been death.

"We carry more than your good wishes to Mars.

"We carry the burden of man's hate, as well as his courage; his evil, as well as his glory.

"These are things for all of us, for all Americans, for all men everywhere, to think about tonight. They are things we could forget but must not.

"Here tonight we have been lucky—so far. The forces of hatred and evil in America and the world may yet spoil this evening for us. We hope not. We know they will, in any event, make at least a few more tries to stop the launch. Of that I think we may be quite sure. We must be ever alert and vigilant against this. We must not relax until Piffy One is on her way.

"Her enemies have not succeeded in stopping her yet.

"They must not be allowed to succeed in the next three weeks."

Applause, thunderous, urgent, overwhelming, endorsed his words. He stood rigid and unyielding while it ran its course, a trim, compact, hypnotically dynamic figure in the lights that bathed his head and shoulders. Old Conn was not doing so badly. He had his audience spellbound and compliant, ready to go wherever he wished to lead them.

But he was an officer in the United States Air Force, an astronaut of the United States, a decent and loyal and basically very conservative citizen, and the dangers that might have been implicit in such another military spellbinder were not implicit in him. When he resumed it was in a quieter, more conversational, more soothing tone.

"Ladies and gentlemen, your job here in Houston in some respects is done; in other respects, particularly those that come under the direction of our dear friend Bob Hertz, here, it is just beginning. You are ready to send us on to the Cape and on our way. You are ready to accompany us with communications and care as we go. You are ready, and I know eager, to welcome us when we come back.

"You won't be half as anxious for that day," he said, and joined in their tension-relieving laughter, "as we will . . .

"To you I say, as my crewmates have said: we appreciate and need your prayers and your support, and with them we cannot fail.

"We go for our beloved country, which needs these days all the help she can get, and we promise you we will not let her down."

And once again the applause roared up. The audience rose, the crew rose too and came to the lectern to stand together smiling and waving, even Jayvee looking excited and proud. The band played "Dixie," then swung into "The Star-Spangled Banner." The anthem ended, the mayor shouted, "This banquet is now concluded, God bless these astronauts, God bless you all!" and the enormous crowd began to file slowly out of the enormous amphitheater.

"That boy gives me the shivers," the *Post* remarked to the *Times* as they stood in the press box watching the happily bemused and excited audience walk out. "I can see him riding a white horse down Pennsylvania Avenue."

"I can't quite see that," the *Times* said slowly, "but I can sure as hell see why he's the commander of Planetary Fleet One."

"How did I do?" he asked, sometime much later that night and Jane murmured in his ear, "You were great. You really were. Just great."

He chuckled.

"I meant the speech."

"I know what you meant!" she said with a mock indignation. "You've been great all the way."

"That's good," he said comfortably. "I try to please my public."

"We're pleased," she said drowsily. Then he felt her body tense, her arms went around him convulsively, and he knew she was suddenly wide awake again, and terrified.

"Oh, Conn," she said, beginning to cry. *"Connie.* I am so worried for you."

"Shhh," he said gently, stroking her hair. "How does that help me?"

"I know it doesn't," she said, "and I'll be brave in the

453

morning when—when you leave. But right now, I'm so scared. It's such a long trip and so far away, and I—I'm just scared."

"Now, I thought," he said, still gently, "that we'd been over all that a long time ago."

"We have," she said, and began to cry even harder. "But now it's here."

"Yes," he agreed with a heavy sigh. "It's here."

But next morning at 8 when they left from Ellington Air Force Base, she and Clare, whose red-rimmed eyes indicated that she too had spent a difficult night, managed to dredge up from the depths where the brave wives of brave men seem to find such things a sufficient spirit and animation to wish them a reasonably cheerful farewell. While they would no doubt talk again several times on the Picturephone before launch, it had been decided by NASA that this time the crew would stay in almost complete isolation at the Cape for the entire remaining three weeks. Sometimes wives had gone there in the past, sometimes husbands had been allowed to fly home for final weekends. But because this was to be the first flight to Mars, the first challenge to what was still essentially unknown, it had been decided that physical isolation, intensive final training, psychological concentration as complete as possible, must be the program. And in their hearts, though it was very hard on their wives and children, both Connie and Jazz felt that this was probably best. And although they would never admit it to them, their wives agreed. The moment had to come, and it was best it come here in Houston on home ground, rather than in the hectic public atmosphere of the pre-launch Cape.

Even so, it was not an easy few minutes at the field, for abruptly, of course, the carefully maintained brightness of the ride up from MSC began to shred away in spite of the best efforts of all concerned. Jazz and Clare's little Joanna almost ruined everything just before they began to say good-by by suddenly wailing, "Daddy, I just don't want you to go!" For a split second all of the children looked as though they would start crying at once.

"Hey!" Jazz said, reaching down and scooping her up into his arms, "what's that over there?" He pointed past their waiting jet, where Jayvee was standing by himself looking suddenly unhappy and alone, to some distant object in the sky. "Isn't that one of those big new rocket planes?"

Joanna blinked and looked and then turned to him with a look of profound disgust.

"Daddy!" she said. "It's a *sea* gull!"

"Well, well," he said, while all the adults laughed very heartily and one or two of the children joined in cautiously. "So it is. What a stupid old Daddy, to think a sea gull was an airplane!"

"It's a sea gull," Joanna repeated. "A silly old sea gull!"

"I ought to be spanked," he said solemnly.

"Daddy!" she said, and began to laugh. "I can't spank you! You're too big!"

"O.K., punkin," he said, giving her a big kiss, setting her down swiftly and moving on to his other two, "you take care of yourself now, and I'll be talking to you soon. You too, you kids! All of you take care of your mother, now!"

"That's my cue," Connie said quickly to Jane, and kissed his own three in rapid succession. Before any of the children really knew what was happening or really had time to start crying about it, the adults were alone together in their own private world.

"Pete," Clare said tremulously, and gave him a hug and a kiss. "Be good."

"Can't be anything else," he said with a rather shaky laugh, returning the kiss and the hug. "I'll keep an eye on the old man."

"Do that," she said with a fair attempt at lightness.

"Jane, my dear——" he said.

"Take care of yourself," she said, holding him close. "Take care of him."

"I will," he promised solemnly. "I really will."

"Good-by, Jayvee!" Jane and Clare called together, waving to his lonely figure by the jet. "Good luck!"

"God bless," he called, waving back. "Take care of yourselves."

"We will," they chorused, and turned again to their families.

"See you at the plane," Pete said quickly turning to Connie and Jazz; bent down and gave each of the kids a quick hug and kiss; and turned and walked away toward Jayvee, his eyes suddenly filled with tears, the flat Texas landscape blurred.

Five minutes later they were airborne with Connie at

the controls; passed once low over the field; dipped wings to the little group on the tarmac that stood looking up, waving bravely; roared away east and were headed for the Cape.

Until the plane dwindled to a tiny dot and disappeared, and for several minutes thereafter, Jane and Clare stood where they were, each with one arm around her children, with the other holding hands in a tight, desperate grip; not talking, not moving, not crying; drained and silent and empty in a world that now also was silent, and drained, and empty.

4.

"Do you read me, Houston?" Connie asked.

"Roger," Stuart Yule replied. "You're looking good, *Santa Maria*. Real good."

"Are we GO for docking?"

"You are GO for docking."

"Roger. *Nina* ready?"

"*Nina* GO," Jazz said laconically over the intercom.

"*Pinta?*"

"GO," Jayvee said.

"Start maneuver," Stu Yule said from Houston.

"Starting maneuver," Connie replied.

Around them space and the silent universe spun slowly as they turned, rolled, fired their rockets, swung gently into position. Far below they caught a fleeting glimpse of Earth draped in clouds, far above the half-moon gleamed. Everywhere the stars exchanged their messages, steady, unwavering points of light in the endless vacuum of the galaxies. The crew of Planetary Fleet One were defiant dots of life, alone in all that fearful emptiness. Slowly, gently, they swung, fired—drifted—fired—floated closer and closer together. There came a nudge, a bump, a slight, reassuring tremor in each of the three spacecraft. They were docked.

"Docking complete," Connie reported to Houston.

"Roger," Stu said. "That was beautiful, babe. You all were just great."

"We thought so," Connie said cheerfully, snapping off the lights, preparing to open the hatch and crawl out into the antiseptic brightness of the Simulator Building where the three mock-ups, each with its cluster of cameras and

457

closed-circuit television transmitters, stood side by side. "I think we have that one down just about pat."

"I hope so," Jazz remarked as he emerged from the simulated Command-Service Vehicle. "I'm pooped."

"So am I," Pete agreed with a grin, climbing out of the Medico-Scientific Vehicle. "When do we get to go home, Daddy?"

"Ten minutes for pee and tea," Connie said, "and then we go at it again."

"We were afraid of that," Jayvee commented, and actually sounded quite pleasant.

"We cannot refrain," the *Times* remarked coldly, "from a passing comment on what seems to us the most peculiar and chauvinistic farewell to Houston given by Commander Conrad H. Trasker of the controversial and disaster-prone Planetary Fleet One.

"We are sorry he felt it necessary to mar so sentimental an occasion with so blatant an appeal to all the most unworthy and reactionary instincts of his countrymen.

"Possibly, being in Texas, he felt he had no choice.

"Still it did not seem to us the time to revive all the most extreme and inflammatory hobgoblins that his less-enlightened and more timorous countrymen worry about. It was not necessary to raise again the specter of a mythical Russian threat to the mission, nor was it imperative to drag forth upon the public counter the bodies of those unfortunate Americans who died in unexplained, but as far as evidence now reveals, entirely accidental disasters.

"Colonel Trasker rabble-roused when he should have conducted himself with calmness and dignity. We wonder once again, as we have on several occasions before, just how fit he actually is to command this mission which now, against all the best judgments of the best minds in the country, is about to fly. . . ."

"O.K., *Santa Maria*," Stu said. "You are cleared for descent sequence."

"Roger descent sequence," Connie said.

"Start maneuver," Stu said.

"Starting maneuver," Connie said.

One hundred miles below the Mars lander, the red-tinged surface of Mars appeared—disappeared—reappeared—in the perpetual drifting fogs that enclosed the planet. Here and there when the mists parted he and Jazz could see a sudden stark upthrust of rock shooting out of the plain like some tortured, jagged exclamation-mark. An impression harsh, hostile, alien came up to them: a living thing, pulsing, malevolent, forbidding. They made the proper calculations, pushed the proper buttons, did the proper things. Smoothly the MLM rushed downward, swiftly the surface of Mars rushed up to meet them. What shall it be? Connie wondered ironically:

"One small step—?"

More likely,

What the hell am I doing here, everybody?

"Retro-rockets firing," he reported laconically to Houston, while Pete, Jayvee and Dr. Freer watched and listened intently at the bank of computers just in front of the mock-up. "Coming in."

"Right on the button, pal," Stu said in a relieved tone of voice. "You've got it made."

"It looks like lovely country," Connie said. "I think I'll build a second home here."

"Get me a lot, too," Stu suggested. "While they're still cheap."

"Sorry," Jazz told him. "General Land Corporation's already in here. We have one condominium left on the waterfront. Only there isn't any water."

"Twenty thousand," Connie said. "Fifteen—ten—eight—six—"

"Looking good," Stu said. "Looking very good."

"Four thousand," Connie said. "Three—two—one thousand—eight hundred—seven hundred—six—five—four—three—two—99 feet—82—73—"

"Looking beautiful," Stu said. "Just beautiful, babe."

"Fifty-four feet—41—30—20—10, 9, 8, 7, 6, 5, 4, 3, 2"—there was a slight vibration, a shuddering, a little bump, a settling—"Mare Cimmerium Base reporting, Houston. Here we are."

"The love feast when the crew of Planetary Fleet One said good-by to Texas," the *Post* remarked, "was just too much. Rarely in America in recent years has there been such an emotional, such a deliberately fact-obscuring— yes, such an *old-fashioned*—display of flag-waving as occurred on that historic occasion. One would have thought this country was rebelling against George III, charging San Juan Hill, taking Iwo Jima and twitting Fidel Castro, all over again.

"Such defiance, such challenge, such breathings of fire and appealings to patriotism! And, we might add, such bugaboos, so skillfully raised, and such fears of the ignorant, so beautifully played upon.

"Planetary Fleet One is not quite the noble, unquestioned, all-American enterprise pictured so stirringly by its captain and crew, it might be well to remember. It is a disaster-ridden project of dubious value whose chances of failure are very great and whose possibilities for genuine accomplishment are very slim.

"Colonel Trasker did his formidable best to arouse his audience and his watching countrymen to a frenzy of 'patriotism' that would hide the dubious nature of the project and the great dangers to world peace and true co-operation with the Soviet Union that are inherent in it.

"Frankly, we hope he failed. The country must see Planetary Fleet One whole and see it clear, for what it is: an ill-advised adventure in pursuit of the outdated bauble of national prestige; an inexcusable and desperately dangerous affront to a great power with whom we must get along in this world; and an exercise in unchecked ego for the President, his advisers in NASA and the little band of glory-seeking individuals who will fly.

"Of course in common humanity we must wish its crew a safe journey and a safe return. But let no one be under any illusions that what they do is as noble and selfless and good for the country as they would have us believe."

Mare Sirenium stretched on every side, naked, harsh and repelling, unbroken save for the occasional jagged peak. Again Connie started his descent, again the alien surface, not quite so strange now, quickly familiar as everything quickly becomes familiar to man, rose to meet him. Beside him a different passenger rode: the second and final descent was the scientific descent. Both Jayvee and Pete were to practice it, not knowing yet whether one or both would make the journey.

"Controls over to Jayvee," Connie reported.

"Roger," Stu Yale said. "Do you read me, Jayvee?"

"Loud and clear," Jayvee said.

"Begin final stages of descent," Stu said.

"Roger final stage," Jayvee said in an impersonal tone, and brought her down exactly on target.

"Controls over to Pete," Connie said.

"Roger," Stu said. "Do you read me, Petros?"

"The voice is magnificent," Pete told him. "Pure opera quality."

"Your target is Mare Sirenium," Stu said sternly. "They have little men waiting there for guys who aren't respectful."

"Oh, I'm respectful," Pete said cheerfully. "And good, too. I'll bet I set her down right on the button."

And so, five minutes later, he did.

"It was not enough," Percy Mercy (Percy Comma Mercy, this time) wrote rapidly on his electric typewriter in *View*'s luxurious offices, "that Planetary Fleet One must be dogged by disasters which would lead the world to suspect that an impatient Deity might be trying to convey the message that it should not fly. Now its commander and crew have attempted to use the occasion of their farewell to Houston to stir up public emotions of the most chauvinistic and detrimental kind.

"Few concerned Americans who saw the extravaganza in the Astrodome—complete, naturally, with a tipsy Texas mayor—can have failed to be appalled by the very obvious rabble-rousing indulged in by the flight's commander, Colonel Trasker. It was a performance that roused sinister echoes of other military figures who have sought to use temporary public fame as a springboard to political power.

"Not only did Colonel Trasker deliberately drag up long-buried controversies such as the fantastic bugaboo of a possible Russian 'attack' on the mission, but he also sought to revive the battle between NASA and its critics over the merits and value of the flight itself. This was unwise, since it must by now be clear to all involved citizens that this disaster-plagued project has even less justification today than it did six months ago when it was first inaugurated by a President whose desire for political advantage is as great as that of Colonel Trasker.

"Affront to the Soviet Union, with which we must co-operate, in space as elsewhere; futile and foredoomed pursuit of the bauble of 'national prestige,' a concept as old-fashioned and outdated as 'patriotism' itself; wasteful robber of funds that had much better be spent on America's domestic needs—such is Planetary Fleet One. Nothing has changed what this magazine said two months ago:

"It is not too late to stop the flight.

"And it must be done.

"It is true, admittedly, that the protests launched in these past several weeks by CAUSE (the Committee Against Unilateral Space Exploration) have not been entirely successful. Two moratoriums have been held. The turn-out, though substantial and worthy of praise for the fine efforts of many involved and dedicated citizens, has been disappointingly small. Much smaller, in fact, than is warranted by the grave nature of the offense to mankind's hopes for peaceful co-operation that all thoughtful citizens of this troubled globe see in Planetary Fleet One.

"Now the mission is in its final days prior to launch. There is time and there is opportunity for at least one more massive nationwide portest which will impress upon the Administration the utter folly it has embarked upon.

"Should this for some reason prove ineffective, then there should be held on the day of launch a peaceful but emphatic demonstration at Kennedy Space Center which will convey to all mankind the deep misgivings, and the apologies, of the American people for what is being done in their name.

"This is the least, it seems to this magazine, that concerned citizens, conscious of their own dignity and responsibility to all mankind, can do."

Informed of all these stern journalistic twitterings later, after they had practiced all day on dockings, landings and finally their return to Earth ("You're coming home after 18 months, and you only have to practice these things two hundred more times before launch," Stu Yule told them. "Act excited." "I am," Jazz said. "I've got a ten-foot beard and a permanent hard-on."), it was Jazz, again, who summed up the feelings of at least three of them in a flat, disgusted tone:

"Oh, Christ, that crap. What relation does that have to us, and the job we have to do?"

5.

T minus one week, and in the steadily mounting tempo of the Cape, Jazz appeared to be right: it really did not seem that the fulminations of Percy and his friends had much relation to the crew of Planetary Fleet One and the job they had to do. Nor did the righteous outcries from certain famous editorial offices appear to have affected the majority of the working reporters who flocked in from all over the world in new hundreds every day. Nor did they affect the general excitement that began to grip Kennedy Space Center, Cocoa Beach and all their contiguous and outlying areas.

While the crew remained in isolation practicing, practicing and practicing again, in Orlando, Melbourne, Titusville and in fact all over the country, the standard and inevitable headlines appeared:

HOTELS, MOTELS REPORT CAPACITY BOOKINGS FOR LAUNCH. KSC OFFICIALS WARN TWO MILLION MAY CLOG ROADS TO SEE LIFT-OFF. HINT PRESIDENT MAY ATTEND AS WORLD VIP's GATHER. CREW WIVES 'TRY TO KEEP NORMAL' IN HOUSTON. PRE-LAUNCH SOCIAL FRENZY MOUNTS AT CAPE.

And among them came those other headlines that always seem to accompany a launch:

HYDROGEN 'ANOMALY' MAY DELAY LAUNCH. SPACE CREWS WORK AROUND CLOCK TO CORRECT 'GLITCHES.' COUNTDOWN PROCEEDS DESPITE WORRY OVER TANK FISSURE. TINY WIRE COULD HOLD KEY TO BLAST-OFF. CREW DOC-

TORS FEAR COLDS, MEASLES, SCARLET FEVER, PLAGUE.

Followed inevitably, after a couple of days of world-wide attention, by:

HYDROGEN 'ANOMALY' CORRECTED. SPACE CREWS CONQUER 'GLITCHES.' COUNTDOWN ON SCHEDULE AS TANK FISSURE HEALED. TINY WIRE IN PROPER PLACE. DR. BERRY GIVES CREW CLEAN BILL OF HEALTH FOR LAUNCH.

At the News Center, at the north end of Cocoa Beach opposite the Hilton, where Marlon Holloway and his colleagues from the KSC news staff tried to maintain some kind of order in the midst of nearly three thousand clamoring newsmen, reporters, broadcasters, commentators, cameramen, still photographers and general press workcrews, excitement and tension mounted almost literally by the minute. Percy and Walter Dobius were there, as were their colleagues from the *Times,* the *Post,* and every other newspaper and magazine of any size and pretension in the United States. AP and UPI had crews of fifty each, NBC, CBS and ABC were equally prevalent. And in the big bright room where the rows of desks and typewriters were separated from the mimeographs and question-answerers by a long counter to which a constant stream of inquisitive newsmen came with their queries, the foreign contingent was also well represented.

Shaggy Englishmen like supercilious unmade beds wandered about with pipes. Blond Germans exchanged their guttural confidences. Neat little Japanese festooned with cameras stood at the bank of telephones along the wall, shouting across the globe to Tokyo. Fortunata and her Italian colleagues made wittily nasty comments about the Americans in their liquid-lightning tongue. A group of burly Russians smiled broadly and turned aside all queries with a practiced ease. ("I say, old boy, is it true that your government is trying to beat this launch?" Ha, ha. "There isn't anything to this stupid American rumor that the Russians might attack Planetary Fleet One, is there?" Chuckle, chuckle.) From Luxembourg, South Africa, India and Israel, from Sweden, Algeria, Brazil and Jamaica, from all the realms and all the climes, they converged upon the Cape. If America succeeded they wanted to report it, and if America failed, they wanted to be there.

If the tone of their comments and their writing was in

general mocking, sarcastic, critical and snide, that was reflective of envy, jealousy and, in some cases, hate; and their hosts fortunately did not see or understand one-tenth of what they said and wrote. So they were made at home with a warm and generous fellowship, given every consideration, treated with every kindness and courtesy, and all was well.

Upstairs on the second floor, walls had been knocked through and a greatly expanded press conference room had been created for the regular ritual of briefings and press conferences that always accompany a launch: the briefing on guidance and control, the briefing on scientific experiments, the briefing on MLM procedures, the press conference on health, the joint press conference held by the Administrator, the director of the Argosy program and the directors of KSC, MSC and Huntsville.

Aided by much reportorial standing along the walls, sitting on the floor and in the aisles, the expanded conference room could just handle the 500 or so who wished to attend each conference. For the biggest conference of them all, the one that would occur this afternoon at 3 with the crew, the room would not be large enough. Special buses would run up to KSC to the training auditorium there. More than 1000 were expected to attend.

Along the Strip in this final seven days, the social pace roared into high gear as it had for all the Apollo launches: an exhausting but enjoyable routine which sometimes prompted the thoughtful and philosophic (usually when they were a little tight) to pause in the midst of some cocktail party at the Hilton or some contractor's bash at the Ramada Inn, and muse: "You know, it somehow doesn't seem right, does it? Those guys up there by themselves at the Space Center getting ready to lay their lives on the line, and us down here eating and drinking and carrying on?"

But nobody ever stopped or stayed home, of course, and in a way this was entirely fitting: Connie and Jazz and Pete, and even Jayvee on a couple of occasions, had all come to the Cape for launches when they hadn't been flying, and many a cocktail party and exclusive Administrator's dinner had known the pleasure of their sometimes well-lubricated company. Up at KSC in their quiet quarters they knew very well what was going on five miles south in Cocoa Beach: to them it seemed perfectly fitting and not at all offensive or upsetting. And so, after those few introspective moments that now and then intruded in the midst of noisy gaiety, the thoughtful and philosophic relaxed. Those moments were a necessary conscience-prodded genuflection to The Serious Side of Things. But they never lasted long, at the Cape.

And how could they, with so much excitement and so many important and fascinating people coming in from all over the world for this most spectacular of all man's assaults upon the galaxy? The roster of the media glittered with names as prominent, and in quite a few instances as powerful, as Percy and Walter. Added to them were all the doggedly surviving veterans of the Cape who had covered space in its fat days and its lean days and were now more deeply thrilled and excited than they trusted themselves to say by this renascence of their beloved program. Mingling with them at the parties, in the restaurants, in the night clubs and bars, were many other veterans of the program: John Glenn, Alan Shepard and Frank Borman; Pete Conrad, John Young, Rusty Schweickart, Gene and Barbara Cernan; Tom and Faye Stafford, Wally Schirra, Walt and Lo Cunningham, Al and Sue Beane, Al and Peggy Bishop; Neil Armstrong, Jim Lovell, Buzz Aldrin, Mike Collins; Chris Kraft, George Mueller, Jim Webb, Tom Paine, Wernher von Braun; and many others famous in the great days of Mercury, Gemini and Apollo, come to lend support to their friends and colleagues of the crew. Government and politics made their contributions also: more than 150 members of the House and 56 members of the Senate were scheduled to be on hand. Virtually all foreign governments were sending official observers, more than 100 represented by ambassadors, presidents or vice-presidents, members of royal families. The President himself, though it had not yet been officially announced, would attend.

Society, too, had its representatives: the heiress to this, the heir to that, were there with their friends and hangers-on. From Hollywood came stars and starlets, In directors and Out directors. From industry came presidents and board chairmen, top managers and top public relations men. It was even rumored that Howard Hughes was there, although, as usual, no one could be sure.

So the flood of the media grew, the flood of VIP's grew, the flood of parties grew; and as T minus seven days raced swiftly into T minus six days, T minus 5, T minus 4 and so down to T minus 3 days, the pace mounted steadily along the Strip. By the morning of T minus 2 days the traffic was so heavy that it sometimes took reporters as much as 45 minutes to negotiate the three miles from the Holiday Inn, the Ramada or the Sheraton Colony in lower Cocoa Beach to the News Center in north Cocoa Beach. Regular press buses traveled the route, but even they had heavy going; and now, on this early afternoon of T minus 2 days, with the crew press conference scheduled for 3 P.M., the atmosphere was becoming slightly hectic as most of the news corps tried to get on board at once. The scenes at the motels and the News Center trembled between slapstick and mayhem as distinguished ladies and gentlemen of the media pushed and shoved and fought for advantage in fifty-eight different languages, including the Tonganese.

In due course, however, as it always does on such occasions, everything got itself sorted out somehow, and by 2:45 everyone who was anyone, and everyone who really wanted to be there, which was almost everyone who was anyone, had found a place in the auditorium at KSC. By some miracle of overcrowding, the total count came to something in the neighborhood of twelve hundred publishers, broadcasters, columnists, commentators and working reporters, plus operators and crews to man the bank of ten television cameras that stood on a raised platform in the center of the room. The hum of conversation, the cries of greeting, the babble of thoughts in a multitude of tongues, raised the decibels to an almost deafening level as the clock moved toward 3. Behind the curtain in the glass cage that NASA had provided for them at the insistence of the doctors, who wanted no chances taken with possible last-minute infections, the targets for today exchanged ironic glances.

"Well, Daniels," Connie inquired, "are we ready for the lions?"

"I feel like eating a few," Jazz said. "Bring 'em on."

"Me, too," Pete agreed. "I hope we won't get into the kind of needling nonsense we did last time. But if we do, I'm ready."

"I hope we won't either," Connie observed, and turned to the silent figure on his left. "How about it, Jayvee?"

Jayvee shrugged.

467

"Can't prove anything by me. I'm just going to play it by ear and see what comes."

"I hope we won't rake up a lot of things."

Jayvee shrugged again.

"You did, in Houston."

"I said," Connie repeated evenly, "I hope we won't rake up a lot of things. It would be nice if the crew could depart with an impression of reasonable unity, it seems to me."

"*I* said, we'll have to play it by ear," Jayvee remarked blandly. "I guess that's about all we can do."

"Hmph," Jazz said. "That's a damned co-operative statement."

"It's all you're going to get," Jayvee told him with a dry little smile.

Pete started to respond but just then Marlon Holloway appeared and moved to the microphone that had been placed to the right of the stage.

"Chins up, guts in and smile, smile, *smile*, boys," he said cheerfully. "Here—we—g-o-o-o-o."

The curtains parted, the lights went down, the hum abruptly ceased.

"Ladies and gentlemen," he said, "in response to many, many requests, the crew has agreed to appear today for this final press conference before launch. We have allotted approximately an hour, and as usual, there are no restrictions on the kinds of questions you may want to ask. Please raise your hand, wait for the portable mikes which will be brought to your seat, state your name and affiliation, and address your question to whichever crew member you wish, or call all of them . . . Yes, Mary," he said, picking out a familiar face from behind the hundred hands that immediately shot up.

"Mary Bubb, Fairchild Publications. Colonel Trasker, do you feel the crew is in a sufficiently good psychological condition, toward the mission and toward each other, to fly this mission?"

Connie smiled, leaned forward, tapped humorously on the glass, which brought a laugh, gave himself a little time.

"Well, Mary," he said easily, his voice amplified by the microphone in front of him, "I think we're in excellent psychological shape as regards the mission. I think we're all of us trained—and practiced—and dedicated—and ready. How we feel toward one another is something each of us will have to answer for himself. If you wish to poll us, go ahead. As far as I'm concerned, and I think this is a fair statement for all of us, I don't see any basic psychological problems that will affect the mission. After all, we're trained for this, you know. We're not prima donnas"—he grinned suddenly—"at least, not to *that* extent."

"Jay Barbaree, NBC. Do you agree with that, Dr. Halleck?"

For a deliberate moment, just long enough to create the effect he desired, Jayvee hesitated. Then he too smiled, a somewhat different type of smile, and answered in a tone as easy as Connie's.

"I don't think it's a matter of agree or don't agree. He has his way of looking at it, I have mine. No doubt the others have theirs. We'll get along, I guess."

"Just 'guess'?"

"Who knows?" Jayvee inquired blandly. "It's a big galaxy." He leaned forward, dropped the smile, spoke solemnly. "I believe we'll get along all right, yes. After all, we have to, don't we?"

"I don't know, Dr. Halleck. I wanted you to tell us."

Jayvee shrugged and sat back.

"Over there on the right," Marlon Holloway said quickly. "Howard?"

"Howard Benedict, Associated Press. Commander Weickert, do you anticipate any difficulty working with your colleagues on this flight?"

Jazz snorted.

"You guys never give up, do you? Stop one of you coming in the back door and another comes in the front. Connie said we'll all get along. Jayvee's just said the same thing. What more do you want?"

"We'd just like to hear it from you, Jazz."

"By George, they do want to poll us, Conn. O.K., I'll say it for you: Yes, we'll get along. Provided everybody—" He hesitated and of course was pounced upon.

"Everybody what?"

"Everybody gets along," he said blandly and turned to his colleague on the right. "Petey, you'd better say your say too."

"Sure," Pete agreed comfortably. "We'll get along. O.K., everybody?"

There was a general ripple of laughter, a tacit concession of defeat. Jules Bergman held up his hand.

"Jules Bergman, ABC. Connie, can you give us some general idea of the mission? I know we've got it all in the handouts, but it might be interesting for the television audience to get it from you direct."

Connie nodded.

"Sure, Julie . . . As you know, the mission really breaks down into two sections—what might be called the practice section and the actual mission. It's been decided by NASA, by all of us working on it together, here and in Washington and in Houston and Huntsville and JPL and Goddard and so on, that it would be advisable to have a very detailed run-through of all phases of the mission before we actually kick off on the flight to Mars. Obviously nobody has ever done what we're going to do before, so we want to be absolutely sure everything is right.

"It has been decided for obvious reasons that the Moon and Space Station *Mayflower* should be the two main practice areas. We're fortunate to have *Mayflower* up, and of course on the Moon, thanks to the Apollo program, we have a lot of expertise in how to behave. So the plan is this:

"We'll blast off from here on Saturday between 9 and 10 A.M., with the first Saturn, carrying me in the *Santa Maria*, scheduled to go at 9:03. The second Saturn, carrying Jazz in the *Nina*, will go at 9:27, and the *Pinta*, carrying Jayvee and Pete, will go at 9:49.

"We will then go into Earth orbit as in the Apollo flights. We will orbit Earth three times and dock the three spacecraft in Earth orbit toward the end of the third pass.

"We will orbit in tandem for two orbits and then, when Houston clears us, fire the third stages to put ourselves into translunar injection. We will then proceed to the Moon on the Apollo schedule of approximately three days, running a great many checks and tests and routine things that have to be done in actual flight before we get to the Moon to practice there. This period will also give us time, I suppose, to adjust ourselves psychologically to the whole idea."

He paused and smiled.

"It still seems a little strange and improbable, even now . . .

"So, then, we reach the Moon, and at that point we

470

proceed again approximately as we did in the Apollo landings. We go into lunar orbit—yes?"

"Anne Killiany, Fairchild Publications. Still in tandem?"

"Oh, yes, I neglected to say that all of this, up to this point, is in tandem—docked. There'll be free passage back and forth: in effect, we'll have three flying living-rooms up there most of the time. It will be relatively free and uncramped, for which"—he smiled again—"we are very grateful. We go into lunar orbit docked and remain docked for twelve orbits. Then we close hatches with me and either Jayvee or Pete in the *Santa Maria*, transfer to the MLM, and practice the first descent, as we will do on Mars."

"Will you actually land *Adventurer* on the Moon?"

"Oh, yes, we're taking plenty of fuel for two landings—in fact, more than plenty, on the final trip out to Mars—and of course in this practice run, we're going to come back to *Mayflower* and refuel. As you know, the MLM is modified from the old LM we used on the Moon. We don't leave the descent stage on the surface—it's all one machine, now. But you're getting me a little ahead of my story.

"We land *Adventurer*, stay on the lunar surface approximately six hours, practice distribution and placing of scientific equipment and experiments, and then blast off, rejoining the orbiting spacecraft where Jazz and Pete will just be finishing their third game of chess—"

"Then you do plan on taking Dr. Halleck with you on the first descent?"

Connie smiled.

"You're too quick for me. Let's say I'm contemplating it but no decision at all has been reached."

"Is that your personal decision?"

"It is."

"Is there any reason," Percy Mercy asked suddenly from the back of the room, "why Dr. Halleck should *not* make the landing with you?"

"No," Connie said patiently, "there is no reason why Dr. Halleck should not make the landing with me. Now may I continue my narrative?"

"Well, then—" Percy began.

"Thank you. We blast off and return to the spacecraft, as I said, and we then make twenty more orbits of the

Moon, during which we sleep and also run through a series of simulated scientific tests comparable to those we will actually perform in Martian orbit.

"This twenty-orbit period on the Moon, I might say, will simulate in microcosm the orbital period on Mars between the first and final landings."

"How long will that period in Martian orbit between landings actually be?"

"Two months," Connie said crisply. There was a little gasp from his audience, all of whom knew this already. But for them, too, it was still a little strange and improbable and hard to grasp.

"Two months, during which the scientific experiments put in place on the first landing will, if all goes well, mature and prove productive. We'll be monitoring them all the time from orbit, as well as from the ground, of course, and the purpose of the second landing is to go down and pick up certain of them that will be programmed to have completed their work by that time and be ready for us to bring home. Others we will leave in place permanently as we have with so many experiments on the Moon. These will continue to transmit to Earth for an estimated ten years' minimum.

"So, then. At the end of that time—I'm back on the Moon, now, in the practice period, so you should make that read, at the end of twenty orbits of the Moon—we will practice our second landing in *Adventurer*, whose crew at that time *may* consist of myself and Pete—or myself and Jazz—or myself and Jayvee—or Jazz and either one of the other two. All of this will be decided in flight, basically on my say-so, but of course after full consultation with Houston—and with the affected members of the crew themselves, of course.

"Then, from the Moon, we will head back to *Mayflower*, where we will dock, board, stretch, relax, take a break, and sleep for, probably, the better part of forty-eight hours. At *Mayflower* the fourth NERVA nuclear engine, which as you know is already there, will be added to the three we will take with us from the Cape.

"We will then reboard, undock, blast off—or rather, more graphically, I suppose, shove off gently from *Mayflower* with a tiny blast of nuclear power, which is all it takes in space—have another firing to place ourselves in transmartian injection, and be on our way. Eight months

472

later we will enter our two-month Martian orbit period and perform our actual landings and experiments. We will then start our return journey, and in about eighteen months from now, will splash down in the Pacific and see all your cheerful faces again. I may say they will look awfully good. Even yours, Fortunata."

He shook his head as if in disbelief and smiled into their delighted laughter.

"Golly, I seem to have been hearing my own voice for a long time. Doesn't anyone want to talk about anything else?"

Spontaneously and with a good-natured warmth they gave him a round of applause. But as he might have known, the friendly mood did not remain unbroken.

"Colonel Trasker," the heavy, emphatic voice said and everyone swiveled about to study the familiar stocky figure from which it came. "Walter Dobius, here. We commend you, as you see, on your most entertaining and competent discussion of your mission. But, Colonel Trasker, what about the deeper implications of this mission? What about the philosophic implications, the political aspects, the things that many thoughtful citizens of the world are concerned about as they contemplate the flight of Planetary Fleet One? What about them?"

For a moment Connie looked both baffled and amused.

"I don't know," he said finally. "What about them?"

"Do you have no thoughts about them?" Walter Dobius persisted. "No comment at all upon the implications of this blatant challenge to the good will and friendship of the Soviet Union? No comments today upon the bugaboo of a so-called Russian 'attack' upon your spacecraft? We were hoping you would tell us *something* of these things."

"Don't do it, Conn," Jazz advised, making no attempt to muffle his comment. "He isn't worth it."

" '*He*' isn't worth it, or *it* isn't worth it?" Walter Dobius demanded sharply.

"I said what I meant," Jazz said calmly. "If you don't like it, complain to NASA."

"No," Connie said slowly, while Marlon Holloway felt nervous and tried not to show it, "that isn't the way to handle him, Jazz. Yes, Mr. Dobius, I'll make a comment, since you ask.

"I have never believed, nor do I believe now, that Planetary Fleet One presents any so-called challenge to any so-called friendship and good will from the Soviet Union. I don't believe the challenge exists and I don't believe the friendship and good will exist either. I wish I were so sweet and naïve and idealistic that I could believe the Soviet Union really wants us to succeed in space, or would really help us with anything but a publicity stunt if anything went wrong; but I'm very much afraid the record of history shows just the opposite. I think they'll mess up this mission in any way they can. I think they've tried already and I think they'll keep on trying. Whether that means an actual attack, I couldn't say. I'd feel better if we were prepared for it. We aren't, so we will have to do the best we can—if we have to do anything. I trust even you, Mr. Dobius, hope we will not."

"And to that," Pete said softly, while a startled silence held the room and Walter Dobius turned several shades of pink and purple, "I wish to be recorded as saying, Amen."

"Me, too," said Jazz.

"But you don't do you, Dr. Halleck?" Walter demanded at last in a choked and furious voice. "*You* don't, do you?"

"Look," Connie said, leaning forward angrily before Jayvee had time to frame what was apparently going to be a careful answer, "they're racing right now to beat this launch. We know that. They've been racing ever since they kicked over the Geneva conference. They make no bones about it. *They* aren't afraid to say they're out to beat us, Mr. Dobius. Why are *you* so afraid to say they're out to beat us? And why are you so afraid to say *we* ought to get out there and beat *them*?"

"I wasn't talking to you," Walter said, still in the same half-strangled voice. "I was talking to the only member of the crew who seems to have an ounce of sanity left about these matters. Do you agree with this—this—*claptrap*, Dr. Halleck, or do you not?"

"Don't try to divide the crew at this late date," Jazz interjected with a deliberately bored annoyance. "We've got enough problems, getting this mission right."

"I repeat—" Walter began, raising himself to his full five feet six; but Jayvee finally held up a hand and forestalled whatever explosion of wounded dignity and affronted pride might have come next. Abruptly the room became very still.

"I don't feel there's any great danger, myself," he said

slowly. "I don't think it matters much whether we're armed or not because I don't think we'll be attacked. I wish we could go in a little friendlier spirit to the Soviet Union, but my colleagues don't feel that way and I'm outnumbered. But I don't really see that it matters that much, one way or the other."

"Well, I——" Walter said, sounding both angry and deflated. "Well—very well."

"That's how it seems to me," Jayvee said.

After that, the press conference descended to the innocuous and insane level of some of the Apollo conferences, in which the crew was asked questions to which there were no real answers, because the answers were so obvious:

"Do you feel frightened at the thought of your long journey? . . . What would your feelings be if the ascent stage of the MLM doesn't work? . . . What would happen if your food supplies ran out? . . . Do you think you will be bored during the trip? . . . Would you be able successfully to handle an abort? . . . Will you miss your families?"

In one sense, however, these were welcome questions for all their inanity because they defused and de-emotionalized a conference which for a few moments had become quite tense.

After Walter's attempt, no one tried any real needling again. Within fifteen minutes Fortunata called out in her heavy accent a tartly bored, "Thank you gentlemen!" Others echoed it willingly and with a certain air of relief the crowd rose, broke up into argumentative, talkative groups and straggled off to the buses for the ride to the News Center.

There were many wisecracks and wittily sarcastic comments as the buses ground back down into the hectic world of Cocoa Beach in the mild October afternoon. But it was generally if grudgingly agreed that the crew had stood its ground and come off fairly well. Not even Jayvee had broken ranks as strongly as many had hoped he would.

"Will you really be glad to see their cheerful faces again a year from now?" Pete inquired as their special antiseptic van returned them to quarters.

Jayvee smiled with a certain wryness and Jazz said,

"I'd like to plant a few of *them* on Mars and see if they'd mature in two months' time."

"Forget it," Connie advised. "They're our last public chore, and it's over, and now there's nothing ahead but Piffy One. Let's have some good drinks and a good dinner and forget it."

And so they did, not even bothering to turn on the television or read the papers any more to find out how hopeless they were.

The inexorable hours raced ever faster toward the launch that now loomed dead ahead.

6.

Friday at 9 A.M., T minus 24 hours, they took off from Tico Airport (serving Titusville, Cocoa and the Cape) in two jets, Connie and Jayvee in one, Jazz and Pete in the other, and spent two hours flying over Florida. This traditional astronauts' unwinder always makes NASA uneasy, considering the cargo and the disaster to the program that could occur from one slight miscalculation, but long ago the crews fought and won that particular battle. It relaxed them, they said, and they were trained to do it, and so why not? For expensive and highly valuable lives, many millions of dollars and the potential cancellation of the mission rode on those graceful loops and rolls and split-second dartings across the Florida skies. But that was what they wanted to do and they did it, just as the Apollo crews had before them.

They plunged south as far as the Keys, shot over and out into the Gulf of Mexico on the west, roared up to the Georgia line, over to Jacksonville, back down to the Cape; circled the busy pads a couple of times with many deep and unexpressed emotions; zoomed out over the Bahamas as far as the outer Exumas, returned to Tico promptly at T minus 22 hours and taxied smoothly to a stop.

They were met by Bob and Vernon Hertz, who had flown in together to spend the day and have their final Earth dinner with them before returning to Houston for the launch. Both looked noticeably relieved at their safe arrival and Connie could not resist giving Bob an affectionate poke in the arm.

"What's the matter, think we wouldn't make it?"

"Someday somebody isn't going to," Bob said, not particularly amused.

"It'll never happen," Jazz said comfortably.

"You astronauts think you're immortal," Bob remarked. "But you aren't and someday you're going to find it out."

"Not this trip, I hope," Pete said cheerfully. "Vernon, how nice to see you."

"It's nice to be here," Vernon Hertz said. "I know this isn't science's weekend but we like to see the action anyway."

"Oh, yes, it is," Pete said. "Jayvee and I are here to carry the banner for you all the way to Mars."

"How do you feel about it?" Dr. Hertz asked, turning to Jayvee with a sudden shrewd concentration. Jayvee did not meet his eyes directly.

"All right, I guess. The experiments are going to be fascinating. I'm glad of that, anyway."

"And he's set them up very well," Pete said with a quite genuine admiration. "Couldn't be better, in fact. We really ought to bring home some marvelous stuff."

But Vernon Hertz was not to be deflected. He again addressed himself to Jayvee.

"You do think everything is going to go all right, then? You're going to be O.K., yourself?"

"Oh, sure," Jayvee said, an edge of impatience in his voice.

"And you're all going to get along all right?"

"Look, Dr. Hertz—" Jayvee began. But Connie interrupted smoothly before he could go further.

"No sweat," he said cheerfully. "We'll manage, Vernon. Don't worry about it."

"I'm not worried about it," Vernon Hertz said matter-of-factly. "I just wanted to bring it out in the open right here and now. It's probably the last chance."

"Didn't the press go into that enough for you yesterday?" Jazz inquired with a sardonic smile. "We thought they did."

"Not quite," Dr. Hertz said. "I wanted to hear it from you." And again, not intimidated or abashed, possessed of his own dignity and his own strength that were quite unshakable, he said, "Jayvee?"

"Yes!" Jaycee said, as close to anger as past deference permitted. "*Yes,* we will get along!"

478

"Good," Vernon Hertz said crisply. "Because you may have company."

"Oh?" Connie said, instantly sober and attentive, as were they all.

"Come along to the car," Bob said. "He can tell you about it while we drive you back."

"This is Kennedy Launch Control." The familiar voice of Bob Ellison, chief of public affairs at KSC, boomed from loudspeakers at the News Center, little black squawk-boxes in all the news bureaus in Cocoa Beach, intercoms at the Space Center, television sets and radios throughout the world. "We have a report just in from the pads that everything looks good. Everything is proceeding on schedule. All systems are GO at this time. T minus twenty hours, and counting."

"How in the hell we're supposed to wade through this stuff and make something coherent out of it," the *Times* said indignantly, gesturing to the pile of releases, statistical tables, mission reports, crew biographies, Saturn photographs, and the like that covered his desk at the Ramada Inn, "I'm damned if I know."

"Yeah," the *Post* said sympathetically. "It's a mess."

"Why don't we all just print their damned photograph?" the *Times* wondered, holding it up. "It says it all, just the way NASA wants it said."

"The image," the *Post* agreed dryly. "It's amazing how that particular photograph always captures it, every mission. Even Halleck looks happy, for once."

And so he did, in the photograph which did, as the *Post* acknowledged, capture the image every time. There they were again—The Crew—white-suited, festooned with equipment, wearing their shoulder patches (this time three tiny golden ships on a deep blue space ocean, PLANETARY FLEET ONE and their names in a small gold band around the rim) smiling directly into the camera as they stood on the simulated moon surface in the bright sun of Houston: confident, happy, infallible; glamorous, superhuman, serene.

Nothing, one felt, seeing that photograph, could stop them. Nothing could trouble them, nothing dismay. There were no human problems here, no doubts, uncertainties, frictions, despairs. Here no human weakness lived in ago-

479

nizing admixture with strength. Here were heroes, demi-gods, children of legend and keepers of the Grail.

"How can you beat an image like that?" the *Times* mused, not without a certain amount of genuine admiration.

"Yes," the *Post* agreed. "You see that particular photo and you always feel that everything's just *got* to succeed."

"This is Kennedy Launch Control," Bob Ellison said, his voice uniting the Cape, the nation, the world. "All systems are GO, no anomalies are reported, everything looks good for the launch of Planetary Fleet One starting at 9:03 A.M. tomorrow. We are presently starting a built-in two-hour hold at all three pads. This is to allow time for crews to rest and for certain programmed delays in certain circuits of the spacecraft. T minus 18 hours, and holding."

"Ja," Albrecht Freer said to the handsome face on the Picturephone. "Ja, we will have it all exactly as you say. We will be delighted to have you with us."

"You mean I'm forgiven for my shortcomings?" the President asked with a friendly mockery.

"Perhaps," Dr. Freer said.

The President chuckled. Then his face and tone turned serious.

"As a matter of fact, I may have an apology for you when I see you. We've been checking a few things lately. An interesting pattern emerges."

"I hope it will not emerge again at this launch," Al Freer said stiffly.

The President frowned thoughtfully.

"I hope not, too, though I wouldn't put any bets on it. In any event, I assume you'll be prepared."

"Can I have federal troops if I need them?"

The President made him an ironic little bow.

"Anything, Al, anything. But we'll hope they won't be necessary."

"We'll hope so," Dr. Freer said grimly. "Meanwhile, we are taking all possible precautions."

"Good. A great deal depends upon this launch."

"Ja," Albrecht Freer said politely. "It is nice to know that this is realized, finally."

"This is Kennedy Launch Control," Bob Ellison said on

the squawk-box, and conversation stopped, typewriters stopped, broadcasts stopped. "We are midway in our programmed two-hour hold on Planetary Fleet One. All systems are still GO. Everything looks good. T minus 17 hours, and holding."

"Our tour will take us first to the Cape," the blue-uniformed driver of the special VIP bus announced, "and then we will return to Kennedy Space Center."

"I thought they were the same," the wife of the Ambassador of Malawi remarked to the wife of the Governor-General of Canada.

"No, ma'am," the driver explained patiently. "Cape Canaveral is the site of the Mercury, Gemini, Atlas and Thor-Delta launches. It is the spot from which man first entered space in the United States. It is still used for a great many of our scientific unmanned launches. Kennedy Space Center on Merritt Island was developed especially for the Apollo and Argosy programs."

"But you do call the entire area 'the Cape,' of course," the wife of the Governor-General murmured.

The driver smiled.

"Yes, ma'am. Americans are very confusing, aren't they?"

"This is Kennedy Launch Control," Bob Ellison said, and conversation ceased wherever his voice was heard around the globe. "The count has been resumed for Planetary Fleet One. All systems continue GO. Everything continues to look good. T minus 16 hours, and counting."

"I think if you don't mind, Stu," Connie said, "we'll run through both landings one last time."

"Fine with me," Stu said from Houston. "We're ready to dish it out as long as you guys can take it."

"I don't want to give anybody ideas," Pete said over the intercom from the Medico-Scientific mock-up, but it *is* 5 P.M."

"And we have been at this since noon," Jayvee noted.

"What party are *you* late for?" Jazz inquired from the Command-Service mock-up.

"Just one more time," Connie said calmly, "if you don't mind. Then we'll knock it off. After all, dinner won't be served until 7:30."

"This is one hell of a well-trained, well-disciplined and

481

well-exhausted crew," Jazz remarked. "I'm going to ask Chuck Berry to let me have five martinis so I can get a good night's sleep."

"You'll be lucky to get one," Connie told him, "so knock it off. O.K., Stuart, let's go on the first descent."

"Roger," Stu Yule said.

"This is Kennedy Launch Control," Bob Ellison said laconically. "A slight glitch has developed in *Santa Maria* on Pad A but there is no indication of serious trouble. It is being taken care of and all systems are still GO. T minus 15 hours, 30 minutes, and counting."

"We've got to be at the Hilton at 6 for a reception for all the visiting Apollo veterans," the society editor of the Los Angeles *Times* remarked in an exasperated tone. "At the Ramada for the Bendix reception, also at 6. At the Sheraton Hall for the publishers' and broadcasters' reception at 6:30. At the Mousetrap for the joint dinner of the Senate and House space committees, also at 6:30. At the Yacht Club in Melbourne for Perle Mesta's party, at 7. At George's Restaurant for the reception for the Argosy program directors, also at 7. And at the Cocoa Beach Country Club for the Administrator's private dinner for the Vice-President. That's at 7:30. Isn't it nice, how quiet things are at the Cape the night before a launch?"

"Impressive," her colleague from the Miami *Daily News* agreed dryly. "Everybody's praying."

The society editor of the Los Ageles *Times* snorted.

"For another drink."

"That's one prayer the Lord always answers, at the Cape."

"This is Kennedy Launch Control," Bob Ellison said. "The glitch in *Santa Maria* has been corrected. No other anomalies are apparent at this time. All systems continue GO. T minus 15 hours, and counting."

"I see," Percy said cautiously into the Picturephone in his room at the Holiday Inn. "Then the plan is, they're mostly coming in tonight."

"Between midnight and 6 A.M.," Clete said. "No rabble. Big names, just as we talked about last week."

"Good," Percy said.

"Many of them will be in the VIP section," Clete said.

He smiled, a sudden, cruel little grimace. "Will NASA ever be surprised."

"But no violence," Percy said nervously.

"Oh, no. Quite dignified. We've screened out the kooks and the crackpots. This will be done in style."

"You're sure," Percy said, still nervously.

"Absolutely," Clete said with a complacent and self-satisfied air. "I'm in charge. It will go exactly according to plan."

"I'm glad it's your plan," Percy said with a hesitant little laugh.

"It is," Clete assured him with a relish that made Percy, for some reason he could not define, even more uneasy. "It is."

"This is Kennedy Launch Control," Joe Stevenick said, Bob Ellison having gone to the publishers' reception at the Sheraton. "The countdown is proceeding on schedule. No further glitches or anomalies have developed. All systems continue GO. T minus 14 hours, and counting."

"I'm sorry I couldn't eat dinner with the crew," the Vice-President said in his quarters at Patrick Air Force Base three miles south of Cocoa Beach. "I would have liked that."

"Chuck Berry is very severe on that subject," the Administrator said with a smile. "And rightly so: he's got to be sure they don't catch anything at the very last minute."

"Vice-presidential germs are certified pure. Oh, well, I guess I can talk to them on the Picturephone."

"I know they'll appreciate it," Andy Anderson said. "I wonder if the President will call them?"

The Vice-President chuckled.

"He should but he may wait until they get to Mars . . . Isn't it about time for us to leave for this shebang you're putting on for me?"

"About five minutes," Dr. Anderson said. "The country club isn't very far."

"Who-all's coming?"

The Administrator smiled somewhat grimly.

"A good many of the most prominent critics of the program."

The Vice-President gave him an ironic glance.

"They just can't stand not being invited when glamour-time comes, can they? They kick the hell out of us for six months but when the parties and the excitement and the headlines come, they all want to be right in there hogging the spotlight and getting the attention."

"They demand their rights," Andy agreed dryly.

The Vice-President shook his head.

"Human nature," he said. "Human nature! And we think we have something to contribute to the universe. Will *it* be surprised!"

"Oh, I don't know," Dr. Anderson replied with a smile. "Maybe not. Maybe it won't be surprised at all."

"This is Kennedy Launch Control," Joe Stevenick said. "We are beginning another scheduled built-in hold which will last for one hour. All three pads report excellent progress on the countdown. Everything looks very good for the launch of Planetary Fleet One, starting at 9:03 tomorrow. Everything continues GO. T minus 13 hours, and holding."

"Hello, Al," the President said, "sorry to pull you out of your dinner-party, but we've just learned that there *is* a demonstration planned for tomorrow. A sort of high-level peaceful-protest, lie-down-in-front-of-the-VAB sort of thing, I gather. Probably due to start in the VIP section with a lot of prominent people involved."

"Violent?" Dr. Freer asked sharply.

The president shook his head.

"No, apparently not. 'A dignified statement,' I understand it's being referred to by those in the know. Of course, you never know for sure, these things get out of hand sometimes. But I would think normal precautions would be enough. And if I were you I don't think I'd even interfere with it too much. Let them have their little show. It probably won't hurt anything and it will send them home feeling satisfied and self-righteous."

"Ja," Dr. Freer said grimly. "I know these innocent, satisfied, self-righteous demonstrations ... You are making a mistake again!" he said with a sudden unhappy desperation. "You are making a mistake again!"

"No, I'm not, Al," the President said comfortably. "Everything is going to be all right. We'll all be on the alert

484

but I don't think we have to overdo it, that's all. Everything is going to be all right. You'll see."

"Oh, yes," said Al Freer bitterly. "I'll see, all right."

"This is Kennedy Launch Control," Joe Stevenick said. "We have completed our scheduled one-hour hold and the countdown has resumed. Everything continues to look good at all three pads. Everything continues GO. T minus 12 hours, and counting."

"The evidence seems to be quite specific," Vernon Hertz said, leaning back in his chair and staring at them candidly across the table cluttered with the remnants of their last dinner on Earth for a while. "Two new shots of the Cosmos series, which may or may not be killer-satellites, went up from the launch site at Baikonur last night, and at approximately 0900 this morning, their time, a large manned shot was launched from Space Station *Stalin* and put into trajectory for the Moon. So, as I said, you may have company. We hope you will be observed and not molested."

"Yes," Connie said dryly into the silence that followed. "So do we."

"Won't it be like the movies?" Jazz inquired innocently. "If something goes wrong with Piffy One, our good old buddies from the Soviet Union will rally 'round and save us in a great spirit of brotherhood, peace and good will out there in big, bad space?"

"So you want to see a movie," Bob Hertz told him, "go to a movie. Meanwhile, keep your powder dry."

"What powder?" Pete asked softly, and again the silence fell.

"Does the President know this?" Hank Barstow inquired finally.

"Certainly," Vernon Hertz said. "I called him within five minutes of the Baikonur shots and even less, I guess, after the Space Station *Stalin* shot. He knows."

"Then why in the *hell*," Bert Richmond demanded, "doesn't he say something about it and let the world know?"

"It would upset the world too much," Vernon Hertz said dryly. "It would throw a ghastly light on the true state of the Communists' attitude toward us. It would

485

appall the naïve and terrify the country. So why should he?"

"And also," Connie said, "to be fair to him: it *would* get everyone terribly upset and what good would it do, really? There's nothing anyone can do about it now. It's too late to arm the spacecraft. And we can't stop the launch at this late date."

"It could be faked," Hank said. "They could run into some mechanical difficulties on the pads. NASA could find a pretext."

"I'm not so sure I want it faked," Connie said slowly. "We don't *know* there's anything hostile planned."

"It's a fair assumption," Hank told him tartly.

"Sure. But wouldn't you take the gamble, if you were in our place?"

For a moment Hank didn't answer. Then he nodded.

"You haven't got a tube of typhoid germs in your pocket, have you, Chuck?" Pete inquired, extending his arm with a show of humor he didn't really feel. "Jab me, pal!"

"No," Dr. Berry said with an unhappy smile. "I'm afraid I don't. You're all as healthy as bobcats, alas."

"Well, this little bobcat," Jazz said grimly, "is going to take some claws along. I don't know what the rest of you did, but I brought a gun and it's traveling in my personal pack whether NASA likes it or not."

"NASA won't know," Hank said quickly. "Nobody here will tell."

"That's right," Connie said in a tone that brooked no argument. "As a matter of fact, so did I."

"And I," Pete said.

There was a pause while some expression they could not read, ironic, secret, almost desperately amused, crossed Jayvee's face.

"So did I."

"Good," Jazz said. "I don't know what good they'll be in space but at least I feel a little less naked."

"I imagine they can do some damage," Connie said. "Anyway, let's hope and pray we won't have to find out."

"You may not," Vernon Hertz said. "It may be all entirely innocent."

"I hope to God you're right," Bert said grimly, "because if it isn't this world is going to be in one hell of a mess in a damned short time."

"If it knows," Bob Hertz said with equal grimness, and again a silence fell as the thought sank in.

"Yes," Connie said finally with a sigh. "If it knows."

"This is Kennedy Launch Control," Les Martin said, Bob Ellison and Joe Stevenick having gone to bed, to be up at 5 A.M. and back on the job. "Work is progressing satisfactorily and on schedule at all three pads for the launch of Planetary Fleet One starting at 9:03 A.M. tomorrow. A minor wiring difficulty on the *Pinta* has been found and corrected. All systems are GO. The project is GO. T minus 11 hours, 30 minutes, and counting."

"Hi," Jane said on the Picturephone, and despite her best intentions she could not keep the worry from her voice or her eyes. "How are you?"

"Tired," he said. "Desperately tired. But"—he managed a reasonably good facsimile of a confident smile—"ready to go."

"They shouldn't have let you get so tired!" she said indignantly. "What kind of people are they, anyway?"

"You know what kind of people they are and you know what kind of man I am. And Jazz is. And Pete is. And Jayvee. We didn't have to stay in the simulators the past two days. NASA cleared us forty-eight hours ago. Chuck Berry told us to rest."

"So you went back to the simulators," she said. "Really, Conn."

"We rested," he said, his voice becoming lighter and more humorous. "We took the jets and toured Florida and the Bahamas this morning. That rested us."

"And then you went back to the simulators."

"Then," he agreed, "we went back to the simulators. But it's all right: we'll get a fair amount of sleep tonight and be up and roaring at 5 A.M. You know there isn't too much to do at launch, anyway: just sit there and let Saturn give us a kick in the tail."

"Unless something goes wrong. Don't get overconfident, Connie. Please."

"I'm not," he said, sounding suddenly more annoyed than he meant to. "Everything's fine."

"No, it isn't. You're worried about something. Connie, what's wrong?"

"Nothing is wrong!" he exclaimed in an exasperated

487

voice. "For heaven's sake, woman, don't give me the pre-launch heebie-jeebies at my age!"

"You've got them over something," she said, unimpressed. "Don't you want to tell me?"

"Nope," he said, suddenly relaxing into a smile that looked quite genuine. "Nope, I do not. You forgot to pack my long undies, that's all. I can't face the other fellows in the morning without them."

"Connie," she said, in a tone hopeless but loving.

"How are the kids? Are you going to let them say hello?"

"Did you want them to? I thought it might be a little rough on all concerned."

"You're right," he said thankfully. "There's my Mrs. Space Program. Where are they?"

"Monetta offered to keep them and the Weickert kids down in Galveston, so I let her. I thought it was awfully kind of her."

"She is kind. What are you and Clare going to do?"

"Get as much sleep as possible," she said with a wistful little smile, "and then she and some of the girls are coming over and we're all going to have a good cry as you take off."

"That's my girl," he said approvingly. Their eyes met, held, widened. "I love you, baby," he said softly. "Take care."

"I love you, too," she said, her eyes filling. "You take care, too."

And she reached over quickly and snapped off her machine, even as he moved to do the same.

"This is Kennedy Launch Control," Les Martin said. "There has been no repetition of the temporary difficulty on *Pinta*. Work is proceeding on schedule. Everything remains GO. T minus 11 hours, and counting."

"Oh, *boy!*" roared the chairman of the House Science and Astronautics Committee at the Mousetrap. "This has got to be the greatest night of them all!"

"I can't stay a minute longer," the society editor of the L.A. *Times* confided to the science editor of the Philadelphia *Bulletin*, who was hanging amicably on her arm at the Sheraton. "I have to get down to the Melbourne

Yacht Club to Perle Mesta's party, and my *God*, this traffic!"

"You see," one of the younger astronauts remarked earnestly to somebody from the AP at the party in Al and Peggy Bishop's suite at the Hilton, "it isn't that there's any real *favoritism* in Houston. It's just that some of us seem to have to wait longer than others before we're allowed to fly. I don't really know," he added wistfully, "quite why that is. I mean, I *understand* it, but—"

"I think we definitely ought to be ready for Planetary Fleet Two three months from now," one of the Argosy program directors assured the chairman of IBM at George's Restaurant. "We've got the bugs ironed out and the old assembly line is really rolling just like she used to. Yes, sir, give us three months and we'll give you Piffy Two."

"I think you men are just the bravest things!" the wife of the editor of one of the more ubiquitous Southern journals told a politely attentive Frank Borman and Neil Armstrong with great fervor at the Apollo Veterans' reception at the Hilton. "Reely, just the bravest *thangs!*"

"How do we know what's going on up there?" Walter Dobius demanded of Percy Mercy as they sat at table with some sixty others at the Cocoa Beach Country Club, having liqueurs after the Administrator's party for the Vice-President. "We're absolutely helpless down here. NASA can tell us anything they want to. 'All systems GO!' How do we know if they are or not? How can we be sure what's happening behind the scenes? Anderson says everything's fine, the Vice-President says everything's fine, the President comes on the Picturephone and tells us everything's fine, *but how do we know?* We're the prisoners of NASA!"

"My *God*, this *traffic*," the society editor of the L.A. *Times* said to the science editor of the Philadelphia *Bulletin*, who was leaning drowsily against her arm as she tooted impatiently on her horn trying to get out of the Sheraton parking lot into the bumper-to-bumper stream that moved slowly along on both sides of the highway. Horns blared, voices shouted merrily, screams of laughter tore the clear, cool night. "We'll never make it to Melbourne in a million years."

"Don't you worry, honey," he assured her with a loose and happy grin. "All these parties tonight are going to be *going* for a million years. The Cape is having a *ball!*"

"This is Kennedy Launch Control," Les Martin said, his voice muted in the background on half a hundred little black squawk-boxes in half a hundred roaring rooms. "We have had a scheduled change of work crews at all three pads. No anomalies, no glitches, no nothin'. Everything is GO for Planetary Fleet One. Have a ball, you-all. T minus 10 hours, 30 minutes, and counting."

In the hushed quarters at KSC, Jazz had stopped by for a brief final chat; Pete had done the same; Jayvee had passed silently down the corridor, returning a terse, "Good night!" to Connie's cheerful, "Sleep well!"; and now he was getting ready for bed. It was past 1 P.M., they would be roused at 5: little enough time to get the little enough sleep he thought they would all probably manage. Not even silent Jayvee would sleep too well, he imagined, though Chuck Berry had given them all a mild sedative to take upon retiring. There had been something in Jayvee's unyielding back as he watched him turn the corner and disappear to his own bedroom that indicated a quiet but almost feral tension. It was going to be a short and difficult night for them all.

Jazz in particular had seemed unusually upset by his farewell to Clare. Apparently it had been an emotional conversation on both sides. He was still blowing his nose and looking bothered when he stopped by to say good night.

"God damn it, Connie," he said, sitting down on the bed. "How do you do it? I suppose when you've made as many trips as you have it gets to be routine. But I'm not used to it, damn it."

"I suppose one gets accustomed," Connie agreed, halting his leisurely undressing with his shirt half unbuttoned, relaxing into a chair. "But I can't say this one was easy. Nor can I really say it was much like the others."

"Did you talk much?"

"Not much, it's too big. The quicker the better, we both felt."

"I wish I'd done that with Clare," Jazz said morosely. "We talked too long. That's always fatal with a woman."

Connie smiled.

"Especially when you're saying good-by . . . Well, Jazzbo!" he said, reaching over and slapping Jazz' knee with an affection that surprised them both. "We're about

490

to do it, by God! I didn't think six months ago we'd see the day."

"I didn't either," Jazz agreed, less morose and beginning to look excited. "I just can't believe it, Conn: on our way to Mars." Then the excitement faded, he frowned. "What do you make of the damned Russians?"

Connie shook his head.

"I don't know," he said soberly. "I just really don't know. I'd feel happier if they weren't up there, but they are and so we'll just have to see what comes, I guess. I don't think they'd dare try to do anything. But they might."

"They'll dare whatever they think they can get away with," Jazz said tartly. "That's for sure."

"Do you think they could get away with our deaths and the death of Piffy One? I don't."

"If they thought they could," Jazz repeated, "I wouldn't put it past them one minute."

"Well . . . we'll just have to see. Anyway, I'd prefer to think they're off on some mission of their own."

"They tried something funny when Apollo 11 went, I remember, and whatever it was they sent up there crashed on the Moon. And nobody ever really did find out who was *really* responsible for whatever *really* happened to Apollo 13. I don't wish them any bad luck but I hope they have bad luck."

Connie smiled.

"I wouldn't be that bloodthirsty. Let's just hope they go their way and let us go ours, and everybody can be happy."

"I suppose that's the proper Christian spirit," Jazz said with an answering smile. "I'll try. But I'll also keep my little gun in my little pocket."

Connie nodded.

"Oh, yes. No point in fooling ourselves that it couldn't be sticky . . . Jazz," he said, on a sudden impulse he couldn't quite analyze, except that they would be flying in less than ten hours and it seemed a time for closing old wounds, "I'm sorry if we've made you feel over the years that we were giving you the short end of the stick. One doesn't mean to be unjust but I suppose after a time, as things change, any sort of judgment can come to be unjust. Anyway, for whatever part I played in it, I'm sorry."

While he spoke Jazz looked first ironic, then skeptical, then pleased, then touched. When Connie finished, he nodded.

"That's O.K., I suppose you guys try to do what you think is right. I don't always"—he smiled wryly—"agree with it, but—I no longer have to, do I? I'm here—I'm going—it's over—we're crewmates. And that's that, right?"

"Right," Connie said gratefully.

"Old Conn!" Jazz said, with a surprising affectionate kindness of his own. "You have to get everything all lined out just right or you aren't happy, are you? I'll bet I would have been on your conscience all the way to Mars and back if we hadn't had this little talk."

"Probably," Connie acknowledged with a smile. "It's the sort of mind I seem to have."

"Well," Jazz said, getting up and preparing to go, "don't worry. I want our commander to be happy. God knows he has enough on his mind without that old hassle."

Connie held out his hand.

"Thanks, co-commander. I think everything's going to go all right."

"So do I, really," Jazz said, returning the handshake. "In fact"—and suddenly he looked surprisingly young for his thirty-eight years, happy and excited—"I think we're going to have one hell of a flight, Conn. I can hardly wait."

"Try to get some sleep," Connie said at the door. "Take Chuck's knockout pill."

"I'll take it," Jazz said, "but I won't promise it will do me any good. Good night, pal."

"Good night."

But after Connie had closed the door and turned back to the silent room, he found that knockout pills, particularly as mild as Dr. Berry had given them, were not much help. He stripped, brushed his teeth, took his pill, slid naked between the sheets, lay flat on his back, breathed deeply. It took him about three minutes to realize sleep was not going to be seduced that easily.

He got up with an impatient annoyance, wandered into the bathroom, recoiled in exaggerated horror from his own tired eyes in the mirror; wandered back out again, picked up the latest issue of one of the more ubiquitous national journals, blinked at four familiar faces on the cover, turned to the four personal sketches inside which

492

began with that arch sort of two-removes-from-reality with which lives of the prominent are treated in print, threw it aside with a sudden sound of disgust; returned to bed. Five minutes later sleep had still not come: he was, he knew, too tired and too tense—not to fly the mission, and not to be alert for all that would be demanded of him in a few hours, but just to relax into a really restful sleep.

He got up again, put on his shorts and T-shirt, threw on a bathrobe, opened his door quietly, stepped into the hall. There was only one other room in his corridor and while he stood looking at it thoughtfully its door also opened. Pete emerged, also bathrobed, tousled and partially sleepy, but not sleepy enough. He grinned and came to mock attention with a mock salute. Then he threw his door wide with an elaborate bow. Connie smiled and went in, dropping into a chair as Pete closed the door.

"God, I'm tired," he said. "But I just can't seem to get to sleep."

"Me either," Pete said, taking the other chair. "We've got to, though. Morning comes and we must take off like big birds. Didn't you try Chuck's pill?"

"They've always worked before," Connie said, "but not tonight. Too many things riding on this one. Too many things . . ."

"That doesn't sound like our confident, infallible commander."

"Oh, I'm confident enough," Connie said, a surprising little edge coming into his voice. "But I hope I'm not a fool."

"I'm sorry," Pete said, instantly sobered. "I was just kidding."

"I know," Connie said. "You like to kid." Then he smiled apologetically at Pete's sudden crestfallen look. "I'm sorry, Petey," he said gently. "I really am. I really must have the jumps, I guess, to talk to you like that. I'd better go back to my own nest and sit on them."

"No, that's all right," Pete said, though still looking a little stricken. "Stick around for a while, if you like. Might as well. Neither of us is in any mood to sleep right now."

"What do you think about this mission?" Connie asked. "Janie thinks we're jinxed. She always has thought so, from the very beginning. Do you feel that way?"

"N—o," Pete said cautiously. "I've tried not to let that feeling take hold of me . . . although sometimes it's been difficult not to. We have had a lot of tough luck, all right." He smiled a wry little smile. "Poor old Piffy One has earned her way, so far ... The thing that bothers *me* most is this dead weight of hostility from many of our own people that I feel we're carrying with us. But I suppose that can't be helped."

Connie nodded.

"We're a political issue, all right, which I suppose is inevitable when you dare to compete with the Soviet Union, and also when you take a conspicuously large amount of money out of the federal budget. There are lots of people who get exercised on both points. When they can put them together in one big package, they really go to town."

"Doesn't the United States mean *anything* to them?" Pete inquired in a wondering tone. "It's been good to me and my family. It means a lot to us."

"Apparently it doesn't mean so much any more to a lot of people," Connie said soberly. "I still think they're in the minority but some of them are in positions where they can make themselves sound like the majority ... and then of course there had been some others who have been actually, physically, hostile, and have been trying to wreck the mission. I don't know what they've discovered in their investigation at the White House but I'm convinced that there has been actual sabotage of this flight. And there still may be. Which is another reason, I suppose, why it isn't so easy to sleep tonight."

"You aren't afraid, are you?" Pete asked, and suddenly his tone sounded so wistful and he looked so much like an earnest little boy seeking reassurance that Connie laughed with a quick affection and reached across and squeezed his arm.

"No, I'm not afraid. And you're not either. Right?"

"No," Pete said, smiling at himself but nonetheless sounding genuinely relieved. "I'm not. But if I ever thought you were I sure as hell would be."

"Well," Connie said, pleased and touched, "that's very flattering. And I shall try to live up to it."

"I hope so," Pete said more lightly. "By God, I hope so! Say: what about the Silent One? Are we *really* going to get along together, as everybody wants to know?"

"Oh, hell, yes," Connie said with some impatience, not with Pete, but just with the whole overemphasized idea.

"He's settled in O.K. Now that we're completely free of people who keep insisting on asking about it, I don't anticipate any problems. He won't join in the community sings around the campfire in the evenings, I imagine, but he'll be all right."

"And old Jazzbo?"

Connie looked amused.

"We had a tender good night a while ago, brought on by the emotional stress of saying good-by to our wives, and also by worrying about the Russians together. Old Jazzbo is quite softened up from his old prickly self, I think. Piffy One has worked a little good magic, there. All's well."

"And your real problem child?" Pete inquired, turning and looking him straight in the eyes—but, Connie could sense, prepared to run for cover at the slightest hint of rejection. So he made his tone gentle and affectionate, because that was how he felt.

"Hell," he said comfortably. "He's the least of my worries. I count on him. I really do."

For a moment their eyes held. Then Pete smiled and visibly relaxed all over.

"Well, that's *good,*" he said softly. "Now I guess maybe I can get to sleep."

"Me, too," Connie said. He stood up and held out his hand. "Good night."

"Good night," Pete said, returning the pressure. He hesitated. "Thanks for everything, Connie."

Connie shrugged.

"Don't mention it," he said lightly, turning away to the door. "It wasn't anything."

"Oh, yes, it was," Pete said gratefully. "Oh, yes, it was."

"Good night, Petros. Sleep tight."

"You, too, Conn. Good night."

Back in his room he stripped again, got into bed, drew three deep breaths and was dead to the world.

In his room Pete did the same.

The crew slept.

"This is Kennedy Launch Control," Les Martin said at midnight. "All systems for Planetary Fleet One are GO. The mission is GO. Your jolly news staff is going to suspend these bulletins for a few hours, now, and get a little rest. We would suggest you leave your squawk-boxes on throughout the night. We will advise you immediately of any emergency should it arise. Assuming no anomalies, we will suspend these reports until 5 A.M., T minus 4 hours and 3 minutes.

"The crew will be awakened at 5 A.M. They will eat a quick breakfast and suit up. Press buses to take all of you who are interested out to the crew quarters for the walk-out, when they enter the van to go to the pads, will leave the News Center promptly at 5:30 A.M. The walk-out is expected to be at approximately 6:30 A.M.

"That is all at this time. Take a quick nap, everybody. We're going to do the same. See you at 5 A.M.

"T minus 9 hours, and counting."

Along the Strip the traffic continued to roar, at all the parties the swingers and the stragglers kept up their hectic pace. Some sensible souls decided to follow the news staff's example and try to catch an hour or two of sleep. More were too wakeful and too aware of the tumbling moments to bother. T minus 4 hours and 3 minutes would come all too soon: most of the Cape really saw no reason to go to bed. From somewhere someone had resurrected and reissued the big white-on-green buttons RCA had distributed for Apollo 8: "The Cape is GO!" Everywhere in the clear, cool night excitement and tension mounted as the hours raced on toward launch.

"Good morning, children," Bob Ellison said cheerfully at 5 A.M. "This is Kennedy Launch Control. Rise and shine! Drop your clocks and grab your socks! We are about to take you to Mars, courtesy of Planetary Fleet One. Stay with us and you will see it all in real, live, better-than-natural Technicolor.

"We are now at T minus 4 hours, 3 minutes, and counting. The count has progressed without a hitch during the night—'night,' what am I saying!—these last few minutes when we have been catching forty winks—or something.

"Press buses will be leaving shortly from the News Center for those of you wishing to witness the walk-out, which is now definitely scheduled for 6:30. Come one, come all.

"Excuse me if I sound a little exuberant, friends and colleagues, but this is the day.

"This—is—the—day!

"T minus 3 hours, 55 minutes, and counting."

"I must say," Pete remarked, "these are among the best scrambled eggs I have ever had."

"Among the last, too," Jazz told him. "At least for a while. What's the time, Conn?"

Connie smiled.

"It's on the clock on the wall. Also your wrist wacth."

"I know," Jazz said cheerfully. "But I won't believe it until I hear it from you."

"It's time to be going," Connie said. "That's what time it is."

"Yes," said Jayvee, and they were all suddenly somber as they stood and prepared to move along to final medical checkup and from there to the suiting room.

"This is Kennedy Launch Control," Bob Ellison said. "The crew has been awakened after a good night's sleep and has had a breakfast consisting of orange juice, scrambled eggs, bacon and coffee. They are now undergoing medical check and will then suit up. First press buses are leaving right now from the News Center. Please hurry if you wish to witness the walk-out at 6:30 A.M.

"Work on the pads is proceeding satisfactorily. A minor glitch on the *Santa Maria* has been corrected. Oxygen tanks and power systems on all three spacecraft are undergoing final safety inspection. Other systems are performing as planned. The countdown continues with all systems GO at this time. T minus 3 hours and 15 minutes, and counting."

"I don't really mind these ungodly early morning walk-outs," the Chattanooga *Times* remarked to the *Guardian*, "because it gives us a chance to see sights like that. Isn't it spectacular?"

Off to the right as the long line of press buses rolled along NASA Parkway from Cape Canaveral to the Space Center, bathed in spotlights that crisscrossed one another against the pre-dawn darkness, looming quite large from this vantage-point, the three white candles were almost unbelievably beautiful. One Saturn V awaiting launch had always been overwhelming enough. To see three was to approach the border line of what the mind could grasp.

"I wonder," the Chattanooga *Times* said softly, "what

old Tycho Brahe and the rest would say now, if they knew we were going to Mars."

"What would the ancient Chinese say?" the *Guardian* responded. "They invented the rocket. A lot of ghosts are riding with Planetary Fleet One today."

And so they were: the Babylonians who first decided Mars was a planet; Lucian of Samosata, who wrote in A.D. 160 the first rudimentary tale of a voyage to the Moon; the Chinese, who developed the first rockets in A.D. 1232, using them against the Mongols to raise the siege of Kai-Fung-Fu; Nicholas Copernicus, who published *On the Revolutions of Celestial Orbs* in 1543; Tycho Brahe, who made many observations of the positions of Mars in the later 16th Century; Johannes Kepler who based his *On the Motions of Mars* on Brahe's work in 1609; Galileo Galilei who published *Messenger of the Stars* in 1610; the Englishman William Congreve, who in 1801 began to experiment seriously with rockets as weapons; the Frenchman Jules Verne, who wrote *A Journey to the Moon* in 1865; the German Hermann Ganswindt, who designed a primitive rocket-propelled vehicle in 1891; the Russian Konstantin Tsiolkovsky who in 1903 published, *Beyond the Planet Earth* in which he visualized colonization of the other planets; the Romanian Dr. Hermann Oberth, who in 1923 published *The Rocket into Interplanetary Space*, proposing liquid-propellant vehicles; the American Dr. Robert H. Goddard, who first studied a liquid-propellant rocket in 1920 and on March 16, 1926, flew the world's first such successful rocket which was approximately three feet in length, flew two seconds at sixty miles per hour and reached an altitude of forty feet; the Germans, who formed the Society for Space Travel in 1927 and began conducting serious experiments; the Germans who created the V-I and V-II rockets in World War II; the American and Russian governments, who employed their captured German scientists to greatly expand and develop rocketry after the war, and so began their race for space; the brave men who flew in Mercury, Gemini and Apollo, and in the Russian cosmonaut program; the many dedicated and hardworking American men and women since who had devoted so much time, energy and skill to the proposition that at some point not too far off, Planetary Fleet One or something like it should stand ready at the Cape to leave for Mars; and the American people, who paid the bill.

From dreams and beginnings, some of them lost in antiquity, some as immediate as yesterday/today/tomorrow, had come the three bright candles, so majestic in their beauty, so awesome in their power. In the face of the Saturn V, a sight that sobers even the most flippant, wisecracks and sarcasms died in the press buses and upon the occupants an intent and brooding silence fell. This was indeed the day, and now at last its full import and implications were with them, unrelieved and inescapable.

Five minutes later they arrived at the training quarters, debarked, clustered in their jostling hundreds in the wide driveway under the enclosed passageway that links the two buildings on the second-floor level. Now they were talking again, the laughs and jokes and gossip rattling back and forth in a dozen languages. To their right as they faced the lighted hallway and the ramp down which the crew would presently come, the van that carried so many to the pads in the great days of Apollo stood backed up to the entryway in its accustomed place. Engineers and technicians wearing fireproof dust jackets fussed around it, uniformed guards patiently shooed back the over-eager who tried to come too near. Television crews sputtered angrily at one another, individual reporters tried to find vantage points from which to use their personal cameras. Above, early-rising NASA employees looked down from their office windows on the brightly lighted area below. Moment by moment the tension grew.

At 6:15 there was a stir inside the hallway where important-looking people came and went. A familiar figure appeared. Bert Richmond stepped forward to the microphone that had been set up at the foot of the ramp. NBC, as representative for the pooled media, stepped forward.

"Bert," he said, "you've just been with the crew. How are they feeling?"

"They're feeling just fine. Everything is GO. They couldn't be better."

"Did they really get a good sleep?"

Bert smiled.

"I don't know. I didn't sleep with any of 'em. But," he added into the laughter, "from what I've seen of them in the last few minutes, I'd say they were well-rested. They look bright-eyed and bushy-tailed to me."

"Anybody show any sign of nerves, would you say? Are they calm as they prepare to start this great adventure?"

"They look just fine."

"Nobody showing any sign of nerves at all?"

"Well," Bert said, a trifle tartly, "you can't expect them to feel the same as though they were about to go down to Galveston and go swimming. Naturally, I'd say, they're feeling a little tension. Who could help it? But these are trained and experienced men, they've got a job to do, and I wouldn't say they're any more worried than you or I would be. In fact, I'd say a damned sight less. Speaking for myself, anyway. I don't know about you guys."

Again there was laughter and after it NBC put his last question in this standard pre-launch ritual.

"Bert, we know you've got to get back in to help with the suiting-up, but one final question before you go: are you fellows in the Atronaut Office satisfied in your own mind that everything is going to go all right?"

"We're satisfied," Bert said firmly. "Piffy One has had a lot of problems, but they're all straightened out now and we anticipate a very smooth mission all the way to Mars and back. Does that answer your question?"

"As much as it's going to be, I guess," NBC said with a smile. "Thanks very much, Bert. You've been a real help."

"Thank you," Bert said, grinned, waved, turned and went back in.

The pushings and shovings, the jockeyings for postion, the outcries in foreign tongues, the gossip, chatter, tension, began again and steadily increased in volume for the next eight or nine minutes.

Suddenly there was a bustle and stir in the hallway, the telvision floodlights went on, the chatter abruptly stopped. A tensely waiting silence fell. New figures appeared near the doorway, formed a line on each side. Heads turned, looking back along the hallway. From somewhere inside came a burst of applause. People began to smile. Bert Richmond again appeared, walking briskly down the ramp.

"Here they come!" somebody shouted and everyone stood on tiptoe, looked, craned, strained.

"It's Trasker!" someone else shouted, and almost before they knew it the white-suited figures appeared, twice as large as life in their bulky suits, wearing their bubble helmets, smiling, waving, walking quickly down the ramp

500

and into the van. The press burst into spontaneous and prolonged applause that continued until the door slammed firmly shut and the van started up and rolled away, the emblem of Planetary Fleet One on its rear glittering and receding in the floodlights.

"That's quite a spectacle, too," the *Guardian* said to the Chattanooga *Times* as they walked back to the waiting bus that would take them to the Press Site. "They looked reasonably calm and happy, I thought."

"It's a job," the Chattanooga *Times* said.

"They're really quite remarkable, you know?"

"They have to be."

"This is Kennedy Launch Control," Bob Ellison said, his voice booming across the rapidly filling Press and VIP sites. "The crew is in the van on the way to Pad A of Launch Complex 39, where Colonel Conrad H. Trasker, Jr., commander of Planetary Fleet One, will debark to enter the *Santa Maria*, which carries the Mars Landing Vehicle of which he is also commander.

"The van will then proceed to Pads B and C to discharge the remaining members of the crew at their respective Saturn vehicles. We will report their arrivals to you.

"We are informed that the President has arrived at Patrick Air Force Base and will telephone the crew to say good-by when they are assembled at Pad A, approximately fifteen minutes from now. We do not know yet whether their conversation will be broadcast. If it is, we will bring it to you.

"We have a very light overcast, as you can see, but it is expected to dissipate within the hour, giving us excellent visibility for all three launches.

"It looks like a perfect day coming up.

"It is now T minus 2 hours, 23 minutes, 35 seconds, and counting."

Above, a photographers' helicopter recorded their progress as they rode swiftly along through the scrub: and though the van was accompanied by the unusual precaution, duly noted by the media, of a four-motorcycle police escort, it looked curiously small and lonely as it traversed a billion television screens around the world.

It felt lonely, too.

"Somebody say something," Pete suggested finally, opening his visor with a fair attempt at his usual cheerful grin. But the suggestion, though appreciated, did not get very far.

"What's to say?" Jazz inquired, staring at the palmettos, the cirrus clouds, the drainage ditches stagnant and placid along the road. "Hey, there, big bird!" he called out to a Great Blue Heron, standing gravely in the mud. "Happy landings!"

"Do you realize," Connie asked moodily, "that it will be eighteen *months* before we see one of those things again?"

Jayvee grunted.

"Or longer."

"Any longer would be never," Jazz pointed out.

"Yeah," said Jayvee, and there was a silence.

"Well, I'm sorry I couldn't get us all to singing," Pete remarked with a rueful smile. "God knows, I *tried*."

"Don't try," Connie suggested, kicking his foot across the aisle. "Just let it bubble up naturally from inside us."

"Yeah," Pete said. "That'll be the day."

And they all were silent again.

On the world's television screens the white van rolled steadily along. At the Press Site, where a big screen down in front of the stand brought the filming of their progress, the hum and bustle mounted steadily in intensity and volume as more and more buses arrived to disgorge more and more reporters. There were the usual greetings by old friends, the usual short, tense and sometimes bitter tussles over reserved seating space, the usual air of picnic and festivity. An electric excitement, an almost hysterical undercurrent of tension, steadily grew. The clicking of a hundred typewriters, the murmur of a hundred dictating voices, provided sibilant accompaniment.

To their left, a quarter of a mile away, the VAB towered alongside. In front, three miles away, the three Saturns stood on the pads, touched now by the growing light of the sun coming up out of the Atlantic. For a moment a sort of reverse sunset touched the clouds, a great pink flush suffused the sky. Against it the missiles looked white, glimmering, ghostly. Then the sun broke through, the clouds began to drift away, visibility swiftly increased. The missiles emerged sharp and clear, glistening in the dawn, little puffs of liquid oxygen venting from their sides to blow slowly away in the soft, cool wind.

502

Santa Maria was closest, on Pad A; to her left stood *Nina*; then *Pinta*, still further left and farthest away. For a moment a hush fell over the Press Site, before the babble of sounds and voices resumed. Suddenly the enormity of what was being here attempted made its own unchallengeable statement against the quiet Florida sky. "Unbelievable!" the *Guardian* said softly to the Chattanooga *Times;* and so it was.

On the other side of the VAB, at the VIP and Dependents Sites, the hush also fell. Among the VIP's the members of Congress, the foreign dignitaries, members of the President's Cabinet, members of the Supreme Court, the military, chatted and visited with a busy, excited socializing. They too watched the van proceeding on the television screens, they too were awed by the majestic missiles as they came into full view. And to their ranks, too, more hundreds were added every few minutes as new buses rolled up and deposited their cargo.

Among these were many of the famous and influential of the world and many of the powerful of America. The newsmen who had been assigned to cover the VIP Site reported them as they arrived, noting with some puzzlement that Percy Mercy, who might normally be expected to sit with the press, had chosen this time to accept the VIP badge offered, with a certain irony, by the Administrator of NASA. Along with him came Senator Kennicutt Williams, Clete O'Donnell, and the publisher of the *Post*. Other Right Thinking folk hovered near. And everywhere throughout the stands, as Clete could see when he stood up for a moment and surveyed the gaily dressed crowds to his right and left, were others, by whom his presence was noted with a little private stirring, a secret electricity through the stands.

But presently Clete sat down. He and Percy embarked upon a long and earnest conversation. The moment passed. At the empty presidential box, two sections over, police and Secret Service stood warily at ease, eying the crowd. Nothing they could see gave them cause for worry. The clouds continued to dissipate, the three stately spires of Planetary Fleet One gleamed ever more brightly in the sun. From time to time, the liquid oxygen vented and blew gently away.

"This is Kennedy Launch Control," Bob Ellison informed the world, and conversation muted to hear his words. "As you can see from your television screens, the van has now arrived at Pad A. First man out is Dr. Halleck, followed by Dr. Balkis and Commander Weickert. There is Colonel Trasker, just getting out ... The crew is greeting members of the launch group at Pad A ... In just a moment they will go into the bunker where they will be placed in Picturephone contact with the President of the United States. This conversation will not, repeat NOT"—there was a loud, indignant groan from the press stand—"be broadcast. This is at the direct request of the President. We do not know yet whether a transcript of their remarks will be available at the News Center after the launch, but since the President has requested privacy, it would seem likely that no such transcript will be available." This time the groans were mingled with boos. "Here in the firing rooms, the launch vehicle test teams are keeping a close eye on the status of propellants aboard the three vehicles. All look good at this time. All systems remain GO, in some cases we are as much as ten minutes ahead of countdown in procedures on the pads. Everything looks very good for the launch of Planetary Fleet One, starting at 9:03 A.M. today. It is now T minus 2 hours, 8 minutes, 46 seconds, and counting."

"Well, gentlemen," the President said. "Here we are."

"Yes, sir," Connie said with a smile. "Ready and waiting."

The shrewd, intelligent eyes examined them slowly and carefully: they felt for a moment like little boys in school. Then he smiled too.

"You seem quite relaxed about it. I wish I were."

"We aren't completely," Jazz said, "but one of our classes at MSC is 'Outward Calmness, Apparent Fearlessness and Graceful Dissembling.' We all passed with straight A's."

The President chuckled.

"They have one like that for Presidents, too. I got the same grade. I think you can rest assured," he said, suddenly grave, "that nothing is going to interfere with the launches. There may be some small demonstration of some sort, probably centered around the VIP Site, but we have exercised every precaution known to man to maintain security on the pads and check out the vehicles.

You know all that, of course, but I just wanted to reaffirm it. Whatever happens in the crowd will be taken care of; don't worry about it. Out there on the pads you won't even know it's happening."

"What about you, sir?" Pete asked. "Are you going to be all right?"

The President nodded.

"Oh, yes. There are plenty of extra guards and a lot of plainclothesmen scattered through the stands. I'll have the usual security, multiplied by ten. And anyway—I don't really think this thing is going to be very much, if it happens at all. Our old friends Clete O'Donnell and Percy Mercy and some of their pals are planning a little protest for the record but that will be about the extent of it, I think."

"It doesn't worry you," Connie said.

"No," the President said. He smiled, "As a matter of fact, it's probably a good idea. Lets them blow off steam, shows the rest of the world we still have free dissent, looks good politically—what more can you ask?" The smile vanished and a grim expression touched the eyes and the strong, determined jaw. "After it is over, Mr. Clete O'Donnell is going to be arrested and taken to federal prison to await trial as a Communist agent, spy and traitor."

"No!" Jazz said into the silence that followed. "Then it's true."

"It is true," the President said. A cold tone that bespoke his power and his anger came into his voice. "And he will pay for it."

"But meanwhile," Connie ventured to state, "he will be allowed to demonstrate and perhaps—"

" 'Perhaps' nothing," the President said in the same cold voice.

"Mr. President—" Pete said, and stopped. "I hope you're right," he added finally.

"Everything's ready," the President said flatly. "Don't worry about it. Now: to end on an up-beat: Planetary Fleet One has been a long time reaching this day. In less than two hours Connie will be flying and in three you will all be gone. The hopes, the pride, the prayers and, I think, the hearts, of most of your countrymen, go with you. Certainly that is true of me. If I have appeared to let you down at any stage of the way, it has not, I think, affected

505

my over-all support for the mission and my basic determination to see it a success. Time will tell whether my decisions have been right. Time, and your own natures—which now, even more than the hardware, hold the key to the fate of Piffy One. I have chosen you, I am sending you. I do not think you will let me down."

"Thank you, Mr. President," Connie said gravely. "That leaves just one question unresolved."

"That's right," Jazz agreed.

Pete nodded.

"What about the Russians?"

"I was on the hot line this morning," the President said, "with the Soviet Ambassador by my side, just for good measure. I told the Chairman that if there was any interference from these new launches we would react in the most definite and most effective ways open to us. That's about as far as one goes in this day and age."

"What did he say?" Jazz inquired.

"Nothing. But I think he got the message."

"We hope you're right, Mr. President," Pete said.

"So do I," the President agreed, somewhat tartly. "If not, then I am prepared to follow through on it. What more is necessary?"

"Fair proof and a lot of evidence," Connie said crisply. "You can't act without it."

"That's right," the President acknowledged. "Bring home all you can find."

"We'll try," Jazz said dryly, "but it may not be easy."

"Anyway," the President said, making his tone deliberately lighter, "what the hell are we all talking about? Nothing's going to happen and we know it. They'll peek and pry, you'll have to expect that, but they won't dare do anything. So stop worrying about it and get back to work." His face became cordial, impersonal, official. "We will all be watching and we will all be proud."

"Thank you, Mr. President," Connie said formally. "We appreciate your confidence and your good wishes and your continuing support."

"God bless, God speed, and come safely home," the President said.

"This is Kennedy Launch Control," Bob Ellison said. "The President has concluded his farewell to the astronauts and Colonel Trasker is now ascending the elevator to enter the command module of *Santa Maria*. We are definitely informed that there will be no transcript of the presidential conversation. Sorry, but that's orders from the big boss, and we don't argue. The van is now proceeding, as you can see on the television screens, to Pad B, where it will deposit Commander Weickert to enter the *Nina*, and from there to Pad C where Drs. Halleck and Balkis will debark to enter the *Pinta*. Everything is proceeding smoothly. Final checks of cabin pressure, guidance systems and emergency detection systems will begin on *Santa Maria* as soon as Colonel Trasker is inside. Colonel Trasker and the launch control crews will be engaged in these check-outs for approximately the next half-hour to 45 minutes. We are now at T minus one hour, 53 minutes, 16 seconds, and counting."

He walked out along the red-painted metal cat walk toward the command module, conscious of the expanse of land and sea stretching away as far as the eye could follow. Far below the VAB looked tiny. Tinier still, the Press, VIP and Dependents' Sites swarmed with little dots yet tinier. When he reached the platform in front of the small "white room" through which he would enter the capsule, he stopped for a moment, so abruptly that Gaudy Gaudet, just behind, almost bumped into him. He turned deliberately and looked east across the placid Atlantic, north along the scrub to the empty beaches, south past the edge of the giant missile to the gantries of the Cape, west across the flatland leading on over Florida, the Gulf of Mexico, Houston, El Lago, the Pacific, the world. From some forgotten reach of college memory a fugitive line came back: "Look thy last on all things lovely. . . ." Impatiently he shook his head and told himself not to be a damned fool. Gaudy touched his arm with a sympathetic smile, he nodded and smiled back, turned and entered the white room. White-suited, white-helmeted figures clapped him on the back, assisted him into the module, strapped him down. Gaudy gave his shoulder a final squeeze, stepped back. The hatch closed, the bolts shot home.

"Good morning, Conrad," said Stu Yule from Houston.

"Connie," said Firing Room I in the VAB, "let's get right to those check-outs, O.K.?"

"Roger," said the machine, and land, sea, family and philosophy vanished as though they had never been. Now

507

there was nothing at all, anywhere in the universe, except the knobs, panels, buttons and blinking lights directly above his face as he lay on his back in the capsule.

"This is Kennedy Launch Control," Bob Ellison said. "Colonel Trasker is now engaged in checking out command module systems in the *Santa Maria*. Commander Weickert has been delivered to *Nina* on Pad B and is about to begin the same procedures. The van, as you can see on the screens, is just depositing Dr. Halleck and Dr. Balkis at *Pinta* on Pad C. They will proceed directly to the command module and will immediately begin the same procedures for their vehicle. For the better part of the next hour these routine check-outs will be proceeding in each of the three modules. Meanwhile, we have been informed from Patrick Air Force Base that the President is boarding his helicopter at this moment for the flight to the VIP Site. We understand he wishes to circle the pads before proceeding to the site. We expect his arrival at the site in about 15 minutes. We're coming up on T minus one hour, 45 minutes, 23 seconds, and counting."

"You understand," Albrecht Freer said on the Picture-phone, "there must be *absolutely no slip-ups*."

"I understand," the director of security said. "We have everything covered, Al, I don't think you need to worry. We began helicopter patrol of the beaches and all approaches at 0600, the Navy sweeps of the sea and coastline have been going all night, the undersea radar screen is reporting all clear all along the coast, we have heavy guards everywhere, security on the pads is airtight"—he took a deep breath—"and in addition to all *that*, we have the Secret Service, the FBI, and a thousand special police in case there really is a demonstration. So! I would say we're pretty well covered."

"Pretty well," Dr. Freer said dourly, "is not always enough."

"So there are kooks among us," the director of security said, somewhat desperately. "You said yourself we can't keep an eye on every crazy man in the world."

"Try harder," Dr. Freer suggested firmly. "There must be *no slip-ups*."

"Yes, sir," the director of security said glumly. "I don't see any signs of any, anyplace."

508

Nor, surveying the happy, excited throngs that now filled the Press, VIP and Dependents' Sites as the minutes ticked steadily away toward launch, was there any visible reason to think the director of security was mistaken.

"Everytheen is lively and bright and exciteen," said CBS' veteran space expert. "This is a happ-py day." And so it appeared to be.

Now as the sun moved higher the clouds had entirely gone. The cool little winds of autumn had faltered and died and vanished. The temperature rose, not humid, not oppressive, a comfortable 72 degrees that made everyone feel pleasantly invigorated. Even the many exhausted veterans of the past week's social whirl seemed somehow to have found a second wind: their lively cries of greeting and exultation filled the air.

At the Dependents' Site, the kids of NASA and the press trampled up and down across the grassy, marshy ground until the area began to look like the livestock section of a county fair. Mothers cried out in admonition, impatience and alarm. Offspring screamed defiantly and happily back. Elders disapproved of youngsters and youngsters, alive with an excitement many barely understood but all enjoyed, ignored them. But the sounds of their exchanges, while raucous, were essentially amicable: it was, as CBS remarked, a happy day.

At the Press Site, in these final minutes before Planetary Fleet One became reality at last, the mood also was amicable and excited. The chatter of knowledgeable voices, the clatter of typewriters, the ringing of telephones, blended in a busy high-pitched uproar. The competing prima donnas of the program held forth in their respective areas: Fortunata keeping her countrymen in stitches, the British contingent puffing on their pipes and peering about, the West Germans dictating industriously to Bonn, the Japanese clicking and clicking, the Russians smiling and smiling, the Americans joking and joking. But for the moment, at least, the jokes were not bitter and the comments, in many languages, were not hostile. A launch always works its own magic on the media: it is an event too magnificent and overwhelming for pettiness to linger long in its shadow. Even the most snide and carping have to pause and concede. They may resume as soon as the missile has finally disappeared down-range but there is a period of an hour or two when they are silenced. They become as eager and excited as anyone.

So it was that when Bob Ellison came on the loud-speaker at T minus one hour, 45 minutes, to announce the President's impending arrival and the departure of buses from the Press Site to the VIP Site, there was a general noisy exodus. Ten minutes later more than half the media were at the VIP Site, busily greeting friends, noting names, buttonholing for hasty interviews that would probably be lost in the fantastic volume of coverage this day, but still had to be done for the record.

Clete O'Donnell, for instance, to the Chicago *Sun-Times*:

"All Americans must wish Planetary Fleet One well. I still could wish that our government had seized the opportunity for genuine space co-operation with the Soviet Union. I would feel much better about the success and purpose of the mission."

Percy Mercy, to the San Francisco *Chronicle*:

"We must all pray for the success of the mission, and we must also hope that once the government has proved to its own satisfaction that it can perform this kind of space adventure, it will then turn to America's own pressing domestic needs and give them the priority they deserve."

Senator Kenny Williams, to the Seattle *Times*:

"Naturally I hope it succeeds, since the Administration is so determined to do it. But we in Congress will have to examine very closely from now on any further requests for things that are essentially just space-stunts. Any further explorations must be undertaken with the Russians, it seems to me, and they must not drain funds from domestic needs that are far more important and far more pressing."

But these were rather rare criticisms, the media found, and actually quite mild. Most of the comments they received were enthralled, enthusiastic, encouraging. Therefore they were quite unprepared for the event which swiftly followed.

It began soon after someone shouted, "There he is!" and a large Air Force helicopter began to spin gently down toward the open field in front of the VIP Site. Everybody in the stands stood up, Clete O'Donnell per-

510

haps a fraction of a minute ahead of the rest, raising his arms above his head as though in an elaborate stretch. Then he lowered his arms, was lost to view among the thousands all around. The helicopter continued to settle gently down.

Its door opened, two Secret Service men got out and came down the steps. The Vice-President appeared in the door and waved: applause and cheers rolled up. He too came down the steps. There was a pause. The President appeared in the door and waved. Again the applause and cheers roared up. He too came down the steps. Somewhere to the right along the stands, a sudden movement began, so swift and well-organized that its participants were on the field and running toward the helicopter before the unsuspecting knew they were there.

"This is Kennedy Launch Control," Bob Ellison said. "The countdown on all three pads continues to go very satisfactorily at this time. The close-out crew in the white room on *Santa Maria*, which has been aiding Colonel Trasker, has been advised by the spacecraft test conductor that they can move out. After they depart, swing-arm 9 of the umbilical tower, the arm that goes from the tower to the command module, will be swung back about 5 feet from the hatch. Once this is accomplished, we will arm the pyrotechnic systems in the spacecraft so in the event of a possible catastrophic condition in the launch vehicle below him, the astronaut can fire the escape rocket and separate from the vehicle. The positioning of the swing-arm 5 feet away is also an emergency measure, so that, if there were sufficient time in an emergency, it could be swung back into place, the astronaut could exit back to the umbilical tower, jump in to the aerial tramway and be carried safely down to the underground bunker. The close-out crew are leaving the 10- and 20-foot levels on *Santa Maria*, and all systems are GO at this time, T minus one hour, 15 minutes, 23 seconds, and counting.

"We are advised that the President has now arrived at —*what? What?* Ladies and gentlemen, we are advised that there is some difficulty at the VIP Site. Ladies and gentlemen, stay where you are! *Stay where you are!* Do not try to go to the VIP Site! Do not try to go to the VIP Site! *Stay where you are! Stay where you are!*"

At first, so innocent is the normal American mind in the Age of Psychotics, most of those in the VIP stands were simply unable to grasp the fact that a rapidly growing mob was actually trying to hurl itself, with an intent which was not yet apparent, upon the presidential party. When the knowledge sank home—verified by angry howls from the racing mob, the appearance of red flags and banners damning Piffy One, the first explosions of Mace and tear gas as the special police and Secret Service began to react—decent men and women began to shout and scream, adding their noise to the rest. The media, running frantically up and down trying to see, trying to report, trying to broadcast and photograph, compounded the confusion. For at least ten minutes, as a hastily formed line of police fought to hold back the shoving, screaming, foul-mouthed demonstrators, it was not clear what was actually happening. All anyone knew for sure was that horror had been unleashed on a day that had been happy but was happy no more.

At the vortex the President and Vice-President, giving one another a brief glance that held not fear but an immense anger, obeyed the tersely shouted commands of the Secret Service and stooped down behind the protective circle of agents that immediately formed around them. They could see almost nothing, and for them the demonstration was a surging—retreating—surging—retreating—surging—wall of sound.

In the mob itself, the front ranks appeared to be composed of the young, suckers as always for the colder and more ruthless minds that formed the rear echelons. From their mouths came the mindless gibberish that passed for thought in their privileged circles, while from behind them their encouraging colleagues tossed rocks, bricks, and the first small bomb, which landed at the feet of an FBI agent and was promptly seized and hurled away into the open field, there to harmlessly explode. Following it came two sputtering sticks of dynamite which were also tossed away. Off to the left, the helicopter started up and although a small section of the mob broke away and raced toward it, it was airborne before they could reach it.

Behind the mob, sufficiently far back to guarantee a reasonable safety, there marched a long, thin line of famous and distinguished people: the president of Yale and the president of Harvard; the poor, pathetic baby-doctor, lost in the anguish of a world he helped to make; the notable archbishop whose social conscience was just too big for his cloth; the insane old ninny who had ruined half a million young lives with LSD; the dreadfully liberal and enlightened auto manufacturer, just back from signing a new deal with Moscow for tanks to kill Americans; the wealthy widow who gave her all, in money and in kind, for anti-American causes; many others of similar nature, character and intelligence; Frankly Unctuous; Walter Dobius; Percy Mercy. And Clete O'Donnell.

Far off there came the sounds of rapidly nearing sirens; out from the VAB came running hundreds of armed guards; valiantly around the presidential party the police and Secret Service fought back. Above, the helicopter moved into position and began scientifically and rapidly bringing the battle to a close.

From one end of the mob to the other it swung. From its open doors the Secret Service men still aboard tossed down cannister after cannister of tear gas. In three minutes' time the mob was broken; in five, its forward members turned and began to run, abandoning their ammunition or hurling it wildly away. Hysterically they screamed, frantically they pushed; now their good friends of the rear ranks were overtaken and tumbled by their desperate onsurge toward escape. And in the field that had been behind them but was now in front, famous and distinguished ladies and gentlemen turned and began running too; one of them, as it developed, not quite carefully enough.

From the helicopter above, his small drama had a certain ironic slow-motion about it as he ducked and dodged and twisted. His whole life had been a fiction of his own devising. Now it concluded with the simple inevitability of a children's primer.

See that funny man.

Who is that funny man?

His name is Clete.

Clete is clever.

Clete hates his country.

Clete wants to destroy his country.

Clete thinks he can destroy his country without being destroyed himself.

See clever Clete!

Look at clever Clete go!

513

What is wrong with clever Clete?
Clete is afraid.
Clete is running.
Run, Clete, run.
See Clete duck.
See Clete dodge.
See Clete blanch.
Hear Clete scream.
Watch clever Clete now.
Clete be nimble, Clete be quick, Clete jump over the dynamite stick.
OOOPS.
Poor Clete.

"This is Kennedy Launch Control," Bob Ellison said, breathing hard. "The riot at the VIP Site has ended. Repeat, the riot at the VIP Site has ended. There has been at least one death and possibly more. We have reports of more than a dozen wounded. They are being removed by ambulance to the hospital in Cocoa. Origin of the disturbance is not known but it was apparently a protest against the flight of Planetary Fleet One. The area has been cleared. Repeat, the area has been cleared. Everything is under control. The disturbance is over. Press buses are boarding at the VIP Site immediately for return to the Press Site. Please board the press buses immediately for return to the Press Site.

"We have passed the sixty-minute mark in our countdown procedures for *Santa Maria* on Pad 3. Countdown procedures are proceeding normally on Pads B and C for *Nina* and *Pinta*. Colonel Trasker has completed a series of checks on the service propulsion system engine that sits below him in the stack. We want to assure ourselves before liftoff that the engine can respond to commands from inside the spacecraft. As Connie Trasker moved his rotational hand controller, that engine did respond by swiveling or 'gimballing.' A series of radio frequency and telemetry checks are now in process for *Santa Maria*. The tracking beacons in the instrument unit that travels as a guidance system for the Saturn V during the powered phase of flight will also be checked. All systems of all vehicles remain GO at this time. Please return to the Press Site. It is now T minus 56 minutes, 24 seconds, and counting."

"Connie," Stu Yule said quietly, "someone wants to talk to you."

"Is it vital?"

"I'm not vital," she said somewhat shakily, "I'm Jane. Are you all right?"

"Oh, hi. Sure, I'm O.K. Why?"

"There was a bad riot at the VIP Site. They think Clete O'Connell was killed."

"Oh?" he said, thinking, *Serves the bastard right.* "Is the President safe?"

"Yes, they didn't reach him. Connie—be careful."

"Listen," he said, amused but affectionately so, "I'm safer up here on top of this bird than anybody on the ground today. Stop worrying."

"I'm trying not to," she said, "but there's been so much —so much."

"Almost over, now," he said; and then, more briskly, "Honey, I've got to get back to work."

"I know. I'm sorry. Everybody here has been so kind. Take care of yourself."

"I will," he said. "I'll be talking to you as soon as we're docked. We'll all be talking."

"Yes, I know, I'll be patient."

"That's my girl," he said. "Stuart?"

"Roger," Stu said. "Run through that last sequence again, will you?"

"This is Kennedy Launch Control," Bob Ellison said, "coming up on T minus 45 minutes, 51 seconds, and counting. We're proceeding with routine checks on *Nina* and *Pinta*, some twenty and forty minutes, respectively, behind the schedule on *Santa Maria*, which of course will launch first. On board *Santa Maria*, Colonel Trasker has been working with the spacecraft test conductor on setting up proper switch settings in preparation for pressurizing the reaction control system. These are the big thrusters on the side of the service module—sixteen of them in four quadrants around the service module. The launch-vehicle people are also keeping an eye on the status of various propellants aboard the Saturn V launch vehicles. At liftoff, we will have each vehicle weighing close to six and a half million pounds on the launch pad. There are now more than one million gallons of propellants aboard the three stages of each of the three Saturn V's. The report

515

here is that the propellants are stable. They did look a little while ago at the RPI on the *Santa Maria*, the high-grade kerosene fuel that's used in the first stage of the Saturn V, to make sure it was at top level. We check out these things with the aid of computers which give us an overall look at the general status. We are now at T minus 40 minutes, 10 seconds, and counting."

He did not know how he had come to be where he was, standing in front of the President in the presidential box between two Secret Service men. All he knew was that it took all his powers of concentration to focus on the stern and unsmiling face before him, and to understand the words that issued from it.

"Sit down, Percy," the President said, not unkindly, gesturing the Secret Service away. "I think you and I better have a little talk. Are you all right?"

"Yes," he managed to say, though his head ached dreadfully and his stomach felt as though seven sailors had it tied in seven knots. "I believe I am."

"You don't look very well," the President observed, studying his profile carefully. "But perhaps," he added, more grimly, "that is a rudimentary form of justice. I understand you were near Clete O'Donnell when he died."

"Yes," Percy said, very low, as the horror of that dreadful moment came rushing back.

"That, too," the President said, "was justice."

His companion looked absolutely shocked, so much so that for a second it blotted out horror and permitted the old arrogant Percy to revive.

"How can you say such a thing!"

"I'll tell you," the President said. "It's an instructive tale, and one I want you to understand. It has been helpful for me, and I hope—*I hope*—it will be for you. He paused and then leaned closer, speaking with a deliberately cold curiosity. "Did he make any outcry when he died?"

As he had known it would, this brought back the horror. Percy shriveled away again, his voice unsteady, his hands trembling, his eyes haunted.

"Just the one word, 'No!'" he said, almost whispering. "Just—'*No!*'"

"Fitting," the President said in a musing tone. "Fitting.

516

He said *No!* to everything good in America, maybe *No!* was the right word for him to go out on."

"How can you be so cruel?" Percy asked, still barely audible.

"How could he be so cruel?" the President inquired. "He never showed any mercy to anyone, Al Freer, Stu Yule, or anybody who got in the way of what he believed in, over all these years. Why didn't he deserve cruelty in return?"

"But he was a *human being*," Percy protested, dimly aware that somewhere in the distance a band was playing patriotic airs, the crowd was chattering again now that the tension was beginning to ease.

"No, he wasn't," the President said. "He was a machine, a time bomb planted in the middle of us. He gave up humanity a long time ago, Percy. He thought humanity was composed of fools. Including you and me. And he was right, too. That's what we've been."

"In what way?" Percy asked, a stubborn, if battered, skepticism showing through.

"Because we refused to believe he was an active Communist agent," the President said, "when he was, every minute of his waking life from age nineteen."

"I don't believe you," Percy said, with a little of the old defiance. But the President lowered his voice and spoke in a hard, hammering tone.

"Listen to me, Percy. This time you are to believe what I say to you, because it is the truth. The time has come for you to stop being a fool, now. An evil and worthless man has died as he deserved to die, and you will listen to me, and you will understand, because it is important for your education and your country that you do so. All right, Percy?"

"I don't see what," Percy began, sounding increasingly stubborn, "what this has to do with—"

"It has everything to do with you," the President said, "because you and I, Percy, represent the fools of the earth who have been in charge of national affairs and public opinion while all the Cletes of the earth have been coming to power. They came to power for many reasons, but basically, Percy, they came to power because we just couldn't bring ourselves to believe that *they always meant exactly what they said*. We liked them, or we found them

517

plausible or justified in some way, and so we couldn't believe. We just couldn't believe.

"Percy!" he said, and he placed his hand on Percy's arm with a grip so powerful Percy winced with pain, while below the edge of the box, reporters and spectators craned curiously at the spectacle of their muted but obviously intense conversation. "I want you to understand, so listen carefully.

"Clete O'Donnell was a Typical American Boy, Radical Division, Later Twentieth Century. He had a 'very liberal teacher' in high school who had a great influence upon him; he had several more at the University of Michigan who carried on the good work. He soon concluded—because that was what he was taught—that the United States was an evil, hypocritical, imperialistic, oppressive, race-ridden society which simply had to be changed to suit the idealistic concept his teachers appeared to advocate. By age nineteen he was ready to become the formal servant of the iron imperialism that lay behind the idealism and used the idealism for its own monstrous ends: this his 'very liberal teachers' did not tell him about. But it didn't matter, because by that time he was ready for it, and conditioned to be monstrous himself."

He paused and looked about thoughtfully at the gaily decorated stands, the excited crowd, the extra cordons of police who now stood all about the area.

"Quite an analysis," Percy said. "Were you there,"

"No," the President conceded. "I came along a little earlier. But all of this is documented, as it is in thousands of other cases. The FBI—"

"The FBI!" Percy interrupted with a growing scorn.

"See that tarpaulin down there?" the President asked, gesturing toward it. "That covers his blood on the grass, Percy. And more. A good deal of what's left of him is still under there, waiting to be scraped up after the crowd goes home. Better pay attention to my tale of the Typical Revolutionary American Boy who found his typical revolutionary ending, Percy. You might learn something.

"So: the FBI has found that he joined the Communist Party, indirectly, through one of its so-called 'New Left' student branches, when he was nineteen. For a time he was involved in the extremely violent sector, the SDS and the Weathermen; then he got smart and dropped out of it. About the time his mentors decided he was capable of

518

really skilled subversion, he knew he was too. By mutual agreement he turned respectable.

"After that he was underground and aboveboard simultaneously. Aboveboard we all know his brilliant record, Percy: you yourself have written many an editorial in support of it, haven't you? The dynamic young labor leader—the active supporter of proper causes—the intimate of presidential dynasties—the enthusiastic campaigner for worthy political candidates—"

"Including you!" Percy snapped with a returning asperity.

"Including me," the President agreed calmly. "Clete was really one of us, wasn't he? Everybody loved Our Clete, and nobody—but nobody—except a few soured old skeptical conservatives—could ever possibly imagine that he might be a deadly enemy of his own country. But we had the signs, Percy. And we refused to believe. That was *our* crime: *we refused to believe.*

"And so on a wave of our scornful laughter and our fervent support he swept through America quietly doing all the damage he could, until the day when it was decided that he must keep his date with Planetary Fleet One. On that day, though he did not know it, his death warrant was signed. And for that, I think"—and the President's eyes returned again with a thoughtful gaze to the tarpaulin, guarded by four policemen, on the grass— "America has reason to rejoice."

"How can you say such a thing?" Percy demanded, so shocked he could hardly articulate. "What kind of Christian charity is that?"

"About what he gave to his enemies," the President said. His expression became ironic. "But don't get me wrong, Percy. I haven't said this in public. I've already issued a statement deploring the death of this fine young man and defending the right of peaceful dissent in this country. I *have* taken the occasion to point out that when dissent is *not* peaceful it can sometimes get out of hand and destroy its creators. But I have done the proper thing about Clete in public."

"And will you disclose the FBI report to the public?" Percy asked in a waspish tone.

"No," the President said blandly. "What good would it do? The man is dead, he has paid for what he did—"

"And to expose him would be to embarrass you politically and lose you votes," Percy interrupted with a spiteful triumph. "And you don't want that, do you?"

"Do you, Percy?" the President inquired calmly. "Consider the alternative."

For a while there was silence, while the excited hum of the crowd grew ever louder and the minutes raced away. Finally Percy spoke.

"Is that all you wished to say to me, Mr. President? May I go now?"

The President nodded.

"Certainly. Just remember the tale of Clever Clete, though, will you? Let it give you a little skepticism about things, Percy. Let it humble you a little, if that's possible. Let it help you grow up. Think about it next time you write an editorial."

"I shall write an editorial along exactly the lines you suggest, Mr. President," Percy said, and his tone was cold and once more self-possessed as he stood up. "It will praise Clete and it will deplore violence. What more can you ask?"

"I ask that you believe the truth about him and learn from it," the President said with equal coldness.

Percy smiled, a bleak and hostile grimace.

"Why should I, when you aren't yourself?"

And without waiting for the answer which might, or perhaps might not, have come, he turned on his heel and left the presidential box.

"This is Kennedy Launch Control," Bob Ellison said, back in the simpler and more innocent world of NASA. "We are now coming up on T minus 26 minutes, 16 seconds, and counting. All systems in all vehicles are GO at this time. We are still in excellent shape for launch. We have just completed a key test in Firing Room I for *Santa Maria*. The launch-control people have made some final checks of the destruct system aboard the three stages of the Saturn V launch vehicle. In the unlikely event during flight that the vehicle might stray violently off course, the main safety officer could take action to destroy the vehicle, which would obviously occur after the astronaut was separated by his escape tower from the faulty vehicle. The check has shown that the signal would come through correctly. We have also checked downrange with Department of Defense support vessels and planes and they are also in readiness should such an emergency procedure be necessary. Everything continues to look good at T minus 22 minutes, 18 seconds, and counting."

"O.K., *Santa Maria*," said Firing Room I. "The crew has its circuit."

"Roger," Connie said, his world bounded by the small cluttered circumference of the command module, the little lights blinking and glowing above his face. "Gee, you guys, this is a thrill. I didn't know you cared."

"Immensely," said Jazz from *Nina*.

"Immeasurably," said Pete from *Pinta*.

"How you doing?" asked Jayvee from *Pinta*, not effusive but at least civil.

"I'm doing fine," Connie said comfortably. "How about you guys?"

"Twenty minutes behind you here," Pete said. "Everything also GO. You heard what happened on the ground."

"Yes," Connie said. "It couldn't have happened to a nicer guy."

"One more bucket of blood for poor old Piffy One to carry into space," Jazz remarked glumly.

"But hopefully an eye-opener for some people," Pete said.

"I doubt it," Connie said. "But anyway, maybe that's the last thing we'll have to worry about on this flight."

"God, I *hope* so," Jazz said fervently.

"Keep your fingers crossed," Pete said. There was a sound of agreement from Jayvee.

"I have everything crossed," Connie said. "Just let us all get up there safely, that's all I ask."

"You're worried about the launches, then," Pete said.

"Hell, they worry me, too," Jazz remarked.

"I'll feel better when we're off the ground," Connie said. "Let's just put it that way."

"Well, Dad," Jazz said. "Back to work for me. Take it easy."

"Roger," Connie said.

"Fly well," Pete said quietly, and again Jayvee made a sound, apparently agreement, in the background.

"You too," Connie said. "See you up there in a couple of hours."

"Roger," they all three said together and the circuit went dead.

"Launch control," Connie said. "We have a little time. Let's check those abort systems one more time, O.K.?"

"This is Kennedy Launch Control," Bob Ellison said. "We are now coming up on T minus 20 minutes, 6 seconds, and counting. Everything still looks GO for the departure of Planetary Fleet One to Mars, starting at 9:03 A.M., Eastern Standard Time, with the launch of *Santa Maria* carrying Colonel Connie Trasker, commander of the mission. There are no signs of any further disturbances among the spectators, and extra guards have been sent in to make sure there will be none. Everything is also GO in the stands at this time.

"To bring you up to date on some of the procedures that have been going on during countdown, a few minutes ago we got by an important test with Connie Trasker checking out the various batteries in the three stages and the instrument unit of the Saturn V *Santa Maria*. We remain on external power through most of the count to preserve those batteries, which must be used during powered flight. We took a look at them by going on internal and then switching back to external. The batteries looked good. The next time we go internal will be at the fifty-second mark with those batteries, and they will of course remain on internal power during the flight.

"The Mars Landing Module *Adventurer*, which has been rather inactive during these last phases of the count also has been on internal power on the two batteries on the ascent stage and the four batteries on the descent stage. Systems in the MLM have undergone check and the telemetry in the MLM has now been powered down to conserve power.

"Connie Trasker is now checking out the abort systems once more ("Why?" someone called out in the press stand, and a sudden new tension was injected into the already profoundly tense and excited atmosphere) and is also going to run through one more quick check of the final pressurization of the reaction control system for the spacecraft. These are the big thrusters on the side of the service module that are used for maneuvers in space. Each of the thrusters is capable of one hundred pounds of thrust and there are sixteen of them. We pressurize the system with helium prior to launch to make sure that all will be in readiness for use in space.

"Going back a bit to the earlier hours of the countdown, the count was picked up at T minus 9 hours. The major portion of some five hours of work on each of the pads this morning was occupied with loading the various propellants aboard the various stages of the three Saturn V's. As we came into the count this morning we already had the fuel aboard the first stage of each vehicle, but it was necessary to bring the liquid oxygen aboard all three stages and the liquid hydrogen fuel aboard the second and third stages. Close to three quarters of a million gallons of propellants were loaded into each vehicle during those five hours of major work at the pads.

"Final checks have also now been performed on the tracking beacons and the instrument unit which acts as the guidance system during the powered phase of flight. Once we get down to the 3-minute, 10-second mark, we'll go on automatic sequence. As far as the launch vehicle is concerned, and this will hold true for the *Nina* and *Pinta* when it is their turn to fly, of course, as well as the *Santa Maria*, all aspects from T minus 3 minutes 10 seconds, will be automatic, run by the ground master computer in the firing room.

"This will lead up to the 8-minute, 9-second mark in the countdown, when the ignition sequence will begin in those five engines in the first stage, the SI-C stage of the Saturn V. At the 2-second mark we'll get information and a signal that says that the thrust is proper and acceptable. We then will get a commit and liftoff, as the hold-on arms of the mobile launch structure release the spacecraft. A vehicle that weighs close to six and one half million pounds will then leave the Earth's surface with some seven point six million pounds of thrust.

"While I've been talking to you, we have passed the 11-minute mark. The Saturn V launch vehicle *Santa Maria* is now on full internal power, the switchover coming shortly after the 15-minute mark. The spacecraft is now on the full power of its fuel cells. Connie Trasker has now armed his rotational hand controllers, which he will use in flight, and we have now gone to automatic with the emergency detection system in case there's any trouble down below with the rocket during powered flight.

"We are now 10 minutes from our planned liftoff of the

523

Santa Maria, first Saturn V vehicle of Planetary Fleet One, Project Argosy, the mission to Mars."

"T minus 10 minutes and counting."

And now all the world quieted down for Piffy One, and the long hard road was almost over. At the Cape, Albrecht Freer and his staff, accompanied by twenty-two astronauts past and present, watched tensely in the firing room. In Huntsville, Hans Sturmer and his colleagues monitored final check-outs to supplement those at the Cape and Houston. At Goddard Space Center they made ready, and around the globe the tracking stations went on alert.

In modest little Space Station *Mayflower*, drifting politely along behind arrogant big Space Station *Stalin*, Americans dropped all pretense of work and stayed immobile before the television screens. In Space Station *Stalin* and at Baikonur, where Academician Alexei Kuselevsky was busy feeding instructions into the computers for the new Cosmos launches and the Soviet rocket on its way to the Moon, Russians did the same.

In New York and Rio, London and Bombay, Stockholm and Cape Town, Katmandu and Nukualofa, and all the cities and towns and lands and nations and oceans and lakes and seas between, the frantic pace of mankind ground to a stop. In El Lago and Nassau Bay, American flags flew and wives, including Monetta, cried with Jane and Clare. And in Mission Control, where the rest of the astronauts mingled with the staff as they moved constantly about the floor checking dials, watching computers and studying television as it brought in the pictures of *Santa Maria* venting little puffs of liquid oxygen and looking awesome and impatient in the bright clear morning, Bob Hertz stood smiling and relaxed beside Stu Yule. And on Stu's shoulder the apparently casual pressure of Bob's hand was growing—growing—growing—

At the Press Site, the VIP Site, the Dependents' Site, the last gossipings faltered, the last bright chatter died. A few typewriters still rustled, a few voices still spoke in hushed tones into telephones connecting to distant offices. Otherwise, the stands were still.

From Kennedy Launch Control, the voice of Bob Ellison boomed out across the silent globe.

"We've passed the 6-minute mark in our countdown for

Planetary Fleet One. It is now 5 minutes, 46 seconds, and counting. We're on time at the present time for our planned liftoff of *Santa Maria* at 3 minutes past the hour of 9 A.M., Eastern Standard Time.

"The spacecraft test conductor has completed the status check of his personnel in the firing room. All report they are GO for the mission and this has been reported to the test supervisor. The test supervisor is now going through some status checks.

"The launch operations manager reports GO for launch. The launch director reports GO for launch. We are now at 5 minutes, 19 seconds, and counting.

"Very shortly that swing-arm at the spacecraft level will come back to its fully retracted position. It should occur exactly at the 5-minute mark.

"We told you a little while ago that we had taken a good look at the Mars Landing Module. The spacecraft test conductor for the MLM reported that the module is GO. The MLM telemetry has now been powered down.

"The swing-arm has now come back to its fully retracted position and it is now T minus 4 minutes, 50 seconds, and counting. Colonel Trasker reports everything fine from where he sits. He is now giving the status on the final alignment of the stabilization and control systems as we now come up on T minus 4 minutes, 20 seconds, and counting. We are still GO at this time.

"The test supervisor has now informed the launch vehicle test conductor everything is now GO for launch. From this time on, the launch vehicle test conductor handles the countdown as the vehicle begins to build up. We are now at T minus 4 minutes and counting. We will go on automatic sequence at 3 minutes and 7 seconds. It is now 3 minutes, 45 seconds, and counting.

"On Pads B and C, *Nina* and *Pinta* are also approaching readiness status for launch, and after *Santa Maria* has been launched we will go to them in sequence for their final countdowns.

"The launch operations manager has just wished Connie Trasker on *Santa Maria* good luck, and Connie says thanks very much, he knows it will be a good flight. We are almost at automatic sequence, and all systems are GO at this time.

"The firing command is coming in now. We are now on

525

automatic sequence. We are approaching the 3-minute mark in the count.

"T minus 3 minutes and counting. T minus 3, we are GO with all elements of the mission at this time. We are now on automatic sequence system as the master computer supervises hundreds of events occurring over these last few minutes. T minus 2 minutes, 41 seconds, and counting.

"The members of the launch team here in the control center are monitoring a number of what we call red-line values. These are tolerances we don't want to go above or below in temperatures and pressures. Team members are standing by to call out any variations.

"Two minutes, 32 seconds, and counting. We are still GO on *Santa Maria* at this time.

"The vehicle is starting to pressurize as far as the propellant tanks are concerned, and all is still GO as we monitor the status.

"Two minutes, 10 seconds, and counting.

"Two minutes and counting.

"Our status board here in control indicates that the oxidizer tanks in the second and third stages have now pressurized. We continue to build up pressure in all three stages here at the last minute to prepare the vehicle for liftoff.

"T minus 1 minute, 35 seconds on the Mars mission. All indications coming in to the control center at this time indicate we are GO.

"One minute, 25 seconds, and counting. Our status board indicates the third stage completely pressurized.

"The 80-second mark has now been passed. We're approaching the 60-second mark leading up to the ignition sequence. We have passed the 50-second mark. Our transfer is now complete to internal power at this time.

"Forty seconds away from *Santa Maria* liftoff. All the second stage tanks are now pressurized.

"Thirty-five seconds and counting.

"Thirty seconds and counting.

"Connie Trasker says everything feels great.

"T minus 25 seconds.

"Twenty seconds and counting.

"T minus 15 seconds, guidance is now internal. Twelve, 11, 10, 9, ignition sequence starts—

"Six, 5, 4, 3, 2, 1, ZERO, all engines running.

"We have LIFTOFF. We have LIFTOFF at three minutes past the hour.

"We have LIFTOFF on *Santa Maria* of Planetary Fleet One, Project Argosy, outbound for Mars."

Even as he spoke, drowning his final words, a great shout went up from the Cape, a compendium of voices, exultant, triumphant, astounded, awed. There occurred the vision of a Saturn launch, a spectacle fantastic almost beyond belief whose full and shattering impact never comes through on television as it does in actual experience.

Just as he reached zero in the count, two great snakes of bright red flame licked out from the base of the vehicle.

Then slowly, ever so slowly—so slowly that at first it did not seem that it would leave the ground at all—so slowly that there shot through the minds of even the most veteran of veterans the frightening question, *Is it all right? Is it going to go?*—so slowly that it always seems an eternity of forevers compressed in fifteen seconds—the beautiful white candle began to move upward.

As it did so there came the first impact of sound, a long, crackling roar like a series of dynamite explosions punctuated by the steady bursting of giant firecrackers.

And then came the physical impact, a long, shuddering wave of motion that felt like a monstrous earthquake, rocked the stands until they rattled, seized the spectators and shook and shook and shook them as though it would never stop.

And slowly, still slowly, but now beginning to pick up speed a little (inside his cocoon at the top, Connie felt as though he were being lifted by an enormous elevator whose pressure upon his body grew steadily heavier and heavier until it seemed it must crush breath altogether) the monstrous beautiful bird began to climb, straight up, while incoherent cries of encouragement broke out at the Cape and elsewhere (including El Lago where Jane and Clare clung together and wept; Firing Room I, where Albrecht Freer clasped and unclasped his hands while silent sobs shuddered through his body; Mission Control, where Stu Yule, his stump propped on a chair beside his desk, shouted, "Oh, baby, GO!" while the tears streamed down his face).

And then it was up and away, steadily increasing in speed as it cleared the top of the tower and began to enter open sky, the long thundering rolls of sound still reverberating, the earth still trembling. When it seemed to stand almost directly overhead, although it was already almost 40 miles high and 55 miles down range, there was a puff of smoke as the second stage ignited. The vehicle tipped, curved into its planned trajectory, raced finally away out of still excited, still stunned, still awestruck voices. And faster until it was gone.

There was silence for a moment. And then the babble of still excited, still stunned, still awestruck voices. And then a general settling, a general quieting down, a general return to the ordinary things of Earth.

But not for long.

"This is Kennedy Launch Control," Bob Ellison said quietly. "We are now five minutes into the flight of *Santa Maria*, T minus 15 minutes, 6 seconds and counting on the launch of *Nina*, T minus 35 minutes, 6 seconds and counting on the launch of *Pinta*. All systems in all vehicles are GO at this time. Right now in *Nina*, Commander Weickert is busy checking out—"

Twice more in the next thirty-five minutes they saw—felt—breathed—tasted—witnessed—experienced—underwent—withstood—the same fantastic experience; and it was no wonder they walked away like drunkards when it was over. Jazz in *Nina* went exactly on time at 9:34 A.M., Jayvee and Pete in *Pinta* left exactly on time at 9:43. Twice more the sky cracked, the earth rolled. Twice more the beautiful terrible birds lifted off to become tiny silver slivers and vanish from the sight of man.

"We have had three perfect launches at Kennedy Space Center today," Bob Ellison said with quiet satisfaction shortly after 10 A.M. Eastern Standard Time. "Planetary Fleet One of Project Argosy, the mission to Mars, is on its way. The President has asked me to express his deepest thanks and profoundest congratulations to all who have made this tremendous event possible: to the crew, to the launch teams and everyone else in NASA who have helped, to the contractors who built the vehicles, above all to the American people whose support, encouragement and prayers have created this triumph. The President hopes the pride and thrill of this great occasion will swiftly obliterate memories of the difficult events of the pre-launch period and that we can all go forward together in the spirit of unity and good will exemplified by this great event today, the triumphant liftoff of Planetary Fleet One. We are now T plus 26 minutes, 13 seconds, into the mission and all is well. All systems are GO."

But on unhappy Earth, the President's hope was of course an idle one. Already typewriters were busy, air-waves were bristling, campuses were troubled and pulpits were about to rock. The world's reaction was momentarily one of awe and wonder but it did not take long for the first sour bellyaching to yap from around the globe at the heels of Piffy One. It took even less time in the United States.

Right on schedule came the solemn statements and somber praises for Clete O'Donnell; the deploring of violence and the ruthless attributing of violence to those whose only desire was to stop violence; the renewal of carping criticisms of the mission; the renewal of bitter complaints concerning competition with the Soviet Union, the renewal of savage outcries about the dreadful failure of the United States to co-operate with that loving power in space exploration; the renewal of hate, banished for a moment by three bright candles.

A sour, sad, spiteful effluvia rose from the world in the wake of the beautiful launches. Those who created it had been momentarily silenced but it did not take them long to find full voice again. In their consistent attacks from the beginning upon the mission they had finally managed to besmirch space, perhaps the last bright jewel in America's crown; and their vindictive caterwaulings, heavy with human hatreds and unkindness, still howled up from Earth and followed Planetary Fleet One, relentless, where it went.

Book Five

1.

Yet for a time—four days, six hours, 16 minutes and 29 seconds,—it seemed there would be no further problems. On third Earth orbit, docking was successfully accomplished; on the fifth, translunar injection. Back from the mission in a constant stream to Houston came the detailed reports that enabled ground to keep a continuing check on men and machinery as Planetary Fleet One streaked steadily outward into space, couched in language sometimes technical, sometimes jesting, always competent:

"Houston, this is Planetary Fleet One. Would you like to copy the alignment results?" ... "Affirmative, One" ... "O.K., NOUN 71 we used 30 and 37, 4 balls 1, NOUN 93 plus 00016 plus 00033 plus 00152. Ground Elapsed Time 00:48:15. Check star 34. Over" ... "Roger, say again check star" ... "Star 34" ... "Roger, we copy and the angles look good ...

"One, we are ready with your TLI 90 minutes abort test." ... "Roger, Houston, ready to copy" ... "Roger, TLI plus 90, SPS G&N 63481 minus 153 plus 132, CETI 064102538, NOUN 81 minus 04761 plus 06001 plus 53361, ROLL 180 193 000. HA is NA plus 002035357-363353349, Sextant Star 34345 0160350, the aboard sight star is not available. Latitude minus 02052 minus 02580 11887 34345 0160350. GDC align Vega and Deneb. ROLL 071291341 no ullage undocks. I have your P37 for TLI plus 5 hours. Over" ... "Go ahead, TLI plus 5" ... "Roger, P37 format, TLI plus 5,00744 6485 minus 165 02506. Readback. Over ... Roger, readback as follows ...

"Houston, this is One. We want to say what a great ride we all had on those birds. Everything was really great" ... "Roger, we'll pass that on" ... "We have no complaints with any of the staging. Everything was beautiful" ... "That's right, everything was nominal. We all had a good ride" ... "Thank you, One, we're glad you made it ... "Roger, gee, thanks, so are we ...

"One, this is Houston. Isn't it about time for you to go into your Astronauts Dazzled by Sight of Earth routine?" ... "Houston, are you taping this for rebroadcast?" ... "Not the question, One. Just the answer. Anybody ready to pour out with the poetry?" ... "We'll let Pete and Jayvee toss for it. Jazz and I have seen it before" ... "Roger. Toss, One" ... "This is Pete, Houston. Right now I can observe the entire continent of North America, Alaska, over the Pole, down to the Yucatan Peninsula, Cuba, the northern part of South America and then I run out of window. Also out of words. Over" ... "You'll have to do better than that if you want to write for *Life* magazine. Over" ... "I have eighteen months to practice, Houston. Try me on the way back. Over ...

"This is Mission Control, Houston, at 6 hours, 52 minutes into the flight. Planetary Fleet One is now 31,565 nautical miles from Earth and the velocity is 10,789 feet per second. The crew at this time is involved in midcourse navigation using their onboard optical system. We have completed the changeover in briefing of shifts here at Mission Control, and the crew activities, until the sleeping period begins, will consist of housekeeping functions aboard the spacecraft, changing out carbon dioxide filters. They will be doing the midcourse correction scheduled for 11 hours 45 minutes into the flight. Right now they are checking onboard batteries, which are currently being charged, a routine operation. This is Mission Control at 6 hours, 54 minutes ...

"One, this is Stu in Houston. They're giving me a little break but I'll be back on the job in about four hours. Bob Hertz says eight but we'll see about that. Take care of yourselves" ... "Roger, buddy. You've done a great job. Get a good rest and come back soon. We'll miss you" ... "Roger, One. It's mutual. Over ...

"This is Mission Control. We don't anticipate a great deal of further conversation with the crew as they are scheduled to get some sleep shortly. We have just advised them through one of the computer programs concerning the deadband for that area, of excursions of the spacecraft that the guidance system will allow before firing the Reaction Control System thrusters to correct it. Since the spacecraft is very stable at this point, with very few wobbling motions, it was felt that a narrower deadband was acceptable. In the event of any larger excursions by the spacecraft, which we would not expect since we are using the passive thermal control mode developed by the Apollo missions, it would be possible to awaken the crew from the ground and have the situation corrected. At this time Planetary Fleet One is 61,509 nautical miles from Earth, traveling at a speed of 7449 feet per second, which would translate to about 5000 miles an hour. At 12 hours, 54 minutes into the flight, this is Mission Control, Houston . . .

"One, this is Houston. Coming at you with the P37 block data, over" . . . "O.K., Gaudy, shoot" . . . "Roger, 02744 5363 minus 165 07314 03744 8016 minus 165 07246 GETI 04644 6141 minus 165 09703 05544 8209 minus 165 09642, do you read? Over" . . . "Roger, read you and will read back in a minute . . . "Good, One. If you have to call us tonight, we'd like you to do it on down voice backup. We're configuring for that mode, and as far as we can see you're cleared for some z's. Over" . . . "O.K., maybe we'll get around to lunch. Anybody for crepes suzette? . . .

"This is Mission Control at 18 hours, 39 minutes Ground Elapsed Time. Planetary Fleet One is now some 79,700 nautical miles out from Earth at a velocity of 6320 feet per second. Cabin pressures holding at 4.7 pounds per square inch. Cabin temperature is 63 degrees. Spacecraft analysis reports coming out of the back room here in Mission Control are almost uniformly good, all systems operating normally. In the spacecraft fuel cells, performance is normal. Telemetry display for the crew biomedical readings show Jazz Weickert and Jayvee Halleck in a fairly deep sleep in their hammocks in *Nina*. They began sleeping after eating a meal, about five hours ago. Under the on-guard system adopted following the emergency on Apollo 13, two crew members stand watch in control of the scapecraft while the others sleep for approximately eight hours. This schedule will prevail until the mission enters Moon orbit and the crew begins preparations for

535

the two test descents and ascents of the Mars Landing Module.

"Connie Trasker and Pete Balkis have the duty now and are standing the first watch. All routine checks have been completed for this phase of flight, all systems are reporting in normal. Connie and Pete have no set duties at this time. Maybe they're reading a good book. This is Mission Control at 18 hours, 45 minutes Ground Elapsed Time into the flight of Planetary Fleet One to Mars."

But they were not reading a book, nor, for the time being, were they even talking to one another. Connie was sitting by a window in *Santa Maria* staring moodily back at the bright blue marble of Earth, Pete was sitting by a window in *Pinta* staring moodily forward into the endless caverns of space. Almost instinctively they had retreated to their own domains when their crewmates had bedded down in *Nina* between them. More than twelve hours of rapid-fire, unceasing work had consumed the energies of all four and left the two sentries in no mood to compare notes on what they had been through. They were too tired to talk, almost too tired to think—except that thinking, here in their tiny world, less than ten trillionth of a ten trillionth of a ten trillionth of a milligram in the mathematical eternities of the universe, was something that could not always be avoided.

For Connie, who had traveled these highways before and knew that at the end of them man still met himself, it was natural to look back and contemplate the place where he had been. For Pete, feeling in some vague, idealistic, earnestly hopeful way that there might lie in store some new answer for old problems, some solace for pain, some saving grace for a still-troubled heart, what lay ahead possessed a mysterious, hypnotic fascination.

He told himself this was foolish, but it was impossible to escape: need insists upon its answers and creates them if they do not exist.

But what need existed for the commander of Planetary Fleet One? What problem lived that he did not have the answer for? What had the world not given to Conrad H. Trasker, Jr., Perfect Astronaut, outbound for Mars? Did not all things move for Connie as Connie's little heart desired?

Well, he thought tartly as he looked back upon lovely,

536

unhappy Earth, you could put it that way if you wanted to, but, personally, he was not so sure. He was not so sure that Conrad Trasker, P.A., in these recent months had been quite as perfect inside as a sizable portion of the world thought him to be outside. He wondered, in fact, with that unhappy, uneasy, unsatisfied self-doubt that sometimes afflicts the outwardly confident, successful and secure, whether he had ever really been what the world thought of as Connie Trasker; or whether there had not always been, hidden behind the smiling face, the competent manner, the swift intelligence and the attractive personality, someone else.

Now as he automatically glanced at the quietly humming computers, the efficiently purring controls busy at their private, infallible, programmed responsibilities, and then turned back to concentrate again upon imperfect, irrational, wildly unprogrammed Earth, he seemed to see himself anew as he walked those fast-receding familiar ways.

He could see himself as a child on the Big T Ranch, largest of the Trasker holdings in Great South Meadow below Denver, playing in the snow; exploring in the spring; riding horses and learning to handle cattle in the high, bright summer; leaving for the Air Force Academy, breaking his grandfather's heart for a while, in the sparkling, golden autumn. He was supposed to stay on the ranch, not his younger brother: the death of his father in a skiing accident at Aspen had made him the heir: why was he leaving? He tried to tell the sad old pioneer who saw him go, found himself unable; was glad his grandfather lived to see his brother take hold in a way that comforted, if it did not entirely appease, the old man; knew that for himself, at least, he had made the right decision, even though South Meadow and the Mountain West would always have first claim upon him, so much so that even now he would repair to them for comfort and replenishment when his glamorous world became, as it sometimes did, too much.

But he had known quite early that he would not spend his life there; he had known quite early that Conrad Trasker was something different, something special. He sometimes wondered, with a wry self-sarcasm, how different and how special: but anyway, different and special enough to know that he had in him yearnings that would not be satisfied by the life of the ranch, hard and wonderful as it was. It was somewhere in his seventh year that he had first become aware of the night sky over South Meadow; and though he had never told anyone, even Jane, he had known at that instant, long before most men were really convinced that it could be done, that he would go there someday. He had no concept of space, no idea of the universe: he saw the sky and he knew. It could not be explained, it made no sense—but he knew. Somebody out in Alpha Centauri, he often thought later with a private amusement when he knew about Alpha Centauri, must have reached down and touched him on the forehead; and the more he knew about space the less inclined he was to be so sure his private little superstition was just a superstition.

Maybe Somebody had.

In any event, being an articulate and effectively demanding child, it did not take him very long to make his interest known. By the time he was ten he had managed to make it generally understood in the family that he wanted a career in military aviation. This caused considerable consternation and dismay—the ranch, nucleus of the six other ranches of comparable size that were later added to it in Colorado, Montana and Wyoming, had been in the family since 1871—and for a time it seemed that his father and grandfather might try to overrule him. But it was so apparent that his heart was absolutely set upon it that they presently gave in; not without some pitched battles he regretted now but could not change, and not without considerable unhappiness all around. But his mother had stood up for him and his own determination had given him strength. Presently they conceded. By the time his father died there was little opposition left. His grandfather was too saddened to battle him longer. And fortunately he had a brother.

What he would have done if Bob Trasker had not been coming along a couple of years behind he hardly dared to think. You didn't just leave a seven-ranch spread and go off to be a fly-boy, even if you were Connie Trasker; though, he suspected, Connie Trasker might. There was by that time a corporation, a general manager, lawyers and accountants in Denver handsomely supported by Trasker Ranches, Inc. He could have run the ranches in absentia. But it would not have been right.

And maybe it wasn't even right as it had turned out: maybe it was all a selfish and willful imposing of his own dreams and desires on the family. Maybe the other Connie Trasker, the one behind the image behind the image, shouldn't have won. But he had and it was too late to do anything about it now. Too damned late, he thought with an ironic expression as he glanced once again at the computers and controls taking him to Mars: too damned late.

So he had gone to the Academy at Colorado Springs, which at least had the saving grace of being less than 200 miles, permitting him to come home often and not seem, for those who had not wanted him to go, too far away. And almost before he knew it had come graduation, Korea, Vietnam, specialization in aerospace, ambition clarified and given final direction as Sputnik ascended and America turned at last with full commitment to space.

He had applied in the second class of astronauts, been accepted, begun immediately to find for himself that leading position in the corps that had been his at the Academy, in Korea and in Southeast Asia. Men gravitated to Connie Trasker as one born to command. He accepted this, gave full loyalty and astute direction in return; never failed anyone who looked to him for leadership; welcomed all challenges, met them with skill, calm and competence; was a model officer, an extremely popular man (except to a few, such as Jazz); and at an early point in his career settled into that glamorous and admirable mold that NASA loves. It was inevitable that he should be selected, inevitable that within six months' time he should have moved into that circle-within-the-circle that runs the astronaut corps. From the first, big things were planned for Connie Trasker and no one planned more astutely than Connie Trasker himself. Big things—the Gemini program. Bigger things—Apollo, the Moon, *Mayflower*. And now, as he had always hoped, intended and made sure would happen, the biggest.

Yet here again, without a single-minded concentration and a fierce ambition so akin to selfishness that they could probably not be separated, he would not have made it. Jane had told him sometimes that his drive was frightening. Sometimes it seemed a little frightening to him. But it had taken him to the place where he wanted to be, the place he honestly felt no one else could fill as well: and so who was to say? Out of the admixture of human motivations had come Conrad Trasker, Commander of Piffy One. And since he gave good service in return for what he got, did it really matter if the motivations were mixed?

And did it really matter if he had drifted into an affair—to be honest, into several, over the years—that in the eyes of the world, if the world had ever known, might in some degree have made a mockery of the smiling, white-suited hero whom adults admired and children worshiped? Did it really matter if he had contemplated, to the point where only a very little more inducement might very well have tipped the balance, something else with his appealing crewmate who thought he needed him, and of whom he was so fond? Did the image behind the image behind the image, the ten trillionth behind the ten trillionth, really matter in the life and career of the honorable, decent, highly trained, beautifully functioning, unflappable machine that was Connie Trasker?

The world, he supposed, as he stared back at it with a curious expression of irony and gloom, might well say yes, it did matter: but that would be the world being disingenuous, dishonest and hypocritical. It didn't matter a damn to the world, which only wanted him to be, for those who liked him, a hero, and for those who didn't, a symbol of all they hated and despised about the space program. That was his purpose as the world saw it: to be hero or villain according to the world's mood and to do the job he was assigned to do. He fulfilled his purpose: what was inside was his own business. The world, he told it from 85,000 miles in space—a safe enough distance, he thought, the irony deepening—could go to hell.

But he couldn't tell Connie Trasker that, or Jane Trasker, or Jane Anne, Buddy and Sue Trasker, or Pete Balkis or Monetta Halleck, or a lot of other people: but most of all, Connie Trasker. Connie Trasker was right here inside him. Will the real Connie Trasker please stand up? He can't at the moment, he answered himself, he'd bump his head. But that didn't make him any less present.

So what did Connie Trasker think of Connie Trasker, child of South Meadow on his way to Mars with a few detours through several other lives that meant a lot to him and to whom he meant a lot?

How did Connie Trasker think Connie Trasker had treated Janie, loyal and decent, generous and kind? How had he treated Monetta, equally decent, equally kind? How had he treated Pete, another facet of the same prism, also decent, also kind? What had he done to warrant their love, and how had he cared for it when it was entrusted to his safekeeping?

He sighed. These were questions Connie Trasker seemed to have to ask himself in this haunted, lonely hour, but they were not questions Connie Trasker necessarily could answer. He thought he had treated each of them as decently as he could, given the circumstances in which he found himself, the limitations of his own character, and the depth of his own need. But hadn't he been selfish there, too? And could anybody in the world who was loved, and who in one way or another perhaps did not return quite as much love as was given, be unselfish? Was it not all a matter of balancing one need against the other? And was there ever a final balance or a final answer?

He sighed again. Suddenly the loneliness seemed more lonely, the haunted hour more haunted still. Abruptly he wanted human company. He turned away from the lovely blue marble, imperceptibly but inexorably growing smaller against the softly glowing dark; automatically scanned the quietly humming machines and satisfied himself all was well. Then he eased himself away from the window and began the hand-over-hand process of drawing his weightless body carefully through the hatch into *Nina*, past his sleeping crewmates, and so through the hatch to *Pinta* and Petros, staring far ahead, his eyes wide, his face touched with an expression of absorption, awe and gentle, indefinable sadness.

Yet curiously he was not aware that he felt sad; at least, not consciously aware. Perhaps underneath, in his mind or heart or somewhere in his body, he was aware of it, but it rarely had definition for him. Now and again a soft little sigh seemed to escape from his lips, not really prompted by anything he might be thinking at the moment: just there. Once in a while when he caught himself at it he would shake his head and tell himself to cut it out, it was no time or place to get dramatic—it was no time, as his older sister sometimes put it, knowing the highs and lows of their mercurial race, to get Greek. It was a time

541

to be little Petey Balkis, Space Buddy, right-hand man to the commander: and that's all, buster.

Which was as it should be, and what was the point in rehashing it at this late date in the mission—or this early date, if one wanted to look at it that way? All of that had been defined, not uncharitably; labeled, not unkindly; and briskly filed away by a busy man who had a great many things on his mind and little time for side issues. If that was what it was. And Pete had never been aware before in his life that it might be anything else.

Thinking back over the years, seeing in mind's eye his own familiar pathways, traced, though he had thought he was getting away from them, against the far, far depths of the galaxy, he remembered himself as a generally sunny child, without any particular problems; filled with a great friendliness and love toward nearly everyone he met; happy and laughing, enjoying every moment of being alive in the Florida sun. In the Greek community of Tarpon Springs, where the ties and customs of the old country still were strong if somewhat touristy, he had grown up, first like some dark-haired, sparkling-eyed little cherub, then like some solid, compact, classic young god or herdsboy straight off the hills of ancient Attica. Everybody knew youngest son Petros of sponge-fisher Milo Balkissilios and everybody expected big things of him. He was dutiful to his parents, loyal to his brothers and sisters, open and welcoming to the world.

The world responded: occasionally, as when cute little Irene Sardassis became pregnant in her junior year in high school and named Petros as one who might have been responsible, with some vigor. But he was able to convince his father that the ground had been well-plowed, and they put up a staunch and lively battle against the sinister Sardassis'. Irene had married Johnny Velakas instead, which she decided she really wanted to do anyway, and now they were all the best of friends. Johnny and Irene and their natally notorious eldest son had been his guests at the Cape for Apollo 17, and all was happiness and jovial, singing harmony.

In those days, of course, the Cape was something far away, at first only a vague presence somewhere off to the east; then, as the program moved on to enter the era of the Atlas missile and the first big launches, something a little more insistent but still remote from the bustling, ingrown world of Tarpon Springs. Several times before he went away to study at Tulane he had happened to be looking east and had seen the sight so many in Florida see, the jagged, snakelike trail of smoke rising rapidly, lingering a while after the missile that produced it, and then dissipating slowly against the placid sky. He had been mildly curious, mildly intrigued. It had never occurred to him then that he would be sitting here now going like a bat out of hell toward the Moon and Mars. It was the last thing on earth, or off it, that he could have imagined.

At Tulane, where he went about his studies with a methodical determination and a refusal to allow himself to be deflected by the surge of well-organized unrest afflicting the campuses, he had decided early that he wanted to be a doctor; and somewhere along the line, he could not say exactly when or how, he had begun to be intrigued by space. The Apollo program was beginning, the Moon goal had been set, the nation was starting to think outward. Somebody in Alpha Centauri may have touched him too, but more likely it was one of his younger professors, a member of the English department who had discovered in himself a great fascination with space and managed to impart it to quite a few of his pupils. None had responded quite like Pete Balkis, who had not expected to at all, at first. But suddenly one day he did: it was almost as though he had awakened with something decided in the night. After that there was no doubt what his specialty would be. He was going to be one of the first lunar space doctors, specializing in the medico-biological aspects of lunar and planetary exploration.

From Tulane he went on to medical school at Duke, though it stretched the family resources to the limit. But he had worked at part-time jobs all through college and had worked every summer. Enough had been saved to put with the modest amount his father could afford. He was able to complete his course at Duke without too much financial strain. He interned in Washington and Philadelphia, returned home briefly on his parents' pleadings to see if he could really be happy marrying Irene's younger sister Theodora and settling down in Tarpon Springs; decided he could not; and resumed the course that was to lead him, though he still had no such conscious ambition, straight to Planetary Fleet One.

By this time he was getting to be a regular habitué of

the Cape, going over for launches whenever he was home, gradually acquiring a wider and wider circle of friends among the younger scientists and technicians he met there. Somewhere around Apollo 16 or 17, during his period of deciding not to embrace luscious Theodora and live in Tarpon Springs, he had been introduced to Vernon Hertz at a Boeing party at the Ramada Inn. They had hit it off immediately. Before the evening was over, Vernon had extracted a promise that Pete would fly out to the Jet Propulsion Lab and look over the job possibilities there. It was not a difficult promise to extract and Dr. Hertz had no difficulty finding the job. Two months later Pete was in Pasadena. Space was a reality at last.

For two years he had remained there, working closely with Vernon, fascinated by the new world waiting, a favored princeling in a fabulous realm. Very soon after his arrival he had met Helen Williamson, a Pasadena girl employed as one of Vernon's secretaries: cute, vivacious, lively, apparently as serene and fun-loving as he was. Or, at any rate, as he appeared to be.

Because inside, of course, he was not all that cheerful. There was a moody streak, a sudden melancholy coming out of nowhere to blight the sunny day. He never knew why, he never knew when. He concealed it well and few around him were sensitive enough to perceive it. Vernon Hertz was such a one, aware that his cheerful easygoing Greek was not always so cheerful underneath. But it never affected his work, it seemed to be gone as rapidly as it came, it apparently represented nothing really deep-seated or worrisome. So Vernon thought and so Pete thought too.

With marriage to Helen, however, the occasional moodiness seemed to change to a real unhappiness that he soon found himself having to fight: a resourceful and deliberate enemy which seemed to thrive on the very things that should have banished it. Despite his high school adventures and a long procession of later conquests who fell before his curly hair and sunny smile, he had always thought with an almost superstitious idealism that marriage must be the perfect answer to all things. He really had thought, in some innocently hopeful way, that he would get married and live happily ever after. Being with Helen should have banished all his melancholies. Instead, it made them deeper.

For a while, however, he did his best, and so did she, naïve and decent and idealistic as he. She did not understand Pete Balkis but she was at first very deeply in love with him and she thought that ought to be enough. So they raced earnestly through the lotus life of Southern California, made friends, (including the Hallecks, with whom they were quite close for a little while), went to the beaches, went to the mountains, spent weekends in Las Vegas, gave and attended parties, sought hopefully, and then desperately, for the will-o'-the-wisp of happiness that ought to have been found somewhere amidst all those barbecues and martinis on the patio. But aside from their first few weeks of intense sexual involvement and an occasional flash of mutual, increasingly desperate kindness later on, it never was. Finally, bewildered, she decided to leave him. Bewildered and by now somewhat afraid, he agreed it would probably be best.

They parted with genuine regret, thankful they had no children although that had been their greatest desire when they were first married. He tried to tell her he was sorry and suddenly almost broke down: he really was and she would never know how much. Her last memory of him was standing on the steps of their apartment building in Pasadena, his still-boyish face abruptly contorted with some deep sadness she could not understand but knew must be terrible for him. Then he jumped in his car and roared away, leaving her crying with a helpless bewilderment in Southern California's eternal smoggy sun.

The antidote was work and for the next six months or so he was the Jet Propulsion Lab's most incessant and indefatigable member. Recognizing his necessity to keep busy, Vernon Hertz piled the work upon him. He responded with a dogged and grateful determination to keep going until he had his thoughts and feelings once more under control. It was toward the end of this period that Vernon reached his decision to send Pete and Jayvee to Houston. There Pete met Connie and had to start the battle all over again: a much tougher battle this time, because now his enemy had declared itself and he realized at last the stakes that were involved.

But he had won and this time for keeps: or so he thought now, staring out into the luminous darkness with a hopeful intensity as though he would somehow become part of it and glide on forever through all eternity until he

545

reached some mysterious and wonderful region of peace where he would be safe and sheltered forever from treacherous, unkindly things. He wanted to serve his country and serve Piffy One; help Connie in every way he could to make their mission the greatest triumph men had ever won in space; help Connie, do all things right, be true to himself, Pete Balkis, a very gentle, decent, good-hearted guy; help Connie and then come home to—what?

What? he asked the pulsating blackness before him. *What?* he asked the stars. *What?* he asked himself. And knew there was no answer.

It was thus that Connie found him as he pulled himself slowly in, hand over hand, through the hatch into *Pinta*: eyes wide, awestruck, completely absorbed; and sad.

He could tell Pete knew he was there, though he did not turn his head or move his body. Carefully Connie eased himself into the seat alongside; put one hand over the microphone to Houston; reached over with the other and squeezed his arm.

"Hi, buddy," he said quietly. "How goes it?"

"O.K., I guess," Pete said huskily, not looking around.

"Good," Connie said. "I need company. Mind if I stay awhile?"

"Please do," Pete said, and managed a small smile, though he still did not look around.

For a long time they sat there side by side, not speaking, not moving, not touching, both now staring far ahead as Piffy One streaked on, inexorable and inevitable, through the endless night.

"Planetary Fleet One, Planetary Fleet One. This is Houston. Is Team Baker up and moving?" . . . "Roger, Houston. Team Baker singing in the showers. Team Able snoring in *Pinta*. What goodies do you have for us this morning?" . . . "We'd like you to do an update on your flight plan and also on your consumables, Jazz. Later on we'll have the morning news for you, if you're interested" . . . "Roger, go ahead on updates. We're debating advisability of news and will let you know later. We sort of hoped we'd left all that crap behind. Read updates, please" . . . "Roger, One. You do sound like your sparkling self today. In your post-sleep checklist and in all other post-sleep checklists, we'd like you to delete the statement that says AUTO RCS jet select 16 to ON, and what we're doing here is to pick this up in the procedure for exiting PTC that's in your CSM checklist. In the CSM checklist on page F-Frank 9-8 it reads to exit G and N PTC, then you've got a PAN 8 change that says AUTO RCS select 12 main A and B. We'd like to move the AUTO RCS select 12 main A and B down to be the second step, so the procedure would read Step 1 Manual attitude 3 excel command, Step 2 AUTO RCS select 12 main A and B, Step 3 would be verified deployed, and so on. Over" . . . "Roger, we copy . . .

"This is Mission Control at GET 25 hours. The flight dynamics officer reports that at this moment Planetary Fleet One is passing the halfway-mark between the Earth and the Moon. The spacecraft are now 104,350 miles from both Earth and Moon, traveling at a velocity of 5,411 feet per second. Commander Weickert and Dr. Halleck have completed a number of routine checks and updates, some of which were broadcast on the color television transmission about an hour ago. As you could see from this transmission, both crew members who are awake seem to be in excellent shape and all things continue GO in this preliminary Moon-phase of the Mars mission . . .

"One, this is Houston. Midcourse correction number 2: SPS G&N 63059 plus 097, minus 020, GET ignition 026 44 57 9 2 plus 00 118 minus 00 003 plus 00 177 Roll 277, roll 277355015, NOUN 44 block is A, delta VT 0021300300168, sextant star 302082370, the rest of the pad is N/A. GDC align Vega and Deneb. Roll Align 007144068, no ullage. For your information your heads will be pointed toward Earth on this burn. If the thought doesn't make you dizzy, readback, please. Over" . . . "Roger, Houston. Not me, kid. Couldn't be dizzier than I am. Readback, midcourse correction No. 2: SPS G&N 63059 plus 097 minus 020— . . .

"This is Mission Control at 25 hours, 40 minutes. The ignition time for this midcourse correction will be 26 hours, 44 minutes, 57 seconds. It will be a service propulsion maneuver. Duration of the burn will be 3 seconds. This midcourse maneuver should reduce the pericynthion of Planetary Fleet One's trajectory from the present 175 nautical miles to 60 nautical miles . . .

"Houston, this is One. It was a little warm in the machine throughout yesterday and last night. It cooled off somewhat with the window shades up, and we've seen suit temperatures of about the high 40s and cabin temps in the low 60s. But this still seems a little bit on the warm side" ... "Are the water temperatures good? Are you getting enough hot water?" ... "Yes, it seems reasonably warm. We made three cups of coffee a little while ago. The last one, when all the plumbing was warmed up, with the hydrogen gun and all, was the warmest of the three. It isn't piping hot, but it beats stone-cold coffee" ... "Who had the second cup, you or Jayvee?" ... "I did" ... "Must be nerves, Jayvee" ... "No, I just like coffee" ... "Roger. What do you want us to do about your cabin temps? Does the heat worry you?" ... "No. Just something to talk about while we wait for the burn" ... "Roger. Glad we can oblige. Let us know when one of you starts drinking five cups. Then *we'll* worry. Over ...

"This is Mission Control at 26 hours, 40 minutes, just under 4 minutes from the midcourse correction maneuver. Colonel Trasker and Dr. Balkis are now awake and have joined Jazz Weickert and Jayvee in *Santa Maria*. All hands are standing by for burn. Planetary Fleet One is now 109,245 nautical miles from Earth. Its velocity is 5033 feet per second ... Stand by, please ... One minute to burn. Duration will be 3 seconds ... Burning ... Shutdown ...

"Houston, burn's completed. We thought we saw 87 or 88 psi on chamber pressure that time. What have you got?" ... "On our realtime telemetry we saw 95 to 97 psi on chamber pressure, but we'll take a look at the recording down here and get back to you. Your residuals are on the order of a half a foot a second or less, and will not be trimmed ...

"This is Mission Control. We have had a successful midcourse burn. Connie Trasker and Pete Balkis have turned in again to catch two or three more hours of sleep before they resume command of the spacecraft to permit Jazz Weickert and Jayvee Halleck to have their next scheduled rest period. The crew reports everybody feeling fine ...

"One, this is Houston. We still have the news down here, if you want it" ... "O.K., Houston, go ahead. Nothing to make us feel more like getting the hell off to Mars than to hear about the mess everything is in down there" ... "Roger, One. We envy you. First of all, skirmishing along the Sino-Soviet border has heated up again. Moscow reports seven troop clashes during the night and claims 47 Chicoms have been killed with a loss of two Russians. No word from Peking. In Washington, the President has met with congressional leaders in an attempt to stave off an immediate showdown vote on his new multibillion dollar tax reform measure. In the Middle East, new raids are reported along the Suez Canal. Israel says two Israeli jets downed six Soviet jets. Moscow threatens severe reprisals if Israel continues to defend itself. Thousands of prominent citizens, including political leaders of all parties, are expected to gather in New York for the funeral of Clete O'Donnell, labor leader hailed by the President and major American media as a great patriotic figure whose loss is a devastating blow to the United States. World-wide interest and considerable criticism continue to focus on the flight of Planetary Fleet One, though its success so far appears to have moderated some of the sharpest attacks. Signals have been received at Jodrell Bank and elsewhere from the two new Soviet Cosmos probes, which apparently are weather satellites. Joe Namath has held his sixth meeting with Commissioner Pete Rozelle in an attempt to iron out their latest dispute. Astronaut wives in Houston report all systems GO on the home front and send love. Over" . . . "Roger, Houston, thank you. Can we activate Command Downlink Special-1 for a minute to ask any word yet on Man in the Moon? . . . "Roger, Special-1 activated. Man in the Moon is continuing appointed rounds which will be completed roughly your GET 40 hours, 30 minutes. He is expected to be in residence when you arrive. Maybe you will see him" . . . "We hope not, Houston" . . . "Roger, we agree" . . . "Any official announcement from Washington on that?" . . . "Nary a word" . . . "I'll be damned" . . . "Roger, we agree on that, too. Back on S-band One, for public chitchat. If you're free for a couple of minutes, we have a procedure here that will let us verify the O_2 flow transducer and at the same time get some more of our cabin enrichment out of the way . . .

"This is Mission Control at 29 hours into the mission. Jazz Weickert and Jayvee Halleck have completed a further series of routine operations following the successful midcourse correction burn at 26 hours, 44 minutes, and are now eating lunch. There is a sound of music in the background, so they have apparently put in one of the microtape stereo decks that have been provided for the mission. There are a total of 200 of these, stored in the Command-Service vehicle, the *Nina*. They are divided into 50 classical music; 50 light popular; 50 novels, plays and collections of poems ranging from the comic to the classical; and 50 of the major philosophical and historical works produced by man, running from the ancient Greeks down to *The Challenges Ahead*, a compilation of the President's latest speeches. Things are fairly quiet at the moment, so we assume Jazz and Jayvee will be taking it easy for a while, getting ready for their scheduled sleep period when Connie and Pete take the duty again. Planetary Fleet One's distance from Earth is now 115,837 nautical miles, velocity 4788 feet per second. They seem to be running a taut ship up there and everything appears to be going well."

And so it was, Jazz reflected as he finished a mushy concoction that tasted like salmon salad and was surprisingly good. Mechanically, that is. And after all, he asked the distant Earth with some sarcasm, what else was there to Piffy One but mechanics?

Mechanically they had accomplished their burn, performed their routines, done their housekeeping, been model little astronauts. Humanly, he was eating in *Santa Maria* and Jayvee was eating in *Pinta*. Between them across the sleeping bodies of their comrades in *Nina* stretched the uneasy tensions of a tenuous truce. He had slipped a stereo deck on the machine to fool Houston, but he had put the relay directly into the S-band. No sound enlivened the spacecraft save an occasional quiet snore from Connie, an occasional little murmur of indecipherable restlessness from Pete. He and Jayvee were by themselves, not talking, not even visible to one another: which was the way they both wanted it, he thought grimly, and the way it was going to stay if he had anything to do with it.

In this, Commander Alvin S. Weickert III was expressing what his colleagues in NASA would have recognized as a characteristic pragmatic impatience; and yet as he finished his meal, slipped his utensils into the electronic washer, got them back clean two seconds later and stored them away in their place against the wall, he reflected that

550

it had not always been so. There had been a time when he had been a calm and placid soul, difficult to hurry, almost impossible to antagonize, patient and forgiving with all he met. What had happened to this model Christian light along the way? he asked himself ironically, and had no doubt of the answer: life. Good old life. Plus Connie and the corps and a few other things.

Yet he really had been such a perfect child back in the days when he was the pride and joy of Alvin S. Weickert II, minister of one of the leading churches in Sioux City, Iowa. He and his two sisters had been everything a kind and patient father and a loving and protective mother could desire. It was drilled into them that ministers' children were supposed to be good, and he was; which accounted, he supposed, for the occasional astronaughty now. And, perhaps, accounted for the fact that, long before he became an astronaughty, he had become a rather wild and unmanageable young man who seemed to find in flying the only outlet sufficiently dangerous and challenging to release the tensions of a tight and complex personality.

But all that came later, after he had gone happily through grammar school an example and an envy to his less well-behaved contemporaries; had moved serenely through high school collecting honors and commendations on all sides; and had started upon an engineering course at Northwestern. At that point something snapped and Alvin S. Wickert III the model student became a model no longer. He did, however, become a human being, and for that he was eternally grateful, rough though it had been upon both himself and those around him at the time.

Looking back now, as he glanced automatically at the dials and buttons and lights and gauges and found them performing perfectly as expected, he could not remember the specific moment or incident that had prompted this abrupt reversal of childhood pattern; unless it was simply that a basically direct and practical nature had decided that it was better to give in to its basic hungers than to keep torturing itself about them. He had been a Very Good Boy—even now he capitalized the words dryly in his mind—up to the beginning of his sophomore year in college, but it had been at a considerable price in self-control and self-denial; a price paid to the point where it was really beginning to affect seriously his studies and

551

general stability. He could remember, with a smile disbelieving yet not uncompassionate toward that long-gone, earnest youth, how he had actually resorted to such homespun remedies as cold showers, pure thoughts, and running ten times around the track. But the showers didn't last and thoughts persisted in remaining impure. Finally he decided desperately that he must do something or go crazy; and promptly found, after his initial hesitations, how easy it was to do something, and how pleasant, if ultimately self-defeating, it was to go crazy in the other direction.

This he proceeded to do for the remainder of his college career. Once the sexual barrier was down, the rest fell fast. Alvin II's little boy Alvin III started drinkin' and whorin' and hellin' around, as he put it to himself, until hell wouldn't have it. He learned a lot of things fast and forgot none of them; let his studies suffer for a while but found them easier to pull back up again as a relaxed rake than he had as what he called a prissy little prude; emerged from college heart-whole, fancy-free and body-ready; again reached a common-sense conclusion—that this was no way to lead a life that would get anywhere; called a substantial if not complete halt; and settled down and went to work.

But the experience left its mark in an essential underlying restlessness that he knew was not going to be satisfied by engineering. A college pal and his country's deepening involvement in Southeast Asia combined to head him in the direction that would ultimately bring him to this particular fantastic moment in time, hurtling toward the Moon at almost 5000 feet per second in the antiseptic white cocoons of Piffy One.

Soon after what he recalled ironically to himself as "the Alvin S. Weickert Self-Liberation Plan" had gone into effect in his sophomore year, he had made the friendship of a lively offshoot of a famous Chicago family whose privately cherished nickname was "Joyboy." Joyboy was as eager as Jazz to find out about the wilder aspects of Chicago, and together they formed an alliance that successfully expanded their knowledge in all conventionally unconventional directions. Joyboy had the money and Jazz usually had the ideas. Together they traveled the town, leaving feminine hearts by the thousands—or anyway, he thought with a certain satisfaction still, hundreds—in shattered disarray behind them. And before long Joyboy contributed something much more important: he loved to fly, had his own plane, and soon began urging Jazz to join him.

The persuasion was not difficult and did not take long: Jazz took to it, as he put it, like a hound dog in heat. "The sky is my limit," he liked to say, not suspecting then that his limit was destined to be far beyond that. He proved to be a supremely receptive pupil, one of those who have a genuine genius for the air. He had his license in record time and soon began to suspect that he had his avocation as well.

By the time he graduated from college he had made up his mind he wanted a career in aviation. The steadily escalating war in Vietnam provided the opportunity. He enlisted in naval aviation, became an officer, served three years brilliantly, recklessly, courageously; decided to stay in the Navy, was ordered home to attend special aeronautics courses; began to be fascinated by space. Somewhere south of Da Nang on a steamy afternoon of his last year in the war he had been chatting with a group of Air Force officers, one of whom in particular shared the same interest. They had talked for a solid two hours, exchanged names and addresses, promised to look one another up Stateside. They never saw each other again until they arrived on the same day at the Astronaut Office in Houston, five years later. But he had not forgotten Connie and Connie had not forgotten him: they were sure they were all set to be buddies, then.

Toward the end of his first year in Vietnam he had gone to Taiwan on leave. At an American Embassy party in Taipei he met a shy, sweet-faced girl named Clare Rosson, whose father was a rear admiral attached to CINCPAC. He could not say now exactly what had attracted him to Clare—probably her unspoiled freshness, which was such a contrast to what he had become used to—but he had been thankful for it ever since, because she loved him in that moment and she loved him still, and he was damned lucky to have her and he knew it. And this was something that had nothing at all to do with being an occasional astronaughty.

So they got married, in a couple of months' time, and with a normal number of ups and downs, lived reasonably happily ever after. The restlessness was still there, the tension and the impatience, and on quite a few occasions,

553

the old pal of Joyboy. But he had made quite sure, he thought, that Clare never suspected this, and he made quite sure, in fact, that it would never jeopardize her or the family that soon came along. Domesticity meant far more to him than he had ever thought it could: Clare was his quiet anchor and the kids were ballast. He might wander from them occasionally at the Cape or traveling the country, but he always came home. He needed them there if he was to do the things he wanted to do in space.

And these were very great; and when he joined NASA he thought he and Connie might do them together. And so they had, for a little while, and so now, ironically, they were again. But the in-between had been a long, often difficult, basically very unhappy time.

Perhaps it was because, during his college years and after, he had developed an innate arrogance of ambition which had taken him as far from the dutifully bland minister's son as his more private activities had done; or perhaps it was because those private activities had given him a certain what-the-hell attitude that made him a little less compliant about fitting into the NASA mold than he should have been; or maybe it was a combination of the two. Anyway, he had been a little too insouciant, a little too independent—perhaps, he could finally bring himself to admit, a little too demanding a little too fast. That seemed to be the principal gripe Connie and Hank and Bert had against him, as nearly as he could figure it out. And they had chosen to pick on things such as his perfectly legitimate interest in playing the saxophone in casual combos to symbolize it. Hell, he didn't disgrace the corps with anything as innocent as that; and his less innocent pursuits were no worse than those of anyone else among his colleagues; and they weren't public anyway.

But whatever the reasons, it was obvious pretty soon that he had rubbed what he came to call, not too privately or discreetly, "The Unholy Trinity," the wrong way; and they had made him suffer for it. He had done all right for a time, and Connie had flown a Gemini mission together with great success and outward amicability, he had later been assigned to a couple of tours on *Mayflower* and been given deserved official praise for it; but the glamour and glory of Apollo were denied him, quite deliberately. His life in recent years had been on stand-by. Out of that had come the bitterness and anger which had helped to disfigure the opening months of Piffy One.

Yet what was he supposed to do, for God's sake, take it lying down and watch the greatest chance of all go glimmering? He had to make a fight for it or lose all self-respect: just as, when he finally realized the kind of vultures who were gathering behind the campaign to destroy the mission, he had to disassociate himself from them and issue his statement standing by the corps. "I'm still an astronaut," he had told that two-bit little Percy Mercy and that stupid juvenile half-ass who passed for a United States Senator, Kenny Williams. And he was, and when the chips were down, that was what he had to remain true to. And out of that, of course, had come his selection for the crew and the start of a new companionship with Connie which might, at last, be somewhere near what they had both originally felt it might be.

Old Connie! he thought with a wry smile as he looked back toward Earth for a second and noted automatically how clear and distinct even now were its troubled continents, its uneasy seas. Was there ever such a moodily conscientious bastard living inside the glamorous protections of a space suit? He had pinned his hopes of getting on the crew for a long time on Connie's conscience, because he knew he had one; and though that had not been the deciding factor, it had certainly prompted Connie to accept his assignment instantly and willingly once it was accomplished.

Connie remarked rather often, Jazz had noted, that he had a lot on his mind; and Jazz knew it was true because he was not entirely without his sensitivities and perceptions, for all his prickly practicality. Jazz knew Connie had all the problems of the mission on his mind; and he knew he had him on his mind; and he was pretty sure, in ways that he was loyal enough not to follow to their ultimates, that he had Pete on his mind; and he also suspected, partly because of Jayvee's one stark outburst, but also because of a hunch that had just seemed to come from somewhere even before that moment, that he had Monetta on his mind; and he sure as hell knew Connie had Jayvee himself on his mind, because how could anybody not have that ornery bastard on his mind?

But Connie carried them all and managed to stay steady, and for that Jazz, although he could not quite bring himself to tell Connie so, but might yet someday, genuinely admired him. He was forced to admit, in fact, much as he had disliked him at times in their fluctuating relationship, that Connie was in many ways a quite remarkable guy. All of Jazz' very great technical abilities and instinctive flying skills were at Connie's service to make of Planetary Fleet One the great historic success they hoped it would be. He was proud to be flying with him and he knew Pete was too.

What that silent character over there in *Pinta* felt about it, he thought with an annoyance that was still strong in spite of his occasional efforts to tell himself he must suppress it, he was damned if he knew. And he was damned if he cared: except as Jayvee's feelings might affect the success of Piffy One.

And they might. Jazz still had a deep and abiding suspicion, in spite of the apparent way in which Jayvee had accepted his obligations to the mission. He certainly hadn't accepted them—fully, at least—to his crewmates, in Jazz' opinion; and he decided now, as he turned once more to check the instrument panels, that he was going to keep right on watching for any false step from across the way. He still didn't like him and he still didn't trust him.

It did not occur to him that Jayvee of course sensed this very well and that this was only part of the heavy burden he was carrying to add to all the other burdens racing swiftly outward with Planetary Fleet One.

Why he should be so burdened was a question he probably could not have answered in any very coherent fashion as he sat now in *Pinta*, staring ahead as Pete had, into the constantly unfolding cosmos. He had asked for it after all, and they had responded. Why did he think he should be free of their suspicions and uncertainties now?

Yet with a certain innate inconsistency that he never quite seemed able to analyze or abandon, he felt that he should be. He was the aggrieved party, after all. It was up to them to accommodate to him, not the other way around. What right did they have to be suspicious of him, who had so many, many reasons for being suspicious of them?

He supposed now, sitting in the quiet spacecraft, soundless save for the small night murmurs of his sleeping crewmates (the one who was awake was keeping his distance, and Jayvee was harshly thankful for that), that it had begun in Greensboro, North Carolina so far back in his life that nobody could remember when. Both his parents had been diligent, hard-working, respectable, quiet. They lived on one of the town's largest and oldest plantations, still owned by the family that had owned their grandparents and given them their names: the white Hallecks and the black Hallecks lived together still, after a hundred years. His father had risen to be an assistant field boss, his mother worked in the mansion as her mother and grandmother had before her—freedom and air conditioning hadn't changed things much. The black Hallecks and the white Hallecks lived in a subtle master-slave relationship to this day: mutually kind, affectionate, helpful, generous—but still the same. It had been too much for Jayvee, and he had left. Yet in some unhappy way, deep inside, its soft and treacherous enchantment held him still.

But he was made of sharper stuff and he grew up in a sharper and more tragic age. The great unrest that seized the younger members of his race in the sixties seized him too, not gaining them full admittance to the world they wanted but spoiling beyond redemption the world they had. A bitter resentment, an angry impatience, an understandable but self-defeating inability to understand the patient yet remarkably rapid processes of democratic change, crippled them all.

Jayvee was like the rest: twice as convinced he had been twice as hurt as he actually had been, twice as positive he was being twice as rejected by those who would not give him what they could not give him as long as he acted as he did: their respect.

He embarked on the vicious and unending circle of returning resentment for resentment, hate for hate; and spun around within it so dizzily he often met himself head-on, coming back.

Thus of all the anger carried in all the young black hearts in North Carolina, Jayvee Halleck's probably was among the most extreme, self-devouring and intractable. But he early learned craft with it, too. He early learned to treasure anger quietly and husband it circumspectly. He early learned that to outsmart the white man you had to play the white man's game. He early learned to keep himself to himself, dissembling his inner turmoil as much as he could, biding his time to take the revenge that he

557

and his fellows were told, by those who played upon them, was their due.

He had not always been successful with this, by any means. Sometimes everything boiled over, as it had in the opening months of Piffy One. Desperate tensions sometimes flared into open hostility: he antagonized the white man's world by being too honest about his feelings toward it. But for reasonable periods of time, and on enough occasions to win white support for his personal ambitions, he managed to be outwardly the responsible black the white world wanted. He was aided in this by a highly intelligent mind. It could have taken him anywhere if it could only have been severed from his fierce, unhappy heart. It was taking him to Mars, he reflected now with a rare touch of irony, and that was pretty far.

And in high school it had taken him, in a sense, even farther, for it had catapulted him out of Greensboro to the California Institute of Technology; and that was a leap almost more significant and important, for one of his background, than the arching leap of Planetary Fleet One. Or it could have been, had he considered it a privilege to be worthy of, and had he not already become so embittered that he considered it instead only a sort of guilty-white-man's reward that was his right for being black.

He could not see it as a privilege, any more than he could see Vernon Hertz' friendship, his selection by NASA and his assignment by the President to Piffy One as anything but uneasy, conscience-stricken attempts by the white world to make amends. Jayvee was one of those who actually believed that all white people felt guilty for things only a small proportion of them had done. He was psychologically crippled to the point where he could not realize that many of them were entirely appreciative of his merits and willing to accord him every advantage he could earn with them. In his mind his Rotary Club scholarship to Cal Tech was Greensboro easing its conscience; Dr. Hertz' friendship was basically a guilty white making himself feel better; his selection by NASA was a further instance of white guilt prompting what was only right; and his assignment to the crew by the President was certainly a white politician making use of Jayvee's color for his own advantage.

And of course there was just enough in each of these assumptions, just enough in each bitter analysis, to keep

558

the assumptions going and the bitterness strong. Fortunately the brilliant mind was too brilliant and too independent to let itself be crippled by the unhappy heart—except on those few occasions, of course, when it really mattered.

Outwardly, however, the quiet and reserved child of his grammar school days moved on to become the quiet and reserved youth of high school and Cal Tech, followed by the quiet and reserved scientist of the Jet Propulsion Lab. Not even to Monetta in the early days of their meeting and marriage had he revealed the depths of the anguish and estrangement in his heart. He was a child of his times, and it had ruined him insde. But to the world's eye, and to hers at first, he appeared to be a steady and admirable young man whose story was living proof of the basic beliefs of his wistfully idealistic and still hopeful country.

But Monetta was a child of her times, too, and it hadn't done this to her. His realization of this, although he only dimly glimpsed cause and effect—or, rather, permitted himself to glimpse it only dimly—was probably the single major cause for the slow collapse of their marriage.

Where he was impatient, Monetta was calm; where he was angry, Monetta was equable; where he was intolerant, she showed tolerance; where he felt at times as though he were living on hate, she seemed to be living on love. It was doubly infuriating to him because he really could not deny, when she pointed it out mildly to him, that he was really doing very well in the world. In some perverse but apparently inescapable way, this made his hatred of it grow even stronger.

There were other things that contributed—his initial rejection from Piffy One had probably been the most decisive—but essentially it was just this difference in attitude that had finally corrupted their marriage. They were compatible intellectually, physically, socially; but they were not compatible emotionally, psychologically or in the degree of their maturity. So it had to end.

But it didn't have to end, he told himself savagely now as he, too, absent-mindedly but efficiently checked the back-up instrumentation systems that were housed in *Pinta* and found them all functioning smoothly, it didn't have to end with the humiliating affront of an affair between his wife and Colonel Smug White Anglo-Saxon Protestant

Astronaut Trasker, sleeping away in there in all his temporarily defenseless arrogance. It didn't have to end with Connie cuckolding *him*, who was ten times as good as Connie ever would be. The white world didn't have to hand him *that* to make it end.

But it had, and he knew it as surely as he knew he was sitting here staring with an increasingly sullen and ominous expression out the window into depths now peopled with the erotic and agonizing fantasies of his own tormented mind. He didn't have much proof, they had been too smart for that: but he *knew*, and the knowledge was capable, when he let himself brood upon it, of driving him close to frenzy. He didn't care so much what they did together, whatever it might be. But he cared to the point of near-insanity what the fact of their being together did to *him*.

He hadn't forgotten it, and he wouldn't—couldn't—even though the necessities of the mission had forced him into an apparent acquiescence in things-as-they-were. He knew how they ought to be, he told himself grimly. And sometime—

Suddenly in *Nina* Connie coughed abruptly, grunted, began gently to snore. Instinctively, furiously, momentarily out of control, unaware of what he was doing until he was halfway there, Jayvee began to pull himself with a blind anger rapidly along the side of the cabin toward the hatch.

As he reached its entrance and looked through, Jazz looked back from the opposite hatch leading into *Santa Maria*.

For several moments they stared at one another, faces tight, tense, wary, many things racing in their hostile, angry eyes.

Then Jayvee forced himself to become calm, forced his expression to become impassive; raised a hand, waved, turned back.

For quite a while thereafter Jazz remained where he was, staring across his sleeping crewmates at the empty opening on the other side. It was not until the downlink to Houston suddenly came alive with Gaudy Gaudet's cheery greeting that he realized that he felt very cold; and that, though he was not an overly imaginative man, the hairs on his neck had risen.

And now the hours began to tumble faster as they drifted toward the Moon.

"This is Mission Control 45 hours, 28 minutes Ground Elapsed Time. Present velocity of Planetary Fleet One is 3799 feet per second at a distance from the Moon of 69,810 nautical miles. Planetary Fleet One is now decelerating as it approaches the point where the Moon's gravitational pull begins to exceed Earth's gravitational pull. The Flight Dynamics Officer tells us this will occur at 61 hours, 39 minutes, 57 seconds GET. At that time the spacecraft-to-Moon distance will be 33,822 nautical miles, spacecraft-to-Earth distance 186,437 nautical miles. Velocity will then have slowed to 2990 feet per second in reference to Earth, 3772 feet per second in reference to the Moon. At that point the spacecraft will begin to pick up speed again. We have begun the clock countdown to the first lunar landing, which as you know is a test landing of the reusable Mars Landing Module *Adventurer*. Our landing clock now shows 57 hours, 17 minutes until lunar landing by *Adventurer*. We still have no decision here or aboard Planetary Fleet One as to who will make the first descent with the flight commander, Colonel Connie Trasker. Consultations will be held in due course and we will let you know. We are now at 45 hours, 30 minutes into the flight of Planetary Fleet One . . .

"One, this is Houston. How are you doing on keeping gas out of the food bags?" . . . "Not too well, Houston. We have these two hydrogen filters which work fine as long as they aren't hooked up to a food bag. But the entryway into some of the food bags is so crumpled that there is back pressure that makes the filters start to lose efficiency. We've found that simply by leaving the filters alone for a couple of hours, efficiency seems to be restored. But it isn't very satisfactory. Suggest you have everybody get busy and work out a deal for keeping those entryways rigid, and send it up to *Mayflower* so we can offload and replace before leaving for Mars. O.K.?" . . . "Roger, Pete, will do . . .

"Houston, this is One. Do you want everybody up for that television show at 51 GET, or shall we let Jazz and Jayvee sleep?" . . . "What's your suggestion, Connie?" . . . "They both seemed pretty edgy when we took over. I'd let 'em sleep, unless you think Pete and I aren't cute enough to maintain the image" . . . "Bob Hertz says you two are

561

so beautiful we don't need anyone else. Over" . . . "Haw, haw. Tell him we love him, too. Over . . .

"One, this is Houston. We'd like to try to correlate your 02 flow in transducer with the flow valve that you've got open. How far open would you say you have the direct 02? Over" . . . "It's hard to give you a good reading without shutting it again, but the arrows are at about the one o'clock position. Now I've reduced the flow and I'll let it stabilize. Right now our onboard reading is about .4 and that's with the arrow in the 02 valve at 2 o'clock position. We're holding steady now at 3/10s of a pound per hour and our cabin pressure now is about 54. I'll close the valve momentarily and then open it again to this position and see how much travel occurs. It's about 30 degrees of travel. Our blowers are stabilized now at .6. Is that enough, or do you want more?" . . . "Pete, that's good enough. We're satisfied now, over . . .

"This is Mission Control at 56 hours, 36 minutes GET. Connie Trasker has been inside the MLM *Adventurer* for a familiarization and check-out period for the past 20 minutes or so, and has now been joined by Pete Balkis. He will do the same with Jazz Weickert and Jayvee Halleck later on. Presently he and Pete will be back in the *Santa Maria* again and ready to start their sleep period, after this rather extended work period they've had. We've sent up word that the spacecraft is to go into the passive thermal control mode at 58 hours. In that mode it rotates at a slow roll of about three revolutions per hour to maintain even heating . . .

"Houston, this is One. Am I right we have now crossed into Moon's sphere of influence? Can you give us update on where we are now, please?" . . . "Roger, Jazz. You crossed the line at approximately 61 hours, 38 minutes GET, at a distance of 186,437 nautical miles from Earth and 32,822 nautical miles from the Moon. Velocity with respect to Earth at the point was 2990 feet per second, with respect to the Moon about 3272 feet per second. From now on your velocity will increase at about 10 feet per second as you accelerate steadily toward the Moon. Don't run into anything. Over" . . . "Only moonbeams. Jayvee has a question. Just a minute, Houston" . . . "Roger" . . . "Are you planning a course correction for us during this work period?" . . . "Negative, Jayvee, we find midcourse number 4 is not required. Over" . . . "Roger . . .

"One, this is Houston. Let's run general check on nuclear engine NERVA, right now, O.K., if you haven't anything better to do. Over" . . . "Stu, you're a humorist, kid. Fire away, over" . . . "Roger. We'd like first check Station 1, JTK 07900367 10 297 6, then Station 2, FML 107896541100 6 8 2B 10 5X 6TBR, multiples you have. Rod 3 and Rod 4 semi-6, semi-7, 5A and 5B. Do you copy?" . . . "Roger, readback: Station 1, JTK 07900367 — . . ."

"This is Mission Control, at 67 hours, 28 minutes Ground Elapsed Time. Jazz Weickert and Jayvee Halleck have completed the routine nuclear engine check of the NERVA requested by Houston and are now standing by to resume a sleep period as Connie Trasker and Pete Balkis come back on the job in an hour or so. We've been expanding both sleep and work periods here as we get closer to the Moon, and after this last formal period coming up, we'll be leaving it pretty much to the crew to catch their own periods of individual sleep depending on the workload and all the final preparations for the lunar orbit injection burn and then the undocking and descent of the Mars Lunar Landing Module that will come along in the thirteenth lunar orbit. The surgeons report everybody seems to be in good shape according to biomedical telemetry received here, and from the crew themselves it's been a consistent report of feeling good, no need for medication, everybody sufficiently rested, and so on. The surgeons report an occasional increase in heartbeat and skin temperature for astronauts on duty during quiet periods when they haven't been occupied with work, but the astronauts report no anomalies so the flight surgeon concludes they were just thinking. Jazz Weickert agreed he was just thinking when we asked him. He said he was thinking about reading a good book in a Japanese bathhouse. There is some skepticism here about this, but anyway, everybody's healthy and apparently having fun. It is now 67 hours, 31 minutes Ground Elapsed Time, and our clock counting down to lunar landing shows 35 hours, 17 minutes to touchdown of *Adventurer* . . .

"This is Houston, One. Connie, we have a few goodies for you: at 71 hours you have O2 fuel-cell purge. At 72 hours, CO2 filter change number 6, secondary radiator flow check, and we'll send you up P37 block data on a two hour pass, pericynthion pass return mode abort. At 73 hours, stop PTC at approximately zero degrees roll. Then perform a P52 option 3 remaining in the PTC REFSMMAT for a drift check. At 73 hours, 30 minutes, maneuver to 000 roll, pitch and yaw. High-gain antenna angles will be pitch 0, yaw 335, and perform a P52 option 1 using the No. 2 alternative landing site REFSMMAT this side of the Eichstadt Crater. Resume the nominal flight plan at 74 hours GET, over" . . . "Roger, at 71 hours you want O_2 fuel-cell purge, at 72 hours— . . .

"Houston, this is One. Special-1, please. What now on Man in the Moon?" . . . "Man in the Moon well-established, One. No indications any anomalies as far as we can see from here" . . . "Is he smiling or frowning?" . . . "Looks like a smile from here, One, but he may be moody. Over" . . . "We'll hope not. Over" . . . "We're with you on that. Over . . .

"One, this is Houston. Connie, have you given any thought who you want for company on your first descent? Over" . . . "Lots. Over" . . . "Can you let us in on your thinking yet?" . . . "Have you done any there?" . . . "Lots. We'll swap you when you're ready" . . . "Not ready yet, over" . . . "Bob points out time is getting short" . . . "You tell him almost 30 hours, and don't worry. I'll call him on Special-1 when I'm ready. I'm really not sure, yet. Over" . . . "Is everything all right up there, One?" . . . "Everything is fine, Houston. Why?" . . . "No reason, Conn. Just wondered" . . . "Tell Bob wondering has no place in a well-run space program, Stuart. Love and kisses. Over" . . . "Give us NERVA check, then, please, Rods 1 and 2, half-5, semi-6, half-9, semi-10 TBS 06846311 X multiple 1, Tab 1, Tab 2, Rod 3 semi-5, semi-zero, do you read? Over" . . . "Keep calm, Robert. I read: NERVA check Rods 1 and 2, half-5, semi-6, half-9, semi-10, TBS— . . ."

"This is Mission Control at 73 hours, 6 minutes into the flight of Planetary Fleet One, Houston has given Connie Trasker and Jayvee Halleck the lunar orbit insertion burn number 1 pad and the crew is making preparations for the burn. The ignition time for that burn is 75 hours, 49 minutes, 49 seconds. Duration of the burn will be 6 minutes, 2 seconds, retrograde, and the change in velocity 2917.3 feet per second. The expected Moon orbit following that maneuver is 169.2 by 62 nautical miles. We will lose signal from Planetary Fleet One at 75 hours, 41 minutes, 23 seconds as it goes behind the Moon. Given a successful lunar orbit insertion number 1 burn, we will acquire the signal at 76 hours, 15 minutes, 29 seconds. Planetary Fleet One's distance from the Moon is now 7331 nautical miles, velocity 4399 feet per second, and increasing. For a while now everybody is going to be pretty busy . . .

And everybody was, as distance shrank in two and a quarter hours from 6522 nautical miles from the Moon to 4625 nautical miles—to 2241—to 1516—to 906—to 309 —and velocity increased from 4483 feet per second to 4765 feet per second—to 5512—to 5981 to 6511—to 7664—

Without a sound, softly through space, Planetary Fleet One fell ever more rapidly toward the Moon. Onboard they worked and worked fast, as they received data from Houston for contingency transearth injection burns if something should go wrong after lunar orbit insertion and they should have to return; ran through checks of radio and telemetry equipment; tested the gimbal platform; tested yaw, pitch, roll; checked camera equipment; checked batteries; checked fuel; made sure all switches, toggles, buttons, handles, were in their proper positions; glanced out from time to time at the desolate, familiar, pock-marked landscape now getting swiftly larger on their right; made sure their machinery was perfect—wondered if they were—placated their particular gods—and hoped to hell everything would work.

For Connie, as for all of them, the things he did were so practiced and routine, so mechanical and familiar, that he could have done them in his sleep. But he did not, of course, nor did they: it was one of those many moments in a spacecraft when no one can afford to take anything for granted. Yet even as he worked, with a swift skill and an unshakable concentration, a beautifully honed and calibrated instrument perfectly tooled for its purpose, some other part of his mind was observing, analyzing, watching what they were doing, making sure all things were right. He was the commander, and careful of his ship.

They began to turn the corner and cross onto the Moon's dark side.

Once again Earth quieted down for Piffy One.

"This is Mission Control (the words boomed out now

565

across the listening globe) at 75 hours, 26 minutes Ground Elapsed Time. Planetary Fleet One is 906 miles from the Moon, velocity 6511 feet per second. We are now 23 minutes away from the Lunar Orbit Insertion burn. The Flight Director is polling the flight controllers here in Mission Control for the GO/NO-GO status for LOI. We now bring you live ground-to-spacecraft communication. It's a little bit fuzzy and cracked, but I think you can get it all clearly:

"One, this is Houston. You are GO for LOI."

"Roger."

"We're showing about 10 minutes and 30 seconds to loss of signal. We would like to remind you to enable the BD roll on the auto RCS switches. Over . . . "

"Roger, and confirm you want PG on low going over the hill. Over."

"Affirmative."

"Houston, do you want to give me a time check and a mark to ignition, please?"

"Roger. I'll give you a mark at 12 minutes to ignition. I'll give you a time hack on the GET at 75 hours, 37 minutes, and I'll show you a bias at about a second and a half to allow for the time of flight."

"O.K."

"Stand by. Mark 75 hours, 37 minutes GET."

"Thank you."

"Stand by for a mark at TIG minus 12. MARK TIG minus 12."

"Thank you."

"This is Mission Control. We are 3 minutes away from loss of signal. Planetary Fleet One is 425 nautical miles from the Moon, velocity 7368 feet per second."

"One, this is Houston. All your systems are looking good going around the corner. We'll see you on the other side. Over."

"Roger. Everything looks fine up here."

"Roger, out."

"This is Mission Control. We have now had loss of signal as Planetary Fleet One goes around the Moon. At that point the distance to the Moon was 309 nautical miles, velocity 7664 feet per second. We are seven minutes, 45 seconds from the LOI number 1 burn which will take place behind the Moon out of communications. With a good lunar orbit insertion burn the Madrid tracking station should acquire Planetary Fleet One at 76 hours, 15 minutes, 29 seconds . . .

"This is Mission Control at 75 hours, 49 minutes. Planetary Fleet One should now have started this long burn which will have a duration of 6 minutes, 2 seconds. With a successful burn we expect an orbit of 61 by 169.2 nautical miles. We're 24½ minutes away from acquisition of signal if the burn proceeds successfully . . .

"We're seven minutes from acquisition. Everyone is very quiet here in the control room, a few brief conversations among the flight controllers and the many astronauts who are here, otherwise quiet . . .

"We're four minutes from acquisition now . . .

"One minute, thirty seconds . . .

"Thirty seconds . . .

"Madrid has acquisition. Madrid has acquisition."

"One, this is Houston. How do you read?"

"Loud and clear, Houston."

"Likewise. Congratulations. Could you give us your burn status report, please?"

"Everything was perfect. DELTA T O, burn time 557, ten values on the angles, BGX minus .1, BGY minus .1, BGZ—"

The slow glide around the dark side, approximately forty-five minutes in duration, neared its end. They joked a little, talked a little, mused much. Tension relaxed.

Then it came back again.

As it did so, an ironic thought, prompted by a worried private report from Jazz a few hours ago, shot through Connie's mind. *One problem has recognized the other. It takes one to know one.*

"What's that?" Jayvee demanded sharply, just as Piffy One came slowly up over the edge of shadow into light.

Far in front, a tiny silver dot in the soft tawny glow, Man in the Moon streaked on ahead and disappeared over the rim into darkness.

2.

And so Earth's hatreds were with them still, he thought with a sad, frustrated annoyance as he and Pete stood the first watch. Why in hell couldn't the bastards mind their own business and leave him and his mission alone?

Why he should have been so certain they would not, he did not know: but instinct, as surely as though he had read the Communist flight plan, told him they were accompanied on the Moon by no friends.

Somewhere back around 61 hours GET he had used downlink Special-1 to ask Houston to give him all it had on the Soviet vehicle. It wasn't much. They were pretty sure it was a fully maneuverable spacecraft, probably with a lander, inhabited by two men. The tiny satellite whose discoveries had started all this six months ago had monitored two heartbeats, presumably human, as the missile left from Space Station *Stalin*. He supposed it would be characteristic of a certain crude, cruel humor to send up two dogs just to make the Americans edgy, but this hardly seemed worth the trouble and expense. More likely it was two Russians bent on destroying Planetary Fleet One. Such, at least, was the assumption on which he had to proceed for the safety of his crew, his mission and himself.

Yet when he came right down to it, what, really, could be done about it? Like horrid little gnomes off on the edge of his mind he heard again the snidely jeering comments, saw again the scathingly scornful editorials—heard Frankly Unctuous unctuously saying,

". . . the question of whether or not the mission should

568

be armed, presumably to guard against some sort of attack by the Soviet Union—an attack, we might add, which seems to be more a figment of rather hysterical imagination within NASA than it is any real, or actual, or even possible threat from the Russians."

—saw the editorial by P.C.M. saying,

". . . the absurd and hysterical proposition that the spacecraft should be armed because the Soviets might, in some mysterious and unexplained fashion, seek to attack them in the skies."

—saw the *Post* and the *Times* and all their dutiful mimics, heard the smooth and oily voices, all, all echoing the same mocking, hostile, death-filled words—death for the crew and death for Piffy One, unless the Lord, Houston and their own abilities managed somehow to produce for them a miracle.

Snug, smug sons of bitches, safely home in bed. Ah, you fools, he thought: you monstrous fools of the earth! If there were only some way to make you suffer what you have done to your country, in this as in so many things.

But there was not, of course—and that was not his problem—and there was nothing to be gained now by letting himself be distracted or weakend by thinking about it.

Connie, purge hate-cells, he told himself dryly; and after a moment of great and deliberate effort of will, was able to answer himself: Roger.

So, they were not armed.

And they had a problem.

And what was he, the commander of Planetary Fleet One, responsible for money, machinery, hopes, dreams, pride, ambitions—national prestige—lives—going to do about it?

His immediate action had been to take it to the crew. It was interesting, he noted in some detached, observing portion of his mind, how they were suddenly "the crew," and no longer Jazz and Pete and Jayvee—except that they *were* Jazz and Pete and Jayvee, and that was what he had to work with, and no more—that and this gleaming mechanism floating softly in orbit around the Moon—and dear old Houston, 235,000 miles away, but, as its magnificent minds had proven with Apollo 13 and a few other things, ready and able, right next door.

After Jayvee's sudden, sharp exclamation, followed by

their quick glimpse of that tantalizing, ominous little silver dot flirting out of sight over the horizon onto the Moon's dark side, there had been a silence in *Santa Maria* for several minutes. Finally Jazz had broken it, snapping off the S-band mike as he did so.

"Well, I'll be a monkey's uncle," he said softly. "And here I am without a paddle."

"Here we all are without paddles," Pete said with a little laugh, and then looked momentarily disgusted with himself because the laugh sounded more nervous than he wanted it to. "You're not alone in that, Jazzbo."

"So what shall we do?" Jazz inquired. "Speed up on the next pass and ram 'em?"

"What would they be doing?" Jayvee asked scornfully. "Standing still?"

"Well, it's an idea," Jazz said. "I think I'm going to go polish my gun for a while."

"Yes," Connie said, "I suppose we might all do that. But then what? Anybody got any ideas?"

"Haven't you?" Jayvee asked, and his tone was not very pleasant. "You're the commander."

"I certainly am," Connie said evenly, "and when I get ready to exercise command, I will. In the meantime I'd like to know what you all think. If you don't mind."

"I think we're damned fools to get excited," Jayvee said with an impatient disgust. "I don't think we have any proof of anything and I think we'd all better just go about our business and not worry."

"Yes," Connie agreed, "I suspect that's going to be the decision when all's said and done. But if anybody has any other ideas now's the time to state 'em. Jazz?"

"Well," Jazz said slowly, "I can see that as a basic mode of procedure. But I also think we might really give some thought to defense maneuvering, and if need be, to offensive maneuvering as well. We don't know what they have on board to throw at us—"

"If they have anything," Jayvee interjected scornfully.

"If they have anything," Jazz agreed calmly. "But if they do, we may be wise to make some plans. After all, we do have three maneuverable units plus the lander. We don't have to stay docked, if worst comes to worst. We can get quite a bit of flexibility here, if we have to."

"That's true," Pete said. "But wouldn't that be pretty damned risky, too?"

Jazz shrugged.

"So it's risky, buddy. Is it your idea of a picnic to have those babies get too close?"

"No, of course not. I'm just wondering if there isn't something we can do on the ground first."

"Such as what?"

"Well, the President did say—"

"The President," Jazz said scornfully. "That crap artist."

"And the man who appointed you, too," Connie said with mock reproach. "Is that gratitude? That's not such a bad idea, Pete. Nor is yours, Jazz. We'll make plans. And we'll call Houston. And we'll keep on doing what we're doing. So you see, Jayvee, everybody's going to be happy. Now," he said, with a wry smile at the disgusted look that comment brought him, "stand by and let's see what we get." And he reached over and snapped on Special-1. "Houston, this is One."

"Roger, One," Stu Yule said quickly, his voice alert. "What's up?"

"Can you put Bob Hertz on?"

"Just a minute. He's talking to Washington."

"You see?" Pete said. "Leave it to our Bob."

"Wait a minute," Connie said. "Don't jump to conclusions . . . Robert?"

"Yes, Connie," Bob Hertz said, calm and pleasant across a quarter of a million miles. "Sorry to make you wait. I've been talking to the President. What's on your mind?"

"Well," Connie said slowly, "we have a—a question, up here."

"I know you do. Your biomed telemetry's still on, you know. About five minutes ago all your graphs went through the roof. That's why I called the President. But you had the S-band off—which is a damned foolish thing to do, incidentally, please don't do it again—so we couldn't talk to you. I assumed you saw your friends, however. At least that's what I told the President just now, so I hope I was right."

"You're always right," Connie said. "That's why we love you. They're roughly a half a moon away, going into the dark side just as we came out. Approximately same orbit, approximately same velocity. Do you have any thoughts about it?"

"One or two."

"Good. We're receptive."

"I'd better tell you what his reaction was, first. It may have a bearing."

"It may," Connie said, somewhat dryly. "And then again, he isn't in orbit with the Reds peeking over his shoulder, and we are. But go ahead."

"He isn't entirely convinced there's danger," Bob said slowly.

"That sounds like him," Jazz said dourly. "Don't rock the boat and make 'em mad."

"To some degree, that's his position," Bob said crisply. "And to some degree, it's mine."

"But, Bob——" Connie began in a disgusted tone.

"Have you got proof they're hostile?" Bob interrupted.

There was a silence from the Moon.

"No——o," Pete said finally. "Have you got proof they aren't?"

"Not the slightest," Bob said.

"Then isn't it a fair presumption," Connie suggested, "that we'd better get ready for whatever might happen?"

"What do you have in mind?"

"Possibly undocking."

"That would be a damn-fool thing to do," Bob said tartly. "You'd be completely vulnerable then, it seems to me."

"Three targets instead of one," Jazz remarked.

"To be picked off one by one," Bob said. "If," he added quickly, "we have to assume anybody's going to do any picking. Our consensus is that you ought to stay together. It also is that until there's some proof, we're all going to have to assume this is a friendly mission. Now, just suppose," he said over the murmur of protest that came clearly across 235,000 miles, "that suddenly you fellows start taking all sorts of evasive action—some of it lending itself to the clear interpretation that it's hostile and offensive—and there they are, just swinging peacefully around in orbit. You're not only going to look like fools, you're also going to look like you're trying to aggress and knock down a perfectly legitimate Soviet space probe. This might cause a few lifted eyebrows in Moscow. You might not even have any Earth left to come back to."

"And suppose they take hostile action against us while we're being good boys and behaving ourselves," Jazz in-

572

quired dryly. "Have they been reminded again by our great leader that *they* might not have any Earth left to come back to?"

"He's going to call in the Soviet Ambassador and reiterate his previous statement," Bob said. "He thinks that'll be enough."

"That's a great help," Connie remarked. "Why will they believe him this time, when they've called our bluff on so many things before?"

"He thinks that will be sufficient," Bob repeated.

"Is he going to make any public announcement of this?" Pete asked.

"No."

"So we're going to be up here," Connie said, "facing possible attack at any moment, and our own country and the world aren't even going to know about it. Right?"

"That's right," Bob said quietly. "And as I said earlier, I'm not so sure I don't agree with him. Because, look, now: what good would it do to get the whole world frantic *when we don't have any proof?* Imagine the climate it would create—instantly—everywhere. It would immediately become a face-to-face showdown. World tension would be unbearable. This country would be in such an uproar the President couldn't move, probably, there'd be so many conflicting pressures. We might quite literally be on the edge of world war. It would be a hell of a thing."

"And there's been no word at all," Connie asked, "anywhere?"

"One or two vague reports from Jodrell Bank about a Soviet launch from *Stalin*, but not a word of confirmation from Moscow or us. In fact, we've denied we know anything and added the assumption that it's simply some sort of deep space scientific probe."

"That was helpful of you."

"Well, I repeat, what would you have us do? Can't you see what I'm getting at?"

"Oh yes," Connie agreed, "we can see. But I think I can speak for all of us—most of us—when I say we'd feel a hell of a lot better if everybody knew the situation. There's some protective value in the public spotlight, you know. As it is, I'm very much afraid you're making us feel like a sacrifice up here—just a nice sitting duck—bait, you might say, for those who want to fish."

"That sounds pretty bitter."

"We are bitter. It *is* a hell of a thing: you're right."

"Well," Bob said. "We're coming up on loss of signal again in about five minutes. The President wants you to continue with the misssion as planned unless and until you have unmistakable proof of hostile intent. And that's our advice here, too. We'll go back on S-band for the second pass and you continue as scheduled. We'll be asking you about what you're seeing and you can tell us. The conversation will be discreet, impersonal and enlightening to the folks back home, who like to feel a vicarious thrill ... I don't mean to sound insensitive, you know I'm not. But at least for the time being, that's the way it's got to be. O.K.?"

"All right," Connie said grimly, "but I understand I am still commander of this spacecraft, right?"

"You are."

"And if an emergency develops, we have a right to meet it as best we can."

"Right."

"And if we see one coming, we have the right to make whatever preparations we deem necessary."

"We don't want you undocked, Connie."

"We won't undock. But we may get ready."

"There is an area, of course," Bob Hertz said formally, "where you have to exercise final judgment and where the ground can't do more than suggest. However, we have given you your parameters, for the time being. We are relying on your honor to stay within them, because if you do not, the international consequences could be ghastly."

"And to us," Connie replied evenly, "as pleasant as a little picnic. Special-1, over and out."

"Roger, and out," Bob Hertz said.

Again there was a silence in *Santa Maria*. Pete broke it this time.

"Well: shall we get ready?"

Jazz started to get up.

Jayvee spoke with a lazily overbearing drawl.

"Not too ready."

"What?" Connie said.

"Not too ready," Jayvee repeated in the same insolent way. "I mean, don't carry those plans for our big dramatic battle in space too far, will you? Because I might have to tell Houston, if you did." He smiled elaborately into their angry faces. "I'd only be following orders."

574

For several moments he and Connie exchanged stare for stare. Then Connie spoke quietly.

"And if we didn't want you to?"

"I'm afraid you might have to restrain me," Jayvee said with a fleering calm. "If you could."

"Well, buster," Jazz said softly, "we might just do that, now. We just might."

Jayvee shrugged.

"I wouldn't advise it. We've got enough worries with *them* without fighting inside here—haven't we? . . . And now," he said, pulling himself out of his seat with an elaborate yawn, "I think I'll get me a few z's. Coming, Jazz-bo?"

"You stay and talk with me for a minute, Jazz," Connie said, forestalling what was obviously going to be a savage retort. "Come on into *Pinta*. Pete, take over, O.K.?"

"Roger," Pete said, watching Jayvee with a speculative glance as he pulled himself into the hatch to *Nina* and disappeared. Then he swung back to the window. "There they come again," he said quietly.

Up into the tawny light, appearing on this pass, because of their relative positions, to be pursuing instead of fleeing, the tiny bright dot moved steadily higher.

Planetary Fleet One slid over the rim into darkness.

Connie sighed.

And now they were back on the bright side, Man in the Moon had disappeared again with a last flick of light that seemed almost derisive, and the chatter which now seemed more than a little inane to him was going back and forth to Houston. But he had his orders and he obeyed them: knowing that he and Jazz had made some specific plans and were in reasonably good shape; knowing also that, so far, there had not been the slightest indication of anything hostile from their ubiquitous company. It made the chatter momentarily a little easier, though it did nothing to remove his underlying conviction that this ominous game of silent tag might yet explode into something desperate and terrible. *Janie*, he said to her in his mind, *you may be right*. But to Houston and the listening world he said with a reasonably cheerful steadiness:

"Houston, this is One. We thought you'd be interested in getting a glimpse of what we're seeing up here as we fly along on this second pass over the bright side of the

Moon" . . . "Roger, One, go ahead. You've got the world for an audience. Over" . . . "Roger, that's flattering. What you see now is Smyth's Sea. We're about 88 degrees east of it, I would estimate. It doesn't look like much of a sea from up here, does it?—devoid of craters and sort of a hilly area. I wonder who named these things? . . . "Obviously not the guys who've been there, Connie. Can you see Manzinus?" . . . "Right, looking back we can see it very clearly right—there . . . We're coming up on Crater Schubert and Gilbert directly below, now. This is close to where we'll be starting powered descent with *Adventurer* later on, when we head down to Tranquillity Base for our first test run. Incidentally, I'll have word on that very shortly" . . . "Good, Connie. Are those the Schubert craters?" . . . "Yes, you can see there's a triple crater with a small crater between the first and third. Schubert N has a very conical inside wall and there seem to be a number of tall craters on the bottom. Now we're beginning to see Alpha 1, which is not a very large crater but a very bright one, relatively recent as such things go. Maybe a couple of billion years. Now we're coming up on the Sea of Fertility, which is about as much sea and about as much fertile as all the others. We're beginning to get a good view of the track leading into the Tranquillity landing site now, and pretty soon we ought to be able to spot the permanent hut left by Apollo 17—yes, there it is, that little bright spot you can see gleaming down there just to the left of that group of small craters. That's where we'll be going in to check some of the scientific equipment left by 17 and previous Apollos, and also to check out some of our portable Mars equipment we're taking along on this flight. Now we're over Tranquillity, directly below. That hut is roughly 10 feet by 10 feet, constructed of aluminum sheets, and probably not necessary to protect anything in the Moon's atmosphere, or lack of it, rather; but I guess man just likes to have the feel of a house around him wherever he goes. How's that for philosophy, Houston?" . . . "You're doing great, Connie. After we finish the tour, we want to give you the data for lunar orbit insertion 2 and we also have the TEI 05 pad ready for you" . . . "Roger. We're very close now to what will be ignition point for powered descent of *Adventurer* tomorrow. We're just passing Mount Maryland, that triangular-shaped mountain you can see in the center. And now we're coming up on Boot Hill, which we'll see about 20 seconds into the descent. Hope this will give you some idea of the terrain here, which as you can see hasn't changed much from the last time you saw it on the last Apollo mission. Somehow those strawberries and corn all of us planted don't seem to have taken hold very well—at least the strawberries haven't. I guess you can see from the commentary that the corn is still flourishing. Ready for LOI 2 and TEI 05, Houston. Jayvee will take. Terminating camera. Over" . . . "Roger, One, thanks very much. O.K. Jayvee, LO1 2, SPS G&N 38320 plus 166— . . .

"This is Mission Control, at 79 hours, 9 minutes into the flight of Planetary Fleet One. We currently read an apolune of 170.2 nautical miles and perilune of 61.2 nautical miles. The time of burn will be 80 hours, 11 minutes, 36 seconds, which should bring us into a tighter orbit of 65.7 nautical miles by 53.7 nautical miles, preparatory to descent of the Mars Lander. The crew is now busy with preparation for this second lunar orbit insertion burn . . .

"Houston, activate Special-1, please" . . . "Roger. Special-1. How goes, Connie?" . . . "Not bad. Jazz and Jayvee are asleep and I've got Pete busy in *Pinta*, so I thought I'd talk. Bob, I think I'll take Pete down with me on the first descent" . . . "You don't want to send Jazz and Jayvee? Or Jayvee and Pete?" . . . "No—I don't think so. In the first place, if there's any skulduggery, I have a feeling it's going to be on the surface and not in the air, so it's my place to go myself and not send somebody else" . . . "You still think there's going to be some. Any signs?" . . . "No. Of course we're blind here. We just catch a quick glimpse, and that's all. Do you monitor anything down there?" . . . "No. The Department of Defense is helping some, but actually we've never really been able to monitor any of their space communications satisfactorily, as you know. I think they're in a deaf-dumb mode anyway. We don't detect a trace of *any* communications. They probably have their orders with them" . . . "That's a happy thought" . . . "Right. But still, no proof" . . . "Roger, still no proof" . . . "Why do you want Pete with you, Connie?" . . . "Because I can rely on him absolutely—as I could on Jazz, of course. But horrible though it might sound to our editorial friends, I would not trust Jayvee with me down there, and I would not trust Jayvee up here with Pete if Jazz and I went down. He's too tough for Pete—or too erratic anyway—if anything happened. I think Jazz, on the other hand—although they hate each other's guts, which poses some problems in pairing them—is too tough for Jayvee, if anything happened. So the only logical breakdown I can see in terms of human material is Pete and myself, and Jazz and Jayvee ... "When you say 'if anything happened,' now, you don't mean from the Russians, right?" ... "Right. I mean if Jayvee acts—the way I think Jayvee might be capable of acting" ... "Any signs of that, either?" ... "The usual: hostile—basically unfriendly" ... "But not incompetent or unreliable?" ... "Not yet, Robert. Not yet. Does Houston confirm Pete for first MLM descent?" ... "Roger, confirm. Again, I think you may be worrying too much. But that's your job" ... "Hmph. Good-by, Bob. Special-1, over and out" ... "Roger, and out ...

"This is Mission Control at 80 hours, 7 minutes into the flight of Planetary Fleet One. We are now 4 minutes, 11 seconds from ignition of the second lunar injection burn, which is to take place near perilune on the far side of the Moon during the present loss of signal period. The burn will not be targeted to place the spacecraft into a precise circular orbit. As we learned from Apollo 10, we want a burn that will take into account predicted perturbations and gradually circularize itself. The burn is scheduled to last 17 seconds and give us an apolune of 65.7 nautical miles and a perilune of 53.7 nautical miles ... It's getting quiet here in Mission Control as we wait for this burn. Mark 30 seconds to burn. Mark 10 seconds. Mark 5 seconds. Mark, planned time for ignition ...

"This is Mission Control. Goldstone tracking station has just acquired signal from Planetary Fleet One. The second burn has been highly successful and Connie Trasker reports we have achieved our planned orbit from which descent will be made. During this next pass over the near side of the Moon we'll have our final familiarization excursion into the Mars Landing Module by Flight Commander Connie Trasker and Dr. Pete Balkis, who will make the first practice descent with him. This is Mission Control at 80 hours, 37 minutes into the flight of Planetary Fleet One to Mars ..."

578

On the fifth pass, two minutes after they came up over the terminator from dark to light, they became aware that the mocking little flash of silver when their company ducked over the horizon had not left the sky empty.

Something was still there.

At first each of them quite literally thought he might have a speck of dust or a fugitive crumb of food in his eye, so tiny and elusive was it, the merest hint of a presence. Then they checked with one another, broke out the binoculars and telescopes, took a really good look just as the new intruder followed its parent over the edge into darkness.

"Houston, this is One," Connie said, his tone more tired and annoyed than anything else. "Activate Special-1, please."

"Roger, One. You're on Special-1."

"Bob?"

"No, this is Jim Cavanaugh, Connie. Your telemetry's getting lively again, I was just going to call you. What is it?"

"They've dropped something. We think it's a lander."

"Any indication of descent?"

"Not yet. Traveling approximately their velocity, same orbit, about ten miles behind the mother craft, as near as we can estimate from here. Advise, please."

"Well," Dr. Cavanaugh said slowly. "Let me call Washington. I'll get back to you in five minutes. Stand by on circuit. Over."

"Roger, standing by on circuit, over . . ."

"Connie, this is Jim again. I talked to the President. His position is the same: we haven't any proof of anything—it may be entirely innocent and scientific—he can't precipitate an international crisis without proof—he wants you to continue as planned unless, or until, you have proof of an anomaly warranting other action. He wants you to know he is in closest touch with NASA and all other intelligence sources at all times and if any proof of hostility comes to him from any source he will immediately react in a way Moscow cannot ignore. But that's the best he can do right now. He is sure you will understand all his reasons."

"What's your opinion, Jim?"

"I really don't know what to tell you, Conn. On the basis of all known factors as of now, he's being scrupulously correct, isn't he? And I guess that's about all any of us can do, at the moment. What's your opinion up there?"

"We don't have much choice, do we?"

"Connie, I'm afraid not. We ache for you down here but we're as helpless as you are, for the time being. Let us know the *instant* anything happens. The *instant*."

"Roger, Jim. We appreciate your feelings. Guess we'd better get back to work, now. Special-1, over and out."

"Over and out."

"This is Mission Control at 95 hours, 25 minutes Ground Elapsed Time into the mission of Planetary Fleet One to Mars. During these past several hours we've had a very thorough and satisfactory communications check with the spacecraft. The crew has been taking individual rest periods from time to time during these hours and performing a number of routine duties. Flight Commander Connie Trasker and Pete Balkis have again gone into the MLM *Adventurer* for some further check-outs and reported back all is well there. To give you an idea of what's coming up in these last few hours as the crew approaches its first major event of the flight, the test descent of *Adventurer* to the Moon's surface at Tranquillity Base, first we'll have a separation burn, scheduled to occur at 100 hours, 39 minutes, 50 seconds. It will be followed on the dark side of the moon by the descent orbit insertion maneuver at 101 hours, 36 minutes, 14 seconds. This will place *Adventurer* about two miles from Planetary Fleet One. Powered descent of the MLM to the Moon's surface will then begin at 102 hours, 33 minutes, 4 seconds, GET.

"Planetary Fleet One is presently in an orbit with a pericynthion of 55.7 nautical miles and an apocynthion of 63.8 nautical miles. Lunar orbit velocity is 5368 feet per second, at 95 hours, 30 minutes into the flight."

"Houston, activate Special-1, please. We've lost it."

"What, Jazz, Man in the Moon?"

"Nope, he's here. His baby. Completely missing on this pass."

"You don't suppose they've redocked?"

"Haven't the slightest. We just know it isn't there any more."

"Assume you're checking surface."

"Absolutely. Negative."

"You're sure."

"Well, as sure as four experienced astronauts can be with the equipment we have available."

"O.K., not challenging. Nothing on infra-red, either?"

"I.R. negative also. There are ways of evading that, though, you know."

"Roger. Well, keep looking."

"You damned betcha. Give our love to the President. Special-1, over and out."

"Over and out."

"This is Mission Control at 98 hours, 20 minutes Ground Elapsed Time. We have just reacquired signal from Planetary Fleet One in its twelfth revolution of the Moon. At this time Connie Trasker and Pete Balkis have entered the Mars Landing Module *Adventurer* preparatory to their descent to the Moon's surface at Tranquillity Base. They're presently completing pressure checks on their space suits. Coming up in this revolution they will be running checks on the guidance platform of the *Adventurer* guidance system. They'll also be running checks on the reaction control system thrusters and their descent propulsion system, as well as the rendezvous radar. Up to this point they report check-out and activation has been moving along very smoothly. Communications are still rather noisy and will probably continue that way until they complete orbital navigation, at which time we expect to be able to get a high-gain antenna and MLM steerable antenna lock and there should be some improvement.

"Jazz Weickert and Jayvee Halleck in *Santa Maria* are preparing to take marks on a landmark near the prime landing site, Tranquillity Base. This information will be used here in Mission Control to update the ground's knowledge of where the spacecraft are. This in turn will assist in getting the precise time for the powered descent.

"We'll be giving Connie and Pete their GO/NO-GO decision for undocking about ten minutes before losing signal on this twelfth revolution. If the decision is GO, which looks probable from all indications coming in so far, the maneuver will occur on the dark side of the moon just prior to our reacquiring the spacecraft on the next revolution.

"Planetary Fleet One is currently in an orbit with an apocynthion of 63.5 nautical miles and a pericynthion of

55.1, as the apocynthion continues to drop and the peri-cynthion to rise and the orbit becomes more and more circular around the Moon.

"This is Mission Control at 98 hours, 25 minutes into the flight."

They completed their suit checks, their guidance checks, their reaction control system checks, their descent system checks, their redezvous radar checks, received their GO from Houston. Piffy One slid over the terminator and entered the dark side. He looked at Pete and shook his head with a slow smile. Pete returned it, much more cheerful now. The little green panel light indicating the direct line between *Santa Maria* and *Adventurer* blinked on.

"How are you guys doing?" Jazz asked. "Had enough?"

"That was quite a little workout," Connie admitted. "But we're happy, aren't we, Petros?"

"Couldn't be better," Pete said cheerfully. "Bring on the Man in the Moon and all his descendants."

"Yeah," Jazz said dryly. "I wish to hell we knew where those bastards are. I'd feel a lot better."

"Wouldn't we all," Connie agreed. "But God knows we've looked and looked."

"Probably gone back to the mother ship and they're getting ready to go home," Jayvee said calmly. "No reason to think anything else. They never have developed a real capacity to land. They probably thought they'd run a scientific probe, get us upset, and then shove off. It's worked. We are upset."

"There speaks the philosopher," Jazz remarked. "Is that the sort of thing you'd do?"

"All right, Jazz," Connie said. "We hope you're right, Jayvee. But if you see 'em coming back, let us know, won't you."

Jayvee grunted, a sarcastic sound.

"Yes, I'll let you know."

"Good," Connie said. "And, Jazz—you two be careful up there, too, O.K.? We want you there when we get ready to rendezvous."

"We'll be here," Jazz said; and repeated with a sudden grimness, "we'll be here."

"Counting on that," Connie said. "Guess we'd all better sign off and get ready now, O.K.?"

582

"Roger," Jazz said. "Don't forget to write."

"You're at the head of the list," Pete assured him.

After the green light blinked off and the circuit went dead they sat silently for a while, studying the glowing panels in front of them, glancing out from time to time at the impenetrable blackness all around, peering down now and then in unsuccessful attempts to distinguish features of the desolate surface streaking away sixty miles below.

Five minutes before undocking, Connie glanced over and smiled.

"Nice to have you aboard, pal," he said. "Everything's going to be O.K."

Pete smiled back. The tension that had begun to creep into his eyes and jaw relaxed.

"If you say so, Dad."

"I say so," Connie said, and prepared to close his visor.

"That's good enough for me," Pete said; and suddenly as he followed suit he grinned, and for a moment looked entirely untroubled, unselfconscious, happy, excited and young.

Many and many a time later, though he did not know it now, Connie would recall that moment and that grin: poignant and touching and possessing the power to hurt forever, when he remembered it against the background of the events that followed, during the visit of *Adventurer* to the surface of the Moon.

"This is Mission Control, at 100 hours, 17 minutes, having just reacquired signal from the spacecraft on the thirteenth revolution. Connie Trasker and Pete Balkis in *Adventurer* are safely undocked from Planetary Fleet One, and in about 20 minutes Jazz Weickert and Jayvee Halleck will perform separation burn which will provide a distance of about two miles between the two craft after *Adventurer* makes its descent orbit insertion maneuver. The separation burn will occur at 100 hours, 39 minutes, 50 seconds, to be followed by the descent orbit insertion maneuver at 101 hours, 36 minutes, 14 seconds. Approximately one hour after that, at 102 hours, 33 minutes, 4 seconds, *Adventurer* will begin its powered descent to the Moon's surface at Tranquillity Base . . .

"Hello, *Adventurer*, Houston. If you will give us 2 and data, we've got the loads for you. We have a DOI pad and a PDI pad" . . . "Roger, ready to copy." . . . "O.K., Pete,

583

here goes DOI: 101361407 981 minus 00758 plus all balls plus 00098 plus— ...

"Houston, this is *Santa Maria*. How do you hear me?" ... "Loud and clear, Jazz" ... "Good. Everything's looking good here. *Adventurer* looks as happy as a clam drifting along down there" ... "Houston, this is *Adventurer*. Two clams" ... "Roger, we can tell things are getting pretty clammy up there. Over" ... "Better say over and *out*, after that one, Houston ... "

"This is Mission Control, at 101 hours, 7 minutes. We're coming up now on 15 minutes to loss of signal with MLM *Adventurer*. The Flight Director has advised all his flight controllers to review data and take a good look at the spacecraft in preparation for a GO/NO-GO decision on the descent orbit insertion ...

"*Adventurer*, this is Houston. We have special greetings and good wishes for you from Dr. Freer and Andy Anderson, who are here in the viewing room. Al Freer says he wished he were with you right now, and Andy says the President joins him in saying be of good cheer, all looks fine from where they sit. Over" ... "Thanks to Doc, we wish he were with us, too. We couldn't ask for better company. Tell Andy and the President since we don't seem to have company, their word is good to have to take down with us. Over" ... "Roger, *Adventurer*. You are GO for descent orbit insertion. GO for DOI. Over" ... "Roger, thank you. Over ...

"This is Mission Control at 102 hours, 12 minutes. We're now 1 minute, 39 seconds from reacquiring Planetary Fleet One, after loss of signal on this latest pass around the far side. If all went well, insertion to our descent orbit has now taken place. We'll reacquire *Adventurer* about two minutes later, on this fourteenth revolution. At the time we acquire *Adventurer* they should be at an altitude of about 18 nautical miles, descending toward the 50,000 foot pericynthion from which point they will initiate their powered descent to the lunar surface. If for any reason the crew does not like the way things look down there, simply by not initiating the maneuver they will be able to remain in a safe orbit of 60 miles by 50,000 feet, and can then attempt powered descent on the following revolution ... The work controller says we now have acquisition of *Santa Maria*. We'll stand by for acquisition of *Adventurer* ... We have *Adventurer*. We

584

are now 19 minutes from the beginning of powered descent to the lunar surface . . ."

The green light was on again, the four of them were linked for one last moment before initiation of maneuver.

"How do you feel about it?" he asked. "Shall we take her down?"

Pete nodded, his face behind the visor solemn and intent.

"Ready if you are."

"Good boy. We'll commit."

"Good luck," said Jazz, above.

"*Adventurer*, do you read? You were garbled, just then. Coming up 3 minutes, 30 seconds to ignition" . . . "Roger, MARK 3:30. Our translation force is balanced couple ON, TA throttle, auto, CDR, Stop button, reset, stop button. Check abort, abort stage reset, att. control, 3 of them to mode control, PGNS mode control is set, AGS is reading 400 plus 1, standing by for arming . . .

"This is Mission Control. That was Pete Balkis reading off the checklist to Connie Trasker . . .

"Hit VERB 77. Sequence camera coming on . . .

"Coming up on 1 minute to ignition, *Adventurer* . . . Roger. We have ignition. Starting descent, altitude about 46,000 feet and continuing to descend . . .

"Everything looks good, *Adventurer*.

"Good here, too, Houston. Altitude 40,000 . . . Altitude 35,000 . . . 27,000 . . . 13,000, velocity down to 760 feet per second . . .

"*Adventurer*, you're looking great at 5200 feet. You're GO for landing" . . .

"Roger, understand, GO for landing. 2000 feet. 47 degrees . . .

"Roger. *Adventurer*, you're looking great at 1600 feet—1400—everything still looking very good . . .

"We're happy, Houston. 750 feet, coming down at 23 . . . 700, down at 21 . . . 500 feet . . . 400 . . . 350 . . . 300 . . . 250 . . . 200 . . . 100 . . . 75 feet, everything looking good . . . Down a half. 6 forward . . . Lights on Down 2½ . . . Forward . . . 40 feet, down 2½, picking up some dust . . . 30 feet. 4 forward, 4 forward, drifting to the left a little . . . Contact light on . . . Engine stop. ACA out of detent. Modes control both auto, descent, engine command override, off. Engine arm, off. Houston, Tranquillity Base here. *Adventurer* has landed. I still see some of those old beer cans we left on Apollo 16. That's a joke, world. We really didn't. Honest, we didn't.

"That's right, world. They really didn't. Good going, Conn. Make yourselves at home . . .

"This is Mission Control, where everybody's happy. MLM *Adventurer* has landed at Tranquillity Base, Moon, and will be on the surface approximately twenty hours. First item on the crew schedule will be a rest period of six hours, after which they'll descend to the lunar surface, take a short test ride in the Mars rover, check on a number of scientific experiments placed there in the Apollo program, and practice distribution and placement of equipment they'll be putting on the surface of Mars eight months from now. We expect things to be fairly quiet for a while, now, both from Connie Trasker and Pete Balkis in *Adventurer* and from Jazz Weickert and Jayvee Halleck in Planetary Fleet One, which is orbiting above the Moon's surface in a near-circular orbit of about sixty-one miles. Jazz and Jayvee have a scheduled rest period too, so we expect things will be pretty routine all around until approximately 109 hours GET, when we'll go on television to bring you the descent of Connie Trasker and Pete Balkis to the lunar surface. This is Mission Control at 102 hours, 53 minutes into the flight of Planetary Fleet One to Mars."

At GET 103 hours, 52 minutes, emerging from the far side, Jazz, standing watch in *Santa Maria*, while Jayvee slept in *Nina*, realized with a start that the silver sliver was no longer visible ahead.

Looking back an hour later as they neared the horizon and began to glide once more toward darkness, he saw with a rising tension that it had reappeared behind him, a good five minutes earlier than it had on previous occasions.

Special-1 clicked on simultaneously from ground and spacecraft.

"What's up?" Bob Hertz demanded.

"They're beginning to close on us."

"God *damn* it," Bob Hertz said.

Jazz snorted.

"You can say that again. I'll wake Jayvee and alert

Connie. Think we better stay on this link, as long as the President doesn't want it made public to alarm anybody?"

"Right. We aren't putting out anything anyway at the moment, since you're supposed to be in a six-hour sleep period."

Jazz said "Ha!" in a wry voice. "At the rate I estimate they're gaining on us, it isn't going to take six hours to decide this thing."

"Well, play it cool and don't do anything until you absolutely have to."

"We won't. But I want you right there from now on. I may need advice."

"We'll be here," Bob said quietly.

At Tranquillity Base the green light glowed again in *Adventurer*.

"Conn," Jazz said, "the bad guys appear to be coming up on the good guys."

"Put me on Special-1," Connie said, and it was an order. "Bob? Oh, Andy. What the hell are we supposed to do now, keep on playing patty-cake?"

"At the risk of sounding monotonous—and heartless," the Administrator said, and an evident strain was in his voice, "all we can suggest here is that you continue the flight plan as scheduled *until we have proof* that this is a hostile approach. At this moment we don't know whether they're coming any closer—what they'll do if they do come closer—or anything about it. Do we?"

"No, we don't," Connie acknowledged, "but we ought to know very shortly, if Jazz' estimate of the overtake is correct."

"Let's see if it is," Dr. Anderson suggested.

"Shall we abort the descent and rendezvous on the next pass?"

"We'd rather you didn't unless we have absolute grounds to justify it."

"We can find some."

"Yes," Andy said, "and then what? Huddle back in Piffy One and not venture out because we're afraid they might do something—*might* do something? Let ourselves be scared by a little psychological warfare? Let them paralyze us from accomplishing our mission just because we *think* they might do something? We can't do that, Connie, and you know it. Furthermore, you'll be on worldwide television and that's a safeguard, right there. And in addition to all that, you fellows wouldn't really want to run away. Now, would you?"

There was silence on Special-1. Finally Connie replied in a slow and thoughtful voice.

"No, I think I can honestly say we would not. But I do suggest this, Andy: since we're dealing with unknowns here—and potentially very dangerous unknowns—suppose we just get this descent over with and get the hell back up there as fast as we can, O.K.? I don't want to spend a lot of time messing around down here while my ship may be in trouble up there."

"Your ship is in good hands," Jazz said; and then added quickly, "But of course you're right. I agree with him one hundred per cent, Andy. How about it?"

"That makes sense to me," Dr. Anderson agreed. "How soon can you get started?"

"One hour and thirty."

"And finished?"

"Plus two."

"Very well," the Administrator said. "Move."

"Yes, sir," Connie said. "Thank you."

Special-1 went dead for a moment; the command link stayed open.

"Well, my friend," Connie said. "Looks like we have our work cut out for us."

"This is a long way from Da Nang, isn't it?" Jazz said.

"Not so far. Not so very far, at all. Same gang, same evil, same war. Is Jayvee up?"

"I'll get him up."

"I'll wake Pete and we'll get to it."

"Good luck to you, pal."

"And you."

"Roger."

"Pete," he said, shaking his shoulder, rousing him sleepy-eyed and drowsy like some amiable, white suited Teddy bear still drowned in dreams. "Seems they want us to perform early."

"Roger," Pete said, instantly awake. "Let's go."

"This is Mission Control, at 105 hours, 16 minutes into the flight of Planetary Fleet One. We've just been notified by Bob Hertz here in Mission Control that it's been decided to go ahead immediately with the moon-walk and scientific-test phase of the mission at this time instead of

588

approximately six hours from now as orginally planned. ("Oh?" said the *Times* sharply as the newsroom abruptly quieted down; but the words went on, bland and comfortable, and the quick, tense puzzlement as quickly receded.) Dr. Hertz informs us that this is at the direct request of the crew, who it seems are wide-awake and eager to get going. Since everybody here is ready, too, the consensus is that there's not much point in an arbitrary wait. So Connie Trasker and Pete Balkis have been given their GO to leave *Adventurer* and descend to the lunar surface about twenty minutes from now. There they'll take a short practice drive in the modified Marsrover that they'll be taking with them to Mars. They will also do some practice placements of various types of equipment they'll be leaving on the Martian surface. Finally they will return to the hut at Tranquillity Base and check out several of the experiments left there by the last two Apollo flights. They hope to show as much of this as they can on television. Meanwhile Jazz Weickert and Jayvee Halleck will be standing by in Planetary Fleet One, orbiting above, looking toward rendezvous with *Adventurer* when she completes her two-hour visit to the lunar surface. ("Two hours?" exclaimed the Denver *Post*. "I thought it was supposed to be six." But Mission Control had an explanation for that, too, and again the momentary wonderment subsided—if it. did not, this time, entirely go away.) There's been a change there, too, as you're probably aware, but again it's a matter of the crew being in real good shape and raring to go. Connie's confident they can complete all their assigned tasks in the two-hour period, so again, Bob Hertz and his flight directors have decided to concur. We'll be standing by now for coverage of the first practice visit of the crew of Planetary Fleet One to the Moon, in preparation for their later visits to the planet Mars. The next voices you will be hearing between Houston and the spacecraft will be those of Connie Trasker and Pete Balkis conferring with Astronaut Stuart Yule, who will be Capsule Communicator for this phase of the mission. As soon as Connie and Pete get their television cameras in place, we'll be bringing you worldwide coverage of their stay on the lunar surface. Stand by . . ."

"Hello, *Adventurer*, this is Houston. How are you coming on cabin depressurization?"

"Fine, Stu. We'll be completed in about ten minutes, I

589

should think. Pete now activating elevator for Marsrover. He'll report in a minute."

"Working beautifully. Just beautifully. There—she—goes—touchdown. Elevator on surface, Marsrover ready for egress."

"Good, Pete. Can you adjust that left camera just a little bit? First test pics coming in a little shady and we find the leg is getting in the way of the ladder about halfway down."

"Roger, adjust. How's that?"

"Much better, thanks. No problems showing up on portable life support systems so far?"

"None."

"Good. We figure you've expended about fifteen minutes of PLSS oxygen so far."

"Roger. Hey, *Santa Maria*, how's the view up there?"

"Contracting a bit as we get toward the dark side, but at the moment not enough to interfere with near visibility."

"That's good. Keep looking."

"Yeaay, boy."

"Conn, we're showing a real low static pressure on your cabin, now, about 1.2 psi. Do you think you can open the hatch at that pressure?"

"O.K., we'll try . . . She's coming open . . . Hatch open. Ah! Fresh air! Nothing like it."

"Don't breathe heavy or you'll take off and turn into a Moonlet. How's suit pressure and portable life systems doing?"

"Fine, perfectly comfortable. Guess we'll be ready to go on network TV for our many fans in about five minutes, if that's all right with you."

"Couldn't be better. We have loss of signal on One, now. How soon do you plan to enter Marsrover after stepdown?"

"About fifteen, I think. It'll take us that long to get TV cable clear and stationary camera placed."

"You're taking a portable with you."

"Right, as far as cable will reach, then we'll leave it and pick up on return. That will be roughly 500 feet out."

"You're GO here for rover trip of approximately two miles, but distance your discretion, Bob says."

"Roger. Think we'll make it about 4000 feet round trip for reasons of time."

"Roger, we copy."

590

"Good. We're activating on-board camera for full transmission now. Pete in charge. Tell us how you read."

"Blurred—now better—better—great, Pete. Just great. See landing site like the palm of your hand."

"Seat of Connie's pants is what you'll see first."

"I'm going to start egress to platform now, courtesy Dr. Balkis, assisting physician."

"That's me. You're lined up nicely . . . To right, a little . . . Now toward me . . . Toward me a little, now down—down. O.K., you made it, all clear."

"Am I centered on platform?"

"Róll to right. O.K. You're lined up on platform. Now move your right foot forward a little . . . That's good . . . Roll left . . . You're still not quite squared away. Roll to the left a little, roll left . . . Right foot just a little to left . . . Got it. You're fine."

"Good. Starting descent."

"Roger, you're coming in great. We see your legs."

"Beautiful, aren't they? Houston, I ought to have something to say. This is the third time for me up here. Give me some noble words, quick."

"Maybe we'd better save them for Pete. It's his first."

"I stand corrected. And humbled."

"That'll be the day."

"Don't laugh, it may happen."

"Never in our time. Those legs are coming in great. Also the gluteus maximus. Better hurry on down, now. We can't take much more."

"Stuart, you're in fine fettle. I'm getting there . . . Just a minute and I'll—be—*down*."

"We see you. Welcome to the Moon."

"Home again . . . Here comes Junior . . . Take it easy, Petros. You almost overshot that second step there. Don't get your small steps and your giant leaps mixed up."

"Houston, that's what's known as a great help. Is he out of the way?"

"Standing back, Pete, open-mouthed with amazement."

"He'll get it filled—with—moon—dust—that—way. O.K., I'm going to pause a minute on the last step. Have you got those words for me?"

"How about, 'I just want to use your men's room'?"

"Stu, you're *great*. And the little Moonman will say, 'I'm sorry, we only give the key to customers.' No, maybe

I'd better just step down. So here goes, I'm—*down*. How about that?"

"Magnificent. We'd think you'd been here a dozen times. Connie, you've got a real gung-ho crewmate there."

"Made a good choice, didn't I? Watch us get busy now and put out the stationary camera and make sure the cable is unwound. Then we'll get the portable camera ready, and then we'll be taking you aboard the Marsrover with us. Stand by."

"Roger. Everything's coming in great, Conn . . ."

"There. Now we're going to get into the Marsrover and my chauffeur here will try to get her started. If Bob Hertz remembered to put in the high-test, we'll be in business."

"Bob says he thinks you two are slightly high on the Moon, right now."

"High on the Moon. Well, I guess that makes sense. How about a song, 'Here we are, high on the Moon—' What's the matter, Pete, power doesn't work?"

"Yeah— . . . I *think* so . . . Just a minute . . . There we go. Funny, for just a minute, there, there seemed to be some sort of interference; kind of fluctuation in the current. But now we're going."

"This is Houston, Pete, you are GO to move off elevator in Marsrover."

"I know that. I just want to be sure that Marsrover is GO. Funny. Well, anyway: she's getting a smooth flow of power now. Hang onto your hat, Connie. Here we go."

"You're looking beautiful up there. We're getting a great picture both from the stationary and the portable as you move off. We've got you on a split-screen transmission down here and it's great. If the portable is any indication, you must be practically floating every time you hit a bump."

"It's not exactly Interstate 80, that's for sure. We're proceeding now, as you can see, toward the rim of that little crater off to the left there which we estimate is about 300 feet from *Adventurer*. That's the crater the crew of 15 named 'Wernher's Wallow," for reasons which escape me now. As we near that, we'll begin to veer toward the right in order to traverse a long trough which runs alongside it, and then move on, still bearing right, toward a much bigger crater known fondly in Houston as 'NASA's Nasty.' It's roughly 5000 feet deep, and it *is* nasty, very

592

steep-sided and full of a lot of jagged peaks rising from the valley floor. So we'll again bear right and move on around its rim to a point where we'll leave the portable, facing after us as we go away so you can watch. We'll then proceed roughly another 1500 feet or so, and then retrace our tracks, pick up the portable and return to *Adventurer*. Then we'll put the Marsrover in the elevator and debark to perform our various tasks on the surface. This will give us a round trip of approximately 2000 feet out and 2000 back, which is quite sufficient to test the Marsrover, which is the purpose of the exercise. Our purpose is not exploratory today, as all this terrain has been thoroughly studied by the Apollo missions . . . Now we're coming up on Wernher's Wallow, as you can see. Kicking up quite a bit of dust, too. Are you still getting a good picture, Houston?"

"Still good, Connie, thanks. Voice signal got a little shaky a minute ago—sort of a wavering—a fluctuation sort of thing. But you're back strong now."

"Fluctuation? That's odd. We got a fluctuation on the rover, too, when we started, didn't we? You're sure we're O.K. now?"

"Yes, fine. Think you'd better stop and check anything?"

"N—o, as long as you say everything's GO again. But let us know at once if it happens again, O.K.?"

"Immediately. You haven't noticed any further anomaly on the rover?"

"No, rolling steady. The voice signal's coming to you through *Adventurer*, though."

"Right."

"Well . . . O.K., we'll shove on, for the time being . . ."

"I'm going to stop the rover about 15 feet ahead, by that little hummock there, and Connie will put the portable in place and then rejoin me . . . O.K., got her, Conn?"

"Roger . . . How's that, Houston?"

"Good, Connie. That's your route in front there?"

"Dead ahead."

"Roger."

"O.K., now I'm getting aboard again and we're moving out. Can you see us all right, Houston?"

"We see you clear, Connie."

"Good . . . Now we're coming up on the little edge along the rim. We'll stop for a minute and take a look down into the crater . . . O.K., no anomalies. On our way again. Are we still visible, Stu?"

"Getting pretty distant and dim right now, but we still catch a little glimpse of you."

"O.K., we'll keep on for about another 500 feet, I'd estimate, before turning back. We'll maintain voice contact, of course."

"Roger. Keep talking."

"Rog. Any acquisition of signal from Jazz yet?"

"Due back in about one minute. Expecting contact momentarily."

"Good. Are we still visible?"

"Lost you now, no sighting. Moonscape empty. Keep up the chatter."

"Will do. Any word from One, yet?"

"Nothing, but expecting soonest."

"Good. We'll shove on, then . . . Now we're coming up on a couple of large rock formations which would appear to have been formed by volcanic. . . . . . ."

"Hello, *Adventurer*? Hello, *Adventurer*? . . . Connie? . . . *Adventurer*, come in, please, we have lost you . . . *Adventurer*, say, please . . . One, this is Houston. Do you hear, One? . . . One, come in, please . . . Jazz? . . . Hello, *Adventurer*, come in, please . . . One, respond, please . . . Hello, One, hello, One, hello, One. Hello, *Adventurer*, hello, *Adventurer*, hello, *Adventurer*. Come in, please, come in, please, come in, please . . . Hello, *Adventurer*? . . . Hello, One? . . . Connie? . . . Jazz . . . Pete? . . . Jayvee? . . ."

"This is Mission Control, at 105 hours, 56 minutes Ground Elapsed Time. We seem to be having a little difficulty here maintaining signal with both Planetary Fleet One and *Adventurer*. However, we're assured by the Flight Director and his staff that this is nothing to be worried about, probably just some temporary interference possibly due to static disturbance on the Moon. We expect to have acquisition of signal from both units any second now, and will keep you on live broadcast so you can hear it when we do. Our flight directors tell us there's nothing to worry about, pointing out we sometimes get these interruptions in space. Everybody here is quite calm,

594

working along, trying to solve this unexpected problem which is a little bothersome but basically quite normal."

"The hell it is," said the AP.

The world stilled again for Piffy One.

3.

". . . to have been formed by volcanic explosion of some unknown date, probably about three million years ago. Up ahead there, you can see the edge of the crater Christopher Kraft, and beyond that the small Hills of the Dawn which form a ridge along the left side of Kraft Crater. We're now about as far out as we're going to go, so in just a minute Pete's going to swing her around and we'll be heading back toward *Adventurer*. We should be back in camera range very shortly. You should be picking us up in about two minutes, coming straight in along the same track we followed out. Houston, have you got anything from One, yet? . . . Houston? . . . Stu, do you read? . . . Come in, Houston . . . Hello, One, are you there? One? Houston? One? Houston? . . . Houston? . . . What the hell? What do you make of that, Pete?"

But there was no reply, and glancing quickly over, he could see that Pete was staring at him through his visor with a frowning concern. He realized with a sudden start which seemed to traverse the entire length of his body that they were obviously cut off from Houston, and apparently cut off from each other.

"Pete?" he said, and tapped his ear with his hand in its clumsy glove.

Slowly Pete shook his head and mouthed the word, "Connie?"

But nothing came his way, either, and he too shook his head.

Pete slowed the Marsrover carefully to a halt and they sat for a moment staring at one another. Then with an instinctive agreement they got out, each on his side, and starting with their eyes straight ahead made slow, thorough turns, 360 degrees, until they faced one another again.

Nothing stirred on the lunar surface, no sign of life was visible anywhere. Gray and desolate, filled now with a sly and subtle menace, the empty moonscape stared back.

After a moment, with a careful caution, continuing to scan slowly and thoroughly as far as they could see in all directions, they climbed back in. Pete put the machine in gear, they moved out: very slowly, very cautiously, tense and profoundly uneasy.

Two minutes later they approached the edge of Wernher's Wallow, found the television camera still in place, the cable apparently intact, everything normal— except that no red on-light glowed on the camera.

Convinced it was futile, Connie made a last attempt.

"Hello, Houston, do you read? Do you see us, Stu? . . . Come in, Houston. Come in Houston. Do you read, do you see? . . . Come in, Houston . . . Stu, come in . . . Stu? . . ."

"Oh, hell," he said in a disgusted tone to Pete, who got the import if not the sound and responded with a grim little smile.

Automatically Pete again stopped the Marsrover, automatically Connie got down, retrieved the camera, attached the cable to the rewind wheel, clambered back aboard. Automatically they moved off again.

A thousand feet ahead, *Adventurer* gleamed white and gold in the light that fifteen minutes before had been unearthly but familiar, and now was eerie and full of unseen things.

Except that now they were not unseen.

Off beyond *Adventurer*, its origin hidden behind hills and hummocks but its motion obviously forward, a small pillar of dust climbed the lunar sky.

"That's funny," Jazz said. "I don't get a damned thing here."

"Try again," Jayvee suggested, calm with a curious, suspended feeling as though he were somewhere else, far away.

"Hello, Houston," Jazz said. "Hello, Stu. Hello, *Adventurer*. Hello, Connie. Do you read? Are you there? One is here, Houston, where are you? Connie, are you there?

Come in both, please. Come in both . . . *Yaah*," he exclaimed, a disgusted sound. "We're out on both circuits . . . Special-1, hello Special-1? Are you there, Special-1? Come in, Special-1. Come in, Special-1. Special-1, come in . . . Hell. Nothing . . . And meanwhile—"

He turned to the window and stared back. Much closer now, perhaps no more than fifty miles away as they came up fully into the light, Man in the Moon maintained his vigil.

"Yes," Jayvee said, with the same dreamlike feeling that he was observing, not living, impending and possibly quite awful events, "meanwhile."

Instinctively Pete reached for the manual speed control, turned the handle to Full On. Ponderously the Marsrover lumbered forward, picked up speed as it rolled, reached its limit of seven miles an hour in roughly one minute. They crossed a gully, topped a rise, saw that they were still roughly 500 feet from *Adventurer*. Abruptly, without a sound they could hear or any physical sensation they could feel, the power died and the rover stopped.

With a sort of desperate anger they took turns working the ignition, yanking the speed control back and forth. There was no response.

Connie hit Pete on the arm, gestured straight ahead with a quick, commanding motion.

With a ponderous haste they clambered down and began to run, jumping and bouncing in awkward, staggering, almost uncontrollable leaps in the one-sixth gravity of the Moon.

Slowly but inexorably the little column of dust continued to come toward them as they neared *Adventurer*.

"What are we going to do?" Jayvee asked. "Undock?"

"Too late now," Jazz said. "We're going to stay on course, make our orbit around the dark side and come back over. If he leaves us alone, we'll leave him alone. If he tries anything funny, we'll reverse thrusters and ram him."

"That could explode both of us and kill us all," Jayvee said, in a strange, dispassionate voice as though he somehow were not involved.

"If you're frightened, buddy-boy," Jazz said coldly, "you go into *Pinta* and close the hatch. The way I look at it, if that bastard is hostile, we're probably going to be killed anyway. If so, I intend to take him with us. If he isn't hostile, we're going to follow orders, assume he's just curious, and leave him alone. But sooner or later Connie and Pete are coming back up to rendezvous, and when they do we're going to be there. Unless signal is restored, which I suspect it isn't going to be, we can't talk to them. So we're going to follow flight plan and be at rendezvous point when we're supposed to be. Does that make sense or doesn't it?"

"It does if they're coming back," Jayvee said.

"Listen," Jazz said in a furious voice that for the first time trembled a little, though he tried desperately to keep it steady, "they're coming back."

With a terrible dragging slowness, in the nearest thing to a living nightmare they would ever experience, they managed at last to reach *Adventurer*, standing innocent and untroubled where it had landed, its hatch wide open, as they had left it, to the lunar sky. Lovely and blue, appearing from this distance totally peaceful and calm, Earth rode serenely on the horizon as three of her unhappy children approached their fateful meeting.

Gesturing to Pete to stay on guard, Connie pulled himself up with a ponderous haste, half climbing, half hauling, to the hatch, and lowered himself inside. One glance told him what he wanted to know: all power was out here, too.

He saw his gun in its niche against the wall, glanced at his monstrous mittens with a bitterly impatient smile, turned away to take a hatchet and a rock-hound's pick off the wall and stick them in his belt; worked himself somehow out the hatch again; missed the platform, grabbed a step with one hand, hung there for a moment; managed to right himself and find the lower steps with his feet, clambered rapidly down; reached the bottom and turned around to find Pete fifty feet out, facing away from him, arms akimbo, every line of his back bespeaking a wary, uneasy and exasperated waiting.

Toward him from a reasonable facsimile of the Marsrover, which had come to a stop beside a hummock perhaps 200 feet away, there slowly advanced the white-suited figure of a Soviet cosmonaut. Behind him the rover stood empty. He was alone.

Connie's first impulse was to take up again his lumbering, leaping, awkward run and get to Pete's side as fast as he could. Then common sense prevailed, he deliberately slowed his pace and made himself walk with a slow, careful dignity which, he calculated, would get him to Pete roughly fifty paces before the Russian got there.

For a couple of minutes he and the stranger concentrated on their walking. He reached Pete as he had planned, touched his left arm, glanced over to offer a brief, encouraging smile which looked a good deal more confident than he felt. Then he turned to face the Russian.

For another minute the latter continued to walk laboriously toward them while they studied him carefully. He appeared to be wearing on his back a portable life-support system roughly comparable to theirs; he too had a pick stuck in his belt; and his hands in their cumbersome gloves seemed to be empty. Nothing visible on his person appeared to be the instrument which had destroyed their power: yet they were instinctively and absolutely convinced that it must be either on him or in his machine.

Connie touched Pete's elbow and casually indicated the pick which hung in his belt close to Pete's right hand. He rested his own right hand on the hatchet.

They waited.

Their visitor came to within two feet of them; nodded his head and smiled; and held out his right hand to Connie.

Slowly Connie extended his right hand and moved to respond.

At that moment, had their visitor been reared in some other place, some other time, their tale would have had a different ending. But he was the child of a frightful philosophy in a dreadful age and it was not to be.

What it was that he saw, or sensed, or feared, or understood, Pete was never to know in the few short minutes remaining to him. But the thing that shot through his mind was so implacable and so certain that it was literally impossible for him to refrain from acting upon it. He did not even have time to express it to himself in words, so swift and overwhelming was it. But the import was inescapable.

He's going to hurt Connie.

So quickly he never knew how it got in his hand, the pick was there; and so quickly it caught the Russian completely by surprise, Pete had lunged awkwardly against him knocking him off balance. He started to fall, Connie started to protest and try to restrain Pete. But Pete's heart, which knew his friend was threatened, had told him truly.

The Russian half righted himself, caught the full brunt of Pete's lunge with his body, jabbed his left hand across Pete's left leg as he attempted to deflect his weight. From the recesses of his glove there shot out a small gleam of steel, apparently some form of switchblade. Across Pete's suit just above the left knee appeared a small, jagged gash.

Carried by the momentum of their struggle, Pete fell to the right, pulling the Russian with him; caught his foot in a crevasse between two small rocks; tried desperately and unsuccessfully to wrench it away as he fell; felt his leg snap, felt the universe go black, collapsed and lay still.

In a tiny, steady stream from the slash above his knee, raising the thick volcanic dust in a small, straight furrow to a distance of approximately one foot, his oxygen, and with it his life, began to vent slowly away.

With an anger so terrible he was no longer a thinking being, Connie raised the hatchet and brought it down upon the back of their visitor's helmet with a strength that cut it virtually in half and split the skull beneath.

Much more rapidly than Pete's, for the rupture was much larger, the Russian's suit began to crumple. He tried to pull away from Pete, flailed futilely and wildly for a second, moved slowly—more slowly—more slowly, as the oxygen left his shattered brain—collapsed and lay still.

From some awful chasm of utter desolation in the very depths of his being a terrible, savage sob welled up in Connie's throat.

Then he was ice-cold and thinking like lightning.

He hurled the bloodstained hatchet away, seized the Russian's shoulders and, struggling awkwardly with the ponderous bulk of his own suit, managed to pull the body off Pete and drag it a dozen feet away. Then he returned to his friend, carefully minding the rocks, the little crevasses, the treacheries of the land in which man would always be a stranger, and managed to kneel awkwardly beside him.

Reaching over as best he could, he pushed together the ragged slash above Pete's knee and tried to hold it while he attempted to rouse him.

Pete, he said aloud to himself, because they had no power and he could not say it to Pete. Hey, buddy. Hey, pal, wake up. Come on, Petros, wake up, buddy. We've got to get you on your feet and get the hell out of here. Come on, best crewmate. Let's move on out.

But Pete did not respond at first, though Connie began to accompany his words with a gentle, insistent pressure on his friend's shoulder. So he tried again.

Petros, he said, and he said it quite sternly. Come on, now. No more of this goldbricking. Got to be up and at 'em. Houston's waiting, the dear old President's waiting, the whole wide world is waiting. *Everybody's* waiting. *I'm* waiting. Come on, now. Wake up. We haven't got all day to stay here talking. We've got places to go and people to see and things to do. Come on, Petey. Let's move, kid. Let's get with it. *Pete.*

And finally there was a movement, very slight at first, then stronger. Pete's eyes opened, looked into his; at first without focus and then abruptly alive with the knowledge of where he was. A sudden fear came into them, they looked from side to side.

Connie mouthed: *he's dead.*

Pete's eyes relaxed. He managed the smallest shadow of a smile.

Good, Connie told him. At least you're with me. I was beginning to wonder.

He reached over, gently tried to remove the pick from Pete's tightly clenched right hand. Pete relaxed his grip, let him have it. Connie held it before Pete's eyes, pointed off toward the dead Russian, pointed down at his own suit, dragged the pick across Pete's field of vision in a tearing, ripping motion, pointed down to Pete's leg.

Pete nodded with a comprehension that suddenly seemed to hold in it something dragging and drowsy again. A cold fear shot through Connie's heart.

Petros, he said, speaking aloud and very carefully, accompanying his words with the action, I'm going to try to prop the gash closed with the pick, now, so don't you move. Let it lie there, O.K., and don't move. I've got to get to his rover—and he pointed and made a small rover, one hand crawling over the other—and find whatever is stopping the power—and he pointed up to *Adventurer*, gleaming and impersonal above—so we can take off. O.K.?

Pete focused again for a moment, slowly mouthed the

602

word *Yes*, smiled and closed his eyes. Again the fear clamped on Connie's heart.

But the oxygen seemed to have stopped venting, for the moment, or be reduced to so small a trickle that it was no longer visible on the telltale surface; and he could feel Pete's chest rising and falling, faintly but still rhythmically, when he put his hand upon it. So he got up ponderously, and said: You lie still now, Petros. I'll be back just as soon as I can. I'll get rid of whatever it is and then we'll take off before you know it. O.K., buddy? You just lie still. Take it easy.

Slowly and carefully he began the laborious walk to the rover, not looking back: eyes, mind, body, entire being, concentrated now upon the tasks that lay ahead if they were to come safely home.

"This is Mission Control at 106 hours, 31 minutes GET. We still haven't been able to re-establish signal with either Planetary Fleet One or *Adventurer* just yet, but everybody here is keeping calm and going about his job and we're confident we'll soon have this annoying little problem licked. Everybody is convinced it's just some temporary anomaly, probably caused by a static disturbance in the lunar atmosphere, and nothing to worry about. We expect to have both craft back on the beam here very shortly now, and as you know, we're keeping all links open so you'll be able to hear acquisition of signal when we do. There's been a lot of conferring and working with the computers and the equipment here in the last few minutes, but everybody's keeping calm and nobody's worried.

"Meanwhile, up there on the Moon, Connie Trasker and Pete Balkis by now should have returned from their trip in the Marsrover and are scheduled to be putting out some scientific instruments near the base of *Adventurer* as a dry-run for what they'll do when they reach the Martian surface. After that, they'll be going in the hut at Tranquillity Base to check on some of the Apollo experiments there, and then they'll be shoving off in *Adventurer* to rejoin Jazz Weickert and Jayvee Halleck, who are up there in One continuing to orbit the Moon. Things right now are pretty quiet for Jazz and Jayvee, because they're really on stand-by until they get word from Connie and Pete that they want to bring *Adventurer* up. We expect rendezvous in approximately one and one-half hours from now.

"Meanwhile, everybody here is doing his job and working away calmly to get this little anomaly on loss of signal straightened out. This is Mission Control at 106 hours, 35 minutes into the flight of Planetary Fleet One to Mars."

They came up again into the light and saw what they had expected to see.

Much closer, probably no more than twenty-five miles behind. Man in the Moon kept them company. They could discern its outlines, now, those of a standard single command module. Through the binoculars they could see that it seemed to possess an unusual array of thrusters and an odd protuberance on one side.

Even as they watched, little puffs of white came suddenly from the rear bank of thrusters.

After that they estimated the gap as no more than twenty miles.

"If Connie and Pete decide to rendezvous on this pass," Jazz said quietly, "we should be able to see them coming up in about thirty minutes."

But when thirty minutes had passed they searched the sky and surface and saw no sign.

Once again Planetary Fleet One neared the horizon.

"What if he tries to knock us down on this pass?" Jayvee inquired in the same curiously detached voice he had used throughout.

"What if he does?" Jazz responded sarcastically. "He won't. He'll wait until we're getting ready to rendezvous, if he has any plans. That's the time to catch us."

"If we rendezvous," Jayvee said.

"God damn you," Jazz said, quite dispassionately. "I don't want to hear that comment again."

Piffy One slid over the edge. Behind them came the small bright glow of Man in the Moon, as distinct and well-defined as theirs in the deep velvet blackness of the other side.

Again he had the nightmare feeling, again time dragged and pulled upon his body as he tried to hurry it across the treacherous surface against the caprices of one-sixth gravity.

And this time it *was* a nightmare, for he had no way of

604

knowing how much oxygen Pete had lost; whether he would remain still and not dislodge the makeshift suture held together by the pick; whether he would be alive when Connie returned; whether Connie could find the mechanism interrupting *Adventurer*'s power; whether *Adventurer* would respond if power were restored, or whether permanent damage had been done; whether he would be able to get Pete up the ladder and through the hatch if Pete were still alive; whether—

He shook his head as he bounced and jumped his way forward, trying to clear it of all these bugaboos that suddenly seemed to close in upon him; succeeded, at least temporarily; put his hand down doggedly; and stumbled on.

About ten feet from the rover, he stopped. Cautiously he examined it, thinking at first it might be mined. Then logic said no, if the plan had succeeded the evidence would have been removed and the murderer would have departed. Two dead American astronauts who had foolishly ripped their suits on rocks would be all that remained of this day's work. Man in the Moon and his buddy would be drinking vodka in Moscow when they were found.

Even so, he proceeded with great caution, stooping to pick up several of the small rocks so beloved of the scientists in Houston, tossing them ahead in an exploratory arc around the vehicle. The dust spurted up, drifted very slowly down again upon the places from which it had arisen: nothing exploded. He stepped cautiously forward, threw several more directly at the rover, its hood, roof, body, tires. The rocks struck, fell off, raised dust, settled: nothing exploded. He moved forward cautiously again. On the seat next to the steering wheel, making it much easier for him than he had anticipated, a small rectangular black metal box pulsated with little lights and gave off a peculiar reddish glow.

At first he thought he could salvage it, aware of how valuable it would be if he could take it home for study and analysis and eventual breakdown into its component parts and capabilities. Once again he used a small rock for testing. It bounced off the thing harmlessly. He reached out a tentative hand, touched it, nothing happened. He tried to pick it up with one hand, found that even in one-sixth gravity it was heavy, lifted it with two, turned it over and examined it carefully. Whatever its mechanism was, it continued working. Lights and glow were undiminished.

There were three buttons at one end. He pushed them, first in sequence, then in all combinations. Each time he said tentatively, "Hello, Houston?" There was no response. The downlinks did not come back on. The power remained off. There was nothing to do but destroy it.

Again he picked up rocks, found one presently that fitted the cup of his two gloved hands; placed the box on a larger, flatter rock beside the rover; began slowly and intently to pound, concentrating on the lights and buttons as being probably the most vulnerable.

He continued for almost fifteen minutes before he broke through the protective shielding of the lights. The result proved him to have been correct.

The lights went out, the pulsating stopped, the reddish glow died and did not return.

He battered it for another couple of minutes for good measure. Then he ran a test.

Because he was under orders, and because he had a mind trained to consider all eventualities, he could still even at this desperate and fantastic moment when he and Pete were all alone on the lunar surface 235,000 miles from home, see the President's argument. This was not going to be easy news to break to the world and it must be done with great thought. Also, it must not be done in any case before they were safely back in *Santa Maria* and on their way to Earth.

So he snapped on the transmitter very carefully, made a sudden, abrupt, indecipherable sound, immediately snapped off the transmitter and snapped on the receiver.

"Hello, Connie?" Stu Yule's excited voice cried instantly. "Hello, *Adventurer?* Is that you, Conn? Connie? Is that *Adventurer?* Connie, is that you, for God's sake? Connie, is that you? Hello, *Adventurer?* Hello? Hello?"

But he did not answer the voice of his good friend crying across almost a quarter-million miles, because he did not want to yet. For all the policy reasons, and because the job was not yet done, he did not want to. It took great will power not to call back joyously, "Yes, it's me!" But great will power was what he had.

It was very good to know, however, that Houston was there when he wanted it.

The fact augured well for *Adventurer.*

Before he moved out he tried one other experiment. He snapped on the private link that tied him to *Santa Maria*.

"Hello, Jazz," he said cautiously. "Connie here. Hello, Jazz, do you read?"

But there was no answer.

That did not augur well for Piffy One.

He closed the circuit; picked up the box in both hands, hoping he had not battered it beyond analysis, determined now that he would, indeed, get it home; and began his awkward, careful trip back.

Everything appeared to be as he had left it.

The dead Russian lay to one side, Pete lay where he had fallen, *Adventurer* loomed white, ungainly and beautiful above.

With a sudden feeling of panic he put the box down and moved as fast as he could to Pete. He placed his hand on Pete's chest, felt the rhythmic rise and fall. But it now seemed definitely weaker, and his friend did not stir at his touch.

He looked down at the makeshift patch. The pick had slipped somewhat during his absence and once again the jet of oxygen, smaller than before but dreadfully persistent, was writing its message in the telltale dust.

Hurriedly he readjusted the patch, stopped the terrible flow. Then he snapped on the internal link again, reached over and snapped on Pete's, spoke softly but insistently. He knew now that neither the world nor *Santa Maria* would hear but he hoped desperately that Pete might.

"Pete," he said. "Petros. Hey, buddy. It's Connie. I'm back. It's Connie, Pete. How are you doing? Hey, Pete. It's Connie. Wake up, buddy. Wake up. Come on, pal, wake up. Wake up. Time to move, now. Wake up, Pete. Come on, wake up. Wake up. That's the boy. Come on, get those eyes open. Get 'em open. That's it. That's my pal. Wide open, now, don't close 'em again. Keep 'em open. That's it. That's it . . . Hi."

Drowsy from some great dream—probably, Connie thought with a shiver, and tried desperately to deny the thought, the last great dream—Pete finally did open his eyes, managed to keep them open, and managed to smile. But his eyes took a while longer than before to focus and the smile was weak. But he did recognize his friend and after a moment he did reply, his voice a whisper in Connie's earphones.

"Hi . . . You . . . got . . . back."

"You're damned right I got back," Connie said, his own smile firm, his voice encouraging. "I got the bastard machine that was doing the job, too."

"Where . . . is . . . it?"

"It's over there. We're going to take it back with us and let Houston find out what it's all about."

Again Pete smiled with a tired gentleness. His voice was very weak, very slow.

"You're . . . going . . . to . . . take . . . it . . . back. . . . I . . . won't . . . be . . . going."

"Now, what the hell kind of talk is that?" Connie demanded loudly. "Of course you're going. We're both going. I can't leave this place without my best crewmate. Hell, I can't do it alone. I need you, pal. Come on now. I'm going to help you up and we're going to get the hell off this Godforsaken Moon and meet Jazz up there. He and Jayvee will be coming over in about an hour, I figure. We're going to be there."

"Good . . . old . . . Connie. . . . But . . . you . . . see . . . I . . . can't . . . get . . . my . . . foot . . . loose. . . . I . . . tried."

"So that's what happened to the patch," Connie said severely. "I might have known I couldn't trust you out of my sight for a minute. That was a hell of a thing to do. Honest to Christ, man!"

"Well . . ." Pete whispered patiently, "I . . . figured . . . if . . . I . . . could . . . get . . . free . . . I . . . could . . . tend . . . to . . . the . . . patch . . . myself . . . until . . . you . . . got . . . back . . . but . . . if . . . I . . . couldn't . . . get . . . free . . . then . . . I . . . wasn't . . . going . . . anyway . . . so . . . it . . . wouldn't . . . matter. . . . And . . . that's . . . what . . . I . . . found."

"O.K.," Connie ordered, "you lie as limp as you can now, and I'm going to see if I can dislodge these rocks and get that foot out. I'll do my best not to hurt, but I may. So be brave."

"I'm . . . brave . . . and . . . so . . . are . . . you . . . but . . . you . . . aren't . . . brave . . . enough . . . for . . . this . . . Connie."

"You let me judge that," he said harshly. "You let me be the judge of that. Now don't say anything. Just lie there."

But though he did his best, tugging and pulling and

cursing, the rocks would not yield and the foot would not come out. Very soon Pete fainted, and at first Connie thought this a blessing. Then when he concluded that his efforts were going to be futile, he became alarmed and desperately anxious to bring him around.

This he presently accomplished but it was obvious that Pete was growing steadily weaker. Nonetheless, he again managed a smile as his eyes finally focused on Connie's.

"It . . . didn't . . . work . . . did . . . it?"

"It didn't work," Connie said simply.

"I . . . knew . . . it . . . wouldn't. That's . . . why . . . I . . . tried . . . to . . . dislodge . . . the . . . pick . . . I . . . wanted . . . to . . . be . . . dead . . . when . . . you . . . got . . . back . . . so . . . you . . . wouldn't . . . have . . . to . . . bother . . . with . . . me."

"*Bother* with you?" Connie demanded and knew he was close to crying. "*Bother* with you? What kind of a friend do you think I am?"

"The . . . best," Pete said, and for a moment the smile went. But it returned. "The . . . best . . . I . . . ever . . . had."

"Stop using the past tense, damn it! There's a way to get you out of this and I'm going to find it!"

"No . . . there . . . isn't . . . Conn . . . we . . . both . . . know . . . that. Now . . . you'd . . . better . . . go. Piffy . . . One . . . will . . . be . . . coming . . . over . . . soon. Give . . . Jazzbo . . . my . . . love. Tell . . . him . . . I . . . really . . . mean . . . it. Tell . . . Janie . . . too . . . she . . . knows . . . I . . . do."

"Pete," Connie said with a desperate calm. "*Pete*. Listen to me. You did this for me and I'm going to get you out of here if it's the last thing I do. I mean it."

The smile came again, and the slow, patient whisper.

"No . . . you're . . . not . . . and . . . anyway . . . I'm . . . not . . . going. I'm . . . going . . . to . . . defy . . . your . . . orders. How . . . about . . . that? . . . Anyway . . . I'm . . . not . . . worth . . . risking . . . your . . . little . . . finger . . for . . . Conn. I'm . . . just . . . a . . . Greek . . . loner . . . from . . . Tarpon . . . Springs . . . I'm . . . a . . . lonesome . . . freak . . . from . . . Cripple . . . Creek. Connie . . . you . . . must . . . go. You . . . must . . . leave . . . me. It . . . doesn't . . . hurt . . . I . . . just feel . . . sleepy . . . and . . . peaceful. Please . . . Connie

. . . I . . . beg . . . of . . . you. You . . . must . . . go . . . Please . . . go . . . Connie."

He took Pete's hands in his and looked around with a wild, unhappy desperation. He saw the Russian, the rover, *Adventurer* calm and impersonal above, the desolate landscape, the empty sky, Earth so far off, beautiful and serene.

He raised his head and stared straight up and cried out savagely to One he rarely thought about and seldom prayed to.

"God damn you, God!" he shouted. "Help my friend and me!"

But there was no help from that quarter either. He felt the hands in his grow limper and held them tighter with his own. He wanted to cry but discipline and training were too strong.

He turned his tortured eyes back to Pete's and found them filled with a serenity that told him beyond argument or appeal that their mission together was almost over.

The eyes looked straight into his.

With a great effort his friend returned the pressure of his hands; said the words he had to say, to die at peace; heard Connie's choked response and understood that Connie accepted and was content with them; smiled and was gone.

Again from somewhere far inside the terrible sob welled up.

Just one, and no more.

Then he reached down for the pick; used it to rip away the mission patch from Pete's left shoulder; put the patch carefully in his pocket and the pick carefully in his belt; stood up and walked carefully to the little black box; picked it up, walked carefully with it to *Adventurer;* climbed carefully with it up the ladder; hesitated for a second on the platform but did not look back; climbed in the hatch, drew it shut, closed it tightly, lowered himself inside, stowed the box under his seat, started the controls.

Rapidly the cabin began to pressurize.

He had, he estimated, roughly forty minutes to keep his date with Piffy One.

"This is Mission Control, at 107 hours, 16 minutes into the flight of Planetary Fleet One. Everybody here is working along calmly trying to solve this little problem of the loss of signal. As you all heard, we did get some kind of input a few minutes ago which we thought at first might come from either Connie Trasker in *Adventurer* on the lunar surface or from Jazz Weickert in *Santa Maria* in her lunar orbit. Astronaut Stu Yule, who is acting as capsule communicator in this phase of the mission, is convinced the noise he heard was a voice, and he says he recognizes it as having been the voice of Connie Trasker. However, as you know there was no repeat of the sound and Stu was unable to establish any further communication with Connie, if that is who it was. Nor has there been any other indication of life—that is, *sound*—from up there, since that initial reception. Nonetheless, nobody here is feeling unusually worried about it, as these things will sometimes happen. Everybody here is going ahead calmly trying to solve the problem and here in Mission Control we're all convinced we'll have it licked very soon. Lots of the astronauts have come in in the last few minutes, and we also have Dr. Anderson, the Administrator of NASA, Bob Hertz and most of the top brass of NASA/Houston and NASA/D.C. with us on the floor or up in the viewing room. The atmosphere here is concentrated and everybody's working hard, studying this little problem, but it certainly couldn't be described as tense or excited. Actually, everybody is very confident we'll soon have full communication again with both spacecraft. There's been some thought of a press conference with Dr. Anderson and Bob Hertz but that would only be if a consensus was reached that there's a real emergency here, and so far nobody is convinced of that at all. It could be if this anomaly continues for another hour or so, we might hold a press conference, but everybody here is convinced it won't be necessary as we'll soon have this problem licked. We're staying on open mike so you can hear anything we hear, and we'll keep on describing the scene in Mission Control to you from time to time, which is calm and confident, everybody just working along busily trying to get this bothersome little anomaly out of the way so we can have full links with the mission. This is Mission Control at 107 hours, 20 minutes into the flight of Planetary Fleet One to Mars."

"Do you see anything?" Jazz asked, and Jayvee, at the window from which he was scanning the lunar surface, said, "No."

"Me, either," Jazz said. "Except that chummy bastard in back of us."

And they turned to stare at Man in the Moon, now no more than ten miles behind and closing rapidly, as every few minutes there came from his rear thrusters the ominous little puffs of white.

"When are you going to use our thrusters and get out of his way?" Jayvee demanded, and now there was a rising note of tension in his voice, a note from which Jazz took warning and made plans accordingly.

"We're going to stay on flight plan until we've exhausted all possible hope that Connie and Pete will rendezvous," he replied evenly. "And if that means we have to have Chuckles here with us for another twenty revolutions, that's what it means."

"But he's going to overtake us in half an hour at this rate," Jayvee protested. "What's going to happen then?"

"If our great leader in Washington is correct, nothing is going to happen but a friendly wave and on he'll go about his business."

"You don't think that."

"No," Jazz said quietly, "I do not."

"Well, then, what—" Jayvee demanded, and the tension was higher in his voice.

Jazz shrugged.

"Then we'll do the best we can, that's all. We'll have to try to take some sort of evasive action, and if that doesn't work we'll have to try to ram him."

"You'll kill us!" Jayvee said sharply. Jazz looked him straight in the eyes with a small sarcastic smile.

"Do you really care?"

"I don't care about you," Jayvee spat out, "but I care about me."

"Yes, I figured that," Jazz said calmly. "But why do you care about you? All I've been hearing for six months is what a hell of a life you lead in the white man's world. Here's your chance to get out of it. And very spectacularly, too. Why knock it?"

"And I don't have time," Jayvee said with a savage annoyance, "to listen to your infantile humor, either."

"O.K." Jazz said with a deliberate blandness he knew would infuriate Jayvee even more and so render him more vulnerable to the plan that was rapidly forming in Jazz' mind, "so it's infantile. At least it isn't sick, like yours.

Look back out at that surface and get to work, will you? We've got to try to find *Adventurer* if she's coming up."

"*Ah!*" Jayvee said with a sullen exasperation; turned back to the window, took up his binoculars and began again his steady left-right scanning of the surface.

Jazz made another of his periodic checks of the circuits, found them all still dead; picked up his own binoculars and resumed scanning from his side.

For several minutes there was silence in *Santa Maria.*

Abruptly Jayvee put down his binoculars and swung around.

"Look," he said. "Why do we wait for them, anyway? We don't see them, we don't know they're there, they may be dead on the surface for all we know. Why should we go through this charade and risk our lives, for them? Why don't we make our transearth injection burn on this next pass behind the Moon and go home? Why should we risk our lives for two corpses?"

At first Jazz did not answer, continuing to scan the empty sky beneath. When he did speak, his knuckles, white on the binoculars, were the only indication of anger.

"I would prefer," he said in a level voice, turning around to face his colleague, "if you would keep your cowardly and unworthy remarks to yourself. Connie is my friend. Pete is my friend. They are also my crewmates on this mission. I shall wait for them as long as there is the slightest hope that they will come back. After I have decided—*I* have decided—that there is no more hope, we will make our burn and go home. Not before. Is that clear?"

Jayvee's eyes narrowed and he returned Jazz glare for glare.

Then he began to ease himself slowly off his seat.

"Where are you going?" Jazz demanded sharply.

"To the can," Jayvee said in a contemptuous voice. "Want to come along?"

"Don't fall in," Jazz snapped. "We haven't got time to purge the waste dump right now."

But that, he felt a moment later as Jayvee pulled himself along the wall and into the hatch to *Nina*, was not a very grown-up retort, even if he was dealing with one he felt to be a long way from grown-up.

He had a much more grown-up answer concealed in his pocket and now he took it out and studied it for a moment. He emptied the shells, spun the barrel, tried the trigger; reloaded and put the gun in the right-hand side of his belt.

Out of sight in *Nina*, he had no doubt whatsoever, Jayvee was doing the same.

So what should he do about it? he asked himself with a sudden, almost ashamed disgust. Hide beside the hatch door and clobber Jayvee when he came back? Tease him along until he could infuriate him enough to catch him off guard and then let him have it? Start a shoot-out in the O.K. Corral, Space Division? Play fastest gun in the galaxy while Man in the Moon gained from behind and Connie and Pete came up from below to seek his help for rendezvous?

He turned away to his window again, the self-disgust still strong.

That wasn't it. Maybe, like the Russian, Jayvee was basically not hostile. Certainly he had received all the training, conditioning, responsibility to make him do the right thing for the mission when the chips were down.

His own best course, Jazz decided, was to try to refrain from any more perosnal exchanges if he could; concentrate on recovering his crewmates and getting them all safely home again; be watchful with Jayvee but give him the benefit of the doubt until he actually had reason to know otherwise.

And keep his powder dry.

He brushed the pistol with his hand, a comforting sensation, as he picked up the binoculars.

Far below but coming up fast, a tiny white spider climbed the lunar sky.

"Jayvee!" he shouted. "*Jayvee!* I've got a sighting on *Adventurer!* They're coming up!"

"Don't have to shout," Jayvee said quietly from behind him, and the mingled tension and triumph in his voice told Jazz what he would see, before he turned around. "I'm here."

And so he was, propped against the hatch door inside *Santa Maria*, his feet braced against a metal shoe-hold on the floor, his left hand holding onto the door.

His right, of course, held his pistol.

Back to Jazz, too, there came the smug, the certain voices:

". . . a black American whose character, maturity, ideal-

614

ism and integrity make him a magnificent representative of his race and of us all," the *Times* assured him. ". . . a fine and wholly admirable American Negro . . ." the *Post* agreed. "The nation may rejoice that a young man of such ability and such human worth was available for this assignment . . ."

For a moment neither of them said anything. Then Jazz spoke.

"You damned fool," he said softly. "Am I going to have to kill you?"

"You don't have to threaten, Jazz," Jayvee said with an equal softness. "Just get away from the controls and nothing's going to happen to you. Except you're going to go into *Pinta* and I'm going to lock the hatch. And then when we get behind the Moon I'm going to fire that burn and we're going home. So just give me your gun, Jazz, and everything will be all right."

"But Connie's coming up," Jazz said, staying absolutely still, careful not to raise his voice.

"Let Connie die," Jayvee said with a curiously impersonal hatred. "He's been big man around my house and around this whole wide world long enough."

"Why should I let Connie die, or Pete either?" Jazz inquired, and now he added a careful amount of contempt to his voice, "just so a sick black child can play God and work out his own twisted problems on us?"

Jayvee's eyes widened, he started to snap back an answer. Then he thought better of it, spoke quietly. But Jazz could see his hands begin to tremble.

"You be careful, Jazz. I don't have to take anything from you. Any more."

"You have a tough problem, friend," Jazz said in a conversational tone. "You have to murder three men so none of us can tell on you later and then you have to kill the Russian. That's a lot of work for one day."

"He won't do anything to me," Jayvee said with a sudden note of pride, "when he sees that I'm black."

"Well, I'll be damned," Jazz said, and he was genuinely astounded. "You really believe that."

Jayvee nodded gravely.

"Yes, I do."

Jazz shook his head, his smile both pitying and ironic.

"You're not a black to him, man. You're an American. You're the enemy. He and his little pal, wherever the hell *he* is, have orders to kill four Americans. They haven't got orders to kill three Americans and save one black. You're in a dream world, Jayvee. Wake up."

"I don't believe you," Jayvee said, and Jazz could see the hands trembling more. "I don't believe you. He'll take me with him," he said, like a little child, "and I'll be happy, and safe."

"I'm sorry for you, pal," Jazz said softly, "because somewhere along the line you got all twisted up. You got everything wrong. You got it all upside down. You got lost."

"*Well, why did you do these awful things to me?*" Jayvee shouted. Jazz could see he was crying, now, his voice ragged and raw with emotion and despair. "*Why has my country done such awful things to me?*"

"Jayvee," Jazz said softly, and he eased himself off the window seat and prepared to pull himself forward. "Give me your gun, buddy. You don't really want to kill anybody, do you? And neither do I. So let's put the guns aside and save them for Man in the Moon, O.K.? Give me your gun, Jayvee, O.K.?"

"*Stay where you are!*" Jayvee said, and although his eyes were red and ravaged and his breath was coming in tearing gasps, there was no doubt he meant it. "*Stay where you are, or you're dead.*"

"I can't stay where I am, pal," Jazz said, still quietly, "because *Adventurer* is almost here, and the Russian is almost here, and you and I have a lot of things to do if we're going to rendezvous, and then get Piffy One safely out of this, and then get ourselves safely home. So come on, let's stop the fuss. Put your gun away and come help me."

"You're going in the hatch to *Pinta*," Jayvee said in a desperate voice that Jazz read as an attempt to convince himself. "Now, get!"

"No, I'm not," Jazz said quietly. "I'm going to get over to the controls and I'm going to get ready to dock with Connie and Pete. If you want to shoot me in the back when I turn around, you go right ahead. But I have my orders and my job to do and I'm going to do it."

And he did actually start to turn toward the controls. But he took the precaution of pulling himself slightly to one side as he did so, and though the movement was slow in zero gravity, it was enough to save him from the direct

616

blast of Jayvee's gun. It was not enough to save him, as he knew instinctively at once, from being seriously wounded.

But for a couple of seconds, long enough to turn and fire his own gun, the full jolt did not hit his system. He continued to function as if he had not been hit, just long enough.

By some fluke his own shot struck home.

At the hatch door, Jayvee's face looked surprised for a moment. Then his gun began to float slowly away from his right hand as the fingers slowly uncurled. His left hand slowly and gracefully relinquished its hold upon the door. His legs lost their grip on the floor and slowly floated up level with his head. Grotesquely and slowly his body began to turn like meat on a spit in the weightless cabin environment. It did not rise, or fall, or shift position, any further. It simply turned—and turned—and turned—and turned. Accompanying it like some horrible little snake, a long thin rope of blood began to wind around, and around, and around it, as it slowly spun.

A searing sledgehammer pain in his right upper back and shoulder hit Jazz at last and for perhaps a minute he blacked out completely. When he revived, he too was floating; but fortunately living instinct had kept his left foot still firmly anchored in a shoe-hold. He was in position facing the controls and in position to look out the window.

Adventurer, much nearer, climbed steadily from below.

Cautiously he shifted position, grinding his teeth with pain and determination. Very carefully he moved his right arm. A savage sword slammed into his head and made him cry aloud. But the arm worked and he could raise it, not fully, but enough to reach the controls. He tried it again, took the jolt of pain, cried out a little less this time. He decided he could do whatever he had to do, providing he did not lose too much blood himself. He passed his left hand slowly under his right armpit, felt gently of his back, winced with pain but satisfied himself of his condition. The shirt-sleeve uniform was wet to the touch but the blood did not seem to be flowing fast or venting into the cabin, at least so far. With a little prayer that it would not, he swung carefully about and with an impersonal attention studied his first and most immediate problem, the body floating gently five feet away.

It was still bleeding slightly, though he could see that

the blood was beginning to coagulate. For several reasons, one of them being the sanitation and safety of the remaining crew and another being the howl of the world he could already hear in imagination in his ears, Jayvee must be disposed of and a story devised to account for his absence. The story would be relatively simple but the disposition might not be so easy.

Whatever it was, he felt it had to be done in the next ten minutes. The urgency, prompted by the imminent arrival of *Adventurer*, gave him the answer.

Carefully he eased himself out of the seat in front of the controls, carefully pulled himself with his good arm along the wall toward the docking tunnel running to the rear of *Santa Maria*. Both the inner and outer doors of the tube were sealed. But if he could open the inner door, let the tube fill with oxygen from the cabin, push Jayvee's body into it and then use the automatic controls to open the outer door with the inner door still open—and then, somehow, God give him and the controls strength, close the inner door again before the cabin became depressurized or he himself got pulled out—the body would be shot into space, to go—somewhere. Into the sun, maybe, or back to Earth to burn up on re-entry, or into an orbit that would carry it, preserved for eternity, out and out, forever.

What a homecoming gift for Connie and Pete he thought with a sudden, grim little laugh, to get Jayvee in the front window when *Adventurer* came alongside for docking. But that could be extremely dangerous if not fatal to *Adventurer* and it could not be allowed to happen. And that meant haste.

He checked the small bank of controls alongside the inner hatch, satisfied himself the outer hatch was fully sealed; opened the bolts of the inner hatch as best he could with his left hand; and very slowly, holding his breath, pulled the hatch inward toward him.

There was a slight rush of oxygen past his body for a second. Then it stopped. The tube was pressurized.

He braced his feet in the shoe-holds below the hatch, grasped a hand bar with his right hand, again cried out with the pain but swore and hung on.

With his left hand he reached out, took Jayvee's left hand and pulled the body toward him. It responded like a feather and he thanked God for zero-G.

Gently he eased it around until the head was close to him, trying not to look at it, trying and managing to be tough and impersonal when he did. It was no time now to indulge in squeamishness or allow himself to become nauseated. It was a job that had to be done. Their lives depended upon it.

He let go of the hand bar with his wounded arm, used it gingerly to reach over and swing the hatch full open. It swung fairly easily though its resistance was enough to make him exclaim again with pain.

Then with both hands, anchoring himself only with his feet, his own weightless body swaying with the effort, he pushed Jayvee head first into the tube, continuing until the body was entirely inside, its head resting against the outer hatch. Then he very carefully and cautiously pulled the inner hatch halfway closed.

And then he took a deep breath, addressed his Deity with something of Connie's bitter desperation on the Moon, and activated the automatic controls that operated the outside hatch.

He caught a split-second glimpse of sky, there was a furious rush of oxygen, he had a blurred and terrible impression of furious, almost living, outward motion in the tube.

He hit the controls for the inner hatch, pulled it toward him as hard as he could, again shouted something stern and incoherent to the Lord, found the hatch slowly and inexorably closing beneath his touch.

In what seemed eternities but were in reality no more than five seconds, it was fully sealed.

He tightened the bolts, leaned against the hatch panting for breath, made himself wait three full minutes by his watch.

Then he activated the controls to close the outer hatch and waited another three minutes.

Then he again prayed in his own exhortatory fashion and opened the inner hatch.

He saw only the empty tube, a long stain of dried blood along one side.

He closed and sealed the inner hatch, waited another two minutes, activated the controls to unseal and open the outer hatch again.

Then he paused and looked around the cabin for a long, grim moment.

"Poor son of a bitch," he said aloud, and briefly felt a genuine regret.

It had all been so unnecessary, such a sad tangle.

Where had it begun, who had contributed to it, how could it ever have been unraveled?

He could not say.

It was a peculiarly American tangle, and therefore, perhaps, there were no real or lasting solutions, on the Moon, or on Earth, or anywhere: only temporary answers, some uneasily viable, some as empty, dreadful and self-defeating as this.

He pulled himself to the window and looked out.

Adventurer was no more than 100 feet away. Through its window he could see Connie, somber but triumphant, raising his right hand in a thumbs-up salute.

"This is Mission Control, at 107 hours, 54 minutes Ground Elapsed Time. It's the consensus here that our little problem with loss of signal may be a bit more serious than was at first assumed, so it's been decided that Dr. Anderson, Dr. Cavanaugh and Bob Hertz, together with Hank Barstow and Bert Richmond of the Astronaut Office, will hold a press conference in the auditorium in approximately thirty minutes to answer your questions about the various plans and possibilities posed by this unexpected anomaly. Meanwhile, there's no sign of panic or tension here in the control room, everybody's working along calmly trying to solve this problem as speedily and efficiently as possible.

"It's the consensus here that there's no sign or proof whatsoever that this situation is caused by anything other than strictly mechanical failure and that once we've got it corrected everything will be back to normal again. Meanwhile, we assume things are going along according to flight plan up there on the Moon, which means that at this point Connie Trasker and Pete Balkis in *Adventurer* are about midway in their emplacement of test equipment on the Moon's surface in a simulation of the exercise they'll conduct when they're actually on the surface of Mars eight months from now. And up there in Planetary Fleet One, Jazz Weickert and Jayvee Halleck are still orbiting around, essentially on stand-by until *Adventurer* comes up to rejoin them about one hour from now. They're performing routine checks, keeping everything in order, getting

620

ready for rendezvous. Everything should be proceeding just about on plan, right now, as we'll find out for sure when we get this anomaly licked and get back in full communication with the mission."

He felt the gentle bump as *Adventurer* aligned with the tube, realized suddenly that he was feeling dizzy; thought he was going to faint; cursed and fought it as hard as he could; did faint, for a second; came to, to hear Connie pounding on the inner hatch. With sheer will power he forced himself to reach over with his left hand, activate the controls and pull it partly open; and fainted again.

Thus Connie found him when he crawled through into *Santa Maria*, his feet anchored in the shoe-holds, his body swaying gently. Connie thought, *Where the hell is Jayvee?* but didn't waste time looking.

Quickly he felt Jazz' heart, lifted his eyelids, satisfied himself it was temporary loss of consciousness and nothing more. As rapidly as he could he worked himself over to the medical supplies in the bay under the left-hand window. Slightly to the rear and less than a mile away, Man in the Moon swung offside. A helmeted face was in the window. He could not distinguish its features but the position indicated interest.

"*Christ*," he said in an exasperated voice; found spirits of ammonia, worked his way back and held them under Jazz' nose.

Jazz gasped, choked, opened his eyes. Relief and chagrin struggled in his smile,

"Well, hello," Connie said.

"Am I glad to see you!"

"It's mutual. What's wrong?"

"You didn't see Jayvee, then. About five minutes ago."

"No, I was getting ready to dock. What happened?"

"He left," Jazz said with a grim humor. "After he shot me."

Connie blinked but there was no time for extended chitchat.

"Are you all right?"

"I'm O.K. for—reasonable operations," Jazz said carefully. "He winged me in the back and may have partially shattered my right shoulder. Mobility's very drastically affected, I've got a hell of a lot of pain and I'm beginning to feel very weak. But I'll do what I can for you, Conn. Where is that Soviet bastard?"

"He's right outside," Connie said, "less than a mile to the left and a little behind. And still gaining."

"It would be great if he were just a pal," Jazz said with a wry smile, "but the way things have been going in the last few minutes—" He stopped abruptly and a cold hand touched his spine. *"Where's Pete?"*

"He's—" Connie began; stopped abruptly and shook his head. A grimace of pain shot across his face. Then it was stoical and calm again. "—not here."

"Ah, Connie," Jazz said in a tired, unhappy voice. "God damn it. I am so sorry."

"It's all right. I haven't got time to talk now but I'll tell you all about it on the way home. And you can tell me about Jayvee. Right now—"

Jazz nodded grimly.

"Right now we have a date with Buster out there."

"That's right," Connie agreed. "One of them tried it on the surface. He had some sort of device that cut the power. It's funny, though—" He paused thoughtfully and frowned. "Down there it cut all links to Houston, the TV, the rover, and *Adventurer.* But up here—"

"Oh, we're cut. We haven't been able to get through to Houston for more than an hour."

"But just the downlinks. The rest of the power's O.K., right?"

"Right."

"That's odd," Connie said slowly. "I wonder . . . He was in a rover, too, apparently coming in from his lander, which was hidden from us, probably behind one of the craters. We were roughly 2000 feet out and I would estimate he was coming up at about the same distance on the other side when our links and TV went out. Yours must have gone at the same moment, because I tried you. But it wasn't until we were about 500 feet away and he was about the same distance on his side that the rover died, and when I got back to *Adventurer* I found she was dead too. Therefore maybe they both had some sort of jamming equipment for communications and then they had those damned little black boxes to knock out the internal circuits."

"Black boxes?"

"I brought one back," Connie said. "It's evidence," he

added confidently, not knowing then how empty his confidence would ultimately prove to be. "So that would mean—"

"That would mean that propinquity is the secret," Jazz said, "and that when old Space Buddy gets within 1000 feet or so, we'll go dead throughout. Connie," he added hastily, "I'm feeling very woozy again. Have you got that—"

"Right here," Connie said, waving the ammonia under his nose. Again he choked and gasped and revived. "Try to stay with me, buddy," Connie urged with some desperation. "We've got a job to do in the next few minutes."

"I will," Jazz promised, "I will. I'm doing my best."

But he was becoming increasingly pale and Connie was beginning to think he might have the job to do alone.

"Here," he said quickly, "you come over to the controls. Can you manage them?"

"Depends on what you have in mind. I tell you, I'll do my damnedest."

"Good man," Connnie said. "I know you will."

He stripped off his spacesuit to its shirt-sleeve essentials, stuffed the suit in the tube and closed the hatch upon it. Then he disengaged Jazz' feet and began to help him toward the controls. Jazz pulled himself with his left arm. Connie pushed from behind, half floating himself. They made it and got Jazz seated. Man in the Moon was closer. The head in the window was still there. It looked both impassive and alert. It did not look friendly.

As they watched, another little puff of white came from the rear thrusters.

He was now, they estimated, about 3000 feet away.

"Taking his time, isn't he?" Jazz remarked dryly. "Playing with us. The son of a bitch."

"Well," Connie said grimly. "We aren't as helpless as he thinks. Sit tight, and if he comes any closer while I'm gone, turn and ram him broadside. Don't worry about me, I'll grab onto something."

"Roger," Jazz said. He smiled, looking keyed up and not quite so pale. "As we say in dear old Texas, hurry back."

And in a surprisingly short time Connie was back, having gone through the hatch into *Nina* and from there into *Pinta*, where he removed binoculars, sextants, extra medical supplies and Jazz and Jayvee's two unused porta-

623

ble life-support systems which now would never be needed on the Moon this trip. After he had pushed them through into *Nina* he returned to *Pinta* and turned all its auxiliary controls to OFF. Then he went back into *Nina*, closed the hatch, secured it; pulled himself back into *Santa Maria*, closed and secured the hatch; worked himself into the seat beside Jazz and took over the controls.

Man in the Moon fired his thrusters again.

His distance now was approximately 1500 feet.

"Hang tight, buddy," Connie directed tersely, hunching forward over the controls. "Our friend is going to get a visitor he doesn't expect."

"Get him," Jazz said quietly. "Let him have it."

And again by some fluke that Connie could never explain to himself satisfactorily later—unless it was that the Lord they had both addressed so sternly had decided to forgive them and stick around—he did.

In the configuration ordered by Houston for reasons the crew had never understood and often complained about, *Santa Maria*, instead of being in the center, was on the right going forward; then *Nina*, then *Pinta*. Now *Pinta* was to be his battering ram. In quick succession he fired the thrusters that would accomplish the plan he had devised half an hour ago when he had come up in *Adventurer* to find the Russian advancing on Piffy One from the other side.

His initial burn of the right rear thrusters swung the combined spacecraft sharply to the left into direct collision course with Man in the Moon. He had gambled that his opponent would fire his own thrusters once more at approximately that moment and he did. Piffy One veered toward Man in the Moon just as Man in the Moon spurted ahead to come parallel. A split second later Connie fired all of his rear thrusters and Piffy One shot forward. A split second after that all power died. But the thrust had been sufficient. The inertial momentum continued. Piffy One met Man in the Moon at just sufficient angle so that *Pinta* took the brunt and gouged straight along the Russian's right-hand oxygen tank.

There was a terrific bang, a terrible jolt inside *Santa Maria*. After a moment that was eternity Piffy One stabilized. But it continued to streak straight ahead, completely off-course and off-orbit.

Now they both prayed, and more respectfully; and

within two seconds, it was answered. Connie's gamble paid off: the power came back on. Instantly several things happened.

Connie hit the controls with an automatic reflex so fast it exceeded thought. He fired the forward reverse thrusters, Piffy One slowed abruptly. He fired the left rear thrusters, Piffy One swung back to the right. He fired the left thrusters, then the right, then the left, then the right, then the left, then the right. Then he paused for five seconds, studied his instruments, fired the rear thrusters. Planetary Fleet One was reasonably back on course.

Simultaneously a familiar voice filled the cabin: "—Mission Control at 108 hours, 6 minutes. We've still got this rather puzzling anomaly of loss of signal, but everybody here is working along calmly to—*what? Hold on, everybody! Hold on! We have acquisition of signal! We have acqui—*"

"Hello, One, this is Houston. We read you now, One. We have telemetry and biomed. Hello, Connie, are you there, Connie? Connie, come in, please. Hello, Connie?"

"Hello, Houston," he said, breathing hard and trying to keep his voice steady, though not succeeding very well. "We have you, thanks. We are O.K. Stand by and we will talk to you shortly. Over."

"Roger, Conn," Stu Yule said, and his voice was shaking too. "There are a lot of happy people here waiting to hear from you. Standing by. Over."

Already approaching the horizon far to their left, venting oxygen in a great white cloud from its shattered right flank, rotating wildly, thrusters firing frantically, Man in the Moon rose steadily away to begin its long, last journey into the Sun.

"Connie," Jazz said in a weak voice, and Connie instantly put his hand over the mike to Houston. "I think I'm going to pass out again."

"I should think so," Connie said with a shaky laugh. "You and me both." He gave Jazz an encouraging smile. "Why not? It won't hurt anything and it'll give you a rest for a while. Take it easy and don't worry. I'll wake you up in a few minutes."

"Thanks," Jazz said, putting his head back and closing his eyes. "I'm afraid . . . you're going to have a rough . . . trip home with me, Conn."

"We'll manage," Connie said with more certainty than

he felt, as the excitement began to ebb and he suddenly realized with a grim little shiver that Jazz might be entirely right.

The thought sent his mind instantly to what Stu had just said and he said sharply,

"Houston, activate Special-1, please. Hello, Bob?—Andy: Andy, you're getting our biomed, right?"

"Yes, Connie," the Administrator said, and Connie knew from the disturbed gravity of his voice what his next answer would be.

"And you're only getting two of us."

"Yes, Connie," Andy said quietly.

"All right," Connie said. "Listen: There is an explanation, and it is a tragic one, but it is not one we can give you now. Jazz and I are aboard. We are alone. We will not, repeat not, discuss it until we see you. Please keep biomed absolutely secret. Please impose absolute secrecy on all doctors monitoring. Please do not fail us in this. It is imperative. Do you copy?"

There was silence for a moment in Houston. Then Dr. Anderson said slowly,

"If you think—"

Connie snapped,

"I think."

Again there was silence.

"Very well, Connie," Andy Anderson said; and there was a note of reservation in his voice that would have alerted Connie, had he been in a less tense and more normal state of mind, to unknown but worrisome troubles ahead. "It will be done."

"Thanks," Connie said, more mildly. "We'll tell you all about it when we get there," and added, almost defiantly though he could not have said why, "The truth is its own defense," not realizing in his peculiar condition of shock, unhappiness and exhilaration, that he would soon be coming home to face all the same enemies of Piffy One who had damned her when she left; and that their renewed and relentless hostility would shortly make of his aphorism one of the more naïve assumptions of the century.

"We'll hope so," Dr. Anderson said quietly. "I'll turn you back to Stu on S-band now."

"Roger," Connie said. "Special-1, over and out."

"Conn," Stu said, "we want you to know how delighted and relieved everybody is here. It would do your hearts good to see all the smiling faces around this place. We were really beginning to get a little uptight about you, boy."

"We were just a little bit uptight ourselves," Connie said, sounding more amicable.

"What's your plan now?" Stu asked, a tentative note in his voice. "Everything go all right on the Moon?"

"Flight plan completed," Connie said crisply. "I think we'll do transearth injection burn on this upcoming pass around the dark side and head on home."

"Well, that's good," Stu said, a little uneasily, Connie thought. "The flight controllers will be conferring here in a couple of minutes, and then we'll know whether we've got a GO or NO-GO for you on that burn—"

"Look," Connie interrupted evenly. "I don't give a good God damn whether anybody down there says I'm GO or NO-GO, we're going to make that burn on this pass and come home. We know what our situation is, so let's everybody down there just stop trying to get into the act and let us do what we have to do, O.K.?"

"Well, yes, Conn," Stu said hastily. "If that's the way you feel about it."

"It is."

"O.K., then, you're GO for burn."

"Thanks so much."

"This is Mission Control, and as you heard in that conversation concluded just before Planetary Fleet One went behind the Moon on this final pass, everybody here concurs that Connie Trasker has a GO for transearth injection burn. When we next acquire signal the burn should have been completed and the mission should be starting its three-day trip back to rendezvous with Space Station *Mayflower*. There, as you know, the crew will rest for several days, undergo medical checks and debriefing, and replenish supplies before taking off once more for Mars. This will complete the preliminary test period of the mission. ("What about that second descent to the Moon?" UPI demanded. "What the hell's going on?" But Mission Control continued its soothing report.)

"Right now, everybody here in Mission Contol is feeling very relieved about the whole situation and all are working along trying to analyze just what went wrong on this unexplained loss of signal we've had for the past couple of hours. Apparently, as you heard Connie report, everything

627

went along fine up there on the Moon, and now it will take some patient and probably lengthy work on the part of all concerned to pinpoint the trouble. We're advised by Dr. Anderson that any debriefing of the crew on that point will have to await arrival at *Mayflower*, as they now have their hands full making this transearth injection burn. Because of this happy change in the situation it's also been decided that there's no need for a special press conference at this time. We expect to reacquire regular signal from Planetary Fleet One in approximately forty minutes when it comes from behind the Moon again. Everything now is getting back to normal and once the burn is successfully completed we'll be entering once again upon a relatively routine portion of the mission. This is Mission Control, at 108 hours, 21 minutes into the flight Planetary Fleet One to Mars."

But despite Mission Control's evident and earnest belief that saying would make it so, neither the journey home nor the welcome that was already beginning to build up on Earth were to prove routine.

4.

"One, this is Houston. We have your transearth injection burn pad for you, if you're ready to copy" . . . "Roger, ready" . . . "Oh, is that still you, Conn? I thought you'd take it easy for a minute and let Pete or Jayvee have the duty. Make 'em work, babe. Don't let 'em get away with anything. Over" . . . "Thanks, Stu, but I'm still minding the store. Fire away on transearth injection please. Time's short. We only have ten minutes to loss of signal" . . . "Roger. We'll give you a TEI 30 and then a TEI 31. TEI 30 SPS G&N 36 691 minus 061 plus 066 135 23 41 56 NOUN 81— . . ."

They passed behind the Moon, lost signal. He made the burn, set Piffy One successfully on her homeward course. They emerged for the last time into lunar daylight, began to pull steadily away from the sear and pockmarked surface.

He did not look back upon it. But for a second he saw again vividly the empty plain, the stranded rover and two dead bodies, one of them his friend: eyes closed, face happy, peaceful and at rest, as he had seen him last.

Thank you, Petros, he said to him in his mind. *You gave your life for me and I don't forget it.*

For a moment his expression was profoundly sad. Then he blinked rapidly, shook his head with an impatient, angry motion, responded with an impersonal calm to Houston when it began chattering to him again after reacquisition of signal.

Finally he got Bob Hertz on Special-1, asked to be relieved of this for a few minutes.

When Bob asked why, he replied sharply, "Because I have some things to do."

"O.K.," Bob said. "O.K." He paused a moment and then added quietly, "Connie, we don't know yet down here, of course, what your trouble is. But *you* know, up there, that we are for you a hundred per cent, that you have our prayers, and, yes, our love, and that if there is anything we can do to help you get over this difficult time and get safely home, we want to do it. So please don't take our heads off. We know you are under great strain but we are only here to help."

Again for a second he came perilously close to breaking down, but *I must not*, he told himself, *I must not, I simply cannot let myself, I have got to get us home.*

So after a moment he managed to speak with equal quietness, though his voice shook and the tensions in it were plainly audible to Bob and to Andy listening beside him.

"I'm sorry. You know I appreciate it. I can't say more right now. Don't worry, I'll be all right. I'll be back on S-band shortly. Just let me do a little housekeeping first and then I'll be back. Ask Chuck Berry and the doctors to stand by. I may need some advice with Jazz. But I repeat, do not worry. We'll make it. I'll talk again in about an hour. Special-1, over and out."

"Over," Bob said in a gravely troubled voice, "and out."

Connie snapped off all downlinks, turned at last to look at his unconscious partner, whom he had not had time to study during the burn sequence except for a hasty glance or two to make sure he was all right.

Jazz' color was still bad but his breathing was steady, his pulse regular, and he appeared to be resting easily.

Connie debated, finally reached over and shook his left arm gently. After a moment Jazz came to; looked around vaguely for a second; focused; shot a quick glance out the window and comprehended at once.

"The burn was O.K. We're going home."

"It was O.K. we are going home."

"Sorry I couldn't help, pal," Jazz said unhappily. "I feel as useless as yesterday's condom."

"That's all right," Connie said, and the laughter that suddenly came was healthy, relieving and most welcome. He realized that it lasted a second or two too long, but he

630

knew that would soon pass. "The important thing is, how are you? How do you really feel?"

"Not really too good, Conn. I really"—and his face twisted suddenly with deep pain as he shifted his right arm very cautiously—"am in pretty bad shape, I think. The antibiotics are beginning to wear off. I could use some more pain-killers. Have we got any?"

"Bushels," Connie said, rummaging in the medical bay. "Thank God. Here—"

"Thanks," Jazz said gratefully, using a water gun with his lefthand and gulping a couple down. "At least they'll keep me from climbing the walls. And maybe they'll stave off infection—let us pray. But Conn: I can't stay here at the controls. I've got to get bedded down somehow. If," he added hastily, "you won't need me, that is."

Connie shook his head.

"What's to do? I have one, maybe two, midcourse correction burns between here and *Mayflower*, and that's all. I can handle both of them with my eyes closed. Strictly by the book from here on." He smiled. "No more little gremlins running around in space. I think we took care of the last one. And anyway: you take it easy for twenty-four hours and you'll be up and around again when I need you. Don't worry about it."

"That's the spirit," Jazz said, a trifle dryly. "Positive thinking."

"I've had my share of the other in the last few hours, thanks," Connie said with equal dryness. "I'll try the positive from now on, if you don't mind. Well: first of all, I think we'd better get some food into ourselves. Think you can manage anything?"

"I'll try," Jazz said doubtfully. "A little."

And he did try, valiantly, but it didn't work. He got down a glass of milk and two mouthfuls of reconstituted mashed potatoes and promptly threw up. Fortunately Connie was waiting with a towel and caught it before it could go into suspension and start to float around the cabin. They could tell that experiment wasn't going to work, at least for now.

"That's all right," Connie said comfortably as Jazz looked both exhausted and disgusted with himself. "We'll try it later. When did you eat last?"

"About three hours before rendezvous."

"Oh, well, no problem, then. You're good for quite a while longer."

"Help me into *Nina*," Jazz requested. "I have to go to the can, if you want to supervise that too, nurse."

Connie smiled.

"That I hope you can manage for yourself. However," he added, and meant it, "if you can't, I'm here. There ain't nobody but me, so if you have to have help, here I am."

"Thanks," Jazz said with a weak but genuine chuckle, "but I don't think I'm *that* helpless, yet."

He was, nonetheless, grateful for Connie's steadying arm as he got up shakily, worked himself along the wall into *Nina*. Connie followed and stood thoughtfully looking out the window.

Jazz gave him a humorous glance.

"What are you waiting for?"

"I want to make sure you don't either float up to the ceiling or go down the waste dump with the bag. Anyway, you know as well as I do there's absolutely no way to do anything gracefully or privately in a spacecraft: no way."

"Well," Jazz said, again with a weak but quite cheerful grin, "I'm glad we're both boys. What do you suppose is the condition right—there?"

And he pointed to the hatch that sealed them off from *Pinta*.

"I think very likely she's ripped away as badly as Man in the Moon if not worse," Connie said. "As soon as you either piss or get off the pot I'm going to get you back into *Santa Maria* and then I'm coming back in here, have you close the hatch, depressurize this cabin, open the hatch to *Pinta,* and find out. After that we'll repressurize and get you bedded down in here. No point in your trying to stay on your feet. By that time I also will be ready to take a small snooze, I think." He yawned suddenly, so deeply he felt as though it would split his jaws. "God, I am tired."

"I should think you would be," Jazz remarked soberly. "Do you realize we've killed three men between us in the last three hours?"

"It doesn't happen every day," Connie agreed dryly. "At least on the Moon. Aren't you through *yet?*"

"I'm through," Jazz said with dignity. "You young student nurses are all alike. Hurry, hurry, hurry, in with the bedpan, out with the bedpan, busy, busy, busy!"

"Come on, Laughing Boy," Connie said, offering his arm. "Let's get you back into *Santa Maria* and then I'm going to check out a few things."

"You be damned careful," Jazz said seriously. "I don't want you floating out into space. I'm getting used to you."

"You know me better than that," Connie assured him. "This will be a strictly routine EVA."

And when he had Jazz safely back in *Santa Maria*, shoe-anchored in front of the controls, it was.

He opened the tube to *Adventurer*, pulled out his space suit, put it back on. Then with a nod and a smile, he worked his way through the hatch, turned to watch while Jazz closed and sealed it behind him, waited patiently while Jazz got back to the controls and started the depressurization of *Nina*. When it was completed, the green safe-light went on.

He worked his way over to the hatch leading into *Pinta*, flipped the catchlocks, activated the automatic release. The hatch swung slowly free.

He looked into the depths of space. Along the right edge a last tiny slice of Moon, going fast, was still visible. Cautiously he pulled himself part way through into what remained of *Pinta*. He was not surprised by what he found.

The vehicle had been sliced almost in half, a long ragged gash perhaps ten feet in width at the forward end, narrowing to perhaps three feet at the rear as they had swung and ripped along Man in the Moon.

The walls had been stripped of equipment as neatly as though someone had gone through with a blowtorch. The NERVA engine was completely gone. All that remained of the redundant set of master controls was a few strands of wire, a sight that disturbed him for a second but was answered with the reflection that from here on home they were virtually guaranteed safe passage. Also, they had *Adventurer*, which, like all the landers since Apollo 13, had been fully equipped for emergency use if needed.

He studied the ravaged spacecraft for several minutes, frowning thoughtfully. Then he closed the hatch and resealed it; half clambered, half floated across to the hatch leading into *Santa Maria;* rapped on it sharply twice. The pressurization light went on at once and stayed on until the cabin was repressurized. He stripped off his suit to shirtsleeve fundamentals again, stowed it under one of the hammocks. Then he rapped three times. From the other side Jazz opened the hatch. He pulled himself back into *Santa Maria*, noting that Jazz still looked pale, his eyes sick and unwell, but seemed to be reasonably steady. He thought, *So far, so good*, not knowing how long it would last but hoping for the best.

"Well?"

"Just what I expected: sheared in two laterally, loss approximately one half, big gash starting front, narrowing to back, redundancy controls gone, everything gone."

"Man in the Moon gone, too," Jazz observed, "for which, Allah be praised."

He worked himself over to the controls again, his face twisting with pain. Connie noted with rising alarm that he no longer made any attempt to use his right arm. It now hung immobile and oddly angled to his side. But his mind was working fast.

"You know," he said slowly, "I've been thinking, while you've been gone, that when we get back we're going to run into a hell of a lot of flak on this. We're going to be back on dear old savage, snarling Earth, where things aren't as simple as they are out here in pure, pristine, blood-filled space. It's just occurred to me we're going to have an awful lot of unfriendly people to answer to. And if we bring *Pinta* back—" he paused and concluded softly, "maybe they're going to believe us, Conn, and then again, maybe they're not."

Connie nodded.

"Yes, I've just begun to have happy thoughts like that, too. What's your solution?"

"Jettison her. We can always say we tried an undocking experiment and lost her. I say, undock and kick her away."

"Onto the Moon?"

Jazz looked grim.

"I expect there's enough on the Moon we'll have to explain someday, when somebody gets back again and starts looking. No, wait until tomorrow sometime and then kick her into the Sun. Get rid of her entirely.

Connie thought for a long moment. Then he shook his head slowly.

"No, I don't think so, Jazz. She's like my black box:

634

she's evidence. And I feel that whether we can justify her or not, whether we can make them understand or not, whether they'll accept what we have to say or not, we've got to hang onto her. Because she *is* proof, for honest men who will believe that we are honest men, of what we say."

Jazz gave him a long, shrewd glance, and again his voice was soft.

"Do you think there are men like that back home, Connie? Outside of our own bunch in NASA, I mean?"

"There've got to be," Connie said simply. "If there aren't, then all of this has been in vain and we might just as well have died where we were—all of us."

"Maybe we'll find that would have been simpler," Jazz remarked somberly. Then without thinking he started to shrug. Instantly his face turned completely white, he gasped and fainted.

Connie got to him as fast as he could, grabbed the ammonia, held it under his nose, once more brought him choking and coughing back to consciousness.

"Don't *do* that," he ordered sternly. "You scare me to death."

"I'm—sorry," Jazz said, still choking but beginning to laugh a little along with it. "I'm sure one hell of a poor, chopped-up, one-winged ruptured duck, aren't I?"

"You are," Connie agreed. "And that's why now we're going to get you tucked into your little trundle bed, sonny boy, and no more nonsense about it. Let me look at that thing."

And he carefully swung Jazz around and for the first time studied the wound in his back with complete concentration.

Coagulated blood covered an area perhaps a foot square, extending from near the right shoulder down almost to the waist.

"I'd say you're damned lucky," he remarked soberly, "that he didn't get you right straight through the lung."

"Might have simplified your trip home."

"And don't say things like that, either, We'll manage. I wonder . . . Apparently a piece of your suit impacted into the wound and stopped a good deal of the blood. I gather the bullet's still in there."

"I haven't noticed it popping out into my hand any time lately."

"No . . . I suppose I ought to cut away the cloth and

clean the wound, but that runs the risk of starting the bleeding again . . . but I suppose I'd better do it."

"Yes, I suppose you had."

"Right," Connie said. "One thing first, though. I ought to check in with our chums in Houston." He flipped the S-band switch. "Hello, Houston, this is One. We've got our housekeeping pretty well done for now, I think"—Jazz mouthed, "Liar," but he smiled and went blandly on— "and so I think maybe we're going to sleep for a while, if that's O.K. with you down there. It's been a long day, and"—he hesitated, but continued smoothly—"everybody here is pretty tired. We'll keep watch as usual, but if you can manage it for maybe the next eight hours or so, don't call us, we'll call you. O.K.?"

"Roger, Connie," Gaudy Gaudet replied cordially. "It's sure great to hear your voice again, but we read you, we'll try to do without it for about eight. Have a good rest. Over."

"Thanks, pal. Can you put me on Special-1 to Bob for a minute? . . . Hi, Bob. Things looking a little clearer at the moment, I think. Jazz has a wound and I'm going to get it cleaned up now, disinfect it, and put on a bandage. Then I'm going to see if I can get a little food down him, followed by a sleeping pill, and I think he'll be coming along all right. Are any of the doctors around, and do they concur?"

"Chuck here, Connie. Can't you tell us the nature of the wound? It would help."

"Not yet, Chuck, sorry. That will have to wait for *Mayflower*. I think I can handle it. If I find I can't I'll get back to you so fast it will make your head spin, never fear about that."

"Well . . . O.K."

"Trust me, Chuck."

"We have to, Connie. What else can we do?"

"Roger, I guess that's right. Special-1, over and out."

"You're a hard-nosed bastard," Jazz remarked. "And," he added, "I hope you know what you're doing."

"*We* know what *we're* doing," Connie corrected. "You can call him any time you don't agree."

"I agree. Let's get to it."

"O.K.," Connie said. "Sit still and try to think about something else."

636

"I have a better idea than that," Jazz suggested quietly. "Tell me about Pete and I'll tell you about Jayvee."

Connie hesitated for a second. Then he nodded.

"All right," he said with equal quietness. "I think that is a good idea."

And while he found the necessary supplies in the medical bay; carefully cut away the blood-soaked suit; gently probed for the impacted piece of cloth, found it and drew it out; staunched the newly flowing blood with towels until it stopped; sprinkled the ugly opening heavily with penicillin powder, placed a heavy bandage over it and strapped it in place across Jazz' back—he talked as clearly and impersonally as he would later at home about the events that had occurred when *Adventurer* reached the Moon. True to his training, his powers as an observer, and his own inclination, he made it strictly narrative, no personalities and no quotes.

It was at least partial catharsis for him and it certainly served its purpose as operational therapy for Jazz: he listened attentive and fascinated, not even wincing under Connie's ministrations until the moment came to remove the fragments of the impacted cloth, when he fainted again and had to be revived. His only comment came at the point of Pete's death, when he said again how sorry he was. Connie confined his response to, "Thanks," and hurried on.

Jazz' own narrative was for the most part equally impersonal, though he could not refrain from showing some anger toward the end. Connie warned him against this and he agreed it was unwise.

"Maybe you and I had better rehearse each other," he suggested, not altogether facetiously; and after thinking a moment, Connie said, "Yes, I think probably we should. After you're up and around a bit."

When he had finished he offered Jazz food again, but again, though he did not vomit, he was unable to get down more than a couple of mouthfuls of bread and perhaps a tablespoonful of hot bouillon.

"That's all right," Connie said calmly, for Jazz looked a little worried for a moment. "You'll feel better after some sleep."

"I hope so," Jazz said. He managed a small smile. "I sure don't feel so hot right now."

"Two of these magic NASA antibiotics," Connie said

cheerfully, tipping them into his hand "and a couple of sleeping pills, and you'll be set for as long as you want to go. Take this water gun and get 'em down."

After Jazz complied, Connie helped him into *Nina* and got him bedded down in one of the hammocks, lying on his left side and strapped in tightly so he would not float out of position. He took his temperature, found it to be 99.8 but was not unduly alarmed under all the circumstances and gave his left hand an encouraging squeeze.

"Take it easy, now, and go to sleep. I'm going to check out everything and then I'll be back and join you. I'm exhausted."

"Do that," Jazz murmured drowsily. "Call on me if you need anything."

"I'll do that," Connie said with a smile. "Good night."

"Good . . . night."

He waited until Jazz' breathing became steady and even. Then he ate a substantial meal himself; returned to *Santa Maria*, checked the controls; set them for thermal control mode, felt the slow, steady rotation begin; listened with a practiced ear to the quietly humming computers, found no anomalies; glanced back at the receding Moon, glanced forward at the oncoming Earth; sighed heavily with premonitions he could not entirely define but knew were beginning to weigh upon him more than he liked; and returned to *Nina*.

Jazz was sleeping soundly.

He crawled into the hammock alongside, strapped himself in, and in three seconds was also asleep.

Piffy One streaked on toward home.

At home, the welcoming chorus grew for Piffy One.

But for two more days he was to be spared the caterwaulings of his countrymen and the carpings of the jealous world. It was just as well, for he had other things on his mind.

Mechanically the flight was as close to perfection as the flight out had been, even though its success now depended entirely upon him as the only member of the crew still functioning. The management of the spacecraft presented no problems, for he had done everything ten thousand times before, during his previous flights and during his endless hours in the simulators. His only personal problem was getting sufficient sleep and he managed to pace himself adequately enough on that until the last twenty-four hours. By then he was near enough home so that he could stand it.

With a combination of guile, vagueness and the help of his friends on the groud, he managed to maintain the fiction that they were all coming back. The Administrator and Bob Hertz had reached the decision that until they could talk to Connie they must protect him; and word had been quietly passed to the key people in the medical, flight control and public affairs staffs. This violated all of NASA's principles but they felt the situation justified it: obviously some great and calamitous emergency had occurred, and since Connie refused to talk they had no choice but to support him. The comments from and to Houston on S-band remained chatty and apparently normal:

"This is Mission Control at 120 hours, 36 minutes into the mission. Planetary Fleet One is now 18,243 nautical miles from the Moon, traveling at a velocity of 4426 feet per second. We haven't heard anything from the crew in the past ten hours, and since everything is nominal and GO on the return trip so far, the flight controllers haven't bothered them. The doctors report crew members sleeping soundly, with the regular emergency watch. Before long we should be getting word from them as they awake and come back on duty. All systems appear to be GO, Planetary Fleet One is coming home after this first successful test phase of the flight to Mars. We'll be having some more direct broadcasts for you when the sleep period is over . . .

"Hello, Houston, this is One" . . . "Good morning, One. You're looking real good. Did everybody get a good night's sleep?" . . . "Fine, thank you, Jazz snored a little, but otherwise all O.K." . . . "Roger, don't let him get away with that stuff. If you're ready to go, we'd like you to do a CO_2 filter change and have the H_2 purge line heater on 20 minutes before the O_2 and H_2 purge. Then we'd like you to initiate a charge on Battery A and leave the charge on until we notify you further. Two hours, waste water dump to 10 per cent. I've also got your consumables updated. Are you ready to copy?" . . . "Roger, understand, will readback on purges, then copy consumables and give you our readings here" . . . "Roger, standing by for purge data and consumables updates . . .

"This is Mission Control at 130 hours, 19 minutes Ground Elapsed Time. Planetary Fleet One has passed across the imaginary line that divides the Moon's sphere of influence from Earth's sphere of influence. At that time the spacecraft were approximately 33,800 nautical miles from the Moon and 174,000 nautical miles from Earth, traveling at a speed of about 3994 feet per second with respect to the Earth. From this point on Planetary Fleet One will continue to accelerate steadily as it nears the Earth. Earth's influence is now the dominant factor in the return of the spacecraft from this first test phase of the mission to Mars . . .

"Hello, One, this is Houston with midcourse correction burn pad. You are now GO on that for 140 GET. Are you ready to copy?" . . . "Roger, ready to copy . . ."

"This is Mission Control at 150 hours, 23 minutes. GET. After successful completion of the midcourse burn, which you heard shortly after 140 hours, Planetary Fleet One has now crossed the halfway mark between Earth and Moon, at that point it was 145,583 nautical miles from Earth at a velocity of 4300 feet with respect to both Earth and Moon. The crew reports everybody aboard in good shape, and all continues to be GO on the homeward journey of Planetary Fleet One . . ."

What the crew reported on S-band about everybody aboard, however, was not what the crew reported on Special-1. Behind the hearty words of Mission Control and the smooth, familiar exchanges which he managed to carry on with necessary blandness, he was having an increasingly difficult time with his wounded partner.

Things had begun to get worse roughly twelve hours after they left the Moon and they had deteriorated steadily since. As they passed midpoint and entered home stretch he did not honestly know whether he would arrive with a live crewmate or the third tragic exaction of the flight of Piffy One.

The uncertainty produced a rapid and drastic revision of what he now saw had been a rather high-handed treatment of the medical staff in Houston. When Jazz finally awoke after almost ten hours of sleep, he stirred, mumbled, rolled over, cried out in pain and instantly fainted again. Shaken, Connie revived him, took his temperature, found it to be 101.2. He went immediately into *Santa Maria* and asked for help.

"Hello, Houston, activate Special-1 please. Hello, Bob?"

"Here, Connie"—without the slightest hint of reproach, only a calm and reassuming confidence—"what's your problem?"

"Jazz is running a temperature of 101.2," Connie said crisply, "as the result of a gunshot wound—"

"Gunshot wound?" Bob exclaimed. Connie did not stop to explain but only interpolated dryly, *"Not* caused by me—entering right middle back laterally and apparently traversing upward toward approximately one o'clock, impacting and probably shattering portions of right shoulder. Bullet still in place, bleeding profuse at first but successfully staunched, wound cleaned, dusted with penicillin, bandaged—I believe I told you anticipated treatment earlier. Two antibotics, two sleeping pills given ten hours ago heavy sleep since then. Great pain on awakening, fainted, I revived him and took his temperature as stated. He has had almost nothing to eat in approximately fifteen hours; vomited when I first tried to feed him prior to sleep period, was able to manage only a couple of mouthfuls on second attempt. In good spirits but weak and worried. So am I. Not weak, but worried. Advise, please. Over."

"Thank God, you're not weak, Connie," Bob said, "that would be too much."

"Call me Iron Man. Is Chuck there?"

"Hi, Connie. Is the wound clean?"

"I swabbed it out very thoroughly, I think, and also extracted some fragments of uniform that had impacted into it."

"I think you'd better keep on with the antibiotics—you have that all-purpose one, don't you, and the penicillin powder. Keep up the internal doses if he can keep them down. I wouldn't disturb the wound again unless you think it's absolutely necessary—"

"You're the doctor."

"I'm the consulting physician. *You're* the doctor. I'd take a look at it pretty soon, if I were you, and if there's any spreading of discoloration or any sign of abnormality, clean it and douse it with powder again and put on a new bandage."

"Shall I try to cauterize it? We have knives and things I might be able to use."

"No, I don't think you'd better try. Let's just put our faith in antibiotics for the time being and see if we can't get him back to *Mayflower*, and then we can put him on the shuttle right away and get him down here and we'll take over."

"How about food?"

"He's got to have some, obviously. Try him again, and if that doesn't work you'll have to put him on intravenous. You have that equipment, too, of course. It's relatively simple."

"Roger, we had quite a lot of emergency medical during training, so I think I can manage that, all right. How it will work in zero-G and in pitch and yaw, I leave you to imagine, but I'll do my best."

"O.K. You may have to work out some sort of pump for it. Just be sure there's a steady flow and not too fast. Give him about half an hour at a time, a full bottle every four hours."

"And run the spacecraft with the other hand."

"And run the spacecraft with the other hand. I'm sorry as hell, Connie, but—"

"Oh, I'm not griping. That's the way the mission crumbles. And by God, it has crumbled. What about temperature?"

"Keep taking it at regular intervals and keep me advised. Talk any time. I've had a cot brought in. I'll be here until you get home."

"Bless you, and bless everybody down there. I'll be talking to you. Special-1, over and out . . . And now, Jazzbo," he said half-aloud to himself as he started back into *Nina*, "let's see what we can do for *you*."

"What's that mumbling out there?" Jazz asked weakly as he reached his side. "Are you beginning to talk to yourself? Am I traveling with a loony?"

"You may be, yet, buddy. I keep hearing little voices saying, 'How about two tickets to the World Series? How about two tickets to the World Series?'"

He placed his hand on Jazz' forehead, took it away after a moment and looked thoughtful. It was still burning.

"What did Chuck say?" Jazz asked. "Does he think I'm going to live?"

"Think you're going to *live!*" Connie exclaimed. "Who said an onery bastard like you could do anything else? The

Lord doesn't want you to die, Jazz, you'd raise too much hell in heaven. Yes, he thinks you're going to live, providing nurse here can get you through. Which," he added firmly, "nurse intends to do. First of all we try some food."

"I'm not sure I—" Jazz began, but Connie ignored him and went blandly on.

"I won't describe how NASA's special regummified Chateaubriand for two looks to the naked eye, I shall simply prepare it out of your sight, place a blindfold over your eyes, hold your nose and tell you to gulp it down. O.K.? It's the only way."

"I'll try," Jazz promised gamely, not looking very optimistic.

He made a valiant attempt but his apprehensions speedily proved correct.

"All right, my boy," Connie said after he finished mopping up, "Chuck says you go on intravenous."

"But it won't flow, will it?" Jazz asked, and for the first time a trace of real fear came into his eyes.

"I'll make it flow," Connie assured him. "As soon as I get through copying the pad for the midcourse correction burn. Let me get that out of the way and then I'll be back and we'll give her a try. Rest easy, meantime."

After he had chatted for a while with Houston, his voice calm, impersonal, and efficient as it came over the loudspeakers to the pressroom and the curious globe, he returned to his medical chores.

First he removed the bandage as slowly and gently as he could, frowned with dismay as he saw the discoloration beginning to spread around the wound, disinfected it carefully again, dusted it once more with penicillin, put on a clean bandage. Jazz groaned and cursed and sweated but did not lose consciousness again, though his protests seemed to be generally weaker. The flavor of Jazz was still there, but diluted.

Increasingly worried, Connie got the bottle of glucose solution, the tube and the needle. He hung the bottle on the wall above Jazz' hammock. He got one of the plastic squeeze bottles that had contained carrots or spinach at some previous meal, unscrewed the top, put it in the electronic washer, pushed the button, extracted it clean two seconds later. He screwed the top back on, punctured the tube between the glucose and the needle, forced the needle and tube through the squeeze bottle, in the one-way valve to admit water and out the one-way valve to emit food. He gave it a preliminary squeeze or two, applying a firm, steady pressure. The glucose solution entered the squeeze bottle and began to travel slowly out again toward the needle.

Jazz, watching drowsily, remarked, "You're pretty damned clever." Connie replied cheerfully, "I think so."

He inserted the needle in Jazz' arm, taped it in place, made himself comfortable in the adjoining hammock and spent the next half hour slowly and steadily operating the squeeze bottle. The liquid dropped approximately one-fourth before he stopped to rest. Jazz, reassured in an almost childlike way by his air of competence, drifted off to sleep before he finished. Connie made sure he was securely strapped in, left everything in place, and went back to report on his medical triumph over Special-1. Everyone was very pleased and he felt very satisfied; except for the look of the wound when he had dressed it, and Jazz' temperature, which instead of dropping had risen to 101.8 when he took it again.

But for the time being, he decided and Houston concurred, the best thing was to leave Jazz alone and let him rest.

"So," he said, sounding relaxed and in good spirits, "with your permission, I shall stop playing nurse and go back to being an astronaut. Midcourse correction burn coming up, and I'd better get ready for it."

He verified the spacecraft attitude by sighting through the sextant the star Houston designated, ran tests on the guidance control system and the reaction control system, received his GO from the ground.

The burn lasted 10.0 seconds, the reaction control system thrusters made a change of velocity retrograde of 4.8 feet per second, the flight path angle was adjusted for re-entry into Earth orbit preparatory to rendezvous with Space Station *Mayflower*. He was at that time approximately 169,000 nautical miles out, traveling at a velocity of 4075.6 feet per second.

Mission Control reported it, everybody breathed easier. He announced a sleep period, fudging the details, and went back to *Nina*.

He pumped another half hour of glucose solution into his sleeping crewmate, felt his forehead again and found the fever still raging, shook his head with an angry worry but knew he must husband his own energies. He set the alarm, strapped himself in his hammock, and slept like a log.

Four hours later, bright and cheerful, he was back again chatting with the ground for the benefit of his listening countrymen and the world as Planetary Fleet One continued the long glide home.

For the next thirty hours, this was essentially his routine. The spacecraft, as he had predicated to Jazz, virtually ran itself.

"The machinery is great," he remarked wryly at one point to Bob Hertz. "It's only the men who have had a few problems."

What they were, however, he steadfastly refused to state in any more detail than he already had; unaware that despite the best intentions and necessary equivocations of himself, Houston and everyone connected with the program, the conviction was rapidly and loudly growing throughout American and the world that something was most gravely wrong with Piffy One.

It is unlikely that even if he had known it he would, or could, have paid much attention, for as the homeward flight entered its final hours, his crewmate grew steadily worse.

Five times over the next fifteen hours he returned to *Nina,* put new glucose bottles in place and fed his wounded friend. The first two times Jazz did not stir. The third time he opened his eyes and managed a feeble grin.

"I'm sorry, nurse," he said in a shadow of his former vigorous voice. "I'm going to have to have that bedpan."

"All right," Connie said. "Let's see if we can get you up and over there."

But Jazz' legs were like rubber and after an earnest but futile attempt Connie eased him back into the hammock and strapped him in again.

"O.K., bedpan it is."

"Hell," Jazz said, and for the first time tears of anger and frustration came into his eyes. "I'm as helpless as a damned baby. You shouldn't have to—"

"But you are," Connie said calmly, "and I do. Hold it and I'll get the bag."

'Hell," Jazz said again and turned his face away. "I'm ashamed to have to make you do this for me."

"Look, pal," Connie said in a no-nonsense tone. "You and I have both raised three little kids and wiped their bottoms, and there's nothing we don't know in this spacecraft about each other's bodily functions, so relax, will you? I'm here to help, that's my job. Now take it easy and we'll get it done."

After it was, he dressed the wound again, found the sinister discoloration had worked its way out in some places to a distance of approximately two inches from the edges of the wound. The temperature was also bad, up to 102.1 now. His patient was obviously failing and in desperation he returned to Special-1 to consult again with Houston. But, calculating the time of less than ten hours to docking with *Mayflower*, and his own inability, despite good intentions and a willingness to try, to do any really effective cauterization or surgery, it was decided that he should continue the same routine of treatment until they got home.

He did so at regular intervals of three to four hours, catching snatches of sleep and managing the spacecraft in between.

Three hours before he sighted *Mayflower*, the area around the wound had become so ugly that Connie, cursing in desperation, fear and frustration, could hardly bear to look at it. By that time, also, Jazz' temperature had climbed to 103. When Connie went back to *Nina* for the last time before he began preparations for docking, Jazz had sunk into a deep coma from which Connie could not arouse him.

"You must live," he said softly to the impassive face, the labored, heavy breathing. "You must live, my friend and my witness."

But there was no answer, and he was not at all sure at that moment that Jayvee's neuroses might not yet prove to have done their final damage to Planetary Fleet One.

Very respectfully, with a genuine anguish for himself and his unhappy crew, he prayed for a safe deliverance. He was humbled now, all right, and he did not know when, if ever, he would be arrogant or self-confident about his destiny again.

Just before Jazz passed out for the last time, he had managed a last coherent remark.

"You're quite a guy, Conn," he whispered. "I mean it. I thank you for all you've done for me. The rest of us carry the hod but you're the greatest. You really are."

And Connie had replied with a bitter, self-directed irony,

"Oh, no, I'm not. No, I'm not. I'm just the fool who thought he wanted to run the show. And the good Lord, bless his heart, said: Yes, little man, you may."

One hour out, when they were safely in orbit around Earth and beginning to close with *Mayflower*, Bob and Andy called him from the space station over Special-1.

"Connie," the Administrator said quietly, "we think you have done an absolutely magnificent job of getting home. Chuck and his staff are confident they can save Jazz, but if they can't, we want you to know that nothing can ever detract from the job you have done for him and for Planetary Fleet One. It has been absolutely heroic and everyone who knows space will always be in your debt."

"It was my job," he replied with a curious combination of gratitude, impatience and a feeling close to resentment that he could not have analyzed if he tried. "I did it."

"Don't downgrade yourself," Bob said gravely. "It was more than a job. It was inspired." Then his tone changed in a subtle but definite way that suddenly alerted Connie to the fact that more than moonlight and roses was involved in this final in-flight conversation. "We have a message for you from the President. He also wishes to express his great gratitude and appreciation to you. He will be speaking to you himself before long. He hopes that in the meantime you will make no public statements of any kind whatsoever to anyone."

"What does he mean by that?" Connie demanded sharply.

"The media have requested that they be allowed to be present at the docking," Dr. Anderson said, "so we have agreed to a pool arrangement whereby you will be met by one pool reporter, a television newsman, a television cameraman and a still photographer. We have brought them up by shuttle and they are now waiting here on *Mayflower*, along with ourselves and the Vice-President and one or two others."

"So?" Connie said and his tone was frigid. "It sounds like quite a Roman circus to me. What do the bastards want to do, photograph Jazz unconsicous with his mouth hanging open?"

"Connie," Bob said quietly, "you must understand that there is enormous interest everywhere in the world about this. I think the President's thought is that anything you say must be very carefully thought out so that there won't be some unfortunate emotional or political reaction that could do you harm."

"*What?* Did I hear you correctly? *'Political* reaction?' Well, I'll be God damned! I have lost half my crew—I am bringing home a crippled spacecraft, a wounded astronaut and myself—I am doing my level best to get us there safely—and that devious son of a bitch is worrying about the *political* reaction? What in the *Christ* am I supposed to be doing up here?"

"All right, Connie," Andy Anderson said sharply. "All *right*. We know you've had problems—"

"*Ha!*"

"—we know you've had problems. But so may he, in defending you."

"*Defending* me?"

"Yes," Dr. Anderson said, "defending you. You don't know what has been going on down here in the last three days."

"No, I don't."

"Let me tell you a little about it," Andy said, still quietly; and proceeded to do so, calmly and dispassionately, presenting without comment or elaboration the situation that waited on the ground.

When it was over Connie said with equal quietness, "Thank you very much, Andy. I understand a little better now. Will NASA stand behind me?"

"Unequivocally."

"Well," he said grimly, "at least that's a little comfort, anyway."

But it wasn't much, really, though he clung to it desperately in the closing minutes of his tragic mission.

He had entertained premonitions on the way home, indulged now and then in dark worries and speculations, occasionally thought gloomy thoughts he told himself he must not surrender to.

But it was only now that he realized how fully he and Planetary Fleet One were about to come once more under the scrutiny, malevolence and attack of their relentless and vindictive enemies.

That sad knowledge, plus the terrible strains he had been under and the terrible relief of getting home, perhaps explained why the photographer on *Mayflower* was able to get the great picture that later won him several prizes: the commander of Planetary Fleet One, just after stepping aboard, crying in the arms of his wife.

The commander might have known, however, that no excuses, however human and reasonable, would be accepted for his temporary loss of control; nor would any charity or kindness be given him by hearts as desolate and uncompassionate as the Moon and minds as sterile and unforgiving as Mars.

Book Six

1.

Hearts as desolate and uncompassionate as the Moon, minds as sterile and unforgiving as Mars: it had not taken them long to launch themselves upon their renewed and savage campaign. Roughly fifteen minutes after loss of signal from *Adventurer* and Planetary Fleet One, in fact.

From then on for three days there had been a steady crescendo of headline, broadcast, commentary and editorial, very little of it favorable in tone or emphasis to the mission or the men responsible for its fate.

First had come the emergency:

HOUSTON LOSES MARS MISSION . . . ALARM GROWS AS MARS FLIGHT BLACKS OUT . . . NASA TRIES STIFF UPPER LIP AS MARS MISSION STUMBLES . . . MARS FLIGHT LOST IN SPACE? NASA CAN'T CONNECT . . . SPACE DRAMA GROWS: WHERE IS MARS FLIGHT? . . .

Then had come reacquisition of signal:

MARS FLIGHT O.K. BUT MYSTERY ABORT ORDERED . . . STRANGE CHANGE IN MARS PLANS STIRS WORLD . . . NASA SILENT ON ABRUPT MARS TURNAROUND . . . WORLD CLAMORS FOR NEWS ON MARS PUZZLE . . . WHAT HAPPENED ON MOON? NASA MUM, U.S. GLUM . . .

Then had come Connie's rough trip back:

MARS MYSTERY GROWS AS MISSION LIMPS HOME . . . HINT HARD-LUCK MARS CREW HURT . . . TRASKER ONLY VOICE FROM SPACE . . . MARS PUZZLE GROWS: WHERE IS CREW? . . . MARS FLIGHT HEADING HOME IN DISGRACE

653

. . . WILLIAMS LEADS SENATE CALL FOR MARS INVESTIGATION . . .

Then had come the word from American's well-wishers in space:

MOSCOW REVEALS SECRET SOYUZ 19 SCIENTIFIC MOON PROBE . . . REDS HAIL SUCCESS OF SURPRISE SCIENTIFIC FLIGHT TO MOON, PROMISE TO SHARE RESULTS WITH WORLD "AT SUITABLE FUTURE DATE" . . . COMMUNISTS SAY SOYUZ 19 MOON-SCAN "MAJOR ACHIEVEMENT" . . . U.S., WORLD SCIENTISTS PRAISE MOSCOW MOON SHOT . . . SENATE SPACE DOVES CALL FOR CLOSER COOPERATION WITH COMMUNISTS AFTER SOYUZ 19 TRIUMPH . . .

And then came the broadcasts, the commentaries and the editorials:

"It is impossible tonight," Frankly Unctuous said gravely in his musings following the 6 o'clock news on the night before Connie reached *Mayflower*, "not to contrast the sad collapse of America's ill-advised and ill-fated attempt to reach Mars with the shining scientific achievement of Russia's Soyuz 19 just announced in Moscow.

"On the one hand a hastily conceived, hastily planned, sadly foredoomed mission seeking only a faded national glory and a less-than-noble prestige. On the other a carefully thought-out, scientifically oriented achievement which does much to enhance the spirit of humanity as it ventures toward the stars.

"No details have yet been revealed by the Soviets concerning the flight of Soyuz 19. But we are assured by Moscow of this: its purposes were humanitarian, its goals were peaceful and its triumph is a shining star in the Soviet crown.

"Not so, alas, our own unhappy mission to Mars, now limping home under extraordinary and unknown circumstances. It would take far more time than we have at our disposal tonight to expound, much less answer, the myriad questions that surround this ill-fated adventure. But one thing is overwhelmingly apparent: the Congress, the country and the world will not rest content until all the facts are put upon the public record, without evasion, equivocation or guile.

"Our responsibility to the world—our responsibility to

654

our Communist friends who have so dramatically shown us once again what true and decent space exploration can be—all permit no other outcome."

"So Planetary Fleet One limps home," the *Times* said on the day of rendezvous, "under mysterious and presumably tragic circumstances. And America's ill-starred attempt to wrest some empty bauble of prestige from a new space race with the Russians is apparently ending in the ignominy all such hostile and unfriendly ventures bring upon themselves and, possibly, deserve.

"We do not know yet what happened on the Moon when the Mars mission made what was originally scheduled to be a series of tests before departing on the main thrust to the planet Mars. But it is clear already that it can only have been something that brought no credit and no glory to the American name.

"In contrast, the news from Moscow of the scientific triumph of the Soyuz 19 mission to the Moon can only underwrite the glaring contrast between the opposing spirits in which the United States and the Soviet Union approach the great challenge of space.

"We do not yet know the full details of Soyuz 19's triumphant visit, and in the Russian fashion, we may never be told them. Nothing has been released save Moscow's bare statement that it has gone, has returned, and has been successful.

"Let it suffice that it was apparently a peaceful mission, designed to bring back new scientific knowledge for mankind. Nothing more is necessary to prove to us that the Soviet Union has again struck a blow for the peaceful and constructive exploration of space.

"And there is one other great aspect of the Russian achievement which must not be overlooked: it will help substantially to reduce the 'imbalance of arrogance' the United States has shown ever since the triumphs of the Apollo program. Soyuz 19's triumphant voyage will place the Russians once again on an equal footing, technologically and psychologically, with the United States. It will destroy the overweening smugness of America in space.

"It, together with the disaster to Planetary Fleet One which has made an early American triumph on Mars impossible, will serve to bring the Russians and the Americans once more level with one another, so that neither can act from a dominant superiority.

"This is a great step forward for world peace.

"We hail it sincerely and pay it well-deserved tribute.

"Now there remains the task of determining what actually happened to Planetary Fleet One, And for that, the crew, the men of NASA who support them to this very hour with a computer curtain of obdurate silence, and the Administration which sent them, must be held to strictest public accounting at the earliest possible time."

"Arrogance and a ruthless shouldering-aside of the decent and hopeful instincts of mankind have produced their just and sorry deserts in the apparently tragic failure of Planetary Fleet One," the *Post* agreed on the same day.

"Seldom has a willful and wrong-headed Administration more flatly flaunted the desires of a larger number of thoughtful and farsighted American citizens. Seldom have the Red Barons of NASA been so adamantly determined that they should have their way with a foredoomed exercise in space futility.

"Well: they have had their way and we hope they are happy with the results.

"Stupidity, false pride, racism and anti-internationalism characterized Planetary Fleet One's beginnings.

"Failure, waste, ignominy and human tragedy, to what degree we do not yet know, accompany its end.

"While the Soviet Union moves ahead with such peace-loving and genuinely humanitarian ventures as the just-announced Soyuz 19 scientific probe of the Moon, America plunges headlong down the blind road of space competition, outdated national pride and a fatuous 'national prestige.'

"We warned against it from the beginning. In one short week we have seen all our forebodings come true. It is not a pleasure to say 'We told you so,' but it is a national duty that all who originally opposed Planetary Fleet One now speak out and emphasize the wisdom of their opposition.

"It is only thus that future space stunts can be forestalled. It is only thus that those responsible for the tragic failure of this one can be brought to book.

"And brought to book, we suggest, is what they speedily should be."

And from the offices of the Committee Against Unilateral Space Exploration, the chairman and his Senatorial co-chairman issued a statement befitting their concern for America and their awareness of their own responsibility to fight for truth and justice in this ghastly and inexcusable episode:

"CAUSE regards with the deepest dismay and the sternest censure that tragic collapse of Planetary Fleet One and its ill-advised and ill-fated mission to Mars," said Percy Mercy and Senator Kennicut Williams.

"We do not yet know the full details of this unhappy venture. We do know that CAUSE opposed it from the first as foolish, futile, anti-peace, anti-international, racist, arrogant and unnecessary.

"CAUSE suggests that from now on the American Government and the present Administration take guidance from the Russians, who have just announced a successful Soyuz 19 scientific flight to the Moon.

"CAUSE does not know the details of this flight, nor does Moscow, apparently, intend to elaborate upon its terse announcement.

"But the announcement alone is sufficiently electrifying: At this late date, despite the example of American arrogance as a result of Apollo triumphs, a great power *can* launch a peaceful mission in space. It *can* act in the interests of all mankind. It *can* go beyond the confines of Earth with humanity, brotherhood and good will.

"CAUSE honors the Soviet Union for Soyuz 19's contribution to the kindliness and humanity of space. It condemns the United States for its own sad and unforgivable affront to that kindliness and that humanity.

"CAUSE now calls for the swiftest and most relentless search for the truth of this tragic episode and the speediest and most inexorable rendering of justice upon those responsible.

"CAUSE suggests that this be done through the most obvious public medium: an investigation by the Congress of the United States.

"CAUSE suggests the timing of such an open, thorough, and public investigation:

"NOW."

2.

Below, its seas and skies and continents shining plain, his native plant turned. Just ahead, only a few hundred feet away, modest little Space Station *Mayflower* drifted quietly along. Far in front, as elusive and now as ominous in his eyes as Man in the Moon, giant Space Station *Stalin* led the way.

Around him were the cramped, familiar quarters of *Santa Maria*. Alongside in *Nina* lay his crewmate, in coma but still his crewmate.

It was a bright sunny morning; and he was reluctant, and rightly so, to terminate his journey.

Some special peace, some special challenge, some exclusive thing that only he and Jazz and Pete and yes, even poor lost Jayvee, had known, was about to be no more.

He did not want to leave the arena where he had been skilled and sufficient and able to do what events commanded of him—the arena where a man could do his job as his job required—where he could be imaginative, be fully stretched, be free.

The wolves of the world were waiting and it was with a sad and inevitable regret that he was home to face their ravenings.

He fired his thrusters, rear, left, right, front, rear, left, right, front; glided to a perfect rendezvous, felt a gentle bump, was docked.

He worked his way for the last time along the wall, opened the inner hatch, saw at its other end three excited faces he did not recognize, pulled himself through the tub and said firmly into the welcoming voices,

"Commander Weickert is in *Nina*. Somebody get him, fast."

At once the white-suited figures went through the tube. Time stood suspended for perhaps five minutes. Then one reappeared, carefully easing Jazz, still in his hammock, which they had simply cut from the wall, along after him. The others came through, lifted Jazz between them, pressed the buzzer that opened the air lock between the weightless section in which they stood and the central section that rotated slowly to create a condition of ordinary gravity.

The first door opened, began to close. The second door opened. Before it shut he recognized a wild glad-unhappy cry: Clare.

He took a deep breath, pressed the buzzer again, stepped through the air lock.

Television lights glared. He blinked for a moment trying to focus.

Then he saw Jane, standing slightly ahead of the Vice-President, Andy and Bob. Suddenly events and memories closed in, the horrible testings of the past four days took their toll.

"Why, hello," he started to say, quite naturally. "So they brought you up here to meet me."

But the words stopped coming halfway when she stepped forward and held out her arms. He entered them and absurdly, awfully but helplessly, began to cry against her shoulder while she cradled his head and whispered softly and managed to shield him—except, of course, for the lucky photographer who would later win so many prizes.

Excited babble welled up, loud, hearty, embarrassed. The moment passed, he dashed a hand across his eyes, blinked into the pitiless eye of the world, managed a smile.

"Mr. Vice-President," he said, holding out his right hand, his left arm tight around Jane, who was crying openly now herself, "Andy—Bob—your wandering boys are safe home at last."

"They couldn't be more welcome," the Vice-President said huskily, and Andy and Bob, for once speechless, shook and reshook his hand fervently while the flash bulbs popped and the camera whirred.

"Jazz—?" he asked.

"On the shuttle already," Andy said. "They'll be leaving

in about one minute. They're going to land at National Airport in Washington and take him straight to Bethesda Naval Hospital. Clare and Chuck are with him."

"What does Chuck think?"

"We'll save him," the Vice-President said. "It may be a long convalescence but he'll make it, thanks to you."

"And Chuck and Houston and all of you," Connie said, and the words sounded corny and were absolutely true. "I couldn't have done it alone."

"Connie!" one of the scientists called excitedly. "There's a call for you!"

Even in the emotion of the moment a sudden ironic little gleam came into his eyes. But fortunately only the Vice-President, Andy and Bob, standing directly in front of him, were able to see it. And for a split second each of them responded in kind.

"If he doesn't mind," he said with a smile, "I will be accompanied by my wife."

He started to step forward but someone cried. "Don't move! We'll bring it over! Stay in front of the camera!"

Again his eyes flicked across those of his three friends but he managed to remain suitably solemn as they handed him a Picturephone and the confident, forceful face appeared.

"Connie, my friend!" the comfortable voice exclaimed. "I shall employ a cliché and say you are a sight for sore eyes."

"And you for a rather sore astronaut, Mr. President," he said with a rueful little smile.

"You've had a tough time," the President said sympathetically. "Jane, you have a very brave husband."

"Thank you, Mr. President," she said quietly. "I think so."

"We all think so," the President said heartily. "Connie, I want you to know how proud your country is of you for your heroic work in salvaging as much of your mission as you have."

"We understand, of course"—and his voice became grave and Connie braced himself for whatever might be coming—"that there have been serious and apparently tragic events. It is obvious to everyone in the world who has just seen the live broadcast of your arrival that your spacecraft is very badly damaged and that you and Commander Weickert have returned alone. We sympathize very deeply with what we know must have been a most terrible and traumatic experience for you both, as we sympathize very deeply with the families of Dr. Halleck and Dr. Balkis, who have evidently been lost.

"These are sad and terrible events which make your homecoming a time of very mixed emotions for us all. At your request, NASA and I have respected your desire that we not ask you to tell us the story of your flight until you could be back home to undergo a full debriefing in person. Such an accounting"—and his voice became even graver and more emphatic—"must now, of course, be given. We will await it at the earliest possible moment with the closest attention and the most sympathetic understanding."

And that, Connie thought bleakly, *puts the monkey on my back. Which,* he added honestly to himself, *is of course where it is and the only place where it can be.*

"Thank you, Mr. President," he responded with equal gravity, while Jane held his hand tightly and his friends of NASA seemed imperceptibly to draw closer and more protectively around him. "I appreciate your greeting, I appreciate your sympathy, I appreciate your understanding. I hope I will have both sympathy and understanding when this is all over.

"Jazz and I and"—he forced himself to say the names, though it was not easy—"and Pete and Jayvee—had a very difficult and, as is obvious, tragic time. The reasons for that are complex and I expect to explain them in my debriefing in Houston.

"It is my own desire that this begin at the earliest possible moment—tomorrow morning, I guess—and I also hope, and am confident, that just as soon as Jazz recovers to the point where he is reasonably comfortable, he will join me in the debriefing. After that, in the usual fashion, I assume NASA will release whatever portions of it are pertinent to a full public understanding of what occurred.

"Isn't that correct, Andy?"

"Yes, Connie," the Administrator said, stepping forward into the light. "That is absolutely correct. I would think, given the importance of the mission and the many questions concerning it which have to be answered, that it would require a very extensive and thorough debriefing to get everything on the record. That would mean, I should estimate, about three weeks.

"I would ask your patience, Mr. President, and the patience of our countrymen and of the world, while we go through this process in Houston. NASA has no intention of concealing in any way what occurred on this tragic flight, but it is necessary that we take the time and do the thorough, patient job that has to be done, if we are to come up with valid answers.

"I think however, as I say, that we can have a full report on or about three weeks from today—if that is satisfactory to you, Mr. President."

The President nodded.

"I think that will be fine. I am sure the country and the world understand the necessity for doing the job thoroughly and doing it right. It seems to me that three weeks is by no means an unreasonable deadline.

"Connie," he said quietly, "you are a brave man and I am proud to know you. I wish you well in this final ordeal of your flight. I know that you know it is a necessary ordeal and that you will come through it with truth as your shield and honor as your guide. God bless you."

"Thank you, Mr. President," he said huskily. "God bless."

The handsome, confident face faded from the screen, there was a little silence. The pool TV newsman smoothly concluded the broadcast, the lights went off, the media withdrew. He and Jane were alone with the Vice-President, the Administrator and Bob Hertz.

"We're with you a hundred per cent," the Vice-President said.

"Doubled," Dr. Anderson agreed.

"More than that," Bob suggested with a return of his cheerful smile. "Now I think we'd better get you on the other shuttle and back to Houston, don't you?"

"Yes," he said, looking at Jane with an expression of mingled sadness and resolution that tore her heart. "Yes. It would be nice—to go home . . ."

But if he, or the President, or his friends of NASA, or anyone else, thought that he would be allowed a quiet passage, they were swiftly disabused in the next few hours.

MARS FLIGHT HOME BUT MYSTERY GROWS . . . TRASKER DUCKS PUBLIC ACCOUNTING OF TRAGEDY . . . NASA TRIES COVER-UP FOR MARS

DISASTER . . . TWO DEAD, SPACECRAFT RUINED:
WAIT, SAYS NASA . . . TRASKER, NASA HIDE
DETAILS OF MARS FAILURE . . . TRASKER MUM
ON RUINED MISSION . . . TRASKER REFUSES
. . . TRASKER DOESN'T . . . TRASKER WON'T . . .
TRASKER . . . TRASKER . . . TRASKER . . .
TRASKER . . .

At 9 P.M.. in the house in El Lago, where the kids
greeted him solemn-eyed but happy, the Picturephone
rang. He went into the study and saw again the powerful,
self-confident face.

"Giving you a hard time, aren't they, Connie?"

"Yes, sir," he said, and his voice trembled a little, "they
are."

"I'm sorry," the President said quietly. "They can be
monstrously vicious sometimes, when the pack gets together." He gave him a shrewd look. "Do I know what
damaged your spacecraft and what caused tragedy in your
crew?"

Connie nodded and said quietly,

"I think you do, Mr. President."

"Shall we tell the world?"

"Do you want me to?"

The President sighed.

"It would be easier for me if you did not. I have to live
with the Communists, somehow. For all of our sakes
—yours and mine—and your wife's and your kids—and
my wife's and kids—and everybody else's—"

"Then you stand by me, Mr. President," Connie said,
and it was not a request but a demand. "You stand by
me, or Jazz and I are going to blow this thing so high it
will get to Mars on its own."

The President studied him for a moment, not angered,
not offended, not frightened, not agreeing—yet. Finally he
spoke in a quiet voice.

"Why would you want to do such a thing, Connie?"

"Because, God damn it, Mr. President," Connie said,
choked with anger and frustration, *"sometime—sometime
—sometime—somebody* in this world has got to take a
stand on *something.* That's why!"

"I won't let you down, Connie," the President said, still
quietly.

Connie gave him a long, anguished look from eyes that
conceded him nothing.

"I'll believe that," he said finally, "when I see it."

"Oh, no, I won't," the President said, miraculously still not offended. "There are ways of doing things, and there is timing, but in the essentials, I won't let you down."

Again Connie gave him a long, steady, unyielding look.

"Good night, Mr. President."

"Good night, Connie. Try to be happy tonight."

And he did try, with Jane, but it was too soon, he was too hurt, there were too many things—too many things. He fell asleep in her arms at last and she held him quietly and tenderly as she would a child, far into the haunted night until she too, at last, worn out with emotion, fell asleep.

3.

Next day, by some miracle of strength and character, he was pretty much himself again, knowing grimly now that he had better be if he wished to survive perils on Earth different but in their own way as deadly as any he had survived in space.

He had no sooner reached his office in the astronauts' building, after a tumultuous greeting in the corridors from Hank and Bert, his fellow astronauts and their secretaries and staff, than Bob and Jim Cavanaugh called to ask if they could come over.

"Don't you want me to come there?" he asked, alerted to something troubled in Bob's voice.

"No, we'd just as soon come there."
hour but that can wait."

"Yes," Bob said, his tone worried and a little odd, "I
"O.K., come ahead. I'm due for debriefing in half an guess it may have to."

He turned away from the machine, stared absently at the enormous pile of telegrams on his desk. He started idly to open a few. They seemed to divide quite neatly into three categories:

They raved:

We are proud of America's great hero. Thanks for your courageous work for our country and for freedom.

Or they raved:

You are a disgrace to your uniform and flag. Incompetent cowards like you are destroying America.

Or they raved:

Space-happy fools rob recent Americans of their envi-

665

ronment, future and livelihood. Why don't you take a trip and really get lost? Power to the people.

He smiled wryly and shoved them aside. They would go the way of all telegrams and letters to the astronauts: into the secretarial pool for the police, impersonal, standard answer, thanking them so much for their good wishes which meant so much to their boys in space.

"Connie," Dr. Cavanaugh said gravely when they were seated, with the door closed and locked, "Bob and I have just been on the screen with Andy, who in turn had just been on the screen with the President."

"He's busy, that President, isn't he? He was talking to me last night."

"What about?" Bob inquired.

"His problems with the Communists. It seems things are tough all over."

"Did he say anything about this clamor for a public investigation?" Jim Cavanaugh asked.

"No," Connie said. "But he did to Andy and Andy did to you."

"Yes," Jim Cavanaugh acknowledged.

"It upsets him," Connie suggested dryly, "and he wants us to give in to it."

Bob nodded.

"That's about it."

"And are we going to? What does Andy say?"

Dr. Cavanaugh frowned.

"Andy is completely and, I gather, adamantly, opposed. However—"

"However," Connie said quietly, "he isn't really the boss."

"That's right," Bob agreed.

"So what does the boss want of me—and why doesn't he have the guts to tell me face to face instead of sneaking through channels all of a sudden?"

"Naturally," Bob said crisply, "he wants you to issue a statement saying you would welcome an immediate public hearing before the Congress and are anxiously, eagerly and willingly available for it."

Connie gave him an ironic stare.

"Am I?"

Bob returned it.

"You are."

"Why doesn't he just issue a statement commanding me

to do so? It's his prerogative. I *am* on active duty. Why does he put the burden of the decision on me? Because he doesn't have the guts to do it himself?"

"That's possible," Bob Hertz said. "That is entirely and absolutely possible."

"Yeah," Connie said. "He told me last night that there's such a thing as timing and that there are ways of doing things. I wondered then if he meant the timing that suited him and the ways that would make him look best."

"Of course, Connie," Dr. Cavanaugh said quietly, "you are not in a very good position to be obdurate, you know. So far as anyone but Jazz knows at this point—"

"How is Jazz?"

"They operated on him yesterday afternoon, removed the bullet, cleaned up the gangrene, pumped him full of antibiotics, continued intravenous, and he's resting easy," Bob said.

"Not conscious yet?"

"Beginning to be, but still pretty woozy."

"In any event," Jim Cavanaugh said, "as far as anybody except Jazz knows right now, you're still under a large cloud as far as this country and the world are concerned. Even here, we don't know yet what happened out there. We in NASA are going along with you because we know you and trust you—"

"Gee, thanks."

"—know you and trust you," Dr. Cavanaugh repeated quietly, "but that doesn't mean that you're home free with anybody else. And it doesn't mean," he added with a certain asperity, "that this chip-on-the-shoulder attitude is going to get you anywhere."

Connie sighed.

"I know, I'm sorry. It isn't really chip-on-the-shoulder. But honest to God, Jim it hasn't been the easiest week Mrs. Trasker's little boy ever spent, you know."

"We know that," Bob said, "and we do sympathize, Connie, you must believe it. But wouldn't it maybe be better to sail right into this and meet it head on? The media aren't going to give up; they aren't going to wait three weeks while we do what they've already convinced themselves and the world is a cover-up job. They're howling and they're going to keep howling. It won't get better, it can only get worse. What's to gain by waiting?"

"And also," Jim Cavanaugh said, "what really would be

gained by having him order you to do it? It would look as though you were afraid to tell the country about it and he had to force you. And that would make you look guilty as hell. Of what, I wouldn't know, but there'd be a real, concerted attempt to make the public think you were, anyway."

"You know all this, Connie," Bob said quietly. "Why stall?"

Jim Cavanaugh studied him thoughtfully.

"You really aren't in a position to bargain. Are you?"

For several moments he did not answer, staring out across Clear Lake and the flat, uninspired landscape that he had not been at all sure, four days ago, he would ever see again. Then he spoke as quietly but no less determinedly than they.

"Maybe not. But I'm not going to make my decision right away. I'm going to talk to Jane and I'm going to do a couple of other things I want to do today, like visit with my kids, and then I'm going to go to Washington and talk to him before I decide. So tell Andy to tell him to expect me tomorrow sometime, if you like. Maybe noon or 1 P.M., how would that be? Then I wouldn't have to get out of here too early."

"Don't push him too much, Connie," Dr. Cavanaugh suggested. Connie shot him a quizzical glance.

"Don't push *me* too much. It may be the last time I control my own destiny. Let me enjoy it."

But inside he felt far from the rueful jauntiness he displayed as they left. He was, in fact, moody and depressed as he called the debriefing staff, found Bob had already notified them, and left his office for home.

Eight or ten reporters were waiting downstairs around the entrance but he brushed past them with a fixed smile that ignored their shouted questions, jumped in the Porsche and roared away.

TRASKER STILL DUCKING, he thought grimly. WHY DON'T THEY LEAVE TRASKER ALONE?

"Oh, hi," she called with a pleased surprise as he came in. "You're back early. How did the debriefing go?"

"It didn't."

"Oh?" she said, coming out of the kitchen, hands covered with flour, face concerned. "What happened?"

668

"Janie," he said, "come in the study and give me some advice."

"Let me get the pie in first." She smiled. "Daddy's treat tonight. Apple pie, just like dear old wife used to make."

"Mrs. Trasker," he said, his mood lightening a little, "you *do* fit the image. By George, if you don't."

"It comes naturally, his lovely wife said modestly. Can I bring you some coffee or something?"

"Please."

He went into the study, shot a savage glance at the Picturephone as he settled into his favorite chair.

You be quiet! he told it sternly in his mind. I don't want to see that powerful, confident, smiling, charming, commanding, dominant, dramatic, et cetera face until I see it live tomorrow in Washington, D.C.

But of course the buzzer sounded at once and he reached over to snap on the machine with an impatient air. The face he saw was not the face he fully expected to see.

"Hello," he said quietly.

"I want to talk to you," she said, with the shy, hesitant look that still possessed the power to move him, even now. "I've got to know—what happened."

"Will you be in Galveston this afternoon?"

"I'll be home by three."

"I'll be there."

"Thank you," she said gravely. "I'm glad you're safe."

"Thank you," he said. "I'll tell you all about it."

After she faded from the screen he spent a minute or two picking up magazines and putting them down. Jane had tactfully removed the newspapers so his public crimes and misdemeanors were not spread before him as they had been last night. He thanked her for that, among many other things. When she came in with the coffee a moment later he had reached one decision, anyway.

"Monetta just called. She wants me to come down to Galveston this afternoon and tell her what happened."

"I think you should go," she said quietly, handing him the cup. "Don't you?"

"Yes, but I wanted to be sure you did."

"I do think so. She must know."

"Thank you," he said gravely.

She nodded, not quite fully relaxed, but meeting his eyes. "You won't be—too long."

He shook his head.

"No. It's not an easy tale to tell but I'll get through it as fast as I can." He smiled and touched her cheek gently. "I'll be home for the apple pie."

"I'm glad," she said quietly, taking his hand for a moment. "And now maybe you'll tell *me*."

"Yes."

And he did, much more fully than he had last night, when broken bits of conversation, almost incoherent and frequently interrupted by the agonized protests of a gradually decreasing tension, had been all he could manage.

Almost dispassionately, now—and I must be dispassionate when I face that committee, he reminded himself, which helped—he retold the tragic story of the flight of Planetary Fleet One. At only one point did he depart from his carefully colorless and straightforward narrative and that was because he was talking to his wife and she had, he felt, a right to know.

"When he—died," he said, and in spite of his firm intentions his voice grew husky and his vision blurred, "or rather, I should say, just before—while—he was dying—he—he—"

"He said something to you," she said, studying his face with sympathetic eyes.

He nodded and told her.

"Dear heart," she said quietly. "I hope you answered."

Again he nodded, not looking at her, his face bleak, his mind a quarter of a million miles away on the empty plain where his friend and the Russian lay side by side.

"But," he said, and now he did look at her, with eyes so sad they almost broke her heart, "I didn't mean that I don't—love—you, too, Janie."

"I think," she said with a shaky little laugh, "that you have enough love for both of us, Connie. I don't feel slighted. And I don't think I would have forgiven you if you hadn't told him that. After all"—and now her own eyes filled with tears—"dearest Pete: I owe him you."

"Janie," he said in a shy, humble voice. "Ah, Jane . . ."

"*Well!*" she said, wiping her eyes, determinedly making her voice brisker, breaking the mood. "You haven't told me about Jayvee, yet. That won't be easy for you this afternoon."

"Jayvee," he said, and he too began to make his voice impersonal, to move away forever from something he would never mention to anyone again, "is a problem. But, then"—and he managed a small ironic smile—"Jayvee always was a problem."

Again his voice became dispassionate, remained so to the end. She exclaimed twice, over the exchange of shots in *Santa Maria,* over the collision with Man in the Moon. For the rest she remained silent and let him talk. When he had brought her up to the events of a few minues ago in his office she folded her hands in her lap and gave him the decided, determined look he knew so well.

"You're going to have to do it, Conn. You might as well do it voluntarily and take credit for coming forward. It would be better than having it appear that he had to force you to do it. It will also make him feel more kindly toward you. He's the President, after all. He's a good friend to have."

" 'With such friends—' " he quoted dryly. "No, you're right, of course. I'm just delaying things to satisfy my own reluctance, I guess." He frowned. "I don't like those sons of bitches in the media and they don't like me. They've been resentful of me from the day I was selected to command the mission. I symbolize all the things in America they don't like: I'm good at my trade and I'm brave and I love my country and I think she should be first. Well"—his eyes narrowed—"I'll give 'em their money's worth and they can have their field day, and then I'll be commander again and the hell with them."

"Commander *again?*" she protested, and he could see she was suddenly, terribly upset. "Connie, you don't mean it? Surely you don't mean it?"

"Now, Janie—" he began, but she was in his arms, crying and clutching at his shirt.

"No, Connie! Oh, please, *no!*"

He knew his best course was silence, so he simply held her tight and let her cry. After the sobs began to recede he tipped her chin up and kissed her gravely.

"Now, Mrs. Trasker," he said softly, "you know very well who you married. You don't really think he's not going to try to vindicate himself, do you? You don't really think he's going to stay on the ground if he can possibly fly again? It would kill him, not to command Piffy Two."

She studied him for a very long time through her tears while he met her eyes directly and without flinching.

671

Finally she managed a very small but gallant smile and nodded.

"I know him," she said. "It *would* kill him. Of course"— and the smile, though still tremulous, managed to increase—"it may kill *me* to have him go again, but *that's* all right."

"I can't help it," he said simply. "You know I can't help it. It's in me and I've got to answer. It's my life, Janie."

"And the kids and I aren't?" she asked quizzically, and then added quickly, "No, that's not fair. I know we are."

"Yes," he said softly, his gaze still straight and unflinching. "Yes: you are."

"Well," she said moving away, drying her eyes, automatically fixing her hair, smoothing her apron, "I must get back to my pie. When are you going to let the President know?"

"I'm going to fly to Washington tomorrow morning to see him. After that I suppose it will probably be a couple of weeks before I have to appear. I'll be back tomorrow night."

"Good." She hesitated and then asked, almost shyly, "When you do have to appear, would it be any help to you if I—?"

He looked surprised.

"I want you with me. Where else would you be?"

"Nowhere," she said, and again for just a second it seemed she might cry, though she did not. "Nowhere . . . Do you want lunch before you go to Galveston?"

"Yes. I won't be leaving until about two."

"Good. I'll get it ready." She paused in the doorway and looked back with a game if rather shaky smile in which he could see many things. "You're something, Connie Trasker. You really are."

He grinned, suddenly feeling happier and more at peace than he had at any time since Piffy One reached the Moon.

"I try to be," he said cheerfully. "It isn't easy, but I try."

And now I hope, he thought as he drove swiftly south to Galveston, that I won't have more tears and upsets to contend with. It occurred to him that they were caused by who he was and what he had to do, but there was no cure for that. As he had told his wife: it was in him and he had

672

to answer. He knew Monetta understood this too, but their meeting would not be unemotional and the story of her husband's death would not be an easy one to tell or take. He sighed unhappily as he reached the familiar apartment building, parked and went, as had been his custom, up the back stairs.

Yet she greeted him gravely and solemnly, not touching him, not letting him touch her: they were good but distant friends, once tender, still respectful, separated now by the events of a journey to the Moon.

They hardly said two words until they were seated, he on the sofa, she across the room curled in an armchair by the window. She studied him intently for several minutes and he returned her gaze as directly and openly as he had Jane's. Then she took a deep breath and asked quietly, "Did he do something bad?"

"Yes," he said quietly. "I'm afraid so."

"Tell me."

And so once again he did, as Jazz had related it to him; and Jazz, he knew, had been truthful, not glossing over his own provocative remarks. Even so, the picture of Jayvee that emerged in those last terrible minutes was not a pleasant one. He knew her own implacable honesty demanded the truth and he did not soften it for her.

She made no comment, showed no emotion, did not frown, sigh, move or cry until he finished. Then after a long moment she did sigh and begin to cry, very softly and quietly, to herself.

He half rose but she made a sharply warning gesture. He sank back slowly in his chair. She continued to cry, staring out the window, uttering almost no sound, letting the tears flow slow and unimpeded down the gentle, high-boned face.

At last the storm began to slacken. He knew she had passed over some fundamental dividing line in her life and was emerging safely on the other side. A calm began to come. At last she spoke, five words:

"Poor Jayvee. My poor Jayvee."

A surprising pang of jealousy, still present though all was over now, struck his heart at the possessive term. Then it was gone and he too felt drained and calm. It was true: the body on its lonely wanderings through space somewhere had been *her* Jayvee, after all. The years were not wiped out so easily as that.

He sighed and nodded grave agreement.

She gave him a long, open, candid look; went through some inner debate with herself that he could just sense; finally reached a decision and spoke again quietly.

"Can I ask you one favor?"

"Anything," he said, and meant it.

"When you go to that hearing—I expect you will—"

Again he nodded.

"—and you come to the part about Jayvee . . . protect him. Don't tell them. Let him rest in peace. Please?"

He did not hesitate. "I will. Of course, Jazz—"

"Jazz will do what you tell him to."

"Yes," he conceded. "I think he will."

"And you will tell him."

"I will tell him."

"Thank you," she said quietly, and stood up. "And now you're going to Washington. And then you're going to want to fly again, aren't you? You're going to want to command the next one. You still want to go to Mars."

"Yes," he said simply. "I want to go."

"I know you," she said, with just the trace of a smile that held in it much of gentleness and understanding. "Jane doesn't want you to, does she?"

"No."

"Neither do I," she said gravely. "But I know you. You'll go."

"If they'll let me."

"I expect they will. There aren't very many in this world like Connie Trasker."

He started to grin but something caught him midway: an enormous sense of desolation and loss, a terrible, scarifying self-reproach, coming oddly out of nowhere to again turn his eyes sad and make his voice husky.

"I don't know," he said with a strange bitterness. "Maybe it's just as well there aren't."

And then they were at the door, she held out her hand, he took it gently, but as a friend.

"Go well, Connie," she said softly, and they both knew it was forever. "Go well."

"And you," he said, still huskily.

He stepped back, she bowed her head gravely in farewell, the door closed. He was down the stairs somehow, into the car, out of the parking lot and on the highway back to Houston before he really began to function with much awareness again.

All the way home he drove safely but almost automatically, as three bright candles in his mind kept soaring, over and over again, beautiful, shining and pure, into the Florida sky.

So lovely a beginning, that it should have come to such sadness for them all.

Yet he knew in all honesty it had not been quite like that.

Bitterly encouraged by many of their countrymen, they had taken the sadness with them and brought the sadness back. The end was in the beginning, and not only unhappy Jayvee but all of them had in one way or another been at fault.

4.

At 9 the next morning, after a reasonably relaxed time
with the kids and, later, with Jane, he took off for Washington from Ellington Field, accompanied by the earnest
good wishes of Bob Hertz and Jim Cavanaugh who came
out to see him leave.

Both offered to go with him. He refused with thanks,
grateful for their kindness but knowing he must face his
formidable friend and/or enemy—he would probably never know completely which—by himself.

He flew fast and alone, hardly thinking at all as he
streaked across the familiar country he knew and loved so
well. Once he wondered: *What do you think of me, down
there? Hero? Coward? Good guy? Bad guy? Little man?
Great?*

But it was the only moody moment of the trip. His
thoughts were devoted almost exclusively to his conversation with the President.

Like most planned conversations, it got off to an entirely different start than he had anticipated. A White House
car was waiting for him at Andrews Air Force Base when
he arrived at 1 P.M. So were almost a hundred newsmen
and photographers. So, inside the limousine, was his Commander-in-Chief.

"Connie!" he exclaimed with a cordial smile, reaching
out a hand and pulling Connie in beside him while the
photographers snapped wildly. "Where were you yesterday? The most famous man in the world and nobody
could find you."

"I was just around home and then down to Galveston

676

for a bit, and then back again," he said, somewhat blankly. "Were people trying to find me?"

"Jane didn't tell you," the President said admiringly. "She didn't want you bothered. You've got a great girl there, Connie."

"Yes," he said cautiously, a little overwhelmed by all this expansiveness as the limousine roared off in the center of its escort of screaming motorcycle police. "I hope it wasn't anything important."

"Not from me," the President said genially. "But I think the press was going crazy."

"Oh," Connie said. "That's all right, then. I didn't want to talk to them anyway."

"Yes," the President said, suddenly thoughtful. "I wonder if . . . Do you think that was entirely wise, Connie?"

"It seemed so to me," he said, a little stiffly. His host relaxed into another cordial smile.

"Well, then, I expect that's really all that matters," he said, and hurried on before Connie had time to shake his head and find that his throat had been slit. "Well, now: what are we going to do about this investigation?"

Connie did not answer for a moment as the entourage screamed along back to the District of Columbia, drawing the startled stares of startled motorists. Then he half turned in his seat to look directly at the President.

"Are you going to support me, Mr. President," he asked quietly, "or sacrifice me to that crew?"

"Well!" the President said with a startled little laugh. "You're direct enough, I must say. And you've earned the right to be, Connie. You've earned it, so keep right on—I hope you will always be direct and honest with me. Of course I support you. I'm here, aren't I? I told the world it had to run itself for a while, I left my office, and I came out here to meet you. That's support in a way that people really understand." He smiled cheerfully. "One presidential gesture is worth a thousand words, you know. Here I am."

"I do appreciate it, Mr. President," Connie said, again cautiously, "and I think it's very generous of you and I'm very grateful for it. But are you going to support me all the way through? Are you going to let me fly again?"

Again the President gave a startled little laugh. This time his answer was not quite so effusive.

"You *don't* waste time on nonessentials, do you?"

"In my profession," Connie said quickly, wondering later how he had had the nerve, "we don't have time for it." It was the President's turn to shake his head and wonder if it was still attached.

But he was, as usual, equal to the occasion.

"There are a lot of aspects to this I want to discuss with you, Connie," he said seriously, "but I think maybe we'd better wait till we get to the house. How did you find the family when you got back?"

Fifteen minutes later, thoroughly chatted out on that subject and a string of others equally innocuous, they pulled up at the South Portico and went into the mansion. After a brisk walk down the corridor, during which many of the staff recognized him and applauded, and several young military aides standing about snapped to attention and spoke his name as well as the President's when they saluted, he and his host took the elevator up to the family quarters and moved on to the President's study.

A table by the window had been set for a salad luncheon, with everything already in place. The President closed the door firmly behind them and gestured him toward it.

"The condemned man ate a hearty lunch," he said, and chuckled. "Beat you to it, didn't I?"

"Oh, I don't know," Connie said, smiling but still on guard. "I'm not so sure that's the way I feel. Having, as I do, such powerful support."

"Ha, *ha!*" the President exclaimed with a delighted expression. "You're quite a man, Connie, now I begin to get your measure. Which, of course," he added gravely, "I have already had a chance to get, in these recent days. Tell me about that if it won't spoil your appetite."

"It may," Connie said, "but I know your time is short so I'll get right to it."

And he did so, while the President listened thoughtfully and intently as they ate; finding that he had a little better appetite than he thought he might have, until he came to the events on the Moon, by which time they were finished and into coffee, so it didn't really matter.

Despite his inner tensions, he did a very calm and creditable job, realizing with a growing confidence that each time it seemed to go more smoothly and impersonally.

The President listened sympathetically but for the most
678

part impassively, his only comment being to remark quietly twice, "Those sons of bitches!"—once when the Russian attacked Pete and again after the climactic meeting with Man in the Moon.

When Connie concluded they both sat silently for several minutes, Connie staring at the President, the President staring thoughtfully out the window over the Ellipse to the Washington Monument, the dark winter Potomac and Virginia beyond.

Finally he sighed and swung back to face Connie squarely.

"I'm still going to have to ask you to play down the Communists, you know," he said quietly.

"But, Mr. *President*—" Connie began. His host raised a hand for silence.

"Understand me, Connie, I do not make this request as any reflection of my own desires in the matter—me: I: the man. It is only I, the President, who feels he must ask this of you. And that only for the highest reasons of policy and world stability."

"But that's *always* the excuse," Connie protested. "They are *always* allowed to go scot-free. We *always* help to strengthen them by helping them conceal the truth of what they're doing in the world. And now," his voice was suddenly sad and tired and disillusioned, "you even want to extend it into space."

"I'm sorry," the President said, falling back upon the last refuge of Presidents, "but I *am* the President, and I *do* have to think of *all* the consequences of *all* the things for which I am responsible . . . I am sorry."

"How can I possibly tell this story under oath and 'play down the Communists'?" Connie demanded bitterly. "You tell me!"

"They'll have to be in there, of course, but Pete *could* have ripped his suit on a rock and the Russians *could* have miscalculated and grazed our spacecraft accidentally in attempting a friendly rendezvous. It *could* have happened that way."

"Only," Connie said quietly, "it didn't."

"No, Connie," the President said gravely, "I believe you: it did not. I believe you because I know you're an honorable man and because it also tallies exactly with my own conception of the Communists. But I repeat again, knowing them and having to live with them in this world—

on the level of policy and razor-thin peace on which *I* have to live with them—we must devise a formula that will save face all around and not precipitate an actual showdown."

"Maybe if we had precipitated a few in the past when we had the chances and were strong enough to do it," Connie said bitterly, "the world would be in a hell of a lot better shape."

"Maybe so," the President agreed quietly. "In fact, I don't think there's any doubt. But we didn't," he concluded quietly, "and so I have to function as the heir of my predecessors, within the steadily narrowing circle of choices they have left me."

"And when it narrows down altogether?" Connie inquired softly.

The President stared down moodily at the table, chin propped on fingertips, eyes narrowed and faraway.

"Each of us," he said finally, with an equal quietness, "must make it last for his own time—in his own way—as best as he can. And that is what I am asking you to help me do . . . Well!" he said, head coming up in its famous challenging gesture, eyes smiling, face again serene and confident, "after we dispose of this little unpleasantness we have to decide what to do about Planetary Fleet Two, don't we?"

For a second time Connie was too stunned to reply. But he recovered, aware that the conversation now was not the conversation of a moment ago.

"Is that the quid pro quo?" he asked calmly, and once again saw he had done the right thing to meet toughness with toughness. The President tossed back his head and laughed with delight.

"As I said before, you *are* direct! . . . It could be. What about it?"

"I marvel," Connie said slowly, shaking his head in disbelief, "at the prisons of power, and the things you have to do when you are inside them . . . Yes, it could be. But I can only tell you this, Mr. President: I will be under oath, I have no doubt I will be asked some very searching questions, and it is going to be very difficult to 'play down' as you put it, the Communists. But I see your point of view and I see your reasons. It isn't necessary to bribe me, although you know perfectly well I want to command Piffy Two. I will do what I can for you, along the lines you suggest, insofar as I can—because I understand and sympathize with you and I see the problem. But," he said grimly, "you understand and sympathize with me, too, Mr. President. I may not be able to maintain it past a certain point. I'll do my best for you but I'm not going to outright lie. Nor am I going to compromise my own integrity past a certain point. I can live without Piffy Two if I have to but I've got to live with me."

The President held out his hand. Connie took it.

"Fair enough," the President said with a firm pressure which Connie returned. "Fair enough. I can't ask for more . . . Well, now," he said, sitting back, his tone practical and pragmatic. "About this hearing, do you think you'd better ask for it?"

Connie nodded.

"Yes, I see that argument, too."

"Why don't you let us issue your statement here, through the press office? That way you can get out of here without being subjected to a lot of needling questions on the way."

Connie shook his head firmly.

"No, I'd rather meet 'em head on. That way it'll look a little more like my own idea. Even though," he smiled wryly, "we both know it isn't."

"No," the President said thoughtfully. "I'm afraid you waited a little too long to make it look voluntary. But it *is* best, really, don't you think?"

"Yes," Connie conceded, "it probably is. One thing, though, Mr. President: I want Jazz with me and that means a delay of probably two weeks until he's fit to appear and take the questioning. They'll howl to high heaven about it. But that," he concluded quietly, "is final."

The President nodded and got to his feet.

"I agree with that and I will support it absolutely, both with an endorsing statement, if you like, and any time they ask me."

"If you will authorize me to say that when I go out—"

"Absolutely."

"Good," Connie said. They shook hands again. He turned toward the door, turned back.

"Will you let them know downstairs—?"

"Right away. I'd suggest you meet them at the Front Portico, that's a good setting. I'll come down and introduce you, if you like."

"I'd appreciate that. And one final thing: afterward, could somebody call me a cab to go out to Bethesda?"

"Cab nothing," the President said. "We'll send you in a White House car, and no nonsense about it. Now, come along." He smiled, rather grimly. "You may find this worse than the Moon."

But though it had its tense moment when Connie refused to expand upon his statement, he found it not too difficult to get through.

"I introduce to you," the President said simply from the hastily erected, red-carpeted dais at the top of the steps, "a brave American who has traveled far on a dangerous journey and has now returned after many deeds of heroism and courage to his native land. He has a very brief statement which I endorse. Colonel Conrad H. Trasker, Jr., commander of Planetary Fleet One. Connie—"

For a couple of minutes there was jockeying and shoving and scrambling for position as newsmen and photographers sought their vantage points. Then they were quiet. The cameras zoomed in on his face, somber and unsmiling.

"Ladies and gentlemen," he said, his words carried live across the seas and continents, "I am here at the conclusion of a tragic mission whose details are of great interest— and rightly so—to this country and the world. It is my earnest desire that those details should be made public at the earliest possible time.

"Accordingly, after consulting with my conscience, my family and my President, I have decided to ask for an early and complete congressional investigation of the flight of Planetary Fleet One.

"It seems only fair to me, and in this I have the approval of the President"—he paused and glanced over, and the President nodded vigorously—"that I should be accompanied by my second in command, the only other"— his voice faltered for a second, but he hurried on— "survivor of my crew, Commander Alvin S. Weickert III.

"Commander Weickert, as you all know, is presently in Bethesda Naval Hospital recovering from wounds received during the flight. (*We didn't think of how to explain those, did we?* his mind inquired dryly.) I am advised by his doctors that it will be approximately two weeks"— there was an uneasy murmur, but he continued, more firmly now—"before he will be sufficiently recovered to

682

stand the strain of testifying. Therefore I would suggest—and in this the President also agrees with me"—again the President nodded——"to whatever committee or committees of the Congress may assume jurisdiction, that we be permitted this delay which is strictly medical and requested on the advice of the doctors.

"During this interim period I will expect to continue with regular debriefing procedures already scheduled at Manned Spacecraft Center, Houston.

"I think I can speak for Commander Weickert as well as myself when I say that we welcome this investigation and will co-operate to the best of our ability with it.

"Thank you very much."

And he started to turn away as the President stepped forward to take his arm.

"But, Colonel *Trasker!*" someone shouted indignantly.

"Come along," the President said firmly, propelling him inside the door. "It's the only way. The car is waiting for you at the South Portico. My Air Force aide will take you down to it and see that you get away unbothered. Give Jazz my affectionate best and tell him I shall be out to see him just as soon as he's able to receive visitors. And Connie"—he paused and extended his hand for one more firm, encouraging handshake—"good luck. It's going to work all right. I'm convinced of it."

"Thank you, Mr. President. Thanks for seeing me."

"Any time," the President said cordially, putting back his public face and releasing Connie to his fate. "Any time."

MARS DISASTER TO GET PUBLIC AIRING, the afternoon editions said. TRASKER ASKS CONGRESSIONAL PROBE . . . CONNIE BOWS TO PRESIDENT'S WISH AT WHITE HOUSE LUNCH . . . TRASKER WANTS TWO-WEEK DELAY FOR WEICKERT AID . . . NASA TO CONTINUE SECRET DEBRIEFING PENDING HILL HEARINGS . . . CONGRESSIONAL REACTION SHARP TO DELAY REQUEST . . . WILLIAMS, OTHERS PLEDGE FIGHT TO BAR TRASKER DELAY BID . . .

The stately tower rose stark and white against the cold windy sky north of Washington, the antiseptic corridors brought him presently to his destination. The notice on the door said NO VISITORS and there were two armed Shore Patrol guards to enforce it, but the director of Bethesda Naval Hospital personally escorted him in, smiled and departed. From her seat beside the bed Clare looked up like a startled deer ready to run. Then she recognized him, put a warning finger to her lips, began to smile and cry at the same time, tiptoed out and closed the door. Then she said, "Oh, Connie!" and give him a fervent hug and kiss.

"Hey!" he said, brushing her tears away gently. "What's all this about? Your boy's doing fine."

"I know he is," she said with a tremulous little laugh. "I'm just so glad to *see* you. And he will be too."

"I'll be glad to see him, the ornery son of a gun. Can he talk?"

She smiled, wiped her eyes and tucked her handkerchief away briskly.

"Practically non-stop today, and mostly about you. Oh, Connie, we are so *grateful*—"

"O.K., O.K.," he said hastily as she began to look tearful again. "He would have done exactly the same for me and you know it. He's a brave man."

"Jane and I have got the bravest in the world," she said. She looked suddenly worried. "Connie, we were listening to the radio just before he dropped off to sleep a little while ago and they sounded awfully critical of you. What's going to happen?"

"I don't know, Clare," he said soberly. "You know I asked for a delay until he can join me, which I think is only right—"

"It's absolutely fair!" she said fiercely.

"—but I don't know. The President agrees with me." He smiled rather wryly. "For whatever that's worth."

"I hope they'll listen! He's got to be with you and he can't do it until he feels better."

"That's right, but we'll just have to see. Is it all right if I wake him up? There are a few things I want to talk to him about before I fly back this afternoon, if I can."

"You go right ahead. He's still very weak and somewhat dopey but he'll pep up for you. I'll go and wait in the family room until you call me."

"You can stay," he said, hoping she wouldn't.

"Oh, no," she said with a smile. "I know you two want to talk. You have an awful lot to talk about. After all"—and she started to get tearful again for a second but shook it off with a little smile—"it's been quite a while since—since he's been able to talk to you, hasn't it?"

"That's right," he said with an answering smile. "Quite a while. About 100,000 miles out, as I recall. O.K., I'll call you. I'll try not to be too long. I won't tire him."

"No one has a better right. Call me when you're through."

He opened the door, stepped inside, closed it quietly behind him, tiptoed over and took her seat beside the bed. For a couple of minutes he carefully studied the sleeping face, listened to the even, comfortable breathing. Old Doctor Trasker, he told himself, I think your patient's going to live.

Jazz' left hand lay stretched along the coverlet near the chair. Connie reached over and took it gently. Jazz started, the rhythm of his breathing changed, he opened his eyes, focused. A slow smile came into his face, his hand squeezed Connie's, hard.

"Well, well," he said in a voice a little slow and labored but beginning to get back to normal. "Haven't I seen you someplace before?"

Connie grinned.

"Yes," he said, releasing Jazz' hand and tipping back in the chair, "I think you have. How you doin', buddy?"

"Not bad," Jazz said, his voice growing stronger as he became animated by the visit. "Not bad at all. I'm not raping my wife yet—or even any of the orderlies, for that matter—but I'm coming along."

Connie chuckled.

"That's good. Think you'll be able to join me in a couple of weeks?"

Jazz frowned.

"Yes, we were listening. If you need me, pal. I'll join you in two days. And that's a promise."

"I doubt if it'll have to be quite that soon. But the day is going to come. That's why I wanted to see you today, because I'm going home this afternoon and we probably won't have a chance to talk in person again until we meet on the Hill."

"Bastards," Jazz said with a weary disgust.

"Not all," Connie said. "We have a lot of friends up there. I don't think we'll be crucified though there will be some who will try. But—" he paused thoughtfully. "We've got to get our story straight and stick to it."

Jazz looked surprised.

"We'll tell 'em what happened." He studied Connie's face with a sudden attention. "Won't we, Conn?"

"If you've been listening," Connie said carefully, "you know I've had lunch with the President."

For a moment Jazz said nothing though his eyes said a lot.

"Well, I'll be damned," he remarked at last. "So that son of a bitch still wants us to protect the Russians. Well, f—"

"Now, just a minute," Connie interrupted calmly. "Just don't sail up through the roof. He has reasons"—he enumerated them—"and he wants us to help him, insofar as we honestly can."

"You think we should?"

"Insofar as we honestly can."

"How does he think we should go about it?" Jazz inquired skeptically. Connie told him.

He snorted.

"How about a gunshot wound in my back? Where does that fit in?"

"Nobody knows the nature of your wound," Connie pointed out. "Nobody knows anything yet."

"But somebody at the hearing is bound to ask."

"Maybe, maybe not. We'll have a little uninterrupted narrative to paint the picture first, I think. And if they do"—Connie shrugged—"do whatever you think best."

"I think I'll tell 'em the truth," Jazz said slowly, "and blow the whole thing."

"I think probably," Connie said, "that moment is going to come, for one or the other of us, before we're very far into the hearing. But I can see the President's arguments and I'm willing to go along and help him, if possible . . . if possible." His expression changed, became almost hesitant. "There is—one other thing I'd like to ask of you, Jazz."

Again Jazz studied his face thoughtfully, trying hard to concentrate through the lingering effects of sedation, and managing.

"You want us to protect Jayvee."

Connie looked completely surprised.

"How the hell did you know?"

"Because I figured you've seen Monetta and she asked

you to," Jazz said simply, and gave him a direct and candid look that Connie did not meet for a moment. But presently he did and replied with equal candor.

"Yes, I've seen her. Not—I mean, that ended quite some time ago. But she did ask me to come down to Galveston and tell her what had happened. I thought she had a right to know and Jane agreed with me. So I went."

"Quite a gal, Jane," Jazz remarked. "She isn't the only one who got a good break in that marriage."

"I know that," Connie said with a smile. "I *know* that, Jazzbo. Anyway, I did see Monetta, and I did tell her, and she did ask me—and asked me to ask you—to protect him when we tell our story."

"Was she surprised?"

"She said very little. Mostly just listened. But I got the feeling she wasn't, really. Very sad about it but not surprised."

"And you think we should agree." Jazz stared at the ceiling, momentarily back in *Santa Maria*. "The twisted son of a bitch came damned close to killing me, you know."

"She knows that," Connie said. "She wouldn't blame you, probably, if you let him have it now. But really, Jazz"—he leaned forward earnestly—"you can't hurt Jayvee, you know. He's probably out in Andromeda somewhere by this time, I guess. All you can hurt is Monetta. And the boy."

"And you don't want to hurt Monetta."

Connie gave him a calm stare.

"No. Do you?"

"I want to hurt the bastards who forced us to take him on the crew," Jazz said with a tired anger. "I want to hurt Percy Mercy and Kenny Williams and all their sleazy bunch. That's who *I* want to hurt."

"Well," Connie said moodily, "you can't even do that. Because they wouldn't believe you. They are so tied in— they are such slaves—to the image of Nature's Noble Savage who can do no wrong as long as he's black—that they simply could not accept the picture of a sick, neurotic, unhappy, unpleasant, immature, unsalvageable Negro. It would drive them mad. So you aren't going to get any acknowledgment from them even if you do blow the whistle on him. They just wouldn't believe you."

For several moments Jazz stared at him. Then he spoke slowly and drowsily.

"It's a crazy world we live in, isn't it, Conn? Do you ever wish we could take our families and friends and start out for some place like Mars and just keep on going and never come back?"

Connie smiled. There was no amusement in it.

"Frequently . . . So what about Jayvee?"

"Whatever you say . . ."

"Good man," Connie said gratefully. He stood up, took Jazz' hand again, gave it a final, encouraging squeeze. "Now, let's talk—often—in the next couple of weeks. Get on the screen any time you want me and I'll do the same. We'll work out the details and get her set. And maybe— just maybe—we can do with honor what the President wants."

Jazz' jawline firmed, his eyes opened wide again and grew cold.

"I'm not going to do it with dishonor, I'll tell you that."

"Nor am I," Connie said quietly. "Now you take care and get your strength back fast. Two weeks isn't any too long to get you to the point where you can appear on the Hill."

"Oh, I would love," Jazz said, his eyes for a moment savage with the relish of it, "I would *love* to be carried in on a stretcher to testify. That would give the bastards a field day they didn't bargain for. We'd see then who could play on public sympathy, by God."

Though they did not know it then—but had they been a little more politically sophisticated, might well have foreseen—they would soon have the opportunity to find out.

The next day's headlines, complete with suitable accompanying editorials, columns, news stories, newscasts and commentaries, said:

IT'S OFFICIAL: TWO DEAD ON MARS FLIGHT . . . HILL DEMANDS IMMEDIATE INVESTIGATION . . . TRASKER DELAY BID DRAWS STINGING ATTACK IN SENATE . . . CRITICISM MOUNTS ABROAD AS WORLD SEES U.S. COVER-UP . . . NASA HIDES TRASKER AS PRESSURE GROWS . . .

The day after that they said:

MARS STALL BRINGS RISING CLAMOR . . . PRESIDENT DEFENDS TRASKER, APPROVES

WEICKERT WAIT . . . NASA FOES THREATEN TO WITHHOLD FUNDS . . . WILLIAMS CALLS FOR END TO "SINISTER EVASION" BY TRASKER, THREATENS BAN ON PLANETARY FLIGHT TWO . . . NASA FRIENDS WAVER, URGE EARLY HEARING . . .

The day after that they said:

SPACE COMMITTEES MEET IN JOINT CLOSED SESSION . . . WHITE HOUSE MAY YIELD TO HILL DEMANDS ON MARS . . . NASA INSISTS WEICKERT UNABLE TO APPEAR . . . WILLIAMS INTRODUCES RESOLUTION FOR SPECIAL INVESTIGATING PANEL . . . NASA FRIENDS FEAR HEAVY BLOW TO SPACE PROGRAM . . . PRESIDENT SEES NASA HEAD ON MARS UPROAR . . . CONGRESS MAY SEEK QUICK SHOWDOWN VOTE ON WILLIAMS RESOLUTION TO FORCE MARS HEARING . . .

On the fourth day the President called Connie in Houston to inform him of the ultimatum he had just received, in a friendly but alarmed fashion, from the chairmen of the two space committees.

An hour after that, the President issued his statement in Washington, Connie issued his in Houston and Jazz issued his in Bethesda.

That night the headlines said:

PRESIDENT OUTWITS CONGRESS, GRABS MARS BALL . . . CREATES SPECIAL COMMISSION TO STUDY DISASTER . . . NAMES V.P., FOUR MEMBERS OF CONGRESS, TOP NASA DUO TO SIFT TRAGEDY . . . HAILS "NECESSARY CLEANSING OF FESTERING WOUND IN SPACE PROGRAM" . . . TRASKER, WEICKERT VOW "COMPLETE DISCLOSURE ALL PERTINENT FACTS" . . . DOCTORS O.K. WEICKERT TESTIMONY FROM STRETCHER . . . WASHINGTON PREPARES FOR MARS EXTRAVAGANZA . . .

Shortly before 10 o'clock on the morning of the fifth day, the commander and co-commander of Planetary Fleet One arrived at the door of the Senate Caucus Room to keep their latest rendezvous with history.

5.

"The Commission will be in order!" the Vice-President said sharply, rapping his gavel hard on the massive committee table at the foot of the tall marble pillars. "And so," he added pointedly, "will the Caucus Room."

Along the high windows to his right the television cameras stared down from their wooden platforms. At the press tables just in front sharp eyes and clever faces from fifty countries gave him look for look. Crouched under the front rim of the committee table, still photographers cursed and shoved and jockeyed for position. In tightly packed rows of seats, and standing in every available inch of space along the sides and at the back, the lucky spectators who had managed to beg, borrow or steal a pass were crowded knee to knee and elbow to elbow.

Many of them he could see were familiar, those inveterate committee goers who grace every sensational show on Capitol Hill: Lady Maudulayne, wife of the British Ambassador, with her inevitable companions, Celestine Barre, wife of the French Ambassador; Dolly Munson, wife of the Senate Majority Leader; Patsy Labaiya, wildly dressed and wildly hatted, wife of the Ambassador of Panama. Other famous wives were there, including those of many members of House and Senate. Scattered among them were officials of NASA, including the Administrator; Dr. Albrecht Freer from the Cape; Dr. Hans Sturmer from Huntsville; Dr. James Cavanaugh from Houston; the editor of the *Times*, the editor of the *Post* and Percy Mercy; a number of ambassadors and ambassadorial wives; and in the first row, in a show of solidarity almost belligerent in its intensity, a number of other familiar faces he had come to know and understand and give his friendship to in the past year; fifteen or twenty of the astronauts, including Hank Barstow and Bert Richmond, Gaudy Gaudet, Emerson Wacker, Roger Webb, and Bob Curtis.

In the center of the first row, flanked protectively by their husbands' colleagues, were three more wives: Jane Trasker, looking tense but also reassuring and comfortable in her fresh and pretty way; Clare Weickert, also tense, shy but quietly determined; and Yo-Shin Yule, gravely beautiful, impassively awaiting events.

So was he awaiting them, the Vice-President thought with some grimness: yet he thought that in a good many ways they had been well-prepared for. The President had done several things in the past four days. In the Vice-President's estimation, he had done them very astutely.

He had delayed taking action until the outcry against Connie and NASA had become so virulent that it had begun to produce a reaction in their favor. Thousands of letters and telegrams were beginning to reach Congress and the White House, approximately 70 per cent of them favorable to Connie, highly indignant toward his critics.

The President had seized the initiative from under the noses—the unwiped noses, in the Vice-President's tart judgment—of Kenny Williams and his thinkalikes on the Hill, and had placed the investigation firmly in his own control.

As a sop to those friendly members of Congress who did not approve of a shotgun hearing yet had nonetheless found themselves beginning to yield to the pressure, the President had chosen his special commission largely from their own ranks, had put at its head his own man and had arranged for it to be held on Capitol Hill in the most historic room of them all.

In the process he had selected a commission heavily weighted (as the media had already pointed out with scathing alarm) with friends of the space program. The Vice-President was its chairman. Assisting him were Senator John Able Winthrop of Massachusetts, chairman of the Senate Aeronautical and Space Sciences Committee; Representative James L. Satterthwaite of Wyoming, chairman of the House Science and Astronautics Committee; Senator Kenny Williams, a member of the Senate Committee and an unavoidable choice because of the resolution he had sponsored seeking an investigation; and that level-headed, intelligent and fair-minded young Negro, a member of the House committee, Representative Cullee Hamilton of California.

To them the President had added two from NASA: Dr. Robert Hertz, director of Flight Control, and Astronaut Stuart Yule.

This, the Vice-President recognized—as there came a sudden electric stirring by the great oaken doors and he knew the big arrival must be about to take place—had aroused the frantic ire of Percy and his pals. But it was a mighty shrewd list of choices and mighty difficult to attack with any show of rationality.

The President had made it even more difficult because he had persuaded Connie and Jazz to issue statements giving every indication of a genuine willingness to co-operate. And he had refrained, as far as the Vice-President could ascertain, from approaching any of the commission members or attempting in any way to influence the course of the hearing.

On this last point, admittedly, the Vice-President reserved some small area of skepticism, since it was out of character for a man of such dominant political instinct to leave the outcome entirely to chance. He would also not put it past the President to have done something to influence the testimony. If so, it was not going to do him much good.

The Vice-President did not know what had occurred at the famous White House luncheon with Connie, but there might have been something. If so he intended to smoke it out, for he, at least, was not here for any cover-up. He was deeply loyal to the space program, deeply upset by the tragedy of Piffy One, deeply fond and admiring of Connie and Jazz: but he was also his own man and an honest one and he hoped to find the truth. He thought the country and the world had a right to know. NASA had a friend in the chair but it did not have a blind partisan.

Nor could the rest of the commission be faulted on that ground. With the exception of Kenny Williams, who had his own axes to grind, its members were fair and honest men who also wanted to find the truth. They were not here to whitewash, the program was too important to them. Connie and Jazz would find, aside from Senator Williams, a friendly atmosphere and a fair examination. They would not find an easy forgiveness if they fell short of the integrity their friends expected of them.

But now the time for reflection was over.

Abruptly the drama was upon them.

The room suddenly roared up into a wild excitement. There came a sudden glare of lights, a sudden rushing forward of photographers, a sudden standing, exclaiming, pointing and gawking from media and spectators alike.

Guards pushed them back and swung open the great doors.

Into the room came two white-uniformed orderlies carrying a stretcher.

From it the co-commander of Planetary Fleet One managed to raise his left hand with a cheerful grin and a thumbs-up gesture.

Walking beside him, right hand resting lightly but reassuringly on his left shoulder, came the commander, a little tension in his eyes for those who knew him but outwardly calm, pleasant, determined and unperturbed.

While the guards shouted and shoved and swore, and the photographers, bent like mindless lemmings upon their noisy, bothersome but necessary tasks, swore back, the little procession moved slowly along the front row of seats to the point where it must turn right and come up to the witness stand in front of the committee table.

As it reached center point it halted on command of Connie Trasker. Both Jane and Clare stood up and came forward to kiss their husbands. (*"God, what corn!"* the *Post* murmured to the *Times*. The *Times* shrugged and said wryly, "It will wow them in Dubuque.") Again the photographers had a field day. Jane and Clare returned to their seats. Connie gestured to the orderlies. The procession moved up to the witness table.

Carefully the orderlies locked the legs of the stretcher in place, gently set it down to the right of the witness chair. Jazz smiled and waved to the members of the commission, who smiled and nodded back, save for Senator Williams, who returned an elaborate scowl which was duly recorded by the television cameras. A committee aide brought two small microphones and hung them carefully around Jazz' neck, and Connie's.

Connie took his seat in the chair, bowed solemnly to the

commission and turned upon the Vice-President a grave and expectant look.

The room became so quiet that only the whirring of cameras broke the silence.

The Vice-President raised his gavel and brought it down sharply. Everyone jumped.

"Colonel Trasker," he said quietly, "Commander Weickert: this commission, appointed by the President to investigate the flight of Planetary Fleet One, is pleased to have you with us. Do you object to being sworn?"

"No, indeed," Connie said calmly, Jazz shook his head and said, "No, sir."

"Very well," the Vice-President said. He stood and raised his right hand, Connie did the same, Jazz raised his right hand. "Do you solemnly swear the testimony you are about to give is the truth, the whole truth and nothing but the truth?"

"We do," they said together, and knew in that moment they could not comply with the President's wishes. But they also knew, though they did not exchange a glance or any sign of communication, that they would comply for as long as they possibly could.

"Good," the Vice-President said comfortably, resuming his seat as Connie did the same. "Suppose, to set the scene for us, Colonel Trasker, you just tell us in your own words—"

But he might have known it was not going to get under way that easily.

"Mr. Vice-President—Mr. Chairman," Senator Williams said heavily from his seat to the Vice-President's right, beyond Representative Satterthwaite, "I wonder if I could put an exhibit in the record?"

There was a little stirring of excitement through the room.

"I think," the Vice-President said, "that a more orderly procedure would be to allow Colonel Trasker to complete his narration and then when it comes your turn to question, Senator—"

"Now, Mr. Chairman," Kenny Williams said patiently, "I don't want the chair to indulge in anything that would hamper this investigation. I have an exhibit I wish to place in the record which I think throws some light on the general mental and emotional stability of this witness. It will help us to judge his story better. I ask that it be inserted in the record at this point, Mr. Chairman."

The Vice-President hesitated. Tension grew. He was obviously pondering whether it was worth making an issue this early. Representative Satterthwaite on his right murmured yes, Senator Winthrop on his left murmured no. He made his decision.

"Very well, Senator. You may submit it."

"Good," Senator Williams said, opening a manila folder in front of him and extracting the picture of Connie crying in Jane's arms aboard *Mayflower*, blown up to twenty by twenty. "I appreciate the chairman's fairness." He held the photograph up and turned it slowly and deliberately toward the audience and the cameras, which obediently zoomed in. Then he shoved it with an air of cruel disdain across the table toward Connie. "I submit, Mr. Chairman," he said as he did so, "that this is not the picture of a man in control of himself. It is not the picture of an astronaut of the United States which most Americans would consider typical of that brave group of men. Any man as weak as that photograph apparently indicates, Mr. Chairman, no doubt *does* have an interesting tale to tell this committee. But it must be judged in relation to his weakness."

"Don't answer the bastard," Jazz whispered savagely. With an effort of the will so great it made him almost physically ill Connie fortunately refrained. His friends were not so restrained.

"Now, *Mr. Chairman*," Bob Hertz said, his voice quivering with anger, just as Senator Winthrop and Representative Hamilton did the same.

The Vice-President ignored them, banged the gavel, reached forward and retrieved the picture, studied it for a moment. Then he passed it quietly to a committee clerk and turned back to face Connie.

"Is that all the Senator has to offer at this time?" he inquired without looking at him.

"That's all," Kenny Williams said in a satisfied tone. "But I intend to refer to it again."

The Vice-President nodded.

"Senator," he said quietly, "you put anything you like in this record. But remember that it plays no favorites. It remembers the weaknesses of Senators as well as the weaknesses of witnesses. If weaknesses they be."

There was a burst of applause, loud and vigorous, from astronaut row, countered by a little wave of boos from elsewhere in the audience. Kenny Williams looked furious, Bob Hertz smiled broadly, the Vice-President gaveled again vigorously.

"The Chair," he said, "will remind the audience that it is here at the courtesy of the commission. We have a perfect right to clear this room if we deem necessary, and will do so if disturbances continue. Colonel Trasker, if you please."

"Thank you, Mr. Vice-President," Connie said, managing to sound quiet and dignified though he was still shouting inside with hurt and anger at the unfairness of it. He paused for a moment. "If I can be permitted, Mr. Chairman, I should like to complete my narrative without further interruption. I think that would be fair. Certainly it would permit me to give you a complete and consistent picture of what occurred on our mission without being distracted by—by side issues. Is that agreeable?"

"That is agreeable and the chair will so rule," the Vice-President said quickly. "Please proceed."

Kenny Williams stirred, the boos obediently rose again, the Vice-President stared calmly straight ahead. Connie proceeded.

For half an hour, while the cameras hovered relentlessly on his face and hands and on Jazz' face and hands, and while the room and a good portion of the world as well followed with hushed attention, he retold once more the tale of Piffy One from her launching at the Cape through her return to *Mayflower.*

His manner was composed and straightforward, his voice level and devoid of emotion. In that tense and historic old room where so many heroes and villains of the Republic's long history have paraded their integrity or lack of it, only the shrewdest ear—and there were one or two—detected on a couple of occasions a subtle change in his voice. But it came and went so quickly they could not be sure it was there.

True to his word to the President, he elided but did not destroy the truth about Pete. He used a phrase that for a moment struck a few as odd—"He then acquired a tear in his spacesuit"—but went on so swiftly and smoothly that it was soon forgotten by most. He did the same for Man in the Moon.

696

"The Soviet spacecraft," he said, "apparently due to a misjudgment on the part of its commander"—there was the faintest little sound, grim and ironic, at his side, but he gave it not the slightest acknowledgment and hurried on—"approached too near the spacecraft *Pinta* and in consequence it became impossible not to have a collision. The collision occured, with the consequences to *Pinta* which many of you saw in the live telecast of our arrival at *Mayflower*. We regained course after the initial shock, the Soviet spacecraft veered away and very swiftly passed out of our sight and out of our knowledge.

"Dr. Halleck was fatally wounded during the unfortunate approach of the Soviet spacecraft and Commander Weickert was very seriously wounded. For reasons of sanitation and health it was decided we could not return the body of Dr. Halleck to Earth. Accordingly it was jettisoned at a point which may very likely have sent it into orbit near the Sun."

There was a horrified gasp from the audience. He went calmly on.

"For approximately the last thirty hours of the flight Commander Weickert was in increasing discomfort, virtually helpless and in need of almost constant care. Approximately ten hours before rendezvous with *Mayflower* he passed into a coma from which I could not rouse him.

"The strain of these events, Mr. Chairman"—and despite his firm intention an acid crept into his voice and he stared with an open hostility at the puffy, aging, baby-face of Senator Williams—perhaps accounted in part for the momentary weakness I displayed upon greeting my wife which so concerns the Senator from Indiana.

"I regret that I feel I had a right to let down for a moment after all that had transpired. But there it is. I do not feel it was the act of a weak or uncourageous man. But I admit I am not so good a judge of weakness and lack of courage as the Senator from Indiana."

There was a delighted hoot and a burst of applause from the astronauts and many others through the audience. A loud and ugly boo replied.

"Mr. *Chairman!*" Kenny Williams protested indignantly. The Vice-President once more resorted to the gavel.

"I would remind the audience again," he said quietly, "—and the witnesses—and the commission—that there is

697

a certain decorum to be maintained here, and it will be maintained. Be guided accordingly."

And with a nod and the barest of winks, which only Connie saw, he added, "Please proceed."

"Mr. Chairman," Connie concluded quietly, "—Mr. Vice-President—Commander Weickert and I have traveled half a million miles to come to this witness stand under very unhappy circumstances. We had hoped to travel 120,000,000 and come here in happiness and triumph. It was not to be.

"Yet, Mr. Chairman, I do not feel that either Jazz or I failed our country or the space program or those who believe in it. This mission operated under great difficulties from the very beginning—as many of you know," he added, while a gasp ran through the room and a little calculating glint came into the eyes of the *Post* and many others at the press tables—"for you helped to create the climate which in turn contributed to so many of the difficulties.

"But we put it together. And we got it launched. And we were on our way to completing successfully the first phase of it, when fate—and the Communists—" ("*Honestly!*" Percy hissed to the editor of the *Times*, who smiled bleakly) "intervened.

"So I do not feel it was entirely a failed mission. Nor do I think the fact that Jazz and I brought it safely home is entirely unworthy, either. We were confronted with a very serious set of circumstances. Some of the most serious were beyond our control. We had to meet them. We did. We lost two men and no one regrets it more bitterly than I. But we brought the survivors and the spacecraft safely home. We did our job.

"And," he finished quietly, "neither Jazz nor I is ashamed of it."

The applause started and grew, the well-organized boos replied. Jazz, grim-faced, raised his left hand, placed it on Connie's shoulder in a gesture of approval and support and let it remain there until the photographers had snapped their fill.

Finally the Vice-President rapped for order. The room gradually quieted again.

"Thank you, Colonel Trasker," he said gravely. "I am sure the commission will give full weight to your account d to your sentiments in making final appraisal of this tragic affair. Commander Weickert, would you care to add anything?"

"Yes," Jazz said pushing the pillow higher under his head so that he could just see the eyes of the commission members over the rim of the table, "I would."

"Very well. You are very welcome to do so. And then we will go to direct questioning by members of the commission. Please proceed. You will not be interrupted."

"Thank you, Mr. Vice-President," Jazz said, his voice a bit faint but amplified satisfactorily through the room. "I'm still a little weak and still under some sedation, so I don't know how well I'll manage—"

("That phony!" someone whispered at the press table. "He'll manage. They've both been briefed a hundred times on this.")

"—but I'll do my best. Which is, I take it, what concerns you here: whether or not we have done our best.

"I don't have anything to add to Connie's narrative. I verify its essential details and I suppose in every way his desire to tell it as he has. We hope these pertinent and essential details of the mission will be of assistance to you.

"One thing only would I like to add, and that is"— beside him Connie, suspecting what was coming, flinched a little: though he shouldn't have, for it was both sincere and deserved—"that it has been my privilege to fly with one of the bravest, kindest and most decent men I have ever known. When the full record of Planetary Fleet One is completed it will be seen that Conrad Trasker was its real hero, Mr. Chairman. He was its heart. And thank God that heart is still beating.

"To him, of course—" and his voice became shaky for a second but he hurried on impatiently and it passed—"I owe my life. I wouldn't be here right now if it weren't for Connie. He nursed me through a very rough time, until I passed out and he couldn't do anything more for me; and then he got me home where the doctors could take over and bring me back. He never complained, he never hesitated; he did everything he could for me. And that for a man he didn't want on his crew, at first. But"—he smiled up at Connie—"I think he got to like me better as we went along."

("God, this is touching," observed someone else. "Are they going to kiss each other right here in the Caucus Room?")

"So, Mr. Chairman," Jazz said, "we managed—*he* managed. He faced what had to be faced when we got to the Moon. He made the decisions. He carried the load. He did the job. The rest of us helped, as long as we could, but Connie kept going when the rest of us had to drop out. He *was* the mission.

"I just wanted to say that, Mr. Vice-President," he concluded quietly as his audience in the room and his audience around the globe listened intently and studied his tired but determined face, "in case anybody here or anywhere has any ideas about making him the goat for this. Any attempt like that"—and some of his listeners had the curious and puzzling feeling that he was making an indirect but definite threat to someone—"could be—rather unfortunate, I think. Yes, sir. It could be rather unfortunate.

"That's all I have to say, except that I will always be proud I flew on Piffy One. We failed in a lot of ways but in some things"—and again there was, for some, that curious impression that he was talking over their heads to someone else—"we triumphed. Connie knows that and I know it . . . and I guess God knows it . . . and it's true."

And he leaned back against the pillows with an involuntary little sigh of exhaustion and pain that came clearly over the amplifiers in the silent room.

"Commander Weickert," the Vice-President said, "we thank you for coming here under such conditions and at such cost to your own health and comfort to support Colonel Trasker in his testimony. He has a good friend and a loyal one and I am sure he knows that and is grateful for it."

"I am indeed," Connie said quietly.

"The next order of business," the Vice-President said, "is questioning by members of the commission. It is almost noon. I think it might be a salubrious idea for all of us to break for lunch. After lunch the order of questioning, unless the commission has violent objections, will be Senator Winthrop; Congressman Satterthwaite; Senator Williams; Congressman Hamilton; Dr. Hertz; Colonel Yule; and the chairman.

"We will stand adjourned until 2 P.M."

Promptly at 2 P.M. the commission reconvened.
Promptly at 2:03 it began to fall apart.

700

"Mr. Chairman," Senator Williams began in an insistent monotone the moment the Caucus Room became silent. "Mr. Chairman. Mr. Chairman."

"Yes," the Vice-President said in an annoyed tone. "What is it, Senator?"

"Mr. Chairman," Kenny Williams said with a nasty relish that would have done credit to his close friend, Senator Fred Van Ackerman of Wyoming, "I wish to make a statement at this point."

"Mr. Chairman," Senator Winthrop said sharply, "that is entirely irregular, unwarranted and uncalled for. The Senator from Indiana has his place in the order of questioning. Let him make any statement he wishes then."

"I agree with that, Mr. Chairman," Cullee Hamilton said. "It seems to me there's an orderly way to conduct this hearing and a disorderly one. Let's stick with the procedure you outlined."

"Well, Mr. Chairman," Senator Williams said as his partisans in the audience began an approving little chittering, "I am not surprised that there should be an organized attempt to cover-up here, because it is obvious enough that there is plenty *to* cover up. I am a little surprised, however, to find the able and distinguished chairman of the Sentate Aeronautics and Space Committee lending himself to it. And I am also surprised at the Congressman from California, who I should think, Mr. Chairman, would be interested in ascertaining the true facts about the loss of a great and most worthy member of his own race."

"Mr. Chairman," Cullee Hamilton said, telling himself to stay calm and managing fairly well, "my race is not at issue in this hearing any more than is the integrity of the Senator from Indiana. It is true that the integrity of the Senator from Indiana may very rapidly *become* an issue in this hearing if he wishes to make it so. If he does, I know how I am prepared to vote."

Again the astronauts left no doubt of their feelings. Again they were rewarded with boos and hisses from elsewhere in the room. Again the Vice-President used the gavel.

"One more outburst of any kind by anyone," he said quietly, "and the guards will be directed to clear this room of everyone except the media. If you don't believe me, try me . . . Now," he said, when he had received and maintained silence for a full minute, "just what is it,

701

Senator, which makes it so imperative to you that you make a statement at this very moment? What is the nature of the statement and why should it take precedence over all the rest of us here?"

Kenny Williams, who, as his colleagues knew very well, was playing the easiest game in America—Manipulating the Media—ignored the Vice-President and stared full into the television cameras as he replied. With an eager concern they stared back.

"It should take precedence, Mr. Chairman, because we were treated here this morning to a carefully prepared, obviously slanted, deliberately unclear accounting of the very tragic and so far unexplained events. I submit that what we got this morning was no explanation: it was the story as the witnesses and their superiors in NASA wanted it to be told. It was not, I submit, the full story of Planetary Fleet One.

"Yet, Mr. Chairman, we are about to go blandly ahead here with everybody lined up to do some nice, polite, pattycake questioning that will have the effect of endorsing and underwriting this deliberately incomplete account. I don't think we ought to wait for the truth to catch up later. I think we ought to get right to the heart of the matter—right now." There was a stirring in the room but in response to the Vice-President's words it was kept under control. "That's my position, Mr. Chairman. Obviously," he added with a sarcastic smile, "it is not the position of my colleagues on this so-called investigating commission."

"Mr. Vice-President," Bob Hertz said quietly before anyone else could intervene, "I will not reply at this time to these egregious attacks upon NASA. But I would call the chairman's attention to the fact that the witness apparently would like to say something."

"Thank you, Bob," Connie said in a dry voice.

"Now, Mr. Chairman," Kenny Williams said indignantly, "this is a most irregular procedure! The witness has had his chance to speak uninterruptedly all morning. What does he want to say now? He is supposed to answer questions now, Mr. Chairman. He isn't supposed to lecture us about anything. This is a matter within the commission, Mr. Chairman. It is nothing for the witness to instruct us on!"

"May I, Vice-President?" Connie asked in the same dry tone.

"Briefly," the Vice-President said.

"All I want to say, Mr. Chairman, is that if it is so vital and important to the Senator from Indiana that you change all your orderly procedure to let him talk, then by all means, Mr. Chairman, let him talk. Commander Weickert and I are not afraid of what he has to say. They train us to face small emergencies."

There was a gasp in the room, and in the White House one member of the watching world knew suddenly, with a rueful shrug and an instant change of plans, that a scheme of high craft and low principle was not going to work.

"Mr. *Chairman*—" Senator Williams began. But the Vice-President turned his gray hair and impressively ample bulk toward him with a bland and impressive stare, and he subsided. The Vice-President turned slowly and impressively back.

"Thank you, Connie," he said, the significance of his use of the nickname not lost upon the audience. "If you and Jazz agree, that's what we'll do. I just didn't want him to railroad anything in on you here, that's all."

"We're ready for it, Mr. Vice President," Jazz said.

"Good," the Vice-President said serenely. "Senator Williams, thanks to the courtesy of these two gentlemen you have the floor. Go ahead."

Kenny Williams gave them a contemptuous glance.

"Smart words, Mr. Chairman," he said coldly, "don't always get witnesses very far on this Hill . . . Very well. I shall proceed.

"Mr. Chairman"—and he began to read from a prepared statement he took from his pocket and placed on the table in front of him—"this commission was given this morning an obviously incomplete and unclear picture of what occurred during the tragic flight of Planetary Fleet One.

"Certain aspects were not even touched upon by the witnesses, Colonel Trasker and Commander Weickert. Certain others were skillfully and, in my judgment, deliberately, shaded over and hurried past in the testimony. For instance:

"Colonel Trasker did not describe how Dr. Balkis happened to 'acquire,' as he put it, the tear in his space suit which, together with his broken leg and trapped foot, made his death inevitable.

"He did not describe how Dr. Halleck received the 'fatal wound' that came 'during the unfortunate approach of the Soviet spacecraft.' He did not really explain the jettisoning of a body which might, Mr. Chairman"—and his voice sank momentarily to a conspiratorial level—*"have been evidence . . .*

"He did not say why it 'became impossible not to have a collision.'" He did not describe the evasive maneuvers he must have taken or the evasive maneuvers the Soviet spacecraft must have taken.

"Incidentally, Mr. Chairman"—and his voice became heavy with irony—"this was obviously the same Soyuz 19 which Moscow has just told us completed a highly successful scientific mission to the Moon. The Soviets do not report any such dramatic encounter as we have heard described here. They do not even report sighting Planetary Fleet One. How are we to be sure this is not all a fabrication of NASA and those witnesses to conceal some sinister error of their own in connection with the spacecraft *Pinta?*

"Furthermore, Mr. Chairman, Colonel Trasker does not describe the nature of the wound received by Commander Weickert which caused so much difficulty in getting home. Granting the heroism of this witness, to which Commander Weickert has paid such touching tribute in his own statement, there still is a serious and in my judgment deliberately unanswered question here.

"And finally, Mr. Vice-President"—and his voice became solemn and grim—"I am advised by sources who place duty and love for country above their own petty ambitions and desires for empty glory, that when the spacecraft of Planetary Fleet One were thoroughly examined at Space Station *Mayflower*, where they are now docked, four days ago, there was discovered in the hatch between the *Santa Maria* and the Mars Lander *Adventurer* an enormous streak of human blood"—there was a sudden intake of breath throughout the hushed room—"approximately six feet in length and two feet in width. I am further told"—the breath was expelled in a long, excited hiss—"that this stain has now been removed on direct orders from someone in NASA. I do not know who—"

704

"Mr. Chairman," Bob Hertz interrupted bluntly. "I gave those orders to prepare the spacecraft for the next mission. The stain was photographed and blood samples were preserved."

Kenny Williams whirled on him sharply.

"You should be sworn to testify."

"In due course," Bob said, "I shall be happy to. Not yet. *Complete your statement*," he ordered in a savagely contemptuous voice and from down the table gave Kenny glare for glare.

"Very well, then, Mr. Chairman," Kenny said after a lengthy silence whose tension became almost unbearable. "Obviously we are on the trail now of a cover-up that *is* a cover-up. Obviously now we are beginning to get to something that really *is* sinister.

"So maybe my statement wasn't so ill-advised after all, was it, Mr. Chairman?" he demanded in a harsh, triumphant, sarcastic voice. "Maybe upstart Kenny is onto something worthwhile after all, right?

"What are you going to do now, Mr. Chairman? Pat these lying witnesses on the back and kiss them on the cheeks with an extra one for NASA? *Or order them indicted for perjury?*"

And now despite the Vice-President's warnings and gavelings and angry attempts to restore order the Caucus Room for a good five minutes was in chaos as press and cameramen scrambled to see, photograph, analyze, describe and try to get comments from, the men at the witness table.

After one quick, somber glance at each other, they returned to gazing straight ahead and sat impassive, expressionless and silent through the frantic moments. At last the furor began to subside. The Vice-President finally re-established order.

Connie Trasker leaned forward and spoke into the absolute hush.

"Mr. Vice-President," he said quietly, while in the White House his most interested viewer braced himself for what he knew was about to come, with your permission we should like to tell you now some further details of the flight of Planetary One. We have told you part of them. Now we should like to tell you the rest."

He turned deliberately and stared slowly around the crowded chamber behind him. His grim face softened for a second when he met his wife's eyes, he almost smiled reassuringly as he glanced along the row of deeply worried astronauts. Then his expression became somber again. He turned back to face the commission.

"May we, Mr. Vice-President?"

"Before you do, Connie," the Vice President said softly, "perhaps you should tell us who it was who suggested your testimony not be complete this morning."

For just a second he hesitated. Jazz stirred beside him.

"The President of the United States," he said quietly, and again there was a great excited expulsion of breath over the room, an excited babble, murmur, gasp and squeak.

He waited for it to subside. Then he turned to his crewmate and said, "Excuse me, Jazz." He reached under the blanket beside Jazz' left arm, extracted a rectangular package wrapped in brown paper, placed it carefully beside him on the table, leaned forward to the microphone.

So he told once more the story of Planetary Fleet One. On one point only, sustained by the knowledge that Jazz would not desert him and with a silent prayer to the Lord to forgive him, did he now withhold a truth he knew that no one, in any event, could ever discover. As he related it now, and as Jazz corroborated, Jayvee had been killed when his gun jammed and exploded as they were preparing for a possible boarding attempt by the Russians.

For the rest he changed nothing, withheld nothing. He opened his package, moved the box forward until it rested halfway between himself and the commission, described in detail NASA's so far unsuccessful attempt to unlock its secrets. He described the tragedy at Tranquillity Base, the encounter with Man in the Moon.

He concluded to find that his account had not altered one single solitary thing in the attitude of his enemies and the enemies of Piffy One.

"Well, Mr. Chairman," Senator Williams said when he had concluded, "that is a stirring tale—if it can be believed."

There was a burst of applause from somewhere in the room. He repeated with satisfaction, "Yes: if it can be believed . . .

"Now, Mr. Chairman," he said, and the sound of the kill was in his tone, "what is the picture we are given here? Let me tell you how it looks to me and I am sure to many, many millions more who are watching throughout the world.

"We have an encounter on the Moon. A friendly cosmonaut from a sister-power in space in a spirit of genuine co-operation and friendliness, innocent and well-meaning, comes up to two American astronauts. He holds out his hand in amity and trust and what happens? One of the astronauts instantly springs upon him with a savage hostility and attempts to bring him down. Naturally he reacts, Mr. Chairman, as any human being having the instinct of self-preservation would react. Bewildered by this attack, unprovoked and inexcusable, from a deceptively friendly American, he strives to protect himself with the only weapon he has, carried for some emergency—but *not*"—and his voice became low and throbbing in the tensely listening room—"*not* the emergency he has encountered at Tranquillity Base. *Not* a hostile attack from an American, Mr. Chairman. *Not* an aggressive and inexplicable attack from those he had approached as a friend.

"So naturally he defends himself. And in consequence what happens? He is promptly murdered by the other American."

A strange, strangled voice cried, "Oh, *no!*" and Connie recognized it as that of his wife. His knuckles turned white on the chair and sweat broke out on his forehead, but he prevented himself from turning around.

The sneering, insinuating voice went on and with a cold and terrifying certainty he knew it was making points.

"So the murderer returns to Planetary Fleet One, where he finds a Soviet spacecraft approaching. Again he, like his companion below, has no proof whatsoever of hostile intent. It is simply a hunch, Mr. Chairman—a guess—a gamble—and potentially a fatal one for the friendly Soviet spacecraft, although we may thank God that Moscow has been able, despite the witnesses' firm intentions, to announce its safe return."

"Mr. Chairman," Jazz said, and his voice too had a strange and strangled sound, "that is a lie. The Soviet craft, as we have told you, was damaged beyond repair. It was rotating wildly, venting oxygen, out of control. It went into the Sun. It did not return to Earth. That is one more Communist lie."

"So the witness claims, Mr. Chairman," Kenny Williams

707

said softly, "but, then, the witnesses have claimed many things, have they not? And how are we to become expert enough to know which of them to believe? It poses a problem.

"But let me," he said, as again there came noisy approval from somewhere in the audience, "let me continue with this scenario as we have heard it develop here.

"The murderer returns—"

"Mr. Vice-President," Bob Hertz said angrily, "how much longer do we have to listen to this foul flood of garbage?"

"The chair will say to the distinguished member of the commission," the Vice-President said patiently, "that the Senator has a right to state his views. He cannot be stopped unless a majority of the commission votes to stop him. And that, regretably, I do not think it will do. So he will continue. You will have your turn, Dr. Hertz."

"But then it will be too late!" Bob protested bitterly.

"Not for the truth," the Vice-President said calmly.

"No, indeed," Kenny Williams said with a cruel satisfaction. "Not for the truth. So, then: the murderer has returned to Planetary Fleet One and now his hunches tell him it is time to murder again. So he inflames and arouses his remaining crew to the same frantic state of mind he himself is apparently in. He does not find this difficult with his white crewmate, who apparently sees things through the same fanatically inflamed spectacles he does. No doubt he finds it harder with his black crewmate—and what a sad spectacle that is, Mr. Chairman! A student—a scientist—a lover of peace and all things of the mind—a truly noble representative of his much-mistreated race—he too must become a fanatical madman under the urgings of his strange commander. Dr. Halleck, that fine, peace-loving soul, forced to prepare his weapon for use against a possible Soviet boarding attempt! *Boarding attempt!* How insane. And so Dr. Halleck, too, earnest, peace-loving, feeling only good will and love for his fellow men, desiring only to be friends with his fellow men, is forced to get his gun. And in the process, tragically, it explodes and kills him.

"Talk of heroes, Mr. Chairman! If there is any hero on this sad ill-fated flight, it is the black hero. There is your hero. Mr. Chairman! *There is your hero!*"

There was a burst of applause, deep, steady, reverent,

respectful. The Vice-President started to gavel it down then shrugged with an air of tired disbelief and let it run.

Senator Williams paused and bowed his head gravely in response to it.

"So we have the Soviet spacecraft approaching, Mr. Chairman," he presently resumed, "and a commander aboard Planetary Fleet One apparently driven out of his mind by fear and evil suspicion. What does he do? He rams the Soviet craft, Mr. Chairman. He does it without warning as he does it without proof. He knows nothing except that he is afraid. And so he acts, instinctively, fearfully, hatefully, but fortunately *not*, as God's good grace would have it, fatally. Moscow has told us of Soyuz 19's safe return, Mr. Chairman. We can thank God for it, for if it had not returned the world would be confronting one of its greatest crises at this very moment.

"As it is we are confronted with—what, Mr. Chairman? Why—" and he gestured with an infinite sarcasm toward the strange black box on the table—"we are confronted with a piece of gimcrackery—this silly box, which no one can prove came from the Moon, or came from the Russians, or came from anywhere—except maybe the fertile imagination of some poor devil ordered to work overtime in the back rooms in Houston.

"And a spacecraft carrying damage which we are asked to believe, Mr. Chairman, was caused by the Russians instead of by the sheer lack of skill, the sheer ineptitude, the dangerous and fatal misjudgments of the Commander of Planetary Fleet One. He tries to blame *them*, Mr. Chairman, for his own dreadful incompetence. That is what it comes down to.

"These are the shabby, the flimsy, the inexcusable things we are confronted with, Mr. Chairman. We are not confronted with triumph. We are not confronted with heroism. We are not confronted with glory.

"We are confronted only with a national shame—a national disgrace—a national wound, if you like, which must somehow be healed.

"I do not know how it can truly be healed, Mr. Chairman," he concluded softly. "But I would suggest as a start the immediate dismissal and court-martialing of the remaining members of the crew of Planetary Fleet One."

Again there was great burst of applause. This time it was the astronauts, the officials of NASA and their many

709

partisans across the room who tried to drown it with boos and jeers and angry shouts.

Their attempt was not too successful. Presently it trailed away into a restless, unhappy silence.

"Colonel Trasker," the Vice-President said with a sympathetic gravity, "is there anything you wish to reply?"

Connie raised his hands to his eyes and rubbed them with a hard, driving motion as though he were trying to rid himself of some malignant sight. But it obviously did not go away.

"Mr. Chairman," he said finally, his voice very low but still carrying distinctly through the amplifiers and coming, along with his bleak, unhappy face, across the lands and oceans to the world, "I feel that Jazz and I are in a madhouse and that the inmates have become the keepers."

There was a sudden jumble of boos, angry jeerings, agreeing shouts and applause. It died in due time and he continued in the same low voice.

"We have told you, now, the final truth of the flight of Planetary Fleet One. We understand a little—I think—the reactions of those who prefer not to believe it. They are terrified of having to face the truth about the Communists, Mr. Vice-President: *they are terrified because if they admitted it to themselves they would have to act. And that would entail terrible risks and they do not have the courage to face those risks.*

"So it is easier to claim it isn't so, Mr. Chairman. It is easier to try to smear us, to concoct some evil cock-and-bull story, to play on emotions and create hobgoblins and use us as the scapegoats for fears and terrors that cannot otherwise be exorcised. That is what is at issue here, Mr. Vice-President; that and the sad truism that in the area of truth, one demagogue is worth a thousand honest men."

Again the boos, ugly, harsh and unforgiving now; and again the applause and angry mutterings of his friends in reply.

He waited for it all to die and went on to his conclusion in a tired and unyielding voice.

"It is obvious to us, at least, Mr. Vice-President, that the Senator from Indiana has accomplished what he apparently set out to do from the beginning, which was to make of this investigation a shambles and a mockery.

"Here is the national shame, Mr. Chairman, here the

710

national disgrace and the national wound—in minds as cold and horrible as his. My crewmate and I are glad we do not live in this madhouse with him. It must be a very pathetic place.

"Commander Weickert and I are of course willing to appear here again if you so desire but we do not really see what good could possibly come of it. We would prefer to continue our debriefing at NASA, where sane men dwell.

"We have told you the story of Planetary Fleet One. What we have told you is the truth. You know the details of our troubles, and you know who is responsible for them. Face that fact as best you can.

"We faced it—and we conquered it—and I would suggest to you that brave men always can . . . *if they will.*"

And he turned in the midst of the boos and applause that now rolled up again in furious competition to gesture sharply to the orderlies, who promptly came forward, accompanied by six of the guards, to take Jazz out.

Connie joined them and they moved slowly toward the door amid shouting photographers and desperately scrambling reporters. When they came to the front row, they were joined by their wives and a protective cordon of angry astronauts.

Outside in the hall more cameras and newsmen were waiting.

The procession paused. Connie stood, surrounded by astronauts, his left arm around Jane, his right hand still riding protectively on Jazz's shoulder.

Frankly Unctuous stuck a microphone under his nose and asked in a dryly patronizing tone,

"Who do you think the commander of Planetary Fleet Two is going to be, Colonel Trasker?"

He looked tired and he looked arrogant, and because he had been through a lot and thought he was probably facing the end of his career and no longer gave a damn, he also looked rather magnificent.

He stared straight into the cameras and snapped his answer into the eye of the world.

"If the President of the United States has an ounce of integrity," he said in a cold and level voice, *"I am."*

6.

MARS COMMISSION VOTES OWN DEMISE AFTER
WILD HEARING . . . WILLIAMS BITTERLY
OPPOSED BUT VICE-PRESIDENT, COLLEAGUES
OVERRIDE HIM . . . HINT PRESIDENT BEHIND
MOVE TO TURN PROBE BACK TO NASA . . .
MOSCOW DENIES STORY OF MOON ATTACKS,
CHARGES "TYPICAL CAPITALIST-MILITARIST
LIES" BY TRASKER, WEICKERT . . . REDS INSIST
SOYUZ MISSION "ENTIRELY PEACEFUL," SCOFF
AT MOON BATTLE STORIES . . . ANGRY DEBATE
IN BOTH HOUSES OVER CREW TESTIMONY . . .
NEW ANTI-NASA DEMONSTRATIONS IN D.C.,
CAPE, HOUSTON . . . SPACE DOVES PLEDGE
FIGHT TO FINISH AGAINST ANY ATTEMPT TO
LAUNCH PLANETARY FLEET TWO . . . PRESI-
DENT MEETS WITH NASA HEADS . . . WORLD
PRESS SKEPTICAL OF MOONARAMA . . .

*Above, the tiny satellite continued its steady rounds and
sent down its steady messages. Below, men of ambition
and power found narrowing circles ever narrower, motives of national interest, survival and prestige ever more
inextricably mixed. The satellite made no judgments,
offered no suggestions, provided no answers. It said many
things in many ways but its essential message was simple:*
Mine are the facts, yours the decisions. *By midnight of the
day of the hearing its reports could no longer be denied,
ignored or rationalized away. Inside narrowing circles there
were new attempts to break out whose success and conse-*
712

*quences no one could foresee. But it was decided they must
be made.*

PRESIDENT CLAIMS SOVIET MARS LAUNCH
"IMMINENT," ANNOUNCES PLANETARY FLEET
TWO ONE MONTH FROM TODAY . . . MOVE EX-
PECTED TO HEAT HILL DEBATE, SPARK NEW
ANTI-NASA DEMONSTRATIONS . . . WHITE HOUSE
CLAIMS PUBLIC SUPPORT "STRONG" ENTHU-
SIASTIC FOR NEW MARS TRY . . . P.F. II COM-
MANDER IN DOUBT. NASA MAY GROUND
TRASKER . . .

"Connie," the confident voice said, and on the screen
the confident face was looking at him with kindly concern,
"I'm sorry to wake you at this hour after such a hard day,
but I want to talk to you and Jazz. Can you be ready to
meet me downstairs in fifteen minutes?"

"Yes, Mr. President," he said rapidly becoming alert.

"Good."

"What on *earth*—?" Jane asked drowsily from the adjoining bed as he hurried about the room hastily getting
into his clothes.

"I don't know what he has on his mind," he said in a
disgusted voice. "I will *never* know what he has on his
mind. But he wants to talk—I talk. See you later."

"Good luck. If there is such a thing any more."

He closed the door quietly, hurried to the elevator,
punched the button, glanced at his watch: 1:15.

In the lobby of the Washington Hilton the last convivial
groups were loudly breaking up, the last partygoers were
finally going home. NASA MAY GROUND TRASKER a
mocking newsstand headline said. Outside on the pave-
ment a tattered memento of the little hairy group that had
paraded against him shortly after 6 P.M. still remained:
TRASKER HATES BLACKS, REDS AND WORLD
PEACE. F— TRASKER.

A modest limousine drew swiftly up under the porte
cochere. No outriders this time, he noticed wryly: things
were being very discreet. The door opened, he hopped in,
the limousine swept away. The President shook his hand
with a cheerful grin.

"This is my I-don't-want-to-be-noticed or sin-in-the-
suburbs car. Not that I ever use it that way but it's fun to

think I could if I wanted to. It drives the Secret Service crazy, doesn't it, John?"

The Secret Service agent sitting beside the driver turned his head with a long-suffering smile.

"You will have your little joke, Mr. President. Some day it may kill us all but you *will* have it."

The President chuckled.

"A President is no hero to his Secret Service men, I always say. He's an ornery, unco-operative son of a bitch who ought to be bound and gagged for his own safety . . . Well, Connie, I *am* sorry to get you out at this hour but I couldn't really seem to get to sleep very well and I suddenly decided you and Jazz were probably just the men I needed to see to regain my peace of mind. It's been a rather wild day, hasn't it?"

"Yes," Connie said dryly.

"At least we got through the commission bit in a hurry."

"Yes," Connie agreed, his tone if possible even drier. "I only came out of it hanged, drawn and quartered, but otherwise it was a very jolly affair."

"You held your own with a lot of people," the President assured him.

Connie shot him a sharp glance.

"Did I with you?"

"That," the President said, nodding at the Secret Service man now studying almost deserted Connecticut Avenue carefully as they sped along, "is one of the things I want to talk to you about."

Obediently Connie said no more. Ten minutes later they were turning in the gates at Bethesda. Five minutes after that they were being ushered into Jazz' room. He had been awakened and, though still a little groggy from sedation, was reasonably alert and ready for them.

The door closed firmly, the Secret Service and the Shore Patrol taking up guard together outside. The President stood quietly for a moment studying Jazz' face.

"Are you awake?" he asked with a smile.

"Just barely," Jazz said, also smiling. He gestured toward a chair. "Be my guest."

"Thanks," the President said. He stepped forward and shook hands before taking a seat. Connie did the same. The President again studied Jazz carefully.

"How did you stand it today? Pretty rough?"

"It wasn't so easy," Jazz said with a sudden deep yawn, "but I found I was hating Kenny Williams so much it pepped me up and got me through it."

The President nodded.

"Insufferable, isn't he? I talked to him last night, you know. I called him in and I carefully explained everything and I asked his cooperation in the same areas that I asked yours. You saw the result."

"Let me get this straight," Connie said sharply. "He knew from the very beginning—"

"Oh, yes."

"And all that phony-baloney indignation and discovery was—"

"Just phony-baloney. Nice guy, isn't he?"

"He's a monster," Connie said quietly.

"In spades and doubled," Jazz said. "Why don't you get rid of him, Mr. President? You seem to be able to do so many other things."

For a second the President started to look offended. Then he laughed.

"Ouch! Maybe I deserved that. Unfortunately, as long as the sovereign state of Indiana in their sovereign wisdom . . . there isn't much I can do. But to get to what I came here for: I want to thank you both most sincerely for trying to comply with my wishes under very great difficulties."

"And now that all of the truth is out," Connie said with a direct and quizzical look, "the Russians haven't started World War III, after all, have they? And so maybe we might just as well have told all of the truth from the very beginning. Isn't that right, Mr. President?"

The President smiled.

"But with the kind assistance of a United States Senator they have managed to convince a great many people around the world that it isn't the truth at all, don't you see. So it really doesn't embarrass them, or make them lose face, or put them on a really dangerous spot from which they'd have difficulty withdrawing. That's the difference . . . And of course—" his voice became soft—"we don't really have proof. We don't . . . really . . . have proof . . . to this day . . . Do we?"

Connie looked at Jazz and Jazz looked at Connie and for a moment it was all they could do to keep from shouting at him. But they managed to conquer the impulse. When Connie finally spoke it was in a voice deliberately flat and impersonal.

"There are two dead men and a rover on the Moon. And we have the box."

"Which, as Kenny Williams says," the President replied in the same soft, regretful tone, "is possibly not enough. It may be years before we get back to the Moon and in the meantime they may get there before us and remove the evidence. And as for the box—well, I don't really agree with Kenny, but on the other hand—it easily *could* have been a stunt fabricated in the labs of Houston."

"Honest to God do you *believe* that, Mr. President?" Jazz demanded with an open anger now. "Do you actually believe that?"

The President's face became still and sharp and shrewd as he looked from face to face with a slow and thoughtful gaze.

"Tell me what I believe," he suggested gently. "Tell it to me all over again from the beginning, just the three of us here all by ourselves . . . and then I'll tell you what I believe."

"Very well," Connie said quietly, though he could not entirely suppress an infinitely tired and frustrated sigh. "Very well. You help me, Jazz, if I forget anything . . ."

And so at almost 2 o'clock in the morning, in the silence of a room in Bethesda Naval Medical Center, he told once more, for the last time, the tale of Piffy One. And because they were alone, in this late hour haunted by so many things of man's courage and man's cupidity, he told it as though he were telling it to himself, almost ignoring his listeners except when Jazz interjected an occasional point or shading of emphasis.

Again the three bright candles roared away in their power and their beauty from the Cape; again the long arching flight took him and his crewmates to the Moon; again *Adventurer* descended, Pete died, Jayvee died, Man in the Moon was sent to the perdition it deserved; again he cared for his wounded colleague and brought him and the spacecraft safely home. And again, for a few brief moments, there was a challenge and a purity, a simplicity and a satisfaction to life that he knew now, with a grinding regret, he and Jazz would never again find on lovely, bitter, hate-ridden Earth.

716

When he concluded it was almost 3 A.M. He and Jazz stared silently at their interrogator.

"And do you swear to me," he said at last, "that this is the absolute and only truth in the matter?"

"We do," said Connie.

"We do," said Jazz.

The President studied them again for a long, somber moment. Then he smiled.

"I believe you. Now I have to prove I have that ounce of integrity. Connie, would you like to be commander of Planetary Fleet Two?"

For a split second Connie started to answer eagerly and joyfully. Then caution and his growing knowledge of this complex man caught the words stillborn in his throat. His answer when it finally came was very slow and very careful.

"On what terms, Mr. President?"

"Terms?" the President said with a sudden laugh. *"Terms?* What do you mean, terms? I'm offering you the job, Connie. Do you want it, yes or no?"

"You know I do," he said while Jazz held his breath and watched him intently. "But I also want to know on what terms."

"I don't have any," the President said blandly. "Maybe you do?"

"Yes," Connie said quietly, "I do. I will take the crew I want to take without any interference from anyone—*from anyone*—and the mission will be armed with sufficient cannon and torpedoes to defend itself against all comers. And the fact will be widely and explicitly publicized."

Again there was a thoughtful silence on the President's part, a pleased smile from Jazz.

"Good for you," he said; and added bluntly, "No honest man could refuse that."

Once more the President started to look offended, thought better of it, laughed.

"We can always count on you to spell it out, can't we, Jazz? What do you think a dishonest man would do?"

Jazz gave him a shrewd, ironic, unflinching look.

"Probably still try to make points with the Communists by refusing to arm the mission," he said calmly.

The President laughed again, not so amused.

"You *are* blunt."

Jazz nodded.

"I have nothing to lose. I'll never recover full use of my right side. I'm grounded forever. I can tell the truth."

"And so," said Connie quietly, knowing it was probably the end of his hopes and dreams, "can I. I will not fly this mission under any other circumstances than those I have outlined to you. I have tried to understand your problem, I have tried to co-operate with it, but I cannot and I will not take another mission and crew into unfriendly skies unless they are equipped to defend themselves. And that," he said, mentally saying farewell to Conrad H. Trasker, Perfect Astronaut, "is final."

But the President, as always, like any astute politician, was not a final type of person.

He surveyed their stubborn faces for a moment. Then he smiled.

"You really *do* understand my problem?"

"I think so," Connie said, rubbing his eyes with a tired frustration. "I do think so, though I find it a little hard to rationalize, now, after what's happened. And I also think the way to handle it is not by being devious but by meeting it head on. That's partly my training and I guess it's partly my character: it's the kind of world I live in. So"—he raised his hands in a half shrug and let them fall—"I guess I won't be commander of Piffy Two."

"Oh, now," the President said genially, rising to his feet and shaking hands, "don't be so gloomy, Connie. We may be able to work something out yet. Don't give up. We'll keep talking. I'll get back to you"—his voice became a little vague—"one of these days . . . Jazz," he said, holding out his hand, "take care of yourself, now. We want you back in NASA in some top post and that's for sure. Give my love to Clare."

Jazz shook hands carefully and briefly with his left hand. Then he looked the President straight in the eyes.

"Why did you tell Senator Williams, Mr. President? Why did you put him up to it?"

The President started to become genial again, dropped it. He returned Jazz look for look.

"I didn't put him up to it," he said quietly, "though I was pretty sure how he would behave . . . Because I had to make it possible for the Russians to get out of it. I had to make it possible for them to make a joke of it. I couldn't afford to make them lose face. I couldn't afford to back them into a corner they couldn't get out of. I'm sorry,

Jazz—Connie. But that's the world *I* live in . . . Good night, gentlemen."

And he was gone, the power of his being and his office lingering for several minutes in the silent room whose remaining occupants, hardly thinking, hardly moving, did not look at one another.

At last Connie stood up and held out his hand.

"Well," he said in a voice that shook a little though he tried to prevent it, "I guess I can always go back to testing jets for the Air Force."

"I'm sorry as hell, buddy," Jazz said quietly.

"Oh, that's all right," Connie said, turning away to the door. "I'll survive. I'm not that weak . . ." He turned back for a moment, a wry and twisted expression on his face. "I like space," he said. "There's no oxygen out there. Men can't breathe. They can't live. You find very few of them around."

"I'm sorry," Jazz repeated. But his crewmate did not answer or look back as he turned quickly to the door again, opened it and went quickly out.

For perhaps ten minutes Jazz lay motionless, his eyes wide and sad, staring at the ceiling. Then abruptly his expression changed, became forceful and intent. He reached over and elevated the head of his bed, snapped on the Picturephone, dialed a number.

When his party came on, sleepy-eyed and wondering, in Houston, he said urgently,

"Gaudy, I'm sorry to wake you up, but we have a little problem for the corps, here."

7.

It was a moment he would never forget. They were on the beach of the island of Eleuthera in the Bahamas, walking over the soft pink sand beside the deep green waters shortly before 7 P.M. on a clear and lovely evening. Suddenly Jane said, "Is that someone looking for us?" Far down the long, deserted shore a boy from the hotel had come running, running, and faintly on the softly rising wind they had heard him shout. . . .

"Gaudy," the Administrator said, his expression somber and concerned, "I'm here with the President. He wants to confirm in person what I told you an hour ago. He has decided to offer you the command of—"

"I'm sorry Andy," Gaudy Gaudet interrupted quickly, "and my apologies to the President, but I haven't got time to talk to either of you right now. I'm about to leave for the press conference."

"Press conference?" Dr. Anderson demanded. "What press conference?"

"The one Bert and Hank and I are going to hold in the auditorium in fifteen minutes. Hasn't Jim notified you of it yet?"

"Jim hasn't said boo," Andy Anderson said unhappily.

"Oh, sure," Gaudy said with an outward cheerfulness, though there were lines of tension around his mouth and more tension in his eyes. "It's all set. It will probably be telecast live, at least I'm told that's what the networks are planning. Maybe you and the President can watch."

"Gaudy," the Administrator said sharply, "what are you fellows up to out there?"

"Just a press conference," Gaudy said. "Maybe you'd better watch."

"Maybe you'd better not hold it," Dr. Anderson said sharply. But he could see from Gaudy's expression that one more perfect astronaut was on the rampage.

"Sorry, old chum," Gaudy said crisply, "but I'm afraid we're committed and all systems are GO. Talk to you later—" his tone became dry—"I'm sure."

And he snapped off his machine and vanished from the screen.

"What the hell do you suppose is up?" the UPI inquired as he sat with the Philadelphia *Bulletin* and the Chicago *Sun-Times* in the rapidly filling auditorium.

"Search me," the *Bulletin* said. "I've heard everything from putting the President in a Saturn and sending him to Mars by himself, to blowing up Cape Kennedy. All I know is, they aren't happy."

"Some of them aren't happy," the *Sun-Times* corrected. "I ran into one of my astroscientist friends a few minutes ago and he said he was sworn to secrecy but not to let ourselves be fooled: not everybody agrees."

"By that he probably means there are about five holdouts against whatever it is," the UPI remarked with more accuracy than he then knew. "That's usually par for the course when the scientists get upset."

"Well," the *Bulletin* said, turning in his seat to survey his gossiping, speculating, jesting colleagues as they came hurrying in, "it promises to be fun, anyway. Never a dull moment with dear old NASA."

Nor was he mistaken in that, for this one definitely was not dull. It was, in fact, "unprecedented . . . unheard-of . . . outrageous . . . and impossible," to hear the editorials and commentaries tell about it later. But like so many things in the space program, it happened anyway.

"Ladies and gentlemen," Bert Richmond began promptly at 10 A.M., his voice disclosing more tension than he realized, "Hank and Gaudy and I have asked you to meet us here this morning to hear a statement from the astronaut corps—or a majority of the astronaut corps, rather. I think we have five, is that right?—yes, five—members, all astroscientists, who have refused to sign this statement. It has been signed by the six other astroscientists and all of the pilot astronauts in the program—except Connie Trasker and Jazz Weickert—or a total of forty to five, which we think," he said, completely seriously, and there was a little titter from his audience, "represents a pretty good cross-section of the corps. Hank, do you want to say anything before I turn it over to Gaudy?"

Just that you've heard the figures on the Corps," Hank said, "and we should of course add that the statement has been signed by Bert and me also. And I am also privileged and pleased to announce that it has been signed as well by Dr. James Cavanaugh, director of Manned Spacecraft Center, and by Dr. Robert Hertz, director of Flight Control."

"Wow!" the UPI whispered softly as they all scribbled furiously and the television cameras zoomed in for closeups of the three solemn faces at the table on the stage. "This may be somewhat bigger than we thought."

"Somewhat," the *Bulletin* agreed.

"*Plenty* somewhat," the *Sun-Times* corrected.

"Gaudy," Hank said quietly, "maybe you'd like to give them the statement."

"O.K.," Gaudy Gaudet said, his voice, too, betraying his tensions: but after clearing his throat a couple of times he proceeded steadily to read the statement through.

"This statement is issued by a majority of the U.S. astronauts. Forty members of the present corps of forty-seven have signed it. Five have abstained and asked that their disagreement be noted. Two, Colonel Trasker and Commander Weickert, have not been asked to sign. All names will be given to you in a printed copy of this statement which will be distributed at the door when you leave. There will be no question-and-answer period because the statement is self-explanatory."

There was a murmur of dismay and annoyance but he went firmly on.

"We will not review the events of the mission of Planetary Fleet One with which you are all familiar. But we will make some general comments:

"We, the undersigned, believe the testimony of Colonel Conrad H. Trasker, Jr., commander of Planetary Fleet One, given in Washington, D.C., yesterday. We believe his account of the attack by a Soviet cosmonaut which resulted in the death of Dr. Petros Balkis. We believe his

722

account of the meeting of Planetary Fleet One with the Soviet spacecraft. We do not believe the Soviet spacecraft was on a peaceful mission and we do not believe it returned to Earth. We believe it was destroyed in space. We believe it deserved to be."

("Solidarity forever!" the *Times* murmured to the *Post*. "And to hell with world peace," the *Post* replied. "Incidentally, what about Halleck? No mention of him." *"Racial* solidarity forever," the *Times* remarked dryly.)

"Furthermore," Gaudy said, "we are convinced that these events clearly demonstrate the widsom of Colonel Trasker and others who wanted Planetary Fleet One to be armed. We believe all such missions should be armed hereafter.

"We are convinced that Colonel Trasker and his co-commander, Commander Alvin S. Weickert III, performed with great courage, heroism and devotion to duty in their conduct of themselves and their mission through its many trying hours. We believe they deserve the highest support and commendation from their country.

"We are proud to say that they have ours.

"The President, as you know, has announced the lauching of Planetary Fleet Two one month from today.

"This morning the President offered command of that mission to Colonel Hugo S. Gaudet.

"He still refused to pledge that he would permit arming of the spacecraft and he refused to pledge that he would take adequate steps to warn the Soviet Union against any further hostile excursions against American spacecraft and American space missions.

"Accordingly," Gaudy said quietly, though his voice trembled a little, "Colonel Hugo S. Gaudet has refused to accept command of Planetary Fleet Two.

("Wow!" said the New York *Daily News*. "Shhh!" said the Cleveland *Plain Dealer*.)

"Further, all other members of the astronaut corps qualified to command or fly on Planetary Fleet Two—namely the thirty-four pilot astronauts presently in the program, exclusive of Colonel Trasker and Commander Weickert—have reached the firm and unchangeable conviction that they will not fly on Planetary Fleet Two except under these conditions:

"1. The spacecraft will be fully and adequately armed

and appropriate public notification of this fact will be given by the President to the Soviet Union.

"2. Planetary Fleet Two will be commanded by Colonel Conrad H. Trasker, Jr.

"Pending acceptance of these two points, the thirty-four pilot members of the astronaut corps will not fly any missions of any kind or participate in any further training looking toward such missions.

"Signed, etc., and you will find the statement with names waiting for you at the door."

"Gaudy—" someone shouted but he shook his head. Looking straight ahead he and his two colleagues marched off the stage and disappeared behind the curtain.

"Of all the corny, two-bit stunts!" the *Post* exclaimed bitterly as the press hurried excitedly out to telephones and typewriters. "Of all the phony—irresponsible—headline-grabbing—worthless—God-damned—*cheap*—"

"That's right," the *Christian Science Monitor* said, pushing cheerfully past. "All they're doing is laying their lives and their careers on the line and I grant you that *is* pretty cheap, isn't it?"

HOUSTON ON STRIKE: ASTROS ISSUE ULTIMATUM ON ARMED MARS FLIGHT, TRASKER COMMAND . . . NO MORE MISSIONS UNLESS WE GET CONNIE AND GUNS, SAY ASTRONAUTS . . . SPACE FRIENDS FEAR END OF PLANETARY FLEET TWO, DEATH-BLOW TO SPACE PROGRAM . . . WORLD SHOCKED BY REVOLT OF "ALL-AMERICAN BOYS" . . . PRESIDENT MEETS WITH NASA HEAD . . . WILLIAMS DEMANDS ENTIRE CORPS BE FIRED . . .

Which of course was infantile nonsense, and as he sat staring out—as so many Presidents had on so many occasions, past the Monument, across the Potomac and on to winter-bare Virginia—he knew it just as well as Kenny Williams did. Sovereign people of Indiana or no sovereign people, he told himself grimly, next election he would have to do something about that little bastard. He had a comfortable majority in the Senate and if his intervention in Indiana cost him a seat, he could afford it. It would be worth it just to get the little psychopath off his back.

How he was going to get the astronauts off his back,

however, was another matter and not quite so easy. They had issued their statement at 10 A.M. Houston time, noon in D.C., and by the present hour of 5 P.M. more than 200,000 telegrams and telephone calls had come in to the White House, nearly all of them both favorable and indignant. It had been more than an hour since the switchboard had been able to function, and that, he reflected with a wry amusement, was probably just as well: nobody could distract him from a decision he and he alone had to make.

That was what they had handed him, these determined and intrepid souls without whom he could not maintain the space program; and they spoke, he knew, from a virtually unassailable political position. The involved reasons why he had handled Piffy One as he had, his rationalizations and explanations which could be given to Connie and Jazz in privacy, were too delicate and perhaps too subtle for the average citizen to understand. The average citizen's reaction would undoubtedly be the same as Connie's: why not tell the truth and sail right into it? Wouldn't you prevail, if the truth was on your side?

For the President, who felt he was bound by his own special imperatives— "But that's the kind of world *I* live in"—this would bring popular pressures that might very well push him into some action toward the Soviet Union that could only have far-reaching and disastrous results to those who most wanted him to take such a line. Connie needn't think he was the only one who felt: tell the truth and full speed ahead. God knows the President did, too, many more times than he could ever afford to let on in public. But living on the razor's edge with the power to tip everything over, you did not deal in such absolutes. You thought a thousand times and did a thousand clever things before you ever, finally, committed yourself to the irretrievable act, the unretractable confrontation.

Yet always the honest simplistics could carry the day in open debate, for theirs was the policy grounded on American principle, American tradition, American gut-instinct. And he had to admit that on the occasions when their view had carried the day the result had not been so bad. It had been pretty much what they said it would be. The truth as they saw it—the truth of the successful, which is the only truth that survives—had conquered. So why not say: tell the truth, and full speed ahead?

This was exactly what he was up against with the astronauts, and it was obvious already that they were entirely in tune with the great middle range of their countrymen. With a violent indignation against the Russians and against himself, they had struck, with what amounted to genius, exactly the right note to muster public opinion behind them. The President knew an overwhelmingly popular position when he saw one. There was not the slightest doubt that the astronauts had taken it this morning. The *Times* and the *Post* and all their faithful band might fume and fulminate, Percy Mercy might stamp his foot and spit, Kenny Williams might demagogue and orate, but the great inert mass of the American people was with its bright-eyed boys in Houston. And furthermore the great inert mass wasn't inert any more: it was moving. No outcry against Planetary Fleet One and the astronauts had ever matched the spontaneous groundswell that was now growing by the minute *for* Planetary Fleet Two and *for* the astronauts. It was threatening to shake the White House itself, if he didn't watch out. And when all was said and done, it could be agreed that where his own political position was concerned—he did watch out.

He would have liked to think that this was all Connie's doing because that would have made it much easier to handle. But he knew it wasn't. Connie and Jane had flown off to the Bahamas this morning for a week of rest in beautiful isolation, but not before Connie had stopped by the White House on the way to the airport. He had not been able to see the President, who was busy in Cabinet meeting, but he had left a letter with the President's personal secretary which she had given him as soon as the meeting broke up. He had it before him now:

"Dear Mr. President: It is with deep regret but with my mind made up that I herewith submit my resignation from the astronaut corps and from the space program. I feel that my veiws are such that for me to remain would be a continuing source of friction and embarrassment for you. Because I believe in the program and also because I think you should not be harassed unnecessarily in the pursuit of your grave Constitutional responsiblities, I am accordingly . . ."

So it was not Connie to be disciplined: it was his entire group of righteously indignant colleagues. And that, as he and Senator Williams both recognized behind the demagoguery, was nonsense.

There also arose, of course, the question of just where his final constituency resided: in Moscow or in America? And there did arise the question, not too often proved by events because not too often did an American Chief Executive press the point: wasn't it true that when a President reflected the gut-instinct of his country the Communists almost invariably backed away from direct confrontation?

The time for this was very late, the narrowing circle was growing ever narrower. But there was still the chance—still the chance.

Studying the reaction from Moscow to the testimony yesterday—a reaction which looked furious and derisive on the surface but which he knew from study and experience was frantically troubled and uncertain underneath—he thought he might be well advised to put himself at the head of the parade. It was a gamble, like all such things: but his own instinct, which was not so far from middle America when he allowed it to operate, told him the gamble might work this time.

And also, he reflected with an ironic little smile, it probably wasn't such a bad idea to firm up that precious ounce of integrity. Connie, he knew, would be pleased.

He picked up Connie's letter of resignation, shredded it slowly and thoughtfully into the wastebasket. Then he called his secretary and began to dictate.

The sun was beginning to slip over behind the central ridge of Eleuthrea, starting to move West across the Straits to Florida and the Gulf. The Atlantic's rollers broke sleeply and placid beyond the coral reef that protected the island's eastern flank, its waters within the reef still deeply green and pellucid in the gently dying light.

For several minutes they had not spoken, strolling barefoot, hand-in-hand, along the curving shore. He knew the major part of his life was over, she knew she must find within herself resources she had never been required to exercise before if she was to see him safely through the terrible testing this would be.

Yet in some curious way they both were content. Already they had accepted, already become calm and ready to face what they must.

727

A shark surfaced inside the reef, a dolphin jumped beyond. A shard of pelicans slipped down the sky. It was almost time to return to the hotel for showers, drinks and dinner.

They turned slowly and started back along the empty beach. Suddenly Jane glanced up, stopped.

"Is that someone looking for us?"

Far down the pink, deserted sands of Eleuthera beside the lovely green water a boy from the hotel came running, running; and through the gentle, lonely evening his voice came clearly on the softly rising wind:

"White House want you, Colonel! White House want you, Colonel!"

And he knew his dreams were not over yet.

ASTROS WIN, PRESIDENT BOWS: TRASKER TO COMMAND SECOND MARS MISSION . . . CHIEF EXECUTIVE ISSUES STERN WARNING TO SOVIETS: SPACECRAFT WILL BE "FULLY ARMED AND WILL TAKE ALL NECESSARY STEPS TO PROTECT ITSELF" . . . CAPE RUSHES WORK ON SECOND TRY FOR MARS . . .

8.

There were in these final days, of course, the bitter cater-waulings of Percy and his friends, of the *Times* and the *Post* and all their spiteful gaggle, of Walter Dobius and Frankly Unctuous and their snide, selfrighteous crew. There were the futile fulminations of CAUSE, unable still to muster more than a few scruffy thousands for its empty but always enormously reported protests around the country. There were the solemn statements from the customary Frightfully Involved campuses, the stern denunciations from the usual Frightfully Enlightened pulpits, the infinitely humorless, pompous and pathetic outcries of the television-encouraged young. There were the nasty snips and snipes in the literary columns, the theatrical columns, the society columns, the "humor" columns, even the cooking and advice-to-the-lovelorn columns—wherever Right Thinkers had a chance to toss in their little knives. There were the harsh, vindictive editorials, the slanted headlines, the slanted news stories, the slanted commentaries, the slanted newscasts in the fashionable major media—and the valiant but hardly noticed rebuttals in their unfashionable smaller brothers. There were the solemn pontifications of Great Statesmen in front of Great Cameras. There were the somber warnings and the vast deplorings.

And at the Cape, where men had a job to do, it mattered not at all.

There as they worked around the clock toward launch the world of their nagging countrymen—who were, as always, just a thin screeching of razor blades on glass atop the vast majority of Americans who supported the mission—seemed far away and unimportant. Occasionally there would be the threatening telephone call which somehow managed to slip through the vigilant switchboard; the vile, condemning letter that somehow managed to creep through the mails; the occasions, few and far between, of personally delivered insult.

Once, when he was driving Jane down the Strip in Cocoa Beach toward Patrick Air Force Base where they were staying with the kids, someone had shouted from the roadside, "We hope you fall into the Sun and burn in hell forever!"

And of course when Moscow announced that its own Mars flight would be armed, he and the President and NASA and everyone else who could possibly be blamed were blamed, and there were great anguished howlings and violent claims from the usual quarters that this would never have happened if the vicious old United States had not driven poor little innocent Russia into it.

But these were marginal things, outside things, faraway things, peripheral and unimportant to the Cape. There the mood was best exemplified, perhaps, by Jane and Clare and all the kids, with whom he and Jazz had frequent evening cook-outs on the beach; by Dr. Freer, who went around with a perpetual smile on his face like some constantly overjoyed old Santa Claus; by Stu Yule and Jazz, who were going to be co-CAPCOMS for the mission; by his new crew, Gaudy Gaudet and Emerson Wacker and Bob Curtis, who went around whistling or singing most of the time while they studied flight plans, worked out in the simulators and talked long talks about what they would find on Mars; by Hans Sturmer from Huntsville and Bob Hertz and Jim Cavanaugh from Houston and Andy Anderson from Washington and all the others who kept dropping in almost every other day "just to see how things were going" and revel in the returning excitement of a new and even more challenging launch; and by the President, who, once committed, did not look back but was on the Picturephone virtually every day to talk encouragingly to Connie, the crew and Al Freer.

This was the real world for Connie and his friends and the other did not matter; and so they moved swiftly through the four short weeks to the launch of Piffy Two, which actually was two-thirds Piffy One. *Santa Maria* and *Nina* of course were still in excellent condition, docked at

730

Mayflower where they had been thoroughly checked out and refurbished. But because of the unhappy connotations that now surrounded the name "Planetary Fleet One," it had been decided that the new mission would carry the new name, though this time there would be only one bright candle: *Pinta II*, which would carry a new NERVA and all four crew members into Earth orbit, where they could dock with *Santa Maria* and *Nina* and then set forth from *Mayflower*.

This time also there would be no tests around the Moon. That too had connotations as well as risks that now were recognized by NASA and the President if they were not by Percy and his friends.

From *Mayflower* the trajectory would be straight for Mars.

Sometimes, playing games with the kids and Jazz on the beach, or sitting in the simulators, it seemed to Connie that his world, from being a savage and troubled place, had somehow changed and become serene and whole again. He was surrounded by his family, his co-workers, his friends. He was doing the job he had been trained to do. He had been tested as few men ever had, he had been stretched to the utmost, he had triumphed over great adversities, he had survived and been able to return—hurt, but stronger in many ways—to do his job again.

It now seemed a very long time ago, that cool spring morning when he had walked across the esplanade at Manned Spacecraft Center on his way to the Astronaut Office to discuss with Hank and Bert the selection of twelve men to fly a years-away Piffy One to Mars. Thanks to the messages of the satellite and the guile of the Communists, everything had telescoped. The faces passed before him: Jane patient and loving; Monetta quiet and kind; Jayvee tense and unhappy; his Greek loner from Tarpon Springs, whose shoulder patch he now wore beside his own, and who would always have a special home in his heart; good old blunt, outspoken, no-nonsense Jazz—and all the many others who had helped or hindered along the way, in Houston, in Washington, in Huntsville, at the Cape—the Russian at Tranquillity Base, the Russian in Man in the Moon—Clete O'Donnell and Percy Mercy—Kenny Williams and his friends, spitting hate—the Vice-President—the President—so many people, so many things . . . and Piffy One had carried them all.

It was a wonder she had ever flown. It was a wonder, hurt and damaged as she was and hurt and damaged as he was, that she had ever come home.

But she had, and he, more than anyone else, had been responsible. And now he was going again, as he wanted to go, on the journey no one had ever taken into mysteries no one had ever seen. A boy of seven in South Meadow, touched by Someone or Something in Alpha Centauri—a man of forty-two at the Cape, leaving for Mars—Connie Trasker, pioneer, explorer, technician—guardian of the Dream, opener of the Way, leader of mankind in its next great step Beyond—Conrad H. Trasker, astronaut: Out There.

So the days whirled on and the excitement at the Cape rose and grew and spiraled up at an ever faster pace just as it had before.

T minus 4 days and the social whirl hit full blast; T minus 3 days and they said good-by to their families and went into isolation; T minus 2 days and they took their jet flight over Florida; T minus 1 day and they spent their last hours in the simulators; T minus 12 hours—10 hours—8 hours—5—4—3—2—1—the President and Vice-President were there, the VIPs were there, the media watched —Jazz and Stu were back in Houston now, ready in Mission Control—on Pad A *Pinta II* stood bright and shining in the sharp January sun, venting liquid oxygen in little white puffs along her sides—in the capsule he and Gaudy and Em and Bob Curtis looked at one another and grinned—

T minus 20 minutes—10 minutes—5 minutes—3—a sudden startled babble of noise on the intercom, the voice of Bob Ellison saying urgently, *"Ladies and gentlemen, we are just advised that the Soviet Union has launched its mission to Mars from Space Station* Stalin!"—and the count resuming matter-of-factly, T minus 1 minute—50 seconds—40 seconds—30—20—10—9—8—7—6—5—4—3 —2—1—ZERO— "LIFTOFF. We have LIFTOFF, ladies and gentlemen, for the spacecraft *Pinta II* of Planetary Fleet Two"— and the great thundering beautiful surge into the sky, away and away and away . . .

One hour later, docking at *Mayflower* for the addition of the fourth NERVA, the final check-out of systems; and one hour after that, as humanity quieted down once again, the prayers in *Santa Maria*, the prayers in Houston, the prayers of men of good heart everywhere—and the final closing of hatches, the activation of thrusters—and slowly, gently, inexorably, the three linked spacecraft pushing away from *Mayflower*, drifting a moment to let *Mayflower* get out of range—and then the firing—and trajectory achieved and the long, long journey begun.

"Hello, Two," the Administrator said over S-band, his voice, trembling a little, booming out around the world. Hello, Connie, Gaudy, Em and Bob. From all of us here to all of you there: Godspeed, a safe journey and happy landings."

And back from space, his voice also disclosing emotion yet steady, confident, calm and clear, the commander:

"Roger, Andy and all. Our thanks for everything. Take care of Earth for us. See you in eighteen months."

And the little white dot on the world's screens growing smaller and smaller and smaller—and eyes, strained from watching, blinking to clear themselves, preparing to return to the cares of everyday—and the white dot dwindling, dwindling, dwindling—

And then it was gone.

It was 3 minutes, 30 seconds into the flight of Planetary Fleet Two, outbound for the planet Mars.

How mighty is man, and how brave in the face of the infinite.

Listen to him, Lord, as he assures You how magnificently he will be housed, how astutely he will conduct himself, how comfortable he will be as he travels across Your universe. Note the perfection of his machines, the beauty of his science. Note how carefully he will be clothed, how efficiently his needs will be tended to, how skillfully he will meet Your problems, how shrewdly he has thought of and provided for every possible threat to his safety and ease—except the threat of his own nature and all the things You can devise to test it.

See him as he prepares to challenge You, wired—encapsulated—suited—unsuited—experimenting—communicating—urinating—defecating—carrying his life about on his back in a portable pack—scientifically eating—sleeping—doctoring himself—peering into Your hidden places—while he glides in unbelievable machines at unbelievable speeds over unbelievable distances just beneath the corner of Your eye.

Look very quickly and You will see him pass through Your shadow. Perhaps he will return and perhaps he will not, but he goes equipped with all the precautions You have permitted him to achieve in all the millennia of his life upon Earth.

Will they be enough?

Don't tell him.

Let him go

He would not believe You anyway.

January 1969—July 1970

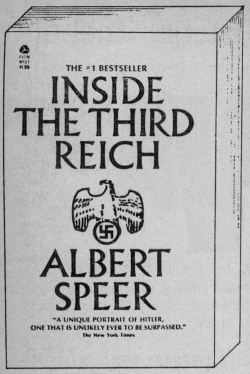